Courage to Fall…

Book #2 of the Courage Series

The heart wrenching sequel to Courage to Fly.

Courage to Fall

Julie Anne Kiley

Dedication

To my new friend Raquel, and all the warrior women out there who live with pain every day.

Before this process we were strangers.

Now, thanks to Silas and Edi we've become friends.

You may be on the 'other side of the pond' but I will be forever thankful for all your support.

This one is for you.

xxxx

ACKNOWLEDGEMENTS

Okay, guys. I'm not going to apologise for the length of this book. There's a reason it's over seven-hundred pages and that reason is Silas Tudor!
Oh, my goodness, what a man!

When I started Edi's story in Courage to Fly, she and I were already well acquainted. She arrived as a fully formed character. I knew her personality, her history and her secrets. Moreover, I understood her.

Silas, on the other hand was a conundrum. I knew bits about him but not everything. However, the more I wrote of Edi's story, the more Silas emerged. He revealed himself to me through Edi's eyes and what a shock it was when I discovered the whole devastating truth.

Silas Tudor, is the reason this book is so long. His story is significant and needed to be told. He's been through such a lot and it was important to me that you all got to know and understand him as Edi, and now I, do.

*

There are some special people I need to thank...
Glyn, for his editing and his *'do you really want to say that'* comments... *Yes, I do!*
Lynn and 'B'. You're the best. Samantha; my beautiful Goddaughter... you may share some feisty character traits with *my* 'Sammy' but physically you are worlds apart. Elaine... enough said!
The ladies from 'Wednesday Vodka Club'... I can't promise your real-life escapades won't inspire further stories! And everyone who read the first book and urged me to complete the second... I'm seriously humbled by your reaction.

Thank you all
Jules

...Falling is like flying, it can set us free.
We just need to have the courage to know; as we tumble through this
life, there will always be someone, somewhere, waiting to catch us...

Julie Anne Kiley

5

by Julie Anne Kiley

Prologue:

Meredith age 14 years six months

This is it. The big day. The party day. I can't believe I've been invited. Nobody ever invites me anywhere. I'm the invisible girl. The plain girl. The one everybody teases because of my plump figure and ginger hair. But today is different. Today, for the very first time, I'm going to an actual, popular girl's, teenage party.

Leoni is the cool girl, the prettiest girl in our year and by far the most popular. Everyone wants to be her friend. Everyone hangs on her every word. She has the best clothes, the best hair, the best makeup, and she's invited *me* to her birthday.

Opening my wardrobe, I flick through the sparse selection for something 'cool' to wear. I have nothing. My clothing consists of Jeans, tee shirts and my school uniform. There are a couple of cast-offs of my mum's that look like they were last fashionable in the sixties, and a short denim skirt I bought from the local market.

Turning my back on the dowdy sad collection, I sit on my bed for a sulk.

If I have nothing to wear, I can't go.

And if I don't go, I'll be back to being ridiculed at school.

And I couldn't stand to go back to being the butt of every joke and the target of incessant bullying.

Reaching beneath my bed, I pull out a well-worn copy of *Teen Magazine*. It's ancient; at least a year old but I live and die by it. All the girls inside look glamorous and stylish – just like Leoni – their hair is perfect and their clothes completely on point to the latest trend, their figures enviable.

As I flick through the dog-eared pages, one picture in the fashion section catches my eye. I've admired the grungy, Madonna 'ish look for ages but there's no way I could pull it off. However, the more I study the picture, and really examine how the outfit is put together, I begin to see, I might just be able to.

Returning to my wardrobe with an open mind, I pull out my denim skirt. What I need is an oversized top and a belt... a shirt. One that's baggy so I can sinch in the waist with a belt.

Nobody else is home. Mum is out shopping and dad has gone to the football. Quickly, I run to my parent's bedroom and open my mum's wardrobe, rummaging through the rows and rows of age-inappropriate clothes, searching for something suitable... there's absolutely nothing. Besides, everything stinks so strongly of cigarettes I'll smell like an old ashtray.

Sighing in disappointment, I slam the closet door on the unsavoury collection. *What would Leoni do in this situation?*

I have an idea. Perhaps not a good one, but it might work... maybe...

In the second wardrobe, I chance a look. Inside the rail is split for double hanging. On the lower rail, there's a selection of casual clothes. Jeans, polo-shirts, sweatshirts and the like. All dated and well worn. However, on the top rail are my dad's work clothes. Jackets, trousers, ties and shirts... Jackpot!

Some of the shirts are a bit loud. Unfashionably so, with large penny-round collars and bright floral patterns; goodness knows how old they are, I've never seen him wear any of them.

Reaching inside, I select a blue and cream paisley patterned, cotton long-sleeved shirt and pull it out. On its own its hideous. Clearly it went out of fashion years ago; but paired with my denim skirt, and a wide belt it might work.

Taking my find with me, I dive back to my room, closing and locking the door behind me. Hurriedly I strip out of my jeans and pull on the skirt. Zipping it up I don't even look at myself until I pull on the musty shirt. Its huge and so baggy I'm sure I could turn full circle inside it.

Grabbing a broad belt from my drawer, I tighten it around my waist over the top of the shirt and roll the sleeves up so they're elbow length. Then I turn to the mirror.

"OH!" The exclamation leaves my lips as a gasp of surprise. I actually look trendy. The blue and cream shirt suits my colouring and by some fluke, the ensemble really works. Turning this way and that to check I've not made any gaffs with my choice; I arrange the stiff collar so it stands up – it looks even better like this.

Riffling in my jewellery box, I locate a long string of fake pearls and loop them around my neck – it's getting there.

"Okay... okay..." I search my room for my hairbrush. Tipping my head, I give my red locks a vigorous back comb. When I flip my head back, my hair is wild and messy, but when I add a jewelled clip, it looks more like the girls in the magazine.

"Makeup," I mutter to myself. I've no idea. I've never so much as used lipstick, never mind anything else. I flick through the magazine to the beauty page. The tutorial is called 'TEEN TIPS FOR AN EYE-POPPING LOOK' and I have none of the things I need.... but mum does.

Back in her room, I find mascara, eyeliner, blusher and lip-gloss – these will have to do. I'm not bothering with eyeshadow.

After a couple of failed attempts and restarts, I check the mirror for the final time. My eyes actually look fantastic. Lined in black kohl pencil and several layers of mascara, the emphasized blue stares back at me. I'm looking more and more like the girl in the picture.

Finally, I root through my mum's shoe collection. Luckily, we're the same size so there's a good chance I'll find something. At the very back of the wardrobe is a pair of high-heeled black patent court shoes. Slipping them on, I open the closet door to its widest for a look in the full-length mirror...

"WOW!" I never knew I could look like this. I'm really pleased with the result. I might not be as slim or as pretty as Leoni and her gang, but I don't look like a complete loser. In fact, I should fit right in.

Enamoured by the new me, I decide there and then never to retreat to the dowdy unfashionable fifteen-year-old. From now on, I will aim for a more sophisticated look.

Nodding once, before I can change my mind, I grab my keys, my shoulder bag containing the card and present I've bought for Leoni, and scoot out of the door. The sun is shining. I'm feeling a million dollars and I'm going to a party.

Leoni and her family live in a really posh area of town. The houses here are private and detached with manicured lawns and expensive cars on the drive. Leoni's house is actually one of the smaller ones but it's still twice the size of our council house.

I walk up to the front door and ring the bell, hearing the Westminster chime inside the house announcing my arrival.

A few seconds later, and I see a tall, broad, shadow approach the door. The sound of laughter, and music is amplified as the door opens, revealing ...

OMG!

... Bobby Price, the most popular boy in the sixth form is standing before me with a huge grin on his face. "Fuck me!" his eyes widen at the sight of me. "If it isn't Meredith Sykes; you scrub up well," he says enthusiastically.

"Guys, Meredith's here," he calls over his shoulder, not taking his eyes off me. "You'd better come in." He smirks, opening the door wider to let me through.

"Th... th... thanks." I mumble shyly. Why did it have to be Bobby Price of all people? What's he doing here anyway? I didn't know boys were invited!

"Oh my God!" Leoni and three of her girlfriends are in the living room, scantily dressed and dancing with bottles in their hands. They look smashed out of their heads. "What the fuck have you come as?" she shrieks, then cackles loudly. Staggering on her platforms she reels into her best friend, Gail, who screeches a high-pitched drunken squeal that sounds like a pig being poked with a stick.

"Oh, my, God... ohmygod, ohmygod!" Her eyes roam all over my outfit. "Where did you get that?"

"Ummm," I blush profusely, wanting the ground to open up and swallow me whole, wishing for all the world, I'd never come.

"Hey, hey, bitches..." Bobby grins and places his arm around my shoulder in a protective manner. "Now, now... I think she looks cool." He smells strongly of booze and now I notice it, it's hard to ignore. Everyone in here is absolutely plastered. I don't feel at all comfortable.

"Mate," another male voice joins the others, "get her a drink, she looks like she needs one." Kevin Kearney, Bobby's mate and Leonie's boyfriend has just entered from the kitchen carrying a bottle of vodka. "Give her some of this, it should wipe the look of horror off her face... cheer up Meredith, it might never happen; Bobby wanted Leoni to invite you. You've caught his attention... though, now I see you dressed up... I can see why," he leers. "Nice tits!"

"HEY!!" Leoni, affronted that the attention has momentarily been stolen away from her, scowls at me meanly, then flings her arms around Kevin and commences to suck on his face like a limpet.

This is horrible. I'm so self-conscious and out of place. I shouldn't have come. I want to leave, but I'm afraid it would make things even worse than before.

Oh, to Hell with it. Reaching into my bag I remove the card and small package containing the beaded bracelet and extricate myself from beneath Bobby's arm. "I only came to bring you these," I mutter, placing the card and box on the marble coffee table beside the empty glasses, cigarette butts and crisp crumbs. "Happy Birthday, Leoni," I mutter. "I need to go... my...er... mum has arranged a family dinner," I lie unconvincingly.

"Thanks," Leoni says, barely noticing the gifts.

"Okay, then... bye." I turn to leave, but my way is blocked by Bobby Price.

"Hey, don't mind them. They're pissed. Look, come and have a drink. We can find somewhere quieter to ... talk."

He rewraps his arm over my shoulder and my stomach flips. He's so good looking, so popular and two years older than me. *Oh goodness!* "Err, okay..." I concede nervously.

Leaving the rest of the party behind, he steers me into the hall, taking a seat half way up the stairs and urging me to sit beside him, offers me the bottle of neat vodka "Here, have a swig, it'll take the edge off."

This I know... My dad's been 'taking the edge off' for the last ten years.

"Thanks." Hesitantly, I take the bottle and place it to my lips. Tilting it back, I screw up my eyes and swallow a huge gulp, spluttering and coughing as the harsh liquid burns my throat. "Ugh!"

"Ha, ha..." Bobby find's the whole thing hysterical. "Try again." He encourages the bottle to my lips once more, using his finger to assist the tilt to maximum effect. This time, I don't splutter, but swallow another large mouthful of the neat spirit. "Well done... that was better. Swallowed like a pro'," he says, removing the vodka from my hand and stroking my face.

Oh God!

A sudden scream and an almighty crash, followed by manic laughter erupts from the living room, startling me out of my wits. What am I doing? I should go home. This party isn't for me.

"Idiots," Bobby whispers, not lifting his gaze from my face. "Your eyes are beautiful..." he praises. "I'm so glad you came." Another loud bang and a cacophony of bellowing laughter, followed by an increase in the music volume, splits the moment as Madonna's *'Like a Virgin'* blares from the lounge.

"It's your song Meredith," Leoni roars from the other room. *"Like a Virgin... touched for the very first time,"* she sings loudly. "You need to go and get fucked, you boring, ugly, fat cow..." The bitter nastiness permeates the whole ground floor.

"I should go." I make to stand, but the small amount of alcohol I've consumed, affects my legs and I stumble, almost tripping down the stairs.

"Woah, steady there." Bobby, makes a last-minute soccer save, preventing me from tumbling head first. "Look, you can't go home like this... come up stairs and I'll make you a coffee. This lot can go screw themselves. Don't listen to them. You look amazing."

Unable to resist, I allow him to support me up the last few steps and across the spacious landing and into a massive bedroom.

"Sit here." I'm guided to the vast bed. "Are you okay?"

He's so kind. I never realized before. I'd only admired him from afar, but he's really nice.

"Yes, thank you," I slur. "I'm okay." My voice sounds weird and distorted to my ears.

Bobby sits beside me on the bed, his arm once again snaking around my shoulder. "Relax, you'll be fine," he says calmly.

I look into his eyes; my vision blurs and I squint in an attempt to focus on his face. It's a challenge.

"Lie back, you look like you could do with a rest."

I feel myself lowering to the soft duvet, my head lands on the pillow and instinctively I close my eyes. "Mmm." That's nice. My head is swimming.

All of a sudden, his mouth is on mine, kissing me. It's hard and uncomfortable and I don't like it. I try to move my head away to release my lips, but I'm stuck in a headlock, his hand on my throat holding me down.

"Shhh, easy now…" he grates against my lips. "Don't fight, you'll enjoy it more."

Suddenly I'm gripped by fear as one hand is thrust roughly up my skirt, tugging at my underwear while the other presses down on my throat; I can't breathe.

"Ssstoppp..." I rasp, terrified and try to push him off, but he's ridiculously heavy and I'm suddenly groggy and weak.

"Oh no you don't... I know what you want and you're getting it right now." His voice has changed from a soothing balm to a harsh guttural growl. "Let's just... turn... you... over." He strains with the effort of flipping my inert body onto my stomach. "That's better... now let's see if we can make this happen."

"N...N..." Try as I might I'm unable to form a coherent sentence. And even more frightening, I can't move. The harder I resist, the more sluggish I feel. My limbs are leaden, my head is spinning. "Ssss...t..o..., plsss…" My words won't come out properly.

"Hughh!" Spreading my legs with his knees and pressing his chest into my back so I'm unable to struggle, he yells in triumph as he forces his way inside and an unholy pain like nothing I've ever felt, attacks me. "FUCK!" he shouts, *"Hughh, hughh, hughh!"* He

10

thrusts violently, over and over again, clutching onto my hair viciously and pressing my face into the unyielding mattress on every juddering, pummelling blow. My insides are on fire with pain and my head spins with humiliation and fear. I'm terrified. This can't be happening to me. Instinctively, I freeze.

Lying limply, with no fight left, tears fill my eyes and I stare unfocussed at the expensive wallpaper. I'm entirely numb. Sensing only the rocking, the lurching movement of my body against the bed, the impaling spear of penetration and the enduring, driving rhythm of him as he forces himself into my unyielding body. I'm powerless.

Eventually, I hear him make a groaning guttural exhale and he rolls off me, leaving me prone on my front.

"Get up," he commands harshly, his voice no longer kind and soothing. "There... you got it."

When I make no attempt to move, he slaps my backside hard. "I said, fucking get up you stupid *cunt!"* Viciously he hisses through clenched teeth, "NOW! Meredith."

Numbly, without any emotion, I slide off the bed onto my knees, patting around me for my underwear. When I eventually do find it, it's in ribboned tatters. Shredded.

For some reason, he finds this amusing. "You'll have to manage bare arsed..." he laughs, zipping his fly and brushing his fingers through his hair. "When we get downstairs... you keep quiet... do you understand me?" Grabbing my upper arm, he hauls me to my shaky feet.

Sickened, dazed and stumbling in my mum's shoes, feeling violated, I trip and stagger on wobbly legs down the stairs. He drags me into the lounge for all to see. "Here she is..." he announces triumphantly to the room. "You can stop playing that song now... it's done."

All the people, stare at me in shock. There's a beat of about a second, then everyone erupts in laughter, jeering and hollering in glee at my dishevelled state.

"Now," Bobby turns me and leads me into the hall. "You be on your way. You wouldn't want to be late for the 'family dinner' would you?" Opening the front door, he pushes me outside where I stand numbly on the step. "Off you pop! I'll call you tomorrow. Be ready." And he slams the door behind me.

Kicking off my mum's shoes, I start to run. I don't look back; desperate to get home, to get away, to put distance between me and what just happened.

Tomorrow... He'll call tomorrow... Oh God! This isn't happening to me...

11

CHAPTER 1

Edi - Present day

The headlights in the rear-view mirror are blinding. My eyesight is blurred from the river of scalding tears that won't stop tumbling from my weeping eyes. I've cried more in the past couple of days than I have in the last – God knows how many years?... It's a lot anyway – more than seventeen; and now I can't seem to stop the relentless flow.

Harshly, I snatch at the button for the car radio… I don't want to listen to that song. *'Two Beds and a Coffee Machine'* – the irony is too much… and the significance too painful, so I switch it off in favour of the silence of the night-time streets.

I have no plan; no destination in mind and no idea what I'm doing. I only know I need to get away and put some distance between me and the horrendous revelations of yesterday, before I physically break down.

The recent chain of events brought me to the edge of my sanity, once more. The primal fear, triggered the primitive part of my brain into fight-or-flight mode. Flight won, and I'm running… again!

Ahead, the traffic lights are changing from amber to red. I consider jumping them, but sensibility makes itself known, and I slow my car. While I wait at the stop light, I pull a tissue from my pocket and wipe my eyes. They're sore from all the tears.

In the rear-view mirror, I see a fast-approaching vehicle. There's no siren, but that doesn't mean it isn't a police car. I watch as it careers towards me at a ridiculous speed. Gripping my steering wheel on reflex, I brace myself ready for the scream of the engine as it hurtles past me and through the red light.

As it gets closer, there's no sign of it slowing down. It must be an emergency vehicle, even without the blues-and-twos. I'm about to pull my car over and out of the way to let it through, when, as it careers by, the driver slams on his brakes. The tyres screech in protest as he negotiates a perfect handbrake turn. Sliding sideways across the lanes, spinning in the road, before thudding to an abrupt stop right in front of me. I yelp in fright, as I watch the now stationery vehicle rock and roll on its suspension with the sheer momentum of the maniacal manoeuvre.

I'm blocked in. I sit gripping my steering wheel so tightly my knuckles turn white. I can't drive forwards and I can't circle round it. The only option is to reverse but my hands and feet won't work. The lights change to green, and I don't move. I just sit, staring as the driver's door of the old Range Rover swings open and a very angry looking Silas unfolds from behind the wheel.

"WHERE THE *FUCK* DO YOU THINK YOU'RE GOING?" he yells, as he strides over to my car, yanking the driver's door open in unrestrained fury. "I asked you a *fucking* question."

"I… I… don't know…" I stammer, my voice is small and weak from all the crying.

"Out of the car…" Opening the door to its full extent, he makes to take hold of my arm, but I recoil. He's so angry, he's scaring me. "Edi… I said, get out of the car."

"NO!"

"Edi, please... Honey-bee. His voice has softened considerably but there's a trace of something in his face... fear?... concern? I'm not sure which.

"I... I... Oh Silas!" I wail, covering my face with my trembling hands; I don't know what I think; I don't know what I'm trying to say...

I feel him lower, crouching beside me, so his head is level with my own. Resting one hand on my thigh, he gently peels my hands away from my streaming eyes with the other.

"Edi, baby..." His voice is soothing and soft, almost a whisper. "Baby... please look at me."

I blink, bringing his beautiful face into vision. One look at him and my brain is immediately attacked with a swathe of recent memories; good memories; erotic memories.

"Why?" he whispers.

"We need to get off the road." The night-time traffic is light, but I'm aware that the traffic signal has changed twice since we've been here and several vehicles have swerved to get around us.

"Not until you tell me why you're running?"

"It's... I'm..." But I have nothing. The true answer is, there's not just one single reason.

"Tell, me. Is it me? Is it the Job? Christina? What is it? Tell me, Edi, please!" He remains squatting beside the open driver's door of the car. The lights have changed again and the traffic has built up while we've been blocking the road.

"No, it's not you, or Christina, or the job... All of those things are great... It's just... *Oh God!*" I wail as the uncontainable tears well in my eyes. Of course, it isn't him... how could he think that... My voice breaks with emotion. "Silas, I can't cope with all the publicity... It'll ruin you and I can't be responsible for that. I should just go..."

"Edi, please... Don't give up on us... Don't give up on me!" Anxiously, he looks around him at the building traffic. "You're right, we need to get off the road." Before I can protest, he's pulled me out of my car, slammed the door and, sweeping me up in his arms, carries me to where his own car is blocking the road.

Dropping me into the passenger seat without a word, he makes quick work of strapping me in before jogging round to the driver's side and climbing behind the wheel. "I'm not letting you go." Turning to face me, he traces the line of my tears with his finger. "I can't let you go... Not now. Not now I've found you." His sincerity is heart-breaking. "We'll get through this. There has to be a way..."

"Oh, Silas... I don't know what to do. Help me..." I collapse forward, weeping into his arms; my tears are an unrelenting flood, soaking his shirt; they just flow and flow. Years of repressed, pent up, emotions are pouring out of me, overflowing in a torrent of scalding unstoppable sobbing.

Silas holds on to me as if my life depends on it. Supporting me, allowing me to release all of the hurt and pain that has been buried so deeply I'd forgotten it was even there. "I've got you. Honey-bee... I've got you. It's okay, let it all go, let it out..."

I'm trembling. My whole system is flooded with adrenaline following my fit of hysterics, and I'm shivering uncontrollably. My leg bounces, as my shattered nerves twitch and tense. But, at last, I've stopped sobbing. Silas is still holding me tightly against his

13

warm body. I don't want him to ever let me go. "How do you feel now?" he asks, unmoving.

"Exhausted…!" I answer, truthfully. I do, I feel completely wrung dry, like an old dish cloth.

"I bet you are." Kissing the top of my head, I feel him shift slightly in his seat. "It's late. Can I take you back now?"

"Yes." The exhaustion is turning in to catatonia. I need to sleep, to drown in oblivion.

Silas twists beneath me, and I feel the brush of wool, as I'm swathed in a blanket. It smells doggy, but it's warm so I'm comforted. "We've not got too far to go… this will do until we get you home. You're shivering." Silas shifts in his seat. "I won't be a minute; I'll just move your car." My eyes close as the door creaks and then clunks shut.

Within seconds he's back. My bag is thrown onto the back seat and he pockets my car keys. By the time he engages the engine, I'm almost unconscious. "Your car will be okay until morning – I need to get you home."

The last thing I remember is the rumble of the car engine as we drive away.

CHAPTER 2

The horrors of yesterday slam violently into my waking brain as I turn over in the sumptuous bed. After Silas brought me home, completely withdrawn and frozen from shock, all I could do was climb beneath the bedclothes and bury my head in the pillow.

I'm not normally a crier, but I couldn't stem the unyielding flow of scalding tears as they streamed from my eyes. I had to let it out, so I did. My thoughts were scattered, my nerves frayed and my wits destroyed. I couldn't hold it together anymore so I succumbed to the numbness of oblivion. I crashed and burned and cried myself into a fitful sleep. Now it's tomorrow, and I need to decide what steps I'm going to take to get through this proverbial shitstorm.

My throat is parched. I need water. That seems like a simple task to get me moving, so I pull off the duvet and swing my legs out of the bed.

It's sunny, the drapes are open but the blinds are drawn. I don't remember doing it, someone else must have been here.

The time on the bedside clock says ten-thirty. I've slept for over fifteen hours. There's a glass of red juice on the bedside table next to the clock. It still has a cube of ice in it so it hasn't been there very long. I pick up the glass and take a long pull on the juice; Cranberry and orange. It's ice cold and refreshing. Draining the glass, I place it back on the table before making my way to the en-suite bathroom.

The sight which greets me as I walk in, is frightening. Gazing at my reflection in the mirror, I barely recognise myself. I look as bad as I feel. And I feel about ninety! My hair is plastered to my head. My eyes and face are puffy from all the crying and there are livid red splodges on my neck and throat. A stress rash. I feel and look hideous.

Stripping out of my tee-shirt, I drop it into the wash-basket before turning on the shower. While the shower is heating, I perch on the loo, head in hands and I try to make sense of my life as it stands this morning. It's impossible. My brain won't work.

I pat myself dry, flush the toilet and collapse into the shower. Perhaps a dousing of hot water will help. Reaching up, I turn the jets on to pulse and flick the power switch to maximum. The high-pressure water pummels my skin but it isn't quite doing the trick just yet, so I raise the temperature so it's as hot as I can stand without flaying my skin off.

Gradually, I feel myself coming back to life. Grabbing the natural sponge, I squeeze on some gel. As I soap my body, the evocative perfume of Tudor Roses and Jasmine permeate the air, mixing with the steam and reminding me of a certain someone, who, most likely, will probably never want to have anything to do with me again.

Slamming the shower off, I climb out. Swathing my hair in a towel, I grab my robe from the hook on the bathroom door and stroll back into the bedroom. Someone has been in, because there is a steaming mug of tea waiting for me on the dressing table.

Flopping my leaden body onto the chair, I heave a sigh as I pick up my moisturiser and daub my face and blotchy neck with face cream. A peripheral movement catches the corner of my eye and I turn to find Christina standing in the doorway, relaxing against the jamb.

15

Dressed casually in jeans and a white tee-shirt; slender arms folded beneath her pert bosom and her expression surprisingly benign she asks, "how are you feeling?"

"What, mentally or physically?" I croak as I fling the hair towel onto the floor.

Treating it as an invitation, she takes a couple of strides into the room and scoops it up. Folding it over her arm, she gives me an appraising look. "Both."

"Well, let me see... Physically, I can't grumble. I'm aching a bit and I have the headache of all headaches but I think I'll live. Mentally... I think I'm a basket case; thanks for asking." I drag a comb through my knotted hair. Maybe inflicting some pain will help.

"Oh dear... Like that is it?" She wanders further into the room and sits down behind me on the bed. Crossing one long lean leg over the other, she stares at me through the mirror.

"Aren't you supposed to be at work?" I ask. I sound sarcastic, ungrateful.

"Day off."

"Humph," I puff in response. "And you got lumbered with babysitting duty?"

"If you like." She's not giving anything away and I wonder if she's here out of concern or because she's been asked to do this.

"How come you have a day off anyway? Aren't you busy with organizing the Gala and all that?" I don't want to discuss the events of yesterday so I'm trying to steer the conversation towards the mundane.

"Worked the weekend... I'm owed a few hours." Her eyes rove over me in assessment.

Swivelling in my seat, I turn so that I'm facing her. "What are you really doing here, Christina?" I may as well ask.

"Silas had a flight chartered for this morning. He couldn't stay so he asked if I would come and keep you company." She sounds matter of fact, as if this is the most normal thing in the world.

"Keep me company? Check up on me, more like!" I wonder what he told her about my meltdown and failed escape effort last night. Picking up the hairdryer and turning to the mirror, I hold her gaze in the reflection.

"He was worried, that's all."

"About what?" I flick the dryer on and tip my head forward, effectively drowning out her response. I don't think I want to know.

The hairdryer is removed from my hand and switched off. She stands beside me like a gunslinger brandishing a six-shooter. "Now you just listen to me Madam... I'm here because we care about you. I care about you. You had a massive shock yesterday. And when he realised, you'd left without so much as a goodbye note Silas was beside himself. He said you were practically catatonic by the time he got you home. He put you to bed but you were completely unresponsive. *Obviously*, he's worried!" Now I've made her mad.

"That was nice of him," I spit. I don't know why I'm being so belligerent, I agreed to come back, didn't I?

"For fuck's sake Edi!" She squats beside my stool, placing the hairdryer on the floor at her feet. "If you want to implode, do it on your own time. That's your prerogative, but at the moment, you're our employee and as such we have a duty of care to ensure your safety." She's sincerer and it makes me ashamed of my earlier rudeness. "Silas was

16

worried. *Christ, I* was worried. Don't you get it. *We...*" she points to her chest, gesticulating between herself and an invisible Silas "were worried. *God...* yesterday was fucking *horrendous*. I can't imagine what you must be experiencing. Can't you just accept we're here to help you through this, not judge you for it?" Yes, she's sincere, but she's also incredibly angry.

"I... but... Oh, I don't know. My head's all over the place. Oh Christina, what am I going to do? I can't get you and Silas mixed up in my shit. It's not fair." I swivel to face her. She takes hold of my hands in hers.

Mine are cold but hers are warm and comforting. She smiles at me. "Edi, you're not on your own anymore. Your shit is our shit! The minute that ex of mine set his sights on you, it was game over... He's an arrogant, single-minded bastard, but his heart is good. I could see it in his face the moment you both met. I've never seen him react like that before and I was married to the man!"

"Christina..." I don't know what to say. His heart *is* good, and kind, and strong and he asked me not to give up on him... *us!*

"C'mon you. My legs are cramping and I need a coffee. Finnish drying your hair and we can go and sit outside. As my old mum used to say, *'all this moping isn't getting the baby washed'*. I'll go and brew up; *you* get yourself dressed." Groaning with the effort, she stands from her crouched position. Her knee joints crack like starting pistols in protest. "God, I'm old," she sighs as she walks out.

I follow her trim physique with my eyes until she's out of view. I remember my gran saying exactly the same thing. She's right. This moping is getting me nowhere fast and I need to shake it off. Picking up the hairdryer, I flip my head forward and recommence drying my hair.

17

Needing comfort, I dress in an old oversized navy hoody and black leggings. Wandering out of the bedroom, the aroma of freshly brewed coffee hits my nose causing my mouth to water and my stomach to grumble.

Christina is striding out of the kitchen with a tray loaded down with mugs, milk sugar, croissants and a large cafetière full to the brim with dark, freshly brewed coffee.

"Ah, you look better. Let's go outside. It's nice and warm. It would be a pity to waste the sunshine, don't you think?"

"Hmmm, yeah, I suppose." I follow dutifully in her wake. She stops at the patio doors, allowing me to take the lead and flick them open before pushing outside and into the brightness of the late summer morning.

The golden sun *is* warm. The balcony is south-facing so it's bathed in sunlight for most of the day. I can feel the heat radiating off the tiles and through the soles of my socks.

Christina unloads the contents onto the glass coffee table before taking the empty tray back inside. When she returns, she's carrying a cut-glass ashtray and a packet of cigarettes. This is a development. I didn't know she was a smoker.

"Don't judge me," she says, plonking down on one of the comfy sofas. "I don't smoke much, but I find that in times of crisis, it helps with my creative thinking; gets the grey cells working and juices flowing, you know? Anyway, a girl can't live on coffee and fresh air alone! I need nicotine to help keep my girlish figure."

Lighting up, she takes a deep inhale before letting it go on a contented sigh. I'm shocked. She seems so... healthy. I feel like I've caught her getting up to no good. I'm surprised she's a smoker. It looks totally wrong on her. She doesn't seem the type. Then again, I've learned little about Christina, other than she swears like a trooper, has power-dressing down to a tee, looks like a super model and is a seriously ruthless business woman! Most of my time has been occupied with learning about Silas!

"Silas hates me smoking." She puffs out another stream of smoke, taking care to aim it away from me. "Shall I be mother?" Leaning forward, she places her manicured hand over the plunger and forces it down the inside of the cafetière. "It was always a bone of contention when we were married. Do you want milk and sugar?"

"Err, yes, both please."

"It's none of his business now, anyway. He can either learn to deal with it or he can lump it."

"Christina, how long were you married?" I don't want to intrude, but have no idea.

"Seven years. Dominic was five when we split." She looks thoughtful and I can't hide my look of surprise. Nic's twenty-two now so they've been divorced a while.

"Surprised huh? Silas didn't mention it then?" She speaks around the cigarette, holding it between her lips as she uses both hands to faff about with the stuff on the tray. A practiced smoker.

"I have to say Edi, I was surprised when it came out who you really were. Silas rang me on Saturday night... or the early hours of Sunday; either way, it was when you were in Paris. He got his knickers in a right old twist over it. Cute really." She pours the coffee and adds a splash of milk and a couple of lumps of sugar. I might need something stronger at this rate!

"Did he?" Of course, he did. That's why he took me back to my own room. He needed to speak to her.

"Yes, he was quite... how can I put it... agitated." Making herself comfortable, she reclines, crossing her long legs, leaning against the cushions. Puffing out another lingering cloud of vapor, she flicks the ash from her cigarette into the glass ashtray beside her. "He said you'd *done the deed* and that he didn't know how he felt about it. I think he was doubting himself. You know... after realizing who you were. He wasn't sure if he was bedding the woman of his dreams or the schoolboy fantasy." God, how mortifying, she's being very candid. If there's one thing I've learned about Christina, it's that she calls a spade a spade; often, and with honest brutality.

"What did you tell him?" This I need to know. If she continues with the honesty is the best policy malarkey, she should spill the beans no problem.

"I told him he was being an idiot. Let's face it, he's not a sixteen-year-old boy with raging hormones. He's a forty-three-year-old man... with raging hormones!" she adds on a wry laugh, blowing out more smoke. "I told him to grow up and smell the coffee. If he wanted you, it was because of who you are now, not who you used to be."

"And what did he say?"

"What could he say? He'd already made the decision on Wednesday; he was taking you to Paris. As I said, the deal was done... no brainer really. The rest speaks for its self, doesn't it? He wants you... not the Unicorn." I look at her totally lost. "I mean to say, it's you - the real you, who he desires. Not some mythical, unattainable, fantasy creature from the pages of history... *you*!" She emphasizes the point by jabbing her finger at my face. "The burning question is, do you want him?" Her voice has toned down as she scrutinizes my face closely.

"Yes," I whisper. I do. I really want him. He's under my skin and in my heart. "Who wouldn't want him?" Well... Christina for one.

Ignoring my quip, she stubs out her cigarette, grinding it into the ashtray before taking another out of the pack. I thought she said she wasn't much of a smoker?

"I knew it... but I had to hear it from you. I feel like Marjory Proops! I'm pleased at least one problem's sorted." She leans back, making herself comfortable. "Have a croissant. They're nice and warm." She gestures to the golden pastries. My stomach growls. I'm hungry. "I'm going to smoke my cig and have a think. You relax and eat that. It'll do you the world of good."

"Are you not having one?" I ask as I take the soft flaky treat from the plate.

"I told you. Coffee and fresh air." She hikes the coffee in one hand and wafts the cigarette in the other, indicating her preferred choice of breakfast.

"Okay." I sip my coffee and watch, mesmerised, as the creative wheels start to turn. I can almost hear the gears shifting. The croissant is delicious and the coffee exactly how I like it and with the sun warming my face I relax into the spongy cushions.

I think I must have dozed off, because I jerk awake at the sound of coffee cups clinking.

19

"Welcome back." She says as she loads up the tray. "You were right out of it there for a minute or two."

"Sorry. I can't seem to snap out of it." This feeling of exhaustion won't shift.

"No worries. It's the shockwave." She gives me an understanding smile. "While you've been away with the fairies, I've been thinking about your immediate problem and I have a couple of ideas that might help." She picks up the tray and heads inside. Calling over her shoulder she raises her voice so I can hear her. "I'm having a glass of wine. Do you want one?"

"Isn't it a bit early?" Checking my watch, I've been snoozing for longer than I thought; It's gone 1:30 p.m.

"It's seven o'clock somewhere," she calls "and anyway, I think we deserve it." She fetches two flutes and a bottle of Prosecco. "Will this do? There's not much choice in there."

"Yeah... lovely... thanks." I take the flute from her hand.

"To 'nutty glitches.' Now, let's shake this bugger down." She clinks her glass against mine. If I didn't know better, I'd bet she was getting a kick out of all this.

"To 'nutty glitches'," I repeat without conviction.

"Okay, it seems to me that there are about five individual issues here." She has a pad and pencil, as if she's outlining a business proposition. "It will make it easier if we list the subjects separately, then come up with an individual solution for each one." I notice she doesn't use the word *problem*.

"The first is undoubtedly the press. I know they can be intrusive bastards, but we need to find a way to work that to our advantage. The second is the children. Both yours and mine I hasten to add. That's a stickier subject, probably best left until later. Then there's the matter of your ex-husband, wherever he is." I go cold at the mention of Bobby...I know where he is. I just don't have the balls to tell her.

"Then there's Silas and the business and me." She itemises all the concerns on her fingers as if they are no more problematic than a Christmas shopping list.

I sit, dumbstruck. Laid out in front of me are all of my worst nightmares. I feel the colour drain from my face; I shouldn't have eaten that croissant.

"Well, what are your thoughts?" she asks, lighting up yet another cigarette.

"I... I... think the North Pole is looking very inviting right now!" I almost mean it too.

"Lord... Dramatic much?" She huffs at me, rolling her eyes in exaggeration.

"Well, I don't know. All I do know is, I've got you into this mess and I need to fix it. At the moment, running away seems the easiest solution for everyone."

"For fuck's, sake Edi!" She spits in annoyance. "Scarpering like Joe Buggery every time there's a slight bump in the road isn't going to help." *A slight bump?* "This is *not* going away. If you run, it will follow and eventually catch up with you again. And once that happens, the consequences will be all the more disastrous. You need to face up to this like the strong, sensible woman that you are. The question is how to do that with the minimal damage to you and your family... and to us for that matter. Anyway, Silas won't allow that... he proved it last night, didn't he? Come on... think."

But I can't think. When I do, I just remember the photos in the paper of me and Silas. Against the tree. On the leafy ground. In the window of his bedroom. And not to mention all the back catalogue of ancient images that could reappear at any time. How can I turn that to my advantage?

I'm jolted from my thoughts when I hear a phone ringing in the lounge. It's my private mobile. The ringtone sounds light and chirpy, completely out of character with my mood.

"I need to get that. It might be Lizzy or David." Christina nods in understanding as I head off to find my phone. I locate it on the kitchen worktop plugged into the charger socket. It's still ringing when I pick it up. Caller ID says it's *The Beeches.* "Hello?" I answer warily.

"Edi, hi, it's Mark." He sounds a bit flustered and nervous.

"Oh, hi Mark. Is everything okay?" I can tell it isn't from the sound of his breathing.

"The papers arrived," he blurts, then goes silent.

"Ah." I rub my forehead with my palm. My headache is back with a vengeance.

"Edi, I'm really sorry. I didn't expect it to be so… candid. I can't believe they printed that stuff." He's speaking in a hushed tone. I expect he doesn't want to be overheard. "If it's any consolation, I wouldn't have recognized you if you hadn't warned me. The pictures aren't very clear."

"Thank you, Mark… but I think they're clear enough. You didn't let the residents see them, did you?" Oh lord, I hope not! My rising panic is clear in my voice.

"No, gosh no… that's what I'm phoning about. The residents have no clue as to what's going on. But I've just had a call from Mr. Prestage – Wendy's dad."

I outwardly groan. "Nooo, oh God, what did he want?" Although I could guess.

"Edi, it's not as bad as you think. He thought the photo's looked familiar, is all. When the penny dropped, he rang to ask me if it was you. I couldn't deny it could I? If it all comes out in the wash, he'll know I was lying and then I'd lose my job." *Fuck, this is bad…* I hadn't even considered the position I was putting Mark in.

"But Edi, he was okay, surprisingly. I think deep down he was quite chuffed about it, 'though he did ask me not to mention it to Mrs. P." *I bet he did!* "Edi, I just wanted to let you know that everything is quiet here at the moment. Nobody has phoned and there aren't any signs of snooping paps. I'll keep my eyes peeled and I'll make certain that Mr. P is on-side. I have a good feeling that he'll be an ally in all of this."

I'm not so sure, but I have to trust someone and Mark has always proved reliable in the past. He really does care about his residents. I give him the benefit of the doubt. "Well… if you're sure Mark. Just keep me updated. How are the boys and Wendy?"

"They're fine. Playing Jenga in the lounge, actually. Do you want to speak to David?"

"No, no. Not today." I know it sounds callous, but I couldn't feign the enthusiasm right now and David would see right through me. "We're supposed to be going to the pub on Friday, but that might have to change if this escalates," which I strongly suspect it might. "I'll call you."

"Okay. Be safe, and don't worry too much. I think this will blow over; you know." I wish I had half his optimism.

21

"Bye, Mark." I hang up and traipse back out to Christina. "That was Mark from the Beeches." Her eyebrows raise in question. "They're okay. No major dramas. One of the parents recognised me in the papers and has been on the phone asking awkward questions. Mark reckons he could be an ally." I shrug my shoulders, not entirely convinced I believe it myself now that I've said it out loud. "The boys are fine," I affirm.

"Lord, this thing is growing like wildfire. We need to find a way of dousing the flames before the whole lot burns down." That has to be the understatement of the year!

I sit beside her on the couch; thinking. Trying to come up with some solution. Then I remember the Gala evening she's planning and wonder if we can use it as a way to get the press on our side. "Christina?"

"Hmmm."

"How do you think it would pan out, if you invited a couple of 'friendly' reporters to the Gala?" It'll go one of two ways...our way, or it could be a huge disaster.

"I was just thinking about that. But the problem is, it isn't for another week or so. We need to do something beforehand, to calm the situation. Then we could use the Gala to fully turn it to our advantage." Her brow furrows. I can tell she's working through all the possibilities of how we can engage the press. She turns to me; a fiendish glint is twinkling in her eye. What's she thinking?

"How would you feel about giving an interview?" *WHAT! No way!* My face must be a picture because, holding up her hands, she shows me her palms. "No... no, wait... just hear me out before you chew my ear off. Think about it. We could invite a pet journalist to the airfield. Give them an exclusive. You can tell your story from your point of view. Just give them enough." She indicates how little by pinching together her thumb and forefinger. The gap she leaves between them is miniscule. I really don't understand, and it must show in my expression.

"Christina... I'm really n..." I don't get to finish.

"No, listen for a moment... What do these turds with cameras want more than anything in the world?"

I don't even need to think about that. "Me... on a plate... preferably naked," is my sarcastic answer.

"Well, why don't you give it to them then?"

Is she on crack?

"*What!*... Oh... no... if you think I'm doing that again you've got another thing coming!" I stand, ready to bolt from the balcony and out the door.

"Sit down and listen... I don't mean that you should strip naked and let them take your picture." She pulls me back onto my seat.

"Too late for that now," I huff sarcastically, perching on the end of the sofa, still ready to do a bunk if needs be. She ignores me.

"How do you deal with a bully?" Her question flummoxes me – where's she going with this tangent? "You give them no ammunition, that's how. You agree with them. You confuse them. You give them nowhere to go." I still don't get it. She sighs, in exasperation.

"You control the interview. *You* contact *them*. Do it on your terms. On your territory. You call the shots; make damn sure you have absolute control over everything they print. Hell, I'll write the bloody contract myself for that matter! You just need to tell the truth.

What they want to hear. Yes, you ran. Yes, you built a new life. Yes, you have a new lover... what of it? Turn the tables on them. Turn their story into a non-story. Once it becomes nothing, the public will lose interest as quickly as you can say knife..." Strangely, what she's proposing begins to make a modicum of sense.

"People aren't interested in the truth, they just want the juicy gossip, so you let the gossip become the truth and eventually..." she holds her hands out in expectation.

"The truth becomes gossip?" I'm still not getting it.

"No, it becomes uninteresting, a dud, boring... in other words, it goes away." She looks as if she's found the solution to world hunger!

"Oh... I don't know Christina." It sounds risky. "What about Silas and the children? How do I skirt around that?"

"You don't... It's that simple. Just say, 'yes, I have two children'. End of. Just say, 'yes, I have a new man in my life'. Period. Give them nowhere to go."

"And what happens when they want a photo of my children?"

"Don't agree to it. Threaten to sue them. In fact, offer them one of you and Silas. You know, posed... boring!" She makes it sound so simple.

"I need to think about this... I need to speak to Silas about it."

"Well, don't take too long. The longer you leave it the closer the circling vultures will get." She picks up the empty glasses and takes them inside, leaving me alone on the balcony with my troubled thoughts.

Could it work? One interview to clear the air and lay all the demons to rest? Oh, Silas, where are you when I need you.

CHAPTER 4

Christina leaves at about four in the afternoon. She says she needs to do some real work before she turns in. I expect she'll be burning the midnight oil again.

I make myself a cup of tea and put a pan of pasta on the stove to cook. I'm reverting back to my student comfort food. Tuna pasta bake should do it.

"Anybody home?" I didn't hear the door, but it's lovely to hear Silas's rich voice. I realise, I was worried he might not want to see me again. I'm so relieved that he's here.

"In the kitchen," I call back. The pan with the pasta starts to boil, so I turn the heat down to a gentle simmer and set the timer as I rummage in the fridge, like Bridget Jones, for the tuna. Unlike Bridget, I locate the tuna and set about preparing the sauce for the pasta.

Silas wanders into the kitchen and drops his keys and phone onto the work top. He's still dressed in his pilot's uniform. My stomach does a flip-flop at the sight of him. He looks incredible. This must mean he's not been into the office, otherwise he would have got changed before coming here. I'd never realised uniforms were so damn sexy. But Silas just looks edible in his. I wonder if he's done it on purpose.

Wrapping his arms round me tightly from behind, he buries his face in my hair and inhales deeply. "Hmmm, you feel good. It's a relief to see you on your feet... feeling better?"

I am now... it's amazing what his touch can do to me. "Hmmm, yes, I do. Thank you for looking after me last night."

He kisses my neck. "My pleasure, Honey... I can smell cigarettes. Has Christina been smoking again?"

I lift my arm to my nose and sniff the sleeve of my hoodie. Yes, there's a faint odour of second-hand tobacco. I didn't notice it before he mentioned it.

"Ughh! I'll go and change." It smells horrid.

"No, it's okay. Let me." Tenderly, he grips the hem of my hoodie and draws it up and off my body, over my head and drops it onto the floor at my feet. I'm stood in just my leggings and white cotton bra. "That's better." He pulls me back into his arms and skates his warm hands all over my back; biting my neck, just below my ear; nipping and nibbling at the sensitive skin.

"Where's Bear?" I ask, breathlessly.

"With a sitter..." His lips quiver against my neck as he whispers his reply.

All the tiny hairs on my body lift in response to his attention. I didn't realise how much I'd missed him and how relieved I am now I'm back in his arms. A delicious thrill ripples through me in anticipation and my heartrate quickens.

His hands find the clasp of my bra and make light work of unhooking it. It lands on top of my hoodie on the floor. "Kiss me," he demands and eagerly, I comply, diving in and taking his lush lips with my own. He tastes of coffee and cinnamon. Curling my tongue under his upper lip, I start lapping at his mouth. "Mmm, now that's what I call a welcome home," he responds, gently.

Feeling his growing erection pressing into my belly, I squeeze myself closer in to him, letting him know I like what I feel. "I'm so pleased you brought me back." I stroke the back of his neck, the reach of my arms causing my chest to flatten against him, rubbing my breasts into the rough gaberdine material of his uniform jacket. "It was wrong of me to run. … I don't know what I was thinking."

He responds immediately, tracing his hands all over my skin until they land on the waist of my leggings. Looping his thumbs into the band, he scrapes them down my legs until they are at my knees. He's unable to reach further without breaking the kiss, so I take over, bending my leg and using my heels to push them all the way down so I can step out of them. Kicking them to the side, I'm now naked in his arms. My skin heats under his caress.

The oven timer starts to ping, indicating the pasta is cooked and ready for the sauce. Silas shocks me by dropping me like a hot potato. "I think my tea is nearly ready… you go and finish it while I go and change." He slaps my bare bottom and turns to stride out of the kitchen.

Stunned and bereft, I'm about to pick up my smoke tainted hoodie when he grabs it from under my nose. "Oh, no you don't… you'll stay like that, I think. Now, go and finish making my meal, Woman. I'll meet you in the dining room in ten." My chin almost hits the floor as I watch him go.

I'm careful as I drain the pasta. I don't want to splash myself with boiling water, so I find an apron in the draw and hang it round my neck. The Apron is black and has a pair of bright red lips bearing the slogan '*Kiss the chef*' written in white on the front. I tie the belt around my waist. The tails of the tie are brushing the cleft of buttocks. It feels sexy and a bit rude and gives me a wicked idea. Tipping the pasta into a colander and leaving it to drain; I've a couple of minutes to spare before I need to add the final touches.

Grinning to myself, I sneak into my bedroom to find my 'Paris' shoes. Silas must be in the shower. His uniform is laid out on the bed where he's left it and I can hear the sound of the powerful water jets coming from the en-suite.

Moving quietly, I quickly locate the shoes and take them into the kitchen to put them on. Once the laces are tied, I check my reflection in the darkened patio window. From the front I look dressed, but from behind, I look… hot! Smiling to myself, I carry on with my domestic goddess duties, aware that I'm flashing my naked arse to the world.

I ladle the penne into a tureen before pouring over the unctuous, creamy, tuna and tomato sauce. I finish by grating some fresh parmesan on top and placing the dish under the grill so it can bubble and brown.

Grabbing knives and forks and glasses, I swiftly set the dining room table with placemats and a white linen cloth I find in the sideboard. I'm just admiring my handiwork, when I hear a stifled groan from behind me. Swivelling on my stiletto heels, I turn to find a gawking Silas frozen in the doorway.

"May I help you Sir?" I ask, giving my best waitress impression. If I keep this going, I might be able to defer the awkward conversation I know must come… well, for a couple of hours at least. Besides, I feel the desire for some physical comfort.

Thankfully, he decides to play along with my party game. "Table for two please," he says gruffly. I notice he's wearing a towel round his waist. It barely hides his huge arousal, which is tenting the front of the fluffy white material.

"Please, take a seat sir." Pulling out a chair, I deliberately angle my body for full effect, ensuring he gets an eyeful of my arse as I bend, and my boobs as I lean over the table. "I'll be back shortly with your food."

Before he can grab hold of me, I twirl out of his reach and sashay out of the dining room, giving him the full-on experience of the dangling apron strings tickling my bum, and the high heeled designer C.F.M. shoes. I hear him gasp as his eyes follow me while I swing my hips seductively all the way into the kitchen.

Once I'm safely seconded, I work swiftly. Switching off the grill I use oven gloves to place the dish onto a tray, alongside a dressed salad and two plates, serving spoons and ramekin containing the rest of the grated parmesan. Carefully, I drape a pot-towel over my arm, before picking up the tray and swaying back into the dining room.

Silas is still where I left him, standing beside his chair, staring at me like he can't quite believe what he's seeing.

"Sir, please take your seat." He looks around, as if he's unsure what he should be doing. Then, he drops his arse into the chair I had pulled out earlier.

After placing my tray on the table, I unload all the contents. Before going any further, I take the remote control and aim it at the music system. The dulcet tones of Chris Isaak's *'Wicked Game'* filter through the speakers. I notch the volume down until it's at a nice, low background level. Silas nods his approval.

Replacing the remote on the table I pick up the serving spoon. Making every stretch and bend count, I twist and turn, tip and tilt; lifting my foot so he gets to see the stretch of my calf and the sole of my shoe. "Would Sir like some salad with his pasta bake?" I ask politely.

"Fuck, yeah," he growls. The sound resonates deep in his throat.

"Thank you, Sir." I take a plate and place it on the mat, in front of Silas. All the while he's eyeing me up, watching me move. I know he wants to touch, but he's restraining himself, allowing me to play out my game to the full.

Brushing in close, I tease him, as I load his plate with the food. The cheesy topping strings between the spoon and the plate as I scoop up the silky, creamy sauce. It makes a plopping sound as I drop it on to his plate; making sure as I lean over him, my apron gapes open and he has a full-frontal view, right down to my Manolo clad toes.

Reaching for the salad I slowly heap a healthy helping onto his plate. The action is like a red rag to a bull. His resolve falters completely and he can't resist the urge to touch me. His hot hand stroked my backside and down the back of my leg.

"Ah, ah, ah!" I scold, "please don't fondle the staff, Sir." I straighten, arching my back so my chest fills the apron and my pert nipples poke out from the sides. His hand drops away as I dodge out of his grasp. He groans and rolls his eyes at my audacity.

Moving quickly to the adjacent place at the table, I load up my own plate, before taking my seat beside him. He still hasn't spoken or taken his eyes off my outfit- if you can call it an outfit, that is!

"How much is this meal going to cost me," he asks picking up his cutlery. His eyes are smouldering and his lush lips are glossy; moist from where he has licked them.

"That depends on how much you enjoy it, Sir," I answer, cheekily, picking up my own knife and fork.

"Well, I might have to sample the wares later. And the staff…" he adds, suggestively. "Let's see." He takes a bite and gives an appreciative nod. "Mmm, very nice." He tucks in and so do I. If someone came in now, goodness knows what they'd think of this bizarre scene.

I decide to keep the conversation as ordinary as possible. Considering how we are dressed and the sexual tension in the air, it might be difficult.

"Did you have a good day at the office?" I ask. I place a forkful of pasta in my mouth as provocatively as I can – with pasta!

"Not too bad. Is that really what you want to talk about?" His eyes are ablaze.

"Why, what did you have in mind?" I hold his burning gaze with my own sultry one. I try to keep up the pretence, well aware I am delaying the inevitable tricky conversation about yesterday and today.

"Edi, I think you know what we need to talk about. This… game is just delaying it." He eats another forkful of pasta and salad.

"Don't you like this game?" I'm still teasing him.

"I like it... but we need to talk - about us. Don't you agree?" He finishes his last forkful and rises from the table to clear away the plates. I notice with disappointment his erection has disappeared.

"I'll help you." I leave my seat, taking the remaining empty plates and stacking them onto the tray before carrying it into the kitchen.

I'm beginning to feel a bit silly in my sexy chef's outfit. The ridiculousness of the situation is falling on me and now I just feel foolish, over exposed and self-conscious. Silas is stacking the dish washer as I lay the tray on the worktop to the side. Standing up beside me, he towers over me, even in my four-inch heels. The closeness of our bodies does what it always does and I feel the prickle of tension start to simmer again.

"I want to talk - but I also want to fuck." His voice is a deep baritone but I can hear the familiar rumble beginning in his chest as I always do when he's becoming aroused. Like a primal mating call, it sings to me and my body responds in kind. My skin heats, my breath hitches, my nipples harden to stiff bullets and a pool of hot damp moisture begins to seep at the apex of my thighs.

CHAPTER 5

"We *do* need to talk. But *I* want to fuck." I answer him. If we can just get this out of our systems, I'm sure that we will have heads clear enough to process all the things we need to discuss.

"Stand here," he indicates to the island in the middle of the kitchen. I don't hesitate. I'm filled with heat and anticipation and a desperate animal desire that needs to be quenched.

I stand with my back to the island, my hands clasped behind me. Silas approaches slowly, without any expression on his face. I notice beneath his towel, he's rigid again. I'm not sure if it's my imagination, or the white material, but he looks bigger than I've ever seen him.

"Turn around." Once again, I don't hesitate. If he wants me this way then that's okay with me. Giving him what I hope is a confident look, I slowly pivot away from him, offering him my back view. "Fuucckk!" He growls. I jump as his hands grip my hips. And for the first time with Silas, I feel the slightest ripple of trepidation. A warning light is flashing on and off in my brain and I don't quite understand why. "Bend forward and spread your legs." Once again, I follow through on his instructions; though this time a little more hesitantly. Leaning over the worktop, it's as if I'm waiting for six of the best. Is this why I feel uneasy?

There's a dull thud, and I see that he's removed his towel and dropped it onto the floor between my feet. I tense again as I feel the palm of his hand sweep across my behind. He's moving the apron ties out of the way giving himself access to my body. Once again, that nagging caution prickles at my brain. I try my best to ignore it, resting my cheek on the cool worktop. I don't say anything, I just listen to his laboured breathing waiting for his invasion.

Nothing happens for about half a minute. My nerves are really beginning to kick in now. Perhaps I'm not ready for this. Perhaps it's too soon after all the upset of yesterday, I need to call a halt before it goes too far.

I'm just about to stand up and stop him, when I feel the searing heat from both of his hands stroke up the inside of my thighs. "Keep still," he tells me as I try not to flinch at his touch. He forces my legs further apart. The tips of his fingers brush over my sex, separating my swollen lips, widening my opening. But I don't feel ready. I'm tense; and I'm not wet enough.

But the honeyed tones of his deep voice and the intuitive need that grips me at the first hint of his firm touch is confusing. It has me completely conflicted. I think I want to stop, but I've lost the power of speech. But I also want to carry on, because it's Silas, and I know I can trust him… but, even knowing it's him and it will be okay - still all the mixed-up jumbled thoughts in my head are telling me that I *must* stop this. I can't talk, my mouth has gone dry.

The warning bell has increased to a clanging claxon and I know I'm beginning to panic. Perhaps it's the position? If I could just turn around and see him maybe I would feel better. I'm so confused, I want him, but not like this.

The mixture of want and don't want are playing havoc with my mind. I barely hear him over the pounding of blood through my ears when he speaks.

"Hang on. This might hurt." The broad head of his erection pierces me. And he's right, it really hurts – I wasn't ready. Can't he tell?

Freezing, the mild panic rising in my throat has struck me dumb. But the feel of him inside me is so good that for a brief moment my desire starts to resurface. If I can concentrate, grasp it, perhaps I can go through with this after all. Shifting my feet, I attempt to relax my muscles and accept his invasion.

He must sense my unease because he stays still for a while, allowing us both to get used to the feeling. "Are you okay?" he asks.

"Hmm," I mumble, offering a hesitant nod. My breathing is ragged and I doubt if I could form a coherent word at the moment anyway. I close my eyes and focus my mind, trying with all my might to calm myself… telling myself that it's okay, it's Silas, and that I want this after all.

"I'm going deeper. Hold on Honey… here it comes." And he surges forward so harshly my hips bang into the worktop.

"N… nnnnuh!" The sudden powerful thrust takes my breath away.

"Shhh," he hushes me. I didn't realise I'd cried out. "I'm going to do that again, hold tight."

I grip the edge of the worktop as I feel him pull out. His hands are still on the inside of my thighs, holding them apart, his grip is strong and harsh. Without warning, he lifts me, using my legs as leverage, he forces me up so I'm lying face down on the cool marble.

"Oh!" I release an exclamation of shock at the unexpected shift in my position. Now my arse is at the perfect height for him. My feet are off the floor and he is forcing my legs wider.

"Now!" he yells as he slams into me from behind. I feel him collide with my womb and I can't tell if I'm experiencing pleasure or pain. All I know is, even with my conflicted state of mind, I'm desperate for him to do it again. "Fuck, you are so tight." He rears back and immediately fills me… hard. His balls slap against my exposed clitoris. Building his rhythm, he's almost violent as he pummels into me over and over.

"Aghhh, Silas," I manage as each of his powerful pounds, forces the breath out of me. "Silas, please." He doesn't hear my plea. I'm impaled to the painful hilt. Moving his hands from my legs, he grips the ties of the apron, using the belt to pull me onto him at a furious speed. "Ahh, Ummm… Sssss, it hurts!" I hiss and wail, my mind is in turmoil.

"Silas!... *No*… Stop!" He's never been this deep or this brutal. My hips are chafing on the worktop, I can feel bruises forming on the bony nubs of my hipbones. "Oww! Silas, please… Aghhh!" I'm in serious pain now, but the heat from my clit is pulsing and my stomach and insides start to quiver and dance… I'm building and I'm close and I don't know how, because now, I'm sure; I want to stop this.

"Yeah, come on Honey… I know it hurts, but when you let go, it will hurt so good!" He rams me so hard that it brings tears to my eyes.

"Silas… *No!*" It's too much. I try to get his attention, but he's lost.

Desperate for breath and release, I struggle against him, trying to push myself up, but his considerable weight is pinning me down. "Silas, please, Aghhh!" I battle the need to

29

move, but I'm beginning to panic. This doesn't feel right. I have no control and I don't like it.

"Come on Edi, now... COME!" He yells the command in my ear and like the puppet I am, I explode around him. Only this time, I don't squirt. This time, it's dry and dirty and my orgasm is over before I can register it. "Agggghh – Fuck." He follows me with his own release. His is quick, and hard and like mine, it doesn't last long and as soon as he has shot his load, he pulls out; stepping back from me as if he's been burned.

Carefully, so as not to cause my bruised body further damage, I allow myself to slide down from the work top. As soon as my feet hit the tiles I spin around, my hand flying out in anger. It connects with his face on an almighty slap.

"What the *fuck* was that?" I scream at him. "That wasn't making love. It was assault... why did you do that?" Angry, resentful tears prickle my eyes. I dash them away, not wanting him to see that his viciousness has made me cry. "I said STOP!" Doesn't he know what he just did?

"*Nooo!*" He looks appalled, stunned even. If he could pale, he would. "Edi, please... I didn't mean to hurt you." His face is ashen. I'm panting in incandescent rage. My anger is palpable. I haven't been treated like that since... well... for a long time... not since Bobby.

"What the *fuck* were you thinking?" He was like a man possessed...

"I thought... Edi... Honey... please, I don't know where that came from." He looks, mortified; disgusted with himself, sickened. And so, he should! "I would never hurt you." He reaches for me, but I snatch my arm away before he can touch me.

"Well, you did," I heave in his face. "I said *NO*, Silas!" Tugging at the ties of the apron, I struggle to undo the belt. He stares at me as if I've gone mad – I think I might have. All of the pulling and tugging has tightened the knot and I can't get it undone. My temper flares even more and I grab the scissors from the knife block.

He takes a cautious step away from me. "Don't you *ever* do that to me again." Waving the scissors at him, I scream in his face. He just stands, watching me warily as I cut through the apron strings, desperately attempting to release myself from its binding restraint. The string falls away and I drag the ruined apron over my head, flinging it on the floor at his feet. I throw the scissors onto the worktop before I'm tempted to do any further damage.

"Edi... Honey?" The fear and confusion on his face is enough to spark my guilt. I definitely gave off mixed signals, but stop means stop...no means no... surely, he understands that much?

"NO!" Waving my hands in his face I turn on my heels and high-tail it into the bedroom, slamming the door for good measure. I want him out of my sight, I can't bear to look at him.

Once inside, I slump against the door. All the breath has been knocked out of me. I can't believe that just happened! Did that just happen? I need to calm down and process this like a sensible human being.

Pushing away from the door, I pace the floor. I'm naked apart from my ridiculous shoes. I don't care, I'm furious. But I don't know if it's with myself for letting it get so rough and not having the sense to stop it sooner, or with Silas, for not realizing that I was struggling with the situation.

As I pace, I fist my hands in my hair, tugging at the strands, tangling the long tresses into knots with my fingers and yanking at my head until it's sore. "Grrrr!" I yell, flinging myself onto the bed and ripping the stupid shoes from my feet. In anger, I lob them at the bedroom door "Gaaagh". They clatter against the glossy wood and tumble to the carpet. How could I have been so stupid? How could I not have seen this coming?

"Edi?" He knocks on the door lightly. His voice is soft, reticent. "Edi, please…"

"NO!" I scream. He must think I'm an idiot.

"Edi, please let me in. We need to talk about what just happened. I could no more hurt you than rip off my own head. Please Edi, let me in."

"Silas…" I don't know what I want to say. I'm so confused right now. Did I miss something or am I being over sensitive? I pull my robe from the hanger on the back of the door and slip it on, tightening the belt into a knot… another knot!

Kicking my shoes out of the way, I can't bear to handle them at the moment, I open the door and retreat, backing into the room.

Silas stands nervously on the threshold. At least he's had the courtesy to cover his modesty with the towel. "May I?" He indicates to the floor in front of him.

I back away further. "It's your apartment." Waving him in, I go and sit on the bed, one cautious eye on the door. Walking towards me, he keeps his pace slow, as if he doesn't want to spook me. I notice he leaves the door ajar so I have a means of escape if necessary. *Well, that's something at least!*

"Edi, I…" he crouches down before me so that we're on a level. "I'm sorry. I was lost in the moment."

"Don't…" Shifting away from him slightly, I close my eyes. That word means nothing in these circumstances. "I've heard it before. Don't you think I've heard it before?" A stray tear escapes. I leave it alone, allowing it to run down my face and drip off the end of my chin and into my lap.

"Edi?" Confusion clouds his face.

"*Sorry! … Fucking Sorry!* … Every time *HE* hurt me. Every time *HE* punched, kicked or… forced himself on me." I can't bring myself to use the word raped! "He would always say he was sorry. He would regret what he'd done, he would apologise, over and over; as if that would make everything alright. As if that absolved him of any wrongdoing. *Sorry!* … It has no meaning in that situation Silas." I stare at him. Challenging him to come up with an alternative excuse for his behaviour.

"Edi, please listen to me." Swallowing, he takes a deep breath. His eyebrows form a furrow as he seeks for the right words. Finally, he looks at me, his steady gaze is full of intent. But I see no real regret in his eyes, just determination. And that worries me.

"I'm not sorry I was rough." I gasp at his frankness. "For God's sake, I was rougher in France… in the garden." I start to shake my head in protest, but I know he's right – he has been rougher. He continues. "Don't deny you liked it, then… I know you did." He's right, I loved it and I won't deny it. But even so...

"You still have grazes from the tree bark." He rubs my back with his hand, stroking over the tender area I know is there between my shoulder blades. "You didn't tell me to stop then." *So, what?* I stare at my hands, my brows knitted in conflict. Does that make me a hypocrite for wanting him to stop tonight? I don't think it does.

31

"I… regret I didn't listen to you. That I didn't pay more attention to your mood." His voice is a soft whisper. "I missed the signals and I was thoughtless." He takes my hand gently. "Edi, please believe me. I would never, ever, hurt you but I won't ever apologise for the way we connect. I know it can be animalistic, but that is *Us*… Don't make this about *HIM*!" I jerk up, my eyes meeting his intense stare. He's making sense, of course. I know he would never hurt me, but tonight…

"Edi… Honey-bee…please… it's about *us*. How we feel when we're together. About what *we* do together. Not about *HIM*… Never about HIM!!"

Clarity hits me like an epiphany. In the midst of all the confusion, I've allowed my brain to control my innermost fear. Once again, I let that low-life get to me. I need to be able to compartmentalize all these burgeoning feelings and emotions. I need to separate the present from the past in order to move forward. Until I can control that side of myself, there's always a chance I will confuse what Silas and I have, with what Bobby did to me and that would be disastrous. I need to explain this before he has me sectioned.

"I was frightened." Not exactly the best choice of words, so I try again. "My mind has been reeling all day. I'm not trying to make excuses. I know I gave you the green light and believe me… at first, I thought that's what I wanted." I'm not making a very good job of this at all. I take a breath and start again.

"You weren't here… all day… then when you came in, I wanted you so much. But my mind, my stupid brain told me I shouldn't. That it wasn't right. I was so confused, but desperate for you at the same time. I love having you; love what you do to me… what we do to each other, is like nothing in the world. But, tonight, it just felt… I don't know. Wrong. All I could see was *Him*. Your hands, became *His* hands and even though it was nothing like what he did to me, the images merged and I panicked." Vocalising all the feelings is helping.

"I wanted to know I could stop it, but it didn't stop… and when you didn't stop… it really scared me." There, I'm being honest. God; only this morning I told Christina I was a basket case and now I've just confirmed it. Now I feel stupid. I told him I wanted to fuck. I gave him the green light. Christ, he must think I'm bat-shit-crazy.

"Edi… Honey-bee. Listen to me." He holds my hand tightly, waiting for me to meet his eyes. When I do, I see something there that I've never seen before. Not in a man, anyway.

"Edi… Your fingerprints are on my soul." *Oh my God!* "You hold my heart in your hands." Covering my mouth, a small sob escapes me. He continues his declaration. Completely unabashed and honest. "I'm irrevocably, completely… unwaveringly, invested in us." He indicates between us. Our threaded fingers waving two and fro. The gesture adds emphasis to his tender words.

"I'm going to tell you something and I want you to listen to me. Are you listening?" My nod is almost indiscernible. "You… are in my life now. You… are the meaning in my life now. Do you hear me?" He's earnest; pleading with me to understand his connotation.

"I hear you." Is all I can say. Though, I'm not altogether sure I understand him.

"Edi… I love you. I would never hurt you. If I was rougher than you wanted tonight, then I apologise for that, but please believe me. I will *NEVER* hurt you like *he* did. I will

NEVER raise a hand to you in anger and I will *NEVER* force you to do anything you don't truly want to do… never!" Whispering the last word, he emphasizes the certainty.

Lowering his head into my lap, he kisses each and every one of my bruised knuckles. They must have been damaged in my struggle. "Let me look," he asks as he goes to open my robe. I don't stop him. I'm still reeling from his heartfelt speech.

"You said you loved me…?" I'm seized by amazement at his unexpected revelation. I've known him for little more than a week.

Gently, he unties the belt on my robe, spreading open the front panels so my naked torso is revealed as the robe falls away. It slides off my shoulders and down my arms. Now my body is exposed, the two, small reddish, bruises on my hipbones are visible. Clearly, they are developing nicely. Leaning forward, he plants a tender kiss on each one.

"I said I love you and I mean it. Edi, I've never felt anything like this before. You have a hold over me like nothing I've experienced in my life - ever. It scares the shit out of me and thrills me to the core at the same time." He kisses across my belly, scattering delicate traces over the pale pink scar that runs along the line of my pubic hair. My skin tingles and heats at his caress.

"I'll never mark you again," he whispers. I'm calming. Just listening to him is easing my troubled mind. "You were spooked. I get it. Perhaps we were both unprepared for what happened." He leans back on his heels. "I don't want you to forgive my stupidity. I don't deserve it. I told you before, when I'm with you, I get carried away, lost… I just can't seem to get close enough… deep enough." He looks away, ashamed by his admission.

I know exactly what he means. When we connect, I just want him as deep as he can go. I can't resist him. I run my palm over his stubbly head. The friction tickles.

"But Honey-bee, I don't want you afraid of me. The thought that I scared you, is sickening. I promise… I will never make you afraid of me again."

"Silas, Silas, I love you too," I whisper. I've admitted it to myself and now I've admitted it to him. "It's me who should be sorry. It's me who needs to apologise."

Jerking his head up, he goes to speak but I stop him, placing my finger-tips to his lush lips, stealing his voice.

"I had no right to align you with that… *creature!* You are *nothing* like *Him.* You never will be. Never could be; I was wrong to think you would ever hurt me the way *he* did. You're right. I don't think either of us were prepared for what happens when we are together. It's amazing and frightening… and… and incredible, at the same time. I love you. I don't want to be afraid of you. You are in my heart and soul and I could no more hurt *you* than rip off *my* own head! *You,* need to forgive *me!*" Taking his face between my hands, I lean forward and kiss his mouth. It isn't a heated kiss. It isn't a passionate kiss. It's an I Love You kiss. An affirmation of my feelings; a lover's kiss.

He reciprocates in kind. Returning my caress, mirroring my embrace, holding my face in his hands, loving me.

"My knees are killing me," he says into my mouth. "Do you think I could get up?"

"I don't know, can you?" I whisper back.

He lifts to his feet, turning and sitting beside me on the bed. "Well… I think we scared each other into an admission. I meant every word, Edi. Truthfully… Can we move forward? Can we forgive each other's stupidity?" He's still holding my hand tightly.

"I forgive you if you can forgive me."

"Ditto!" Leaning in, he kisses me again – sealing our lips; confirming our promises; affirming our love. "I want to go to bed... I want to make love. I promise, I'll be gentle."

"I think I want that too..." I'm no longer freaking out about his forceful loving. I know that I need time to come to terms with what has happened and I am in no doubt that my overreaction was due to my subconscious warning me to be on my guard.

Taking his hand, I lead him to the bedside. He observes me quietly while I pull back the duvet one handed. Then I climb in, pulling him in beside me. It's my turn to be in charge. To be the one to show affection.

I roll over him, swathing him in my body, wrapping him tightly in my arms. I crawl all over him, straddling his hips, stroking and caressing him everywhere. It's my turn to love him... so I do... my way.

CHAPTER 6

Silas lies impassively beneath me. Observing me as I trace my fingers lightly over the bumpy contours of his muscles and ribcage. My untidy hair swings round my face as I lean over him. The tips tickle his flesh and cause goose bumps to appear, peppering his dark mahogany skin.

He splays his long fingers over my thighs. Although his touch remains light, I can still feel the growing heat radiating from his hands. Occasionally, his fingertips give an involuntary squeeze, letting me know that he's affected by my ministrations.

He's being so careful not to hurt me and is desperate not to scare me. Our previous encounter this evening almost had me fleeing again in sheer panic. My brain was overwhelmed with anxiety, still trying to process the disturbing events of yesterday. His forceful lovemaking brought on the melt-down of all meltdowns. And that lead us to confess our deepest most personal feelings and emotions, which in turn has led us to where we are now.

I've been sat here, straddling his hips for what feels like hours. Sometimes I sit up as I am now; sometimes, I lie flat, on top of him. Pressing my chest to his, just so I can feel our heartbeats synchronize in that incredible way they do when we are bound together so closely.

We haven't had sex, but we *are* making love. Making love in the most incredible way. Exploring each other's bodies. Kissing warm skin. Skimming eager, searching hands over tendons, joints and muscles. Touching. Feeling. Being. Just allowing ourselves the intimacy of sensation. Each of us taking the time to just learn; to know the contours of the other's body. It's almost spiritual. It's an incredible feeling and I'm brimming with an oceans worth of emotions I can't describe.

"When we're old and grey, I still want this," he whispers, stroking along my legs.

"Hah! Even when I'm so fat and flabby and my stomach is squidgy and I'm so heavy that I squash you when I sit on you?" I trace the shape of a heart on his chest with my index finger.

"Yes... I'll still want this - even when my belly is so big, I can't see my cock for my gut. And my back is bent. And your breasts swing like spaniels' ears and your arse is huge," he teases, squeezing my cheeks to emphasize his point.

I grin at the image. "Ha, ha -when you're so stout and I'm so overweight, and both our bellies are so wobbly that we can't reach each other to fuck, we will still have this." I toss it right back at him.

"Edi, even when my prostate is so large, I have to get up ten times a night to pee; when my dick has shrivelled to the size of a chipolata and I need Viagra just to get hard. Even when your crow's feet are crinkling round your pretty eyes. Even when your teeth are soaking in a glass by the bed... I'll still want this; want you... I love you." Gently he traces my face, "I want to be the reason for every wrinkle and every laughter line... I. Love. You."

He wins, I can't think of any more derogatory images to counter with. I smile as he disparages us both with his imagination of how it will be a hundred years from now.

Silas's hands smooth up and down my thighs. He heaves a heavy sigh before speaking. "I know it's a cliché, but I don't want to go to sleep. I don't want this night to end." His voice is hoarse and barely above a whisper.

"I know what you mean," I reply, my own voice is as hushed as his. "If we could just stay like this. Let everything else just disappear... I love you, Silas," I affirm my declaration.

Knowing he knows and knowing that he loves me too, doesn't make those three words any less meaningful. I pour every ounce of sincerity into them.

"I know you do. And I love the bones of you too, Edi Sykes; My Honey-bee."

He lifts my roving hand from his chest and commences a string of light feathery kisses around my wrist, giving each little bumble bee its own special brand of attention before kissing from my wrist and up my forearm. Circling his tongue in the groove of my elbow, I watch in fascination as he licks all the way up my arm until he's at my shoulder. Very tenderly, he draws me towards him, moving his other hand to the nape of my neck, brushing my mated hair out of the way so he can kiss the sensitive skin just below my ear.

It's exquisite and tender and soft. A legion of tiny butterflies has alighted on my skin and are caressing me with their delicate wings.

"Lie back." He pushes me so I'm flat on the bed. Rolling on top of me, he cradles my face in his palms and commences to kiss me blind.

Accepting his weight, it isn't until I feel him enter me that I realise I've unconsciously opened up for him, like an unfurling rose. Sliding slowly inside me, I feel him at an incredible depth. He's hard as before, but this time, he's being so gentle. Rocking in and out, he kisses me as we make incredible love.

Tipping my hips, I meet his every thrust. My fingers curl, gripping the sheets beneath them for purchase. I flatten my feet on the bed and lift, pushing up and forward, encouraging him to move just a little faster.

When that doesn't work, I bend my knees so they are almost touching my elbows, forcing my hips high and off the bed, meeting his groin with mine in open invitation. Crossing my ankles around his waist I draw him deeper.

"Edi..." he warns, not wanting to change the pace, choosing to keep his rhythm slow and regular. "No... relax." I feel his hand grip my ankle, removing it from around him and flattening me, pinning me to the bed.

"This way... just lie still and let me love you." In and out he glides. My insides are beginning to ripple and pulse with each move he makes.

"Silas, love me..." I whisper in his ear. "Make me come..." Oh, I want to come so hard for him. "I'm close."

"I know... stay still, Honey." He moves out of me and I feel him descend my body, kissing all the way until his head is at the apex of my thighs.

"Open for me baby..." Blowing a cool stream of air over my scorching centre, he inserts a finger and hooks it so he is grazing my front wall. I grip onto it with all my internal muscles, sucking it inside.

Lowering his mouth, his lips find my clitoris and kiss it. Then he sucks it into his mouth, clenching the tender button between his teeth, nibbling and sucking. Moving his finger in and out, circling and caressing, he sends me higher and higher until I can barely breathe from the ecstasy.

"I can't hear you but I know you're going to come."

"Ahaa!" I cry, my bated breath has finally released and the sudden rush of blood to my head and other extremities is making my whole-body tingle and fizz. Any minute now, I'm going to go off like a firework.

"That's it Honey… let it go."

"Ahhhh! Ohhh!" And I come. It's beautiful. A cascading ripple of life engulfs me from head to toe, flooding my entire being with an incandescent light and heat.

Silas has crawled back up my body and has re-entered me. I feel him come inside me, joining me in my euphoria. I'm glowing like a living flame and I'm pulsing round him as he continues to pump into me. I don't just feel it in my centre, but in every muscle, every nerve and every cell of my body.

An aura of intense bright, white light is glowing and pulsing around us, binding us together, engulfing us in a tsunami of sensation and elation. And as the intense orgasm gradually recedes, I'm saturated with a feeling of such overwhelming love so devastating it brings me to tears. Not from sadness but from sheer unbelievable joy.

Clinging onto Silas, I am awash with emotion; attacked from every conceivable angle by the enormity of what just happened. I hang on to him for dear life, as if to let go of him would release him from my world and he would disappear forever… I can't let that happen so I hold on tighter, weeping into his neck and panting into his ear.

"Jesus, God!" he breathes, there's a cadence to his voice that I can only align with reverence.

"Did you feel it too?" I need to know it wasn't my imagination. I'm brimming with light and a dizzy, heady feeling I can't name.

"Am I still alive? What the hell *was* that? I feel like I died for a minute there." His eyes, too are moist, flooded with unshed tears of emotion.

"An epiphany, a revelation? An affirmation, I think?" I can't stop my own tears as they roll away and slide onto my pillow. The incredible release I felt at the moment of climax is still echoing. Every nerve and cell of my body is singing with it.

"I feel like I've left my body and been launched into orbit! Did that happen to you too?" There's wonder in his words.

"Yes… I was bathed in light, as if heaven had appeared around me. That sounds ridiculous, doesn't it?" I'm still sniffling and clinging on so tightly that my arms are going numb.

"No, that's exactly it… my body feels like it's filled with electricity. I've never experienced anything remotely like that before. Are you okay?"

I know precisely what he means. I'm clinging on so tightly I can feel every single vibration as his rigid body trembles and heaves its way through the rapture, fighting to find some semblance of calm. Eventually, he manages to disentangle himself from my vice-like grip so he can look at me.

"What are you doing?" The fact that he's freed himself causes me to panic he might walk out. "Don't leave me."

"Silly girl. I'm not going anywhere."

37

"Do you promise?" I sniff.

"Cross my heart and hope to die in a cellar full of rats." Smiling, he strokes a finger over his chest, marking out a cross over his heart emphasizing his vow. I sniff a laugh at his sincerity.

"Silas, that was incredible. I've never felt that close to anybody in my entire life before."

"It was biblical," he states simply. "A life affirming moment, and I want that and more every day with you." He kisses me tenderly. When he pulls back to gaze into my eyes, my tears have dried and I'm just awestruck by the intensity of our connection and his beauty. It's hard to believe this stunning man is mine.

"I know we don't want this night to end, but it's..." He looks at the clock. "Three-thirty," he groans. "And we have work today! Turn onto your side so I can hold you."

"Okay, Boss-man." I'm not going to argue. I'm dead beat. We'll be up in less than four hours. "Good night, Silas... I love you."

"And I love you too... good night, Honey-bee."

I close my eyes and I'm asleep in ten seconds...

CHAPTER 7

Wednesday dawns bright and clear. It's only when I'm in the shower I replay all the horrid things that happened on Monday, and then again on Tuesday evening. Those thoughts are quickly replaced though, when I remember our amazing connection last night, and the magical feeling that came from our intense coupling and mutual declaration.

Silas is in the kitchen. He's grilled some bacon and tomatoes and used the Hovis loaf to make some whole-wheat toast. Riffling through the cupboard, I find the HP Sauce and commence plastering it, before adding a couple of rashers of crispy bacon. I'll give the tomatoes a miss. I finish by slapping on another layer of sauce before adding the toasted lid.

Silas watches my ritual in mild amusement. "You can do another one of those for me, please." He pours out the tea and hands me a mug, just as I'm plating up his tomato, bacon and brown sauce butty. We swap over, his plate for my mug.

"We might run into the pap's today. They were camped outside the fence all yesterday apparently."

"I thought you were away flying yesterday?" I chew and sip.

"I was, Spanners told me. They had a boring day though. Nothing to see was there?"

Wiggling his eyebrows, he takes a huge bite out of his toastie; a glob of brown sauce appears at the corner of his mouth. I lean in and lick it off. "Hey! I was just about to get that," he says, affronted, wiping his mouth with the back of his hand as he finishes his breakfast. "Anyway, the papers were pretty devoid of anything new yesterday. Just a re-hash of Monday, thankfully."

I test the water. "Christina thinks I should give a controlled interview."

"Does she now?" He picks up his cup and drains the last inch of tea before loading it into the dishwasher. "I'll need to think about it."

Now that comment just pricks at my irritation nerve. "Hmm, I understand your concern, but surely the decision lies with me?"

"Yes, it does, but I don't think a little thought is a bad thing. Do you want to go out for dinner this evening? We could go into town?" His sudden change of direction almost gives me whiplash.

I know it's a distraction tactic but I might be able to work this to my advantage. "Alright. That would be nice." Picking up my own plate and cup, I add them to the load in the dishwasher. "We can discuss it over dinner. Anyway, I have two more people to interview today and I need to prepare for the new girl starting on Monday."

"Yes, we can, and yes, you do. Come on – teeth then work."

In the bathroom, we each use one of the his and hers sinks to clean our teeth. I quickly brush my hair and tie it up in a ponytail. Silas is dressed in his uniform again so I'm assuming he has another flight today. It feels like a week since I was at work rather than just one day. So much has happened.

We walk down the stairs hand in hand. The old dear on the floor below is locking her door on her way out. She gives us a cheery "Good morning ducks" as we pass.

Outside, there's no sign of any reporters or photographers. It would seem they aren't aware of the apartment, which is a good thing. It makes me smile when I think about the long hours they spent outside the airfield yesterday, and probably outside Silas's barn last night, hoping in vain for a photograph, or some further saucy, alfresco action to report today.

But as we approach the airfield, it's a different story. My hands are cold, a clear sign my nerves are kicking in. The muscles of my thighs are so tight with tension they're trembling. I begin to feel anxious.

Silas visibly stiffens beside me. "Fucking leeches!" He hisses under his breath. Three black transit vans are parked nose to tail along the perimeter fence. About six photographers are standing, shooting the breeze, smoking and drinking coffee from Styrofoam cups. This is going to be interesting to say the least.

Silas clicks the remote on his keyring and the metal gates slide open. Unfortunately, this draws the attention of the paparazzi and they all quickly stamp out their cigarettes and drop their coffee cups in favour of their cameras and flashbulbs.

I duck my head down as we pass through the gates. The paparazzi don't follow us. They can't, it's private property. But that doesn't stop them attempting to flash their cameras in my face, trying to get a shot of me through the windscreen of the car. You'd think from all the unwanted attention I'm getting I was a notorious serial killer, rather than a washed-up page three glamour model. It's ridiculous.

"I'm going to drive round to the fire exit. You can jump out there and walk through the hangar to the office. It should make it harder for them to take your picture from that angle." True to his word, he skirts around the side of the main building and into the open doors of the nearest hangar, where Sparks is awaiting our arrival. Efficiently, he opens my door for me and shows me where the fire exit is. The old boy is acting like my personal bodyguard.

The ginnel between the hangar and the main building is only about three feet wide. Both fire doors are located halfway down so I can go out through one, and in through the other without much exposure. I still hear the jeers and clicks as the scum at the fence vie for my attention, desperate for the money-shot.

"Halloo!" Christina sings as I enter my office. "You look a million times better than you did yesterday my lovely." She hugs me in greeting.

"Hi, yes. Thank you so much for yesterday. I do feel better. Still a bit nervous, but I'm not letting that lot get the better of me." I look around, something seems amiss. "Where's Bear?" I ask, realizing that we do indeed have a missing member of staff.

"He's around here somewhere." She seems unperturbed that the dog is missing. "He's not speaking to me. Apparently, it's my fault that Silas is flying two days in a row."

At her voice, a pointed black muzzle appears at the door. "I know you're there. Don't be giving me the cold shoulder. You're going to have to get used to this." She speaks to the dog as if he understands her every word. It's comical.

Bear skulks into the office, the epitome of dejection. He looks so sad and down hearted it makes me tilt my head to the side and croon. "Aww. Look at him."

Christina, tuts and shakes her head. "Stop it with the puppy-dog eyes. They won't work on me." And then immediately drops to her knees to give the poor dog a big fuss. He looks up at me all forlorn – but he can't prevent his tail from wafting the air on an involuntary wag; indicating that his self-pity tactics have had the desired effect.

"You're such a diva! You should be on the stage." She roughs through his coat as she stands up. Bear rolls onto his back and waves his paws in the air like a dying fly. "I'm not falling for it," she tells him, turning her attention to me.

Conceding defeat, he returns to his front and yawns, stretching his paws in the familiar downward dog position, before getting up and giving a single loud bark - the last word goes to Bear - before trotting off in search of his next victim. "Right, what's on the cards for today then?"

After reviewing the agenda, Christina leaves me to it. I check the schedule. Silas has another internal flight this morning, but it is only to Manchester. He'll be back by three-thirty. My interview candidate is due in at eleven, so I have a quick read of my notes and questions and another review of her C.V. Everything looks in order.

Grabbing a coffee, I settle at my desk. My peripheral vision is prickling as I try my best to ignore the crew of photographers and reporters standing around the gates. This will never do. The candidate is due within the next hour and that lot are enough to scare off even the most intrepid of contenders.

I know they can't see me, but it is distracting me from concentrating on the job at hand so I cross the office and twist the pull cord on the blinds, effectively blocking out the view from that window. I am still able to see the runway and the apron; it's just the view of the main gate that has been shuttered out. I feel better immediately.

At eleven o'clock on the dot, my work mobile phone rings. An unknown number, flashes up on the screen. Tentatively I swipe the screen to answer. "Royal Tudor Charters, good morning."

"Err, hello. Is that Ms. Sykes?" The voice is small, nervous and female. It doesn't sound like a reporter. "I'm really sorry I'm late. This is Nasima. I'm due to come for an interview this morning but I can't get in. There's a crowd at the gates and I can't get through."

Oh, the poor girl! This is getting beyond a joke. "Hi Nasima, yes, this is Edi. I'm really sorry about the idiots out there. Stay in your car and I'll send one of the lads to come out and fetch you." I hang up and immediately tannoy a call through to the hangars. "Spanners, could you collect Miss Ahmed from the front gate please and escort her to my office. She's surrounded by the *walking dead!*"

"On my way… do I need to get the hose out again?" I can tell that he's itching to give the brainless herd another dousing, but I don't think it would do our reputation any favours.

"No, just ignore them and they might go away. I just need Miss Ahmed to get through unscathed, if you could manage that, I'd be grateful."

"Will do." He can't hide his disappointment.

I quickly call Nasima back to let her know that help is on the way, before flicking on the kettle and grabbing my interview questions, a note pad and a few pens for good measure. Scanning her C.V for the millionth time, I set my desk up ready for the interview.

Two very enlightening hours later, I have all I need. Nasima is perfectly qualified for the job and has sailed through the interview with flying colours. I like her as much as I liked Susan and I think they both will make fantastic additions to the team.

Nasima is tiny. Fragile, reed thin with flowing jet-black hair she keeps off her small, pretty face, with a satin Alice band. She's demurely turned out in a black trouser suit and a cream polo-neck sweater. Even with the warm weather, she seems dressed for winter.

She tells me she's twenty-five, but she looks about sixteen, and when we shake hands on a farewell, my hand swamps her tiny bird like one and I'm afraid I'll squeeze too hard and crush her delicate fingers. Her hand is cool, but her handshake is surprisingly firm for such a slight person. I get the impression she's a lot tougher than she looks.

"Thank you so much for coming in. I'll be reviewing all the interviews later today and I'll get back to you by the end of the week. I hope that will be alright?"

"Yes, thank you for the opportunity. I think I'll be okay on my way out. It was just a shock to see… all that lot at the gates." I can tell she's curious as to what's going on, but I'm not up to explanations.

"Oh, just ignore them. They think there are some celebrity's flying in today and are hoping they'll get some good pictures. I think they'll be disappointed," I lie.

"Oooh! Who is it?" Her interest is piqued at the thought of David Beckham or Ed Sheeran making an appearance.

"Oh, it's nobody special, believe me. They've had a wasted journey today." Her small expressive face clearly shows her disappointment.

Well, never mind Nasima, there'll be plenty of other times when you'll get to see the odd minor celebrity or newspaper fodder.

As if on cue, Spanners arrives at my office door in time to escort her out. He's really earning his keep today. He nods at me as they leave the office. I suspect he's still keen on giving our unwelcome guests a freezing cold shower. I just shake my head at him. It really isn't worth it.

The second they're gone; Christina pops her head round my door. "Well? How was she?" she asks, as if I was test driving the latest model Jaguar.

"Really good actually. I think she'll be perfect".

"She looked minuscule. Are you sure she'll be able to manage all of this?" she indicates round us as if we are standing in the lion's den, or some kind of underworld lair.

"Absolutely. There's much more to her than her size. A real pocket battleship. I imagine she's had more than her fair share of being underestimated because of her stature. I'll bet she's a tough cookie when she wants to be." Even as I say the words, I know I'm right. There's a lot more to Nasima Ahmed than meets the eye. Yes, she'll definitely fit right in here.

"Well, so long as, you're sure." She seems happy enough with my decision. "Look, can you hold the fort for an hour or two? I want to pop into town and then I'm going over to see Dominic. I said I'd take him for supper. He likes Italian, so we're off to *Gusto* on the high street. Is that okay?" I have no idea why she's asking me. It's her business. Surely, she can come and go as she pleases?

"Of course, I will… have a wonderful afternoon. Oh – if you see David, tell him I'll see him on Friday. We're taking them all to the pub."

"Sounds fun! If you're sure you'll be okay... the dog's sulking under my desk by the way."

"Yeah," I laugh. "I'll be fine. Shoo, off you go and enjoy the afternoon with your boy." I wave her out of my office.

By five o'clock the Muppets at the gate have got bored. There's only one van left. The others have drifted away, obviously fed up of waiting to see if I'll make an appearance. All this hanging around must be costing them a fortune.

I flip the blind open, just so it's wide enough for me to see out without leaving my chair. Silas still hasn't returned from his Manchester flight, but he's contacted me to say there was a delay because the flight before his had to wait for something or other… anyway, he'll be here by six, which is cool.

My office phone startles me. The ring volume seems louder somehow. I lean over and pick it up. "Good afternoon, Royal Tudor Charters." There's silence at the other end. "Hello, Royal Tudor Charters. Can I help you?" There's a click, and the phone goes dead. I stare at the receiver for a beat. Then, deciding it was a wrong number, I drop it back into the cradle.

No sooner have I put it down, when it rings again. Grabbing the handset and as if on instinct, I look out of the window, and up at the cloudy sky. There's a small black dot on the horizon - the Cessna. Smiling, I answer the call. "Hello, Royal Tudor Charters, can I help you?"

"Now, there's a far better welcome." The frigid chill that hits me at the sound of *his* voice shocks me through with terror.

My heart skips a hundred beats and my mouth floods with saliva. Seized by panic, I slam the phone down so hard my fingers hurt. My better judgement kicks in and in a pique of sanity I pull the handset from the cradle and drop it onto the desk so it can't ring again.

No, no, no – it wasn't him… it *wasn't* him… it wasn't him… I repeat it in my head; if I say it enough times it'll be true.

Cowering, I back myself into the corner seeking safety. I stare disbelievingly at the offending piece of equipment, as if it's the phones' fault Bobby has just reared his ugly head.

Wiping the back of my hand across my mouth, my stomach gives an involuntary lurch. Inhaling deeply, I fight to dispel the sudden urge to vomit. *"Shit!"* I feel sick. Recognising the need to sit down before I collapse, I skirt the edge of the office, hands held out, seeking the back of my chair. Grasping hold for balance, I swivel it until it faces me, then flop down, trembling in the seat.

Outside the gates, another of the black vans has returned. Apparently, it only left to fetch more coffee. One of the journo's is handing out Starbucks cups from a recycled cardboard holder and passing them to the guys hovering around the perimeter fence. "Fuck…" I whisper, startling myself.

A sound at the door draws my attention away from the window. My senses are turned up to eleven – I'm on high alert. But it's only Bear, he's appeared at the sound of my voice. He must've been lying outside my door. The vantage point in the corridor gives him a perfect view of all the offices and who might or might not be in them.

"Come here you." I pat my leg in invitation. He doesn't need coaxing. In two second flat, the gorgeous creature is at my feet, head in my lap. I've never felt more relieved to see him. Bending down, I rub my face in his soft fur. His warmth permeates round me like a hot blanket. "Good boy," I whisper in his ear and kiss his majestic head. "You are such a good boy." I feel safe with him nearby.

My mobile phone chirrups, causing me to jump about nine feet in the air. Bear lets out a single bark. "Sorry boy," I apologise for startling him. Still anxious I check the screen, it's a withheld number so I let it ring. If it's important, they'll leave a message. The ringing stops, a double chime indicates a voice message but I just stare at the phone as if it's going to explode.

God, Silas...please hurry up.

As if he's read my mind, Bear leaps to his feet and dives to the window. His hearing is far more acute than mine, so I'm not surprised when, a few seconds later, I hear the low drone of an approaching airplane.

Squinting my eyes, I watch in blessed relief as the Cessna nears the runway, just as the radio announces her approach. "Charter field, requesting permission to land. Hi Honey-bee, are you there?" I grin at his informal request.

"Yes, I'm here Boss-man. You're clear to land. The welcome committee is still at the fence though, so take care, babe."

"Is that my Honey-bee? God, I've missed you." His voice is so warm, he's smiling.

"Honey-bee, is receiving you loud and clear. Now get that fine arse down on the ground so we can go and get some dinner."

"Fine arse, eh? Well, Roger that." I don't know if he realizes what he's just said there.

"*Really!* Roger that did you say!" Tongue in cheek, I'm laughing at him and he knows it.

"Hey, don't knock it till you've tried it, baby... Coming in to land, in five, four, three, two, one..."

Bear lets out a string of welcoming barks and rears up to the window, resting his paws on the glass for a short second before leaping down and bounding out of my office, in the direction of reception.

The Cessna has executed the perfect landing and is taxiing along the runway towards the apron. Spanners and Sparks are out, ready to guide him back in. Mesmerized, I watch in awe as the sleek aircraft makes its approach before gliding to a steady stop. It's my man that's driving that!

My mobile phone begins to ring again; reminding me of the unwelcome caller not twenty minutes ago. I don't answer it. I don't even look at it. It's gone five thirty and technically I'm off the clock. That's my excuse and I'm sticking to it. It rings off. Again, the double chime indicates yet another voice message. I pick the phone up and drop it blindly into my bag.

Grabbing my stuff, I make my way along the corridor and out to the fire exit that will lead me to the hangar opposite, and my man.

Pausing only to call the dog away from his vigil by the entrance, I open the door and step outside... and there he stands... looking like the safe haven that he is; Uniform on, cap tucked under his arm, he's waiting on the threshold of the fire door for me to dive into his arms, so that's exactly what I do.

44

CHAPTER 8

My bag, laptop case and shoes clatter to the floor as I scramble to get myself as close as I can to my human refuge. In my haste to wrap as much of my body around his I've almost knocked him clean off his feet; he jerks and takes a long step backwards to brace himself while catching me up against his body. His hands cup my bottom as he kisses me to death.

"Wow, that's a welcome and a half," he hisses in my ear as he walks me towards the back of the dimly lit hangar. His cap has hit the deck, added to the pile of other stuff. "In here." He opens a frosted glass double pane door with his elbow and backs us through it. Refusing to lower me to the floor, I continue to kiss his neck and grapple onto him, reluctant to let go.

Swinging me round so that he can close the door, I hear the lock click into place. "Now, we're alone." The hollow mechanical noises of the hangar are muffled by the closed door, but I can still make out the murmurings of the boys and the occasional bark from Bear, as they manoeuvre the aircraft back into its designated spot.

The sounds echo and reverberate off the cement walls inside the vast space. The room we are in now however, is much smaller. An interior office of some kind. I don't really take it in. To be absolutely honest, I don't care where we are as long as we're together.

"Here, stand here." He drops his hands and I lower my feet to the worn flooring. It's cold underfoot. My shoes are outside in the hangar, along with my bag, lap-top case and his cap.

The floor's covered with industrial grey linoleum tiles. The room smells vaguely of diesel oil and sweat. It's cooler in here and there are no external windows, apart from one, thickly frosted, set high up in the external wall. An extractor whirs as it filters air through the sealed pane. The walls are painted a dull matt grey and the fluorescent lighting is harsh and factory like.

There's a desk, with a basic office chair in worn denim-blue material. Foam stuffing is spilling out here and there where the stitching has split through years of hard wear and tear. There's a steel safe. A couple of metal filing cabinets lean against the back wall; on top of the cabinets is a stack of lever-arch files and an old plastic, in-out post tray come desk tidy. On the wall there's several black and white framed photographs of people and aircraft, posters of super-cars as well as the obligatory girly calendar and an annual wall planner.

It's sparse and barely furnished, unlike the plush offices in the main building. This is the working-hub of the Airfield; where the guys do their thing. Nothing fancy about it at all. It's exactly what it looks like. A back office serving the mechanics and planes, nothing more.

He takes hold of my face with both hands and kisses me. It's urgent and frantic. Like an addict desperate for his next fix, he eagerly consumes my mouth, delving with his tongue, tasting until his initial thirst is quenched.

Once he calms, he pushes me back so my backside hits the desk. "Take your knickers off." Undoing his belt, he releases his huge arousal from his uniform pants and starts to work himself in long firm strokes. "Now, Edi... what are you waiting for?"

With trembling hands, I fumble under my skirt until I find the top of my underwear. Yanking them down, I make quick work of stepping out of them. He takes them from me and slips them into the breast pocket of his jacket. They cause the perfect tailoring to bulge; a little lump spoiling the smooth lines in the expensive fabric.

I'm panting in anticipation. The noises outside the office have grown louder as the guys carry out their routine of putting the plane to bed. They know we're in here; they saw him carrying me inside.

"Open your legs and sit on the desk." I follow his orders, lifting my skirt so that I'm exposed to him. He wastes no time with foreplay. He's on me in a second. Forcing my legs further apart and sliding his smooth silky cock deep inside my hot, wet channel. SLAM!

"Oh!" I yelp, the sudden powerful force of his penetration, punching the sound out of me.

"Oh yeah… I've been waiting for this all day." He stills and kisses me. "You okay?"

"Silas… Ohhh!" My elbows give and I recline backwards on the desk. My knees lift and he grabs me round the tops of my thighs. This is going to be fast; I can tell.

"Edi, are you okay?" He asks again. I know he's still concerned because of my reaction to his forceful approach last night, but I couldn't be more okay.

"I'm okay… fuck me." I hiss. Digging my fingers into his biceps, I hold on, waiting, ready. "Now Silas, fuck me."

The desk creaks as he starts to move. The metal legs screech on the linoleum, as with each thrust, he propels it an inch at a time towards the far wall, where it eventually comes to a halt. The rhythmical bangs as the desk collides with the bare brick resound and resonate through the small room. It sounds like the furniture is being hurled against the wall.

"Everything alright in there?" I hear Sparks shout as he rattles the door knob.

"Yeah, fine." Slam, bang, crash. Silas doesn't slow his thrusting; he just shouts back; though he does sound a little breathless.

"Oookay then!" Sparks replies, clearly curious.

I'm oblivious. I'm teetering on the edge and I need him deeper. I bend my knees further, but Silas stops me by taking my ankles and lifting them up so my calves rest on his shoulders and my legs straighten. This causes my thighs to close further together, narrowing my passage and tightening the grip I have on him.

"Oooh! That's deep," I groan, my breath catching with every pound.

"Yeah? You like that." SLAP!

The sting of his palm catches me unaware and I yelp loudly. Releasing my hold of him, I throw my arms over my head and grip the edge of the desk behind me. SLAP! He hits me again. This time, I'm ready for it and I push down, forcing myself onto him, clenching with all my might and squeezing his cock as tight as I can… it's his turn to yell.

"*Jeeze!* Fuck, that's tight." I feel him drag himself out of me before ploughing back inside. It must be just as sensitive for him; because he pulls my right leg out at an angle, effectively flipping me, so I am lying on my side on the desk with my right leg bent at the knee, and my left over his shoulder. This opens me up to him both physically and visibly.

I can see movement at the door; heads bobbing as they walk back and forth outside, unaware as to the goings on behind the frosted glass.

"Ahhhh!" Silas is relentless, I'm building fast now. Any minute and I'm going to come all over him. "Please…" I pant. "Silas, I'm… Ohhh!"

"Fuck, I'm there." Increasing his pace, I feel him thicken and lengthen. My own climax is building in conjunction with his and in the second it takes for him to land a final stinging slap, a direct hit on my exposed clit, we both yell our release at the same time. "Fuucckk… Edi."

"Aghhh! Silas," I scream his name; so loudly, there's no chance the guys in the next room didn't hear it. I'm pulsing and coming hard. My juices are running down my thigh and dripping onto the blotter beneath me. I've ejaculated again, only this time, it's all over his uniform pants and the old wooden desk.

My skirt is rucked up around my waist, so it's been saved from the wetness, but as Silas pulls out of me, a river of liquid escapes, flooding the teak wood grain of desktop beneath me and dripping over the drawers and onto the floor. "Ughh! That's sticky." Pushing myself up on my elbow, I close my legs so I can sit up. Silas is staring at the wet messy puddle we've made.

"Err… yeah, that's one way of putting it. Jump down, let's get this cleaned up before the Chuckle Brothers call the fire brigade to break down the door."

He lifts me to my feet. The residue of the warm liquid runs down the inside of my leg. I have to stop myself from using my skirt to wipe between my thighs. "Here," he hands me a Kleenex from a box on the side. I take it gratefully and begin to mop up the gloopy river soaking through my skirt. "Do you think we'll ever be able to do this without making a mess?" he asks, though not without a grin.

"No," I laugh as I rearrange my crumpled clothing. "Would you want to?" Suddenly I'm worried he thinks I'm disgusting, the way I squirt every time I come. He snatches up some more tissue from the box and soaks up the puddle on the desk, before dropping the bunched-up paper onto the floor and skating over the escaped drips using the toe of his shoe, while at the same time, fastening his pants and tucking his shirt in. Multi-tasking. Who knew?

"Fuck, no!" he laughs. Bending to pick up the soiled tissues, he tosses them into the wastepaper basket. "I think we rearranged the office." The room looks like a twister has hit. The desk is wedged up against the wall and the chair is tipped on its side against the filing cabinet. The force of the collision has caused all the lever-arch flies and post tray to tumble to the floor. Papers are scattered everywhere. It looks like the place has been ransacked.

"Oops!" I say on a cheeky grin. No wonder Sparks was checking everything was okay. He must have thought there was a brawl going on inside.

"Let's straighten this lot and then get off home. The hound will be wondering where we are." In my haste to get at Silas, I'd forgotten about Bear. To be truthful, I'd forgotten about everyone.

"Do you think they're still out there?" Meaning Spanners and Sparks.

"Not if they know what's good for them."

After pulling the desk back to its original position and righting the chair, he puts the last of the binders on top of the drawers. The office looks as it did when we came in; before the hurricane hit. "Come on, let's get out of here. I need a shower and I promised you dinner."

We almost trip over the dog as we exit the office. He's lying across the threshold, seemingly on guard. There's no sign of the others. They've obviously seen sense and left for the night.

Silas's Range Rover is exactly where he left it so we can jump in unseen by the mob at the gate. I scooch down in my seat covering my face. Silas laughs at my antics as he rounds the front of the building. "They've gone," he announces with some relief.

Sitting up in my seat, I see he's right. There isn't a soul around. The car park is devoid of any vehicles and the black vans from this morning have thankfully disappeared.

"They must have thought we'd left. Empty car park."

"Phew! Thank goodness. Let's hope two days without anything to report has put paid to them." It's a pleasant thought, but I'm doubtful. The press can be relentless when they're after blood. I've seen it before. It's nasty.

"Humph!" Silas isn't convinced. "I'll believe it when I see it."

We drive home against the main flow of traffic. We aren't heading to the apartment, so I assume we are going to the barn. When I see the familiar hedgerows and wild flowers, I know we're close and start to relax a little. He pulls into the drive and jumps out. Bear bounds round the back of the house, barking at top note at a flock of pigeons that have taken up roost in one of the trees, startling them into flight. He trots back to us, pleased with himself. Can dog's look smug?

"Show-off." Silas rubs the dog's head as he slips the key onto the lock and lets us in. "Would you like a brew?"

"Ooh yes please." I'm spitting feathers. "A cup of tea would be lovely, thank you."

"Champion. I'll put the kettle on, you go and have a shower. I'll be up in a mo'." I love the way he speaks. It's northern and comforting.

"Okay." Climbing the stairs, I fish around in my bag for my mobile phone. I'll listen to the messages when Silas is having his shower.

Tossing my bag on the bed, I strip off my messy skirt and top and look around for a washing basket. Spying it beside the bedroom door, I drop my soiled clothes into it and make my naked way across the landing to the bathroom. Turning on the shower, I sit on the toilet and have a wee, while the bathroom fills with a steamy vapor. Once I'm done, I dab myself dry, flush the loo and step into the steaming jets of water. Bliss.

Silas enters the bathroom as I'm exiting the shower. "That was quick." He's right, I don't hang around. Three years sharing the smallest bathroom in the world with two other people has made me super-efficient at showering. "I was hoping to join you." I grin at his obvious disappointment.

"You'll have to be quicker next time, then, won't you? Oooh, tea. Thanks." Greedily I grab my mug and head into the bedroom as Silas starts to remove his uniform.

CHAPTER 9

Flopping onto the end of the bed, I find my mobile phone. I don't know why I'm suddenly worried about this. If *he's* left me a voice message, I'll just delete it; I don't need to know what he has to say.

I scroll to the icon for the answerphone and press dial. The phone tells me I've two new messages. Pulling in a deep breath, I press play.

"Hi Edi, It's me… Christina. Thanks for covering for me today. The boys are great. David came to the Italian with us. He has a healthy appetite, hasn't he?" He certainly has. I smile mildly at the image of David, tucking into his spaghetti. "I just wanted to let you know that we've had the best time this afternoon. No need to call back. I'll see you tomorrow. Bye-ee!"

That's nice. David loves pasta and pizza. I'm sure he'll tell me all about it on Friday. I press four to skip to the next message.

"Meredith?" My heart leaps to my throat and my blood turns to ice in my veins. His voice is a deathly warning. Menacing. With that one word, all of my earlier terror has returned with a vengeance.

Anxiously, I glance at the bathroom door across the hall. I can hear the shower running. "You have something of mine," he states, calmly. "Something I want back. Something you stole from me, something that didn't just belong to you." *Oh God!*

"I know where you are Meredith. I know you think you're safe, with your new man. I know lots of things about you; 'Edi' isn't that what you're calling yourself nowadays?"

I can't swallow, my mouth has gone dry but that doesn't prevent the sudden surge of bitter bile rising up into my throat. My hand's trembling so much I can hardly hold my phone.

"Just remember, I can cause a lot of trouble for you if you don't cooperate. I'll be in touch… *soon!*" The message ends but I remain frozen in place, my phone still pressed to my ear. His barely veiled threat rings loud and clear; still resonating through me like the clarion call that it is.

How the Hell did he get my number?

Lowering the phone to my lap, my hands are shaking as I go to delete the message. But for some reason I don't; instead of pressing three for delete, I press two to save. An insurance policy maybe?

I know what he thinks I *stole* from him, but thankfully, she's safely out of the way in America – for now at least.

I need to buy myself some time; some time to think before I'm forced to speak to him again; I know I'm going to have to face him, to meet his wrath head on. It's unavoidable.

The shower has stopped. I can hear Silas humming some tuneless melody as he moves around, drying himself, collecting his things together, before he comes out of the bathroom.

Hastily, I switch off my phone; powering it down so it can't ring again. Placing it face down on the dressing table, I jam the charger into the socket, a fair excuse to leave it switched off until morning. By the time Silas re-enters the bedroom, I'm the embodiment of composure, perched demurely on the bed wrapped in my fluffy robe, sipping my scalding tea - let the Oscar-worthy performance begin!

"I thought we'd go into the village tonight." Dropping his towel into the washing basket, he doesn't seem at all surprised to see my clothes already in there. "There's a new Tapas restaurant just opened. I thought we could give it a try." Picking up a clean pair of boxers from the chest of drawers he drags them up his fine muscular legs.

"That sounds lovely. I hope they don't mind casual dress. I think I've only got my jeans and tee-shirts here." They'd better not mind.

"As long as you have that sexy underwear on, I don't care what's over the top." He starts to splash on his aftershave. *Hmmm!* Sandalwood and musk. I inhale deeply, appreciating the now familiar heady scent. It comforts me. "I'm sure you'll look beautiful whatever you decide to wear."

Dropping a playful kiss atop my head, he strides to the wardrobe and fishes out a hanger. Meticulously, he straightens out his uniform, smoothing down the front of the jacket before hanging it up. The shirt is unceremoniously screwed into a wad, before it too is tossed, overarm, like a basketball, directly into the laundry basket. "I'm just going to load the washing machine." He picks up the hamper. "You, okay?" He asks, finally noticing my reticence.

"Yeah, just a bit tired." I force a smile, trying to remain calm. He gives me a curious look but doesn't pursue it.

"Dry your hair and get dressed. You'll look beautiful," he reaffirms as he walks out of the room, leaving me to it.

With a reeling mind and mixed emotions, I'm still replaying Bobby's voice message while rummaging for something half-decent to wear. Tia, Silas's sister has been very astute and brought a mixed selection of my clothes to the Barn. I choose a black zip-up cap-sleeved top and a floaty black and grey skirt I've had for years, but hardly ever worn. I wouldn't normally put them together, but they look fine and more importantly, they're clean.

Deciding to add a touch of glamour, I strap on my new black 'Paris' shoes and check myself out in the mirror. I actually look half decent – not quite 'Christina chic', rather more 'boho-chic' but the style suits me, so I find a broad leather belt and buckle it loosely so it drapes around my hips. Finally, I give my hair a blast with the hairdryer so that it looks a bit shaggy and flicky.

I'm still faffing about with it when Silas returns to the bedroom. "See," he announces, appreciatively. "I told you you'd look beautiful." Wrapping his arms around my waist from behind, he gives me a peck on the cheek then goes to his wardrobe to choose his outfit for tonight. Black jeans and a white oxford shirt. Tan loafers and belt. He looks fantastic in about sixty seconds' flat. "Ready?"

I nod as I switch off the hairdryer. "Almost; just let me do my face and I'll be right with you."

"Don't overdo it. I'll wait downstairs. Ten minutes, okay?" Again, he leaves me to it. I quickly apply some tinted moisturiser, blusher and a flick of mascara before dabbing my lips with pink lip balm; they feel chapped. A last flick of my hair and a glance in the mirror tells me I'll do, so I grab my clutch and a lightweight grey cardigan, then follow in his tracks down stairs.

Silas is in the kitchen. He's filling up Bear's water bowl as the dog is chomping noisily on his dinner, paying us no attention whatsoever.

"Someone's hungry," I muse, pointing at the bobbing head buried in the food dish.

"Yeah… me." Silas places the water bowl on the floor beside Bear, who doesn't even bother looking up from his meal as Silas gives his head a stroke. "See you later boy."

"Are we driving?"

"Yes, it's a few miles into the village and you can't walk in those." He points at my feet, a salacious smirk playing on his lush lips. He's right, I'd fall flat on my face if I had to walk more than a mile in these darlings.

"Thank you," I smile back as he takes my hand and leads me out of the kitchen.

'*La Torre Tapas Restaurant*' looks no more than a large café. The name isn't imaginative and the décor even less so, but the delicious aroma greeting us as we enter suggests we're in for some serious culinary delights.

We choose our own table. The young waitress looks about sixteen, but she's efficient and well trained. She offers us a drinks menu and points to the blackboard, which details the specials and dishes of the day. There is a varied choice on offer, but not that varied that it'd have to be pre-prepared in advance.

"Can I get you something to drink?" she smiles sweetly at me. With her curly blonde hair and willowy figure, she reminds me of Lizzy, and that, in turn, reminds me of the nasty, threatening voice message Bobby left on my answerphone. My stomach gives a lurch and I shiver. It doesn't go unnoticed by Silas, but he remains quiet, studying the menu.

"I'll have a Bud Light please… Edi?" He looks at me questioningly.

Quickly, I scan the selection of drinks on offer. Sangria. They have Sangria.

"Erm… Sangria please." I hope they do it by the glass.

Jotting our drinks order on the pad she points to the board. "All of our dishes are freshly made to order. I'll fetch them out as the chef cooks them. They're a decent size, so you should be good with three each," she enthuses. "I'm sure you won't be disappointed. I'll leave you to choose while I get your drinks." Off she trots towards the bar, where a young guy with long hair in a ponytail is mixing cocktails and pouring wine.

"This is really nice." I look around the small room. There aren't that many covers. It's reminiscent of the Bistro we ate at in Paris. There's a few more tables in here though - about twenty - and most of them are occupied with either groups, families or couples. The music is subtly muted to background level, but I recognise Enrique. It's a strange combination of British Coffee House - come Spanish Wine bar. It's lovely.

Ignoring my nagging mind, I sweep the disturbing thoughts away so I can enjoy my night with Silas. Rubbing my hands together, I check out the specials board. "What do you fancy?" I ask.

"You…" His eyes burn into mine; his voice is warm and suggestive. "But let's have something to eat first." Sitting back, he picks up the menu as if he hasn't just lit the blue touch paper that is my simmering libido.

Scoffing at his cheek, I try to hide it, but know exactly what he means. The atmosphere is an epitome of foreplay. I can feel a familiar tingle, rising in my body at his promising words. "Okay then…" I cough slightly and decide to make my selection. "I think I'd like the roasted asparagus with truffle oil and shaved Manchego… ooh! and could we have the lamb chops with basil and mint pesto?"

"Mmm, sounds delicious. How about the Potato and Chorizo in tomato sauce and the citrus and pomegranate salad?" I'm not a huge fan of Chorizo, but I'm prepared to try it. "Yes. Should we get two more dishes, or do you think that will be enough?"

"Do you like black pudding?" Any northerner worth their salt, loves black pudding. I grin my approval. "So that's the black pudding with roasted red peppers – one more?"

"Mmm? Okay, the prawns?" King Prawns in garlic butter – delicious.

Silas waves at the waitress, who's on her way over with our drinks. "Have you decided?" she asks as she places our glasses on the table. The sangria looks lovely - packed with fruit. Silas reads back our order and I listen intently. It sounds like a lot of food for two people, but I'm hungry so I'll give it my best shot. Once she has our order, the waitress dances off to the kitchen, which is through some really jaunty saloon doors at the rear of the bar.

"Now… are you going to tell me what's up?" Silas can't be fooled. He knows there's something not right with me.

But me, being me, I still try to hide it. "Oh, it's nothing." Shaking my head, I plaster on a too broad smile and evade his question, but he's no fool, he knows something's up.

"Edi…" he warns taking my hand. "God, your hands are freezing." Using this as an opportunity to be vague, I just nod.

"Yeah… I don't feel too clever. I think I might have a cold coming on or something." That seems to pacify his curiosity slightly.

"Well, in that case, we won't stay out too long." He gives my hands a rub to warm them up. He's being so kind and attentive. But he doesn't look completely convinced as he takes a pull of his beer and I sip at my Sangria.

"Here you are…" The cheery young waitress glides up to our table carrying a tray, laden with the first of our sizzling plates. "Chorizo, the prawns and the salad." It all smells divine and my stomach growls, reminding me I'm starving. "The rest is on its way." She sings as she places the steaming dishes in the centre of the table. A second waitress is close on her heels with the rest of our banquet. Once all the plates have arrived, they leave us alone to devour our food.

I'm quiet as Silas shares the food between our plates. Although I'm hungry, my appetite has vanished. I know I need to eat and I'll feel much better with some food in my stomach but I just can't seem to muster the enthusiasm to actually put it in my mouth and chew. Warily, I glance around the restaurant at the other diners. I feel as if I'm being watched, but everyone seems oblivious to us; probably just my imagination working in overdrive.

"Edi, for fuck's sake what's wrong?" Irritation is clear in his voice. He's not happy with me. Frustrated, he's really trying to stay calm. But my mind is reeling. I have no idea what to tell him or what to do about the message on my phone. Desperately I try to get a grip.

52

"Nothing, I'm okay, honestly," I lie through my teeth.

"Well would you be surprised if I said I didn't believe you?" He picks up a prawn and starts systematically peeling the shell off the succulent meat.

No, I wouldn't...

"I'm fine. It's just the..." My voice trails off into silence. It's just the what? Why can't I find the courage to tell him what's going on? I'm such a coward.

Perhaps it would help if I picked up my knife and fork; forcing myself to make the effort and eat something. Copying Silas, I also choose one of the sizzling prawns. The task of pulling it apart helps. Popping it into my mouth, I manage to get the succulent flesh past my lips and once I taste its salty sweetness, my appetite is resurrected and I chew appreciatively.

The food is lovely, not too spicy, thankfully. "Mmm," I hum, trying to make all the right appreciative noises as I struggle my way through my dinner. "It's very nice." Getting a grip on myself, I go for a change of subject. "Oh, by the way - Christina left me a message earlier. She visited Dominic this afternoon and took both of the boys for lunch. It went down well apparently." The shift in conversation seems to get him back on side and distracts him from asking, yet again, what's bothering me. "I mentioned that we were taking them to the pub on Friday."

"Crap! I forgot about that. I'm sorry Edi, I've an overnighter on Friday. I'm off to Paris again and won't be back until Saturday morning." I'm disappointed he hasn't thought to invite me to join him this time. Perhaps he's fed up with all the drama I'm causing.

"No worries," I sulk.

"Jesus! What now?" he hisses at me. The waitress picks this precise moment to check our food is okay. "Its fine... thank you," we chorus in unison as Silas waves a dismissive hand in her general direction. She spins on her toes and skips away, satisfied.

Silas spoons some black pudding onto his plate. "I wish you'd just tell me what's wrong." He offers me a spoonful. I nod my acceptance. "It's really frustrating that you don't trust me, you know."

Oh, that's unfair... he knows I trust him. "I've just got a lot on my mind. How do *you* think I should deal with all this shit? Should I just ignore it?" I spit sarcastically.

"You know, fine and well that I don't think that. Perhaps Christina's idea is a good one. Perhaps you should give a controlled interview."

"I... I, don't know." Yesterday, the idea was appealing, but after the events of this afternoon, if I give an interview, it will certainly expose me to Bobby, and that will just complicate matters further. It's not just the press I need to be concerned about. "I'll think about it." I've eaten enough.

Sulkily, I pick the pomegranate seeds off the salad leaves and nibble on them one at a time. Silas eyes me speculatively.

Choosing not to look at him, I scan the restaurant again, only this time my gaze is drawn to and settles on the window. Misted with condensation, I'm unable to see outside properly, but that disturbing sensation of being watched is back. Instinctively, I drop my eyes to my lap.

Silas is simmering away gently underneath that cool exterior. After our disclosures yesterday, this feels like an impasse; I know I need to tell him about the phone calls.

"Fuck this…" he mutters under his breath looking away.

Taking a cleansing breath, I speak softly. "Before you landed tonight, I received a phone call..." Returning his gaze back to me, he waits expectantly - still bubbling. "It was Bobby." I squeeze my eyes together, not sure if the simmer is going to turn into a full-on boil. When I risk looking at him, I can't read his expression. "I didn't speak to him… I hung up." I won't mention the threatening voice message.

"Is that it?" he asks. "Is there more? Are you hiding something from me?" I shake my head fervently – no. "I'll give you the benefit of the doubt, but remember, I'm here and I can help you."

My eyes brim with tears again. I doubt that anyone can help me with this hideous situation. All I know is, if I tell Silas what's happened; if I tell him about the threats, then he'll have to make a decision between me and his business and I can't let that happen. Bobby might be a thorn in my side, but to Silas and Christina, he's the stability for the future of their company.

Sitting there, in the small restaurant, I clam up. My mouth seals and I can't eat, drink or speak. I just stare into space.

It's more than Silas can handle. My sudden shut down tips him over the edge. "That's it… I've had enough; have you finished?" Knocking back the remains of his beer, it's clear to me he wants to get out of here. "Perhaps tonight was a bad idea. I really wish you'd tell me what's wrong with you."

Sighing, I wipe my hands on my napkin and pick up my drink, tipping it to lips so quickly the fruit at the bottom surge's forwards, the momentum causing the red wine to spill out, all over my chin, splashing onto my shirt and trickling down my front - soaking me right through to my bra. *"Jesus!"* I curse, loud enough to draw the attention of the other diners. Tearfully I start to mop up the mess.

"Excuse me." Choking back my embarrassment, I push to my feet, the chair legs screech loudly on the floor tiles, drawing even more unwanted attention. Removing myself from the table, "I need the ladies…" before he can protest, I run towards the small door at the rear of the restaurant that indicates the toilets.

"Edi…" he calls after me, exasperated. Ignoring him, I fly through the door and lock myself into the cubicle. Thankfully there's only one toilet so I have the restroom to myself.

Leaning over the wash basin, I look at myself in the mirror. "What the fuck are you doing… stupid woman." I look completely ruffled. My hair is a damn mess and my face is flushed and blotchy. My shirt is clinging to me where the sangria has soaked it through. Letting out a huge sigh, I run some water into the basin and grab a couple of paper towels from the dispenser. I need to get a grip. This is ridiculous. It's unbelievable that even after all this time, Bobby can still have this effect on me.

When we were together, I lived in a continual state of nervous apprehension and turmoil; never knowing which of my apparent misdemeanours would set him off onto one of his abusive rants. Living in a persistent state of stress, I became a shell of myself. The reaction I'm having now is reminiscent of that time. Try as I might, I can't get past it. I thought I had; but no. I thought my time in the wilderness years had made me safe; I thought my recent awakening with Silas had made me stronger. But the events of the last few days have knocked me sideways; straight back to square one as far as confidence is concerned.

I splash my face with water. When I look at myself again, I have smudges of mascara under my eyes and there are pale patches on my cheeks where the blusher has partially washed away. I take another paper towel and scrub off the remaining makeup. Christ, I look a fright! There's no denying, I've worked myself up into a frantic state and I need to seriously contemplate what my options are… and I mean seriously!

Before I can consider what to do next, I need to first get out of this restaurant and back home. Tomorrow is Thursday. There's only one more working day after that and I'll have the weekend to decide what to do.

Taking one last look at myself, I huff out a breath as I drag my fingers through my hair in an attempt to make it look better. It doesn't work. "Bollocks to it." I give up and head back into the main restaurant where Silas is paying the bill. Turning to look at me, the concern in his eyes is only slightly masking his aggravation. Clearly, he's fed up that I've managed to spoil our evening - yet again.

"Thank you, sir, I hope you visit us again soon." The smiling waitress waltzes off towards the till.

"All sorted?" he asks me, not waiting for an answer and not taking my hand, he walks over to the door and exits the place, releasing the door behind him, so I have to catch it before it swings shut in my face. I just follow dumbly in his wake unsure of what to say. He must be seething.

Once outside, the evening has darkened and the air is chilly. I wrap my arms around myself in an attempt to retain some body heat. Silas ignores me as he gets into the car, leaving me to struggle with the stiff latch, and climb in. The overenthusiastic slam of his door leaves no doubt as to the state of his disposition. He's furious and it's my fault.

Silas completes a U-turn in the road and as the car sweeps round, I catch a glimpse of a guy in a dark hoodie ducking into a shop doorway opposite. That chilled feeling washes over me again and I hug myself tighter - paranoid!

We drive back to the apartment in complete silence. I notice it's to the apartment and not to the barn, a clear indication he wants nothing more to do with my contrary mood tonight. In fact, it'll be a miracle if he ever wants to see me again. Perhaps it's for the best. It may even make my next decision much easier.

As we pull into the carpark at the apartment block, he remains silent, brooding.

"Silas… I…goodnight. Thank you for dinner." I climb out of the car and he doesn't even look at me. I just stand there like a plumb on the gravel waiting for him to say something.

Eventually, after what seems like a year, he lets out a resigned sigh. "Edi, whatever is bothering you… you need to deal with it. I know you've had a shitty few days, but this… closing yourself off… shutting me out… isn't going to make it any better." I just stare at him. I feel catatonic. When I don't answer, he just shakes his head in frustration. "Just… sort yourself out." He slams the car into gear and streaks off, out of the carpark. The wheels of the Range Rover spin on the gravel, loose chippings flying up as if to emphasize his point.

All I can do in my current state of misery, is watch him leave. It's dark, there's no moon and no stars. It's as if the night's sky is mirroring my dismal mood and my dark, though now exposed secrets; ominous, threatening, gloomy. Slowly and with a heavy heart, I make my way up to the apartment.

CHAPTER 10

Inside, an air of flaccid emptiness surrounds me like a damp blanket. Of course, it isn't really cold; it's me.

As soon as I enter the living room, the land line rings. I ignore it. I can't bring myself to quicken my pace enough to get there before it rings off. Standing in the doorway, I just stare at the offending telephone. I feel exhausted. The desire to just crawl into bed and sink into mindless oblivion is overwhelming.

However, the sound of the house phone reminds me I don't have either of my mobile phones or my lap top. I've left everything at the barn. I groan, knowing I'll need them tomorrow, but the thought of driving over there and collecting them tonight is agonizing.

After screwing up our date with my moody behaviour, I doubt very much if Silas would even answer his door to me, let alone allow me in to collect my belongings. Anyway, I've had a glass of sangria - so I shouldn't drive.

The feeling of abandonment is palpable. I fling my bag onto the sofa and head into the bedroom. The phone in the lounge starts to ring again - but I ignore it - again! How many disregarded calls is that today? Five? Six? At this moment, I don't care. I'm in a massive sulk and I know that once I start sulking, it'll be a few hours before I can shake it off. *God!* I'm an embarrassment to myself!

Unwillingly, my mind drifts to the phone calls I received earlier, replaying the nasty voice message from Bobby; just the memory of his menacing tone is enough to trigger the shakes. And all that being watched rubbish, is just that… rubbish. Why would he bother to watch when he knows where I am and he can use intimidating phone calls? Am I being paranoid?

I can't quite believe how stupid I've been. In less than two weeks my well-constructed, happy little utopian life has smashed to smithereens by my own selfish, egotistical ambition. Now I'm well on the road to destroying not just myself, but my career and my children's lives. Not to mention the flourishing business Silas and Christina have worked so industriously to build.

If Bobby knows where I am and where I work, that means he's seen the pictures in the tabloids; that means he knows about my relationship with Silas. And knowing Bobby as I do, I may just as well put a target on Silas's back.

Bobby doesn't want me, but I'm under no illusions; he doesn't want me to be happy either. His warped impression of our toxic relationship has always been the same. He's a psycho' and I can't have him back in my life, or Lizzy's life again. Knowing all of this, I have no choice; I need to leave before this gets completely out of hand. But the thought of leaving Silas causes me actual, physical hurt.

Like a knife in my heart, the brutal stabbing sensation takes me completely by surprise; causing me to gasp aloud and pound my chest with my fist. What the Hell am I thinking? I could probably walk away from the job, but I could no more walk away from Silas, than I could abandon my own children.

Jesus! What the fuck am I going to do – I'm damned if I do and damned if I don't!

Wearily, I strip off my clothes, discarding them on the floor like so many unwanted rags and climb into bed. I can't even imagine how Silas must be feeling. Clearly, he's had enough of me for one night, or else he wouldn't have left. I think I'm being punished for my bad behaviour.

My hand drifts between my legs, touching my damp folds with featherlike fingertips, and subconsciously I start to stroke myself softly. But I hesitate; my customary method of self-soothing, is failing. It feels wrong somehow. I still my fingers but leave my hand where it is. I don't seem to be able to ease myself this way anymore; I've always been able to do so previously, whenever I felt anxious or worried. But I haven't felt the need for self-comfort until now, because now I'm alone. For the first time - since I met Silas - I'm alone, and I can't give myself what I need.

Rolling onto my side, I close my eyes and will myself to escape the heavy feeling of wretchedness engulfing me. As usual, oblivion takes me, within ten seconds.

It's dark and there's a weight. It's heavy and its bulk is pressing on my legs; forcing them into the mattress beneath me, preventing me from moving my feet. I'm lying on my side and there's a tight, vice-like band encircling my arms, trapping them against my ribs, ensnaring me, caging me. I'm completely immobile, bound to the bed and totally helpless.

Gripped with panic, I taste acid in my mouth as the sudden terror forces bile up into my throat. Fear growing, I start to struggle against my restraints. Panting loudly, I push and pull, fighting at the weight, the ropes, the straps; desperate to escape the bonds holding me down.

Abruptly, I'm free. My arms are released and the weight restricting my movement has suddenly disappeared. I thrash about in the bed, flinging my arms wide and out of the sheets, drawing my legs up to my chest.

What the Hell?

The bedroom is instantly flooded with a bright searing light. My eyes are stabbed with shards of it as it invades my semi-awake brain. Squinting to protect my eyes from the harsh glare, I take advantage of my sudden freedom and leap off the bed, springing from the mattress and flying towards the bedroom door, not looking where I'm going; desperate to escape my captor.

"Edi! – wait!" The panicked voice halts me in my tracks. Freezing on the spot, I'm shaking and shuddering from head to toe in distress. "Edi?" His questioning voice is quieter, soothing.

Slowly, I pivot my shivering body in the direction of the familiar voice. Allowing my eyes a few seconds to adjust to the light, I try desperately to control my frantic breathing and clattering heart.

"Silas?" My voice is croaky with sleep. I sound hoarse.

Gradually, it begins to dawn on me. Silas is sitting in the bed, the duvet pooling round his waist, a look of sheer panic on his beautiful, *stupid,* face. "Silas!" My tone is harder now I've realised what's going on. *"ARE YOU A COMPLETE FUCKWIT?"* I yell at the top of my lungs - *Good God, the man's an idiot…* what the hell is he thinking, creeping into my bed in the middle of the *fucking* night? *"WHAT THE FUCK???"* Suddenly furious with him; I pick up the closest thing to hand and hurl it blindly in his direction.

Only when he ducks, and it collides with the headboard behind him, do I notice it's one of the scented candles from the chest of drawers. Silas manages to duck out of its way; but he can't prevent it ricocheting off the padded material behind him and catching him with a resounding thwack, on the back of his head, before landing in his lap. *"ARE YOU A COMPLETE MORON? WHAT THE HELL WERE YOU THINKING?"* I'm livid!

"Edi, stop… wait… ouch!" Rubbing the back of his head with his big hand, he picks up the offending missile and gives it a thoroughly disgusted look, before placing it on his bedside table. "That hurt," he mutters curtly.

"GOOD!" I heave. "Serves you right for sneaking into people's bedrooms in the middle of the night and binding them to the bed!" My breathing is calming down, but I'm still on the verge of hysterics.

A sudden movement in my peripheral vision catches my eye. The apologetic fan of a fury tail wafts in surrender from the side of the bed nearest the wall. There's no sound, but a dark tan head, tipped with a shiny, black, button nose peeks out from its hiding place. Rounding the end of the bed, Bear keeps his head dipped low in submission, as he approaches me warily.

Huge chocolate-brown puppy-dog eyes meet mine, his tail, keeping up its gentle swaying rhythm, fans the air around him. Silas remains still, watching me, watching Bear. *What's he doing here?*

"I thought there were no dogs allowed?" I snap, uncharitably. It's the only thing I can think of to say. This explains the crushing weight on my legs, he was lying on the bed over my feet. I must have really startled him when I started thrashing around like a beached whale because he was gone the moment I started to move.

"We didn't mean to scare you," Silas deems to speak. "I just went to pick him up - bring him back here. I never intended to leave you on your own tonight."

"Well, you could have fooled me!" The way he left seemed clear enough.

"I tried ringing, but you didn't answer your mobile. It was only when I got back to the barn, I saw it was on charge in the bedroom. I tried the land-line, but you didn't answer that either." He's almost accusatory.

"I went to bed."

Bear has finished his stealthy approach and is sat beside me, leaning against my bare leg. It's only now I realise I'm completely naked! Instinctively, I shift my hands to cover my modesty.

"I know," his eyes follow my actions. "What are you doing?" dropping his eyes to where I'm hiding myself. "You look beautiful. Don't hide yourself from me Edi." Even in my post-panic state, I can feel the desire in his voice. "I didn't mean to scare you," he says again; this time his voice is a seductive whisper. "Open the door and let him out," he commands, inclining his head towards Bear, "he can sleep in the lounge." He nods towards the door, as he holds out his hand to me.

Reaching behind me I open the bedroom door. Bear takes the hint; obediently skirting round me and trotting outside, making himself scarce. I close the door after him on a gentle click, never once removing my eyes from Silas.

"Come back to bed," he sighs.

"Don't think I've forgiven you for scaring me half to death," I grumble. Though now I just feel a bit silly at my over-reaction. I should have realised it was Silas, and not some mad maniac kidnapper. How would they get inside anyway?

"Here, climb in and let me hold you." The duvet is opened, exposing his stunning physique in all its naked magnificence. His mocha skin, a mesmerizing, stark contrast to the pale tones of the creamy white cotton sheets.

Padding across the thick carpet, I reach the bed but I don't climb in. I perch on the edge, beside Silas. "That was a stupid reaction," I tell him. "I should have realised it was you." My brows knit together in a frown. Why didn't I realise it was him? "Is your head okay?"

"It doesn't matter. Come here." Stroking the inside of my arm gently in encouragement, he draws me in. The tone of his voice, however, tells me that it does, actually matter. He's affronted. My body should have recognised him, even if my brain didn't. And quite frankly, so am I. "You were obviously beat. I should have spoken to you so you knew it was me but you were out cold. It probably didn't help the hound took it upon himself to sleep at your feet."

"On my feet, actually! It was probably his weight that caused the fright. I'm not used to it. Your arms, however; I could very easily get used to having them wrapped around me at night." I stroke him back, the vein travelling the length of his muscular arm just adds emphasis to the taught bulge of his bicep.

But enough of the sitting, I need to lie; preferably beneath Silas, all night. Lifting my feet from the thick carpet, I elegantly slip them beneath the duvet and turn into him before he envelops me in the luxurious sheets and his strong welcoming arms.

"Go back to sleep, Honey-bee. I have a hunch you might need some energy tomorrow." He strokes my cheek softly and kisses my lips.

For now, my meltdown is forgotten and my brain is temporarily silenced from its jumbling confusion. I'll think about it tomorrow. Silas is right. I will need energy, and common-sense, and resolve, and... I'm asleep in ten seconds.

CHAPTER 11

'WOOF!'

"NO! – Bear… Oh for fuck's sake…" The exasperated voice tells me it's morning and I need to get up. Stretching my arms over my head in satisfaction, I roll onto my side to check the time. Six a.m. Not as early as I thought it was, but not so late I couldn't steal a couple of extra minutes.

'WOOF, WOOF, WOOF!!' The urgency of the barks has me curious as to what's going on.

Getting out of bed, I grab my dressing gown and make myself decent before going to find out what's causing the commotion.

Silas is nowhere in sight, but the drapes to the balcony are billowing gently, which suggests the patio doors are open, so I head in that direction.

'WOOF!' It's coming from outside, so I step through the curtains. The balcony is empty. I'm confused. I could have sworn the barking was coming from out here.

"Morning…" Still perplexed, I look around for the owner of the disembodied voice, but I can't see him. "Up here," he calls. Registering which direction his voice is coming from, I look up to see him hanging over the wall of the roof terrace. "Come and join us." He disappears from view. Smiling, I make my way up the curving steps to the roof garden.

Silas is sat at one of the tables reading the morning paper. Coffee cups and a cafetière are spread out on the tablecloth, along with cereal bowls, fresh fruit, milk, sugar and all the condiments. It looks like room service has been and gone.

Picking up a croissant and pouring myself a cup of coffee, I take a seat on his lap. I feel a weird sense of déjà vu, until I realise, it's almost exactly like the breakfast scene from *Pretty Woman.* Rolling my eyes at my silly epiphany, I shift off his lap and find my own chair. Julia Roberts, I'm not!

"Where's Bear?" I can't see him anywhere. I know he was barking earlier. It's what woke me.

"Bear!" Silas calls, and as if from nowhere he materialises from his hiding place behind the hot tub. The rubber chicken is lolling from his mouth and his glorious tail is wagging joyfully. "Come here boy, come and say good morning to Edi." The dog happily greets me, before settling at Silas's feet.

Stuffing my mouth full of croissant, I take a sip of my coffee. Mmm, I was ready for that. "What was all the shouting about?"

Silas drops his paper and gives me a lovely warm grin. "Bin-Men." Shaking his paper, he disappears behind it, leaving me with a frown and a puckered brow.

"Bin-Men?" I'm curious. I can hear the distant rumble of a dust cart, but it sounds miles away.

"Yeah… we don't like Dustbin Men… do we, lad?" He drops the paper again and shaking his head gives Bear a dirty look. Bear ignores him and continues torturing the poor rubber chicken, which wails mournfully with every chew.

"I thought he was going to go throw himself off the edge of the balcony. He hates the truck. Don't ask me why. That's why we're up here. It's safer. He can't see them from up here." The thought of Bear launching himself from four stories is alarming and it must show on my face because Silas rubs my hand in comfort.

"Don't worry, they've gone now." Folding his paper, he places it on the table before standing up and stretching. "There's nothing in there today, by the way." He nods at the paper, tapping the folded tabloid with a long elegant finger. *Phew!... that's a relief.* It sounds as if the press is finally giving up, thank God. "As it's early, do you fancy a work out?"

I screw my face up. "Not really." I'm feeling lazy.

"Come on. It'll do us good. The gym's always pretty slack at this time in the morning."

I suppose some cardio *would* do me good. I haven't been to the gym in over a week. "Yeah, okay," I relent. "Let me go and get changed." Dropping the remains of my breakfast on the plate, I run down the stairs and through to the bedroom to find my gym kit.

Silas is right on the money. There's only a handful of people in the gym this morning. He goes off to the weights corner, leaving me by myself near the treadmill. I plug my earphones in, and set my iPod to shuffle. I've got so many songs on here, it's always a surprise when the next one comes on; just as it is now… this is one of my most favourite songs ever. *'You to Me Are Everything'* by *The Real Thing,* starts to fill my head and I hum along as I build up to my regular pace.

Nine more surprising songs later, and I'm still going strong. I've been in a world of my own and haven't noticed the time passing.

I'm not a particularly good runner, although I'd really like to be. But my short stubby legs are not really made for long distance. I'm built more like a sprinter, or a Rugby prop forward maybe! But I'm delighted with myself when I check the dials on the treadmill. I've managed thirty whole minutes and have run nearly 6.5 Km. That's a personal best and a really great achievement for me. The machine starts the cool down, so I take the opportunity to wipe my face with the towel and have a long slurp of water from my bottle.

As I gradually recover, I remove the earbuds and take a look around me. Gosh! I must really have been in my own world because the place is now buzzing. I recognise the same two women from my first visit, chatting away on the cross trainers.

The music's pumping loudly and the array of TVs on the back wall are all tuned into different stations. Some displaying the latest news, some shopping channels, advertising various gym and health products and equipment, and some playing music videos that have little or no bearing on the ear-splitting music blasting through the gym speakers.

Jumping down from my treadmill, I take extra care not to catch my legs on the rubber belt; one burn is enough, thank you very much! The reddish-brown mark is still visible on my shin, even more than a week later.

Paying no attention to the goings on around me, I walk over to the cooler to replenish my water. Completely lost in thought, I stand to take a drink of the refreshing liquid.

It's abundantly clear that something has caught the full attention of the people in the room, because several of them are staring at me in a strange and enquiring way. Self-conscious all of a sudden, I look down at myself, checking that I haven't got a massive hole in my leggings or a stain on my tee shirt… no… nothing. What's up with everyone? Why are they giving me funny looks?

As soon as I glance to the rear of the room, I know. There on the middle TV is the local morning news, and projecting from the screen, loud and proud, is a photograph of … me!

It's an old picture from my modelling days. The image has been digitally altered, or strategically cropped, to make it suitable for TV. You can't see my nipples, but even so, it does little to hide the fact I'm topless. There's a rolling caption underneath the picture which reads: '*Meredith Frost – 18 years after going missing – the famous glamour model reappears at Paris Fashion Week.*'

What the…? Why is this even news? It's stupid. But then reality hits, when I realise about twenty pairs of curious eyes are focused directly at me.

Currently, they're not sure; my resemblance to the old air-brushed photograph on the screen is minimal. Hopefully, they'll decide it's a coincidence and the frumpy woman in the baggy leggings couldn't possibly be one and the same.

Well, hope clearly isn't a strategy in this circumstance, because the two gossipy women on the cross trainers have dismounted and are making their way over to where I'm standing.

Swivelling on my trainers, I dip down and pick up my towel, throwing it over my head, feigning drying my hair, but in reality, hiding my face. I dodge the nosey parkers and skirt quickly round the edge of the gym, aiming for the weights section and the security of Silas - I can hear him grunting loudly as he powers through his lifts.

The moment I enter the weight room, I realise I've made a humongous mistake; it's full of men - hefty, steroid inflated, body builder types - all sweaty and groaning with the colossal effort of lifting such impossibly heavy weights. The odour of testosterone is overpowering.

Every head turns towards me as I walk in. Every single muscle on every single body, flexes as I pass; pecs twitch, biceps curl, quads tighten to snapping point and leery eyes follow me greedily; but I keep my eyes focused directly on my own mesmerizing target.

There's only one motivation for me, only one head I'm interested in turning, and that head belongs to Silas Tudor; and there he is, right at the back of the room.

Sensibly, the others have kept a respectful distance. He's completely in the zone; effortlessly power-lifting about ten tons at the bench-press. The only indication of strain is the rigid concentration on his beautiful face, and the tension in his glistening biceps as he slides the resisting weight up and down the supporting bar. He looks fucking *deadly*.

In here too, the TV is tuned into the same local news channel. The screen is spilt and the sub-titles relay the words of the presenter as the pictures flick between the running montage of old photographs and what's happening in the studio.

The old nude picture has been replaced by a more recent one. It's black and white, but this time, it's clearly me. It's the photograph from the paper, the one from the other night - of me, standing at the bedroom window - peering into the darkness. Again, it's been doctored so as to hide my nakedness, but it's still obviously me, and I'm still obviously naked. I look more like the 'now' me, in this picture. I feel sick… this is hideous. I need to get out of here before someone really recognizes me.

Keeping my head down, I traverse all the men who are now staring at me with renewed interest, and get to Silas in about three seconds flat. He looks up at me from his prone position on the bench. Replacing the weight bar in the stand he sits, his face full of concern. "What's up, Honey-bee?" He reaches for the towel draped round my head and commences wiping himself down.

"Silas, we need to go. The news... the TV," I whisper, my eyes darting over to the array of screens adorning the wall. It gets worse and I'm horrified when I see Lynda seated demurely beside the news reader, preening and pouting at the camera. Finally, she has her audience.

What the hell?

The sight of her, in all her Technicolor glory, heightens my anxiety. I'm keen to hear what she has to say, but the pressing desire to remove myself from this situation and get out of here is a much greater driver, and I snatch at Silas's arm in an attempt to get him moving. It's impossible, I can't budge him, it's like trying to shift a steamroller. "Now, Silas... please." I urge, quietly, frantic not to draw any further unwanted attention.

"Hey... hey... yeah. We can go." Bemused, he glances round the room, taking in the curious looks of the now blatantly staring body builders. Rising from the bench, his eyes land on the bank of screens on the wall. "Oh fuck!" he hisses. "C'mon." Grabbing my hand, he turns me quickly and drapes his arm round my shoulder, pulling me into him and shielding me from the prying eyes of the gorillas surrounding us. Hastily, we make a break for it - me breaking into a light trot to keep up with his long strides - out of the weight area, through the gym and into the fresh air of the carpark.

"Christ... Are you okay?" My shoulders are grabbed and he looks deep into my eyes checking for any signs of the inevitable meltdown.

"I'm... yes... no... I'm fine. Can we just go - before someone puts two and two together, please?"

"Yeah... yeah, sure. C'mon, Baby." He places me in the Range Rover and we zoom off in the direction of home before anybody has a chance to raise a question.

CHAPTER 12

Back in the relative security of the apartment, we shower and dress. Both of us are silent, both of us thoughtful, both of us unsure of what to say.

If the pictures have made the local TV news, then the press must really think they're on to something with this story. If they've found Lynda, then they'll find Bobby; He's bound to have seen the article. They've played right into his slimy hands with this and, without doubt, he'll use the opportunity for publicity to his full advantage.

I really don't expect he'll leave me alone now. I need to tell Silas about him and quickly; about who he is and what repercussions it could have on all of us, and the business once it all blows up. And I need to contact Lizzy and explain before she finds out some other way.

As if on cue my mobile rings. I thought I'd left it at the barn. Then I understand... Silas must've brought it back with him last night. I allow it to ring off. I'm not killing myself by trying to locate it. If it's important, they'll either ring me back or leave a message.

I drag on my navy trousers and cream shirt. They're clean, but I really should invest in some newer clothes, especially now I have two new glamorous assistants to keep up with.

Workwise, I've still not decided if I'm staying - which is ironic - because now it mightn't be my choice anyway. That's another discussion I need to have as soon as possible. God, my mind is a riddle of contradiction because of this ridiculous charade.

In the living room I quickly locate my phone. Checking the number, I'm relieved to see it is a call from Nasima. I make a mental note to ring her back once I'm in the office.

It's getting on for eight o'clock and we need to be off. Regardless of all the media rubbish, I'm conscientious and I still have a job to do.

"Silas, are you nearly ready to go?" I call through to the kitchen, where I can hear him loading up the dishwasher.

"Yep, all ship-shape and Bristol fashion." I can't believe how calm he sounds; as if my near naked form hasn't just been plastered all over the morning news. Bear follows at his heels, clearly ready to get out of here.

We take the lift. I think it's a ploy to hide Bear from the old dear downstairs; I'm guessing there're no dogs allowed. Once in the Range Rover, we head to the air field. The traffic is light and we arrive in no time at all.

The queue of black transit vans is becoming a permanent fixture against the fence, as is the gaggle of increasingly dishevelled reporters. Feeling hunted, I do my trick of shuffling down in my seat and hiding my face with my hands while Silas drives straight through to the rear hangar, as he did yesterday, thus avoiding the ever-increasing committee of circling vultures at the boundary fence. This whole performance is becoming a three-ring circus, with me as the main attraction.

The Chuckle Brothers are in the hangar repairing something or other; and as we exit the car, Bear leaps out, his enormous paws landing silently on the concrete floor. Trotting happily by my side, he decides he's coming with me today. As I did yesterday, I enter the office through the fire door, pausing only to give Silas a chaste kiss goodbye.

Christina is, as usual, on the phone, her feet up on her desk crossed casually at her ankles. When she sees me, she quickly straightens herself up; dropping her feet to the floor and smoothing down her black linen pants. Cutting her call short, she places the phone into the cradle and follows me into my office, quietly closing the door behind her.

This startles me, because it's the first time she's done it. Usually, the door remains open unless we're having a scheduled meeting. But I don't remember scheduling a meeting for today, so this is odd.

"Are you okay?" The question's out of her mouth before her arse hits the chair. She shakes her head on a frown. Clearly, she thinks it's a silly question. "I mean... I saw the news this morning... you must be feeling crap." Getting back up, she pours us both a coffee from the fresh pot on the credenza.

I take it willingly. It smells divine. "Hounded more like, but to be honest, I don't know what to think." I take a welcome sip. "God Christina, my mind's whirling with all sorts of thoughts. I can't seem to settle on one without another barging in and knocking it out of the way. It's like the dodgems in here." I give my temple a firm tap.

It's true. I'm so confused right now I can't decide what to do. One minute I'm leaving, and the next I'm staying. Then I'm brave and facing up to it, then I'm a coward and denying it; the next thing I know, I'm having a meltdown. The whole thing is a ridiculous, mind-fucking, shitstorm and I just want it to go away so I can get on with my life... but after seeing the news, especially now Lynda has reared her not so ugly head, I know it won't go away, unless I do something to make it... oh and then there's that arsehole Bobby, just to add fuel to the fire.

She looks at me with such an expression of kindness and understanding, for a brief moment I think I've said it all out loud. "I saw that awful woman on the news; she jumped on the band wagon quickly enough, didn't she?"

"Lynda," I say on a resigned sigh, "yeah... we 'bumped' into her in Paris. Collided, more like... but she was so high and pissed, I didn't expect her to remember it." Ha, wishful thinking - clearly after seeing me in the paper, she just couldn't resist the golden ticket to get her face back in the media again.

"Have you given any further thought to holding a press conference or controlled interview?" She blows some steam off her coffee but doesn't drink. "After this morning, it might not be as bad as you think."

I give a nasal humph, exhaling my frustration at the whole thing. "No..." I roll my eyes sarcastically at the thought. "I don't know if it will do any good anyway." *Not now Bobby's on the scene.* Rubbing at my forehead, I can feel the beginnings of a headache coming on.

"Well, you know my views on that. I think you should just do it... get it over with... like pulling a plaster." She mimes whipping a band aid off her arm.

"Hmm, maybe." What would happen though? "Christina, there is something I..." Her phone rings, halting our conversation and me in my tracks.

Checking the screen, she frowns. "I need to get this... sorry." Pushing her chair back she stands and leaves my office; her phone firmly wedged against her ear. It seems our conversation is over for now.

Huffing out a resigned sigh, I place the empty cups on the tray before taking my seat to get on with some work. The first order of the day is to return Nasima's call.

She answers on the first ring; she must have been waiting for me. "Hi, Edi... It's Nasima." She sounds nervous. "Umm, I saw the news this morning." *Ah!* "Umm, I just wanted to let you know that I still want the job."

This comment startles me... I never thought anybody would be *that* concerned; but then again...? "Oh, err... yes. Please don't pay any attention to all that silly nonsense. We're dealing with it." I try to remain professional but this is way beyond embarrassing.

"Well, no. It's not that, it's just... well... I don't want my parents to find out. They're a bit... strict ...old-fashioned... you know, and would probably stop me from working with you. I'm sorry... that sounds terrible. But they are quite... traditional."

Oh no, the poor girl. How could I not realise this? Once again, my stupid history is affecting far too many people!

Think Edi...

"Look, Nasima. I really want you to come and work for us. There's no reason why your parents should worry... it really is old news and complete rubbish; blown out of all proportion." But if I've learned anything in the last couple of weeks, it's that you shouldn't hide things if they aren't meant to be hidden. In this case, perhaps honesty is the best policy?

"Perhaps you should tell them. They may surprise you." Even as I say this, I know there's not a snowball's chance of them understanding!

"Umm, I don't know. I'll think about it. But I just wanted you to know, that's all. I'll be there on Monday unless anything drastic happens." She still sounds chirpy and confident.

"Thank you for calling. I look forward to seeing you on Monday. But promise me you'll think about speaking to your parents... okay?"

"I will. Bye Edi."

"Bye Nasima." I really hope she finds a way of discussing this with her family. She's so strong - well mentally - but physically she's like a fragile bird. It must be difficult to always need the approval of your parents; especially if they have strict traditional beliefs.

Refocusing, I plough my way through the morning's tasks, thankful for the distraction. Everything is coming together. Both the new girls are starting on Monday and Christina has informed me she's offered the job of IT consultant to a guy called Jasper Holt. I wasn't aware we'd advertised the vacancy, but if we're growing the business then I suspect we will need an IT person too.

When Silas pops his head in at midday, Bear completely ignores him. And it's only when I notice he's wearing his uniform, I understand why. He didn't have it on this morning so there's obviously been a change of plan.

I'm right, there's been an unexpected request from a client in Birmingham who needs to fly to Glasgow for an important meeting this afternoon. It's an acquaintance of Silas's, so he called him direct but I manage to secure a flight plan without too much trouble. Silas will leave for Birmingham, at 13:00hrs. As the flight only takes 90 minutes, he should be back by 6:30pm this evening, so I tell him I'll wait here for him to return and baby-sit the dog. He kisses me swiftly and firmly on the mouth, before picking up the flight plan and heading out to where the Cessna is prepped and waiting on the runway.

By mid-afternoon I'm starving hungry. Christina hasn't returned to finish our conversation, but I need to tell her about Bobby before it all gets too out of hand.

Finding myself in the staff kitchen, I make two tuna and tomato sandwiches. The tuna filling looks a bit dubious; a little off colour, because it's from yesterday, but if we die of food poisoning, at least we won't have to deal with the marauding press anymore! Grabbing the plates, I head towards Christina's office, ready to pay the piper.

I can hear her on the phone as I approach. I'm not sure who she's speaking to, but her tone is quiet and calm. As I knock, she calls for me to come in, so I find my way to the chair opposite and hand her the plate with her sandwich, just as she's saying her goodbyes to her caller.

"What's all this?" she asks, examining the sandwich, cautiously picking up a corner of the bread to peer at the contents like it's a failed science experiment.

"Tuna and tomato," I answer, whilst picking the tomato off my own snack. Like Lizzy, I'm not good with raw tomato.

She puts the plate on her blotter. "I'll eat it later, if you don't mind." Using one finger, she slowly inches the plate further away from her, so it's out of her eyeline, and I expect, odour receptors - something tells me, she won't be eating it. She wipes her hands on a napkin, before dropping the napkin into the wastepaper bin at the side of her desk. "Is there something on your mind?" she asks.

It's as plain as the nose on my face there's something on my mind. "I need to speak to you. It's probably easier to do it now while Silas is flying." My appetite disintegrates and I give up on my own unappetizing lunch.

"What about?" Leaning back in her chair, she takes a sip of water. "Do we need to close the door?"

Nodding, I cross the room and lightly push it to. I would prefer it if we weren't overheard. "I don't know where to start really." Sitting down, I reach into my pocket and bring out my phone.

"The beginning is usually the best place," she says calmly, though, plainly, she's unsure of where this is going. She doesn't want me to leave, she's made that fact clear; but before she decides, before she fully commits to being on my side, she needs to know the truth. It will undoubtedly change her mind.

Dialling my voice messages, I hand her the phone so she can listen for herself. Tentatively and with a little frown she holds the phone to her ear. I study her face closely for any signs of recognition. Her brows tighten as she listens to the message. Pulling the phone away from her ear, she gives me a curious look. "This is me… telling you I'm taking the kids for supper," she says, clearly confused.

"Keep listening… it's the next one." I sit - statue still - waiting for her to respond. My eyes don't leave her face. In hers there's no hint of acknowledgement, or suggestion of emotion whatsoever, about what she's hearing. She just sits, serenely, calmly and as quietly as I am, passively returning my gaze across the desk.

After what feels like an age, she drops her hand. Looking at the phone, she swallows, composing herself... composing her words. Eventually, she takes a deep breath. "Well..." There's still no trace of emotion. This woman is usually so animated, so over the top, that the controlled stillness she's displaying, scares me almost as much as hearing Bobby's voice did last night. "This is a turn up for the books, isn't it?"

"Yes..." I just sit and stare at her, unsure of what else to say. I pick at my cuticle, worrying it. It's a sign of nerves and I'll be drawing blood next if I don't stop. In a forced effort, I clasp my hands together tightly, resting them in my lap.

"Is this the first time he's contacted you?" she asks quietly. I still can't gauge her reaction.

"Yes... well... yes, it's the first time he's actually contacted me. He had no idea where I was... but... I saw him last week. I don't think he saw me though."

I'm unsure, but I don't think she's fully made the connection. It's only now that I realise, I want her to get there on her own; as if her working it out for herself will somehow make it easier for her to digest.

Screwing her face up in cautious interest, she reveals the first suggestion of tension since she listened to the phone message. "Last week? Where Edi? Where abouts did you see him last week?" But I know from her hardening expression it's beginning to register.

"Here... he was here." My whispered words are enough. I don't say more. The tears roll down my cheeks as finally she gets there on her own.

"Robert Price? ... *Fucking Jesus!*"

CHAPTER 13

The office clock sounds like a ticking time bomb. It draws my attention. Four o'clock. Silas won't be back for several hours. I don't know quite why I'm fixating on the time; perhaps it's to prevent me from thinking about the crucial decision Christina must make about my employment. I hate to put her in this position, but I'm such a coward. The truth is, it'll be a relief for someone to make the choice for me.

In my head, I'm already leaving; my bags are packed and I'm ready to go. A vision of Silas floats through my mind as if reminding me what I'd lose if I went. His smile, his deep brown eyes, his glorious body, the way he's loving me and the way I'm loving him.

I feel the growing wetness on my cheeks and close my eyes against the relentless torrent. These are tears of loss, of anguish - not tears of anger or humiliation. I've not yet left, but the excruciating pain growing in my chest can only be grief, can't it?

Once again, I've managed to ruin my life. When will I ever learn?

"I'm sorry," I whisper, more to myself than to Christina. I start to haul my increasingly heavy body up and out of the chair. It'd be better if I went now, while Silas is away and can't come chasing after me. Christina can break the news. Once again, I'm taking the cowards way out.

"Where do you think you're going?" The sharp edge to her voice has me stalling, hovering over my seat.

Opening my damp eyes, Christina's stern face comes into focus. "I… I." Unable to finish my sentence, I drop back into my seat.

"Who was that woman on the TV this morning?"

Confused by her question, I answer honestly. "Lynda Summers. We worked together. Years ago."

"And can I assume, from your reaction, she has some connection to this 'Bobby' person too?" Her, referring to him as I know him, gives me some hope she's allowing me some benefit of the doubt.

"He… he worked with her manager… Bobby only really managed me at the time, but he was trying to build his reputation - gather a stable of girls. He saw Lynda as the next addition to his portfolio." This is true. Bobby didn't hide his lofty ambition from me. His desire was to create the most lucrative and enviable establishment, and thus, with financial backing from his father, Wayland, become the most powerful man in the industry. His intentions were very clear.

"Portfolio; of what, exactly?" Christina has reverted to a business-like curiosity.

"Bobby wanted to grow the business, add to his collection; diversify into other areas." I watch as Christina's eyes flash with growing clarity. "I knew exactly what he meant by *'other areas,'* he wanted to expand into adult magazines… produce movies… you know… pornography." Even saying the word, all these years later, it nauseates me.

That was the final straw. I couldn't, wouldn't, get on that slippery slope. But my constant protestations, my unwillingness to comply to his demands, just earned me further brutal beatings. I knew if I wanted to survive, to save my life, and that of my child, the only option was to get away… to escape the downward spiral once and for all and leave.

"As soon as I realised his true intentions, I had to break free of him before it was too late." I thought I'd buried all of the hurt and humiliation of my past years ago, but the simmering anxiety I feel in my chest only goes to prove the dreadful memory wasn't too far away from the surface, waiting to bubble to the top like a seething cauldron of putrid poison.

My bitter tears have dried on my cheeks; the skin tightening with the salty remnants. I rub at my face instinctively. My hands are freezing cold.

"What an unbelievable bastard," she hisses through clenched teeth. "I understand now why you're so concerned about coming into contact with him again." She's missed the point completely!

"Christina... no... don't you see. This will cripple the business. If he comes after me - and he will - this will drag you and Silas into something that has nothing to do with you. Your other clients will be affected. Nic, Silas's family, his parents, his sisters..." I don't even know if Christina has an extended family, but this is all snowballing out of control and it needs to stop. "The only definite way to end it is for me to leave now, before it becomes overwhelming." Even as I say this, I know I'm delusional. Bobby won't stop, not now; not now he's found me.

"What are you talking about? Has nothing I've said to you sunk into that thick skull of yours? You're going nowhere. Even if it bankrupts us, I won't have this business associated with such... such... a chauvinistic, perverted, megalomaniac. I knew there was something dubious about him the moment we first met, but I couldn't put my finger on it. He was such a charming businessman - or so I thought - he covered his tracks well. No, I'll renege on the contract before I let you leave and ruin both yours and Silas's lives. You're staying and were dealing with this sensibly."

I'm astounded. Never before has anybody been so vehemently on my side. Only my late grandmother was as supportive, and that support went, along with her beautiful mind, over the long years she struggled against the ravages of Alzheimer's.

A feeling of incredible warmth travels through me like I haven't felt in such a long, long time. This isn't just an employer taking care of an employee; this feels like family taking care of family.

In an instant, my mind is made up. The gratitude I feel at this moment is overwhelming. I'd do anything she suggested to rid us of this evil presence - anything.

As if reading my mind, she raises her head. "I'd not normally be prepared to risk the business, but if that's what it takes, we will. We have the funds to fight him in court, but it won't come to that. Something tells me that Mr. Robert Price has more to hide than he's letting on. I can't believe he simply gave up on his sordid ambitions, just because his wife disappeared."

There's one thing I need to tell her before this gets out of hand though, "Christina... Silas doesn't know..."

Waving off my comment as if it's irrelevant, she starts to pace the office floor in contemplation. One hand on her slender hip, the other caressing the fluid gold chain that slithers silkily around her throat. "Edi, leave this with me. I'm taking it to *The Rose Council*, we've dealt with his type before."

The Rose Council? What's the Rose Council when it's at home?

My puzzled expression prompts her to elaborate. "Sorry Edi, 'The Rose Council' is just the board of directors... it's what we call ourselves," she explains, hastily.

"Don't worry, I have a couple of ideas swimming around in my head, but I need you to promise me you won't do anything hasty - you need to trust *me* now - I need some time to digest this. But I promise you... we are on your side. This will be resolved." The last bit is said under her breath, before focusing determined, shrewd eyes on mine. "Promise me..." she demands forcefully.

"I promise..." I comply willingly. She's right, Bobby wouldn't have abandoned his lofty ambitions just because I left him. In fact, my leaving may have made it easier for him to expedite his plans.

While I was there; while Lizzy was there - we were effectively acting as his conscience, a visible reminder, a talisman of decency. Once we'd gone however, there was nothing preventing the debauched and corrupt side of him from taking over.

But taking it to the Directors though? I feel terrible this is affecting their business.

"Silas should be home in a couple of hours." She looks at her watch as she strides over to the coat stand. Removing her jacket, she jolts me from my inertness and back into action.

"Go and get your things, and the Hound. I'll drop you off at the apartment, I need time to think about this. If we want the full support of the Council, then I have to present it in such a way they can't veto the motion."

"What about the arrival procedures? The flight... Who's going to do that if we're not here?"

"Who do you think? The people who did it before you; Spanners and Sparks... and the night supervisor Johannes." I look at her bewildered. *Who's Johannes?*

Recognising my surprise, she puts me out of my misery. "The night '*Manager*'..." her fingers draw quotation marks in the air. "What? ... You thought we closed up at night? He's been here as long as the other guys, you just haven't crossed paths yet."

"Oh," yet another member of the team I've still to meet. That's two new names I've learned today. Jasper Holt in I.T. and Johannes Whateverhisnameis, the night supervisor.

She grins at me as she threads her willowy arms into her sleeves. "Johannes Müller. He's South African and wonderful!" *Ah... so he's wonderful!* Anticipating my wayward thoughts, she laughs lightly. "And yes, he's mine... and before you ask, we have an open relationship. I'm better at that than monogamy!"

"Oh," I repeat. Although, I did wonder. She overshares where her personal life is concerned, so I can't say I'm surprised by this new snippet; just surprised this is the first time he's been mentioned. Oh well, I've only been here three weeks or so, so I suppose there's still much to learn.

"Go and get your stuff." She waves me on my way.

Quickly, I remove myself from her office and head back to mine to collect my belongings. Bear stretches into his customary downward dog position, releasing a satisfied whine as he waits patiently for me to gather my bits and bobs. The warm feeling, I had before, is still there, soothing me, protecting me. I feel like I belong, and this growing group of new people truly care about me.

I'm still musing over my new found resolve about things when my office phone rings. Unconsciously, I pick it up. "RTC, Edi Sykes speaking."

"I saw you." The menacing growl has an instantaneous effect on me. The warm, comforting feeling dissolves and I'm abruptly swathed in an ice-cold blanket of fear. "You were at his home... I know where he lives."

The world stops and the phone goes dead - the ringtone reverberates down the line, filling my ear with a continuous brrrrr. I had no time to form words, no time to gather my thoughts and no time to process the voice; but I know it was *him*.

Instantly my reactions change. The shock and coldness subside into a brilliant flash of burning, fiery anger - *how dare he?* This time, strangely, I'm not so afraid; rather, I'm furious. I'm suddenly fizzing with it - seething with incredulity - *how the hell dare he threaten me like that?*

"You ready?" Christina's voice snaps my attention to the door. She must see the look on my face because she straightens up immediately. "What happened?"

"It was *him*... on the phone... just now!" I hiss.

"Hmm, well I expect he's trying to intimidate you. Are we going or what?" Is that it? She's not flown off the handle, or protested against his threatening behaviour - just - nothing.

Her dismissive reaction to his blatant intimidation tactic forces my own brain into a confused state of calm... again, she's right; I need to take a leaf out of her book, several leaves in fact, and be rational. There's no point in allowing him to get to me. He can threaten me all he wants but until he actually does something, makes a move or reveals his cards, there's absolutely nothing to fear. This is emotional bullying and I refuse to be intimidated.

At the moment he thinks he has the upper hand, but after this morning, I'm positive things are about to change for Bobby Price in a way he won't be expecting.

CHAPTER 14

Christina drives like a complete maniac. For self-preservation, I grip the sides of the car seat; my fingernails digging into the soft pliable leather. I'm wearing my seatbelt, but my instincts tell me Christina is as reckless with her driving as she is with her love life! However, even at this speed, the Mercedes is a smooth ride and I feel quite safe, even on the narrow country roads.

She has her music turned up to a deafening level. Her taste is not dissimilar to mine it would seem, but still, I try not to wince as, *Roll with It* by *Oasis* blasts from the speakers at about a hundred decibels.

"What exactly did he say to you?" She takes a bend at about forty-five miles an hour. She clearly knows these roads really well.

"Um, he just said he'd seen me today, and he knew where Silas lived."

She looks over at me, her neat eyebrows disappearing under her choppy fringe. "Well, in that case, we'll stay away from the barn. The security's better at the apartment anyway." Turning her attention back to the road, she shifts down a gear and lowers her foot, accelerating closer to fifty.

I press myself into the seat, my head welded to the headrest. I still don't feel unsafe, but neither I, nor Silas, drive as fast on these roads; but then again, our vehicles aren't of the same calibre as Christina's swanky Merc.

"Do you really think he'll try something?" she asks, skirting yet another blind bend with ease.

"Honestly, I don't know. He was pretty handy with his fists when we were together, and not shy about using them either, but I've no idea if he's still the same – 'though, if it's at all possible, he sounded even worse." In truth, he sounded murderous, but my own ineffaceable fury helped quell the effect of the deliberate intention of his words.

"It's his animal instincts coming out. Like any predator, if he feels threatened, he'll attack. What you need to do, is be prepared for it."

It's a fair point, well-made, but far easier said than done. *My* primal instinct is to gather my children and run, but we've established, in no uncertain terms, that isn't an option anymore.

I need to fight fire with fire, and if Christina's suspicions are accurate, it means his baser proclivities have only become more debouched and indulgent over time. There's no doubt he's bold; he truly believes he's infallible, completely above the law even. More worryingly than that, though, is his delusional, idiosyncratic belief that now he's found me again, he still has the right to wield control over me.

"What's your suggestion then? What should I do?" I've no ideas, so I hope she has.

"Nothing, for now at least. First, we need to confirm our suspicions, which won't be easy." She rounds another bend on what feels like two wheels. "I have some contacts. I should be able to make some subtle enquiries without causing too many ripples in the water... oh, and don't mention it to Silas yet... I need to think."

My instinct is to ask how she has contacts able to uncover such things, but I keep my mouth shut. Perhaps I don't need to know this. And don't tell Silas... why?

We're arriving at the main road; the junction is up ahead and I begin to relax my vice-hold on the car seat. My fingers are stiff with gripping so tightly. Thank goodness, we're almost home.

"Pigs in space!" she curses, under her breath. I follow her gaze to see a large white transit van parked in the apartment car park. I'm immediately on alert for the paparazzi, though it shouldn't have been able to get through the secure gates without the pass-code.

"I'll let you out. Go straight up to the apartment and wait for Silas there. Have a glass of wine, phone the kids, have a bath, play with the dog, do… whatever it is you do… but *do not* leave the apartment again tonight. Is that clear?"

"Crystal," I whisper, quite taken aback by the sudden forcefulness of her instructions.

She clicks the fob and the gate swings open. Hurriedly, she drives into one of the guest parking spaces. "Bear, out," she orders. Obeying, he bounds forward as soon as my door is open, snaking his sleek body through the narrow gap between the front seats with ease. "Keep him with you. If anybody says anything, tell them he's an assistance dog or something. He'll look after you until Silas gets back."

"Okay. Bear, come; will I see you tomorrow?"

"You will. Oh, and Edi…" leaning towards me, she smiles softly, "we'll get through this. I promise." Returning her reassuring smile with my weaker one, I close the car door.

Skidding on the gravel, she completes an impressive wheelspin, and has left the carpark before I can raise my hand to wave goodbye.

"Come on then, you." Hovering on the doorstep, I fish my keys out of my bag just as two huge burly men are leaving the building. Curiously, I watch them as they climb into the white Transit. The van has blacked out windows, so once they're inside, I can only see them through the front windscreen; I stare as they strap themselves in.

They're definitely not paparazzi and they certainly don't look like removal men, with their wraparound sunglasses and smart black suits - they look more like nightclub bouncers. Then it occurs to me… they must be the security patrol Christina mentioned earlier. Immediately, I feel safer.

Entering the foyer, I take the stairs. With Bear, it's easier than going in the lift. When I reach the third floor, the door to my elderly neighbour's apartment is wide open.

Aware that the old dear may have accidentally forgotten to close it, I poke my head in to check everything is okay. "Hello?" There's a hushed mumble of voices coming from the lounge area. "Hello? Is everything alright in there?... stay," I instruct Bear, and he obediently drops his rump to the floor.

I'm about to walk in, when a fluffy cloud of white hair and a flurry of floral material bustles down the hallway towards me.

"Oh goodness me! Yes, everything is fine my lovely." The old dear moves fast! "I'm alright, I have visitors... just my… err… grandchildren, come to visit. They must have left it open." Giving Bear a wary look, she starts to shut the door on me, but not before I catch a fleeting glimpse over her shoulder, of a tall, slim, Asian man, as he quietly closes the internal door to the living room.

He looks familiar, but I can't place him. The apartment block is exclusive, and there aren't that many folks living here. Like all private people, they keep themselves to themselves, but if he's visited his grandmother before, it's possible I've seen him around, I just can't remember where.

"Bye-bye, lovely." She draws my attention back to her. "Thank you for your concern, but I'm alright." And without further ado, the door closes on my curiosity.

"Well, so much for being a good neighbour!" I grumble to Bear. He gives a passive wag of his tail, and starts bounding up the next flight of stairs towards the penthouse.

After letting us in, I disable the alarm and head into the kitchen to carry out the first of Christina's many instructions; pouring myself a large glass of Sauvignon Blanc. I take a huge gulp, practically draining the glass of the deliciously cold liquid. Topping it up again, I root around in the cupboard for a suitable bowl to give Bear a drink of water.

Once he's served, I grab my glass and head into the lounge; Bear is instantly trotting at my heels, and I lower myself onto the sofa to wait for Silas's return.

I must have dozed off because when I come around, my feet are resting on the sofa and I'm covered in a snug fur throw. My half-full glass of wine is sitting on the table in front of me. Bear is lying on the floor, snoring lightly, but his twitching ears show signs that while he's dozing, he's still alert and ready to spring into action at the slightest sound.

"Hi."

Covering my mouth, I yawn deeply. Looking around, I see Silas standing by the window with a glass of scotch in his hand. He looks relaxed, his other hand casually hidden in the pocket of his dark blue jeans. He's wearing that light cream sweater again; the one that defines his perfectly toned, broad shoulders.

"Hi yourself," I drawl, stretching my arms over my head and elongating my crooked spine like a cat. "What time is it?"

"About ten o'clock." Slowly he paces over to where I'm lying, snuggled on the sofa. Bending at the waist, he brushes my hair from my forehead and gently places a tender kiss on my brow. "You were snoring." He strokes my face before kissing my nose tenderly.

"No, I wasn't!" I scoff in mock indignation. The truth is, I probably was, but I'm not going to admit it.

"No, you weren't," he concedes, grinning. "Budge over." I'm shifted so that my spine is pressed along the back of the sofa. Silas places his glass on the table and steps carefully over Bear, lying himself snugly beside me on the cushions. I drape the blanket over him and snuggle into his chest. He's so comfortable, even with all his solid muscles. "You looked exhausted. I didn't want to wake you." His hand gently strokes my back.

"How long have you been home?"

"Oh, about an hour or so."

"That was late. I thought you'd be back by six'ish."

"I was, but Christina called an emergency Board Meeting. Luckily the rest of the board were able to attend… it took some time." He doesn't stop stroking me and his tone doesn't alter, but I think I know what the 'emergency board meeting' was all about.

"Ah…"

"Quite." I'm gently lifted with the expansion of his ribcage as he takes a deep inhale. "You need to know, that the board agrees with Christina on this. We can't be associated with the likes of Robert Price," he sounds far too calm for someone who's just discovered his girlfriend's ex-psycho has been revealed as their businesses lucrative new client. Christina can't have told him the whole truth.

"We've engaged someone to have a subtle dig around in his affairs. We should know soon enough if he's legitimate, or if the sports agency is just a cover for his other businesses."

"Who?" I'm curious.

"Oh, just someone we use from time to time when we need to… be sure."

"That sounds sinister." I grin. "I mean, why would you need to look that closely at people?"

"Edi, some of the people we deal with are extremely wealthy, some obscenely so. We need to ensure there's no corruption involved, and whatever business they're hiring us for is legitimate. I wouldn't want to suddenly be arrested for smuggling diamonds, or cocaine!" He's so matter-of-fact, but the thought had never occurred to me before. A private airline charter is just perfect for that kind of operation. No wonder he gets people checked out.

"Oh, Lordy. I never knew."

"Well, now you do." Kissing the top of my head, he releases me from his hold. "If we can get something concrete on this arsehole, it'll be an open and shut case and we won't need to involve external lawyers to dissolve the contract. Anyway, Christina has it all under control. Come on, let's go and get some sleep. You must be dead beat."

"Yeah, I am a bit." My limbs are stiff from being curled up for so long. I stumble to my feet dropping the blanket on top of Bear as I stand. He doesn't move so much as a muscle; only a slight twitch of his ears shows he's still breathing. "How many people are on the board?" I ask. "I thought it was just you and Christina." There was no mention of any other partners when I Googled the company before accepting the job.

"Well, this is a slightly different board - for the wider business - The International Board, if you will."

"International?" I wasn't aware of an international connection.

"Yeah, 'though some are just advisors nowadays, they still have an authoritative vote where important decisions are concerned. My mother and father - as founding members - Gerard and his father Charles, and Johannes - who you've yet to meet." At the mention of Johannes' name, he performs an exaggerated eye-roll, "me and Christina make up the seven."

I'm surprised. This is a turn up for the books, Johannes and Gerard… and Gerard's father. "Was Marcus on the board too?" I remember the discussion about Gerard's late brother and wonder where he fits into all of this.

"Yes. Before he died, he was number six on the board. In other words, he had the sixth vote. Afterwards, Christina moved to six and the remaining members voted Gerard to take her place as number seven."

CHAPTER 15

We enter the bedroom at a leisurely pace, and at once, Silas begins to remove my clothing. Standing before me, he undoes the buttons on my shirt.

But even with this obvious attempt at distraction, my curiosity won't let go. "So, there's a pecking order?"

He slips the shirt over my shoulders and it drops to the floor. Taking me gently by my shoulders he turns me so I have my back to him. "Yes, there's an order, as there is to most things... a hierarchy so to speak."

"So what number are you?" I roll my neck to release the knots in my taught muscles.

He unclips my bra and slides it down my arms, sending it drifting to the floor. His strong arms encircle my hips as they reach around me, dexterous fingers seeking out the zip on my trousers. Pressing his front against my back, he continues to slowly remove my clothing while whispering the mundane details in my ear, as if he's narrating a tale of exotic seduction.

"I'm number four," he murmurs, sensually as he slides the zipper down. "Dad's number one," he traces the shape of an infinity symbol on the soft sensitive skin on my lower belly with his finger. I shiver in anticipation. "Charles, Gerard's father, is number two." My trousers skim down my legs, dropping to the carpet. "My beautiful mother, Sylvana, is three." The heat from his mouth grazes my ear and I jerk when I feel his thumbs tuck into the band of my knickers beside my hipbones. "I'm four," his lips skim the column of my spine as he lowers, taking the whips of satin and lace with him. "Johannes is five," his scorching breath flutters over my now naked bottom, and I shiver some more, clamping my teeth onto my lower lip to keep from groaning in pleasure. "Christina's six," he rises, stroking his heated palms up the backs of my legs. "And Gerard makes seven." When his hands reach my shoulders, he spins me around so suddenly I don't have time to take a breath before he smashes his mouth onto mine greedily.

Even though his sweater is made from the finest cashmere, the friction from the soft knitted fabric still has my nipples stinging with tenderness at the sensation. Pulling at the hem, I soon have his chest bared and flattened against mine.

Oh, the feel of him, I can't get enough!

Briefly breaking mouth contact, he yanks the crumpled jumper over his head and flings it in the corner. Propelling me backwards, he lowers me onto the bed before backing away and making brisk work of his jeans, shoes, socks and boxers.

I don't have time to admire his fine physique; he's on me in a nanosecond. "Ooof," I expel as he lands full length, on my body. "You're heavy," I complain.

"I know." He doesn't move, but just nudges my legs apart with his knee. "Seventeen and a half stone at the last weigh-in." *Wow,* that is heavy! I calculate he must have at least seven stone on me in the scales department... that's a whole other person!

Giving me some slight relief from his bulk, he supports his weight on his elbows. I love that he's so heavy, the weight of him is such a comfort. "Stop complaining, lie back and think of England!" Gazing into my eyes, he watches me as he slowly slips inside.

"Ahhh!"

His head drops and his forehead touches mine. Withdrawing slightly, he drives forward again, this time a little deeper. "Bend your knees." I'm lying flat, my arms reaching out from my sides, my hands fisting the bead covers.

Gingerly, I bend my legs, knowing what will happen the second I do.

Oh, that's deep!

I feel him sliding into the furthest part of me. The higher I raise my legs, the deeper he goes and I start to rock my hips, meeting his gentle thrusts, riding the smooth wave of our lovemaking.

"That's it. Do you know how beautiful you look right now?" he whispers. "My god, you're glowing." Collecting my hands from where they're gripping the sheets, he lays them above my head, threading his fingers through mine, our palms touching. "How lovely you are."

Dropping his gaze to my lips, he doesn't kiss me, instead, he just watches, as I slowly unravel beneath him. "I can feel you pulsing. It's incredible - like small electric shocks up and down my cock." His eyes are beginning to close; he's getting close... so am I. "Speak to me, Edi." he whispers. "Tell me what you feel."

"Silas, I..." I don't know what to say... what he wants to hear. I'm not good at pillow talk and I'm afraid I'll sound silly if I start. "Ahhh," I breath, settling on moans of pleasure instead of actual words.

"There, there... Shhh, Honey-bee, I have you."

"Ohhh, please..."

"Is that good?"

"So good, oh, so good..."

"Are you ready to come?"

"Nearly there..."

"Well then, we need to get you there.... come on Honey-bee. Give it up for me."

And under his gentle persuasion, I fall... gently at first, but then as he continues his thrusts and increases his pace, I quicken once more, the ripples of pleasure building and building until I can no longer contain it, releasing on a breathless yell of pure unadulterated rapture; pulsing and throbbing my way through the most intense prolonged orgasm, until I can no longer sustain it.

My legs drop and I release the vicelike grip on his fingers. I'm loose and lax, my legs are wobbly and I couldn't move now, even if the building were on fire.

"Oh, Man... that was intense." His head drops to my chest and his body blankets me. I can feel every ounce of his seventeen stones now and his sheer weight has me wheezing as I struggle to push the air out of my lungs.

"God, you're heavy," I pant.

"You're beautiful." He kisses me and rolls off. He's still hard. He hasn't come.

"You didn't finish." I roll onto my side and start to stroke up and down his ribcage.

Tilting his head sideways, I'm met with a wicked grin. "I thought you could do that for me. It's about time you did some of the dirty work."

"Oh!" I gasp, "you cheeky bugger." Leaping up I straddle his thighs. "Let's see how long you can survive this then."

Swiftly, before he can protest, I grab his manhood and lower my mouth around the shaft. Forcing him deep into my throat, I draw back, then surge forward. I can taste myself on him and it's a huge turn on.

"Woah! Steady, there…" His yell of surprise is an even bigger turn on though, and only encourages me to increase my pace; shielding my teeth and squeezing my lips together as I slide him in an out of my greedy mouth. "Oh God, Edi… slow down, I'm gonna come." He pushes at my slippery shoulders to get me to release my hold, but determinedly, I resist, keeping him deep in my mouth and sucking furiously. I won't give up my prize. I calculate it's been about twenty seconds and he's gonna blow his load… any… second… NOW! One last deep plunge, and a rendition of my deep-throat swallow and he's a goner, exploding into my mouth on a ragged roar and an eruption of creamy, salty cum. I swallow and lick like the cat that's got the cream… well, I have I suppose.

Smugly, I release him and lift my head. He's staring at me in disbelief; lying flat on his back, sweating and panting as I just perch there on his thighs. "Did you say something?" I question cheekily.

"Why you little…" he grabs me and pulls me down on top of him. "You're heavy," he chides, nuzzling my hair.

"Shut your face," I giggle back.

"I love you." The words tumble from his lips, unexpected, but so welcome.

"I love you too, Boss-man. Shall we sleep now?"

"Yes, Honey-bee, we can sleep now.

I jerk awake. Silas is snoring gently beside me. Bear is nowhere to be seen. Looking at the bedside clock, it's only just gone 4am, but I feel wide awake. What is it with me and waking up at stupid o'clock these days?

I'm restless and I know I won't be able to go back to sleep, so I creep out of bed and find my swimsuit. I may as well make use of the facilities, and I'm bound to have the pool to myself at this hour.

Leaving a quick note beside the bed, so Silas doesn't freak when he finds me gone, I pull on my fluffy robe and step into my flip-flops, then make my way down the stairs to the swimming pool.

The building is quiet but for the hum of the fluorescent lights in the stairway, and the occasional rumble of the lift as it moves between the floors. People must be up and at their business, but I don't see a single soul on my way to the solarium.

However, once there it's clear I won't have the swimming pool entirely to myself, as I first thought. The old dear from downstairs is here, swimming a stately breaststroke; the water around her barely rippling as she glides through it with her steady pace.

Ditching my robe and towel on a nearby chair, I cross to the steps. An almighty splash from the opposite end of the huge pool stops me in my tracks. Someone has dived into the water and is propelling along under the surface like a subaquatic torpedo. They pass by the old dear, who pays them no attention, and zoom towards me at a rate worthy of an Olympic champion.

When they reach about half way a dark head lifts from the water, tilting sideways to take a measured breath, before continuing smoothly in a perfect front crawl, to complete the length of the pool. This is some serious swimming.

On arriving at the top, the swimmer completes a flawless flip turn then powers off in the opposite direction. Once again, the self-propelled missile quickly approaches the old dear - who's still only halfway to the other end - and streams past her in a flurry of arms, legs and minimal splashes. Again, she ignores it and just keeps pushing herself through the water at a steady pace.

Refusing to be intimidated by the blatant display of male dominance in the pool, I climb down the steps and choose a lane. Kicking off from the wall, I build gently into a steady freestyle stroke. I'm not a particularly fast swimmer, but I'm a strong one. My personal skill is endurance, I'm able to swim for long periods without tiring - so distance swimming was always my preference over racing when I was in the school swim team. I'm still good, although I don't often get a chance to use my talent these days.

Fly-boy streaks past me on his return up the pool, and I manage to lap the old dear. We fall into a neat parade of swimmers, each going at our own pace; slow, medium and Speedy Gonzalez!

After about half an hour of this bizarre race, fly-boy stops at the edge of the pool to recover his breath. I'm heading in his direction, and from about ten meters away, I realise he's the old dear's grandson, which explains her indifference to his performance - she's seen it all before.

Leaning his elbows on the rim of the pool, he rests his back against the tiles and watches my approach with curiosity.

He's muscular but lean; far too lean, in fact, for a boy of his height, and his chest bones are prominent between his modest pecs. He flips his dark hair off his face with a long-fingered hand and stares at me as I swim towards him. His almond eyes follow me as I reach the edge of the pool.

"Hello." His voice is high pitched and soft. Not very masculine at all, but then, nothing about this boy is very masculine; he's androgynous, almost. I give him a half smile as I start to turn and head back up the pool. His grandmother is at the top end, making her way to the steps, clearly on her way out. "Have we met?" His speech is softly accented. Asian? European? I'm not sure, but there's a definite accent there. Vaguely, I wonder whether it's from his father or mother; because grandma - Mrs. Thingy - is definitely English.

"Erm, no, I don't think so... I live on the floor above your grandmother." Again, I try to break away and continue my swim, but he seems bent on conversation.

"Ah, my... grandmother. Yes..."

"Well, nice to meet you... Err...?"

"Liam."

"Nice to meet you, Liam..." "And you are?"

"Oh, sorry. I'm Edi." I dive beneath the water and swim away before he can ask any more questions.

Liam, hmm? I still have a strange feeling I've seen him somewhere before; I just can't put my finger on it.

By the time I reach the bottom of the pool, both Liam and Granny Thingummy, have gone and I'm alone. I complete a few more lengths, but before long, I decide I'm missing Silas, climb out of the pool and head off for a shower.

Back in the apartment, I'm greeted by a sleepy Bear. Patting his head, I fill his water bowl before filling the kettle, then head off for a hot shower. As I pass through the bedroom Silas is still sleeping, his head under the pillow, so I try to be as quiet as I can on my way to the bathroom.

An hour later, I'm showered, dressed and back in the kitchen. I'm just plugging my hairdryer in, when Silas appears in the doorway. "Did I wake you?" I ask.

"No, no… the alarm did that," he strolls over to me and takes my half-finished mug of tea from the worktop. "Did you enjoy your swim?"

"There's fresh in the pot… yes, I did thank you. But I thought I didn't wake you?"

"You didn't – my bladder did!" Sipping my tea, he scrunches up his face in disgust. "This is like ink!"

"Hey!" I manage to rescue my cup a split second before it's tipped down the sink. "I like it strong… don't judge me - I'm Mancunian," I whine. He might like his tea a bit fortnightly, but I like mine strong. As my nanna used to say *'strong enough so you can trot a mouse across it'*… which reminds me… "Mrs. Thing, from downstairs was in the pool. Her grandson's staying with her. Did you know?" I tip my head upside-down and switch on the dryer, blowing a hot stream of air over my head, and drowning out Silas's reply. The dryer is removed from my grasp and unplugged before I can stand up straight. "Hey," I whine again. I'm whining a lot this morning.

"Yes, I did. You can use the bedroom to dry your hair - I'm up now." I'm herded off towards the bedroom. "Eggs, okay?"

"Yes, thank you, Eggs would be good." I'm ravenous after my swim.

I put the finishing touches to my makeup. My hair looks nice and shiny this morning and I feel energized after my exercise. Silas calls from the kitchen, the eggs are ready, so I join him at the breakfast bar.

"Mrs. Whittham." He bites down on a piece of toast as I look at him in utter confusion.

"What?"

"Mrs. Whittham… not Mrs. Thing… her name is Mrs. Whittham."

"Ooh!" The penny finally drops and I realise were talking about the old dear from downstairs. "Well, Mrs. Whittham swims a mean breaststroke."

The eggs are perfect, fluffy and peppery, just as I like them. I also have a fresh cup of mouse-supporting tea! I take a welcome sip of the steaming liquid. Silas can't resist shaking his head at me.

"Oh, shut up you! I like my tea dark and strong. What's wrong with that combination?"

"Like your men?"

"Ha, ha, Tommy Cooper!"

"It'll put hairs on your chest!"

"And won't you be upset when that happens?" Draining my cup, I slide off my bar-stool and load my plates in the dishwasher. "Anyhow... Mrs. Whittham's grandson tried chatting me up in the pool, so he's clearly into hairy chested women!"

"Did he indeed?" Silas joins me at the sink. "He needs to be careful."

"Why... are you going to bash him up for me in a jealous rage?" I'm flattered.

"No, he won't know what's hit him – what with your enormous weight, dexterous hands, magnificent vagina and talented mouth." I'm grabbed round the waist and hauled against his hardening body. "Not to mention the hairy chest and the builder's tea - he couldn't cope with a woman this real - he'd be mincemeat; dribbling and gibbering in five minutes... you'd eat him alive!" His lips meet mine in a hot kiss.

I should be offended by his words, but I'm not. He's right, I am a lot to take. The changes in me since I met him are subtle but nonetheless mesmerizing, even to me. Every day I feel different, like another hidden part of me is emerging from deep inside.

All too soon, the moment is over. "C'mon, let's get this dog out of here before he shits on the carpet!"

"Ooh, you silver tongued devil, you... you're so romantic."

"I know... you're a lucky bitch."

"Wanker," I mutter at his retreating back. I love the bones of him so much!

CHAPTER 16

"T.G.I.F."

"Hmmm?" I feel like I've been awake for hours.

"T.G.I.F?   Thank God It's Friday?" Silas looks at me as if I'm thick.

"Oh, yeah… Friday." The happy glow of this morning's domestic bliss is rapidly turning into a chilly nervousness. I'm no longer worried about what Bobby will do, but I am concerned the business is going to be affected. And Silas still doesn't know who he is!

"When do the new girls start?"

"Monday. Why, you looking for a trade in already?"

"Nah… they might be less trouble, but why make life easy eh? Besides, we've only just got started. There's loads to do yet."

"Humph!" Still loads to do, and lots still to know I would say.

Thankfully, there are no dubious vans parked near the gates, and no sleazy photographers waiting for us to arrive. We've dodged a bullet this morning. There is, however, a sleek vintage Jaguar in the carpark and a beautiful glossy Jetstream sitting on the apron outside the hangar. I don't recognise it as one of ours.

"Gerard's here," Silas cries with a huge grin as we park up. Wasting no time, he leaps out of the Range Rover.

Gerard is waiting in the foyer with Christina. They're chatting quietly with another man. Each of them holds a black folio in their hand. I don't think I would recognise Silas's old friend Gerard, if he didn't have a leather folio case with him!

"Here they are now," Christina announces, noticing our arrival. Bear greets each one in turn. He seems to know them.

"Mon-amie, Tueur-Noir. Good to see you - and you too, beautiful Edi." Gerard gives me his customary European welcome and plants a kiss firmly on each of my blushing cheeks. "Silas, my friend." He repeats the gesture with Silas.

"Good to see you, Gerard. We're pleased you can be here." Silas looks relieved to see him. "I'm forgetting my manners… Johannes, let me introduce you to the lovely Edi Sykes… Edi, this is Johannes Müller." Silas's approach to the stranger is professional; reserved and polite, rather than warm and friendly. I get the sense they aren't that close.

"Charmed, I'm sure." Johannes, lifts my hand to his lips and coolly kisses it.

I don't think I've ever seen a man with eyes so intensely blue or hair so luxuriously golden and thick. He's very tall and lithe in appearance. Soberly dressed in a smart charcoal grey three-piece suit, with a black shirt and silver tie - the word monochrome springs to mind.

"Very nice to meet you, Johannes." I glance at Christina, who's standing demurely beside him. It's a new look for her, one I've not seen before anyway.

"Shall we?" Christina opens her arm, signifying we should follow, and we all troop off in the direction of the board room.

"Have I missed something?" I whisper to Silas as we reach the double doors at the rear of the open foyer.

"No, we just need to update Gerard on the details of last night's meeting. You go ahead, you must have a ton of work to catch up on. I'll see you later for lunch. Okay?"

"Err, yeah, tons… see you later then." I'm left on the periphery of my office as the rest of them head into the boardroom. Bear stays with me, and looks at me balefully. He knows the score. "You can shut up too," I say to him ungenerously. He's done nothing wrong.

As the group sidle through the double doors, I get a fleeting glimpse of the rest of the board members, all evenly distributed around the large oval table. From that brief moment, it's clear to decipher who's who. Silas's elegant mother, her silver-grey hair, cut fashionably short; his father, solid and stern-looking but fiercely handsome, just like his son. Gerard's father, Charles; short in stature, but strongly built like a compact French bull dog.

Their eyes divert from a fourth person I can't see, to the four newcomers entering the board room, before the doors swing to a silent close, locking them inside, and me, distinctly on the outside. I feel excluded. Vaguely, I wonder who the eighth person is? I know there's only seven board members, so this is someone who's been invited.

I've no right to feel left out. It's a private executive meeting for goodness's sake. But for some irrational reason I'm feeling snubbed; probably because there's someone else in there who I don't know.

I pull myself together sharpish. "Oh well, we'd better get some work done; c'mon boy." Bear and I trundle into my office, determined to have a productive day.

By lunchtime, the meeting is still in progress. Silas said it was just a debrief from last night, but it appears there's much to discuss.

Making myself a cup of tea, I'm glaring at my office door with growing consternation when I hear raised voices. They must be finished. With my curiosity suitably piqued, I place my mug on the credenza, and look at Bear. He must want to go out surely? I bet his legs are crossed underneath the desk. "Bear, come…"

Clearly, I was right. The poor dog doesn't hesitate, leaping to his feet and trotting eagerly to the door. When I open it, the voices become louder. I'd assumed the meeting was over, but it seems it's still in progress, just a more heated discussion.

Silas's voice booms from inside the sealed room. "Why the fuck wasn't I told?" Oh crap… I think he just heard about Bobby. Hastily, I sneak out of the office and down the corridor, tripping on tip-toe so as not to make a sound. I think this is best left to Christina.

Once I'm outside I enter the field to the left of the building behind the hangar. Bear charges off to do his business and I wait patiently, eyeing the shiny planes and aircraft. I really fell on my feet with this job. I absolutely love it here. I absolutely love my Boss-man and I absolutely love the new assertiveness he's brought out in me. If only we could sort out the tangled mess I've caused, we could all get on with enjoying this wonderful life.

"*Edi!*" The spell shatters with a resounding crash, and I'm ejected from my pipedream by the angriest voice I've heard in years. "Where are you?... *Edi?*" There's an undercurrent of panic, or is it nervous concern?

Silas steamrollers around the corner like a bat out of Hell, colliding with my body and knocking me flat on my back. "Ooof." I'm instantly winded.

Without hesitation, Bear launches at him; his protective instinct taking over, he bowls into Silas, forcing him away from my prone body. "Bear, NO!" I manage to heave through my wheezing lungs. Instantly, he drops into submission at Silas's feet. Recognising his master takes the wind out of his sails and the aggression out of his attack. I'm astonished, I never would have expected him to defend me like that - not from Silas.

"Good boy," Silas praises his actions, rewarding him with a huge pat, before turning his attention to me. "Jesus, Edi... are you okay?" Dropping to his knees beside me, I'm scooped up to a sitting position. "Honey, I'm so sorry. I didn't see you. Are you alright? Are you hurt? Let me look."

"No, no, I'm okay."

Silas helps me to my feet, and I brush the flecks of freshly mown grass from my clothing. "Shit... you're bleeding." Lifting my arm, Silas examines a nasty graze on my elbow. "Christ, I'm so sorry Edi."

Holding my palm to his face, I shake my head. I don't want sorry. "Honestly, I'm okay. Anyway, what's so urgent that you need to plough me down?" as if I didn't know...

Gathering his senses, Silas's mood turns from concern to fury in a split second. "*Robert Price.*" He snarls his name contemptuously through gritted teeth. "Robert. Fucking. Price."

"Christina told you then?" As I speak her name, she appears around the corner, skidding to a breathless juddering halt in her three-inch heels; taking in the sight of us, me dishevelled, Silas seething, before bending at the waist and exhaling her relief. "I told him..."

"Why Edi? Why didn't you tell me?" He's quivering with barely suppressed rage. I glance at Christina seeking support.

"Silas, it was me. I knew you'd react like this; I couldn't allow Edi to tell you herself. If you need to blame someone, blame me." Reaching out, she places her hand on his arm, offering comfort. "Silas?"

"You should have told me..." Jet-black eyes, blaze into mine and for a split second, I think he's going to envelope me in his arms, but he doesn't. Turning his back on me, he stalks away; his pumped body rippling with intent and anger as he rounds the corner, Bear trailing obediently in his wake.

"Silas..." Starting after him, I wail to his retreating form.

But Christina halts my progress, placing her arm across my chest, barring my way and preventing me from following. "No, leave him... he needs time to digest this."

Incredulous, I stare at her in disbelief. "You knew he'd react like this, didn't you?"

"He hates injustice. I knew he'd blow. It was better he heard it from me... seriously."

"Injustice?" I'm bubbling, simmering with anger. She should have let me tell him. I'm sure I could have pre-empted this, preventing him from diving off the deep end. "You told me to trust you, was I wrong?" The question hits her in the face like a mallet.

"No... you can trust me. It's Silas... he..." trailing off, she hesitates.

"He what?... He what Christina? What don't I know? What haven't you told me?"

Dropping her gaze to the floor, she looks crestfallen. "Lots of things, Edi... there's lots you don't know."

I go cold, the warm afternoon sun turns to an icy winter on my skin and I shiver. *There's lots to know?*

Draping her arm round my shoulder, Christina leads me back indoors. "I can tell you some of it… but please, hear me out before you judge."

Back in the relative quiet of Christina's office, she grabs two tumblers and fills them with three fingers of Scotch.

"It's going to be that kind of conversation then?" Remembering the last time I drank Scotch in her office, I don't relish what I'm about to discover.

"Hmph." Placing the glass in my hand, she eye's me warily. "Most likely," she confirms my worst fears.

"I'm listening…" Taking a sip of my Scotch I stare levelly at her, waiting.

"When you first came here, I didn't know what to expect." Sitting at her desk, she reclines in her chair and returns my stare. "No, that's not right; when you arrived, I knew exactly who I wanted you to be. I needed someone… unremarkable… uncomplicated… quiet and compliant. Someone who wouldn't draw too much attention but who could be trusted. That's who I expected you to be." Her expression doesn't change as she reveals this. "You came highly recommended."

"You already told me this. My letter of commendation from my professor… remember?" I try not to bristle at her bland description of me. I'm all of those things to an outsider… one who doesn't know my history… I wear the illusion well.

"I remember. But the truth of it is, he brought you to me, not the other way around; not the way you think."

I take another sip as I allow this bit of information to take hold. "I applied."

"Yes, you applied, but who suggested you should? Who gave you the details?"

"My professor." Now I'm wary, I applied for the role, based on his advice. "He gave me the details."

"He found you for me."

This isn't news, he was very supportive when I was looking for the right job. "Am I missing something?" For the second time this morning, the sense I've been kept in the dark is ticking at my brain. She needs to be clearer. Either I'm being dense, or she's being purposely vague.

"Edi… I needed someone specific. Someone who fitted a certain… profile and a certain criterion. More importantly, it was imperative the qualified person was of a certain age. Believable. We have connections all over the world, use people all over the world… your professor has been working with us for years."

"I don't understand… what do you mean… you use people?" I'm getting annoyed with all the cryptic data.

"Edi, this will be hard for you to hear so please don't be upset."

"Upset… try fuming… try murderous… tell me before I explode Christina."

"You came to us for a very particular reason."

"Go on…"

"Silas needed a cover. We needed someone who would be workable and provide him with the right kind of … concealment so he could carry out his job unnoticed."

"I'm not following."

"*Jesus*... Edi, Silas isn't who you think he is. He wasn't meant to fall in love with you. You were supposed to be nothing more than a diversionary tactic, a pawn to detract attention from a job in hand. This wasn't meant to happen... you..."

What?

Holding up my hands, I halt her in her tracks. I don't want to hear any more of this claptrap. "Stop!" She stops. Silently she waits for me to speak. Now it's my turn to get there on my own. I do, and quickly... "I'm a scapegoat? An excuse?"

"It wasn't supposed to happen this way," she whispers.

"Then what, Christina? What? You tell me what was supposed to happen; because as far as I was aware, I was starting the job of my dreams..."

"You were perfect on paper; highly qualified, academic, unassuming. You fitted the bill precisely. Someone who'd be there but not be the centre of attention. Someone who understood the business but would be so nondescript, they'd fly under the radar." The irony of that statement just takes the biscuit. "Someone who Silas could be with, without drawing unwarranted attention."

"So, you employed me because I was older and boring? Is that it?"

"They're your words, not mine... but ... yes."

"Well, that came back to hit you in the face, didn't it?" The level of sarcasm and venom in my retort surprises even me.

"In more ways than one..."

"What's that supposed to mean?"

"Paris."

"Paris." I physically deflate. Apart from the hideous party, the rest of the sensual experience will be etched on my memory for a lifetime.

"Yes, Paris. It was supposed to be a cover for a job. You were there as decoration, nothing more. The green dress? Did you seriously think you'd get away with standing out so vividly at a black-tie event?" She eyes me sheepishly. I feel embarrassed. I thought I looked good, but she's just smothered all the good with that one disparaging statement. "But yes... it came back to bite us in the arse; ferociously, I would say..."

I'm unbelievably hurt. She pushed us together, wanted us together. Now it's as if it was all an illusion. My heart's too fragile for this. Silas said he loved me... we made love... a lot. Not just in Paris, but since. All my pain and anguish bubbles to the surface.

"What... did you think would happen? Did you think I'd let him fuck me just to be grateful, because I was flattered, he showed some interest?" I did, but she doesn't need to hear that. I was a gullible sap! I should've smelled a rat; I should've known it was too good to be true... but he told me he loves me... just this morning... he told me he loved me. "What happened? What changed?" I spit.

"You weren't who you were supposed to be. You were far, far, more. You were smart, funny, warm, and... human. You were Meredith Frost, returned from the wilderness and he fell in love with you... that's what happened."

"I fell in love with him too," I whisper. Christina looks at me as if I've just confessed to a crime. I have fallen in love with him. It isn't my fault, it was easy, he's an amazing man. "So, this 'job'... did it happen, or did I ruin that too?"

"No, everything was delivered."

"Delivered?" Realization hits me like a thunderbolt… shit, he's a criminal - a smuggler or something - he uses the aeronautical business as a cover for his illegal activity. I don't want to know what it is, but I can guess. There was definitely a furtive undercurrent when I met Gerard; now it all makes sense. They're an international smuggling ring, and I've inadvertently landed smack bang in the middle of it all.

Fucking Hell!

"Yes. And now… this exposure could be crippling. I wasn't aware of who you were. This is all my fault." She's distraught, but I won't concede.

"Yes, it is." I'm not denying it. It is her responsibility, her doing, her damage, her fault. Bobby found me because of her and now we have a huge mess. And to think I was concerned about their business?... fuck that!... Bobby will be in his element. "What's next?" I'd love to know what she proposes to do about all this.

"Christ knows… we get pissed?... I kill you?... you kill me?" Rubbing her hand over her forehead, she huffs an ironic laugh, "pigs in *fucking* outer-space… this is fucked up!"

"Yeah… it is." Knocking back my drink, I extend my glass; getting drunk right now being my preferred option of the three. "Where's he gone?" she knows I mean Silas. I'm hopeful he's gone to cool down, but I'm doubtful.

"Probably to hit something…"

I bridle at that. Hit what? God, I hope he doesn't do anything unwise. "What?"

"The gym… he'll be at the gym beating the crap out of something or lifting something heavy."

I'm placated, but not by much. The fact he's venting his spleen at the gym is little consolation, when I've been treated like a commodity to be used and manipulated at their whim. I should be the one beating the crap out of something.

"I want to go home." Standing, I slam my empty glass on the table. If he deems to come back, he can do some explaining. I don't care how angry he is. I'm the one who's been cheated and coerced, I have every right to be mad too.

CHAPTER 17

I pace the apartment like a prowling lioness, unable to dispel the notion once again I've been used. A man's plaything, manipulated and moulded until I'm compliant and willing to do anything and everything asked of me.

Of course, this time is different. This time, I was more than willing to be consumed by the hedonistic, overwhelming desire that grew inside me, day by day, minute by minute. This time it was Silas and this time I truly loved him.

But Christina has sewn a seed of doubt and I can't prevent my mind from seesawing between fear, anxiety, anger and sadness. I'm all over the place with my emotions. I need to get a grip and face up to what I need to learn. I need answers and I need them from Silas.

It's four o'clock. I've been home for an hour and as yet, I haven't sat down, preferring to stalk the apartment from room to room, killing time with my seething thoughts.

My mobile rings, my usual ringtone and I dive to the kitchen where it's charging on the counter.

"Hello," I snap, not even looking at the caller I.D.

"Whoa…, easy there, tiger." It's Lizzy.

My heart leaps with joy at the sound of her voice and my eyes fill with tears. "Oh… oh, baby-girl, I'm so pleased to hear from you…" I croak breathlessly, trying to prevent my voice from cracking and giving away my distress.

"Mum?... What is it?" She's perceptive enough to know there's something up.

"Oh, Lizzy, baby… I miss you so much. It's so long to be apart. I thought I'd cope, but I'm not doing too well. I miss my Squidge." Hoping her baby-name will cause a diversion and draw some humour, I wield it unashamedly.

"That's not going to wash, mother." It doesn't work… I'm rumbled. "Tell me… what's wrong? Is the job horrible? Are the people rotten?"

I manage to smile through my sorrow. "Huh! The people are fine." Some of them are more than fine. "I'm just being dramatic. You shocked me calling out of the blue, that's all." *Dramatic!* That's an understatement.

"Hmmm, well, if you're sure it's nothing?"

She offers me another chance to come clean, but I'm steadfast. "Honestly, I'm tired and it was such a lovely surprise to hear from you - it made me realise how much I'm missing my little girl - I'm fine… really."

"Pfft!" That did it, she hate's mushy stuff. "Well, get over it… I've got some news."

"Oh, what's she been up to now?" It has to be Sam. She's either been arrested or has landed a job as an exotic dancer. I wouldn't be surprised by either.

"We're coming home." Lizzy drops the bomb and waits for my response.

"*What*, why?" My voice has risen several octaves in surprise.

Coming home?

"Yeah… the truth is, we've had enough. I think six weeks was overambitious for two British birds who've never been further than Benidorm." *Goodness…* "This long-haul business is okay, but to be honest, I'm really missing you and the Carrot."

Oh, David… crap! We were supposed to be taking the three musketeers to the pub tonight. I'd be surprised if that happens now. But the girls coming home though? How many more complications do I need today?

Sensing my absence from the conversation, Lizzy barks down the line for my attention… "Hello… hello, are you there?"

I can't speak. I'm desperate for them to come home, but I need this mess cleared up. With the girls away, it was one less thing to worry about. "You're coming home? That's brilliant. Umm, when?"

"Well, we thought we'd stay one more week. Travel to Florida, and fly home from there. I think we'll have just about done everything we want to; until the next visit anyway."

"Next week." That doesn't give me much time. "Are you sure? You've only been there a fortnight. Surely, you can stay a bit longer?"

"Nope… The deed is done. We're going to Florida tomorrow and the following Saturday, we're flying home. I thought you'd be pleased?"

"Oh Baby-girl, I am, I am… it's just… work's so busy… you know."

"Yeah, I know what kind of 'work' you've been up to. And I can't wait to meet him… Look, I need to go, this call will be running into the millions if I don't hang up. But I'll call you with the flight details next Friday. Ciao Mamma."

"Bye, bye darling… I love you."

"More than Coco-pops." As the phone goes dead, I hear the keys in the door. Silas is back.

Unable to settle on a mood, I'm nonplussed when he enters the kitchen… armed with a beautiful bouquet of pale-yellow roses! "Peace offering."

Ignoring him, I skirt around the counter, walk through the lounge and on to the terrace outside. I need fresh air, I'm suffocating. There's far too much to think about, discuss and argue over and I don't have patience for romantic gestures here and now.

"Edi… can we talk?" Abandoning the flowers, he's followed me into the cooling afternoon. "Edi?"

"Talk…" Speaking to the view, I refuse to look at him. "Let me get this straight. I need to make sure I have all the right words before I start." Then, whirling towards him, I lean on the perimeter wall, crossing my arms over my chest in order to prevent myself from lashing out. "*Cruel, conniving, lying, manipulating, thoughtless, selfish, user!*" He recoils at the might of my anger. "You used me and abused me and now I'm in love with you and I hate you for it!" Rising with every word, my voice has become a screech and my fists are slamming into the wall behind me.

"I thought Bobby was an evil bastard, but I don't even know if there's a word for how I'm feeling about you and Christina right now. You *used* me, Silas. You're a criminal and I've been sucked in to it all without the first notion of what I was letting myself in for… seriously, how could you? You must think I'm something else!"

"Criminal? What the Hell are you talking about?" I'll give him his due, he looks confused.

"You. You and your *'International Business.'* Christina told me about it. I'm not so stupid that I can't work out what the business is… smuggling. You use the Air Business as a cover. You used *me* as an alibi in Paris, didn't you? What did you bring back huh? What were you and Gerard doing all that time you were away from me, hmm?" The confusion on his face has transformed into a look of astonished incredulity.

"I stood there like an idiot, sticking out like a sore thumb, in that stupid green dress, while people pawed at me, while Lynda recognised me. All to draw attention away from whatever dodgy deal you and Gerard were cooking up in that back room!" They had to be up to something dodgy, what else could it have been? *God I'm stupid!*

Would you ever have told me? Or did you expect I'd remain oblivious forever? I may have taken my clothes off for a living, but Christ, give me *some fucking* credit… I still had a mind of my own. How the Hell do you think I managed to look after myself and two children for seventeen years. I'm not a complete idiot Silas." Boiling tears of shame are streaming down my face, I'm incensed with humiliation and fury and totally unable to control it.

"Well, you're not as smart as you think you are, because everything you've just said is utter bollocks. Do you know how ridiculous you sound right now?" He meets me volume for volume and head-to-head. He's as angry as I am and probably twice as loud. But I don't care who can hear us, we need to have this out.

Storming past him, I fly back into the lounge, Silas following hard on my heels. Grabbing my arm, he spins me so we're nose to nose. "Take your hands off me." Flexing my arm, my fingers curling into fists by my side, I'm ready to punch him - it'll be ineffective, but I'm prepared to fight back. With a heaving chest, I hiss into his face "Let. Me. Go." I'm not afraid of him, I know he's not Bobby, and he won't hurt me but at this moment, I don't want to be distracted by his touch.

When he drops his hand, I immediately feel bereft, 'though I'm grateful he's yielded to my demand.

"I'm not a criminal," he whispers. "I'm not a smuggler."

"No? Then what Silas? I know whatever you do isn't completely 'legit', so what are you?"

"I'm not a criminal," the concerned furrow of his eyebrows, as he murmurs his denial, have me on edge.

Ignoring my request for an explanation, he continues. "I admit, initially you were employed to assist me in a difficult… transaction - but the moment I saw you, I knew - I wanted you instantly; I couldn't dismiss the feeling that we were meant to be together." His sincerity is calming.

"What are you, Silas? Hmm, If you're not a smuggler, then what?" It's with some difficulty I resist his compelling words.

"Honey-bee, please. We need to talk about this rationally. Don't let one argument tear us apart - we're stronger than this."

"Argument." Is this an argument? It feels much more than that to me.

Silas turns and walks to the kitchen, leaving me standing confused and none the wiser in the middle of the living room. "We said we'd take the kids to the pub for tea." Just like that, it's as if the last ten minutes didn't happen. A switch has flicked and his temper has abated considerably, but I'm still simmering with questions.

"And how are we going to do that when we're fighting like this?" I've followed him into the kitchen where I find him rummaging in a cupboard.

Collecting the cut glass vase that just last week was holding my beautiful peonies, he fills it with water and starts to expertly arrange the yellow roses. "Edi, I think I've just as much to be angry about as you do. But my main concern is your safety. I can't stand by and watch *him* rip your life apart again. Not now. Not now you're mine." The last bit is said in a whisper so faint that I barely hear it.

"Silas…"

"Please Edi… there's stuff about me you need to know, but believe me when I tell you, honestly. I. Am. Not. A Criminal!"

I believe him… How could I not? My relief at hearing this is palpable. Covering my face with my palms, I collapse to my knees and sob. I sob and sob. The tears just keep coming.

I've never cried as much as I have since I met Silas, yet he's without a doubt the love of my life. I've never felt so alive as I do when I'm with him.

When he makes love to me, I forget every bad thing that ever happened to me. There's only him and me and our incredible connection. The world doesn't exist when we're together and it frightens me that I feel so deeply for him.

Even if he is a notorious organized crime boss, I couldn't give him up… I could forgive him anything. "I'm sorry…" I sob the words that mean so little to me, but it's the only thing I can say. The only thing that is right, here and now.

"Don't you dare say you're sorry to me. There's no need." Stooping, he scoops me up as if I weigh nothing and carries me to the sofa. Dropping me onto the cushion, he leaves me there to gather my thoughts while he goes into the kitchen. I can hear him, going through the motions of making tea.

Five minutes later, he's back and I'm considerably calmer. "Mouse supporting tea." He hands me the steaming mug.

"Thank you." A weak laugh escapes my lips. I appreciate the gesture.

"We need to talk about the scumbag." He says it quite calmly, even though I know he's seething just thinking about it.

"The scumbag… I couldn't think of a better name for him!"

"If the cap fits."

"He'll do his best to discredit you."

"He can try."

"Silas, he has no scruples… none. He has no conscience; he won't give up on this - ever."

"We'll see."

I sip my tea. It's strong and hot and distracting. "These things… I need to know about you… are they bad?"

"Some things…"

"Have you done bad things?"

"Some things…" He looks so sad suddenly it wrenches my heart. He's too good to do bad things.

93

"Silas?" I place my mug on the coffee table and swivel in my seat to face him. "I think I need to confront Bobby. If I can face my deepest fears, face Bobby, could you tell me some of the bad things?"

"Some of the bad things…" He's wistful, his eyes drifting and misting over.

"Silas?"

"Oh, shit! C'mon, we need to get moving if we're going to the pub with the kids." Abruptly, he's back in the present, once again evading my questions.

"Silas?"

"Yeah? We'll be late. Hurry up. We can talk later."

"Silas?"

"We. Will. Talk. Later…" I'm guided through the door and out of the apartment, the subject closed, but only temporarily. I have no intention of letting this drop. Making a mental list of questions, I trail down the stairs to the next landing.

CHAPTER 18

The kids are thrilled to see us. David and Wendy sit side by side on the rear seat. I squash in beside them so Dominic can sit next to his dad.

"We just need to collect Bear from the barn," he tells them when they complain the dog is missing.

Satisfied, they chatter on about all the things going on at the Beeches. Apparently, Wendy's parents have arranged for an entertainer to come in and play some singalong songs for her birthday. It's a few weeks away yet, but he's very popular so it's best to book in advance.

At the barn, the rest of us wait in the car while Silas collects Bear. With him securely settled in the hatch, we get going again.

The pub's quiet for a Friday, so we don't have any trouble finding a table. We quickly order, and while we wait for our food, Nic, Wendy and David take Bear to the adjacent field to play catch, leaving me and Silas alone.

"Are you going to sulk all night?"

"I didn't realise I *was* sulking," I retort, sulkily. "And yes, I just might!"

"Edi," he warns.

"What?"

"We promised the kids a nice pub dinner. Can't you at least *pretend* to enjoy yourself? By all means rip into me when we get back, but for now, just straighten your face will you?"

The harsh tone of his voice is like a slap and I'm immediately on the defence. "Don't speak to me like I'm a child," I hiss.

"Well, stop fucking behaving like one."

Our puerile sniping is cut short by the kids returning to the table, warm and glowing from their run-around the garden with Bear. I notice Nic's smiling. It's the first time I've seen his smile and it's beautiful, just like his dads.

Sheepishly I look at Silas through my lashes. I want to make amends for my behaviour. He's gazing at me just as thoughtfully. "I love you!" I mouth, silently.

Tilting his chin, he acknowledges my contrition, "you too," he mouths back whilst nodding his gentle acceptance of my weak apology. "Oh look, here's the food… it looks great."

"Two fishfinger sandwiches, one cheese and onion pie with mash, one cod and sweet potato fries and a sirloin steak with triple cooked chips." We all raise our hands in turn as the server announces our meals.

"Mmm, I'm hungry." David grabs the cutlery from the wooden caddy and hands it round the table.

"Will that be all?"

"Could I have some vinegar please?" David and I chorus in unison, then giggle as the waiter takes the bottle from the pocket of his apron.

"Vinegar, ketchup and some tartar sauce." They magically appear, as if he's performing a conjuring trick; thrilling the kids with his charm and cheek.

Silas slices the end from his steak and drops it on the floor for Bear, who's salivating at the sheer abundance and tempting prospects going on above him on the table. "Good lad."

"When's your Birthday Wendy?" I'll get her a nice present. Something girly, perfume perhaps.

"September the seventh; I'll be twenty-six," she announces proudly.

"Mine's in September too. The fifth." David, always keen to be heard pipes up. "Mine's before yours. I'm going to be eighteen."

"Yes, you are. What would you like for your birthday? Anything special?"

The fishfinger sandwich is scrumptious; David is tucking in too. Licking ketchup from his fingers, he finishes his mouthful before answering. Placing his knife and fork on the table, he becomes serious. "Yes."

"Well, what is it?"

"Mum, can you tell me about my dad?"

His comment floors me… literally… I freeze with my sandwich suspended halfway to my mouth as time stalls. Suddenly my head is swimming and the wind is stolen from me; the beer garden seems to shrink to an infinitesimal speck on the horizon, drawing away from this point in time; a point in time I want to rewind as if it hasn't happened.

"Mum! Mum! Please, mum." I'm on the grass and I don't know how I got here. "What happened?"

"Edi? Edi? Oh Christ, Edi?" Strong arms are lifting me to a sitting position. "You passed out and slipped off the bench. Are you okay? Did you bang your head?"

Am I okay? I check my vital signs, I feel okay. I've never fainted before, it feels strange, like time disappeared and I ended up on the floor. "Yeah, yeah, I think so…"

"Let me help you." Silas assists me to my feet, pulling the chair so I can sit down. "Steady."

"Mummy!" David flings his arms around me. "Mum, I don't want to see my dad. I'm sorry."

"What… no…" This isn't his fault. I attempt to shake some of the fuzziness from my head.

Nic and Wendy are looking on in concern. Wendy has her arm around Nic's shoulders giving him comfort. The picture's comical; he's easily a foot taller than she is.

"Edi?" Silas is crouching before me, the remains of my fishfinger sandwich are scattered on the floor where they must have fallen when I fainted. "David, go and fetch some water, will you?" Silas, hands over a ten-pound note. David takes it but doesn't move, hovering beside me, worried.

"David darling, please can you go and get me some water?" If I ask him, I know he'll do as he's bid. And as I knew he would, he jogs off to into the pub for my drink.

"Wendy, Nic, please will you go and help David?" Silas asks quietly.

"Yes, come on Nic. Let's go." Wendy understands immediately and takes the hint. Tugging the sleeve of Nic's sweater, she urges, "we need to help David," apparently more than happy to be out of our way. "Your dad has this under control."

"Thank you." Silas watches them go before rising and sitting beside me. "Jesus, Edi. What's going on with you tonight?"

"I... he's... where did that come from? He's never asked about his dad before, I've no idea how to handle this."

"Look, just let's get home. Here's David with the water."

David passes me the bottle and I take a long refreshing drink. "Thank you, love. That's better."

"Mum, are you alright now?"

"Yes Davy, I'm good. Let's just get going. I think I need to get some sleep. I'm tired love, that's all."

"Well... okay then," he concedes, though I sense reluctance in his manner. "Silas, can you take my mum home please?" He's uncertain, but I know he won't question me further.

Nic and Wendy hover with Bear on the edge of the beer garden. Clearly, they're eager to go too. "Yes, come on guys, let's get Edi home."

We drop the kids off at the Beeches. On the journey, Silas placates them by making light of my fainting performance; dismissing it as tiredness. Extracting chuckles from the guys with his routine; I'm working too hard when I'm not used to it; he's a slave-driver; Christina's cracking the whip; that kind of thing. By the time we arrive at the Beeches, they appear to have accepted it as just one of those things. But all joking aside, Silas may well be right, I've never had such a dramatically eventful day in all my life; and there's been several since I started working at RTC, but this one takes the cake.

I'm dead on my feet as I shuffle into the foyer with Silas by my side. "Edi, I need to leave." He looks at his watch, "I'm running late... will you be alright on your own?"

"Why... why do you need to go?" I thought he was coming in so we could pick up our discussion where we left off.

"Remember... I have an overnight to Paris. I told you."

"Oh, yes I remember now... I'll be fine. I just need to sleep." I'm sulking again, though it's half-hearted. I really am exhausted. Perhaps we should leave it until tomorrow when we're both fresher and more receptive.

"I'll see you up."

"No, no, I'll be fine... you go. Don't be late for Gerard."

"If you're sure, I don't like leaving you like this. Should I call Christina?"

"Jesus, Silas, just go will you. I'm fine. I'm tired and I don't need a babysitter!"

His face is etched with concern, but he doesn't push it. "I'll see you tomorrow then?"

"Yeah, in the morning." Nodding, I dismiss him on a wave. I don't kiss him, or even look at him, I just sidle through the door to the stairway and start a slow steady climb to my floor.

Arriving at the second landing, I stop and lean against the wall to catch my breath. The door to Mrs. Whittham's apartment opens, and the young Oriental guy walks out... with a stunning willowy black woman.

WHAM! Recognition hits me, and I'm zapped from my stupor in an instant; Liam Zaio and Django are striding towards me, arm in arm and utterly oblivious to the frayed woman stood panting in the corridor! Blinking in disbelief at what I'm seeing, I don't trust my eyes. The last time I saw these two together was on the TV, the morning after the Paris fashion week wrap party, the morning after Pierre Adrax was found dead in his hotel room. The morning they were arrested!

So engrossed are they in each other, they barely give me a passing glance as I meld myself against the wall, allowing them right of way.

No wonder he looked familiar when I saw him in the swimming pool. I didn't recognise him in the water. Who would have? It's the very last place I'd expect to see him. But now he's with Django, they're unmistakable. Individually, they're striking, but together, they make an unmistakable combination, impossible to ignore.

What the Hell are they doing here? I gape after them, contemplating if I should follow. I wonder where they're going?

Quickly, I sprint up the remaining flight of stairs, almost dropping my keys in my haste to get into the apartment. Leaving the door to close on its hydraulic hinge, I charge onto the balcony and lean over the wall, looking down into the carpark. Where are they?

A shiny black Jaguar is parked in the visitor's space, its engine idling. It's reversed in, so it's ready to drive out at top speed.

I hear them before I see them. High affected laughter and chatter echoes from below, though I don't catch any specific words.

When they come into view, Liam supports Django gently by the elbow, attentively guiding her towards the Jag. Then the driver's door opens, and... *Oh my God!*... It's Johannes!

Opening the rear door of the car, he scans the area with keen eyes, checking for watchers. *Don't look up, don't look up*... but he does, briefly flicking his eyes skyward and towards me. Startled, I jerk backwards, hoping I was quick enough and he didn't notice me.

Standing on the balcony, I slowly count to ten, before taking a tentative step forward, daring to risk a surreptitious peek over the edge. Holding my breath, I quickly glance down at the Jag, which is now pulling out of its parking space and exiting the double gates.

Releasing an audible sigh, I watch as it manoeuvres into the flow of traffic and glides smoothly down the road.

Stepping away from the wall, I sit in the nearest chair, which just happens to be one of the sofas, and stare, unseeing, at the coffee table. Now I'm really confused. *Just what the Hell is going on?* I have no idea what I've got myself involved with, but I'm determined to find out.

Before I know it, I have my laptop set up on the dining table, a cup of strong black coffee steams on a coaster and I've found a lined notebook and several pens. Both my mobile phones are set neatly to the side and I've slid the security bolt and chained the door; just to be sure. I don't want any unwelcome disturbances.

Now I have all my stuff, I don't know where to start, or what exactly I'm looking for, so I sit and sip my coffee, hoping for some divine inspiration.

Deciding on a quick Google search, I type in 'Liam Zaio' and get about fifty-thousand hits; all to do with his modelling career and mostly arty images of him, stalking moodily along various catwalks looking pale, gaunt and drawn, draped in wisps of sheer designer fabric.

I scroll through the list, searching for a hint of the story from last Saturday, but there's nothing. *How strange?* Perhaps I'm not using the right combination of words, so I quickly type in 'Liam Zaio, Pierre Adrax, Django' and hit the search key.

Again, I'm presented with a series of photographs of the models; occasionally there's one of Adrax alongside them, but there are no stories. *Weird.*

I stare at the screen. I don't understand why there's no details about the incident last week and the mysterious death of Pierre Adrax - then I glance at the top of the frame, and realise I have selected images. *Idiot!* I aim the mouse at the news tab, and click. Suddenly the screen changes and I'm bombarded with thousands of results; from the BBC Headlines, to the latest top stories from around the world.

And there it is, the latest update on the 'Unexplained Death of Fashion Mogul, Pierre Adrax.' Clicking on the article, I start to read.

Last Saturday the fashion world was rocked to its foundations by the sudden, unexplained death of design house mogul, Pierre Adrax.

Mr. Adrax's body was discovered in his hotel bedroom in the early hours of Saturday morning by his ward, the top Japanese model, Mr. Liam Zaio.

Results of a post-mortem, performed by the renowned pathologist, Monsieur Benoit Babine, have so far proved inconclusive and the preliminary examination revealed nothing to specify the exact cause of death. Earlier today, a spokesperson for the coroner's office, said the current position remains, Mr. Adrax died of natural causes as yet undetermined.

In a further statement, a police representative confirmed, while the exact reason for the death remains unclear, detectives have yet to rule out the possibility of foul play; and while initial investigations have failed to uncover any evidence to support their suspicions, French Police will continue with their inquiries until such time the coroner deems the case to be closed.

Mr. Zaio and his companion, the Somalian supermodel Django, remain in protective custody, although, currently, their whereabouts are unknown.

So, whereabouts unknown, and an inconclusive post-mortem? Well, I know where they are. They're here - with Mrs. Whittham - their 'Grandmother'. And with Johannes appearance and furtive behaviour, it's beginning to make some sense.

No wonder Silas said I sounded ridiculous when I accused him of smuggling. For goodness's sake! He's not a criminal, he's a saviour! His side-line isn't importing illegal drugs, or trafficking, it's helping vulnerable people. How wrong was I, suspecting him of criminal activity, when all the while he's providing a safe house, a refuge for two people who have absolutely nowhere to go? He's a hero, a man of honour, not a villain. What a joyous revelation.

I sit in stunned silence for a few minutes deciding what I should do next. There's only one thing that springs to mind... '*The Board*'. Clearly, I need to understand more.

Moving the cursor to the search bar, I type in '*Rose Council*'. Nothing comes up other than a load of sites referencing Lancashire Borough and Yorkshire Councils and a whole raft of *'Wikki'*, about the *'War of the Roses'*, but there's nothing specific about the *'Rose Council'* as I know it - I could be here all night.

Changing tack, I type in 'Johannes Müller' and click enter. Several results fill the screen. Along with details of his Linked-in profile, Facebook page and Instagram account there's a hyper-link to his international logistics business. I click on it.

Johannes is the Director of JM Logistics and Transport FCA, which I know stands for free carrier in the air transport industry, so a valid association to RTC is conceivable and would make sense. The business concentrates on transportation between Europe and the rest of the world, and has been incorporated for over two decades – so quite established.

The next click joins the dots, and does indeed, connect the two businesses. It briefly mentions the international association with Royal Tudor Charters, and shows a very professional photograph of Silas, Johannes and Christina. Silas is frowning as usual. Christina looks radiant, and is wearing her customary gold chain. Johannes appears cool and handsome, with just a trace of a smile on his lips.

Other than a comprehensive list of services and connected businesses, there's little more to read. The original was founded by Johannes' father, Johan Müller. The current headquarters are located at Port Elizabeth in the Eastern Cape Province; one of the major Sea Ports in South Africa. The Air business operates out of Port Elizabeth International Airport.

Picking up my pen, I make some notes on my pad. Nothing too detailed, just bullet points. If I'm going to remember all this stuff, I need to write it down.

So absorbed am I in my research, when my mobile rings, I answer it on impulse.

"Hello?" I underline the address of Johannes head office with a double line.

"I saw you…"

"What? Sorry, who is this?" I'm not paying attention.

"I said, I saw you." *Bobby!* "Since when did you do charity work?"

Charity work? "I have nothing to say to you. You need to stop ringing me and leave me alone."

"I saw you… with the retards in the pub." He's putrid.

My anger bubbles at his disgusting arrogance. He has no idea David is his son, and I vow he'll never find out. I ignore his comment, not willing to rise to the well strung bait. "Leave. Me. Alone." Surprising myself at how calm but determined I sound; I hang up and switch off my phone.

Losing interest in all things Johannes, I don't bother clicking on his personal details; it can wait for another time when I have more energy for concentration.

What a day! I've had enough, and Bobby phoning was the ultimate last straw. I need sleep. Switching off my laptop I unplug everything and pack it all away. Grabbing my phones, I enter the bedroom, suddenly bone weary.

Stripping off my work clothes, I leave them where they land and crawl into bed. I can't even summon the energy to brush my teeth. Switching off the light, I'm asleep in ten seconds.

CHAPTER 19

Someone is hammering loudly. The relentless banging and thudding won't stop. I wish whoever has decided Saturday morning is the perfect time for a spot of DIY would pack it in.

Reluctantly, I open my eyes. I was having such a lovely deep dreamless sleep as well. Rolling onto my back, I listen to the incessant racket, only to realise it's coming from my front door!

Shit! I forgot to remove the security bolt when I came to bed last night. If it's Silas, I've managed to lock him out. He'll be fuming.

For some reason the image makes me giggle, and I clamber from my pit, chuckling at the thought of him standing outside the apartment, making enough noise to waken the dead.

"Alright, alright… I'm coming," I call as I drag on my dressing gown.

The hammering doesn't stop, but is joined by an impatient voice shouting my name. "Edi, come on will you. I'm bursting for the loo!"

"I'm here." Releasing the chain, I unfasten the bolt, and step back just in time, as the door swings open and a clearly desperate Silas forces his way inside and dashes off in the direction of the bathroom. "Whoa… someone's in a hurry," I say to his fleeing back as I close the door.

"Yeah."

I follow him, but don't enter, choosing to allow him some dignity. "Have you been there long?" Glancing at the clock, I see it's gone eight. I slept well.

"A couple of hours, I didn't want to wake you." The toilet flushes and I hear the running of the tap. A couple of seconds later and Silas appears, drying his hands on a towel. "Why was the door bolted? I had to sit on the mat outside, until I was desperate for a pee." He frowns, hanging the damp towel over the radiator.

"I was on my own. I feel safer with the bolt on," I lie convincingly.

"Hmmm, well I tried phoning, but there was no answer."

"Oops, I switched my phone off." Backing into the bedroom, I pick it up from the bedside table and switch it on. Immediately, it starts to chime, telling me I have several missed calls and text messages. "Looks like you tried a few times."

"I may have left a couple of messages and the odd text," he says, sheepishly.

"Well, you're here now… breakfast?" It's the least I can do after he's been sitting, cross-legged on the welcome mat for the last hour or so.

"Mmm, yes…" He stalks towards me, intent clear in his eyes. "I'm starving." Reaching out, he grabs the belt of my dressing gown and uses it to draw me towards his waiting mouth. "Kiss me wench," he demands softly.

"Why, sir… I'm not suitably dressed," I tease, as he takes my lips gently.

"Really?" Silas tugs lightly on the belt, so that the knot slips through his fingers and unravels. Once the ties are hanging free, he sweeps his hand across the front of the robe, unwrapping it and draping it open so my naked torso is unveiled. "Well, it looks like you're suitably *undressed* to me." Sliding his hand inside the material, he strokes my belly, just below my navel, ever so lightly, the slight friction causes me to shiver.

"I've missed you..." His hand travels downwards, "...so much." Lower it goes, until he's brushing his fingers through my damp pubic hair. "So, so, much."

Retreating half a step, he reacquaints himself with the contours of my body. His eyes travel, over my breasts, along my sternum, until he's raptly studying his hand as it caresses and traces the cleft leading to the entrance of my moist centre.

Dropping to his knees, he looks up at me as I look down upon him. For a few seconds we stay like that, just gazing into each other's eyes. Him exploring with gentle fingers as he watches my response; me holding onto his shoulders to prevent myself from toppling over as I absorb the heady sensations of his attention.

"Silas," I start to tremble with want.

"I'm here." Leaning forward, he kisses me. Gently, his fingers separate my folds and his lips land softly on my tender clitoris. I mewl with desire.

"Shhh."

"Ahh, please, Silas." Oh Lord, this is heaven.

"Be still Honey-bee. We're nearly there." He introduces his tongue, and inserts two fingers. "Open your legs, baby." I widen my stance so he has better access. "That's it. Now sit on the floor."

Gently, I'm lowered until I'm sat on the floor with him kneeling between my legs. "Now, lean back - go on - lie down." Tilting backwards, I recline, focusing on the ceiling, waiting for my next instruction. "Now, stay still, and enjoy..."

My arms fly above my head at the first strike of his hot tongue. "Ahh!" the sensation is incredible. I bend my knees and curl my toes into the plush carpet.

Silas continues to suck and nip while at the same time, returning two fingers deep inside me, pumping slowly in and out, at a steady relentless rhythm.

"Oh, God," I wail. I'm building up to an intense release. "Please..." Silas latches on to my clitoris and starts to flick backwards and forwards with his tongue. The change in tempo increases my desire and I writhe on the floor. "Silas, I'm coming." Plunging deeply with his fingers, he laps at my sensitive nub, encouraging my orgasm forward.

"Come for me, Honey-bee."

And with his final demand I shatter, splintering into a thousand glittering pieces, I come, trembling and shaking; I squirm and spasm on the carpet, my legs juddering with the sheer stimulus of uncontainable tension. "Agggghh!" I scream, my breath releasing along with my glorious climax. Oh lord, he's so talented. I love his mouth on me.

"How was that Honey?" A smug looking Silas lifts his head from between my thighs, and rests his chin on my pubis. His lush lips are glistening.

"It was alright," I smirk cheekily.

"Just alright?" He feigns hurt. He's stupidly skilled at cunnilingus, and he knows it.

"Meh! it was fine I suppose..." I shrug on a cheeky grin. I'm risking a good hiding at this rate.

"Well, if it's just alright, I'd better give it up as a bad job. No point in pursuing something if you're never going to be any good at it," he huffs sarcastically, heaving himself to his feet.

"No, no…" I laugh at his sulk. "It was amazing, the best… earth moving. I love your mouth. You're brilliant… I love you," I sooth, taking the sting out of my previous tart comment.

"That's better; now get your arse off the carpet and make me some breakfast woman, before I tan your hide and fuck you into submission."

"Ooh, you silver tongued Devil." I'm hauled to my feet, my belt retied and I'm frog-marched into the kitchen, where I'm deposited in front of the stove.

Silas takes a seat at the breakfast bar. "On you go… don't let me stop you."

Two eggs, grilled bacon, tomato, mushrooms, fried bread and a slice of black-pudding later, he leans back in his chair and pats his flat stomach. "I'm stuffed… that was lush. You can't beat a fry-up on a Saturday morning."

"You're welcome. Anything for my Boss-man."

Loading the dishwasher, I flick on the kettle and drop two tea-bags into the teapot. Sweeping by him in a flutter of fluffy purple fur, I take the milk from the fridge, but don't get very far. Silas traps me in his vicelike arms and hauls me in to his chest, pulling me against him tightly and burying his face in the crook of my neck.

I wait patiently, clutching the milk bottle, allowing him to inhale my scent and get his fix, before I'm freed so I can finish brewing the tea.

"How did the trip to Paris go?" I hand him his milky tea, "fortnightly, as you like it," as I take a reviving sip of my own, preferred, dark tan, builders brew. "Hmmm."

"Thank you; it was uneventful. There and back, just a quickie, not a lay-over."

"For what reason?" I have an idea, but I need confirmation from him.

"Dropping something off."

"What 'something'?"

"Nothing important." He's evasive, I'm not happy.

I know it's not really any of my business, but I need to know what's going on. The subliminal snippets and dribs and drabs of information are driving me bonkers. And what with Bobby crawling out from under his stone and making my life a misery, I need at least this part of it, to be constant. I just need clarity, not this fuzzy evasive *hooey* I'm being drip-fed.

I decide to go for it. He'll either tell me or he won't. "Silas, I saw Johannes… last night after you left. I saw him, and I saw *them.*"

Silas stands and places his empty plate in the sink, his face a mask of indifference. Facing me he folds his arms over his broad chest in a mocking parody of my balcony stand-off yesterday. "Who do you think you saw, Edi?"

"I don't *think* I saw anyone. I *know*, I saw them… Liam and Django. They were here, staying with the woman, Mrs. Thingy, down stairs."

"Whittham."

"Yes, Whittham. Whatever her name is, her - they were staying with her."

"And?"

"What do you mean, and? What's going on Silas? I love you, but if you don't tell me what this is all about, so help me, I'll… I'll, kick your arse!"

He falls about laughing, bending forward and clutching his stomach as he roars with mirth at my impossibly weak threat.

Clearly, he's not for telling me anything… "Twat!" Oh, he's a complete arse today. I flounce off, in a flurry of purple fluff and stomp into the bathroom to take a much-needed shower, shouting my insults as I go. "Knob!"

Slamming the bathroom door, I chunner as I shake my arms free of my dressing gown. "Wanker!" I mutter, under my breath, flicking on the jets and stepping under the powerful spray. "I could kick your arse if I wanted to." But it's a joke, he'd make mincemeat of me. "Knob-head!"

"Edi, try as you might, your insults just bounce off. You couldn't hurt me with your words. You're too kind, and the name calling is endearing. I love you; even when you're trying so hard to be angry with me… I love you." He steps into the shower with me. "Shift over fatty…" Now who's name calling? "Besides, you love me and I know you don't mean it."

"I do so… I do mean it… you're a knob."

"Oh?" he picks up the natural sponge.

"And a Twat!"

"Ah-hah!" Crowding me, he loads it with body wash and purposefully massages it into a white foam with his big hands. My mouth goes dry.

"You're… a… a… wanker." I'm repeating all the derogatory terms I know for men, but I'm speedily running out of insulting adjectives and fast losing momentum.

Mesmerized, I watch as he slowly squeezes the sponge against his damp, hard chest so the peaks of white foam coat his dark skin. The bubbles drift between defined pecs and slide downward towards his flat stomach; I follow their path, hungrily.

"Git…" Another insult trips off my tongue, but I'm smiling now. He's right. I can't help it. There isn't an affront, slang or derisory jibe, sharp enough to pierce his beautiful hide. My words ricochet because I love him. And, in all honesty, I don't mean any of them.

"Wanker, am I?" Lowering his hand, he takes hold of his hardening length and begins to pump, slowly. Blinking lazily, he impales me with his molten gaze. Challenging me. Taunting me.

"Yes…" I whisper. Oh, this isn't fair. I need to keep my annoyance going. I need him to explain what's going on, but he's distracting me.

"You could help me out here you know?" The sponge falls to the floor of the shower, forgotten. The pace of his hand remains steady, but his breathing is becoming heavy. He's close.

"Hmmm. C'mon, Edi. Give a Boss-man a helping hand…"

Resistance is pointless. Desperate to touch him, I place my fingertips to his throat and stroke down the centre of his chest until our hands meet. Placing my palm over his fist, I encourage him away, and take over the long, slow, rhythmic strokes, never once removing my eyes from his blistering gaze. Standing this close, the tip of his penis grazes my midriff, causing him to gasp.

"Shh, you asked for help, and here it is."

"Edi…" hissing my name, he closes his eyes and tilts his head so it collides against the shower wall. Raising his arms, he braces them on the tiles. Oh, this image is incredible.

"You're a Wanker..." *pull*... "a Twat..." *stroke*... "an Arse..." *slide*... "a Dick... but you're mine, and I love you..." *pump.*

"Yesss..." His hips are beginning to thrust against my massaging palm. Swaying gently, back and forth, building a rhythm, in preparation for the imminent eruption.

"Is that good Boss-man?"

"Fuck, yeah."

"Are you ready to fire?"

"Edi... do me..."

"Oh, I will," and I do. Stepping in even closer, so the head of his glans rubs against me, I pump and squeeze, building the pressure, revelling in his pleasure. Taking hold of his ball-sack with my other hand, I pummel and kneed him towards his climax.

When it arrives, it's spectacular. "Aghhh!" A jet of white-hot larva hits my stomach, scorching me, covering my hand, dripping over my belly, coating me in his essence. "Edi."

I'm enveloped in his embrace and his mouth is on mine within seconds of his release. The water pounds against us, battering against our heads and bouncing off our entwined bodies. A reprisal of the rainstorm in Paris.

"That was amazing." Touching his forehead against mine, I'm kissed, gently, reverently. "I'm taking you somewhere special this afternoon." Although I'm not side-tracked from needing to know more about what's going on, my curiosity is instantly piqued at this news. There's no hiding the glint of mischief in his eyes. "Dress pretty."

"Wait, what?" Dress pretty. I don't have pretty! "Silas, you've seen the extent of my wardrobe. Pretty isn't in there." It'll be jeans. It's weekend.

Turning me away from him, he starts to wash my hair. Thick fingers massage my scalp. "Well, we don't need to be there until four, so we have time to find you some pretty."

I'm lathered up, shampoo cascading into my face, I scrunch my eyes shut so they don't sting. "No, I don't need anything," I garble through a mouthful of soapy water. "Ugh," I'm directly beneath the showerhead.

"Believe me, you need pretty today."

"Where are you taking me?" Perhaps it has something to do with *The Board* and Liam and Django? This may be his way of explaining things. Now I'm nervous as well as puzzled.

"It's a surprise... a good one. You'll like it." Rinsing out the conditioner, he combs his fingers gently through my hair. I'm intrigued to know where this skill for hair maintenance comes from, given his own is clipped so closely to his head. "Come on, out you get." My bottom is slapped and I'm guided from the shower.

Silas gathers a towel from the heated holder and swathes it around me. I feel like a mummy. Dropping a smaller towel over my head, so I'm temporarily cloaked, he rubs at my hair so vigorously I have to clutch onto his hips to stop myself from falling over. "Ow!"

"Oh, stop whingeing." Removing the towel, he pitches it into the hamper. "See, nearly dry." Lifting my fingers, I run them through the now tangled knots on my head. They are indeed almost dry. "It won't take long for you to finish it off now. C'mon, let's get dressed." He strides out of the bathroom completely butt naked and dripping wet, totally unashamed and unabashed.

Twenty minutes later and we're both dressed in jeans and trainers. His are swanky black and white Adidas Campus, mine are a well-worn pair of Tesco's finest! His jeans are Gant, mine are Florence and Fred! Fashion wise, we are miles apart. He's stylish, cool and trendy, I'm boring, dowdy and frumpy. When I look at the two of us together, I have no idea what he sees in me, but whatever it is, I'm glad he does. I can't wait to see what he finds 'pretty', but one thing's for sure, I'm positive I won't be able to afford it.

"There're a couple of good boutiques in town. You should find something suitable there." He makes it sound simple.

"Are they expensive?" I'm screwed.

"You let me worry about that. We're not talking top designer, just damn good quality. One of the shops creates their own lines. They don't compete with the big-league designers, but they have some lovely individual pieces. Or so Christina says," he feigns a camp gesture, flicks his hand and bobs his invisible hair. I look at him in astonishment – the man speaks about women's fashion as if he's in the business – what the Hell? "Seriously... I have three sisters, a glamorous ex-wife and a mother, who's the epitome of elegance and sophistication... credit where it's due please?"

I puff a relieved, but still slightly veiled laugh. "Okay." I've no idea what constitutes 'pretty' but I've seen his sister and Christina, and they're both flawless. The slight glimpse I had of his mother yesterday, does nothing to stem my anxiety either. I've spent so many years in the comfy-clothes wilderness, I've absolutely no self-awareness in this area.

As we walk by the huge ornate hall mirror, I take a critical sideways glance at myself. Apart from the good haircut, I look like every other normal woman on the street. My clothes are nondescript and boring, badly put together; chosen for affordability and comfort rather than making a statement. Although, I suppose I am making a statement of sorts - it says, don't notice me - perhaps it's time to change. Silas deserves to be supported by the woman on his arm, not hindered. I vow to find something pretty and make him proud.

CHAPTER 20

All in all, the shopping experience went well. We only had one slight disagreement, when Silas insisted, I buy a leather biker jacket, and I insisted I didn't. Consequently, I'm now the proud owner of two new day dresses, two occasional dresses, two summer ones, and a formal skirt suit, which can interchange with black trousers for an alternative work outfit. Two sleeveless blouses, three tops, several casual tee-shirts and vests and some new Levi jeans and my own pair of black and white, Adidas Campus – oh, and a black leather biker jacket!

Silas takes me to the barn so I can change into my pretty summer dress and my black, Paris CFM shoes. Apparently, we also need to pick up Bear, as he's coming with us to wherever we're going.

I unpack my purchases and hang them up. The shop was called *McGillis Man and Woman*, and was as wonderful as Silas promised. All the items were bespoke designs, so I'm secure in the knowledge I won't see anybody else wearing the same dress. And as Silas said, the prices were reasonable, considering the individuality.

Now everything is out of the bags, it doesn't look like much, but I've been assured, by the stylist, Lorraine, it's the perfect starter, capsule wardrobe.

I dab on some light makeup and zip myself into my new summer dress. A mustardy yellow lightweight jersey, with a scattering of flowers in reds and blues. It didn't look anything on the hanger, but when I tried it on, the colour was perfect for my skin tone, the delicate fabric skimmed my curves and the cold shoulder feature added some interest, without being too flouncy. Finished at the perfect length, the handkerchief hem flatters my legs and even adds the illusion of height; I sound as if I know what I'm talking about - I don't - I'm quoting the stylist.

Brushing my hair, I step back and admire my new look. Wow! I thought I looked okay in the old green dress, but this is a totally new me and I like it. "Okay girl, you've got this." Tucking a wayward strand behind my ear, I grab my new jacket and suede clutch and I'm ready to go.

Silas and Bear are outside in the garden. I can hear Bear barking enthusiastically as they play catch with the gnarled Frisbee. I hang on to the door jamb as I call to Silas, "hey you guys!" In unison, they lift their heads in my direction. "I'm ready when you are, Boss-man."

"C'mon boy, let's go." He ruffles Bear's glossy mane, indicating the game is over and it's time to make a move. "Wow... you scrub up well!" His dazzling smile sends welcome sizzles through me; it's an incredible feeling to have these genuinely admiring compliments. He's the only man I want to hear them from.

As we meet on the doorstep, his hand lands lightly on my waist, charging the sizzles into a full-blown jolt of electricity. "You don't look too bad yourself," I gasp, a little too breathily.

Kissing me on the cheek, he winks, then walks on. "Edi, I'm just going to nip to the loo. Could you find my wallet and keys for me please? I think I left them in the lounge; I won't be a sec.'" Pulling the kitchen door shut, he drops the latch and flicks the bolt, as he sweeps past me and along the hall to the downstairs cloakroom.

"No worries." Bear trots behind me as I go in search of Silas's things. I spy the keys on the coffee table. His wallet is on the sofa. Being too lazy, and trying to be clever, I reach out for both at the same time; catching the keys, I miss the wallet and knock it on to the rug. "Oops!"

Bending to pick it up, the wallet's fallen open. Tucked into the window on the inside leaf, is a faded photograph. Even though it's in colour, the iffy fashion confirms it's several years old. It's a picture of a family. A mother, father and two cute grinning children.

Smiling, I pick it up for a closer look at a childhood picture of Silas, his parents and sister. They both look really young on here. Silas can't be more than five and Tia looks about three.

As I bring the picture towards me, a thought strikes, Silas's mother looks remarkably like Christina in this photograph, albeit there's a distinct difference in fashion sense. And his dad could easily pass for Silas's double, with the head of thick black hair.

Wait! – it *is* Christina… *and* Silas… *and* two small children! "Oh!" I gasp aloud, surprising myself; my hand covers my mouth at the unexpected realization.

Checking over my shoulder, ensuring he's not on his way back, I draw the small picture towards my eyes. It's a thumbnail of each face, but I can just make out the little boy's eyes – pale green, smiling, engaged – its unmistakably Nic. And what's more, he looks… *fine*; happy and healthy with no sign of the crippling autism he lives with today.

"Sorry about that. You ready?"

Jumping at his voice, I attempt to quieten my suddenly galloping heart. "Yeah." Subtly folding the wallet as I turn to face him, "yeah, I'm ready… found them," I jingle the keys, lamely.

"Thank you." Holding out his hand, he reclaims his belongings, sliding the wallet into his back pocket and tossing the keys into the air once before catching them and twirling them around his finger. "Bear, come."

As we walk through the hallway, I pay a little more attention to the array of photographs, which adorn the wall. And there it is; the very same image. It's definitely Christina and Silas and I'm convinced the adorable, bright-eyed little boy is Dominic, but who's the girl? Then I remember Silas mentioning his youngest sister is several years behind him in age, perhaps it's Chloe then? But surely, she's older than Nic, not younger? This little girl definitely looks younger, I'd say by a year or so. I'm totally confused. But I don't have time to mull it over, I need to put my curiosity to one side for now, as we climb into the Range Rover and head off on our mystery tour.

I've no idea where we're going as we drive through the village and out into the suburbs. The quaint country cottages and outlying semi-detached houses soon make way for substantial detached villas, rambling estates and majestic stately homes, with manicured gardens behind trimmed laurel hedgerows.

The scenery is beautiful, the traffic quiet, as we trundle along the B-road, dodging the pot-holes. A pair of magpies rise in the field as we pass. Two for joy. I'm not really superstitious but instinctively, I offer them a salute and bid them a good morning. Silas notices and gives me a sideways glance on a wry smile. I smile back.

After about twenty minutes Silas takes a left into a gravel driveway, bumping over the cattle grid between two towering gateposts each topped by a sphere of ancient granite.

The drive is narrow, but not overly long. A modern well-appointed two-story house is set in a large but modest garden. A triple garage stands to one side and there's enough space to park at least five cars. I know this because there are three cars already here, and easily space for another two.

Silas pulls in, switches off the engine and steps out, all without saying a word. Bear - who seems to be familiar with his new surroundings - runs off and around the back of the garage, barking his arrival at top note.

"Where is this?" I feel the need to whisper, it's so tranquil.

"You'll see soon enough," he grins.

I don't need to wait long. Bear comes charging back towards us, but he's not alone. He's being closely pursued by a miniature jet-propelled ball of white fluff, which in turn is being chased by a young, willowy girl.

She runs towards us laughing loudly, happily waving her arms in our direction. By the time she reaches us, she's breathless.

"Si!" flinging her arms round his neck, she bends her knees and hangs on to him, swinging her legs and kicking up her heels. She's wearing a floaty pink skirt, white gypsy top and gold gladiator sandals. "You came!"

"Yeah, we came." Silas prizes her arms from around his neck and lowers her to the gravel, where she immediately turns her beaming face towards me. "This is Edi. Edi... meet my little sister, Chloe." I can barely hear him over the cacophony of barking and yapping that accompanies his introduction. Bear and the fluff-ball are careering and leaping around in an over-excited canine jumble.

"Pleased to meet you Edi," she yells over the ear-piercing racket, "shut up Margo!"

I'm expecting a hand shake, but instead she lunges, and before I know it, I'm in a tangled hug with his baby sister. "I've heard so much about you... *Margo Leadbetter!* will you behave!" The little ball of fluff immediately shuts up the yapping and meekly trots towards Chloe, suitably reprimanded. "I should think so too, madam; showing yourself up in front of guests... that's better." Sweeping the small dog under her arm and taking my hand, she starts to lead me towards the entrance porch. "The others are already here. Mum's faffing as usual. She can't wait to meet you."

"Mum?" I mouth at Silas as I'm drawn through the front door.

Silas nods, his mischievous smile turns into a full-on shit-eating grin, "yep!"

Oh, crap, I'm meeting his family!

The house is stunning, as I've come to expect from all Tudor properties. Although, as beautiful as it is, it's clearly a well-loved and lived in family home, rather than a cold clinical showpiece like the apartment.

"This way." I'm led through the inner hallway, decorated with a mass of family photographs, highly polished tables and collections of antique bric-a-brac, on to a contemporary, functional kitchen. In complete contrast to the hallway, in here it's all mod cons, double ovens, grey units and sparkling marble worktops - then out through bi-folding doors to the decked and terraced rear garden.

The garden's far from being modest, though. It's stunningly manicured and expertly planted, nothing plain and ordinary about it; skilfully landscaped to incorporate the many natural features and established trees. Whomever has designed this outside space has a sympathetic and keen eye for detail. Several seating areas are strategically placed to take advantage of the sun and shade, as well as a wooden pergola entwined with climbing roses and draped with twinkling lights, above a sandstone dining patio. The whole thing catches my breath, it's simply gorgeous.

"Oh, wow."

"I know. Mum's the green fingered one. She designed and planted the whole thing herself." The sense of affection and pride is clear. "It was a great garden to grow up with." I look at him fondly. I can imagine all the fun they must have had as children, romping around in this fantastic place. "I broke my arm falling out of that tree," he says, pointing at a distant Oak.

Several people are milling around, either sitting at the dining table, stood in small groups talking or walking about carrying trays, plates and glasses. A tall, slim woman is placing a large bowl of salad in the centre of the table. The whole family group portrays an image of happy, chatty, polite society. The atmosphere is one of suburban homeliness, even with the majestic house and grand garden. I halt in my tracks; suddenly feeling very shy and self-conscious.

"Mum, dad, everybody, there here!" Chloe lowers the small dog to the ground, calling the family to arms. I feel like a new curiosity; everyone stops what they're doing as one and focuses their attention on me.

"Mum, dad, this is Edi." Silas has nudged Chloe out of the way, and sensing my trepidation, he wraps a protective arm around my shoulder, waiting for the onslaught.

Within seconds, I'm surrounded by Tudors… all speaking at the same time, all desperate to be the first to shake my hand or kiss my cheek, or tell me that they're delighted to finally meet me.

"Whoa, whoa, give her some space. Edi, I'm sorry, my family can be a little full on." Silas waves them back, allowing me some breathing room. "Let me introduce everyone." The initial excitement has died down as one by one, they step forward to greet me. "This is my mum."

"Darling girl. Call me Sylvana… our home is your home." I'm kissed on the cheek tenderly by his mother. Her hands are soft and she's dressed in a simple silver-grey cashmere sweater-dress, with a silk scarf tied around her hair to keep it off her barely made-up face. Her clear skin is smooth and wrinkle free.

"Hello," I stammer, "the garden is beautiful."

She gives me a demure nod in acceptance. "Thank you - This is my husband, Leon."

A solid wall of a man wearing a barbecue apron and carrying a giant fork, steps forward. His likeness to Silas is striking, the same mocha skin tone, the same gleaming smile; only older. I get a glimpse of Silas's future, and I'm pleased. He's extremely handsome and still trim and fit for his age. Refraining from shaking my hand with his greasy fingers, he bends and kisses my cheek politely. "Welcome, Edi. Please excuse the get-up. My wife insisted I chef today, before it rains," he rumbles, waving the fork around at the cloudless sky.

"Leon," Sylvana scolds, "it won't rain. I hope you like sausages and jerk chicken?"

"Err, yes, thank you," I mutter as I wait to meet the next family member.

"I'm Jasmine. Call me Jazz. He's saved the best 'till last," she quips at her brother, who's still clinging to me like I might fall over, "you've already met Tia." Jasmine has long fingers with short nails, painted electric blue to match her wide leg satin trousers. She's wearing a cropped, cream and white striped jumper, slouching off one exposed shoulder. Her hair is piled into a tight top-knot and her bone-structure is to die for. I'm surrounded by a family of super-models!

Tia raises a lazy hand to me in friendly greeting. "Hi babe!" she drawls. She's the only one who's still seated. Apparently in her eyes, as we've met before, I'm no longer a novelty.

"Come on, come and sit down and have some Pimm's." Sneakily, I'm removed from Silas's grasp - Chloe's clearly a Ninja.

"Chloe," Silas warns.

"Oh, shut up. Come on Bro', there's a place here for you too."

Good-naturedly, everybody shuffles round, moving down a seat, making room for us. We're just taking our places at the table, when a familiar voice rings out from the kitchen. "Sylvana, where do you want the bread rolls?" *Christina?*

"Oh, out here please, darling," Sylvana answers. I'm not sure what I expected, but I didn't expect that. I knew Christina maintained her relationship with Silas's family, and I'm pleasantly surprised to find she's here today. Instantly, I feel myself relaxing, knowing I have an ally.

Christina appears with Nic walking steadily by her side carrying a basket of bread, slowly and with determined concentration. "Oh, hi there, Edi – you look gorgeous," she calls, distractedly. Her attention isn't on me really, she's just being polite. Lovingly, she guides Nic with his allotted task. "Here we go… you just put them on the table for me love, carefully now."

Gently, he places the basket squarely in the middle of the table, before acknowledging his dad with a brisk nod. "Thank you, sweetheart. Now, do you want to help Grandpa with the burgers?" Nic, his expression flat, nods once again, then wanders towards the barbecue.

As he reaches us, he pauses by Silas, tipping his head in his usual head-butt greeting, touching his brow with Silas's, before continuing on to his grandfather, who's busily cooking some delicious smelling goodies on the smoking grill.

Watching Nic I'm taken back to earlier, and my discovery of the old photograph in Silas's wallet. Observing him now, there's barely a trace of that engaged, smiling little boy. I wonder what happened to him. What event or illness could cause this significant change?

"Penny for them?" Silas whispers in my ear. He's clearly noticed my silent interest in Nic.

"Hmm, no… I'm just in awe of your family. They're very special. It must be nice to have so many of them still around." I take it all in as Christina joins the throng. They

111

mingle and mix, chatting easily with each other, no tension, no arguing, just plenty of smiles and laughter.

Seeing them like this, I'm saddened by the absence of my own family and I have a sudden longing to see Lizzy and David. "I only had mum, dad and grandma, growing up. I think I'd have liked a sister," I say wistfully.

"Well, you have now… look," he nods towards the table. "You can have mine… willingly!"

CHAPTER 21

Lunch is a lively affair. Everyone speaking at once, or so it seems. Leon's burgers are cooked to perfection, and I notice Nic is happily tucking into his third hot dog of the afternoon.

Nestled snugly on the bench-seat between Silas and Chloe I'm pleasantly full and replete. The food was plentiful and moreish, the Pimm's is delicious and I'm on my third glass.

The dogs are sleeping on a patch of warm grass in the middle of the lawn. Margo has climbed on Bears back, using him as her own personal cushion. He doesn't appear in the least bothered by her presence. "Why do you call her *Margo Leadbetter*?" I ask Chloe.

"Because she's a spoiled little diva, who rules the whole household and thinks she's superior to everyone else," Chloe explains with affection, "but underneath, she's as soft as shit... her barks worse than her bite... literally."

"She's cute. The name really suits her." The little dog certainly seems to have the upper hand.

"Hmm, well, she has her moments."

His family are lovely. Although my initial thought was my presence here is more of an inspection to warrant my worthiness for their precious son, I no longer feel under close scrutiny. Everyone has been so welcoming and kind. I don't think anything could spoil this wonderful occasion.

"So, what's all this I hear about a stalker?" Well.... anything except that!

Leon is speaking, and at the sound of his rumbling baritone, the entire table falls silent. Every face pointed in my direction with interest, expectantly waiting for some coherent explanation from me. Of course, they all know... that's why I'm here.

My sense of security was short lived. It's been replaced by acute embarrassment tinged with guilt. So...I was right, this is a test of some kind. An examination of my moral personality, my suitability.

Leon isn't smiling anymore. The physical alteration in him is quite frightening. Gone is the warm genial, kindly grandfather. Standing before me now, is a man more reminiscent of a feared patriarchal don.

"Oh, err, I'm not sure... I don't know..." I stammer, no idea what to say.

"Dad!" Silas's tone is a warning.

"Son, if this is going to be a problem, it needs addressing."

"Dad, please, not here. It's not appropriate."

The girls and his mother are flicking nervous glances between Leon and Silas. Clearly this isn't their first stand-off. Christina is examining her perfect fingernails as if nothing untoward is happening. Nic is rocking back and forth in his seat, aware of the change in atmosphere.

"Then where?"

"Dad... just not here... please."

Leon stands and removes his apron, dropping it onto the table. Squaring up to his son... a challenge. "If not here, when we're able to speak freely, then where?" Everyone is hanging on to Leon's words with bated breath.

The air is suddenly charged with an invisible force, reverberating between father and son like a ricocheting atom. I'm unnerved by the sudden shift.

"Dad, Sir, it's neither the time, nor is it the place," Silas growls through gritted teeth. "We spoke about this yesterday... remember?" I want to crawl under the table.

A distant rumble of thunder peals from afar, and an ominous breeze flutters the napkins and lifts the edges of the tablecloth, as if in caution.

"I told you it was going to rain." Using the impending shower to her advantage, Sylvana breaks into the conversation between Silas and his father. "All hands-on deck, come on darlings, let's get this lot cleared and take this party inside before the heavens open."

Glad of the distraction from the awkward moment between the two men, everyone jumps to their feet tidying the table before the rain arrives.

"Not you two," Leon's command is levelled at Silas and I, "you need to come with me. This way." Left with little option, I leave the table and watched by the scurrying family, nervously follow Silas and Leon inside and through to his home office.

"Dad, do we really need to speak about this now?" Silas's anger is barely restrained, I can hear the growing tension in his voice. He doesn't like being told what to do.

"Yes, Son... we do." Leon closes his heavy oak office door and indicates to the seats in front of his antique writing desk. "Sit down. Both of you."

We sit. Me, fearful; like a frightened child, waiting for a dressing down from the head master; Silas, like a cornered predator, ready to spring and fight for freedom at the first opportunity. He's not taking this power struggle well.

Leon pours us all a glass of the good stuff, not asking whether I like it. He clearly knows I do. Handing the goblets to us, he takes his chair and inhales deeply, gathering composure.

It must have been killing him, the pretence of the barbecuing father; this character seems a much more comfortable role for him.

"Now, I need honesty, from both of you. In order to clear up this disaster, we need truth, transparency and a plan."

"Dad, we have this under control. Really, there's no need for you to involve yourself," Silas tries but fails to hide his irritation. He's submitting to his father out of respect but his underlying fury is brisling below the surface. Leon isn't having any of it.

"Now you listen to me, boy! We became involved the minute Christina brought this to our attention."

His reaction seems over-the-top. Christina and I were dealing with it. Bobby's a jerk. I'm sure we can manage this and move on. "Mr. Tudor," I start, but one look from Silas and I stop. Clearly, it isn't my place to speak.

"Does *she* know about our business?" Leon's voice is cold, his words carefully measured.

"Yes." "No," Silas and I chorus in unison.

"Yes, I do! I understand what's required. I'm building a team. It's growing," I say, indignantly. How can he say that? I'm affronted.

"Yes, I mean yes, she does." Silas gives me a sideways glance. I'm placated, but only slightly.

"Mr. Tudor, I know my past has dredged up some unpleasantness, but it's my issue, and I'm dealing with it. Christina and Silas have been amazing. But I know, consequently, the problem is mine and I need to be the one to clear the mess away. And I will."

"Edi," Silas growls.

Leon looks at me quizzically, scrutinizing my face, seemingly seeking reassurance my stupid problem isn't going to damage his reputation or the company.

"I'm going to go on record," I say with determination. Until this minute, I was uneasy about speaking out, but now I know I have to. It's the only way forward.

"No, Edi… no, you can't do that." Silas grasps my hand tightly, crushing my fingers. "I don't think it's a good idea."

"Hang on, hang on a minute here, both of you…" Raising a hand, Leon leans back in his chair. "It might not be a bad idea. We need to mitigate any damage. Divert the attention away from us, so we can… continue our operations. I can't have an association with the likes of this man. He's the dregs of society, and you know my feelings about that kind of lifestyle, boy."

"Dad…" Silas really is struggling with his father's dominance of the meeting.

"No. Edi and Christina might be right. If she can control this, we can use it to our advantage."

"I can… Silas, I need to do this, please. Not just for me, but for David and Lizzy too. I just want them to have a happy life, and that won't ever happen, if I can't get past this."

"If, you're sure?" Finally, Silas concedes. He's not going to win this argument and he knows it.

"I am." I've never been surer of anything in my life – other than my love for Silas and the protection of my children – my determination is sealed.

Sensing victory, Leon is suddenly all business. "Right, I need to expedite the investigation into his affairs. I'll contact the service company and chase it up tomorrow."

Eh? What's this now?

"Dad, are you sure? We're grateful, but it isn't necessary." He's exasperated.

"Silas." It's the first time I've heard him use his name – and it is as loving as any good father could possibly be. "My Son, I needed to meet this lady. I needed to see for myself. Call me a doubting Thomas, or an over protective father if you like. But I know there's been a significant change in you. Everyone, even Christina, said it was because of this girl, here. But I needed to see it for myself." He turns his attention to me.

"Edi, you've made my boy happier than I've seen him in decades. Complications and history aside; I didn't think he'd be able to find true happiness again… not after… anyway… you're nothing short of a miracle."

"I… me… no, it's Silas who's changed me. He's the miracle," I whisper, astonished at the turn of events and the abrupt change in Leon's demeanour. Silas is truly his father's son. "I can sort this out. I promise."

"Oh, my dear, I know you can. And you will. Give me a couple of days, and I'll hand you what you need." *What I need?* I can't help but notice, there's a trace of warning in his words. "Now we've sorted that out, I think there's some cake with my name on it." Knocking back his whisky, he stands and gestures for us to do the same. Silas and I down our drinks, placing the empties on the desk, before following his father out of his office.

"I'm gonna fix this," I whisper in Silas's ear as we enter the kitchen.

"I know you will Honey-bee, but you'll need help. And you have us now." His steely eyes don't leave his father's back for a second.

When we enter the kitchen, a cheer rises. Everyone is gathered around the windows watching the rainstorm.

"At last, here's the birthday boy!" Tia yells in mock exaggeration. "Where've you been? Plotting something, no doubt!"

"Tia, that's quite enough. Make yourself useful and fetch the cake." Sylvana's dark eyes flash a warning at her eldest daughter.

"Cake!" Nic mumbles, clearly delighted with the notion.

"Yes, cake – for Grandpa's birthday," Christina enthuses, kissing Nic on the cheek and hugging him into her side. "Let's find the candles."

"Oh God, the house is gonna burn down. Where's the fire extinguisher," Chloe laughs as she rummages in the kitchen drawer for the lighter.

"Cheeky little bugger," Leon chides fondly. "Where's my cake?"

"I didn't know it was your birthday!" I exclaim. Not that I'd be expected to know. "Silas didn't tell me." Elbowing him in the ribs jokingly, I follow it up with a Paddington-hard-stare Lizzy would be proud of. Silas kisses my cheek and pinches my bottom, his mood immediately lightened by the benign activity.

As the family gathers round the table ready to sing happy birthday and blow out some candles, Nic is hovering next to Silas, warily watching as the small flames are lit.

"It's okay, look, Tia has it all under control." Silas kisses the top of his son's head tenderly, and I wonder, once again, what happened to this beautiful gentle boy.

Happy birthday to you,
Happy birthday to you,
Happy birthday dear Leon,
Happy birthday to you.

"And many mooorr!" finishes Chloe in an impressive fake baritone.

I'm handed a slice of cake and take it over to the table where Christina is sat, sipping coffee and quietly observing Silas and Nic as they devour theirs.

"So, this was the acid test," she says as I sit beside her. "The family, Leon, Sylvana – I think you passed."

So, I *was* being assessed after all. I look around at the Tudors. Happy, involved, loving. "Leon and Sylvana are quite terrifying." I'm not going to lie; the last few minutes were a jolt to my nerves. "Why do you say that anyway? Why would I need to 'pass the test'?"

"He's a wonderful man, you know, my ex-husband." Silas and Nic are eating cake off each other's plates now. They've such a strong bond.

116

"I know." I love him, it's that simple.

"Don't you dare hurt him, Edi." I'm shocked by the warning. It's like she's slapped me. Silas is a grown, man. I could never hurt him. "He's been through a lot. More than you could ever comprehend. He's strong, yes, but his feelings for you are new to him. It's dangerous for a man like Silas to become… attached." Leaving me with that thought, she rises from the table and takes her cup to the coffee machine for another hit.

Left alone with my thoughts, I quietly observe the family. Leon, the prominent father figure, a veritable mountain of strength and supremacy. Fiercely protective of his family, while at the same time, striving to maintain dominance over his equally powerful son. Sylvana, the supportive matriarch. Loving and giving, creative, beautiful – the perfect wife and mother. Tia, with her acerbic tongue and sarcastic wit. Jasmine; gentle, kind, thoughtful, as reflective, as Tia is impulsive. And Chloe; she reminds me so much of Lizzy; happy in her skin, the wry sense of humour, killer dress sense.

Christina returns, her coffee cup refilled, she smells vaguely of cigarettes. I notice her hair is slightly damp. "Fresh air," she mumbles. "So, what do you think? I know you passed their test, but do they pass yours?"

She's a sharp one. My silent ruminations have obviously not gone unnoticed. "They'll do," I quip. "What happened between you and Silas, Christina?" It's transparent to me, the family means a lot to her. I'm curious as to why they didn't stay together. "I mean, I'm not complaining. After all, I'm the one who's benefitted, but why?" I can't imagine ever wanting to give up a man like Silas.

"I already told you… we weren't compatible."

"There has to be something else. I've been warned by Leon and now by you. I'm not stupid… what's the deal?"

"It isn't something we talk about." Her eyes are suddenly sad as she watches Nic and Silas. I don't get it. They looked so happy in that old photograph.

The old photograph! Should I risk asking?

"Christina, tell me if I'm overstepping the mark, but earlier today, I saw something that had me wondering."

"And what was that then?" The sadness is replaced by a glassy challenge.

Swallowing my nerves, I allow my question to form. "I found a photograph. It was in Silas's wallet. It's the same as the one on the wall in the barn, so I wasn't snooping." I rush on. "Who's the little girl?"

Christina's face droops. Suddenly she seems aged, tired. However, she doesn't look away, but continues to hold my gaze. "Maya," she sighs, as if I should already know. I'm not going to get an explanation; I can see that. *Maya.* Where have I heard that before?

Rising from her seat, she glides across the kitchen to Nic, placing her hands lightly on his shoulders. "I think we should get going," she says to Silas. "Sylvana, Leon, it's been a wonderful afternoon but I need to get Nic back."

"Darling, thank you for coming – Ooh, Nicky, treasure, give granny a kiss." Sylvana reaches towards Nic, hopeful in her attempt to glean some affection. Nic drops his head in his now familiar acknowledgement – the only way he knows how – they touch foreheads lightly.

117

"Now me." Leon, the doting Grandpa, is given the same treatment before Christina guides Nic from the room. The whole family follow them into the hall, bidding their farewells.

Only Silas and I remain in the silent kitchen. "Who's Maya?" I ask gently.

CHAPTER 22

Silas's lips part as if to speak. The flash of pain that slices through him is devastating to see. Closing his mouth, he drops his head, hiding his clouded eyes from mine.

"Silas," I leave the table and reach him within seconds, "Silas?" Clutching the tops of his biceps, I dip, seeking out his face, I need him to look at me. "Baby... please."

The family are returning, I can hear their clattering heels on the parquet flooring of the hallway.

I can't allow them to see Silas in pain like this. "Come on, let's go into the garden." I tug his sleeve, encouraging him to follow me outside. "We need to check on Bear anyway."

Thankfully, he doesn't resist. He follows, numbly, obediently – like Nic – as I lead him onto the patio.

The rain has stopped. There's a cigarette butt in the ashtray on the table. The red lipstick indicates it's Christina's.

I check the cushion on the wicker patio chair is dry, before guiding Silas into it. He sits without hesitation. I'm worried, I've never known him to be so quiet, so compliant. "Silas, please?"

"Maya's my daughter. Our daughter. Mine and Christina's. Nic's baby sister." His voice sounds calm, though I'm not at all convinced. "She passed away."

"Oh Jesus." I'm not as shocked as I should be by this revelation, though I know I should be horrified. The jigsaw pieces were beginning to slot into place earlier. There couldn't have been any other explanation really – I think I'd suspected as much when I saw that old photograph. "Do you want to tell me what happened?"

"No." When he raises his head, his dominance has returned. The lines of his face are harsh, his eyes clear and empty of emotion. "Let's go."

"Okay."

Transformed, standing before me is once again, the cold, brooding, closed off statue of a man I was presented with the day we first met.

Gone is the gentle giant, with the chipped-away corners, the softened edges. Every trace of the warm protective man I've come to love and cherish is hidden. He looks like he's hewn from granite.

"Bear." The command is so harsh, it causes me to physically flinch. This is his armour, his protection against the pain and suffering that surfaces every time he thinks about that beautiful little girl.

Bear appears from wherever he's been sheltering. His fur is only slightly damp, not soaking, so he's dry enough without needing a rub down.

Margo Leadbetter, on the other hand, is filthy. Her once, snow-white coat is caked with sludge and stuck through with soggy leaves. Her paws are black from digging in the mud and her face is splattered with flecks of dried-on dirt. She's taken full advantage of her unexpected freedom, letting herself down badly, enjoying the inclement weather.

"Oh, my God!" exclaims Chloe. "Look at the state of you – where've you been?"

Bear waves his tail knowingly. She may have a grand name, but underneath all that bouffant well-groomed fluff, she's just as prone to misbehaving as the next pampered pooch. Margo yipps happily at her mistress, spinning a circle on her hind legs, clearly delighted with herself. "Oh, gosh, stop it... you're going in the bath... now." It'd be hilarious, if it wasn't for the solemnness of Silas's mood and my worried state.

"We're leaving. Thank you for the food." Silas kisses his mother on the cheek. "Dad," he nods at his father. "Happy Birthday. I'll see you at the office on Monday." Not bothering to say goodbye to his sisters, Silas leaves them, fussing over a very soggy and dirty Margo.

"Good bye, darling." Sylvana doesn't seem to be aware of the shift in Silas's disposition. "It was lovely to meet you, Edi. Come again soon. We must do lunch," she adds as an afterthought. I can't imagine 'doing lunch' with his mother.

"Thank you so much, it was lovely to meet you all, goodbye," I splutter.

Silas strides purposefully through the front door and climbs into the Range Rover. I let Bear in, and before I've fully closed my door, Silas skids off the driveway, wheels spinning, spitting up the small stones and hurtles down the path towards the road.

"Silas!" My grip on the door handle is painful, my seatbelt is digging into my shoulder and I'm being bounced around in my seat like a ping-pong ball. "Silas... please, slow down."

I'm jolted when he skids to a screaming halt, about half a mile away from his parent's gate. We're in a damp country lane. Puddles of water have accumulated in the pot-holes skimming the grass verge and the overhanging trees are releasing heavy droplets onto the roof of the car. They make a *dink, dink, dink*, sound as they hit the rusting metal.

"Get out..." he growls, under his breath.

"Wha... no... I...."

"I said, get out."

He's fearsome. Uncertainly I climb out of the car. Looking back down the lane, I know where his parents' house is, but if he abandons me here, I'll be damned if I'll go back and ask them for help. I'd rather risk thumbing a lift, or walk!

I hear the car door slam and step back, expecting him to speed away, leaving me stranded by the roadside, but when I look up, Silas has also alighted from the car and is standing, staring at me with clear intention. My stomach flips. That look. It kills me, every time.

"Come here," he whispers softly, his body is rippling with barely suppressed need.

I don't hesitate. Skirting an extra-large puddle, I round the rear of the car. Silas meets me as I cross the tailgate, taking my arms, guiding me so I'm facing the back window. "Palms flat on the glass," he instructs, and I follow through without thought or trepidation. I know what's coming and I don't care. He can take me wherever he wants.

Unspeaking, he stands behind me on the wet road. Lifting my dress, he reaches beneath me and nudges my legs apart with his knee. I can't even hear him breathing over the rush of blood in my ears.

A light gust of wind ripples the trees, and a fat raindrop splatters onto my head. Another one lands on my face. I hadn't realised I was looking upwards. The tree canopy is swaying, wafting the iridescent green against the backdrop of blue sky. The lane is silent apart from the rustling leaves, the sound of the birds and my own pounding heart. A car could come by at any moment, but I don't care – he needs this.

Silas's hand reaches beneath my dress and he hooks a finger into the seam of my underwear, drawing it to one side. I feel him fumbling for his belt and fly. "Lean forward, give me your arse," he hisses in my ear.

Bending, I lean my weight on the car, my cheek pressed to the window. If he needs this, then he can have it.

Slam! He's inside me without warning. My stomach collides with the spare wheel, his dick collides with my womb and we both yell at the depth of penetration.

"Grrr."

"Oh."

Nothing more is said by either of us. No gasp, no noise, no sound. Silas thrusts into me relentlessly, and I accept him, willingly, needing respite from this most conflicting of days.

Once, twice, three times, he slams into me. It doesn't take long, I'm so close, I'm about to explode. But then I feel him. A hot wetness fills me and he stills, collapsing heavily into my back so my chest is pressed tightly against the car.

Pulling out, he spins me round so now my back is up against the rear window. Glowering into my face, with eyes as black as Whitby Jet, he delves his hand into my soaked knickers.

Spreading my moist folds, he quickly finds what he's seeking, and without even a blink, mercilessly begins to flick rub and massage my clitoris. Defiantly, I hold his black stare with my own icy one, my blue eyes drill into his, challenging; neither of us prepared to give in to the other.

Rolling the heel of his hand against my sensitive bud, he inserts two fingers, while with his other hand, he lifts my leg, draping it around his waist. Still, we don't speak, no words are needed.

Relentlessly, he finger-fucks me, until I can stand it no longer and I come, silently; the remnants of his own ejaculation are slick on my thighs, as he rams his fingers deep inside me, feeling the pulses he's so expertly commanded.

Withdrawing his hand, he lowers my leg, then as if the whole encounter meant nothing, walks back to the driver's door, fastening his zip as he goes.

Climbing into the cab, he sits, waiting for me to get in beside him. When I do, he pulls away before I can fasten my seat belt. Silent and brooding, we drive home without uttering a single sound.

Back at the barn, I leap out of the car and run towards the door. His silent treatment for the last half an hour has given me space to think and I've managed to work myself into an indignant fury.

Mostly it's to do with the way his father spoke to me. How dare he? I'm not a member of his family to be pushed around and ordered about. I hated the way he tried to belittle Silas in front of me. I hated the way he threw his weight around and changed the subject and brandished his mixed messages and cryptic commands. My feathers have been severely ruffled, and the more silent Silas was on the way home, the angrier I became.

Bear joins me on the doorstep. I don't have a key so, as much as I'd like to flounce through the door and slam it in his face, I need to wait for Silas to unlock it for me.

When he does, I push by him and into the corridor, but I'm halted in my tracks at the mess that greets me. The place has been trashed!

All the photographs adorning the walls have been smashed to smithereens and lie broken and scattered on the floor. Instinctively I grab Bear's collar, pulling him back, preventing him from walking on the splintered frames and shards of broken glass, strewn across the tiles.

Silas pushes by me, taking in the chaos. "Wait here," he instructs, the low mood of earlier has been replaced with something different.

Suddenly he's alert, watchful, acutely aware of his surroundings, switched on. "Go outside and get back in the car... *NOW!*"

Turning on my heels, I drag Bear out with me. He's not keen to come, rearing up onto his hind legs, twisting, straining to be released. Overpowered by his strength, I can't hold him and have to let him go.

Too afraid to call after him, in case the intruder's still inside and hears me, I climb into the car and watch as he sweeps past the open doorway and around the side of the house towards the rear. He's heading for the back door.

This only heightens my concern. What if the burglar is in the kitchen, waiting, biding his time? What if he attacks Bear?

Suddenly I hear barking. A barrage of fierce growls and snarls splits the silence. Then nothing. Oh, no! He's been hurt.

My hand hovers over the door handle, contemplating whether to follow the noise, what should I do. I don't know if I'll be of help, but I need to do something. I fumble with my clutch bag, rummaging for my phone, I'll call the police – at least I can do that – I'm surprised Silas didn't tell me to do it before.

Just as I'm about to press nine for the third time, Silas and Bear come walking round from the back of the house, looking all the world as if they're returning from a gentle stroll.

They stride with purpose towards the car, towards me. My thumb is still hovering over the number nine, as Silas opens the car door, and takes the phone from my hand. "It's okay. They've gone."

"Oh... but..."

"We don't need the police. Nothing's missing. I think it was either kids, or an opportunist. The back door was open." *Oh?* "Come on, it's just a bit messy."

"If you're sure..."

"Yeah, c'mon. Look, Bear's happy enough." The dog is sniffing around the front garden. I'm not sure whether he's trying to locate a scent, or re-marking his territory, but he raises a leg on the root of a tree, so he seems relaxed.

"As long as, you're sure." I climb out of the car on shaky legs. This day has just been one thing after another.

The clear up takes us all of half an hour. The only casualties are the photographs in the hallway. Strangely, nothing appears to have been stolen. Even my new clothes are where I left them, hanging from the picture rails in the spare room. If the sole intent was to make a mess, then they succeeded, but only partially.

Silas said they got in through the back door, but I distinctly remember him bolting it, just before he asked me to find his wallet and car keys.

After I've swept up the shards of glass, and thrown away the broken frames, I stack the pile of rescued photographs on the kitchen counter. Absently, I flick through them, searching for the one of Silas, Christina and the children, but it isn't there. I look again, perhaps I've missed it? No, it's definitely missing.

"Silas, I think they did take something…" Cautiously entering the lounge, I approach him, unsure of how he'll react. "They've taken the picture."

"Which picture?" he looks up at me, his expression as weary as I feel. This day has taken its toll on him too.

"Umm, the one of you all. The same as the one in your wallet."

Groaning, he drops his head into his palms. I see his shoulders begin to shake. His back is trembling, hunched over, collapsing in on himself. He's crying, sobbing silent tears of utter anguish.

My heart breaks for him. I can't stand it. The excruciating pain he must be feeling at this moment is unbearable to imagine. Rushing across the living room, I envelope him in my arms, swathing him with my love, pouring my compassion into him. All I can do is hold him while he weeps.

As the minutes pass, the silent tears escalate into wailing cries of fierce agony. Howling. Debilitating. Relentless. Try as I might, I can't console him. My dress is soaked through, his face is a crumpled mask of suffering. I rock and cajole, muttering nonsense words, soothing sounds, but all to no avail.

Wrenching himself away from me and lifting his head, he screams at the ceiling, fisting his knuckles into his eyes, gauging at them, desperately rubbing away the wetness in an attempt to stem the river of tears streaming down his cheeks. And all I can do is try and hold on to him, clinging to him in sheer terror for his sanity, desperate to keep him aligned with me; certain, if I let go, he might just disappear into a vast ravine of his own grief so profoundly deep and dark, he'll never find his way out.

More time passes. My legs are numb from being folded beneath me, but I refuse to move. It feels like hours; but in reality, it's minutes.

Then, very gradually, his hacking sobs begin to subsided, his eyes are closed in preservation. An attempt to block the visions of Lord knows what horrors. His arms are around my waist, his head collapsed and heavy on my chest.

"Baby?"

Another five minutes go by and he's ominously silent. Risking movement, I look down at him and find he's succumbed to an exhausted sleep. He's still, clinging on to me tightly, seemingly in oblivion. Carefully, I unbend my legs, stretching them out on the sofa so I'm lying beside him, his head resting on my shoulder.

With one hand, I reach over, tugging at the woollen throw and drape it over us, so we're both covered by the musty smelling blanket. Exhausted, I close my eyes and I'm asleep in ten seconds.

CHAPTER 23

I awake with a start. Something wet has touched my face. Something warm and a bit smelly. Opening my eyes, I see Bear, he's licking my cheek, encouraging me to wake up."

Okay, okay." Lifting my head, I feel nailed to the sofa, crushed under some enormous weight.

Silas is lying still, on top of me. But in his sleep, he's shifted, so now I'm trapped beneath the full weight of his huge body.

"Silas." Shaking his shoulder, I, like Bear, go for gentle encouragement to waken him.

But Bear becomes impatient and rears up on to his hind legs, landing his front paws squarely in the middle of Silas's back. He's a considerable weight himself, and I feel the depression in my spine as he adds his own six stones to the ton of solid man-muscle already smothering me.

"Huh!" A crinkled face appears from beneath the throw. Red eyed and dry mouthed, Silas gradually regains consciousness, scraping a hand over his stubble, scratching his chin.

I'm thankful, he seems to have recovered from his awful breakdown; but I know the moment the realization crashes over him. The memory is reflected in his face like replaying a movie. "Honey-bee?" His voice is hoarse, sandpapery from sleep and emotion.

"I'm here."

"Oh, my God." Swiftly, he sits up, dropping the throw to the floor. Bear barks at the sudden movement. "Jesus…" Rubbing his hand over his head, he draws it down his face, as if the friction will eradicate the pain.

"It's okay… Silas… Baby… it's okay," I sooth. "You made it." He did, he got through what must have been a living Hell, and he's come back to me.

"It was like losing her all over again." And there it is, the unimaginable recall. It's as if the grief was too great, the memory too powerful to be real. Even though so long ago, it was clearly etched into the deepest recess of his mind, biding its time until some incident, some trigger, discharged; where it exploded only to destroy him all over again.

"I'm here." I repeat, it's all I can be. Here. For him. For us.

"*WOOF!*" Bear barks, reminding us there's someone else who requires attention.

Levering himself off of me, Silas stands and stretches his arms over his head. His shoulders crack in protest, his limbs unfurling stiffly. "I'll let him out." Bear barks his appreciation, as they head to the kitchen.

Leaning back against the cushions, the exhausting events of last night replay in my head. The unnerving sounds Silas made as he howled through his grief. Tears well in my eyes as I recollect my own devastating inadequacy, my heartache, as I ineffectively tried to sooth his fears.

There's no escaping it. Silas needs to talk about Maya and what happened. It's the only way he'll come to terms with it. I know from experience, he'll never get over the loss, but there is light at the end of the tunnel if you can learn to accept it; and if necessary, you can forgive.

"God, the poor bugger must have been bursting." Silas comes back into the living room carrying two mugs of coffee. Setting them on the table, he bends and picks up the throw that's tangled on the floor, before draping it over the back of the settee.

"I know how he feels," I say, suddenly desperate for the loo myself. Swinging my legs onto the floor, I take my stiff body to the downstairs cloakroom.

When I return, Silas is slumped on the sofa. He looks like he's aged about twenty years overnight. "Should we have a bath?" I ask. I know I need one.

"Yeah, that'd be good. After this. Here, drink up."

I run the hot water into the large tub and swish in a good measure of bath soak. I can't wait to get into the steaming water and relax my aching muscles.

Silas strolls in, still looking exhausted. He's naked and so am I, but there's no sexual tension whizzing between us. No, we just need to be close, touching but not frantic.

"Climb in," I say, switching off the tap.

Once he's settled, I swing my own leg over the edge, hissing as I lower myself into the scalding water, my back to the taps. Silas has the other end.

"Why are you over there?" he grumbles. Waves slosh over the side as I manoeuvre myself around so my back is against his front and we relax in the steam. "I think I'm going to fall asleep again. I don't remember ever being this tired."

"It's the adrenalin."

"Hmm?" he yawns.

"The adrenalin. It wipes you out." This I know for an absolute fact. There were times, in my past, when I could barely keep my eyes open, I was so exhausted with the sheer effort of keeping body and soul together, let alone supporting the children - which reminds me - "Lizzy and Sam are coming home." Perhaps some nice news will lift the mood.

"Oh, when?"

"Next Saturday I think."

"We can pick them up. They can stay at the apartment. You'll stay here with me," he announces with some certainty.

"Silas, I don't know if I can move in with you. After last night, we need to talk. You need help." I say it as gently as I can, tenderly brushing my hands up and down his lower legs.

"What about last night? It was an emotional day."

"Silas," I sigh. Ignoring the episode won't make it go away.

"Alright… but I'm not speaking to a professional. I'll talk to you."

"But…"

"It's Sunday. We'll shack up and hunker down and I'll tell you about Maya… and Nic."

"If, you're sure?"

"I've never been surer of anything in my life." Kissing the top of my head, he yawns deeply, then pushes me forward so he can get out of the bath. "Enjoy your soak Honey-bee. I'm going to have a shower. I don't think I'm a bath person." He leaves me, immersed in the hot water, pondering. Brimming with uncertainty, I do want to know about Maya and Nic, but I'm not sure I'll be any use as a therapist. Silas seems to believe I'll be able to

125

guide him through this. I'll try, but I'm cautious. I don't think I could support him through another breakdown like last night.

We sit on the floor in the centre of the lounge. Even though it's warm, Silas has lit a fire and we have the scattering of a make-do carpet picnic laid out on the rug. Crisps, chocolate, cheese and bread, as well as our obligatory bottle of Scotch at the ready, in case of an emergency.

Bear's slavering, looking longingly at the cheese with a hopeful expression. "Leave," Silas commands. "If he eats any of that cheese, we'll suffer the consequences later." Bear slinks away with his tail between his legs, seeking out his dog-chew.

"How do you want to start?" I ask. "Do you want to do it the same way I did?" Harking back to when I revealed my secrets to Silas; the relief when I unloaded my burden was palpable. I wonder if he wants to adopt the same approach.

"I don't know if it will work for me," he's pensive, hesitant. "Let me start, then you can come in and ask questions if you need to."

"So long as, you're sure."

"I've never been surer," he repeats in affirmation.

I settle against the sofa and cradle a freshly poured tumbler of scotch to my chest, allowing him the time to compose himself. This will be difficult enough without me whittling away at him for details.

"How much do you know about organized crime?"

The question throws me. "Absolutely nothing!" I say in alarm.

"Well, I know quite a lot about it. Or I should say, I know a lot about the kind of people involved in it." He takes a sip of Dutch courage. "Several years ago, there was a spate of gangland activity. A crimewave of mega proportions involving numerous unsavoury, underworld characters.

"It was briefly mentioned in the media at the time, but the Government weren't happy with all the negative publicity the country was receiving and effectively glossed over it.

"They did everything they possibly could to silence it without physically outstepping the boundaries of the law; embroidering the truth, distorting the facts, creatively misrepresenting the details; basically, a cover-up so the people remained ignorant to the true scale of the threat. Information was withheld and reports in the media were so far from reality, even the ministers involved in the charade began to believe what was being reported. Most of the incidents were either swept under the carpet, or reported so vaguely, people didn't really know what was going on."

"I had no idea." How Silas fits into this is worrying.

"No, well, neither did the rest of the population, but I'm telling you now; it was rife," he says gravely. "At the time, I was in the Police Force."

"Oh." This surprises me. I never thought of him as anything other than the man I know now.

"Yes, well, I say the Police Force, but I was actually part of a small specialized team, an undercover unit, if you will." He swallows another sip of Scotch.

"Was this when you were married?"

126

"Yes. Christina and I were both in the UK Branch of the Elite International Detachment. She was in Forensic Intelligence and I was in the Armed Combat Division. Both groups were created for one specific purpose - a clandestine branch of the Armed Response Unit; brought together to eradicate organized crime. That's how we met. The university story is just that – a story." He pauses, allowing me to digest what I'm hearing.

"Personal relationships within the squad were discouraged for obvious reasons, but as often happens when a small group of dedicated, like-minded people work together in close proximity; especially under such stressful circumstances, the inevitable happened.

"Initially it was just a physical release for both of us, a way to blow off steam. The whole unit worked hard, played hard and fucked hard. Christina and I were no exception; our sexual appetite was only subjugated by our appetite for justice." I inwardly cringe at the description of their sex life. Though it does answer some questions in regard to his enthusiasm to the act.

"So, you got married?" I'm surprised it was permitted.

"It was unexpected but when she got pregnant, after the initial shock and discussions about what we should do, we took it as a positive omen and made the decision to keep the baby."

He turns to face me. "What you need to understand is, in our line of work, normal relationships were practically impossible. Our lives were… unpredictable. Who knew if we'd ever have the opportunity again? Fate had decided for us I suppose.

"I know that sounds cold hearted, but you have to understand in our field, people were either married to the job, or married to somebody in the job. Civilian relationships didn't stand a cat in Hell's chance - they had a limited shelf-life - so, stupid as it sounds now, we got married."

"And you had the baby?" *Idiot, of course they did!*

"Yeah, when Dominic was born, it changed my outlook on everything." His eyes mist at the fond memory.

I understand completely - the first touch of that little human; tiny fingers and toes, the unique baby smell - it's the original love at first sight.

"From the first moment I held him, I became obsessed. My focus sharpened; my main purpose in life was to help cleanse the world of underworld activity. But more importantly it was now my mission to make the planet a better place to live for my child.

"Within months, Christina became pregnant again. By this time, she'd left the service. One thing we agreed on was at least one parent should be there to concentrate on the children. Having two parents in such a hazardous occupation would have been stupid and irresponsible, but she was still firmly in support of my decision to remain in the force.

"We both held the same views on organized crime – had seen too much of it to step away completely. So, she joined my father in the Aeronautical business. It fit in with our growing family, and my mother was only too happy to play the devoted Grandmother."

"They were close in age."

"Yeah, less than twelve months between them - Irish twins," his lip twitches at the old-fashioned euphemism. "Nic was only just walking, when Maya was born. They were a handful, that's for sure." Looking wistfully into the distance, he smiles properly for the first time in ages. "They certainly kept us on our toes - but that only made me more determined to succeed in my goal."

This all paints a pretty picture of an ideal family life; beautiful children, doting parents and proud grandparents. So, I have to ask, "what happened, Silas?"

"I think I need to take a break." This isn't what I'm expecting, but if he needs some time, I'll give it to him.

"What do you need?"

"More of this," handing me his empty tumbler.

Unscrewing the cap, I pour him a large measure, topping up my own glass before replacing the cap and handing his drink back to him.

My head's getting fuzzy from the neat scotch and the heavy confession, but we're making progress so we need to persevere.

"So, what happened?" I ask again.

His eyes crinkle. This is clearly becoming increasingly painful to tell.

"She… they…" shaking some distraction away, he searches for the right words. "The children were our lives. Maya, Nic, they were our reason for living, our driving force for good." Another large sip of scotch. "God, this is too hard."

Touching his hand, I wait patiently for him to gather himself.

"Maya was the light of my life, the apple of my eye, they both were… but… I know there's no such thing as having a favourite child; but there's just something about a little girl," he looks at me, pleadingly. "You love then both equally - but a daughter - you love *differently*. You know what I mean?"

"I know what you mean." I do. I know exactly what he means. It's something that can't be explained unless you have both girls and boys, because, quite simply, it's unexplainable – but I know exactly what he means; you just love girls, *differently*.

"I'd had some success, a major breakthrough with one of the O.C. Syndicates. I'd managed to penetrate the cell and was in the process of destroying one of the main avenues for people trafficking between France and the UK." His eyes close at the recollection.

"I'd been undercover for months; barely been home. Living in the City, I'd finally infiltrated the organization - proved myself, gained their trust - gathered all the intelligence needed to make our move. I played my part well. It was a scary time especially for Christina.

"I had some leave coming, so took the opportunity for a weekend away with the family. Just the four of us. I orchestrated some ridiculously convoluted reason for my absence; it was a huge mistake; I was so stupid. So utterly stupid - but I needed to see my family. Be normal. Catch my breath before the final push."

Silas continued. "You see, I knew we were close and I had to focus all my attention on the final sting." Lowering his head, he inhales. "I knew, once the thing was in motion, I wouldn't see them for quite a while. As part of the pretence, I would be arrested along with the rest; we had to maintain the illusion to gather all the evidence. The idea was sound. From the inside, I could get them to talk."

I wait in complete silence. I have the feeling we're reaching the climax of his story. Even though I'm apprehensive, unsure about hearing the rest of this harrowing tale, I don't want to interrupt him and stem the flow of words, so I sit, silently, anxiously willing him to continue.

"We rented a cottage in the Cotswolds. It was blissfully quiet, set deep in the Gloucestershire countryside, as far away from the world of organized crime as we could possibly get. I was convinced we would be safe... but I was wrong."

"Oh Jesus," my hand covers my mouth, my eyes widening. I don't think I want to hear this, but I know, in order to save Silas's sanity, I must. Bile rises in my throat and I swallow it down with a large gulp of scotch.

"We were walking. Just walking, in the park. Nic was holding Christina's hand. Maya was getting tired. I remember it was sunny, not a cloud in the sky."

"Somebody had lost a kite, its strings were entangled in the treetops, the sail pulling to escape. Maya was fascinated by the bright colours, it's odd what stands out in your memory. I don't recall the sound of the car as it approached." He shakes his head. "I don't remember what we were laughing about, but we were laughing. It was idyllic, just the birds, the breeze and that tangled-up kite, high in the treetop and us... laughing."

More scotch slips down his throat. His eyes are focused on the patterned rug, as if the spiralling swirls of red and gold are forming images of his memories.

"At first, I convinced myself someone was letting off firecrackers, although deep down I knew it wasn't. I'd recognise the sound of a gunshot as clearly as I recognise my daughter's laughter. Instinctively, I swept Maya into my arms, lifting her up and away from danger. But I was too slow. The second shot hit her on the upswing; square in the chest."

A momentary pause, then Silas continued. "The velocity of the bullet was so powerful it snatched her out of my grasp, out of my protection, throwing her into the air and across the park where she landed face up on the ground. She was a month away from her fourth birthday."

I can't breathe; I know this... "I remember." I do; it was all over the news at the time. The little girl brutally murdered in a drive-by shooting while out with her family in the park. It affected me so badly... I was paranoid. She was similar in age to Lizzy. It was all I could think about for weeks... the poor parents. "That was you?"

He only nods.

"I made Lizzy sleep with me in my bed, too terrified to allow her out of my sight. It was shocking."

Laying down my scotch, I move closer so I can touch him. "Oh, Silas... you incredible, amazing man. How do you survive something like that? How do you live with it day after day?" Moreover, how does Christina cope?

Continuing, Silas is deadpan. "I couldn't move. This couldn't be happening. Christina was hysterical, kneeling on the floor. Then I see she's cradling Nic to her breast.

"He was limp, completely lifeless, blood was everywhere and all I could do was stand there, waiting for the next round, the kill-shot that would take me away from all the carnage and horror erupting around me... at that moment, I would have welcomed it."

Silent tears are streaming down my face; this is unbearable. I smother my cries by fisting my knuckles into my mouth. He doesn't need me screaming too when all he can hear is the echoes screaming inside his head.

"As the car screeched away anarchy ensued. The Park resembled a warzone. People were yelling, shouting as they fled, scattering in fear, running in every direction. And Maya was lying lifeless on the cold, cold ground.

"I wouldn't allow anyone to touch her - I needed to get to her - she needed me," his voice vibrating with the sheer emotion of recollection. "I knelt down beside her, howling at people to get back, keep away, leave her alone.

"She was beautiful. Her eyes were open, focused on the kite in the tree. There was a hole in her tiny chest the size of my fist, exactly where her heart should have been beating. But there wasn't a trace of blood on her face."

"Oh Christ, Silas... I..." nothing I can say could help him. I have no words. It's intolerable to think what this family have gone through. "Silas," reaching out, I tentatively place my freezing cold hand over his. He recoils; so much so, he drops his glass. The tumbler rolls on the rug, spilling its contents; a brown stain seeps into the red swirls.

Silas springs to his feet, sprinting to the door before I can stop him, lurching and stumbling then retching into the downstairs cloakroom. Before I know it, I'm by his side as he heaves and spews and cries into the toilet bowl, purging his stomach of the bitter contents.

Placing my hand in the centre of his back, I smooth the fabric of his tee-shirt, pointlessly ironing out the wrinkles. Beneath the damp cotton his skin is on fire, sweat is soaking his shoulders, beading on his neck.

I'm terrified he's going to choke, or have a seizure or heart attack. "Silas?" I whisper, "Silas, Baby... please." I'm crying uncontainable tears of grief for this man who's just imparted the most inconceivable piece of his history to me. "Silas, oh, God... Silas..."

Eventually, he sits back on his heels, his hands trembling nonstop as he wipes his mouth. Falling against me, he weeps, silently, resting his head on my knee. I stroke his hair, his face, his back, his shoulders, desperate for him to feel the tenderness of my caress; he needs calm and reassurance.

"It was my fault. All my fault."

"No, Silas ... no. It wasn't your fault; you couldn't have known. You weren't to blame." He's not, he isn't, I won't believe he's guilty. He's carried this burden for so long, convinced he was culpable, but it isn't true. The only person responsible is the coward who pulled that trigger.

"Yes, I was. They followed me. I was so stupid. I should have known better. Of course, they didn't trust me. They knew. They'd known for weeks. Someone had informed on me. Someone on the inside, a corrupt copper. I was wearing a target from the moment I stepped into their world. I'll never forgive myself."

Now I see it. For years, he's been crushed beneath the weight of guilt and grief. It's the level of guilt he's carried; is still carrying... the belief he doesn't deserve forgiveness or happiness that's moulded him into the man he is today.

He remains curled in the foetal position, on his side on the bathroom floor, his head in my lap, his arms hugging his chest. "It was me they wanted, but because I lifted her... *Oh God!*" he cries, "... because I lifted her up, *she* shielded me, *she* took the bullet that was meant for me."

"Baby...," *no, no, no –* I can't bear it.

130

"Nic was collateral damage. The first shot collided with a tree, but somehow ricocheted and hit him in the temple. The bullet lodged in his brain. It was too dangerous to operate; he would have died. The injury left him with severe learning disabilities, autism and lasting communication problems."

Another short pause, then he continues. "His brain damage is due to the bullet being in there. They still won't contemplate surgery; the risk is too great. So, you see, that's my fault too. I lost them both that day. Maya gave her life and Nic his mind... and Christina... has never looked at me the same, since."

"Silas, *no*... *no*, you didn't *lose* them. Nic is still very much alive and he loves you, more than anything. I see it every time you're together." I have to make him understand this wasn't his doing. "Maya is still with you too; she always will be." I place my hand over his racing heart. "In here." Slowly he lifts his head to look at my hand on his chest.

"If she were still alive today, she wouldn't blame you - she'd adore her daddy - as much as any little girl ever could; you'd be her hero. And Christina... she's a woman who's found her own coping mechanism. I know she doesn't blame you." After all, he didn't pull the trigger!

"Oh, Edi..." he covers his face and weeps. Not the howling animalistic sounds of yesterday, but soft, cathartic, tears of acceptance, of suppressed heartache. Finally, he's grieving openly for his lost daughter.

CHAPTER 24

It's Monday morning. A working day, but I've absolutely no idea how we're going to get through it. I have no capacity for thinking about work, or schedules, or new starters. My entire brain is filled with thoughts of yesterday. How Silas is going to survive today is beyond me.

We went to bed and fell into a fitful, restless sleep. Silas cried out several times during the night, waking me from my own distorted dreams. Neither of us looks rested, neither of us looks fit for anything.

Breakfast has a meditative air. We're tip-toing around each other, not wanting to shatter the delicate atmosphere; bearing the weight of Silas's burden equally on our shoulders.

Bear, who was ignored for most of the yesterday, has managed to forgive us our sins. His unconditional love for Silas is the one redeeming feature in an otherwise melancholy morning.

Reaching down, Silas drags his fingers idly through Bear's glossy coat; drawing strength from the warm silky fur, just as Jason did from the mythical golden fleece.

Heaving an almighty sigh, he level's his beautiful eyes on me and attempts a watery smile. "You ready?"

"Yeah, as I'll ever be," I reply, with equal lacklustre.

"Let's get this over with. The sooner we go, the sooner we can be home."

Squaring my shoulders, I recover a bit of my strength, "Okay, c'mon Boss-man. Let's do this."

We lock up and leave the barn, each of us putting on our best game-face; a facade, if ever there was one.

Arriving at the airfield, there's no sign of activity. The place looks deserted. I have to say, I'm grateful; the last thing I need today is more drama.

Silas parks in his spot and we all climb wearily out of the Range Rover. Even Bear seems less enthusiastic than his usual bouncy self. The only other car in the carpark is Christina's. Silas throws it a disdainful look, before kissing me swiftly on the lips and slouching off towards the hangar, with Bear in hot pursuit.

I don't know what his day entails, but I do know he isn't flying. When we left this morning, his uniform was in the wardrobe fresh from the drycleaner.

Walking into the foyer, I'm instantly swathed in an abundance of calm serenity and my concerns are mollified slightly. I love working here.

I'm wearing one of my new outfits today, along with a pair of *Kurt Geiger* nude patent stilettoes. My heels click on the tiles as I walk through to my office. The sound echo's, rebounding off the walls and high ceilings.

When I catch a glimpse of Christina sitting at her desk, I pop my head round the door to say hello, and check the time for our usual Monday briefing.

I'm immediately shaken by her appearance. She looks as though she's pulled an all-nighter in a sweat-shop! Her typically perfect hair is scraped back from her tired face, piled high atop her head in a messy bun. Where the hair is too short for tying, there are straggly wisps drooping over her brow and around her ears. Missing is the elegant work outfit and the gold chain, traded instead for a baggy grey sweatshirt, which only helps drain the colour from her usually glowing face, making her appear sallow and ill.

"Err, hi!" I announce my presence, tentatively. "Are you okay? You look as tired as I feel."

"Oh, Edi, morning… yes, I'm not a hundred percent today - I worked the 'graveyard' shift - sorry, I must look a sight." Rummaging through her bag, she locates a compact mirror and flips it open.

"Ughh! Goodness, this will never do." She pulls at the bun, releasing the rest of her hair, which immediately falls in a perfect halo around her face. The transformation is instantaneous; despite no makeup and the drawing effect of the hideous sweatshirt.

"Can you hold the fort for a couple of hours? I could do with a shower. To be honest, I could do with a complete spa break, but I don't have the time!" She's aiming for jovial, but it comes out as wearisome; another clue to her current state of mind.

"Err, yes, sure. I've got the new girls starting today. They're due in at nine-thirty, so that'll keep me occupied."

"Oh, *fucking*, pigs in space!" Clearly, she's forgotten. "That bloke's starting today too, whatever his fucking name is, the IT guy. Oh, for fuck's sakes what's he called?"

"Jasper Holt?" I pull from nowhere!

"That's it! Jasper Holt. I'll never remember it. Can you sort him out when he comes in? Just point him in the direction of the server room and tell him to get on with it. He'll know what to do."

"Oh, err, yes, of course." I'm not even sure where the server room is.

"Right'o then, I'll leave you to it. I need to go and drink the blood of a couple of virgins and make myself human again." Thankfully, her wry sense of humour is returning.

"Christina…" my voice breaks as I say her name. I don't think I'll ever be able to voice the level of overwhelming sympathy and admiration I have for this strong woman. "I'm… I… he…" Words fail me.

Her soft smile lets me off the hook. "Can I presume from the way you're looking at me, he's told you what happened?" Her eyes become moist and her voice catches. "Almost seventeen years and he hasn't allowed anyone to penetrate his shell. I'm just glad he let you in," she sighs in gratitude.

"It isn't something I'll ever forget. I live with it every day… the pain I mean. I can only describe it as a chronic, lingering ache; always there. Sometimes it'll flair. There are still days when one can barely function…"

"I… Oh Christina, I'm in awe of you." Dumbly, I hover in the doorway as she starts to pack up her bag.

"Don't be… sixteen years, eight months and thirteen days is a long time…" her words may be accepting but her manner exposes the nerves. It will always be painfully raw.

"Silas needs help. He's made self-flagellation an artform." *Oh my God!* "He won't allow himself to be forgiven. Now you've cracked the surface, there's some hope. Did he tell you everything?"

"Err, yes, he told me. He found it a strain, but he told me." I'm not going to reveal quite how much of a strain; that it almost broke him and he almost collapsed in the process. For some strange reason, I feel that should remain between Silas and I.

"Good," she exhales. "He needed to talk. He's kept it bottled up for too long. It was killing him." I'm stunned by her candidness. "It worked then."

What's this now? "What worked?"

"Oh, come on, you didn't really think there'd been a burglary, did you? The only thing missing was *the* photograph. I had to do something. It was becoming dangerous for him to stay so closeted."

Opening my mouth to speak, I find I'm lost for words again. *It was her?* She was the one who broke into the barn and made all that mess? Christina? I'm astounded.

"Why?" Re-entering her office, I close the door behind me; leaning against it, so I'm blocking her exit. She's not going anywhere until she explains. "Why would you do that? You must've known what it'd do to him!" I'm incredulous, taken aback by her duplicity; how could she?

"Look, I'm not sorry I did it. It was the only option left to me. He was destroying himself with all the suppressed guilt. He needed to acknowledge what happened. I knew taking the picture would trigger something - when I saw his reaction yesterday - when you admitted you'd found the photograph in his wallet.

"He overheard you asking me about Maya, and the look on his face made my mind up for me, gave me the idea - I had to try - fuck knows I'd tried everything else!"

I stare at her in stunned disbelief, my lips unable to form any shape other than a shocked 'O'.

"Did it work?"

Did it work? Let me think about that for a second. "Jesus, Christina, he was beside himself."

"He told you, didn't he? About us, about Maya, about Nic?"

"Yes, it worked." It worked, but the cost to Silas... his distress was almost too great.

Physically deflating, I sag away from the door, my shoulders slumping under the weight of her admission. Stepping forward, I use the chairback for support as I struggle to come to terms with the brutal way Christina has forced Silas into divulging his deepest darkest horrors to me.

"Well then," sniffing once, she slings her bag over her shoulder and passes behind me. "You know; it wasn't just Silas who lost her," she whispers in my ear as she passes. "We all suffered, me, Nic, our families - we all endured the same loss."

It's true, she's right, they did, but I'm fighting for Silas here; they were all affected by the devastating events, and endured the unbearable heartbreak only losing a child can bring.

Lifting my head, I find her eyes swimming with anguish. I've never seen her cry, and she doesn't allow me to see it now, defiantly dashing away the tears with a flick of her hand.

"All I've ever done is try to bring him out of his self-imposed hell. You helped me with that. He loves you. It's all you need to know; be sure of it. You can do the rest. I'll see you later."

As she leaves the office, I vaguely register she's wearing baggy joggers and converse. The pants are far too loose, hanging off her slender hips. From behind, she looks like a gangly teenager. Allowing the door to swing closed, she leaves me alone to contemplate my options.

I sit at my desk, replaying our conversation in my head, debating with myself over and over whether to tell Silas it was Christina's actions prompting the chain of events leading to his breakdown and subsequent admission.

It's a dilemma. On the one hand, he's opened up to me. I now understand so much more about his history and what makes him tick. On the other hand, what she did was nothing short of cruel; a brutal clumsy attempt to crack him open, to induce the most painful, frightful, memories from him, subconsciously forcing him to re-live what must have been the most horrific day in his life.

It was a malicious act; driven from a place of desperation to release the man she once loved and shared her life and family with, from his innermost purgatory. And while it was undoubtedly wicked, it worked.

I'm jolted out of my quandary by my phone. It's the internal line, so it can only be Spanners or Sparks.

"Hello?"

"Mornin' Twinkle." It's Charlie. "There's a couple of *twirlies* in reception. I fink they're for you. There's a shifty looking geezer in the gallery too, 'e looks like 'e might be up to no good; got a ponytail and everyfink 'e 'as." Poor Charlie, he sounds flustered, he's been confronted by the lot of them all at once.

"Oh, sorry - it's the new starters. I'm on my way. Don't panic."

"No panicking going on 'ere sweetheart. 'Vey don' call me 'laid-back Sparky Charlie' for nuffink yer know!" He hangs up, clearly panicking. I chuckle to myself thankful for a moment of light relief. I doubt anybody has ever called him that in his life!

In reception the girls are seated side by side on the leather sofa, chatting politely, getting to know one another. The contrast in their appearance is striking; they couldn't be more different.

Susan Smith, tall, sturdily built, wearing a colourful floral miniskirt, block tartan wedges and red gypsy top. Her hair is dyed bright pink! I'm sure she was brunette last week. Oh well!

Nasima, by distinction is her polar opposite. Demure, in a navy trouser suit, white blouse and flat shoes; a cream Hijab, covering her hair; she looks doll-like in comparison to the statuesque Susan.

As they chat away, I'm in no doubt I've made the right decision about these two. They may be oceans apart physically, but I'm convinced they'll soon be as thick as thieves. I've seen the dynamic before with Lizzy and Sam.

A bookish looking young guy is hovering around the foyer exhibits, feigning interest in a stripped down bi-plane propeller. I'm unconvinced by his apparent absorption, as every now and again I catch him glancing over the top of his horned rimmed spectacles at Susan. I sense an equal measure of devotion and heartbreak may be on the horizon.

135

"Good morning, everyone," I smile broadly, hoping my nerves aren't showing and I sound welcoming. "I hope you haven't been waiting too long? If you'll all come with me, I'll start with a quick tour and introduce you to the rest of the team - well, the ones that are in today." I laugh lightly, suddenly aware that 'the team' as it currently stands, consists of Silas, Sparks, Spanners, Christina and me. I know there are a couple of apprentices in the workshop, but I've no idea what their names are.

"Hi Edi, I'm so excited. So's Nasima - I don't know who *he* is though." Susan whispers the last bit behind her hand, casting a suspicious eye in the direction of the young, geeky guy, skulking around the models.

"I… I'm Jasper. Jasper Holt. IT" Jasper stammers, walking towards us on long skinny legs. By the time he reaches me, he's holding out a slender-fingered hand in greeting. I take it, expecting a limp handshake but I'm comforted to find his grip, firm and reassuring. "Nice to meet you, Ms. Sykes."

"And you Jasper; well, we may as well start with the new team; this is, Nasima Ahmed, she's our new finance expert and this is…"

"Susan Smith, Administration," Susan jumps in, finishing my sentence and introducing herself to a very starstruck, Jasper. He blushes to his roots, before gathering his senses and shaking hands with both of them.

"I can't wait to get started," enthuses Nasima, "I've loads of ideas for bookkeeping and I've created a new formula that can project the estimated profit for the next five years. I'd love you to see it." She' practically fizzing with energy.

"Well, okay then, let's get going. Oh, I need to check… are any of you afraid of dogs?" I remember my own reaction when I first met Bear. It's hard to believe I found him so frightening.

"No."

"No, no, I love dogs."

"Umm, I don't really know any, but I'll be okay." Jasper, Susan and Nasima, all speak at once, looking around them, searching for said dog.

"Well then, I suppose we'd better go and meet the most important member of the team then."

The meeting with Bear went well, he greeted everyone gently. Spanners and Sparks were their congenial selves, complete gentlemen, keeping the cheeky banter to a minimum with the girls and making Jasper feel like one of the guys.

The meeting with Silas was less successful! He was moody and curt and slouched away into the back office as soon as he could. I tutted at him and shook my head; he really is rude when he wants to be.

"Don't mind him, his bark's worse than his bite." It's exactly what Christina said to me, after our first meeting. "Silas is a fantastic Boss and an accomplished Pilot."

"Is he your boyfriend?" Susan asks, bluntly. *Where did that come from?*

"I… well… err, yes, we are in a relationship so I suppose he is." How weird. Boyfriend makes us sound like lovestruck teenagers, but I suppose it's the right context.

"I'll show you the office; and Jasper, I think you know where the server room is? Christina mentioned you'd already been given an overview?"

"Yeah, I know where to go. I've a list of things to sort out today. Apparently, the wiring is in a complete mess and she wants me to set up a regular back-up and defrag' schedules."

This all goes above my head. He may as well be speaking Greek. "Yer, well, umm, okay. We'll see you at lunch then," I say with minimum confidence. He looks the type to forget to eat when he's deeply involved in databases, wiring and server output.

We watch as Jasper all but skips off in the direction of the server room, which I now learn is behind reception. I have the feeling he's relieved to be on his own, surrounded by the veritable safety of buzzing switches and flashing lights.

"Right, up we go...if you'll follow me..."

The girls are happily seconded in the main office. Discussions about who should have what desk, and which area is best suited to what department are quickly resolved, and I leave them to get on with logging in to their computers and setting up passwords.

Jasper is happily jogging up and down the stairs transporting cables, wires keyboards and monitors; arranging work stations and assigning lap-tops. He's in his element.

Nasima has practically exploded with excitement at the prospect of implementing the new finance system. I've never seen anybody so enthusiastic about a spreadsheet. And Susan has already made herself at home, personalizing her work station with a colourful desk tidy filled with a selection of neon-bright pens and pom-pom topped pencils. The pink spotty mug on her desk, declares *'It only takes coffee and makeup to be this fabulous'*. Her mouse mat has a photograph of a group of elegantly dressed girls holding glasses of champagne – Susan's hair is purple in this picture. If I wasn't so certain of her abilities, I'd be apprehensive she's a flibbertigibbet.

Yes, everything in the workplace is coming together nicely. Now if I could only sort out my own personal catastrophes, life would be well on the way to being perfect.

CHAPTER 25

Considering everything that's occurred today, I'm relatively calm. As much as Christina's disclosure sickened me, I can accept her heart was in the right place and she meant well, but talk about brutal.

Silas has been seconded in the outer office all day. Locked in the hangar, he's filled his time cleaning and servicing the aircraft, finding solace in the physicality of manual labour.

The few times I've spoken to him have been strained, his mood hasn't lifted at all. If anything, he's become more withdrawn and surlier as the day progressed, while I on the other hand, have remained worryingly tranquil.

I don't really understand why I'm so sedate. Though I have sympathy, I should be furious with Christina - deep down, I suppose I am - but callous though her actions were, they provoked Silas's emotions in a way I could never in a million years have anticipated.

The new girls have gone home and Jasper's managed to wangle himself an invitation to the pub for a *'welcome to the boys club'* drink with Spanners, Sparks and the apprentices.

I'm sat alone in my quiet office, waiting for Silas to finish whatever it is he's doing before we too, can go home.

Carefully I begin to examine all my newly acquired knowledge. But there are still so many unanswered questions. Like, what happened after the shooting? Who was responsible, and are they still at large? That thought alone terrifies the Hell out of me. I daren't even consider the deprived mindset of cold-blooded psychopaths, who can mercilessly murder children in broad daylight.

How can a person learn to survive with the knowledge that somebody deliberately stole the life of one child, and irreparably damaged forever the existence of another?

The answer is, they don't - they can't. Silas coped the only way he knew how; by burying it in a pit of hellish darkness, the same way I did; only my troubles appear petty and insignificant in comparison to what he's had to tolerate.

Yet, my problems, trivial as they now seem, are still there, niggling away at the edges of my world; chipping the varnish and threatening to allow the rot to set in. The sooner I find a way to rid my life of my past, the sooner I can help Silas face his future.

I'm desperate to understand the connection between Silas and the two models I first saw in Paris, and then back at the apartment - what were they doing there anyway? Who's this Mrs. Whittham and where does she fit into all of this? What about the *Rose Council*? Why was his father asking all those probing questions yesterday?

"Hey," Silas enters my office. He looks knackered; exhausted by all the physical work he's done today. "Are you ready to go?"

"Yeah, sure." Checking the time, I'm surprised to see it's pushing seven pm. "Gosh, I didn't realise it was so late, aren't you hungry?" I know he missed lunch.

"Bloody starving. I could murder some fish and chips." I physically flinch at his careless choice of words, but thankfully, Silas misses it.

"Fish and chips sound good to me. Is there anywhere open on a Monday?"

"Yeah, I know a decent place; they should still be serving."

As we enter *Babette's Café* I laugh. Silas gives me a quizzical look.

"What's so funny?"

"I came here on my first day. I got lost and needed the loo, so I came in here. The waitress directed me to the airfield."

"Ah."

We quickly find a table and the same waitress who assisted me a couple of weeks ago, takes our order. If she recognizes me, she doesn't let on.

I didn't realise I was so hungry. I devour my supper in record time, even though the fish was the size of a whale and the chips could have fed a small army. Silas has done the same, barely speaking to me as he chomped his way through his own substantial plateful.

"I needed that," he says, leaning back in his chair and sipping his mug of tea. "You never cease to amaze me - I don't know where you put it all," he muses at my clean plate.

"My dad used to say I had hollow legs." I had a decent appetite as a child; probably why I was a chubby kid.

"Well, if you've finished, we should get going. I can't leave Bear in the car for much longer. And I've something to show you when we get back."

"Ready when you are, Boss-man."

Back at the barn, I'm feeling stuffed from my huge meal. Silas takes a quick shower and I change into my sweatpants and baggy tee. I need comfortable clothes to allow my stomach to expand.

I'm in the kitchen making us a coffee when I hear an out-of-place, yet familiar noise. It sounds like a child's voice; laughter and a squeal! Yes, it's distinctly a child's voice - coming from the lounge.

Quickly, I pick up the mugs, taking care not to spill the contents as I pad across the hallway and into the living room.

Silas is crouched on his haunches in front of the TV stand. Bear is sitting beside him panting steadily; his head keeps cocking to one-side at the unfamiliar high-pitched sounds. On the screen there's a grainy image of what appears to be a kid's birthday party.

Fiddling with the controls, the image on the screen begins a staccato zoom through reverse as Silas rewinds the old video tape.

"Take a seat," he says, over his shoulder. "I'll be there in a bit, as soon as I can get this thing working properly."

I place the steaming mugs on the coasters, and get comfortable on the sofa. I'm not going to spoil the evening by asking probing questions tonight; there's plenty of time for that. And I'll be careful to pick my moment before revealing what I've discovered about the break-in, or should I say, staged break-in.

Silas joins me on the sofa and Bear squashes himself into the remaining space, squeezing on the edge, resting his head in Silas's lap.

"I wanted to show you this. I've not watched it for such a long time. I couldn't bring myself to look at them, as they were." He gulps back the emotion. "You should have seen them... they were the most beautiful children... full of life and mischief." His voice is low, loaded with love and sorrow in equal measure. "Happy, funny, bright… oh God, I miss them… I wish they were still here!" A single tear rolls down his cheek.

"They are, Silas." He has to know they've not gone. Nic, although damaged, is still very much alive, and Maya will always be such a huge part of his heart. He still has two children - he needs to acknowledge that. "Show me your beautiful babies. I want to know them."

Swallowing, he faces the TV but hesitates. His hand's trembling uncontrollably as he holds the remote. "Will you help me?" he pleads. "I can't seem to get this thing working…"

"Of course." Gently I cover his shaking hand with my own, placing my finger atop of his on the switch, applying pressure. I kiss his lips as the button depresses, offering him some strength to see this through.

Snuggling together, we watch as the homemade credits begin to roll.

Dominic Leon Tudor: 4th Birthday Party

The picture changes to a young Christina in the kitchen of a family home I don't recognise. She's sticking candles into a *Thomas the Tank Engine* cake. Four candles. "Goodness, she looks so classy," I whisper quietly.

On the TV Silas is providing a running commentary. "And here we have the piece de resistance, the masterpiece. Courtesy of Miss. Jasmine Tudor - thank you Jazz - the cake is amazing, he'll love it."

"Sure will, thanks Jazz," Christina smiles her thanks to Silas's talented sister.

The shaky camera travels through to a dining room, the long table is set up for a children's party. Plastic tumblers, paper plates, party hats and streamers adorn the setting. Hanging silver banners declare *'Happy Birthday Dominic'*. Multicoloured balloons litter the floor and float freely beneath the ceiling. It's all very congenial and typical of a kiddie's birthday celebration.

A shrill shriek causes the camera to swing wildly in the opposite direction, focusing on the garden, through a patio window. A crazy, overexcited gang of mini-humans are racing around the lawn, screaming and laughing in sheer glee.

"Oh no, here we go!" Silas' warm fatherly timbre says through the speakers.

"Oh, Christ…" the real Silas quivers beside me, averting his eyes from the inevitable sight. "I don't think I can do this."

"Yes, you can baby… I have you, I'm here. You can do this," I sooth. "Maya needs you to do this. She needs her daddy." I know it's clichéd, but I believe every word. Silas can't abandon his little girl; she still needs her daddy. She needs him to remember her, to love her, to protect and preserve her memory, not bury it. "Look, she's there now."

Heaving a juddering sigh, Silas risks a tentative look at the screen. "Oh, Lord…" he prays to the Almighty for strength. "She's so small…"

On the TV a miniature tornado hurtles towards the camera, Nic runs in utter abandon as only a four-year-old boy can - a direct beeline towards his daddy.

Cantering in hot pursuit, close on his heels, is a tiny ball of fire; giggling and laughing, arms flapping in unmitigated joy, braids bouncing. "Daddy, I'm a pony…"

Maya's voice chimes, like a tinkling bell; deliciously sweet as honey and effervescent with childlike joy and wonder.

My eyes immediately fill with tears at the wonderful sound. I'm catapulted back seventeen years, to Lizzy at the same age. The innocence, the unabandoned bliss of life, the unconditional love and above all, the security and safety.

"Oh, my God, Silas, she's precious," I cry, unable to hide my heartache. "Oh my, just look at them both…" my hand goes to my heart, in a feeble attempt to prevent the dagger from piercing it any deeper. The stabbing pain I feel there, at the sight of these two stunning children, threatens to kill me dead. God only knows what it's doing to Silas.

I risk a glance in his direction, terrified of what I'll see. He's smiling, damp eyes glazed in wonder at the images of his children, so full of vitality and life.

His focus never leaves the screen, staring in awe at the images as they reflect in his dark eyes. I watch as he does, as Nic runs and rolls and spins in the garden. Surrounded by his little friends and his baby sister, the Birthday Boy is revelling in the attention and adoration of everyone around him.

Silas watches intently. It's like he's never seen the video before, though I know he must have watched it over and over again in the past.

Seeing his children, alive and full of vigour is wondrous; but to know this is all history, and an impossible reality, is heartbreakingly sad.

These delightful free spirits are no more – gone. Their light, extinguished before it could shine so brightly. The knowledge is almost unbearable.

Silas points at the screen, drawing my attention to the images. "Look, the candles." The picture shows the whole family, friends and parents, performing the most popular and often repeated song in the world - to a four-year-old shining little boy - Dominic. Oh God, to imagine what he must have endured in his life.

On screen I watch as Leon, Sylvana, Chloe, Tia and Jasmine enjoy the childlike antics; singing happy birthday, blowing out candles, playing noisy rounds of pass the parcel, musical chairs, what time is it Mr. Wolf? Limbo, corners, every party game imaginable is captured on film.

"Ha, ha, listen to her singing… she never could get the words right." Maya's childish voice carries above all the others. Perhaps it's an illusion that it stands out, perhaps I'm more tuned in to her frequency, but I can distinctly hear her over all the rest.

"Abby, birfbay doo yooo, abby birfbay, doo yooo, abby birfbay, near Nicky, abby birfbay doo yooo," she claps away with everyone else…

"Watch this bit, it's hilarious…" Silas is engrossed, remembering every minute detail like it was yesterday.

"Daaad! She blewed out my candles!!!" Nic wails as Maya, quick as a flash, blows all four of the candles out before he has a chance. "It my bifday - not hers!"

Nic's complaint rips at my heart. These days he's barely capable of stringing a coherent sentence together, let alone complain about the injustice of someone blowing out his birthday candles.

Those callous bastards took away Maya's short life and heartlessly deprived Nic of all the joy's open to a young man. My sadness instantly migrates to a fierce anger and hatred for those responsible.

"She was a right little monkey; so jealous when Nic got the attention." Silas is engrossed in his children. "*Oh,* Edi, I'd forgotten. I was so steeped in horror; I'd forgotten how wonderful she was. And Nic, can you see? Isn't he amazing?"

"Yes, darling, he's still amazing. Look, at them, there they are. They will always be there; they will always be in here," I sigh, placing a tender hand over his heart, sensing the beat so strong and fierce; a manifestation of his physical love for his children. A love that will never die or diminish, as long as his heart remains beating.

"Thank you for sharing this with me." I kiss his lips in gratitude. It must have been difficult for him. "They're wonderful."

"Thank you for watching it with me," he sighs. "I haven't had the nerve to look at that video in about, seventeen years... I couldn't, it was too ... difficult. But you've helped. I'm so glad I watched it, with you."

The screen has changed. The birthday party is over and a new stream is playing. It's a different day. Nic is on the top rung of a slide. The lower end is wedged into a child's paddling pool.

It's summer. The sun is shining. Christina is tripping around the garden, dead-heading the petunias, wearing a miniscule white bikini and holding a glass of wine, while the children play happily together.

"Daaad! Those are *mine* shorts..." Nic complains, pointing at his baby sister who's sitting in the paddling pool, scooping water in a yellow bucket and pouring it over the head of a bedraggled doll. "Mine!" he whines, then sits down on the top step of the slide, before letting go on a squeal and splashing down into the pool, causing a tidal wave of grassy water to drench his sister and, unfortunately, his mum's bottom as she bends over examining a rose bush.

"That was a good summer... It was just before I went deep undercover. Less than six weeks after this was filmed, she was gone."

Silas freezes the image. It stalls, fixing on a still of Maya, soaking wet and laughing, sat in a grassy paddling pool, playing with her Barbie and dressed in her brothers red swim-shorts. It's too much.

"Silas, baby, let's watch some more tomorrow," I say calmly, attempting to extract the remote from his fingers. This can't be good for him. I want him to accept what's happened and embrace the memory of Maya, but I fear overexposure could have a negative effect.

Reluctantly, he releases his grip on the control and I quickly stop the video before switching off the TV completely.

"It's late... let's go to bed." I stroke my hand over his head, enjoying the mild prickling sensation his stubble brings.

"You go on up. I'll let the dog out and be there in a few minutes." Leaning forward and out of my embrace, he stands, forcing Bear to jump off the sofa with him. "Come on boy, outside." Bear obediently follows his master's footsteps, into the kitchen and out of the back door.

I wake with a start. I have no idea what I was dreaming about, I only know it has disturbed my sleep. I'm disorientated. The room is pitch dark, and I'm alone in Silas's bed.

Reaching out, I try to locate my watch on the bedside table; three a.m. Where is he?

Swinging my legs over the side, I grab my dressing gown and stuffing my feet in my slippers, I head downstairs in search of him.

He's in the living room, sat on the floor surrounded by boxes of video tapes. They're scattered all around him in small piles. He's engrossed in the images playing out on the silent TV.

The volume is muted so as not to disturb my sleep but the sheer fact I was alone was disturbing enough to wake me.

Slowly I walk across the carpet and drop down beside him. If he needs to do this tonight and watch every film of his children, then I'm prepared to do it too.

Resting my head on his shoulder, I loop my arm through his as we stare at the screen. Although it's just gone three a.m. it looks as though neither of us will be sleeping.

CHAPTER 26

I'm jiggered. We didn't go to bed, but stayed up watching the old home movies. The more we watched the more strength and resolve Silas somehow absorbed from the past images. It was psychologically exhausting, but observing him reconnect with his children was encouraging. He appears to be healing, although it remains to be seen if this acceptance will last. I'm still worried about him, but at least while I'm consumed with Silas's situation, I'm not fretting over my own.

I've still not plucked up the courage to tell him what Christina did. It's Tuesday, he's flying and with his fragile state of mind, I'm not happy about it; neither's Bear. I just need to trust he's an accomplished enough pilot to manage the levels of stress he surely must be experiencing.

I need to speak to Christina today. I'm more determined than ever to clear up the mess about Bobby and put my version of events out there; in other words, 'the truth' once and for all. However, after pulling an all-nighter I'm punchy and out-of-sorts. I don't think I'll be very effective today.

The new guys are already set up and working; you'd think they'd been here for months; it's reassuring to know I've appointed great people. After bidding them a good morning, I leave them to it and grabbing a cup of industrial strength tea, I go in search of Christina. A very dejected Bear skulks along by my side.

I find her in her office. Surprisingly, she looks as fresh as a daisy, dressed impeccably once again. A delicate gold snake chain skims the white silk blouse she's wearing. You wouldn't recognise her as the woman who only yesterday was mooching around in baggy sweats.

"Oh, hi Edi… come in…" Her demeanour has changed too, there's no hint of contrition or guilt about her actions at the weekend. The cool business woman has returned with a vengeance.

"Morning, you look brighter today," I say with a fake enthusiasm even I'm not fooled by.

"Thank you; yesterday was very productive. I heard from Mrs. Whittham," she says, giving me a critical once over. "You look how I felt yesterday," she muses at my shattered appearance.

"Yeah, I'm a bit done in," I'm not telling her why, "but I'll be alright after I've drunk this," I gesture with my mug.

Christina takes one horrified look at my mug of molasses and wrinkles her nose in distaste at the inky liquid. "Ugh, I don't know how you can drink it that strong; anyway, Elaine sent me over her findings, it's interesting stuff."

At first, I'm confused; but then it dawns on me, Mrs. Whittham, or Elaine, has been digging for information about Bobby. "She was successful then?" I ask tentatively.

"Oh, like you wouldn't believe. You know, I've worked with Elaine for donkey's ages, yet she never ceases to amaze me. The woman is a master sleuth - could get blood out of a stone without even breaking a sweat - I don't know how she does it."

"It sounds interesting." Placing my cup on a coaster, I take the seat opposite. "What did she turn up?"

"I think we'd better get comfortable - this could take a while..." Picking up a buff manila folder she indicates I should follow, and heads off in the direction of the Board Room.

I've never been in here before. I get a weird vellichor feeling when I enter - like I'm stepping into a library, or archive repository, it's very odd. There's a wistful sense I need to keep quiet, be serious, as if I shouldn't really be in here at all.

The strange aura's uncomfortable and makes my skin prickle with suspicion. Goose flesh rises on my arms and the small blonde hairs stand to attention. Shivering involuntarily, I've the distinct awareness some significant decisions have been made in this room.

"Come and take a seat. I'll sort this stuff out. If we lay it all on the table, we should be able to digest it better." I observe Christina sift expertly through the contents of the file.

Nervously, I pull out one of the high-backed leather chairs and sit down. The room has an ethereal calmness about it, but I feel anything but calm. I have no clue what Mrs. Whittham has discovered. Moreover, I'm uncertain whether I want to find out.

Clearly Bobby was resourceful enough to get on with his life and business after I left; looking at him last week, he's definitely prospered. Still, even with his current interference in my life, I don't think it's my place to snoop and pry. All I want is for him to leave me alone. I thought we were simply going to draw up some kind of public statement, maybe a press conference or interview, something to make it all stop for good.

"There..." Christina has finished sorting through the paper and photos, "it looks like our Mr. Price has been a very busy boy!"

Curiosity gets the better of me and against my better judgement, I lean forward. My interest is spiked when I look at the familiar images spread out on the table. Lots and lots of photographs of young girls; very young girls; all provocatively dressed and suggestively posed. I'm appalled at what I see. This can't be anything to do with Bobby, surely?

"What the *fuck*?" I blurt, insulted by the shocking pictures. "Where in God's name, did she find these?"

"All I'll say, is Mrs. Whittham has her sources. I have to admit, I was shocked."

Shocked? *Bloody hell*, these pictures are unbelievable. "Seriously, Christina, Bobby wouldn't do this..."

"Wouldn't he? How old were you exactly, when you first met, hmmm?"

"I... he was eighteen..." I stumble.

"I didn't ask how old *he* was; I asked how old *you* were."

"Fourteen," I whisper, unable to drag my eyes from the disturbing images before me.

"Fourteen..." Christina repeats, as if it answers all the questions.

Tapping the first picture with her shiny manicured finger nail, she enlightens me. "Alyson Sato." The first girl looks young, but it's difficult to tell as she's Asian, dressed in Harajuku costume; Japanese I presume. It's sickening. "She's Anglo-Japanese heritage. Her mother is British. Her father is a Japanese banker. In this photo she's fourteen. Coincidence?

"The next girl," she moves to the second picture and gives it the same treatment. "This one is a little older, Caroline Russell, sixteen years of age; moved out of the family home and hasn't been seen since."

My mind can't decipher what I'm hearing. There's no way Bobby has anything to do with this.

"Wait… I can see all of these… but what do they have to do with Bobby?" This is all wrong.

"They're his," she sweeps a sedate hand across the photographs, as if I should understand.

I shake my head, hoping to clear it of the disturbing thoughts that are forming. "No, he… he… wouldn't."

"Oh, he would, and he did… does… all of these girls work for him. Let's just say he's diversified in the last nineteen years or so. Yes, our Mr. Price has been a very busy boy indeed."

They work for him… it doesn't take a genius to realize in what capacity - Glamour Models. All these girls are provocatively dressed, they're all young, slim and pretty. The photographs look professionally staged, well-lit, expensively produced and developed. If it wasn't for the subject matter, they could be in Vogue.

"Jesus, Christina… how… where?" I'm so tired, my mouth isn't working properly.

"How did she find them?" she asks. "As I said before, Elaine has her ways; but I suspect she asked for a catalogue. You can do that you know; if you know where to look."

"Jesus," I repeat, unable to focus on the enormity of what she's uncovered.

"My question to you is, what do you want us to do about it?"

"What?... me...why?" What is there to do… this is his business. I don't understand.

"Yes, this may seem unbelievable. But the evidence and ammunition we have here is enough to put him away for a very long time."

"Wait…" my head hurts from lack of sleep, and the inability to process what I'm digesting. "What exactly is this a catalogue of? All I see here, while disturbing, is a bunch of young girls and women working for a model agency – alright, they're presented in a provocative and sexualized way, but nevertheless, they look like models to me."

"Escorts."

"Sorry… what?"

"Escorts… companions… prostitutes… hookers; call them what you will. This is a magazine advertising high-end prostitution. More disturbingly, we have intelligence at least three of these girls were sold to an Arab Prince – so we're also looking at people trafficking, or if you prefer, the sex trade… he's a very bad man Edi. A very bad man indeed."

"No, no… that's not right… he wouldn't… he… I…"

"Yes, yes, Edi, he has. After everything he's done to you, why are you still defending him? You're in denial… look…" I don't need to. "… it's all here, the evidence speaks for itself." Taking my hand, she offers me some comfort; allowing me time to digest what she's just divulged. I'm shocked beyond belief. How has he come to this?

146

"That could so easily have been you..." her eyes stray to a pretty blonde girl of about fifteen; blue eyed, pink cheeked and dressed in a virginal, white satin nightdress leaving nothing to the imagination. She looks innocent, pure.

Gasping, I cover my mouth with my hand – it could've been me – it even looks like me – like Lizzy – Oh lord, this is my fault; if I hadn't left, none of these girls would be in this horrendous situation – I caused this – me!

"*Nooo...*" I wail, "I didn't know... if I'd stayed... he wouldn't've... oh God, *Nooo*," I'm panicking.

"What... no, no, no... stop, Edi, stop... look at me." Christina grasps my shoulders, pulling me forward on a shake, getting into my face. "Edi, no, stop... this isn't new... look here, at this girl – this picture's twenty years old. This is a collection spanning several years, some of these girls are in their late thirties now... like you. Didn't you ever wonder what his father's business was?"

"Wha'...they..." no, that means... that means, this was going on all along, under my nose; it's not possible. "I didn't know..." I whisper, the reality of it all is hard to grasp, "I never knew..." It's all I can say.

I'm appalled, horrified beyond measure. His family was wealthy but I never questioned how. I shared my life with this man and I didn't know the half of it. I thought I had it bad - but those poor girls. *Oh Jesus!*

"He's a very, very bad man," Christina soothes, rubbing my back, "and Silas will kill him when he finds out."

I can't believe it. I need time to absorb and analyse this revelation. Folding my arms on the table, I drop my head. Christina continues to stroke my back.

"Shhh, it's okay," her voice is tender, softer than I've ever heard it before. "Shhh."

It's only now I realise I'm weeping. Exhaustion and emotion overwhelm me. Forcing my heavy head to lift I push away from the table. "I think I need to go home. I need to think about what I'm going to do with all of this."

"Of course, your car's ready," she smiles for the first time in hours. "The boys have done a great job. Silas won't be back for some time; will you go to the Barn?"

Obviously, I'd love to go to the Barn, but I don't possess a key. "No, I'll go to the apartment." Silas will find me. He always does.

"Okay, do you want to take the dog or leave him here?"

I hadn't even given Bear a thought, but I realise now, I want him with me. It's bizarre how attached I've become to him – he makes me feel safe. "I'll take him." I don't hesitate, he's coming with me whether he's allowed in the apartments or not; I need him there.

"Go and get your stuff; I'll tidy this."

"Thank you," I whisper weakly. Bear follows me into the corridor, close on my heels, his doggy super-senses on high alert – protection duty.

I've been so absorbed with what we've discovered, I've forgotten it's still only mid-morning, so I'm startled when Johannes and Leon walk around the corner, followed closely by Sylvana and Gerard. The four of them are deep in hushed conversation, strolling meaningfully towards the Board Room.

When they see me, they halt as one; Leon alone continues walking, stepping forward, smiling broadly, arms held open in welcome. "Edi, darling girl – how nice to see you." He

147

surprises me by taking my arm and kissing my cheek fondly. "We were just on our way to a meeting." Stooping, he gives Bear a solid pat, scratching behind his ears. Bear, as is his way, tilts his head into the sensation, leaning into Leon's hand. "You look after this lovely lady," he speaks directly to Bear, a gesture which surprises me, "no rolling in mud, mind," he scolds, hinting at the debacle with Margo Leadbetter on Sunday. Leon winks at me conspiratorially. "… shall we?" he aims at his colleagues, gesturing they should move on into the Board Room.

"Nice to see you Edi." Gerard is uncharacteristically cool in his greeting.

"Good morning." Johannes is business-like, nodding curtly in my direction as he crosses the threshold of the heavy oak door.

"Ummm…" I've no time to respond.

"Darling." Sylvana air kisses my cheek quickly; she's gone before I can reciprocate.

"Go home, Edi. Have some rest. Things will be better in the morning." Leon follows his wife through the door, closing it firmly behind him.

The urge to gate-crash is almost overwhelming. Suddenly I'm alert and desperate to know what they're discussing behind that sealed barricade but I know I wouldn't be welcome. The meeting is private – although with two significant members missing – whatever's being discussed can't require a vote.

Exhaustion finally catches up with me, and after picking up my bag, phone and lap top I head out to my waiting car.

I've not driven it for well over a week. It's been serviced by Spanners and valeted by the apprentices; it's looking pretty good. The rust patches have gone and it's sporting four brand new tyres. It looks like a new pin – I'm thrilled.

"Come on boy." Opening the rear door, I let Bear into the back. Dropping my bag onto the passenger seat I strap myself in, then turn the ignition.

Appreciatively the reconditioned engine roars to life; a sound I've not heard for so long, and I can't help but smile as my old rusty bucket revels in its new lease of life.

Putting my shades on, I pull out of the airfield and speed off in the direction of the apartment.

CHAPTER 27

The flat is quiet, museum-like. The contrast between here and the Barn is more startling by the day. I'm staggered by how comfortable I've become at Silas's quiet country retreat; although, I'm not completely surprised I still feel like a fish out of water when I'm here.

Even though I'm tired, I'm still restless. I can't relax. Every time I try to close my eyes for five minutes, my mind reverts to this morning's discovery and won't allow me to sleep.

Accepting I'll never fully settle until Silas returns, I decide to take Bear on a long walk I change into my old trainers. It'll be good for both of us to get out into the fresh air and if I tire myself out, there's a slight possibility I'll sleep tonight... just a slight one.

"Bear, come." Sensing freedom, he's at my side in a nanosecond. "Good boy." I clip on his lead and set the alarm before heading off.

We walk in the direction of the village. I'm not confident in finding the canal footpath when I'm alone. I'm sure Bear knows the way like the back of his paw, but I'll stick to the main street and do some window shopping; I might even call in to *Babette's* for a frothy coffee.

Bear sets the pace, a brisk trot for him and a lively stride for me, which soon has me breathing deeply and swinging my arms in time with my purposeful gait.

The walking is cathartic and I'm soon feeling better. It's good to be outdoors in the sunshine. As I walk, I mull everything over; am I really in denial about Bobby's capabilities? Was I really so firmly under his thumb all those years ago? How could I have been so oblivious to the full extent of his families' dealings?

I suppose financially we were well-off. Considerably well-off if you believe he only had one model – me – on his books at the time. Come to think about it, I must've been earning a pretty penny for us to afford the nice house in a good area, the fancy cars, the flashy clothes. *No... think about it, Edi...* obviously it couldn't have been from my earnings alone. Clearly there must have been funds coming in from elsewhere. I was popular and in demand, but there's no way I was pulling in that much revenue.

My head begins to pound at the unsavoury realisation. How did I not work it out at the time? And moreover, what made me different from all of the other girls? Was it just that I was the first? I seriously doubt it.

Bobby wasn't particularly attached to me... how could he be? I'm under no illusion. If he truly loved me, surely, he wouldn't have been so handy with his fists. That hints at frustration, resentment; if he really loved me, surely, he wouldn't have wanted me parading around in my underwear or semi-naked in newspapers and adult magazines for all the world to see; so why was I so different?

The answer hit's me like a wrecking ball; realization pulling me up so short. I stop dead in my tracks, jolting Bear to a puzzled halt as I stare at my feet in understanding... *I was different only because I had Lizzy... 'you have something that belongs to me,'* that's what he said on the phone.

The whole time, behind my back he was secretly building a stable of girls; most likely in preparation to one day take over his dad's business… I always knew he had ambition, but I mistakenly thought it was for a model agency; clearly the prostitution and white slave trade was a much more lucrative industry. That's why the beatings, that's why the cruelty and the brutal sex. He resented the fact I had a hold over him and that hold was our daughter.

The harsh brutal reality of my past is finally sinking in. Any one of those girls could have been me… *no Edi, stop lying to yourself, stop making excuses for his depravities*…it *was* me… the only difference is, I had something the others didn't possess... his baby... his little girl.

That was the single significant difference. She was the one reason I wasn't sold to the highest bidder like these poor wretches on those glossy, pages... Lizzy, my Lizzy!

A surge of adrenalin floods my system like a starting pistol and abruptly I start to run. Bear, excited by the sudden increase in speed, keeps pace with me stride for stride as I steadily build up to a sprint.

I don't know where I'm going, I'm not seeing straight, I'm just running; a subconscious desperate attempt to escape the crushing blow I feel at the thought, had it not been for Lizzy I'd have been sold, owned and most probably dead by now.

Bear lunges forward, bounding ahead of me and dragging relentlessly on his lead, jarring my shoulder in the process. But I know I mustn't leave go of him as we career full pelt down the High Street; dodging shoppers, mums with push-chairs, school children carrying satchels and bags that look miles too heavy for their small frames to carry. I run, seemingly aimlessly, following Bear, focussing my eyes on his tail, blindly allowing him to guide me.

Several long minutes later and I'm still running at top speed. Vaguely, I'm aware we're no longer on the street, but have veered off onto a narrow country road – a dirt track – parallel to the highway. Bear seems to know where he's headed, so I continue to follow in his wake, trusting him implicitly.

I'm sweating and panting, my legs are leaden and my shins hurt from relentlessly pounding the pavement, but still I continue to run. I've never run so far at this speed in my whole life, but I'm unable to stop or slow down. I can't quit the treadmill; I just keep going, pounding the tarmac like it's a running track; I can't feel my feet anymore.

Suddenly, Bear veers off the path swinging wildly to the right. Dragging me with him, he slips through a narrow gap between two Hawthorn hedges. Blindly, I follow, the vicious barbs spiking out from the branches whip across me, slashing my arms, my shoulders, my legs. They grasp onto my body and clothing like the hooked talons of a wild beast, clawing at my face and piercing my skin through my tee-shirt.

Then there's a gate, a lawn, a gravel drive way – he's brought me home to the Barn – to his home. Sensing my distress, this wonderful creature has acted entirely on instinct and guided me to safety.

Skidding to a halt by the front door, he performs his usual ritual, cocking his leg on the base of a tree, then sits panting at my feet, red tongue lolling, looking up at me expectantly; waiting to be let in.

Dropping his lead, I fold over at the waist, gripping my knees and almost collapsing in exhaustion. Gulping in heaving breaths, desperate for oxygen, my lungs are burning, ready to explode, fit to bursting. My legs tremble uncontrollably as my muscle's spasm in protest at the abrupt deceleration. My eyes and nose run relentlessly. My mouth fills with saliva, and I spit, unladylike, unable to swallow it down for fear of choking.

Eventually, unable to take my weight any longer, my legs give way and I tumble forward, pitching heavily onto the ground, the small sharp stones embed into my knees and heels of my hands as I kneel, retching and heaving on the gravel path.

Above the pounding in my head and the hammering of my heart, I hear a familiar crunching sound. Turning my head sideways, I see the wheels of a thirty-year-old Range Rover as it glides slowly up the driveway. The world spins and tilts on its axis, my shoulder smashes into the floor and my temple bounces off the pebbles. The last thing I remember is a pair of Adidas Campus, as they land on the ground and start running towards me – Silas is home.

I come around on the sofa, my back is to the cushions and I'm covered with the tartan throw. On the floor beside me is a red plastic bowl, I think it's from the kitchen.

"Specialist equipment," Silas quips, "just in case." Smirking he gets up from his chair and sits beside me, stroking my hair. "That was quite a run for a first attempt. Six miles is a long way when you're not used to it… or have the right footwear!" Glancing at my feet, I notice my shoes and socks have been removed. Plasters are stuck on my toes, my instep and my heels. "Those blisters will take some time to heal," he motions to the tape with obvious concern. "What were you thinking Honey-bee?" he whispers tenderly.

"Not thinking…" my voice is like gravel, forcing me into a coughing fit, which causes my stomach to gripe, tightening like a fist and I heave over the side of the sofa into the red bowl.

Now I understand why it's there – *God,* I don't think I'll ever be able to breathe properly again – I've caused irreparable damage to my lungs.

"Don't try to speak, Baby. Just breathe. In through your nose and out through your mouth, slowly."

I endeavour to measure my hurried breath, as Silas coaches me through my shallow breathing. Gradually, my heart calms and I begin to regain control; slowly but surely my rhythm re-establishes itself and my breathing steadily returns to normal.

"That's it Honey-bee, you have it, in and out… in and out… slow and deep… in and out."

When I open my eyes, it's dark and I'm lying naked in Silas's bed. Turning on my side I groan, my muscles protesting at the movement, before I clumsily manage to re-position myself. Silas is sleeping beside me. Calmed, I close my eyes and fall back into a welcome deep dreamless sleep.

The next time I open my eyes its morning, but my vision is blurred, so I can't decipher the time on the clock. I'm lying on my stomach, my arms folded beneath the pillow and I'm reluctant to move.

Feeling the bed dip, I try and turn my head, but find my neck is so stiff, it's almost frozen in place. "Ahh," I groan as the pain hits me.

"Shhh, hey, stay still." A firm hand begins to stroke my back, moving across my shoulders, massaging the discomfort away. "Give it a few minutes. You'll be as stiff as a board this morning so don't try to move too quickly."

Silas continues to rub me back to life, gradually increasing the pressure until my muscles are warmed up enough for me to risk any substantial movement.

"Jesus, I feel like I've been run over." Tentatively, I try to push myself up onto my forearms so I can turn over and rest on my back. "What time is it? I can't see the clock," I ask on a moan.

"It doesn't matter what the time is, you're not going into work today," Silas informs me sternly.

"No." Finally I've managed to turn over. A Timpani is beating behind my eyes, threatening to deafen me. It's probably the result of my stiff neck; and my arms and legs ache horribly - It's like the worst case of DOMS in the history of the world, ever!

"I need to get up and go to work," I protest, but remain motionless on the mattress. I'm paralysed with pain. *Who am I kidding? I'm unable to sit up, let alone go to the office.*

"No, you're going nowhere. I've already phoned Christina." Silas leans over me, bracing his arms either side of my shoulders on top of the duvet, effectively trapping me underneath it with only my head showing over the folded covers. "You look like a Chad," he says, kissing the tip of my nose; it's the only part of me that isn't screaming in agony right now. "Christina sounded upset when I told her; what the hell happened to freak you out like that?"

I don't know what to tell him. I've no idea why my body reacted the way it did, I just know I needed to get off the street and find somewhere safe; I suppose I felt exposed – how else do I explain my sudden desire to run a marathon? "Umm, I need the toilet." I evade his question and try and wriggle out of my cocoon.

But he's not having any. "Edi," he warns; however, he does ease back so the covers loosen and I'm no longer trapped.

"Oh God." Just sitting up is excruciating. I'm never running again. Bellowing like a baby buffalo, I swallow a breath as I try to sit up without success.

"Here, no, no, wait." Silas places his arm under my aching shoulders, supporting me; then, looping my arm around his neck, he gently eases me forward so I'm in a sitting position.

Immediately my calf's spasm into a rancorous cramp, knotting into solid boulders on the backs of my legs. "Ah!" reaching down I rub at my aching limbs in a feeble attempt to release the knotted muscles. "Christ! This fucking kills," I gasp.

"Take your time." Silas removes the duvet, replacing my hands with his own firmer ones, lifting my leg and massaging me through my cramp. "Okay, are you ready to try again?"

"Yes, thank you." Very slowly, I swing my legs off the bed and lower them to the floor. "Aren't you going to be late for work?" I know he was supposed to be flying again today. He seems more himself, even if I'm not.

"No," he doesn't elaborate.

"Oh, I thought you were flying?" hissing through my teeth, I manage to stand. My knees let me know they're not happy and my quads are strung so tightly my toes raise up off the carpet so I'm effectively balancing on my heels. Jesus, I'll never walk without support again!

"Not today." His arm curls around my waist. "Come on, I'll help you. I bet you won't be doing this again in a hurry."

"Ha, ha, you're hilarious, you know that?" I grumble as he assists me while I shuffle like a hobbled donkey to the bathroom.

"Comedy gold right here," he mutters. "I'm not working today either - we need to talk."

"I know," I whisper. We do need to talk. I know about Maya, but there's still so much more I need to know; so many unanswered questions and so much for me to tell him, now I know the horrifying truth about Bobby.

"I'll run you a bath." I'm perching on the loo, watching Silas filling the bath with water and adding a generous measure of Epsom salts. "There, are you okay on your own, or do you need my help?"

"Thank you," I say again. "I should be able to take it from here."

"Okay, I'll go and make a brew," he adds, leaving me to it.

Standing slowly, my muscles still protest loudly, but I'm not giving up the fight to move, so they're gradually relenting, my joints steadily loosening.

Once I'm on my feet, I hold tightly on to the wash basin and examine my face in the mirror. My vision is still blurry. I'm looking through a pinkish cloud, and I can see why. My left eye is completely bloodshot, the surrounding tissue, bruised a bluish purple. A livid scratch scars my cheek beneath my eye, and my face is flecked with small red pin-pricks, the remnants of the Hawthorn splinters, embedded under my skin. Silas must have sat all night, tenderly digging them out of my cheeks with a needle.

I look like I've been dragged through a hedge backwards – technically I have – but it isn't a laughing matter; I look an absolute fright. The thing that scares me most about my face is it looks exactly as it did, when Bobby took his fists to me. I'm battered and bruised, once again *his* victim.

Turning away and groaning in pain, I manage to coax my leg high enough to step into the bath. Clinging onto the sides, I lower my aching muscles into the healing water and slip down below the surface.

My arms smart, where the talons and thorns have stabbed the surface of my skin. My thighs sting and burn, both with muscle fatigue, and the million lashes left by the whip of the branches.

Closing my eyes against the sharp stings, I rest my thumping head against the back of the tub and allow the soothing magnesium sulphate to work its magic, reducing the inflammation lying beneath my skin.

An hour later, and the salts have done their trick. My body can finally move again, albeit a little stiffly, and I no longer feel like my limbs are tethered together with barbed wire.

153

I've thrown on my joggers and a baggy tee-shirt. My face still feels swollen and blotchy, the red pin-pricks stand out lividly against my pale skin.

Silas is in the living room nursing a mug of tea, his ankle crossed over his thigh, flicking through an Aviation Magazine. He looks up when I enter. "You look a bit better, come and have a drink."

I stagger to the sofa and collapse beside him, a sack of potatoes with a spotty face, scarred arms and blistered feet – I'm a mess.

I down my tea in one. It's tepid, strong and bitter with tannin, but it's refreshing and I was absolutely parched. Silas pours me another mug from the teapot on the table. It's stewed to within an inch of its life and its perfect. "Ugh, I don't know how you drink that," he grimaces, reminiscent of Christina's reaction yesterday when she saw my inky brew.

It reminds me of why I'm sat here in this shocking state. "Silas," I say, placing my empty mug on the table, "I need to explain what happened yesterday… what Christina... I mean, Elaine found out about Bobby.

"But there are so many other questions I have for you too. So many loose ends that I don't understand."

"I know," he answers, his expression blank and resigned. "I know Honey-bee, I know."

CHAPTER 28

"Did Christina explain anything?" I broach the subject the only way I know how – feet first.

"Only that you were upset when you left. I know I've been a lot to take lately, what with what happened, you know, my meltdown - Maya and Nic and everything else, but I'm better now - I promise." He touches my cheek tenderly.

"Oh Silas... it's not just your history that's the issue. If this is going to work, we need to be completely open and honest with each other," I say on a sigh. "I have so many questions, I don't know where to start and my baggage is getting heavier by the day – I'm only just learning the full extent of Bobby's hidden life – a life I had no idea existed, until now." I shudder at the thought, my stomach turning over.

But Silas looks confused. "What about it?" he asks, his eyebrows knitting together on a frown. "I know he was a scumbag... are you telling me there's more?"

"Shit..." I curse under my breath. This is all becoming a knotted ball of twine. I need to take care when I unravel it, otherwise I'll cause further damage. "I thought she would have told you... you know... what Elaine found?" Crap, this is getting messy.

"What did she find?" The frown has gone and in its place is the blank, stonewall expression he wore at his parents' house; the game face; unreadable, unemotional, detached, cold.

I realise now, this is his coping mechanism; things get serious or problematic and he pulls down the mask.

"He's not just running a model agency."

"Well, I know that; we knew about the sports stars and the promotions. That's what he needs us for."

"No, no... listen..." I interrupt, twisting in my seat so I can face him; my back tweaks, giving me a swift reminder that I'm still not on top form. "Ooof..."

"Are you okay?"

"Yes, yes, I'm fine... listen… Bobby uses the legitimate businesses as a cover up." Blurting it out before I swallow helps. "He's running an undercover stable. They're not all models, or footballers, or athletes..." I allow it to sink in. Surely, he isn't this dense? "People trafficking, white slave trade, prostitutes... you name it, he's knee deep in it... oh God, Silas... what am I going to do?"

His expression doesn't change, but the twitch at the corner of his eye tells me he understands – perhaps more than I gave him credit for – he was a vice cop for God's sake!

"Silas... what am I going to do?" I repeat, hoping he'll have a magical answer to my problems.

"Nothing... not yet anyway," he grinds through his teeth. "If Christina and Elaine are correct in their findings, then he won't be working alone. He has to have connections, someone who he can use as a filter, a middle-man, someone who he off loads the *goods* to."

Goods? I feel sick; hearing the term *'goods'* in reference to those poor girls is so inhuman, humiliating - they're not a commodity, they're people - it sounds so wrong coming from Silas's mouth.

"He needs to be stopped, and quickly." From the way his eyes are flickering from side to side, I can tell his mind is working at the speed of light; calculating, creating, deciding on a strategy, a plan of action. "You need to do that interview," he announces, "as soon as you can; an exposé. The world needs to know the kind of man he was... is... what you ran from and why you did it."

"What?... lord, look at me... I'm a complete mess; how can I go on TV looking like this?" My reaction is pure instinct. Fighting against Bobby is all I know, and if looking like a walking accident is enough of an excuse to keep me off the telly then I'll weald it like a shield.

"Edi." He looks me over, at last his expression changing to one I'm more accustom to. "This is just superficial and you know it; you ran a marathon – well a small one – yesterday." He rubs my arms; it doesn't hurt in the slightest. "This is just the result of colliding with an unfriendly bush for Christ's sake; you weren't hit by a juggernaut." Bear chooses this precise moment to enter the lounge, "and here he is - the 'U-Haul' king - it must've been a challenge dragging you all the way home."

"Hey," I kick his shins, even though it hurts me more, "he was doing his job, weren't you boy?" Bear growls in warning at Silas. It's low and half-hearted, but it's the thought that counts. "Good lad," we chorus together.

"He really is a fantastic dog, Silas; how long have you had him?" I'm sure I've asked this before, but anything to change the subject.

"I thought I said? After we divorced Christina was worried, I was becoming a recluse. She was probably right. Thinking about it, I was happier on my own... especially after... well you know."

"You need to say it out loud if you're going to accept what happened to her," I urge gently.

"After Maya died... there... I've said it..." He rubs his hand over the stubble on his head; betraying his nerves. "Christina turned up at the office one day with this ball of fur. He looked like a cross between a baby grizzly and a lion cub. I think she'd had enough of my moods. She just handed him over and walked away – left me to it – I'd never had a dog before. Now I don't think I could live without one."

"There must have been a few years in between where you were so lonely..." he must have felt desolate.

"There were... lots of them. I submerged myself in the business, I was so consumed with guilt, I became a husk of a man – an emotionless shell. The things I did bore little meaning. I did them because they were necessary, because they needed doing. I did them without thought or feeling."

Reflecting, Silas continued. "Christina became concerned I was losing my mind, my true identity; so, on a whim, she found Bear. He was supposed to be a connection, a kick-start to my dead emotions, someone who needed my full attention, to give me what I needed in return... unconditional love."

He explains this with such depth of feeling, I know he has a profound connection to his canine companion.

He did a great job, but he could only bring me so far... you did the rest." My stomach flips over, not with pain, or nausea, but with an indelibly good, warm sense of compassion; compassion for this man whom I've come to care so deeply about.

"Six years... I waited for you for six years. That's how long he's been with me; and now he cares more about you than he does about me... don't you hey, you turncoat." Roughly, he pummels Bear on his ribs, pulling his scruff, and wrestling him onto his back so he can continue to play-fight.

Bear relishes in the attention, leaping to his feet and bounding around the lounge, barking, wanting to rough-house, chasing his tail. "I'll just let him out; I can't believe he still has this much energy after yesterday."

"Neither can I," I muse to myself as they leave the room.

My feet are sore, but taking the empty mugs into the kitchen I feel much better now my muscles are no longer in spasm.

While I flick the kettle on to make another pot of tea, I smile as I watch Silas and Bear cavorting around the back garden. Bear is leaping gazelle-like over the foot-high grass and wild flowers as Silas throws a tennis ball for him.

The trill of my mobile phone disturbs my observations. I know it's around here somewhere, but I can't see it. It rings off.

I go on a bean-search around the living room, hunting it down. Where can it be? It starts to ring again, and this time I know I'm closer. Lifting the throw off the sofa, I locate my phone beneath a cushion.

The screen tells me it's Lizzy. Hastily, I swipe to answer. "Hello? Hi Lizzy, baby-girl, is that you?" I'm breathless with excitement at hearing her voice.

"Hey, hey, hey... mamma! Yeah, it's me..."

"Oh, Lizzy, darling girl, I'm so pleased to hear from you." I sound like an overprotective fussy mum.

"Don't be a 'smother', we spoke on Friday you nutcase!" she laughs. "I was just ringing with our flight information."

Oh, how could I have forgotten my baby girl is coming home. "When," I ask eagerly, "we'll collect you from the airport, oh I can't wait to see you."

Silas has returned from the garden, listening intently; 'Lizzy' I mouth, 'ah' he replies, then gives the universal gesture for a cup of tea, one hand vertical, the other placed horizontally over the top, I nod and mouth 'yes please,' all the while listening to Lizzy jabber on the other end of the line.

"So, you see, we can't make Saturday, the Florida direct flights are astronomical, so we're on standby for vacant seats on Monday from JFK... MUM! are you listening?" she scolds.

"Yes, yes, I'm listening, so it's a week today then?"

"Yeah, unless we can get a cheap standby. I knew you weren't listening, is that Silas distracting you?"

"Like you wouldn't believe," I grin at her cheek.

Silas has returned to the room, and catching the tail end of the conversation, he indicates he wants to say something. "Hang on Lizzy, Silas wants me."

157

"Oh, he does, does he?" she giggles. I hear Sammy sticking her two-penn'orth in, in the background. I can only imagine what she's got to say.

Removing the phone from my ear, I press mute. "What?"

"We could always go and fetch them." Silas slides the fresh tea onto the table before straightening up. "I mean, we can take the jet – it's mine," he adds, as if I didn't know.

"Oh." I'm surprised, I would never have expected that. "Oh, no Silas, I can't exploit your business like that; it wouldn't be right."

"Why ever not? You'd use a company car easily enough, wouldn't you?"

"Yes, but..." Is there a difference? I mean a car's a car and a plane is a plane. Why am I debating? it's a fantastic idea. "If you're sure..."

"I've never been surer," he smiles and kisses my forehead. "Let me go and check with the local airports. It'll need to be one of the smaller ones, the girls will need to make their way there once I have confirmation – they should be okay to do that, right?"

"Err, yeah... right... thanks...it's New York... not Florida by the way..." I fluster.

Silas disappears into the other room, presumably to check flight plans and I unmute my phone. "Umm, guess what?" my voice sounds wavy and hesitant.

"Err, you got married, they found Glenn Miller, the Queen is really my secret grandmother... I don't know... what?"

"We're coming to get you..." I say, leaving it hanging there for a moment, hoping she'll catch it before it drops.

"Whaatt!" her screech is deafening. "Oh wow! In a plane?"

"No on a magic carpet – of course, in a plane..." I say on an eye roll.

"You've got to be *shitting* me... a plane? A real private plane? *SAM!!*... Sammy, did you hear that? We're going to be on a private plane... Silas and mum are coming for us! Oh mum, that's amazing..." I think she's crying.

"Lizzy, Lizzy... listen to me. Silas will work out the details, but you'll have to find the airport, do you hear?" She's bouncing up and down, squealing with delight – of course she can't hear me! *"ELIZABETH MARY PRICE!"* I yell down the phone, pulling her attention back to me with her Sunday name. "Listen, please... You will need to find your way to whichever airport can accept an executive flight."

"Teterboro Airport," Silas has returned, "New Jersey, they shouldn't have a problem getting there and they can stay at the Airport hotel – there's a Rodeway inn nearby."

"Oh, Lizzy, did you hear that – Teterboro – I'll text you the details."

"Brilliant, we're stoked. It'll be a fantastic way to end the holiday. When will you come?"

I look at Silas for inspiration, and reading my mind, Silas continues. "We'll set off on Saturday afternoon. It'll take us about six hours, but we can have a twenty-four-hour layover in New York, before flying back on Monday, how does that sound?"

"Oh, Silas..." I've never been to New York. "It sounds perfect." I'm overwhelmed.

I convey the message to Lizzy, who's overjoyed we'll be meeting them for a few hours in the city that doesn't sleep. I can already imagine her planning our day. "Good bye sweetheart, I'll see you on Saturday."

"Bye mum, bye Silas... and thank you so much... this is unbelievable... thank you!"

After the phone goes dead, Silas gives me all the details the girls will require; times, dates, hotel suggestions and, more importantly, the address of the Airport – I can't wait to see them – it's so exciting.

"I can't believe you did that," I say once I've forwarded all the relevant information, and Lizzy has confirmed receipt.

"She's your girl, and you need her home. What else am I going to do huh?"

"But, New York..."

"New York... *'Concrete jungle where dreams are made of',"* he sings in his best Alecia Keys impersonation. *"*It's a strange lyric don't you think? But I suppose, *'Concrete jungle of which dreams are made,'* wouldn't rhyme, would it?"

"I love you..." I do, with every beat of my heart, every breath I take, every burning flame; with every corny love song lyric ever written in the world, I love him. He cripples me, I love him so much it hurts. "You are my heart, don't ever let me forget that."

"And you are mine, Honey-bee." Gently, he takes my hand and lifts it to his lips. Holding my glassy gaze firmly with his own, he kisses each and every one of the tiny buzzing bumblebees encircling my wrist. "And this is mine," pressing his mouth to the void, the blank space, where the bees don't meet, he sucks until the only bruise I ever wish to see, has been restored to its rightful place, filling the gap.

"Yours," I whisper, and in that moment wonder if it's possible to love another human being more than I love this man.

We eat a light lunch of tuna salad. Silas has confirmed the flight details with Christina, who seems totally unconcerned we'll be unashamedly abusing our business perks by absconding in the company jet to New York for the weekend.

"It's all sorted. I'm looking forward to it. We'll take the Gulfstream; I don't think you've flown on her yet, have you?"

"Err, no." *Gulfstream?* I wasn't aware we had one in our fleet!

"She has a longer range than the Cessna so we won't need to refuel on the way."

"Ah, okay." I'm familiar with the statistics, but a *fucking* Gulfstream? Wow!

"Now, let's think about our other problem... by my reckoning we have five days to get your story out there; are you willing to let Christina make some calls?"

"I suppose so. There's no alternative really, is there?"

"No." It's an emphatic flat 'no', one that won't be overruled, ignored or disobeyed. I have no choice. I'm going to do this; *he* needs to be stopped.

"Right then, I'll speak to her and get the ball rolling. I mean it Edi; this thing can't continue. If what you're telling me is true, then the rest of the world should know."

It's true; I absolutely loathe Bobby for what he's done to me and those other poor girls, but what terrifies me more than anything, is my self-doubt and whether I have the level of conviction to follow this through to a conclusion; to consciously go out on a limb and deliberately ruin him.

There can't be a positive outcome for him after this. Exposing Bobby for what he truly is will irreparably destroy his legitimate business, career and reputation; he'll undoubtedly be arrested and sent to trial. Do I have the strength of character to do that to him, even after everything he's done to me? I don't know if I can face it; especially a court case. And worst of all, if he falls from grace, I'm absolutely positive he'll try and take me down with him.

But I know I must do it, it's my moral duty. Silas is correct, he can't be allowed to carry on like this; for virtually twenty years he's been abusing, using and discarding these innocent young girls, including me. He's destroyed lives, broken homes, ripped out hearts and crushed people, all shielded by legitimised business...

No more... I'll find the courage to bring him down, and if I have to, I'll find the courage to fall along with him. The only saving grace, the one shining certainty in all of this, is when I do eventually fall, Silas will be there to catch me.

CHAPTER 29

I don't know how I'm feeling today; my emotions and thoughts are all over the damn place. I didn't sleep very well last night and not only because of the aches and pains. To be honest, most of the discomfort has gone and physically I'm fine, it's all the other stuff that's causing the problems. The mental conflict.

Silas spent most of the night on a conference call with Christina and more surprisingly, Montgomery Philips.

It turns out Philips is an executive at a National TV station. He's mainly involved in the political arena, but also has a hand in producing the occasional current affairs program covering human-interest topics, which is why he's willing to help us.

Philips isn't a foolish man; he knew fine and well who I was the minute he saw me, and was champing at the bit to get a slice of the action when it came to spilling the beans on Robert Price.

Apparently, Bobby isn't particularly well liked within the industry, and it came as no surprise to Montgomery that Bobby has other darker 'business' interests.

Monty has agreed to a slot on the same breakfast programme Lynda Summers was interviewed on last week. It's not an ideal solution and to me reeks of media sensationalism. But it's short notice and beggars can't be choosers so I have little option if I want to get this over and done with. Unfortunately, the fly in the ointment is, it can't happen until we return from The States next week. Blockbuster Movie hype being such, promoting the new *Brad Pitt* film takes precedence interview wise; and Marina Esposito, the presenter on the programme is busy traversing the press-junket circus for the next few days.

On a positive note, I'm ridiculously excited about my pending trip to New York. I really can't wait to see Lizzy and Sam. They've been away far too long and if I have my way, they'll never again be this far from my sight.

Silas has handled the flight arrangements and hotel reservations; in Manhattan of all places. Christina has also called a meeting of the *Rose Council* to keep them abreast of the situation – when things start to move around here, they certainly move quickly.

To keep them abreast of what's gone on I've called a team meeting for the new troops. They don't need to know the finer details, but I'd hate for them to see the interview on TV and have a massive shock; I'd rather they were prepared.

Susan is beside herself with excitement at seeing her boss on the telly; Nasima isn't so sure; her strategy will be to keep her parents as far away from the TV as possible so as not to upset them. Jasper is indifferent to the whole thing. If it doesn't have a hard drive, RAM, motherboard or micro-processor he isn't interested; unless it looks like Susan, then he could be tempted.

Silas is flying today, so I'm occupied with organizing his departure and flight plan. With all the drama of the last few days, I'm content to finally have the mundane normality of an everyday routine.

At mid-morning, whilst delivering some mail to Sparks I'm not surprised to see Johannes and Gerard in the lobby. They've arrived for their meeting with Christina and the *Rose Council*.

Leon and Sylvana are already here and apparently, Charles, Gerard's father will be attending via video link direct from Paris. Although he no longer holds a vote, his opinion is still very much valued.

Silas is also attending the meeting. His flight doesn't leave until later this afternoon. It's Paris again, but this time I'm not going. He has Gerard to keep him company.

On entering the hangar, I hear Sparks in the back office, his dulcet tones echoing around the cavernous space, the pitch-perfect acoustics pinging his tuneful tenor off the walls and ceilings as though it were an auditorium.

Hearing it causes me to blush. I'm recalling my passionate tryst with Silas in the inner office; anybody who was within ten miles of the vicinity would have known precisely what we were doing – the noises alone would have given us away!

In a ridiculous attempt to be professional, I knock politely on the blue door but when I don't get an immediate answer, I pop my head inside on the hunt for Charlie. "Hello?" I call out, pushing the door a little wider. The singing and shuffling are still going on inside the strong room, so I call a little louder, "Charlie?... Sparks? Are you in here?"

"*Let the stormy clouds chase, everyone from the place...*"

"Sparks?"

"Oh, 'ello Twinkle." Charlie comes out of the strong room, releasing the heavy metal door so it clunks closed behind him and locks automatically; understandably so, as there's millions of pounds worth of expensive equipment inside and security is paramount.

"'Av you got that paperwork love?" Putting himself between me and the metal door, he removes the envelope from my hand and walks round to the overstuffed swivel chair that sits behind the desk. "I'll, err, sort this later, I'm just finishing an inventory – stock check – you know what I mean." Unlocking the draw, he drops the unopened envelope inside before relocking it.

"Would you mind signing?" I proffer the receipt book. "Sorry, I know it's a faff but it's the easiest way to keep track," I explain.

"No, no, that's fine." Sniffing, he squiggles an illegible signature against the date before returning the book to me. "I'll get back to it if you don't mind love?"

"Sure... I'll let you get on then," I smile as I pass the old desk; an image of my encounter with Silas plays in my head, and I flush a thousand shades of crimson as I realise Sparks is watching me with a barely hidden smirk on his face.

Embarrassed beyond belief, I scurry out of the room, but not before I hear Spark's dulcet tones as he starts to sing, "*he loves you, yeah, yeah, yeah...hmm, yeah, yeah, yeah!*"

Shaking my head in exasperation, I can't help but smile, hastening my pace so I'm quickly out of earshot and in the quiet sanctuary of the main building.

When I get back, Bear is skulking under my desk. He's not happy and I soon know why when Silas strolls in. On the other hand, I'm delighted – he looks a million dollars in his uniform.

"Hey gorgeous, I'm about to go into the lion's den; are they all here?"

"Hey yourself," I sigh, failing miserably to disguise my heated gaze as I stare in unadulterated appreciation at my man. My Boss-man! "I think so... I saw Gerard and Johannes earlier; I think the others are already in there."

"Well, wish me luck," he takes his time kissing me before pulling away, and I immediately miss his lips on mine. "I'll see you later... and you!" he raises his eyebrows at Bear, who yawns noisily, demonstrating he's bored with the whole *'master goes flying'* deal.

"See you." I take a seat behind my desk, and resting my feet on my furry footrest, settle into the tasks of the day.

Two hours later, there's a babble of voices as the members troop out of the Board Room. Leaving my desk, I stand in my doorway bidding everyone farewells, silently wishing I knew what the Hell was on the agenda!

"Ah, come on then *Pinocchio*... I'll fill you in." Christina crosses my threshold and drops into her favourite chair. "Come... sit..." she pats the seat beside her, "this isn't getting the baby washed!"

If I'm honest, I'm not relishing this. I know she'll have particulars regarding the TV interview, but I feel unprepared and wary. I'm certainly not ready, I could do with another few weeks to get my head around it, but time's a luxury I don't have. It's now or never.

"Okay then Baldrick, what's the cunning plan?"

"*Who?* Oh... yes... right... well..."

The next few hours are utilised going over the interview process. We're attempting to prepare me for what probing questions may be asked, only breaking for thirty minutes so I can send Silas off on his flight, and for Christina to take Bear out onto the field for some 'fresh air'. Then we picked up where we left off; with me trying to sound professional and calm and Christina patiently coaching me through my statement responses. I'm so not ready for this!

The interview will happen on the Wednesday following our return from New York, and I've been blessedly reassured it will be just me and Marina in the studio. No audience, thankfully, only the director and a couple of camera men; so, it'll be as intimate and as private as they can make it; well, apart from the expected ten million viewers that is! *Oh God, what am I doing?*

With the plans for my interview underway and under the circumstances running as smoothly as they can, I'm about to upset the apple cart, because the next item on the agenda is to call The Beeches and warn Mark.

As usual, he's on the ball, and says he'll ensure all the TVs are tuned into another station. Even with his assurance, I'm still nervous about it. There's nothing stopping the resident's from flicking the channel over and accidently coming across 'David's mum', on TV. No, it's clear I need to speak to David face to face, though I have no idea what I'm going to tell him. I decide to go and see him this evening; Christina says she'll come too and I'm grateful for her support.

At five thirty, we pull into the familiar car park of The Beeches. Bear settles in the back seat on his blanket and I crack open a window for him. We shouldn't be here too long.

After signing in we go looking for our respective boys, but surprisingly, we can't find them. Usually, they'd be in the conservatory but today they're conspicuous by their absence. The place is suspiciously quiet.

"Hello," Wendy calls, looking up from her book. "If you're looking for David, he's in the gym."

"Oh, hi Wendy." Not wanting to be rude, I walk over to where she's curled up on the sofa. She looks snug and comfortable, dressed in baggy pink joggers and a warm sweatshirt. "Hello darling, how are you? No don't get up," but I'm too late. Wendy uncurls from her seat, closing her book gently before dropping on the cushion, then engulfs me in a welcoming embrace.

Oh, it's lovely... encircling her in my arms, I hug her back fondly, resting my chin on her shoulder and closing my eyes... I needed this. She smells of strawberry shampoo and fabric softener. It's so comforting.

"It's okay Edi," she whispers into my ear, "you'll be okay."

Startled by her perceptiveness at my mood, I slowly draw back, releasing her from my hold and gaze into her knowing eyes. "Thank you, I needed a hug," I smile softly.

"I know. We all need a hug sometimes; I could tell you needed one. Is Nic's dad away? Is that why you're sad?"

Sad? Am I sad? I hadn't thought of it. Anxious? Yes. Concerned? Well, yes. Stressed? It goes without saying; I'm definitely all of the above, but I hadn't considered I could be sad too! How bizarre. Wendy's Spidey-senses are on high alert this evening.

"Ah, darling, I'm just a little tired. You know Christina, Nic's mum?" Swiftly, I change the subject, but as I glance at Christina, I know she's digested everything Wendy's said. Her shrewd eyes betray her every time. She doesn't miss a trick.

"Wendy, sweetheart... did I hear you correctly? The boys are in the *gym?"*

"Hiya... yeah, it's funny. They think they need to get buff." Wendy starts to giggle. "David thinks I'll love him more if he's got big muscles... like Nic and his dad!"

"Oh... erm?" I don't know what to say to that.

"No, it's funny, really. I'd love David even if he was a seven-stone weakling... he's silly." Wiping her eyes, she leads us out of the conservatory and through the hallway to a part of the building I haven't been to before.

"Oh, lord... this I've got to see..." Christina comments under her breath. But when I give her a look, I can tell she's not being judgemental, just curious.

In the workout room, David is being closely supervised by a stocky young man in a navy-blue training kit and baseball cap.

Attentively, he observes as David bends to lift a barbell. The bar has weights on either end, and David concentrates on his trainer's instructions, focussing his eyes on his reflection in the mirror as he bends his knees and straightens his back. I'm impressed.

Stealing a glance at Wendy, I can see the love glowing in her eyes as she watches her man work out. Is that what I look like when I admire Silas? I do hope so.

"Well done, Davey, lower and up... keep your back straight. Three... four... five... and, down."

"That's Adam," Wendy whispers. "Davey thinks I fancy him." She smiles cheekily. "I don't though. He's not as handsome as Davey."

164

David has spotted her. She gives him a demure little wave as he wipes his hands on a gym towel. He looks satisfied with himself, and so he should. I had no idea he's been working out; and seeing him now, I recognise new definition in his arms and shoulders. He *is* looking pretty buff, even though I say it myself. My little boy is not a little boy anymore!

"Well, there's a surprise," Christina breaks the silence. "David, you're looking rather ripped!" she announces, "well done you." She doesn't miss the daggers from Wendy at that comment. "Oh please... I'm old enough to be his grandmother!" Rolling her eyes, she sweeps past us and over to where Nic is jogging on the treadmill.

Another personal trainer, this one's a girl, is standing beside the rolling road, her eyes never wavering from Nic as he glides effortlessly through his cardio session.

"How long has he been on here?" Christina's tone has gone from mirth to concern.

"Erm?" the girl checks her watch, then notes the time on the equipment clock. "About thirty minutes," she confirms nervously. "Once he's on here, it's a challenge to get him to stop. He seems to have stamina to spare," she explains.

"I know," Christina acknowledges. "Nic?... Baby, it's time to slow down."

"I've been with him the whole time..." the poor girl looks worried, as if she's in trouble.

"It's not your fault love," Christina says, moving into Nic's line of sight, "you weren't to know."

Nic?... Dominic, it's mum." Desperately, she tries to engage with her son, but his focus is elsewhere, buried deep inside behind that impenetrable barrier of his trapped mind.

The girl looks mortified. "I... I'm sorry, he seems so stable on here... happy. He's not even sweating, look."

Christina flicks her eyes to the badge on the girl's chest. "Eve?" For a moment, she's startled, but recovers quickly, "Eve, it's okay. Clearly, you're not aware. Nic will run until he drops. He has no sense of pain and doesn't feel fatigue. He'll just keep going until his legs give out."

"Oh shit... I mean, oh no... I wasn't... I'm so sorry... what can I do?" The poor girl looks terrified. I know how she feels; Silas never mentioned this compulsion.

"It's okay. If he's been on here half an hour, then you need to start to slow the run down gradually.

"How does this thing work?" Christina looks at the buttons and arrows on the machine.

"I'll do it..." Eve reaches across and lightly taps one of the arrows in an effort to reduce the speed of the treadmill.

Christina looks instantly relieved, but quick as a flash, Nic's eyes dart to the adjuster, and he immediately places a finger on the up arrow, increasing the speed even further.

"I'm sorry, I'm sorry..." Eve stutters, "I'll try again..." Reaching out, her finger hovers over the down key, but Nic's too quick for her, slamming his hand over hers, ensnaring her fingers beneath his own on the speed dial.

"Ow!" Eve exclaims. "Nic, please let me go." It makes little difference; her hand is pressed firmly under Nic's trapped in place – he's not releasing her.

"*Shitting Pigs in space!*" Christina hisses under her breath. "Nic, baby... you need to let Eve have her hand back," she coaxes gently. "Nicky, sweetheart. Give Eve her hand."

The rest of the gym has stopped what they're doing and are focussing all their attention on the drama going on at the treadmill.

Wendy cups her cheeks in her palms, a look of horror plastered on her face. David has his arm protectively around her shoulders; for the first time, he seems unable to perceive of a way to help his best friend.

"David, why don't you take Wendy to the kitchen. You must need a drink." I widen my eyes and jerk my head, indicating that he should get her out of here. Thankfully, he takes the hint, nodding at me wildly, before turning her around and leading her out of the gym.

Meanwhile, Nic still has Eve's hand trapped beneath his on the dial. Adam has cleared the rest of the room, and managed to track down Mark. Both men come jogging through the door wearing a similar expression to mine – concern.

"Nic!" Christina tries again, more forcefully this time. "Nic... can you hear me?"

"Christina, what can I do?" Mark asks, but Christina ignores him.

"Nic... Nicky..." she's becoming frantic.

Suddenly, Nic releases Eve's hand and she stumbles backwards, colliding heavily with Adam. "Ow!"

But it isn't the breakthrough we're hoping for. With Eve's hand no longer covering the dial, Nic jabs his finger on the up arrow, increasing the speed to a ridiculous sprint.

"No... Nic... no..." Christina is shouting now, desperate to get him to focus on her, on anything other than this punishing regime.

"Christina, let me try," I say gently, taking her narrow shoulders, and pulling her away. "Take her," I say to Mark, who sweeps Christina into his arms where she stares in utter anguish at her son.

Stepping in front of the treadmill, I know I need Nic to make eye contact before I can even start to slow down the machine.

"Switch it off..." Mark barks at Adam.

"I can't. If I switch it off, it'll stop dead and that'll cause more harm than good," Adam replies loudly over the sound of Nic's pounding feet.

"God, I wish Silas were here," Christina wails, "he'd know what to do..." I'm in no doubt he would, but he isn't, so we need to resolve this ourselves - I've never seen her so distraught.

Ignoring them all, I take a deep breath. *Okay*, I coach myself, *take a step back... observe...*

Nic's arms and elbows are level, his fingers aren't fisted but relaxed, his stride, while fast, is even and steady, his eyes are focussed seemingly on nothing, but his stare is sure, aimed at a poster on the wall. *Okay... alright... he's alright.*

"He's okay," I try and make my voice as reassuring as possible. "Look, watch him, he's alright – for the moment."

Christina visibly flinches in Mark's hold. "He needs to slow down," her anxious voice says it all, she's terrified her son will be irreparably damaged from this brutal excursion.

I need to pacify her. "Christina, listen to me," I say as calmly as I can, over the constant beat of Nic's feet. "He's steady, look at him, he's not even perspiring."

"But he doesn't," panic rises in her voice, "he has hypohidrosis, it means he doesn't sweat, his body can't regulate that way, not since the accident..."

Oh, fuck no! I've completely misjudged this. Nic's body doesn't sweat, which means his temperature will be escalating rapidly. At this rate, he'll overheat and have a seizure before we can get him off the damn machine! *Okay, okay... don't panic... just think... engage him, you've got to engage him...*

"Nic," I coax, "Nic, it's Edi..." Nothing... I try again, aware that I need to keep my voice as normal as possible; getting frantic now won't help anyone. "Nic, it's Edi... Do you remember me? I'm your dad's friend..." Nic blinks once, but still doesn't break concentration.

Frantically I search my brain for something else. *David!* Yes, let's try that... "Nic, David was asking if you'd... you'd...erm..." I stumble over my tongue, seeking for something that David would want him to do, "...like to help him make dinner?"

"Yes, that's it," Eve has her hands clutched together under her chin.

"How long is it now?" Christina asks.

"Forty-five minutes..." Eve answers instantly, she has her phone set to stopwatch and is steadfastly timing every second.

"He's past the safe limit... thirty minutes, after that, he can have a seizure... stop him." Christina's panic has risen to critical levels, I need to stop this now.

I have to think of something... Silas... when I mentioned his dad, there was a split second where Nic's eyes moved... Silas... he has to be the key to unlock this.

"Nic? Your dad will be here soon," I lie, "he's coming to see you." Nic's eyes flick over to mine, momentarily, before refocussing on the poster...*Yes!* "Nic? You should really have a shower before he gets here... so you're ready..." Nope! Again nothing. *Fucking Hell, I'm failing!*

"Keep trying Edi," Christina encourages from beside me.

If only I could hit on something tangible, something Nic can relate to, I know I'd break through this.

"Coming up to fifty minutes," Eve says.

Suddenly inspiration hits me and I know I have it, the one thing he can't resist, the one thing he always engages with... "He's bringing Bear..." If necessary, I'll get him from the car.

Nic's eyes blink rapidly, as if someone has waved a hand in front of his face. There's a glimmer of an opening and I jump on it. "They'll be here very soon. Bear's coming. He'll want to play with you." He blinks again. It's like a fog lifting.

"Berrr!" Nic's voice is hoarse, but he's acknowledged; finally, he's acknowledged Bear.

"Yes, Nic. He'll want to play catch... frisbee, or a tennis ball... but I don't know where to find one. Can you help me?" Still making it up as I go along, I gauge his expression, there's definitely a change.

"Berrr, ball, catch." His feet pound hard on the belt.

"That's fifty-five minutes," Eve informs us.

I hear Christina audibly gasp beside me. She's holding her breath.

"Nic, I think you should stop now. Your dad and Bear will be here any minute." Tentatively, I hesitate, observing his reactions, allowing him to make the sensible decision.

If he slows down in the next two minutes, he'll be fine... I don't believe I've resorted to bargaining!

If he stops in the next thirty seconds, there'll be no damage done and I'll tell David the truth about Bobby...

Very slowly, Nic turns his gaze towards me. *Yes!*

"Hey there... Hi Nic... can you slow down now huh?" I smile, hopeful that he's understood me.

Nic reaches out with his hand, and presses the down arrow, once, twice three times, reducing the speed to a steady jog.

"Oh, thank you Jesus!" Her relief palpable, Christina's words release as a reverent prayer.

"That's it... can you go slower?" Nic presses the key again, reducing the speed even further, so he's now speed-walking on the treadmill.

Two lividly red spots have appeared on his cheeks, a danger sign his blood vessels are dilatating, seeking the surface of his skin, desperate to get rid of the excess heat.

"That's good, great..." I try my best not to rush him, but he needs to get off this treadmill, and quickly, so we can cool him down. "You should be able to stop now." But Nic just keeps on walking.

"He walks," Christina whispers, "when he's stressed, he walks."

Clearly, we're not out of the woods yet. I'm beginning to think Nic will only stop when he sees his dad and Bear walk through the door.

However, just when I think all is lost, and my only option is to go to the car and collect the only ally we have, David re-enters the gym carrying an old-fashioned tartan flask.

"Nic, I've got your protein drink, Man," he announces, as if it's the most normal thing in the world to have his mum, two personal trainers, Christina and the Beeches' head honcho, hovering in anguish around his best friend as he walks himself into oblivion.

Quick as a flash, Nic bangs his hand on the stop button and the treadmill ceases action.

"You need to get showered before your dad gets here," David continues, muscling his way between Mark and Adam, so he can reach his friend. "I'll hold onto this until you get down."

"'tein..." Nic mumbles, climbing off the treadmill and almost collapsing to his knees from exhaustion.

Adam lunges, catching hold of him before he hits the floor. "Pass me the towels," he barks as he lowers Nic on to the rough carpet. "Quickly, we need to get his temperature down."

Mark and Eve start to spread damp towels over Nic's prone body. They've been soaked in cool water. David kneels at his head and begins to open the flask.

Christina is weeping softly, observing her son's inert form with justifiable distress. In an attempt to offer some reassurance, I cross to her and place a supportive arm around her shoulder.

"He'll be okay now Christina..." I sooth, "look, it's all under control."

As I say this a paramedic enters, carrying his medical kit... somebody had the presence of mind to dial 999.

"Is this Dominic?" he asks.

"Yes," David answers, calmly. "My mum managed to stop him, but he needs to be made cool," he explains authoritatively, assisting Nic with sips from the flask. "That's his mum, Christina... he won't talk to you."

Once again David has shown the ultimate in common sense and phoned an ambulance. I'm so proud of him.

"Come on, let them do their job."

Christina is slumped limply against me. "Edi, thank you... you saved him... thank you." Unwavering gratitude sweeps across her face like a gentle breeze. In an instant, the torment she's displayed over the past half an hour has started to abate and in its place is an expression of sheer exhausted relief. "Thank you," she murmurs, "I'll be forever in your debt. I'm so glad we found you. For Silas, for Nic and for me... I'm... we're so *lucky* we found you."

"No, I'm the lucky one... believe me." Tenderly, I kiss the top of her head, offering comfort to my Boss-man's ex-wife... who'd' have thought it?

The ambulance crew have managed to re-stabilise Nic's body temperature. Christina won't allow them to admit him to hospital, insisting instead that he remain at the Beeches under the expert care and supervision of Mark and his team. Reluctantly they agreed, but only after David explained Nic needed to keep calm; that being in a hospital environment would have exactly the opposite effect on him, and when Mark produced his certificate confirming he's medically qualified to manage Nic's condition should there be a flair up, they finally signed him off as clear.

I suspect they're quietly relieved. Hospital beds are a scarce commodity these days and I'm certain they can find better use for one than blocking it with, apart from his obvious difficulties, a very physically fit young man.

After a quick check on Bear, Christina goes with Nic to settle him into his room and try to place a call to Silas. Meanwhile, I ask Mark if he wouldn't mind waiting, until I've had my chat with David. After all, it's what I'm here for, all other drama forsaking.

169

CHAPTER 30

Mark allows us use of his office. He sits behind his desk and keeps quiet, choosing to observe rather than advise.

"Goodness, that was frightening." My hands are trembling as the residue of adrenalin flooding my system gradually dissipates. "I didn't know about his condition." In all our conversations about the children, Silas has never mentioned it.

"I know; Nic likes to walk... I shouldn't have let him go on the treadmill." David's unerring instinct to shoulder the blame for the incident troubles me.

"No David, it most definitely wasn't your fault," Mark admonishes. "If anything, it's mine... I should have been there."

"What is this... beat yourself up day? Clearly it isn't your fault David, and Mark, you can't be everywhere at once; of course, it wasn't your fault either - The PTs should have been more vigilant." They were there after all.

"And therein lies the problem." Mark's demeanour says it all... the PTs didn't know; ergo, Mark's accountable.

The severity of the situation isn't lost on me... but something tells me it won't be progressed. Silas and Christina have as much faith in Mark's capabilities as I do. In my humble opinion, he's a marvel with his residents and they all love him.

Insofar as this incident is shocking, episodes of this nature are decidedly rare at the Beeches. It's a slip, not an avalanche, but a slip-up nonetheless. It may not be a big one, but it's enough to rock the boat if it gets escalated.

However, I doubt that will happen. Christina's an understanding woman. She knows the consequences outweigh the outcome... losing Mark would be a disaster all round. No, I believe Christina was placated. And Mark will learn a valuable lesson from the incident; more importantly, so will the PTs.

Lowering his voice, Mark speaks softly. "Edi, remember why you came tonight... David should be your focus now."

Nodding at Mark, I concentrate my attention where it belongs, on my son. David is looking warily at us. He's afraid of what he's going to hear.

"David, I came here tonight to tell you something important." I glance at Mark who nods he's in full support.

"Is it about Nic?" David asks, concerned as always for his best friend's welfare. "Is he going away?"

"What... no, no darling... Nic's fine, isn't he Mark?"

"Yes, Nic's fine David..." The reassurance smooths out David's worried expression.

"David, I need to tell you something, let's sit down."

We both sit. Settling into my chair, I ensure I'm facing David, we need eye contact. Our knees are touching as I lean forward taking his warm hand in my chilly one.

"Wow... your hands are freezing mum... are you okay?"

Huffing a smile at his everlasting concern for others, I speak softly, squeezing reassurance into his hands. "David, do you remember when you asked me about your dad?"

"Yes, last week..." his eyes go wide. "Why, am I going to meet him?" He's eager, clearly anticipating some good news.

Knowing I'm the bearer of bad news, and what I'm about to say will probably break his heart causing him to hate me, I press on. "No Darling... I'm sorry, but no..." Keeping a tight hold of his hand, I'm unsure if the comfort it brings is for David or for me. My desire to soothe him is crippling.

"Your dad - he isn't what you think..." I faulter, searching for the right turn of phrase; the right intonation. "He's not really a very nice man." Miserably, I fail! My abrupt delivery is heartless and unkind... a slap... "he's not good," I add, compounding the issue. As hurtful as it is to hear, it's the truth... a vast understatement, but the truth nonetheless.

"*My* dad?" Jerking backwards into his chair, his hands slide out of my grip, and he stares at me, puzzled. "My dad... is bad?" Bewilderment and disbelief flood his face as what I've divulged begins to sink in.

"Oh, darling, I'm so sorry." If I could take it back I would... my poor boy. But he needed to know, I couldn't run the risk of him discovering this any other way. It had to come from me.

The lightning speed at which David rises to his feet has the chair legs screeching in protest on the wooden floor. Backing away from me, his legs collide with the chair and immediately it topples over, crashing to the ground, startling us all.

"NO!" His yell is as loud as I've ever heard from him. "NO... MY DAD IS NOT A BAD MAN!"

"David, please listen to me."

"NO!" Retreating further he reaches for the door handle. "NO... YOU DON'T SAY THAT!" He's screaming. I've never seen him like this and I'm scared.

"Please!" Slowly, I rise to my feet. I'm not handling this well, but honestly... how else could I explain. "David, you need to know... you need to listen to me..."

"NO!"

Turning on his heels, he yanks the door open and runs from the room before I can say any more.

"*David!!!*" Calling after him, I make to follow, but Mark's rounded the desk and is blocking my way. "Let me go," I wrench at my arms, trying to release myself from Mark's hold, but I'm going nowhere, I'm gripped tight. "Mark," I growl into his face, "let me go now..." I demand, but he just remains steadfast.

"Edi... give him some space." Mark's calming gentle tone, which I've heard countless times before when he's speaking to the residents, resounds. "He'll come around. He's just had a huge shock, let him go."

"But..."

"Edi... please..."

I know he's right. David needs to calm down. I need to let him digest this before I can explain further. If I try now, he won't listen properly. Mark's right, I need to give him time.

"Shit Mark, what've I done?" Slumping into my chair, I watch as Mark calmly picks up the other one from the floor and straightens it up so he can sit beside me.

"Edi, David isn't stupid."

"I never said he was!" Snapping my head up, I bridle at the word I hate.

171

"Sorry... no, I know you didn't... but he *isn't* stupid. He's sensitive and curious and like any young man, he's looking for a male role model. In his eyes, he's built his dad up to be a hero. Now you've just told him he's a villain. Don't be discouraged by his reaction. It's normal."

Christ... the thought of Bobby being a role model gives me the creeps. Covering my face with my hands, I lean forward, resting my elbows on my knees and groan loudly.

"*Grrr,* I think *I'm* the stupid one." Why on God's green earth did I think it would make things better if I told him the truth? "What should I do?"

"Nothing... as I said before, he'll come around. Be patient."

"*Christ*, it's a mess. I'm supposed to be giving that bloody TV interview next Wednesday, and my son won't listen to me."

"Edi, how necessary is it for David to know? I'm not prying, I don't want you to tell me anything, but I was surprised by your approach."

"Oh Mark... I don't know any more!" Dropping my hands, I look at him. He doesn't know the half of it about Bobby, but he will; just as the rest of the country is going to find out soon enough.

"You know, I've always striven to do the best for David. I think I've made a mistake today. You're right, as usual... he doesn't need to know."

"Do you want me to speak to him?" Mark's kind offer is tempting, but what could he possibly say? "I can embroider the story a little if you like; make something up about his dad leaving you – something like that?"

"I don't know." Shaking my head, I just want the whole nasty business to be over. "I left him; he never knew about David, and if I get my way, he never will. God Mark, how do I fix this?"

"I think, it'd be best to just say he wasn't very nice to you, so you left. Or you could apologise and say it came out wrong. Or you could just say that truthfully, his dad wasn't in the picture and has never known about him."

"Yeah, I suppose so," I sigh in defeat. All are acceptable options, but none are the complete truth.

"Mum?" David is leaning around the doorframe sheepishly, his fingers gripping the front of his tee-shirt, an unconscious sign of his distress. "I'm sorry I shouted at you." The tremor in his voice is heart-breaking.

"Oh darling... it was my fault." Unable to contain my relief, I stand. Rising quickly from my chair, I meet him as he enters the room, flinging my arms around him, hugging him tightly. I would never hurt my boy. The love I have for him is indelible. Our hearts pound as we hang onto each other so tightly.

"I'm sorry David."

"Was he *really* a bad man?"

I nod into his shoulder. "Yeah, he wasn't very nice to me, so I couldn't stay with him."

"Does he know about me?" Clearly, David was eavesdropping.

"No, he doesn't know about you. But I have to speak to some people, to tell them some things, so he might find out."

"Who do you have to speak to?"

"David, you know I'm your mum and I love you... but I used to be quite famous for a while."

"I know!" His stark statement pulls me up short – I didn't expect it.

Holding him at arm's length enables me to gauge his expression. "What do you know?"

"You were a model," he shrugs his shoulders, as if it's no big deal. "You were very pretty – I saw the pictures – in the paper."

I shoot Mark a look that could stab out his eyes. "I warned you to keep the papers away from him..." I hiss.

"I did." Mark is mystified. "David, where did you see the paper?"

"In the pub. It was on the table in the pub. And I read about mum. Her picture was in the paper. She was pretty." The pure innocence in his tone is humbling. "She was a model," he tells Mark, daring him to challenge the statement.

Oh Christ! Of course, it was. Every person in there had probably read it.

"Well, then..." Mark mumbles, unable to find words.

"Mum, I don't mind. You *were,* I mean, *are* very pretty," he repeats, emphatically, "I'm proud of you."

My heart explodes. How the Hell did I not see this coming. My son has been exposed to my sinful history, and in his innocence all he says is *'you were pretty'* and *'I'm proud of you'.*

I'm such a numbskull! I tell myself every day how amazing my boy is, yet I don't think I fully appreciate it. He's a marvel and I love him all the more for it.

"Oh David... not as proud as I am of you..." Taking hold of his face, I kiss him as only a mother can.

"Ugh, no sloppy stuff..." he wriggles out of my clutches. "I won't ask about my dad again. If he's a bad man, I don't think I'd like to meet him. And anyway, if you marry Silas, he'll be my dad and Nic will be my brother," he says cheerfully, the prospect clearly very appealing. "I think I'd like Silas to be my dad!"

Choking back a cough, I wonder in disbelief at the imaginative twists and turns of David's mind. "Um, let's not get ahead of ourselves, shall we?" I gasp.

Mark is smirking, arms folded over his chest, his usual stance... He can bog-right-off too! "Role model," he mouths, silently. I have to admit, I could think of worse.

"Is everything okay?" *Oh great!* Now Christina's arrived to stick her oar in.

"Everything's fine." Swiftly changing the subject, Mark straightens up. At the sight of Christina, the glint of apprehension is back. "How's Nic?" Mark walks around his desk. "I need to write a report on the treadmill incident." Rooting through his drawer, he locates the accident book and starts to flip the pages. "I'll type it up and send you a copy. I'll also be speaking to the staff, and the PT's so they are aware of Nic's condition. I'll make sure this doesn't happen again."

"Thank you, Mark, I appreciate it. Nic's good. He's sleeping." Frankly, she looks exhausted herself. "If you could let me have a copy of that, I'd be grateful." She's clearly not happy though.

"I've informed Silas; he'd like to know exactly how Nic managed to access the treadmill, even with staff present."

Mark shrinks in his chair, visibly intimidated. Christina is a formidable character when she wants to be. I'm sure Mark hasn't heard the end of this.

"Christina, I take full responsibility for the whole episode. The gym staff are new. They weren't made aware of Nic's obsession with running. I hold my hands up, it was my error. You have every right to ask for my dismissal."

I'm shocked, she wouldn't, would she? Surely not. The Beeches can't afford to lose Mark! My head is swinging between Mark and Christina, like I'm at Wimbledon.

"Nooo!" David protests loudly. "You can't make him leave!"

"Oh, for Christ's sake! No one is going anywhere. If I'd wanted your head on a silver platter, believe me, I'd have had it by now. You didn't do it on purpose." Although, that said, she still looks mighty furious. I'm not fully convinced she means it; and if I'm not convinced, there's no hope for Mark... one look at his ashen face confirms it.

"Pigs in fucking - pardon my French, David - space! Nic's fine... he'll recover."

Mark's relief is tangible. "Christina, I can't apologise enough, I really mean it. Speak to Mrs Derbyshire, she'll want to hold a disciplinary."

Oh Heavens! Could today get any worse?

"Mark!" Christina barks; authority dominant in her voice, "I've said my piece. Nic would never forgive me if you were to leave... you're staying... there will be no investigation and no disciplinary for you. I'll speak to Doreen." *Doreen?* "We have an understanding – if I say I don't want to take it further – she'll listen to me." *Ah... that'll be Doreen Derbyshire then!* "The report will suffice and if you say you're going to train the staff fully, I'm satisfied." Turning towards me, she refocuses. "Are you ready to go?" And just like that the matter is closed!

"It's okay mum... you can go... I'm fine."

"Christina, Mark, please could I have five minutes alone with David? I won't be long."

"No problem. Mark, we can go and speak to Doreen; let me handle her." Mark and Christina leave the room, allowing me some much-needed privacy with my son.

"Now then... be honest with me... how do you really feel about the stuff in the paper?"

David hangs his head; he looks forlorn and it breaks my heart. "Mummy, I *am* proud of you... but I think I want to talk to Lizzy... I *miss* her." It's as if a veil has been lifted, this I can achieve...

"Well, you won't have to wait too long..." I smile softly at him, this news is good news, and I can't hold it back. "She's coming home... Silas and I are going to pick her up on Saturday and I know she'll be so excited to see you."

David's smile is dazzling. He can't hide his joy at the thought of seeing his sister. "Really? Oh mum, I can't wait to see her."

"You can tell her everything, she'll listen and she'll understand," I hope. I still need to speak to her, which could prove to be more problematic than speaking to David was today. "When she's home, we can all sit down together and I promise, I'll tell you anything you want to know... I love you, David."

"I love you lots."

"More than Jelly-tots?"

"More than cocoa-pops," and I'm engulfed in his arms.

"Seriously, David. If I've embarrassed you in any way, I didn't mean to. I'm going to fix this – next Wednesday – I'm going to fix this for well and good and then we can all get on with our lives."

As amicable as our parting is, I'm still full of trepidation when I think about David's blow up over the news about his dad.

The effect on him was frightening and my decision to withhold information was completely misjudged. I should never have hidden things from him all these years. My son is quite capable of making decisions. I'm the guilty one here; guilty of underestimating him, guilty of lying and guilty of being selfish. And now I'm even more determined to sort this mess out.

Christina drives us home to Silas's barn. My head's pounding, my hands are cold and my cheeks are burning; all conclusive to the stress of the last couple of hours. I can't wait to get home and have a shower.

"What time's Silas due back?" With all the drama, I'd almost forgotten he was flying.

"Oh, it'll be tomorrow. It's an overnighter, didn't he say?"

Well, that's just ruffled my feathers. "No... he didn't." Why didn't he tell me? He said he'd see me later, but now he's not coming back until tomorrow.

"Oh? That's odd. Perhaps he thought he'd mentioned it."

"Christina, can I ask you something?"

"Fire away..."

"What was Johannes doing with Django and Liam Zaio at the apartment?"

Even though I timed my 'out of left field' question to put her off balance, Christina doesn't react; not a blink nor a flinch. Cool as a cucumber doesn't even cover how unruffled she is... completely unmoved.

"Edi, one of the things we do as a business is help people. Johannes was assisting in relocating them. They needed our aid, and we obliged. It's as simple as that."

I let it go. I'm sure there's more to it than just 'helping them out' but for now, I'll give her the benefit of the doubt.

"Here we are..." she sings as she turns into the drive. Sensing our approach, Bear sticks his nose between the seats.

He's been so good, waiting in the car and then waiting while we drove home. He deserves a good long walk, but as we're both thoroughly wiped out, I imagine he'll be disappointed yet again.

"Out you get..." Christina opens her door, and Bear leaps out; immediately cocking his leg on the alloy wheel, indicating his distain at being ignored for most of the day. "I love you too," she grumbles as she rummages inside her bag for her keys.

Looking at my disapproving face, she sighs, then unhooks her key and hands it to me. "Silas would want you to have this," she says, handing it over.

Inside the barn we ditch our handbags, shoes and jackets in favour of large wine glasses, a bottle of red and the remote for the music system.

175

Flopping on the sofa, we sit together in an exhausted heap. The tones of Twenty-One Pilots *'Stressed Out'* say it all for us... It's been a day!

CHAPTER 31

"Two dresses, two tops, jeans and underwear..."

"Are you sure that's going to be enough?" he calls from the bathroom.

Now I'm concerned. Apart from my impromptu trip to Paris with Silas, I've barely been further than a weekend in Bath since I was an impoverished student. We stayed in a youth hostel and all I took were jeans and sweaters. This trip is so different. I've no idea what to pack.

"You do it then..." flopping on the bed, I give him a sulky Paddington stare, hoping he'll take pity and make all my clothing choices for me.

"Ooh no... I'm not falling for that one, just pack for one evening and a day in the park. Jeans should be fine...you'll be perfect whatever you wear." Silas wanders in from the landing looking like the Greek God he is, fresh from the shower, a minuscule towel is all that's hiding his substantial modesty; I'm instantly distracted from my mood.

"You make me sound like Mary Poppins..." I say as I accidentally catch the towel with my finger as he passes, causing the scrap of cotton to drop to the floor.

"No way... she was only 'practically' perfect," he growls, seductively. "Now... you need to do something about this..." Standing before me, he slowly strokes his length.

With all that tantalising delicious flesh at eye level, my mouth begins to water in anticipation. "Only, 'practically' perfect, eh? Well, I need to ensure my reputation remains intact..." I match his voice in the hushed whisper department.

Every time I look at him, he takes my breath. I can't believe he's mine. This beautiful man is mine...

Reaching out I take him in hand, stroking along his length, watching in wonder as he grows ever harder and longer under my touch.

His skin is silky and warm, his girth, as impressive as always, my fingers, stretch around him, but are unable to meet.

"Take it deep, Edi," my fascination is broken by his gruff instruction. Stepping closer to me, his feet are planted between mine on the plush carpet. His hands rest on his hips, emphasizing his physique. "I love your mouth on me..."

My hooded eyes burn; I imagine my pupils, large and dilated as I gaze at his amazing face. His own pupils are barely detectible, so large are they in his caramel eyes they appear black and shining.

Trapping him with my stare, I lean forward, my lips prickling with hunger, my mouth flooding with saliva in anticipation of his taste. Oh, this will be good.

"Are you ready to be eaten?" I whisper, licking my lips, coating them with a flick of my tongue, "because, I'm ready to eat..."

He gasps at my crudeness, but I don't care. What else do I call it. I'm definitely hungry for him and I want to gobble him up.

Very tenderly, I kiss his tip. A bead of cum appears and I stroke it over my pouting mouth, slowly spreading the essence of him along my top lip, around the sides and over my bottom lip as if he's my own bespoke brand of lip-gloss.

"Jeeezz..." Silas tips his head back and moans at the ceiling. His hips thrust of their own volition, nudging into my lips, which part willingly.

Slipping him into my mouth, I support his sack with my hand, caressing the taught skin, flicking my finger along the seam.

He's deep now, stroking the back of my throat, I resist the need to swallow; that comes later.

Removing my hands from his manhood, I grip his buttocks, digging in with my nails, inducing a strangled cry from his throat. *"Yeah..."*

His hands seek out the buttons of my blouse, and once they're undone, he grasps my breasts harshly in a vice like grip, forcing me to moan around him. My vocal cords vibrate, sending a symphonic tremor all the way down his shaft to his base. The resultant shudder tells me he can feel it in the pit of his stomach.

"Aggh, Honey-bee, please," his hands force the cups of my bra down, so he has a breast in each hand.

Gradually, he massages, pummelling and squeezing in rhythm to my mouth's working. The sensation urges me on.

Drawing back, I slide him through my lips until only his glans are in my mouth. Furiously flicking my tongue across his slit, I watch in awe as he begins to tremble and his knees threaten to give way. He's close.

I slide my hands so they are holding tightly on to his buttocks, and very gently, I ease them apart. Instantly his eyes find mine. He knows my intention and he doesn't resist...

Seeking out the rim of his anus with my pinkie, I inset it up to the second knuckle, massaging his prostate, I pump it slowly in and out. "Agggghh! Edi, yeah, fuck me..."

His begging is my undoing and I slam my mouth on him until I'm choking. Once he's at the back of my throat, I perform my piece de resistance; I swallow, the suction is squeezing so tightly, he has no option but to come... pumping loud, hard, and wet; spilling jet after jet of salty sweetness down my throat. "Fuucckk yeah!" he roars to the heavens in release.

His chin drops to his chest, and his hands release their grip on my breasts, landing on my shoulders. The relief is instant, I didn't realise he was squeezing so tightly until he let go.

Steadily, breathing through my nose, I allow him to deflate in my mouth, holding him there, the vacuum sucking my cheeks hollow.

Silas cups my face, his fingertips stroking beside my lips, a look of wonder on his glorious face as he caresses the seal where my lips meet his flesh. The tickling sensation causes me to smile.

The inevitable opening of my mouth, brings an audible pop as my tongue relaxes. My engorged lips pucker, still coated with the remnants of his pre-cum, I grin, jutting out my chin. I know that was a good one.

"Ummm, do you think you could take your finger out my arse?" he wiggles his hips, encouraging me to remove my probing digit. "Only, it's beginning to smart a bit!"

"Huh," I laugh, "sorry." Gently, I remove my pinkie.

Silas reaches down and grasping my arms, hauls me to my feet. Swathing me into his chest, he kisses the top of my head then rests his cheek there. "It's gonna be okay you know?"

My euphoria of seconds ago, dissolves into a sort of mild sorrow. I know what he's getting at. The last couple of days at work I've been in and out of moods, but this cloudy feeling doesn't seem to want to lift.

I'm conflicted. One minute I'm ecstatic, we're going to New York to collect my baby girl and Sammy, but at the same time I'm aware when I get back, I have to run the gauntlet of the press. I'll be judged.

Flowing hot and cold doesn't cover it – I feel like I'm riding a see-saw of emotions right now.

"I know..." I mumble in response, even though I'm not wholly convinced.

"Hey, do you think that's why she's only *'practically'* perfect?" Silas quips.

I stay where I am, tucked under his chin, but my brow creases in a frown... "Who?" I'm lost.

"Mary Poppins..."

"I'm not with..."

"It has to be... think about it... her BJ's must be rubbish, or at best mediocre, that's got to be the reason... Bert isn't a happy chimney sweep!"

"Oh God... can you imagine?" I laugh as I unravel myself from his naked clutches, chuckling at the image of the wholesome nanny on her hands and knees, measuring Bert's length before opening her pert mouth.

"Where do you think you're going?"

"To the bathroom," holding up my hand, I curl my pinkie finger at him, waving, "I need to wash my hands...

"Ooof." My breath is knocked out of me, as I'm swept off my feet and flung onto the bed.

"My game, my rules... you've not been dismissed." Rummaging under my skirt, he has my knickers off in a split second and before I know it, my legs have been parted, and I have a seventeen stone Neanderthal glowering over me.

His dark eyes flash with mischievous intent, as I stare blatantly into his handsome face. "So, what is this game then?" As if I didn't know.

"Now it's my turn..." he starts to hum as he lowers himself down my body in his search for the promised land. *"Chim chiminey, Chim chiminey, Chim, chim cher-ee! Silas is lucky as lucky can be..."*

"Oh Lord..." I place my hands over my burning face as he goes down on me, the undefeated master of his game.

Two hours later, and our bags are standing side by side at the front door. This time tomorrow, we'll be in the air and I'll be having my first flight in a Gulfstream. But for now, we're preparing to take Bear on his last walk before we drop him off with Silas's family.

Christina has Nic for the weekend, and quite rightly doesn't want any distractions. Still a little wobbly from his exertions on the treadmill, he needs calm.

179

They'll visit Silas's parents on Sunday, Nic can see Bear then. I dread to think what he and Margo will get up to while we're gone, but that's going to be Chloe's problem.

"Ready?" Silas removes Bear's lead from the hook behind the door.

"Yeah." I tie a double knot in my Timberlands just to be sure, then grab my jacket. The evenings are beginning to cool down.

Out in the garden, we don't head for the road, but walk instead to the rear of the property and into the small copse behind the house. I smile shyly up at Silas as I remember a more... stimulating visit to these trees.

"Grrr." He pinches my bottom and pulls me in to his side. "Don't tempt me..."

"What? I'm sure I don't know what you mean." I do, but I'm not admitting it out loud.

"I could have your jeans down and your knickers off in ten seconds... and you know it."

"Okaaay..." I tweak my lip in acceptance. He could, and I'd let him but unfortunately, we don't have the time.

"Now look what you've done!" He makes a show of adjusting the bulge in his groin. "I can't fucking walk straight."

Laughing out loud, I snake my arm around his neat waist, my thumb hooking subconsciously into the beltloop of his jeans.

Following a natural worn track, we cross the rickety old style and enter the fields beyond. Bear bounds ahead, gazelle-like. The crop is almost waist deep, so most of the time, the only part of him visible is his tail, rising like a periscope above the ears of wheat.

The farmer hails a greeting as we pass. "It's a public right of way, part of an ancient roman footpath, actually," Silas explains to my puzzled expression.

"Ah."

"Bear loves it here, it's so quiet and peaceful." I can understand why; it's idyllic.

Holding hands, we stroll through the field, with no sound but the rhythmic swish, swish, swish of sweeping stalks against denim; enjoying each other, taking our time, walking the perimeter, so that Bear has a good long snuffle and run around.

"If I forget to tell you, I had a wonderful time in New York..." I snuggle into him, stuffing our joined hands into his jacket pocket.

"You ain't seen nothing yet Honey-bee..."

"I love you for doing this for me," I whisper.

"And I love you for letting me... C'mon, let's get this dog to my parents."

The house looks much the same as it did last time we visited, only without the balloons and birthday decorations. Sylvana is alone when we arrive. Apparently, Leon has a 'meeting' – what's with this family and their meetings? – but should be home soon. Chloe and Jasmine are at yoga and Tia is working late.

"Come through, dear's... Edi, can I offer you some wine?" Sylvana already has a chilled glass sitting beside her chair on a small side table.

It'd be rude to refuse. "Oh, thank you, that would be lovely."

"I'm okay mum, I'm driving. I'll stick to water."

"I have iced tea?"

"Oh, yes then, please... peach if you have it."

"Of Course, no problem; excuse me for a moment," she leaves us in the living room.

"This house is beautiful." I walk around the lounge, absorbing the abundance of photographs and pictures. Artworks adorn the walls, paintings of all kinds from landscapes to modern art. It's an eclectic mix and suits the room beautifully.

"Here we are." Sylvana hands me a glass of white and passes a bottle of Iced Tea to Silas, who immediately removes the cap and downs a long swig.

I sip my wine. It's crisp and cold and I know instantly this is no cheap supermarket plonk. "This is lovely," I acknowledge, taking another longer mouthful.

"Why yes, I'm pleased you like it. Charles is dabbling... quite successfully if you ask me."

For a moment I'm confused... Charles?... the name rings a bell, but I'm not sure where from. My face must be giving away my muddle because, Sylvana elaborates. "Charles has a vineyard in Burgundy - in Auxerre, actually - this Chablis is a delight. I expect he'll be winning medals next season."

Ah, finally I remember. Charles is Gerard's father; of course, he produces phenomenal wine... why wouldn't he!

Silas rolls his eyes at me. The clang from the penny dropping a million feet must have sounded like a gong! "Well, this is delicious. I wish him every success."

"Cheers," we clink and drink.

"Now, where's that dog?"

Bear's been conspicuous by his absence since we arrived. I vaguely remember him slinking off into the kitchen behind Sylvana, but he's been so quiet I'm beginning to think he's fallen asleep.

As if on cue, Bear and Margo dart in from the kitchen, careering a neat circuit around the coffee table with decided precision, missing every trinket and ornament, before charging back the way they came, through the lounge door.

Sylvana indulges them with a huge smile. "I don't know... those two!" she absently takes a sip of her wine and sits on the sofa, patting the space beside her indicating, I too, should sit. "Now, have you brought his bed?" she asks Silas, on the tilt of a head.

"I'll get it... it's in the car."

Finishing the last of his peach tea, Silas leaves us alone and heads out to collect Bear's overnight bag.

The room is quiet, except for the ominous ticking of the antique grandmother clock standing in the corner. Sylvana observes me mildly. I sip my wine and gaze around the imposing space, feigning interest in the variety of intricate knick-knacks, hoping I'm not going to receive a lecture from her as I did from her husband.

"You do know he's smitten, don't you?" she announces coolly. Her manner is unnervingly similar to Christina's. "He's invested." That strange comment grabs my attention, *invested,* an odd turn of phrase.

"So am I..." I'm not fooled. I know I'm being judged. This formidable lady is making her own assessment of me, discounting anything she's heard elsewhere.

"Good... he needs you to be," she states sternly. "Silas is a complicated man. His history, his trauma, makes him so. I know you know the depth of his sadness." Her expression is unwavering. I can only put myself in her position; a mother protecting her child.

"I do..." I understand completely, in another circumstance, I'm her.

"So, you're invested?"

"I am," I answer, without a moment's hesitation, because it's true. I am invested. I love him. I want him and I need him.

"Then we understand each other?"

"Yes, we understand each other."

"Good... Ah, here he is..." Silas stumbles into the living room carrying Bear's rather large dog-bed, piled high with bowls, biscuits and dog food, not forgetting his rubber chicken. "Just drop it in the hall dear... Chloe will sort it all out later."

As Silas reverses out of the door, Sylvana turns warm eyes on me. "You know dearest, I think you're just what he needs," the warmth soon turns to an ice-ray, "but hurt him at your peril... more wine?"

"Ummm?"

"No, sorry mum, but we really need to be off. We have an early start tomorrow."

How much did he hear?

Silas removes my empty glass and places it on the table. "Ready?"

"Yeah," I'm so ready... get me out of here please. "Thank you for the wine... and the chat," I say, pointedly.

Sylvana looks at me warily, unsure of where I'm leading. The 'chat' was supposed to be private. "Yes, well... err..."

"And just so you know... my investment, as you put it, is one hundred percent. I have no intention of hurting him, letting him down, or deserting him. This is real..."

Silas eyes us each with suspicion. "What did I miss?" he asks.

"Oh, just your mother, being a lioness..." I smile at Sylvana. We have an understanding. I'm a lioness too.

Sylvana visibly relaxes, her eyes softening in the wake of my disclosure. "Dearest... I love her..." she kisses Silas on the cheek tenderly, "she's perfect."

"That she is..." he whispers. I don't miss the smirk and cheeky wink as his eyes flick to my sealed lips.

"Practically," I grin. "Sylvana, thank you for taking care of Bear. When we get back, I'd love for you to meet Lizzy and David, that's if you'd like?"

"Oh! Yes, how wonderful... I can't wait." Her joy at the idea of meeting my children is genuine and I'm grateful for it. They need stability.

"Come on, let's get gone, before the rest of the crew arrive. We'll never get away if Jazz and Chloe see you. Bye mum... see you in a day or two."

"Bye dears."

"What the bloody Hell was all that about?" We're on our way home in the dusk and Silas is desperate to know what went on in the fifty seconds between him leaving to get Bear's stuff, and returning to a decidedly frosty atmosphere. "Did she threaten you?"

"No..." I lie, "she just wanted to be sure I knew what I was letting myself in for. I think she's more afraid for you than she is for me..."

"Ha, that'll be the day... what did she say?"

"Oh, you know... the usual motherly stuff... '*Don't hurt him... don't cheat on him... suck his dick every day...*' that kind of thing."

Silas swerves, nearly mounting the verge as he looks at me open mouthed... it's comical.

"Oh, come on... it was a little funny."

"You can be really crude sometimes... you know that?"

"You only have yourself to blame there boy... I was all meek and mild until I met you... now listen to me."

"I've unleashed a monster... and my mother is scared of you... double points... brilliant!!"

CHAPTER 32

"Morning sunshine..." my nose is kissed, and I'm drawn from my comfortable, warm slumber, by a grinning Adonis pinning me to the mattress.

"What's the time?" I yawn, wiggling my way down the bed face down.

"Time you were up and dressed." He whips back the covers, and slaps my arse. "Come on, we have places to be."

In a flash, I'm out of bed; my sleepy brain, instantly alert with thoughts of Lizzy and Sam, New York, Silas and flying...

Silas is left lying in the heap of a warm vacated duvet, laughing at my sudden burst of energy. Rolling onto his back, he watches in amusement as I fly around the bedroom grabbing underwear, jeans and my jumper. "Relax... take your time... we'll make it," he calls at my retreating back as I head for the shower. "Do you want some eggs?"

"Yes please," I reply as I dive into the steaming jets. We have time for breakfast, that's good.

At the airfield, Spanners and Sparks have guided the Gulfstream onto the apron. She's stunningly beautiful. A Gulfstream G500, capable of travelling over five-thousand miles and, so I'm told, every discerning pilot's wet dream.

"Wow!" I gape in wonder at the sublime craft. Inside, I know she'll be every bit as impressive as she looks from the outside. Her skin is silver with dark blue striped embellishments, her tail fin bears the identification GMM-253 along with a now familiar Tudor Rose emblem.

"Beautiful, isn't she?"

"God, yes..."

"Gerard's father bought her after Marcus died. He wanted Gerard to be safe. This is his way of ensuring Gerard's protected."

"So, this is Gerard's plane?"

"Yeah, essentially it belongs to the business fleet, but each of us have our own particular favourite. This is Gerard's baby. He loves her. He'll be my co-pilot today".

"Oh? You never said."

"Didn't I? Oh well, it must've slipped my mind," he says, evasively. "Ah, speak of the devil..."

Gerard strolls towards us, arms spread wide in greeting; his right hand clutches the ubiquitous leather folio. His brown hide pilots' jacket is worn in places with faded patches, signifying its age; but he wears it so well. I can't help but admire his charm. He's looking dapper and handsome in that effortless, Gaelic way he has.

"Edi, mon ami, you look incroyable, splendid as usual." My shoulders are gripped and I'm embraced fondly and kissed on both cheeks.

"Tueur noir..." Gerard moves his greeting to Silas.

Raising my eyebrows in his direction, I detect his slight flinch at my reaction to the usage of such an archaic term. I still find it uncomfortable when Gerard voices this

184

distasteful reference to Silas; I doubt I'll ever get used to it. In every other way, Gerard is charming; but this is one aspect of his personality I really don't like.

Sensing my discomfort, Silas leans in close and whispers, "it really isn't what you think," before turning and heading towards the awaiting plane.

Remaining stationery, my eyes follow him incredulously as he leads Gerard away from my death stare. *Black Tudor!* What part of that isn't what I think?

The interior of the aircraft is every bit as exquisite as I imagined. It's undiluted over the top luxury, and I love every inch of it. From the plush cream leather armchairs to the rich crimson carpet, even the gold-plated trim on the walnut tables screams bad taste; in every good way possible. The décor's more in keeping with a luxury cruise liner than an aeroplane.

Settling into my seat I prepare for take-off. In less than six hours, I'll be in the Big Apple. I can't quite believe the turn my life has taken. In the last couple of months, I've gone from a humble student, barely making ends meet, to… this. I gaze around in awe.

To say the shift in my circumstances was unforeseen would be a vast understatement; the biggest surprise of them all, being the man sitting not thirty feet away from me behind a walnut veneered door. He's a man I couldn't have created, even in my wildest of dreams; a man who has turned my world upside down, inside out and changed my whole perception of myself for the better. There's no doubt I'm a stronger person for meeting him; stronger in every way.

Only by being with him, could I ever have found the courage, confidence and resolve to accept my past and challenge it head on. Only being with him, has nurtured my self-belief into worthiness… just knowing I'm enough, is enough; even with all my baggage, hang-ups and imperfections… So what? Whatever happens in my life, where ever it leads me, from now on … I matter…I'm worthy.

I shake my head at the sheer wonder of it all. It's true when they say you don't know what lies around the corner. Magical things happen every day to ordinary people… and I'm living proof.

The barely detectible sound of the engines draws my attention to the window. Sparks is sat astride his trusty red steed, guiding us out.

Spanners windmills his arms, waving his paddles in the direction of the runway. Idly I wonder who's manning the departure desk?

I raise my hand at Charley, and he gives me a cheery salute in return; then settling onto his seat, he pulls his ear defenders in place as Jim takes his place beside him on the tow truck. Expertly, Charley uses one hand to spin the steering wheel, whizzing the vehicle around on a sixpence before driving off in the direction of the hangar, disappearing from my line of sight.

Once airborne, I unclip my safety belt and head to the cockpit to check if the guys would like a coffee or anything to eat.

"She 'ees, ze one then, yes?" Gerard's question permeates the small door way as I draw it open. Perhaps I should've knocked?

Tentatively, I reclose the door before I hear Silas's reply. I really don't want to hear him speaking about me to his friends… it doesn't sit well and gives me an odd invasive feeling. Tapping my knuckle lightly against the polished wood, I wait for the invitation before reopening the door.

"Come in…"

"Hi… err, I was wondering if you'd like a coffee?" The brilliant azure of the vast open sky greets me as I step through into the small space.

The view through the window, it's clear, bright and cloudless… a magnificent vista of the brightest blue, and I'll never tire of it.

"Hey, gorgeous… yeah… two espressos please. I'll be out in a few minutes. We just need to clear UK airspace and then Gerard will take over for a couple of hours and I can rest."

Gerard is speaking into his headset. He acknowledges the offer of coffee with a thumbs up gesture.

"I'll fetch them," I say, backing out of the cockpit.

In the galley, I quickly locate the coffee machine and some cups and saucers. I chuck a couple of Lotus biscuits onto a plate for good measure while the rich, bitter-sweet aroma gradually permeates the cabin, denoting the quality of the beans.

As I potter about, I can't help pondering over what Silas may have answered in response to Gerard's question. Am I the one? Silas has told me I am, and he's certainly the one for me, but in my experience, what a man says to his mates differs greatly from the way he speaks to his woman… although, I am considerably limited in experience, so what do *I* really know?

Lizzy knows more about men than I do! That thought is unnerving, so I swiftly shut it down. I don't want to be thinking about my daughter and her experiences with men… my shoulders shudder involuntarily at the mere notion … *Ugh!*

"Here we are, two espressos." I shimmy my way through the swinging door of the cockpit, saucers in hand. Silas twists around in his seat, reaching his arms forward, taking both cups from me and placing them on the small console between the two pilot chairs.

"Thanks, Honey-bee."

The back of Gerard's head shifts in Silas's direction on hearing the term of endearment. "'Oney-Bee… zis is your name?" he contorts himself so I'm in view. "'Eez nice… it suits you."

"Um…" I mumble, looking at Silas for reassurance.

"Yeah, you don't get to use it, Gerard… me only…" Silas growls at his friend. "Seriously, Gerard… do you hear? I mean it." The warning is clear. Silas is the only one who's allowed to call me by that name.

I offer him a grateful smile… yes, I'm *his* Honey-bee, nobody else's. I think I have the answer to Gerard's question!

"D'accord! Pardonne-moi, il ne se reproduira pas." Gerard nods in my direction, "Pardonne," he repeats directly to me.

"Well… okay, but just be warned…" Silas eases at Gerard's apology. "Are you alright to take her for a couple of hours?"

"Oui, oui...vous reposez, aller," Gerard replies; his English seems to have deserted him for some obscure reason.

Silas rises from his seat and removes his headset, picking up his coffee cup and following me through the cockpit door.

"What was all that about?" I ask as we re-enter the main cabin.

Silas finishes the last dregs of his coffee and reaches around me to drop the cup into the small sink. "Huh!" he grunts. "He's nervous. He reverts to French when his courage fails him."

"Why would he be nervous?" As if I don't know.

"I'm not sure... but my educated guess would be, because he's shit-scared of me and knows when I'm serious... and I *am* serious about you, Edi." His face softens, "Really, really serious."

That does it. I melt into him. My legs turn to jelly at those words and I can't support my own weight, so I wrap my arms around his neck. "I love you, Boss-man," I murmur; Oh God, I love him so much.

"Come on, let me give you the tour." Unhooking himself from my grasp he swings me around, holding onto my wrists from behind, he propels me forwards and out of the tiny galley space and into the main body of the cabin.

"I've seen it," I grumble, as I'm nudged onward towards the rear of the plane.

"Not all of it," he rumbles suggestively in my ear, "mile-high club here we come..."

"Silas!" I squeal, as I'm hoisted up in front of him, his arms around my waist so my feet dangle off the floor like a wayward child.

"In here," he whispers, as he elbows open an unremarkable plain white door at the rear of the cabin...

Oh My Gosh!

It's a bloody bedroom! A full-sized double bed, dressing table, wardrobe and everything...

"Wow... Silas, this is amazing!" My feet are lowered to the plush emerald green carpet and I'm jostled forwards towards the bed as Silas closes and purposefully locks the door behind us.

"Yes, it's a bedroom. And we're going to christen it... right now." I'm spun around and his lips slam against mine hungrily. "Honey-bee, you're so sweet. My Honey-bee."

"Yes, yours... only yours."

"Can you feel my heart? It's going ballistic. That's what happens when I imagine another man thinking about you... your sweetness... your honey."

"Were you serious when you threatened Gerard... were you serious?"

"Abso-fucking-lutely," his lips travel to my neck.

"Is he really afraid of you?" My eyes roll with pleasure at the feel of his mouth on me.

"Terrified," he murmurs with intent as he nips my sensitive skin, then kisses his bite.

"Why?" My hands are fisting his shirt, the grip unyielding in my need for him.

"He knows my capabilities," he hums against my throbbing vein.

"Capabilities?" I chuckle. "I know your capabilities..." but I doubt we're speaking of the same capabilities here.

187

"He knows… I'm deadly…Lie on the bed…"

I'm released and pushed backwards into the room, towards the cream satin dressed bed. I recline and lean on my elbows, watching him as he unbuttons his shirt.

It's reminiscent of that first night in Paris, where he took me so perfectly and unapologetically for the first time. Where we made love on the balcony in the pouring rain, and where, for the first time, I felt the full intensity of what a real man can do to a woman when she's willing and compliant.

"You're so beautiful," I mimic his words from that night, thinking I'll have some fun at his expense, "remove the shirt…" I quip; my lips failing to suppress the hint of amusement threatening to morph into a full-on grin.

I see the moment the dots connect as he realises the direction I'm taking. "I don't know about that… I'm not very good at this…" it's his turn to mimic me.

"I think I'll be the judge of that… now…I said, remove the shirt…"

"But…" he demur's, stammering, trying not to express delight at the turned tables.

"Either you remove the shirt or I will."

Keeping his blazing eyes firmly on mine, he rips the shirt from his body; ensuring maximum flex as it skims his shoulders; stretching his neck, emphasizing his firm pecs and gorgeously defined six-pack. I'm dribbling!

Leaning down, he goes to pull off his loafers. As quick as a flash, I remember his barked instruction to me… "No, the shoes stay," I demand firmly. Again, I imitate his words.

Raising one eyebrow he grins as he acknowledges my game, but it's impossible, he's unable to quell his mirth any longer. "Seriously?" he coughs, "you want me to leave my shoes on?"

Incapable of restraint, I laugh out loud. The image of him keeping his shoes on is so comical, I fall about; unable to keep up the seduction routine… it's just too funny.

Holding up my hands, I concede defeat and surrender to his mastery of the game… I'm useless, I'll never beat him!

"Oh, you're sooo, dead…" he drawls; his smile beaming in the glow of victory as he lowers himself over me.

I don't care I've lost the game; I'm a million miles in the air, on a luxury plane, on the way to see my baby girl in New York… I'm in Heaven… literally flying!

CHAPTER 33

We land at Teterboro Airport, New Jersey with little drama or fuss. It was an uneventful flight, unless you count the 'mile high' initiation ceremony that is!

I'm reliably informed we'll be confirming our membership on the return journey! Although I'm thrilled at the prospect of another sky-high tryst with Silas - the experience was exhilarating, possibly due to the cabin pressure and altitude - I'm not entirely sure I'll be as willing to repeat it once Lizzy and Sammy are on board... no matter how much of an exhibitionist Silas is, I'm not up to performing in such close proximity of my daughter and her best friend. One thing I've learned about myself is I'm not a quiet lover!

We didn't really eat on the flight. Silas and Gerard were more than happy to stick to the excellent quality coffee and I was so nervous and excited at the pending adventure, my stomach was full of butterflies rather than hunger pangs.

But now we've landed and unloaded our bags, I'm beginning to feel light headed and a little sick; a sure sign I'm peckish and dehydrated.

"Once we've collected the car, I'll take us to a diner I know," Silas says, reading my mind.

"Drop me at the 'otel... I 'ave some things to attend to," Gerard says, gruffly.

He's still smarting from Silas's rebuke earlier; and I expect from hearing our vocal performance in the bedroom. I didn't miss the sulky expression and look of mild incredulity cross his features.

On Silas's return to take over the controls, Gerard huffed his way into the rear of the cabin, and choosing the seat furthest from the galley, closed his eyes going straight to sleep, making his point and annoyance known.

"Yeah, we do need to complete that bit of business," Silas confirms. "I'll take Edi for a spot of lunch, then she can meet up with the girls for a reunion drink. I'll join you in the hotel lobby later?"

"Oui, zat should work," Gerard nods in affirmation as we reach the car. "Just drop me at the front door; I'll check us in and grab room service. You go and enjoy your lunch."

Gerard opens the rear door of a huge Lincoln town car. "Edi, your limousine awaits," he smiles at my open-mouthed disbelief.

"Oh Lordy!" I exclaim as I climb in. I was expecting a yellow cab not Donald Trump's personal chauffeur!

After supervising the loading of the bags, Silas speaks to the driver before climbing in beside me. Gerard takes a seat up front, riding shot gun.

"Oh, wow Silas, this is amazing. How on earth did you plan all this in such a short time?" I ask, as the penny drops.

"Christina!" we chorus together. The woman is an absolute marvel.

"Now sit back and enjoy the sights. We should be at the hotel in about thirty minutes or so."

"Okay," I mumble, already mesmerised by the height of the towering buildings and jaywalking pedestrians. It's like being on a film set.

As Silas predicted, thirty or so minutes later, we're at the hotel. The Sherry-Netherland is on 5th Avenue, directly opposite the entrance to Central Park… it really is a film-set. Gerard jumps out, hailing the bell-hop, who scuttles to collect the bags from the trunk.

Silas rolls down the window and Gerard pops his head inside. "I'll see you in a couple of hours oui?"

"Oui; a plus tard. D'accord," Silas responds in fluent French, "faire les arrangements. L'heure est fixée," he concludes, before closing the window.

"Can you take us to Brother Dell's please?" Silas leans towards the driver, as I watch Gerard enter the hotel, the bell-hop in his wake, carrying all our bags.

"Sure, boss," the driver replies, his Brooklyn accent is so strong, for a moment I think he's putting it on for my benefit. "He does the best Sloppy Joes in Manhattan," he informs me, "you'll love 'em."

"You will…" Silas confirms the statement with a sideways glance.

I have no idea what a 'Sloppy Joe' is, but if it moos or grunts or clucks and is wrapped in bread, then I'll eat it… I'm starving.

"Why don't you give Lizzy a call and let her know we've landed?" Silas wipes his lips on the white paper napkin dabbing at the remains of the rich sauce. The driver didn't lie, the food is unbelievable, considering it's basically a minced beef sandwich!

"Oooh, yes!" I texted the girls when we landed, so they know we're here, but we've yet to arrange where to meet. "Should I say the hotel?" Lizzy would love the luxury after all the nomadic, budget places they've stayed in.

"Yeah, that'll work. We can go back and you can have a relax before you meet them." He waves at the server, performing the universal sign-language for the bill. "Have a nice soak and take your time to get dressed. The girls are booked into the hotel for the night, so I'm sure they'll want to do the same."

Silas insisted the girls stay at the same place as us. There was no budging him on that score. He'd said we'd been separated long enough and he wanted their last night in the Big Apple to be a memorable one.

"Remember to charge whatever you have to our room." Silas hands the server a generous tip, before lifting his jacket off the rear of the chair and draping it over his shoulder. "I expect you to drink your body weight in cocktails. Gerard and I have plenty to keep us occupied… there's some business we can conclude while we're in the city, so this evening belongs to you and the 'girly reunion'."

"You're so generous." He is; not just with his money but with his time, his compassion and his attention.

"Honey-bee, it's been a long time since I've wanted to be. Just let me… you deserve it." He drapes his arm around my shoulder as we head out of the deli.

The car is waiting for us, the driver, standing on the sidewalk, leaning against the door finishing his own Sloppy Joe. At the sight of Silas, he stuffs the last bite into his mouth, before crumpling up the greasy paper and tossing it into an overflowing waste bin.

"I'm sooo, stuffed," I sigh, patting my bloated belly as I climb in the back seat. The flight and the car journey are catching up with me and I could do with forty winks, never mind a bath and cocktails. At this rate I'll be asleep by ten!

"Ring Lizzy!" Silas reminds me of the reason I'm here.

Pulling out my phone I notice I've already missed two calls from her. Quickly, I press redial and she answers, almost before the first ring sounds. "Mamma!" she screams down my ear, "where are you? We can't wait to see you?"

Hey, baby-girl... I'm in the car on the way to the hotel. Where are *you?*" Perhaps we could pick them up on the way.

"We're already here!" she exclaims, her voice full of awe and wonder. "This place is amazeballs!"

"Edi, it's the dog's," I hear Sammy's not so dulcet tones in the background as she makes her qualified assessment known.

I smile fondly at Silas, as a warm feeling of contentment fills me... God how I've missed them. "I'll be about..." I widen my eyes at him, realizing I haven't the first clue how long we'll be...

"About twenty minutes," he whispers, sensing my question.

"Twenty minutes," I repeat, mouthing a 'thank you' to Silas and blowing him a kiss.

"Brilliant, we're gonna have a shower and we'll see you in about an hour?" Lizzy suggests.

"Sounds good to me," I answer. "Oh, baby, I can't wait to see you. I have so much to tell you." More than I really want to, I think to myself, hanging up the phone.

My mood plummets at the thought and I'm hit with a decidedly melancholic feeling. It must be reflected in my actions, because Silas draws me to him and tucks me under his arm.

Kissing the top of my head, he murmurs "Honey, it'll be fine... you'll see."

"Yeah, well, I'm not holding my breath..."

How can it be fine when I'm about to break the news to my little girl that her dad is a people trafficking pimp, and possibly a paedo', hiding his wickedness behind legitimate business; who used to beat me black and blue, force me to take my clothes off for money and make me feel worthless. And who is imminently forcing my hand into making a public statement on national TV about my past life?

As if he knows my thoughts and can read my mind, Silas seeks to reassure me. "Edi... stop! It *will* be alright... you'll see."

"Hmmm." I wish I had half his confidence.

Two hours later I'm bathed, prepped, preened and fragrant, and dressed in my new flutter sleeve blue satin casual cocktail dress. It feels lovely and comfortable. I've teemed it with my black Paris shoes; ever hopeful they'll do the trick and make Silas's mouth water. Silas and Gerard are still out. Apparently, they have *'business'* to attend to; although what it is, I have no idea. Part of me wonders if the whole thing is fabricated, so the girls and I can enjoy our emotional reunion audience free.

I take the elevator to the lobby. The journey down is swift and silent, only the chime indicating I've arrived at my destination.

Walking into the bar, I gaze around me, searching for the familiar shaggy mass of blonde and unruly tufts of jet-black curls, but they're nowhere in sight. Concluding they must be running late, I sidle up to the bar, picking up a cocktail menu to occupy myself while I wait.

"Bugger me!" The abrupt exclamation startles me. I'm taken by complete surprise and whirl around on my bar stool seeking out the culprit – and there she stands – beautiful, tall, slim and dressed immaculately!

Her hair is piled in a sleek bun, atop her head. Loose tendrils artistically skim her throat, emphasising the length of her neck, not to mention the deep plunging 'V' neckline of her pink chiffon gown. A gold filigree collar finishes the look.

All eyes are turned in her direction – why wouldn't they be – she looks stunning.

"Fuck-a-duck!... Edi... wow!" There's no mistaking Sammy's voice as she enters the room, covering the distance between the doorway and the bar in two seconds' flat.

She too, has had the works! Gone is the messy tangle of frizz and in its place are an array of bouncy glossy waves, cascading over her shoulders onto the cream satin blouse, enhancing her curves in all the right places. The black leather trousers are cinching in her small waist and cupping her Monroe hips and peachy bottom. Even the red heels are a revelation. I've never seen Sammy wear anything other than trainers or boots.

"What the Hell happened to you two?" It's the first thing that trips off my tongue! Not, 'hello,' or 'I'm so happy to see you,' or even 'you look amazing', which is really what I should have said...

"We've been 'made over'!" they screech in unified glee. Well that much is obvious, but I'm confused. "It came with the room," Lizzy states, as if I should know this.

"Oh Gosh!... you two..." at last I remember where I am, who I am and why I'm here... more importantly, who's standing before me.

Slipping down from my stool, I open my arms and we all fall together in a coiffured, tangled embrace. Crying, sniffing, laughing, we cling to one another. Three bonkers English women, dressed to the nines, causing a scene in a posh hotel bar, in the middle of posh Manhattan.

"So, where did all this come from?" I ask, once we have calmed down and ordered our first round of cocktails.

Lizzy takes a sip of her Pornstar Martini, and places her glass on the coaster, with an appreciative hum and an exaggerated eye roll. "Same place you got yours," she eyes me up and down, clearly bemused by my appearance.

I scoff at her cheek, and take a welcome glug of my Long Island Iced Tea – *Mmmm, sooo, good!* "Silas has a lot to answer for..." I tut, thinking he'll be laughing somewhere at the thought of us here, dressed in our finery.

"Well, I think we've all scrubbed up really well..." Sammy sniffs, straightening her back and making a point of focussing her eyes on our reflections, which stare back at us from the ornate bevelled mirror hanging behind the bar. "C'mon, selfie time..."

Fishing her phone out of her bag, she orders us about like a mini–Sergeant Major until we're arranged to her liking, before we all pull ridiculous faces at the camera.

"Ladies, please allow me," says the barman, "now, say New York!"

"New York!" we squeal and laugh, holding up our drinks and clinking our glasses together.

"So, this man then…" we're on our third round of cocktails and the conversation is becoming serious. Lizzy bores her eyes into me, delivering one of her famous Paddington hard stares. "Go on, spill the beans."

"Oh yes… tell us Edi… he sounds gorgeous… and he must be sooo rich…"

"Sammy!" I scold, although she's not wrong. He is wealthy, but it's not his wealth which attracts me; surely, they must know I'm not that shallow? "Seriously, girls… I've been swept off my feet in the most incredible way… it sounds surreal; far too good to be true, but it is… he says he loves me, and I believe him!"

Lizzy scowls, and looks at her feet. A sure sign she's ruminating, making a judgement and mulling things over.

I don't blame her for being dubious. I'm her mum and I've never had a boyfriend… ever… in the entire history of her childhood; or adulthood for that matter. This must seem incredibly weird and uncomfortable for her.

"Is he kind?"

Her question comes so out of left field and takes me by surprise. It isn't what I expected her to ask. "I mean, if he's kind to you, it's all that matters. The money's nice, but it doesn't make up for kindness, does it?" She nibbles her bottom lip; naturally she's concerned, but on this point, I can instantly put her mind at rest and without doubt.

"Oh Baby-girl, he's the kindest, loving, most protective man I could wish to know. He's endured enough suffering in his personal life to last a lifetime, but he's trying so hard to accept it; to learn to live with it." The parallel between our two lives isn't lost on me. My own hardship is nothing in comparison, but it's tainted my outlook all the same. "I'm supporting him through some stuff right now. So, in a way, we're actually helping each other to draw a line and move on."

It sounds trite; as if I'm making excuses for suddenly having a life. I shouldn't be making excuses for living… "Lizzy, this is what I want. It's the only thing, apart from you and David, that's made me happy in such a long time. I'd forgotten how that felt."

"And so had I…" his warm hand lands on my shoulder. "Hello Lizzy, I'm delighted to meet you at last. I'm Silas."

Lizzy reaches out her small hand, and takes Silas's proffered introduction. "H…hi!" she whispers nervously, "I'm Lizzy."

"I know; and you are definitely your mother's daughter. Apart from the colouring, I mean. Although, with a mother as beautiful as Edi, it isn't surprising."

Lizzy and I glance at each other; no one's ever mentioned a resemblance between us before, but then, we've never been seen together as well-groomed as we are right now.

I look at our reflections in the mirror. Posed side by side I can see the similarity, it's uncanny! I've never in my life noticed it; we do look alike. The only difference, as Silas pointed out, is our colouring. I'm astounded.

"Wow…" Sammy chips in, "I can see it too!" All three of us stare with new-found focus at the familiar faces staring back. "Hmph! I wonder how the guys at Uni' didn't put two and two together?... I'm Sammy by the way," leaning across me, she introduces herself to Silas.

"Hello, Sammy. You look lovely."

"And I'm Gerard..." his voice trails away as his eyes come to rest on my daughter. She too is lost for words.

Without removing his focus, he gently takes her hand and holding her gaze in his, kisses the back of it tenderly. She's instantly enchanted, like a delicate butterfly drawn by the charms of the predatorial spider and I'm catapulted into the highest stratosphere of motherly anxiety! *Oh crap!* The chemistry is off the charts – I should have known this would happen.

"Hi Gerard; lovely to meet you," she purrs, her voice is kitten soft.

"Ahem!" Sammy interrupts the tension, "who wants another drink?"

The spell momentarily breaks as we all shout our orders to the barman. Sammy saves the day as usual!

CHAPTER 34

About a hundred cocktails later, we sway our way up to our room. I'm more than a little tipsy and the jet lag is beginning to get to me.

"I can't believe Gerard!" I exclaim as we wait for the lift.

"He's a Frenchman," Silas offers by way of explanation - as if that's an acceptable excuse for making my daughter go weak at the knees!

"But he has no shame…" I grumble, offended by his unapologetic derision towards the fact I'm her mother.

"He's… A… Frenchman!" Silas spells it out in block capitals; a clear message I should understand and accept the inevitable. Frenchman equals no shame!

"Humph! He's rude…" He isn't, but I'm feeling belligerent, and old! What's that all about all of a sudden?

"I think someone has had a few too many cocktails," Silas whispers in my ear as the tuneful ping announces the arrival of the elevator. Huffily, I shuffle in, sullen and disgruntled at the weight of my considerable age.

Silas strokes my bottom, giving it a squeeze as we step back to allow another couple to enter. Through my beer goggles, I squint at the reflection of the couple in the copper mirrored interior. They're handsome. Maybe a little older than us, but still, stupidly attractive. I conclude it's an American thing.

The guy is dressed in a tux; his tie has been unravelled and is hanging loose, James Bond style, beneath the winged collar of his dress shirt.

He has stubble, and short black hair, with a bit of a silver fox thing going on, and with his ebony-coloured skin, he's not a million miles away from Silas, in the ridiculously handsome department.

His wife's equally as stunning. Tall! Slim! Gorgeous! She's wearing a black structured gown, masterfully cut to accentuate her perfect figure and skimming the floor as if it's been made to measure; in fact, it probably has.

Silas chuckles from beside me. Wondering what's so funny, I catch his humoured expression in the mirror, before my eyes drift to my own face in the reflection… Good Lord… I'm gawping!

My mouth hangs open, I'm rocking on my heels openly staring at the couple. Blatantly giving them a critical up and down once over as if they're in a magazine photograph, and not just standing right there!

Silas laughs again, giving me a little nudge with his shoulder and, for good measure, my bottom another squeeze. Leaning sideways and shooting him a hard stare, I wobble in my shoes, causing him to place a supportive hand on my elbow.

Eventually, I'm relieved from any more of my exaggerated observations, the lift pings to a halt and the man escorts his wife out.

"Good evening," he nods in our direction, offering a beaming smile as he leaves.

Huh! well that's a surprise, he's British… I frown.

As the lift door closes, Silas can contain his mirth no longer and bursts out laughing. I look at him with scorn… "what's so funny?"

"Ha, ha, ha… you!" he guffaws, "you're hysterical."

"Why? What did I do?" I sway, in my attempt to face him.

"Do you know who that was?"

I turn and examine the closed elevator door, as if by some miracle, I've developed the power of x-ray vision and can now see the man and his wife through a foot of solid metal… "Some bloke and his fancy missus!" I mumble unkindly.

"Ha, ha, ha…" Silas is bent double. "Some bloke and his fancy missus? Really… you didn't recognise him?"

"Should I?" *Sway, sway…Oh dear!*

"That, my wonderful Edi, was none other than Idris Elba!"

For a moment, I'm puzzled; attempting to connect the name to the face… "Oooh!" *Clang!* "Oh, shit… I was just staring at him as if he was a nobody in a posh suit!"

"Yeah, it was classic!"

My brow furrows. "Yeah well, he might be in line for an Oscar, but he's still not as hot as you…"

The elevator pings to a halt, and with the jolt, my knees give way and I crumple in a heap on the floor. "Oof… sorry," I look up at him, as he bends to assist me to my feet.

"Come on you… I think you need to sleep."

"Idris Elba, eh?... well, he'd better look out… I love you Silas… thank you for bringing me to my baby girl." They're the last words I speak, until the following morning!

At four-thirty a.m. I spring awake. The jet lag has kicked in and my brain is convinced its morning. Turning over in bed, I watch as Silas slumbers soundly beside me. I'll never tire of looking at him. I have no idea what I did to deserve it, but I'm so thankful he's in my life.

Silas mumbles something incoherent and snuggles deeper into the pillow before settling into a light snore. I smile to myself, enjoying the quiet peace of my secret observations.

I'm reminded of a time when I would tiptoe into Lizzy's bedroom late at night and just watch her sleep. Once Bobby had passed out, I would leave our bed and seek out the sanctuary of my baby's room. There I'd curl up on the floor beside her cot and watch in awe at the gentle rise and fall of her tiny chest.

Most nights I'd remain there, unable to leave her, needing her to be safe; until the dark of the night began to melt away and the first hint of a navy-blue dawn filtered through the curtains. Only then would I sneak back to my own room and climb beneath the duvet.

If I was lucky, I would grab an hour of sleep before Bobby awoke and the whole cycle of cruelty would begin all over again. Looking at Silas, sleeping so peacefully beside me, makes me feel safe. I never felt safe when I was with Bobby.

He was controlling, vicious and mean. The more I think about it, the more resolve I gather. I know I'll have the fortitude to face him on Wednesday. The time I've spent with Silas has been enlightening in so many ways. I no longer feel weak and feeble, afraid of my own shadow… I'm discovering a strength I didn't know I had, and it's all due to him and his stoic belief in me.

I don't know what will happen on Wednesday, and I refuse to worry about it. For now, I'm in New York. My baby girl is here, and I'm with the man I love.

Turning to face the window, the light of a golden dawn begins to filter its way through the blinds. Morning has broken over Manhattan, and in a few hours, I'll be strolling hand in hand with my man through the most famous park in the world. Closing my eyes to the lightening sky, I try and grab another hour...

"Morning Starshine... you look gorgeous," Silas urges me to wake with a kiss on my head, and a red-hot poker nudging at my bottom. "Do you fancy a workout?" I can feel his grin as he seductively blows a stream of heated breath over the shell of my ear.

"I thought you'd never ask," I purr. Stretching my arms over my head and arching my back into his welcome erection. "Is that a pistol in your pocket or are you just pleased to see me?"

"Oh, you never know with me... but I think I'm *very* pleased to see you," he growls, placing a hand between my shoulder blades and purposefully rocking me onto my front. "Knee up please," he requests, most politely.

I dig my hands under the pillow to support my head, and raise my right knee as instructed. Sighing deeply, I relish the feel of his warm palm as it strokes the inside of my thigh.

My stomach presses into the firm mattress, as I revel in the pressure of his touch. "That's nice," I coo in satisfaction, unable to prevent the moans of appreciation from escaping my lips.

"Oh, I think we can make it more than just nice." His voice has taken on the deep resonance I recognise when he's becoming more and more aroused. It causes my belly to ripple in anticipation. "Are you ready to be fucked?"

"Yesss!" I hiss, my own arousal surging forward with every anticipated sensation.

"Hold on tight Honey-bee, because here I come..."

"Aghhh," my breath is knocked out of me as he surges forwards and upwards; entering me in one swift movement. "Oooh..." I exhale on a sigh, as I allow him to take me to heaven.

"Oh, Edi, you're so hot and wet. I could stay buried inside you forever." Silas pumps his hips, drilling into me, "Can you feel that?"

"Oh Lord..." I moan, "too good..."

"I'm here to please, but I need to do something..."

Silas removes himself from my willing centre and I'm immediately chilled by the loss of his body-heat and exposure to the airconditioned room. Flinging the duvet onto the floor, he stands at the foot of the bed, and grabbing my ankle, draws me towards him, so I'm swimming along in reverse.

"What are you doing?" I screech, as my arms flail for purchase on the silky sheets. It's impossible, he's far too fast, far too strong and far too determined, to get me off the bed. Giving in I allow him to drag me onto the floor. "Oof!" I grunt as I land with a bump face down. "That wasn't very gentlemanly." I kick at his lower belly in an attempt to break free.

"Oh Edi, you should know by now, I'm no gentleman when it comes to sex with you," he laughs, lifting me gently to my feet and turning me to face him. "Lips," he demands and I offer him my eager mouth. I love his kisses.

While we kiss, his caress travels from my shoulders, down my arms, to my wrists; he takes a firm hold and draws me with him, reversing across the bedroom floor. As is my usual wont with Silas, I follow willingly.

His kiss is fierce and blistering, so meaningful, I'm unable to focus on anything else. "Turn around," he urges.

I do, and it's only as I open my eyes, I see we're outside; literally dwarfed by the petrified forest of concrete giants surrounding us as we stand on the huge paved terrace overlooking the magnificence that is the city of Manhattan.

"Oh, wow…" It's incredible.

The iridescent morning sun is reflecting off the mirrored windows of the skyscrapers, the brilliance rebounding between buildings. Everywhere I look the view is sensational.

"Walk to the edge; it's okay, you're safe…" I'm urged forwards.

The buildings are stacked sky high, tightly packed together, their structures appear to virtually touch; and I'm struck by the distance between our terrace and the buildings nearby. Incredibly, we're almost isolated. Even in this jungle of tower blocks, there is an oasis of calm.

"Silas, this is stunning…"

"You're stunning…" he takes my mouth gently, kissing me deeply, reverently.

Drawing away, he looks down at me. The golden sunlight reflects in his chocolate eyes, turning them a hypnotic shade of amber. "You are my heart…" he says with meaning. "You are my world…"

"And you mine…" He is, there isn't any doubt.

"Shall we?"

"Oh, please," I breathe in desperation. I need him to take me now.

"Over here." I'm guided to the centre of the terrace, where the day-bed and outdoor furnishings are arranged so beautifully. "Lie down," he gestures to the wide recliner, large enough to accommodate two.

My body lowers of its own volition, and I spread my legs invitingly.

Silas stands beside the bed, looking down, his gaze skates over my reclining form. "Touch yourself," he orders, his eyes flashing with desire.

Placing one hand above my head, I use the other to stroke my body. Smoothing my fingertips over my erect nipples, I pinch, tease and torture my skin until goose bumps begin to pebble my flesh.

"What are you doing?" I ask, keeping my eyes locked onto his, as he observes my exploring fingers.

"Remembering," is his cryptic answer.

"Remembering what?" His concentration never wanders from my form, as I continue to arouse myself.

"Remembering you." His voice is filled with an emotion I can't place. I don't know if he's sad or wistful, but it scares me… until…

"I want you branded into my memory. I want you, looking like this, every time I think about you. I want this to be my everlasting thought... just you... like this. I want this, when I'm old and dying to be the last thing I remember ... I will go to my grave with this image of you in my head... I never want to forget how you look right now."

My hand stills; now I understand the emotion on his face.

Reaching towards him, I urge him forward, drawing him closer until his knees have no option but to bend and lower onto the bed. "I love you Silas," I whisper as I cup his cheek, "you are my life and my love and I will forever remember how you look in this moment. But know this... even old and grey, you will always be beautiful to me, because your beauty is in here." I cover his heart with my palm. "You are worth more than you know. You are valued more than you think, and you are and always will be, my everything."

"And you are mine," he says as he lowers into me.

Our lovemaking is slow and gentle. We may be outside, and we may be on show for the world to see, but incredibly, we are as one. We move as one. He shifts and I lift. He thrusts and I rise to meet him. He strokes my cheek and I caress his lips. We undulate and writhe together, soaring into a bright blue ether... our heaven.

"Edi," he cries.

"I know..." my response is clear; he's coming and he needs me to be with him, as I need him with me.

"I love you..." he calls as he pours his soul into me.

My legs grip his waist, tightening around his ribcage until I have no feeling in my thighs. The final thrust tips me over the edge, and I may as well be falling off the balcony as I'm hurled into an abyss of undiluted pleasure; I tumble, spin and sore through the clouds towards the ground.

"Oh... My... God!" I pant, catching my breath as I recover from my high.

"I know!" Silas's words are barely audible, "I know..."

CHAPTER 35

Rummaging through my handbag, I locate my little tin of Vaseline. My lips feel chapped so I dab on a film of the cherry flavoured lip balm. Massaging at the chapped skin, the relief is instantaneous as the oily film absorbs, and smooching my lips together I drop the small tin into my bag then head out of the bathroom to find Silas sitting at the desk browsing through his lap top.

As he catches sight of me, he lowers the lid and stands. "You look refreshed," he says on a smile. "Are you ready for a New York breakfast?"

"I'm starving!" The morning exertions have taken it out of me and now I could eat a horse.

After we made love slowly, Silas insisted we performed an encore standing on the edge of the terrace overlooking Central Park. It was both liberating and decadent and I loved every second. "Shall we go and find the others?"

"After you Ma'am."

Silas opens the door and we step out into the massive hallway. I must've been smashed last night because I don't remember it at all.

Noticing my confusion, Silas grins and puts my mind at rest. "You weren't that plastered; just jet lagged. Do you remember anything after the bar?" he asks with a puzzled look on his face.

"Umm? A bit," I lie, unconvincingly.

"Ha, you really don't remember do you?"

"No," I mumble truculently… I hate jet lag!

As we reach the elevator, Silas presses the button and we wait patiently for the lift to arrive. Checking my watch, I see it's just gone eight in the morning. Earlier than I thought, but then, my body clock is screwed.

"In you get."

I'm escorted into the lift and we head down. At the next floor, the lift pings to a halt, and the doors open… a couple get in and I blush a million shades of scarlet, because I recognise the man immediately.

Idris Elba! *Fucking Idris Elba!* My mind is blown and I'm instantly hit by fan-girl fluster.

"Good morning," Idris says. "You look decidedly better today."

My head whips to Silas, who's wearing a particularly dubious expression; he's trying but failing to look innocent, as if butter wouldn't melt… shame I know different!

"I am, thank you," I reply politely. "I was very tired," I explain.

I have no idea what's going on, but I can imagine… I must have been really out of it, last night if I met Idris Elba, and don't remember!

"Well… have a nice day," he offers as he exits the lift, his palm placed protectively in the small of the woman's back.

Spinning on the spot, I'm thrilled as I look at Silas. He's watching me in high amusement. "That was Idris Elba, wasn't it?" I hope it was… he's gorgeous.

"Yep; and I have it on excellent authority, that I'm far better looking," he retorts with an air of superiority.

"Huh," I scoff in derision… "who told you that?"

"Someone of great importance and impeccable taste… someone who knows all about these things…" he says mysteriously, turning his back on me and heading to the dining nook.

Catching him up, I try to keep pace. "Who? Who said that…?" I mean he's a great looking man… but Idris Elba… come on!

"Wouldn't you like to know?" he winks at me, as I crumple my brow in disbelief.

"Here they are… morning guys…" Sammy is standing with a plate piled high with scrambled eggs, bacon, pancakes and hash browns. "Sleep well?" she asks, not really waiting for an answer. "I went out like a light. I was knackered," and she wanders away towards the table, where I spy Lizzy sitting far too close to Gerard.

Both of them are engrossed in conversation. Lizzy stirs lazily at her coffee cup, gazing dreamily into Gerard's dark eyes! *Lord Give me strength!*

"Morning everyone," I all but shout, causing them to spring free of each other's magnetic pull and focus their attention towards Silas and me.

"Oh, hi mum, hi Silas… good morning," Lizzy stammers.

Sammy sits down knowingly. Picking up her knife and fork, she digs in to her plate, though not before ladling on the ketchup and maple syrup.

We watch her performance in bemused silence as she precisely slices a piece of pancake, layering it expertly with eggs and bacon before dunking it into the ketchup and syrup and stuffing the whole lot in her mouth. "Wha…?" she asks, mouth full, noticing she has an audience.

"Well," I say on a shake of my head, "I'm going to help myself to the breakfast buffet… anyone coming?" I stare pointedly at Lizzy, willing her to get the message and get off her arse and follow me.

"Oh, yeah, I'll come," she says, receiving loud and clear. "See you in a bit," she whispers to Gerard.

"Enchante, Mon cher." Gerard's response is seductive and intense.

I turn my back on the whole performance and march mulishly towards the warming counter. As we reach the array of food, the pure cornucopia and vast selection on display before us is overwhelming!

"I only want some fruit, and maybe some yoghurt…" Lizzy mutters at the sheer volume of abundance.

"Never mind that Madam, what's going on with you and Gerard?" I stage whisper as I pick up a ladle and begin to scoop fresh fruit salad into a bowl.

"Nothing," she replies, far too quickly.

"Seriously?" I snap. She's not fooling me in the slightest.

"He's gorgeous!" she rolls her eyes in mock exaggeration. As if I hadn't noticed; he's a fox.

"Yes, I know he is… but he's also very French." Even I don't know what I mean by that statement!

"Oh, for fuck's sake, mum… it's just harmless flirting. Get a grip!"

"Just be careful that's all. He's a lovely chap, and extremely charming but I don't know too much about him."

"He's really nice." She flips her hair affectedly, picking up a miniature croissant and sniffing it. "Does this have nuts?"

"Almonds, I think." She hurriedly puts it back on the stack.

"Lizzy, you can't do that once you've touched it… here, give it to me."

"Sorry…" she mumbles as she sheepishly remembers her table manners and places the manhandled croissant on my plate.

"Well, he does seem nice; but surely… isn't he a little old for you?" I'm not entirely sure why I'm uncomfortable with this, but for some reason it isn't sitting well.

"It's a bit of fun," Lizzy whispers, "and anyway, for all you know we might have been shagging our way around America!" That comment was snide and completely uncalled-for.

"Lizzy!" I scold, "you know exactly what I mean. You've known him less than five minutes."

"Ha! That's rich!" She's beginning to lose her patience with me, "and anyway, it's been almost twenty-four hours; for your information, we met yesterday while you and himself were off enjoying your lunch!"

I ignore her barbed jibe and attempt a gentler approach. "Seriously, Lizzy. Just take it slowly…please."

"Typical!" Lizzy snaps, dropping her empty plate back on the bar in temper. "You have no room to talk! Look at you… shacking up with the first bloke who pays you a little bit of attention!"

I'm shocked by her sudden outburst. Turning my back on her, before I say something I'll regret, I continue along the breakfast buffet, picking up a plain yoghurt and sprinkling some dried cranberries and toasted seeds onto the layer of fresh fruit. "I was only saying it out of concern for you," I hiss, "and, for your information, Silas is more than just some 'bloke' who's paid me 'a bit' of attention." That comment stung.

"Well, you should know me better. You're my mother after all."

"And you should know me better too…"

Pivoting on my heels, I stalk back to the table with my light breakfast.

Slamming my dish down, I pick up my napkin and give it a vigorous shake, dropping it onto my lap before picking up my spoon and starting to eat.

I'm aware of questioning eyes on me, but I refuse to acknowledge them. I'm annoyed with my daughter, and I need to calm down before I engage in polite conversation.

"Alright?" Silas asks.

"Fine!" I grumble, filling my mouth again so I can't speak.

"Oookaaay!" Sensibly, he leaves me alone and addresses his chat towards Gerard.

I don't know what's going on with me at the moment but that's both of my children who've had a strop with me in the past week! As a family we rarely argue. Usually, we just pal along; bumbling through life together. But now things have changed. I'm no longer good old reliable mum; I've become an interfering old bag! And what's more, I'm a bag with baggage! I still need to tell her about the TV interview and what's going on in regards to Bobby!

Shit! After our 'little disagreement' I've no idea how I'm going to remain calm when broaching the subject with her.

Lizzy sidles up to the table and quietly takes her place beside me. I continue to shovel down my breakfast, still reluctant to join in the chatter.

"I'm sorry mum... I shouldn't have said that," Lizzy whispers so only I can hear. "You deserve some happiness. It's just..."

Shaking my head in exasperation, I exhale through my nose as I try not to bridle at her again. "What, Lizzy?" I turn to face her, not the least bothered we have onlookers to our spat, "What?"

"It's just... I'm sorry, okay?"

Turning to face her, it's like I'm having a repeat of the conversation I had with David. Taking her hand in mine, I use the other to stroke a stray curl behind her ear as I focus her attention towards me. "Look, let's just forget it. I know you didn't mean what you said. But you also need to know that Silas is in my life now," I say this as I glance his way across the table. "He's wonderful, and I can't imagine my life without him in it... and Lizzy, you know too well, the only people I could say that about before were you and your brother..."

"Gee, thanks..." Sammy announces in an attempt to break the tension.

"Seriously, Lizzy... I mean it. You and David are my world, I love you unconditionally and I will protect you with my life.... Silas is my heart... he will never replace you, but he is here to stay; and you need to accept that."

"I know... It's just... difficult."

Baby girl; you and David will always be my priority... no matter what. You always have been and you always will be... but what happens once you no longer need me? I think I deserve a little life of my own, don't you?"

"Oh Mum... yes... I'm sorry... I'm being selfish... I'm sorry Silas!" Lizzy colours as she looks towards him; reminding me of her immaturity.

Silas rises from his seat and rounds the table. Crouching between Lizzy and me, he places one arm around my shoulder and rests the other on top of Lizzy's.

"Lizzy, I know this must seem like a whirlwind," he looks at me on a soft smile, then gives my daughter his undivided attention, "and to be honest, I wasn't expecting it either, but it's happened and we're incapable of stopping it. Your mum is the best thing that's happened to me in a very long while..."

Lizzy looks at me in confusion, but just as quickly returns her attention to Silas.

"Lizzy, I know you have questions," Silas continues kindly, "and believe me, so did I... we... we both had questions and still do. There's a lot to digest. But for now, please can you be happy for us?"

Lizzy passes watery eyes over to me, clearly, she's struggling with the situation and her defence mechanism was to flirt unashamedly with Gerard. I think she was trying to prove a point... shame it misfired!

"Lizzy, please sweetheart, this is it... my chance... please understand." I aim to reassure her; at twenty-one, I shouldn't need to do this, but it's been just us for so long, and we've been through so much... it must seem very strange.

"Yeah... I suppose I'll get used to it," she mumbles sulkily. "Does David know?"

"Yes, David knows; and what's more, David is more than happy about it. But you can speak to him yourself tomorrow can't you... because we're going home!"

Thankfully, her eyes begin to clear. She's coming out of her sulk. Once she recovers her equilibrium, she'll be mortified by her behaviour, but for now she needs the gentle touch so I'll relent.

"Oh mum... I've missed you. Don't let me travel this far away on my own again... I'm not old enough!"

"Oh, thanks a million! I like that..." Sammy's dulcet tones break the mood," who am I, Scotch mist?"

"Oo is zis Scotch meest?" Gerard asks, totally confused.

"Nothing... I'm sorry everyone!" Lizzy concedes. "You must think I'm behaving like a spoiled brat."

"Yes..." Sammy agrees with her best friend, "but you always do, so what's new. Now can we all finish our breakfast so we can get out and explore Central Park before we have to climb onto that luxury jet and fly home?"

CHAPTER 36

Central Park was sultry, hot and humid, and I'm covered in midge bites from sitting on the grass by the baseball pitches. My ankles look like I have fleas and they are red and blotchy from where I keep scratching at the itch!

"Keep still and let me dab this on!" Silas has hold of my right heel and is attempting to apply antihistamine cream to every tiny mark.

"I think it had fangs!" I moan as I watch him diligently dotting on blobs of white ointment. "Do I have to rub it in?"

Silas passes over the box so I can read the instructions for myself. "No, it just needs to absorb slowly. There, that should do it."

Looking down at my feet, my ankle is decorated with a delicate abundance of tiny white spots; reminiscent of the patterns on the top of a pair of kiddie's lace ankle-socks. "Ooh, missed one…" Silas announces as he spies another bite, hidden behind my knee. "Well, you won't be wearing your fancy shoes anytime soon I reckon," he complains disappointed.

"I don't know… the laces should hide the marks very well." I'm very attached to those shoes and for good reason! And I'll still be wearing them when I'm ninety if they continue to have such a beneficial effect on Silas!

We're back at the hotel, all packed and ready to leave. The plane is on standby but we still have a few hours before our designated departure slot.

As first impressions go, I've really been blown away by our whistle-stop visit to New York. A couple more days would have been wonderful, but I know we need to go home, get the girls settled and press on with the next hurdle… my TV interview.

I still haven't found the strength to tell Lizzy. After our fall out this morning, I've been treading around her on eggshells; trying not to rekindle the argument, but it's been a challenge.

As much as she acknowledged her childish diva behaviour, it again managed to resurface a couple of times; first when we were ordering lunch at the Central Park Café, and they didn't have the flavour of Iced Tea she wanted, and secondly, when we were waiting for a cab to bring us back to the hotel. Lizzy became impatient and tried throwing her weight around until I reminded her about her earlier behaviour and she reined it in.

While the three of us were enjoying the sights, Silas and Gerard were busy, dealing with some company business on the other side of the city.

I was aware they had some work to attend to, but a little disappointed all the same. Maybe next time I'll have him all to myself. It's an indulgent thought, and one I'm not prepared to let go.

Now we're reunited we can have some quality time together before we depart this amazing metropolis.

"What do you want to do for the next hour or so?" Silas asks on a jiggle of his eyebrows.

"Ummm…" I recline on the bed like a Cheshire cat; stretching out and arching my back; I'm totally rubbish at this seduction lark, but I'll make an effort for him! "I don't know… what did you have in mind?" I ask suggestively, knowing full well what he has in mind.

"Shopping?"

Oh… I read that wrong then!

Sitting up, I straighten myself out, feeling a little foolish at my 'Mata Hari' performance. "Err, yeah…" I have no money, so I won't be buying anything.

"C'mon… I have a surprise for you."

Half an hour later and we're on Wall Street. I'm bowled over by the sheer magnificence of the place. I can see Brooklyn Bridge in the distance as we jump out of the yellow cab and take our chances with the other pedestrians, crossing the main road.

Silas takes my hand and leads me left down a narrow side street, heading towards a tall marble building with huge picture windows. The windows are covered over with security shutters; the place doesn't look open.

As we reach a locked metal door, Silas buzzes the intercom. A voice from inside asks us our business, and Silas gives his name and announces he has an appointment.

"You do?" I ask quizzically.

"You'll see…" he winks his mysterious, I have a secret, wink as the door buzzes a release and swings open to reveal a smartly liveried gentleman.

Standing aside, he greets us as if we're expected. "Welcome back Mr Tudor. Very nice to see you again, sir."

"You too Anton; thank you…" Silas takes my hand and leads me through the huge security door.

Inside the corridor the walls are white veined marble; it's chilly, long and narrow with muted lighting and a high vaulted ceiling. It gives nothing away in relation to the function of the building. Perhaps this is something to do with his business and I'm meeting the US arm?

Anton leads us towards another internal security door. There is a digital key lock and thumbprint identification pad; very mysterious and very secure.

Anton keys in the code, presses his thumb to the pad and the door clicks and whirrs open to reveal… a staffroom!

Now I'm even more confused, because I most definitely didn't expect this.

At the end of the vast room is yet another security door.

"Where are we?" I whisper, feeling decidedly conspicuous as we creep across the open area.

"This is the employee entrance Ma'am; the main store isn't open today," Anton replies cheerfully heading to the staff entrance.

My forehead creases as I lower my voice even further. "Store?"

Silas keeps a tight hold of my hand. "Yes… shopping… I told you."

He grips my hand even tighter as if he's afraid I'll bolt, and I'm drawn towards the entrance to the main store.

This door has a card swipe lock. Anton lifts his ID from the lanyard, and runs it through the reader; the door swings ajar. "After you, Sir," Anton places the flat of his hand on the turquoise painted wood and pushes.

Instantly, I'm blinded by bolts of bright lightening, triggered as the vivid contrast between the muted illumination of the staffroom is overshadowed by the dazzling glory of the store proper. "Oh!" I gasp, unable to take it in fully. It's incredible.

Patterned gold accents glisten and sparkle off the clear glass display cabinets. Shards of iridescent light are reflected by the faceted glass beads, trailing from the arms of the many crystal chandeliers hanging on chunky golden chains from the Art Deco ceiling. Its timeless beauty is heart-breaking.

"Where is this?" I ask in awe as my eyes become accustomed to the wonders laid out before me.

"Guess," Silas whispers, spinning me in his arms.

"I can't," I cry, my smile is huge and my eyes wide with childlike wonder; the place is incredible.

"Okay, I'll give you a hint... where did Audrey Hepburn have her breakfast?"

My breath leaves me as I stare around in disbelief at the beautiful surroundings. "Tiffany! We... we're in Tiffany?" *Sheesh!*

It's a good job Silas has hold of me, because I feel my legs buckle!

"You said we were coming shopping! Silas, I can't afford anything in here," I exclaim.

I don't care what Anton thinks; there's no way I'm spending my salary on trinkets and jewellery when I have bills and a student loan to pay back!

"Calm down... I've something for you."

I start to push away from him and protest. There's no way... but then I hesitate; my eyes grow large... no... he wouldn't, would he? I've only known him a few weeks... there's no way he'd be buying me a ring!

Clocking my horrified expression, he starts to laugh. "Relax, Edi chill... it's not that... not this time, anyway," he adds on an eye roll. "I had something made... something individual, something significant, something meaningful. And I commissioned it especially for you." He lowers me down the length of his body and gazing into his eyes I land gently on my feet.

His grin is replaced by the softest of smiles. His irises shimmer with the reflection of the sparkling light. Leaning forward, he kisses me deeply, slowly. I lap at his mouth, taking my time to savour the lushness of his lips. My eyes close instinctively, blacking out the harsh lights and I'm catapulted into the warm sensation that is kissing Silas.

"Ahem!" We're rudely interrupted by a polite cough. "Sir, if you'd like to come this way, I will bring the item for you." Anton indicates we should follow him to the private viewing rooms towards the rear of the store.

"C'mon; now you're over the shock, I can't wait for you to see this..." Silas has his wicked smile back. He seems excited with the prospect of showing me what he's bought. It'd better not be ridiculously expensive. I'm useless with jewellery. I've never really owned anything special and I'll no doubt lose whatever it is in about half a day!

"Please come through." Anton opens a heavy wooden door and we're led into a plush viewing room. "Champagne for Madame?"

"Oh, yes please…" I might need it.

"Sir?"

"No, thank you, but I'll have an espresso if you have one?"

"Certainly sir."

With that, Anton departs, leaving us alone in the snug room.

"Where is everyone?" The store is devoid of any other customers or employees.

"We have the place and Anton to ourselves. I made sure of it." Silas slips his arm around my shoulder as he kisses me softly on the temple. "I wanted this to be a unique and private experience."

"Silas, you know you overwhelm me every time. I'm not worthy of all this." It's so out of my comfort zone, I'm beginning to worry it'll all fade.

"Hush. Just enjoy it, will you. I'll be the judge of who is and isn't worthy. I need to do this; let me do this."

Somehow, this feels like compensation, as if he's making amends for something. I don't know what he's compensating for. There's no need for any of this. All I want is him.

"It's just so much. The job, the apartment, Paris, the shoes, the watch… and now here… in New York… in Tiffany for goodness' sake… it's just…"

I don't get to finish. Anton is back with a tray, containing a champagne flute, a gold and turquoise cup of espresso and a traditional turquoise Tiffany giftbox!

Oh Lord!

Anton places the tray on the table, and Silas releases me from his hold. I'm handed the glass and before I can think, I take the biggest, unladylike, gulp of bubbles. Spluttering my thanks, I place the half empty flute on the table. I'm nervous and my legs are shaking.

Silas places a hand on my thigh; a sure attempt to calm me. "Hey, it's okay. I want to do this." He kisses my forehead and turns to face Anton.

"Now, Mr Tudor. We received details of the commission, and I believe you have discussed the proposal with our top designer, Jules."

"Yes, that's correct. She sent me the images by email, and we debated slight alterations over the phone."

"So, you have not yet seen the competed item?"

"No, only in a photograph."

Anton smiles, unable to hide his delight at being the one to reveal the finished article. "Sir, having witnessed the artistry and skill as the piece came together, I'm certain you will not be disappointed."

"I'm sure I won't, but it isn't me who you need to please," he says, looking directly at me.

I shrug, embarrassed by all the intrigue and fuss. I really hope he hasn't gone too overboard.

"Allow me." Anton lifts the pretty box from the tray and places it on a velvet cloth.

My heart begins to pound so strongly it feels like it's going to jump out of my chest. My jiggling leg goes into overdrive, the top of my thigh catching the underside of the table every time.

"Hey… stop!" Silas soothes.

"Okay." My voice is so small. I'm terrified.

Anton lifts the hinged lid and smiles at the contents. Swivelling the box to face us, he relishes the look on both our faces at the big reveal.

O.M.F.G!!!!

"Oh!" Exquisite is the first word that springs to mind to describe the contents. Swiftly followed by delicate, intricate, unique, and… perfect! "Silas." Glassy tears form in the corner of my eyes and I quickly reach to dash them away. "It's unbelievable." Shaking my head, the tears continue to roll in an unstoppable release of emotion. I can't believe he's had this made for me.

"It could only be one design for you," he speaks softly, reaching into the box and lifting out a stunning bracelet.

Seven buzzing, golden bumblebees are strung together on an intricate, woven chain. Each tiny bee is flying towards his neighbour on delicately spread white gold wings. The body of each bee is crafted from pure yellow gold, with contrasting stripes of white around the middle; each stripe holds a row of tiny diamonds.

I'm stunned by its sheer beauty. I can't speak. The tears just flow in a continuous river.

"I'll leave you for a moment, to enjoy the piece," Anton says. Subtly rising from his chair, he leaves us alone in the viewing room.

"Oh, Silas… I don't know what to say."

I'm overwhelmed by his generosity. The bracelet may not be a two-carat diamond ring, but it is, none the less, an individually commissioned piece by one of the most renowned goldsmiths in the world… from Tiffany, for goodness's sake!

"Here, let me…" he lifts my right arm and places the bracelet around my wrist. Fastening the clasp, he allows my hand to hover there for just an instant, the light catches the bees wings, the shimmering diamonds offering a perfect illusion of flight, glittering with every tremor and quiver of my shaking nerves. "See," he says softly, "it's perfect… just as you are perfect… perfect for my Edi… perfect for my Honey-bee!"

"Thank you," I whisper, my voice thick with emotion. "I'll treasure it… always."

"Just as I treasure you," he says, the sentiment in his own voice matching mine. "Just promise me, you'll always wear it?"

"Oh… I'll never take it off… I love it… thank you so much."

It must have cost him a small fortune, but I'm not complaining. I've never in my life owned something so uniquely me; so perfect, and as Silas said… perfectly me!

"This is staying on, forever… I love it."

Silas breathes a huge sigh of relief. Secretly, I wonder if he expected me to decline the gift? Yes, it's extravagant, yes, it's more than I deserve, but the lengths he's gone to… the sheer detail and care he's taken to ensure every tiny intricate element is just right…just so… there's no way I would refuse.

This is more than an exquisite piece of jewellery; this gift has significance; it has meaning. And that meaning is worth more than any twenty-carat diamond. This means he knows me, warts and all. This means he loves me, warts and all. And this means he wants me, warts and all… no, I would never refuse this gift.

"Kiss me Boss-man!" I demand.

I'm brimming with love and I need him to understand. "I'll never be able to match this you know," I murmur into his mouth.

Pulling away slightly, he stares at me in contrition. "You already have… you made me believe in happiness again. You made me believe in humanity… I love you… Edi, you are my greatest gift."

CHAPTER 37

I sit in my plush leather seat by the porthole window, absently tilting my hand, mesmerized by the glittering string of bumblebees; I still can't believe it belongs to me.

My mind strays to thoughts of insurance, and wall safes and security. Then I scold myself for being foolish. Silas will have thought of everything. I sit back and relax, resuming admiration of my new baby.

"That's pretty… let's see then." Lizzy dumps her skinny arse into the empty seat beside me.

I lean my arm across my body, twisting my wrist for effect, showing off the bracelet.

"God; it's gorgeous," she exclaims as the full effect hits her senses. "He must've spent thousands!"

Snatching my arm back, I'm appalled by her mercenary attitude… she's been brought up better than that! "Lizzy!"

"I'm sorry… but shee-it. Just look at it. Mum, this is an amazing piece you know."

Drawing my arm back protectively, I admire the beautiful jewel. Lizzy seems to understand more about this than I do.

"Seriously? I know he had it made, but it's a gold bracelet, not a huge diamond."

"God, mum… sometimes I wonder at how naïve you really are." Leaning into me she lets me have it with both barrels.

"This," she strokes a long finger over the delicate wings adorning my wrist, "is 'Tiffany'," exaggerating the word Tiffany with sarcasm and finger quotes. "This," once more she strokes the gold, "is not only 'Tiffany'," again with the quotation marks, "but it is bespoke, hand crafted, personally designed, one off 'Tiffany'."

"I know…" Am I being dense or what? I know all that.

"Fucks sake Edi…" Sammy has joined the 'pick on Edi' party, sitting on Lizzy's knee and reaching over to get an eyeful of my jewellery. "The minute it was commissioned, it went up in value. The moment you walked out of that store this little gem substantially increased in worth."

I look from Lizzy to Sammy and back again. Surely, the minute I stepped onto the street; its value decreased?

"It's not a car… though, if it were a car, it'd be an Aston Martin…"

"Or a vintage Roller…"

"Or a one-off Ferrari."

They're having fun at my expense and my ignorance. How rude!

"Seriously, Mum. This little trinket is worth more now than it was this morning. Believe me. This is no little keepsake. You need to look after it. Bespoke Tiffany pieces, with a provenance certificate like you have, are very rare and highly coveted. It's a desirable piece. Silas knew what he was doing when he bought this for you. It's an investment… you'd better leave it to me in your will!" she laughs, shoving Sammy off her lap, so she falls in a crumpled heap on the carpet.

"Anybody fancy a drink?" Sammy asks, scrambling to her feet, completely unabashed by her tumble.

"Oooh, yeah… Mum, can we open a couple of those little bottles of champagne?"

"Help yourselves," I mumble, dismissively; I'm far too preoccupied by my now, very precious heirloom!

I enter the cockpit, carrying two steaming mugs of coffee. Silas and Gerard are relaxed and comfortable, taking it in turns at the controls as they did on the outward flight.

"Ah… coffee, thank you Edi." Gerard is being incredibly polite.

"Lovely, thank you Honey… have you spoken to Lizzy yet?"

My face gives me away, and I wrinkle my nose at him. "No, not yet, but I will. I think I need to do it here where there's no escape. She can hardly run away from me at thirty thousand feet can she."

"Go and do it now. We still have a couple of hours before we land. It'll give her some time to digest it."

"Hmm, you're probably right. It's the terrible twin, I'm bothered about. We can't seem to get a minute to ourselves."

"Tell her as well… she'll find out soon enough, and she can act as a buffer… you know... the voice of reason?"

"Clearly, you don't know Sam very well!" I scoff, as I re-enter the cabin.

"Who doesn't know me?"

"Silas… he thinks you're the voice of reason," I quote.

"Humph… I am… he knows me well enough." As usual, Sammy is unmoved by any insult I can throw. She's armour-plated and hard to disappoint. She doesn't hold grudges and other than Christina has the best self-confidence of anybody I've ever met!

"Okay then, voice of reason, where's Lizzy? I have something I need to tell her, and you're going to stop her from parachuting out of this plane when she hears it."

"Oooh, sounds intriguing…LIZZY!"

"What?" Lizzy exits the bathroom at the rear of the jet.

"Baby-girl. We need to talk."

"Oh-Kaaay," she says warily.

"Let's go and sit by the window."

I choose the seating area with the facing sofas, so the girls can sit together opposite me. Once seated, I lean forward, nervously. My hand drifts to my bracelet where I finger the tiny bees, and I wonder if this will be my new tell-tale fidget?

"Mum, you're scaring me. What is it?" Lizzy looks panicked. She hates bad news and doesn't cope well with upset and disruption. "Is it David…" she cries, sitting up poker straight in her chair, clasping her hand over her mouth in fear.

Quickly, I move to dispel the worry about her brother. "No, no… he's fine. Honestly, this isn't about him."

"Oooh, goodness; you had me going for a minute there." She lets out a sigh of relief – though I don't know how long it'll last.

"No, baby, Davey is absolutely fine. He's besotted with his girlfriend actually…"

"*Girlfriend??*" The girls chorus.

"What, the carrot has a bird? Way to go David!" Sammy claps her hands in glee.

"Seriously, Mum. You have to tell us all the gossip," Lizzy screeches in delight.

Realising I'm deliberately changing the subject to avoid telling them the horrid news, I haul myself back on track. "I can tell you about that later," I smile and nod at my inadvertent use of the 'shit sandwich'. Nice work Edi!

"Lizzy, this is going to be hard for you to hear, but you need to know, because things have happened in the few weeks you've been away."

"What on earth are you talking about?" Her puzzled expression says it all; I'm making a hash of it as usual.

"When I went to Paris… you remember… Silas took me?" I start again. A little less garbled. A little more assertive.

"Yeah, we saw the pictures." She grins and Sammy winks, nudging shoulders with Lizzy conspiratorially.

Now it's my turn to frown; they saw the pictures? But then I realise, they mean the ones I sent them, my selfies from the hotel room!

"Yes, well… while I was at the party, I err, bumped into an old friend… acquaintance really… from my past."

I pause, checking she's absorbing what I'm telling her. There's no immediate response, so I continue.

"The woman… she was someone I knew a long time ago. When I was still with your father. She made a huge scene. Saying she'd found me and I…"

"Wait… what? What do you mean… found you?" The confusion shifts between them like a hazy fog. They have no idea what I'm on about… of course they don't.

"Lizzy… when I was younger, I made some bad choices in my life."

She opens her mouth to interrupt, but I hold my hand to stop her. I need to continue.

"I did things I'm not proud of. I was unhappy and thought I knew what I was doing, but I didn't. I took my clothes off for money!"

There, it's out.

"WHAT!?" Lizzy stands, then sits, then stands again. Sammy's chin has hit the floor, and all she can do is watch her friend as she performs a comic imitation of a jack-in-the-box. It'd be funny if it wasn't so tragic!

"Lizzy, please, sit down… I haven't finished." I reach out to her, desperate for her to hear the rest before she judges me.

"No…," she makes to shimmy past Sam, sidling through the small space that is only a couple of inches wide.

Sammy seizes the opportunity, and flings herself forward, wrapping her arms around Lizzy's knees, trapping her in a strange wrestling hold and halting her in her tracks.

"Gerroff me," Lizzy snaps and she batts at Sammy's head with flailing arms.

"Oww! Stop it you psycho bitch! Sit down and listen to what she has to say… stop hitting me!"

"No, leave me alone…"

"LIZZY!" I rarely shout at my children, but I've had quite enough of her bad behaviour, "SIT DOWN!" I insist.

The look of alarm on Lizzy's face is amusing. She's not used to being told what to do and it clearly must feel like a slap, because she instantly stops smacking Sammy, and shuffles back to her seat.

213

"This better be good..." she grumbles, folding her slender arms and giving me daggers!

"That's better. Let's all just calm down," I say, taking control of the situation.

"Now, I need you to listen... ap, ap ap...!" I raise my finger when she tries to interrupt, "You. Will. Listen," I inform her forcefully. "For once, you will sit there and listen to me; because I have no intention of repeating myself... do you understand?"

Silence.

"I said... do you understand?"

"Yes mum."

"Yes Edi."

I look at their little faces. One sulky, the other flushed with intrigue and I will myself not to blurt an ironic laugh. Because truly it is *fucking* laughable... the situation is ridiculous.

"I was a topless model for a while. Before you were born, and then for a year or so after... no, Lizzy please..."

She slaps her hand over her mouth; wide eyed she listens.

"Your father had big dreams, big ambitions and I was a stupid gullible schoolgirl who believed every lying, conniving, bull-shit story he fed me.

"He was my manager. I was so young. Only fifteen when you were born. I know you know that, and I know you don't judge me for it; but the truth is, I should have known better but I didn't."

I continue. "It took me three years and a ton of courage to get away, but I did. I left him. The day of your great-grandmother's funeral, I walked out and never went back."

Keep going Edi! "I was well known and my disappearance made the papers. But I deliberately hid myself away from society – I didn't want the attention. I had priorities, to look after and protect you and David. Eventually the hype over my disappearance died down and I thought no more about it – it was behind us – until I started my new job and one of the clients turned out to be Bobby!"

She remains quiet, her hand clamped to her mouth; a solitary tear escapes from the corner of her eye.

Sammy too is transfixed; though not teary, she looks shocked.

"Yes, Bobby appeared out of nowhere, the day we flew to Paris. Then, that *Bloody* woman, Lynda started shouting her mouth off at the party, and all Hell broke loose. By the time I came home, I was on the TV news and in the paper. Bobby started leaving threatening messages; demanding I see him, that I come back. It's a mess."

I'm shaking. "I'm so sorry Lizzy... I couldn't tell you over the phone. It had to be in person..."

"Mum," her voice is soft with shock. "I'm sorry... I remember..." The fear in her face has me sick with worry.

"Nooo," I didn't mean to rake up any bad memories for her... she can't remember... it's impossible...she was three for Christ's sake!

I do... I remember... I remember us leaving... you crying... the car ride... just bits, but I remember..." She looks at me as though a revelation has been unveiled. "What are you going to do?"

This is the hard part… she needs to know the threat Bobby is to us… to her. "He has no clue about David." At least I can put her mind at rest there.

"Is he David's dad too?" I'd almost forgotten Sammy was here.

"Yes," Lizzy and I reply in unison.

"I do remember Mum, even that…" she gasps in horror at what her infant mind must have filed away. She saw what he did to me that afternoon… she was there. An image like that is not easily forgotten.

"Oh, baby, I'm sorry…"

"It wasn't your fault. He was horrible. The monster under the bed, a wicked evil person."

"Yes, but now the monster is back and he's not going to go away again without a fight. Because, you see Lizzy… he believes I've stolen something from him. Something precious."

Her head tilts to the side in confusion. "What, what does he think you stole?"

"You, baby girl… he thinks I stole you. And he wants you back…"

CHAPTER 38

In the fraction of time it takes for her to digest this bombshell, Lizzy's ashen face morphs from confusion, to shock to fear to panic.

"Baby girl, listen… listen to me… you need to focus."

Her hands cover the lower half of her face as her eyes widen in terror. She remembers that night. She knows what Bobby's capable of and she's scared.

"Nooo, Mum… please. I can't… don't let him…" Standing, she looks around for a means of escape; there isn't any.

The irony isn't lost on me. Lizzy's reaction to fear is to run; exactly like mine, flight is her mechanism when threatened… a family trait, or a learned behaviour I'm unsure, but my instinct is, or was, exactly the same…

But since meeting Silas I have gained a new resolve. Now I understand that fear, no matter how great, can't be allowed to win.

After hearing Silas's story, and what he's endured, my own circumstances seem insignificant in comparison.

Over the years, I've learned to shy away from anything that could present a potential danger. I've spent the last nineteen years unconsciously looking over my shoulder, living in the shadows in the pretence of safety. Protecting my children from any perceived danger was my number one priority; but in doing so, I've inadvertently passed on my irrationality.

This has to stop now! I don't want my children living in fear of a threat that may never happen. I want them to have full lives of freedom, excitement and positivity.

It's taken time, but meeting Silas has been a revelation. I'm no longer afraid of my own shadow. I still have a way to go, but standing up to my greatest fear, my nemesis, is the first step to complete freedom from the past.

Silas has helped me think differently, to look at life in another way and to begin to enjoy living again. I have a new strategy; now I intend to fight.

"Lizzy." I need her to calm down, I need her to listen. "Baby… nothing is going to happen. He can't do anything to take you away, or hurt you. I won't allow it."

Sammy has been uncharacteristically quiet, but breaking her silence, she takes hold of Lizzy's shoulders, forcing eye contact. "Liz, listen to your mum… I'm hearing what she's saying, and you have to, too!" She gives Lizzy a little shake, "hello, are you in there?"

"Y… yes," Lizzy begins to nod her head. The fear is subsiding, but the shock is still present. "Yeah, I'm okay…" she stammers. "I'll be okay."

"Look, I think you need a few minutes… go and lie down in the cabin and I'll bring you a drink."

Hopefully, a few moments of quiet will allow her to digest the news without combusting. I've never been more grateful being in an enclosed unescapable place!

Sammy supports Lizzy by the elbow as if she may tumble, guiding her to the bedroom at the rear of the cabin. I head to the galley. A cup of hot sweet tea is required, I think.

As the kettle settles in to boil, I lean my backside against the narrow cupboard and ponder my own reaction to what I just divulged.

It's strange; the more I talk about it the less worrisome it becomes; its diluted. I've gone from being absolutely terrified, to a feeling of seething anger at what he's done, and is continuing to do. And now I've retold the story for the umpteenth time, I'm experiencing more frustration and irritation at the injustice of it all.

The fear is definitely dissipating, and in its place is a growing sense of duty, the record needs to be set straight and my side of the story should be heard; I can no longer stay mute on the subject. Justice needs to be served and he needs to be exposed for what he truly is, and only I can do that.

I enter the bedroom to see Lizzy lying on the bed. She's on her back, lying flat, hands over her chest, staring up at the ceiling. As I close the door, she turns her head in my direction but doesn't move to sit up.

"Tea?" I smile reassuringly, placing one of the mugs on the bedside table. "Do you mind?" I point to the bed, asking if I can sit beside her.

Lizzy shrugs her shoulders, but shuffles a couple of inches over so I have some room to sit beside her.

"I'm sorry it was such a shock," I say softly, stroking a wayward curl from her forehead.

Lizzy turns on her side and bends her knees. Shifting closer, she rests her head on my lap and allows me to soothe her.

I'm catapulted back in time, to when she'd come home from school, usually upset by one of the bullies, and we would lie like this. Her, with her head on my knee and me stroking her hair.

We remain like this for a few minutes. I'll allow her to indulge in some self-pity then I think I need to instil some tough love.

I blame myself for her insecurity. All those years of my jumping at invisible ghosts and hiding in the shadows have rubbed off on her. I'm not surprised she wanted to call an end to the trip so soon. Sammy must be furious.

"Here." I hand her the tea, and she heaves herself up and sits cross-legged on the bed.

"Thanks." She takes a long drink, then winces at the amount of sugar. "Ugh, that's sweet," she complains.

"It won't do you any harm; drink up."

Reluctantly, she drains her cup, then hands it back to me so I can put it on the table.

"How are you feeling now?"

"Still shocked, but a little better. Why are you so calm? It's not like you."

No, it isn't… or wasn't… but I'm learning not to react so violently to stress, and that's what we need to address now.

"Well, let's just say the last few weeks have been … enlightening."

"Clearly…"

"No, seriously, Lizzy… it's been quite a revelation. I'm changing… for the better… and I want you to know you don't have to fear every little thing. I was wrong to make you feel like that and I'm sorry.

"I've learned a lot, and I'm still learning. But one thing I've learned with certainty, is the only thing to fear, is fear itself. We create our own limitations and boundaries. We can

217

be our own worst enemy. Fear can take hold and ruin our lives but only if we allow it, and I'm not prepared to let fear rule me anymore. You need to do the same."

"Huh!" she shrugs, dropping her eyes to the silky pattern on the duvet. "That's so easy for you to say, isn't it?" She starts to twist the ring on her little finger. "Here you are, dropping bombshells and throwing out advice like a therapist. So, you're cured, are you? You know everything there is to know… Silas has transformed you into this brave, fearless amazon, huh? You're Wonder Woman?"

Oh, she's so angry.

"I didn't say that, but yes… if you must know. I'm not fully cured, but I'm getting there. One thing I've come to realise, is, no matter how difficult my life was, there's always someone else who's suffered more; endured more, and worse things. Horrific things; and Silas has helped me to see that."

Her head snaps up. There's a perceptive look in her eyes. Putting two and two together.

"Yes, before you ask… he's been through a lot. I'm not at liberty to tell you because it's not my story to tell, but just believe me, he has."

"But…"

Before she can interrupt further, I continue. "You remember when we visited David? The last day before you went to America?"

"Yeah?"

"Do you remember his friend, Nic?"

"Yeah… the one with the teddy… the stuffed dog?"

"Yes, that's him… well, Silas is Nic's dad." I wait a beat for that snippet to sink in before continuing. "It was a complete coincidence," I add.

"So, let me get this straight… Silas… your Silas…" she nods in the direction of the cockpit, "is the dad of David's friend, Nic?"

"Yep."

"And you didn't know… before you took the job, that is?"

"Nope."

"That's crazy."

"Yep." I nod once.

"Does Davey know?"

"Yep."

"Does he mind?"

"Nope." This is getting repetitive.

"Wow… so what happened to him… I mean, did he have an accident or something?"

"Yeah, something… so now you know. Some people have it worse than we do… a lot worse."

"Yeah, I suppose…" she drifts off into her own thoughts.

"Anyway; I'm going to do something about it."

She looks at me puzzled. "What can you do? He was in an accident."

"No, silly, not Nic." I brush the hair from her face. "Bobby… I'm not going to let him drive a wedge between us," I indicate from her to me to emphasize the point. "He's not going to intimidate us anymore. He is due what's coming and I'm going to make sure he can't do this to anybody else… ever."

"What are you going to do? How?"

"On Wednesday, your mother, assisted by Christina - my new boss and Silas's ex-wife, by the way - is going on national TV to put the record straight, it will be my version of events. My story."

"Oh My God! Seriously," she's lighting up. Today must be blowing her mind with all the information bombarding her. "Does Davey know?" As always, the concern for her beloved brother comes first.

"Yes, he does. And what's more… he's all for it."

"But," her brow furrows. Something is troubling her. "My dad doesn't know about Davey, does he?"

"No, and he never will." That much is certain; I'll never tell him.

"So, what are you going to say?"

"I'll open myself to questions. I'll tell the truth; that I left of my own volition and the reasons why. If he doesn't leave us alone after that, I'll get an injunction. I'm sick and tired of being afraid he'll come back. Now he has, I want him gone and this is the best way to achieve that… I just want my life back. I'm fed up of running scared. I need to have courage… remember what you said to me at the airport?"

"Yeah… courage to fly…"

"Courage to fly…" I nod in agreement. Silas has given me wings and I'm going to use them to break free from the hold Bobby has over me.

I hold Lizzy in my arms. Hers slip around my waist and she buries her head in the crook of my neck. "You're the bravest person I know… I love you mum."

"And I love you too Baby-girl."

Now all that's left is to convince myself. Words are all well and good, but truth be told, I'm doubting I'll be able to summon my courage when the time eventually does come. What is evident and empowering is, Lizzy has belief in me, as does David, Christina and more importantly, Silas.

They have all found the resolve to believe in me, so perhaps I should believe in myself too. It's time to stick to the courage of my convictions. I will endeavour to brazen it out on Wednesday. After all, what could go wrong? I'm the one with truth on my side. I have all the evidence, and the images to prove it. All I need now is belief in myself, as they believe in me. I can and will do this!

CHAPTER 39

The landing is smooth as always. Silas is an amazing pilot, so natural you'd think the wings were attached to him. It's nearly seven pm, but that would be midnight in New York and my body clock is all over the place.

My brain is telling me I need to sleep, but my eyes are saying different. I need to eat. I think that would help ward off the impending jetlag.

As we disembark, I'm comforted to see both Spanners and Sparks are still here, and the sight of Bear in his usual spot behind the automatic door is heart-warming.

A surge of delight engulfs me at the presence of the beautiful creature. I never would have thought I'd become so attached to a dog; but then, Bear isn't any ordinary dog.

"What the Hell is that!" Sammy has caught sight of Bear too, and is having a very similar reaction to the one I had when I first clapped eyes on him.

"Oh, WOW! He's gorgeous!" Lizzy on the other hand is instantly besotted. "Who's is it?"

"That, my darling girls, is Bear!" I smile as we tow our wheelies towards the reception.

Bear seems to grow larger before our eyes. The nearer we get, the bigger he becomes, it's like an illusion.

"He belongs to Silas, and he's an absolute gentle giant," I say.

Sammy clearly isn't convinced. "Fuck me sideways... it can stay on the other side of that glass... it's not coming anywhere near me... I quite like my arms and legs where they are, thank you very much!"

"Oh, don't be such a coward... he's beautiful." Lizzy laughs; for once she's braver than her friend. It's refreshing.

"Come on, I'll introduce you..." Silas has caught us up, and is eager to be reacquainted with his best buddy.

Overtaking our leisurely pace, he drops his case and jogs forward, his weight automatically causing the doors to glide open as he meets the range.

As soon as the gap is wide enough, Bear snakes his lithe body through the sliver of an opening and jettisons free like a cork out of a bottle.

Sammy stops in her tracks and screams in terror. Thankfully, Bear has only one object in his sights, and that's his master.

At his approach, Silas plants his feet firmly on the ground and prepares for the attack. Bear doesn't disappoint. Five feet away from Silas, he launches himself in the air at full pelt. Silas braces for impact, catching the full weight of him directly in the chest as if he was no bigger than a Jack Russell!

"Nice to see you too lad!" He leans away as Bear squirms in his arms, determined to lick every part of his face. "Down you go." He drops Bear to his feet, where he immediately spies me and the whole fuss making scene begins again. Only this time, I come down to his level. He's far too well-mannered to jump up at me; he'd knock me for six if he did.

"Jesus! That thing is a monster..." Sammy hisses.

"Oh, he's not… he's a puppy, aren't you?" Lizzy drops to her knees and Bear introduces himself; he's keen to make a new friend and rolls over onto his back for a belly rub.

"Pigs in Space!" I look up to see Christina striding towards us with a bemused look on her face. "Some guard dog you are," she says to Bear, who completely ignores the insult as he rolls on the ground at Lizzy's feet, ears flopping and pink tongue lolling out of the side of his mouth. "Welcome home beautiful people…" she cries, flinging her arms around me and giving me a hug. "And you must be Lizzy?" She offers her hand and Lizzy takes it. "Nice to meet you."

"And this is Sammy," I indicate to where Sam is frozen solid, eyeing Bear with trepidation.

"Hi," she says, offering Christina her hand, her eyes remain firmly on the dog.

"Well, come on in. I've ordered some food; you must be starving!"

Although the workplace is closed for the evening, the signs of a productive day are everywhere. While waiting for the Deliveroo to arrive, I gave Sammy and Lizzy a quick whistle-stop tour, culminating in my office, which was accompanied very satisfactorily with plenty of appreciative 'Oooh's' and 'Ahh's' at the sheer gorgeousness of the panoramic view from the window.

"I can't believe you work here!" Lizzy steps up close to the glass bubble and peers out; training her head left and right so she has a full view of the airfield and runway. "It's the nuts!"

"I know…" I'm still reeling with the wonder of it all myself. Every time I come in here, I'm reminded of just how fortunate I've been.

"So, you know how all this shit works?" Sammy runs enquiring fingers over the equipment.

"Of course, I do… it's my job."

"Well, I think it's amazeballs!" Lizzy gives her assertive opinion.

"Yeah," Sammy yawns, reminding me they've probably not eaten or slept much in the last few weeks.

Thankfully, the food order is on time. "Come on… Let's go eat, then I can show you where you'll be sleeping!" If they think the office is the dogs', I can't wait for them to see the apartment!

Gerard and Lizzy have moved to the sofa, taking a large pepperoni pizza with them. Currently, Lizzy has her legs curled beneath her and is picking the circles of processed sausage off the cheese and dropping them in her mouth. Gerard is biting through a huge double stack, clearly unperturbed with Lizzy's way of pinch-eating.

Sammy is flopped on one of the leather armchairs, head tilted back, snoring lightly in a pizza induced coma. She's wiped out.

So, how was New York? Christina poses her question at Silas.

"New York was eventful!"

"How so?" Christina takes a piece of tissue and dabs at the greasy cheese atop of her small slice of pie.

"Oh, you know… business went okay." Silas glances sideways at me, before continuing. "Edi enjoyed the midges in Central Park, oh and the recommendation… you know… Jules at Tiffany… excellent! Please thank Elaine for me."

"Oh! So, let's see it then!" Christina is distracted from all business talk at the thought of my gift. "Oh, wow… it's stunning! And if I may say so… absolutely fitting for you."

I tilt my arm, so she can see the full effect.

"I love Tiffany," she muses. Absentmindedly, her hand drifts to the customary gold chain she always wears around her neck, and I wonder if it's also a Tiffany piece? It certainly smacks of exceptional quality.

Suddenly, she's animated. "Well, this isn't getting the baby washed…" Standing and gathering all the empty plates, stacking them together she continues. "You lot need to get going; it's a big day tomorrow."

"Yes," I stand too, the movement disturbing Gerard and Lizzy, who gives Sammy a quick kick, waking her so she jerks to attention. "I'll help."

"No, no, this can wait until morning. I'll stack them in the kitchen. You go and collect your stuff. Silas will meet you in the carpark."

"Oh… okay. C'mon girls…" I encourage their weary forms to follow me. "I'll take Bear outside for a wee."

"Thank you… I'll be there in a few minutes." Silas kisses my nose, and pats my bottom, as I pass.

"Bear, come," I call.

Bear obediently follows on my heels as I head through the office to the main entrance at the foyer. Lizzy and Sammy accompany us on fading legs.

"Does that happen often?" Lizzy yawns as we step outside into the cooling evening.

"Does what happen often?"

"Oh, you know… that Christina bird sending you off like that… it's as if she doesn't want you to hear what's being said." Lizzy, even in her ravaged state of exhaustion, is still as sharp as a tack.

I hadn't really noticed it; not consciously anyway, but now she's mentioned it… "No," I fib. "Not often. Just when it's high-level company business."

"Well, I thought she was rude," Sammy pipes up, yawning.

"No, she's not like that," but they may well have a point. "She's just… business like… efficient."

Bear snuffles around the grassed area, tail wafting. Eventually, he finds what he's been searching for; the wheel of Silas's Range Rover, which is on the edge of the car park. Cocking his leg in a very self-satisfied way, he completes his business, trots back to me and sits patiently by my side.

"That beast is huge… where does it sleep?" Sammy muses.

"With me and Silas. He's very loyal. Once you get used to him, you'll be fine."

"Yeah, well… I don't think he'll ever be my best friend; are you sure it's a dog… it looks more like a horse!!"

"Oh, Sam, he's a darling." Lizzy drops to her knees, enjoying another cuddle with her new pal. Sam stands back, eyeing them with disapproval. I feel this new love triangle could be a challenge.

222

"Are we ready?" Silas strolls from the door, duffle bag in hand, followed by a now quite dishevelled Gerard.

As Gerard runs a tanned hand through his hair, I can't help notice, even in this tousled state, he looks so damn soave! Crumpled, but in a sexy kind of way! Lord help me... this is Lizzy's type of man to be sure.

I sneak a sidelong her way... yeah... she's noticed. I wonder where he'll be sleeping tonight?

"We'll take the girls first." Silas throws his house keys at Gerard adding, "we'll meet you at the barn." So that's clear then; whatever Gerard may have thought, he's staying with us tonight and not at the apartment.

I'm grateful for Silas's protective nature. Charming though Gerard is, I can't help thinking he would be very dangerous for my girl; especially in her current vulnerable state.

Gerard raises a hand and blows the girls a very Latino air-kiss. "Oui, bon... I will see you again soon, ladies." I don't miss the look he passes to Lizzy; loaded with intention. Oh yes! I need to watch him very closely.

"Bye," they chorus as they climb into the back seat.

"Gerard, take Bear!" Silas sends the dog off towards Gerard, who reluctantly opens the door of his Mercedes, so he can jump in.

Gerard raises a one hand salute, climbs in his car and screeches away, clearly not at all happy with the arrangements. I, on the other hand, am delighted. That's at least one more night where I can keep them apart... Gerard will be on his way back to Paris tomorrow and I can properly relax. Even if it's only for a couple of days!

CHAPTER 40

We have to wake both of the girls when we arrive at the apartment. The drive is short, but it was long enough for them to nod off. Wearily, they stumble out of the car and up the steps, barely awake sufficient to absorb their surroundings.

Lizzy leans against the wall of the foyer and Sammy leans against Lizzy while we wait for the lift.

"God, it's like the Walking Dead!" Silas chuckles as they shuffle in side by side.

"They'll wake up once we're inside."

"I hope so; I don't relish hefting these two lumps into the bedroom!" Silas winks, amused. There's no doubt he could carry them both at the same time, and still be able to manage the bags.

The lift pings our arrival at the penthouse, and I nudge a very sleepy Lizzy in the back, encouraging her to walk forward and into the lounge. Silas does the same with Sam.

"This way Missus!" I steer her by the shoulders towards the bedroom.

Once there, I guide her to the bed, where she flops down, fighting and kicking as I try with varying degrees of success to remove her converse and socks.

"Nooo," she complains. "Gerroff!"

"Okay then, have a good sleep and ring me in the morning." I give up, and unfold the throw, draping it over her now snoring form and tucking her in. Undoubtedly when she awakes, she'll have no clue where she is.

Hastily, I scribble a short note on the bedside pad, urging her not to panic and to give me a call. Then, just as quickly, I realise how predictable I'm being; reproaching myself for fussing so much, she's just returned from two weeks trolling around the States... obviously she'll cope with a luxury apartment for goodness's sake!

"Good night baby girl," I drop a light kiss on her forehead.

"Are you ready?" Silas whispers from the doorway. "I've left sleeping beauty in the spare bedroom; do you want to check on her before we go?"

"Yeah, I'd better. I'll leave her a note, so she can find Lizzy in the morning without going into a complete melt down."

Sammy is barely visible, nestled beneath the duvet, the top of her curly head resting on the fluffy pillow... butter wouldn't melt... yeah... believe that and you'd believe anything.

I write a quick note with instructions for the alarm and how to navigate the apartment and kitchen... it's almost an essay! Then, I repeat the good night routine, kissing her head, stroking her hair and tucking her in. "Nighty-night chuck."

Silas is waiting patiently in the living room, standing before the picture window and staring out into the dark night.

His silhouette is impressive. If I was unfamiliar with it, I'd find it intimidating, but I'm well accustomed to it, so I just take the time to admire him for a minute.

But as Silas always does, he senses my presence and turns to look at me. "God you're beautiful," he breathes. "Shall we?"

"Yes, I think they'll be alright now."

"I should bloody well hope so!" he says, looking around him.

That wasn't what I was meaning, but he's right. Who wouldn't love it here?

"Let's go. I'm knackered."

He must be. After flying all that way, he must be feeling it now.

"Yeah, come on."

We exit the apartment with Silas's arm draped around my shoulders. My thumb naturally finds its way into the loop of his belt.

"Ohh… gosh…" I yawn, the weariness finally hitting me, now I know the girls are safely tucked up in bed.

"I know…"

The drive to the barn is a breeze. Traffic is light and the roads are relatively clear. "Work in the morning," I sigh.

"Yep… no rest for the wicked."

"Why would you say that? You're the least wicked man I know."

"It's just a saying…" but his smile is weak. Clearly, he's feeling the fatigue of the long day. "Here we are." He turns into the driveway and parks up beside Gerard's car.

"What do you make of Gerard?" I frown at the sight of the shiny vehicle. "I mean, you know him well… do you think he'll make a play for Lizzy? They seemed a bit cosy."

"Edi," Silas finds the spare key under the plant pot, "Gerard is a Frenchman, with an eye for a pretty girl. But truthfully, if he harmed one hair on her head… friend or not… his life wouldn't be worth living; and he knows it."

My mind is eased by his protective words. I know he means it and I'm thankful. Lizzy isn't his daughter. But, knowing what happened to his beloved Maya, I can fully appreciate where the deep-rooted need to shield her has come from; I get it!

"Thank you, Boss-man!"

"My pleasure, Honey-bee… or it will be in about four minutes time!"

Swiftly, and silently, he scoops me off my feet and glides soundlessly up the stairs; somehow managing to miss the one creaky tread, and into the bedroom.

The house is silent with not even the slightest hint of a grumble or snore from Bear, or from Gerard for that matter. Just the seductive sound of Silas's heavy breath as he strips me of my clothes and lays me on the bed.

"I've waited all day for this," he hums against my throat.

I'm drowsy and sleepy, but the moment he speaks my libido is lit on fire. Just the soft caress of his lips ignites a flame, which once aglow, won't be fully extinguished until I'm truly satisfied. Accepting his caress, I tilt my head so he has better access to my neck.

"I need to taste you." Kissing from the hollow beneath my ear, he takes his time, nipping and sucking his way over my tender skin. "Mmmm, you taste divine." I seriously doubt it; I've been travelling for most of the day, holed up in a plane.

However, the proximity of his body has me squirming. He's the same… he too has been travelling. His skin is warmed by the artificial heat, his clothes, stale and yet somehow, I find the musky scent drifting through my senses intoxicating. It's a pheromone which calls to me on a subconscious level, a beacon, a pungent lure, just for me and I can't get enough of it.

Pushing his shoulders, I force him to release me. The heat at my core is searing and I'm soaking wet with anticipation.

"What?" His brows furrow as he whispers his question. He thinks I'm pushing him away. I'd never push him away.

"Lie down beside me," I instruct. I need him close. Willingly, he climbs onto the bed and reclines. "You must be so tired... here, let me do this."

Kneeling beside him, I gently take the hem of his sweater and draw it up revealing the taught glistening flesh beneath. And with it, another heady wave of that manly odour.

"Mmmm!" Unable to resist, I lick the planes of his chest, lapping at the salty skin, revelling in the succulent sweetness of his warmth. "God! You smell incredible..." My nostrils flare, widening in an attempt to inhale even more of him. "Jesus, I want to lick you all over!"

"I'm not stopping you Honey-bee!"

Keeping my lips on his body, I smooth them downwards until I find his navel. Swirling my tongue in the shallow divot, my mouth waters savouring the zing of his personal flavour.

I fumble with inept, eager fingers to unfasten his belt, pausing only briefly to whip it from the belt loops and hurl it to the floor. Once his belt is off, there's no stopping me. I pull down his zip, and undo the button, yanking on his trousers desperate to remove them and have him bared to me.

"Hey, hey, ouch... careful there, that zip's sharp," he grabs my shoulders. In my haste to rid him of his clothes, I've caught his foreskin on the zip! That must have hurt.

"Oh God... I'm sorry." Quickly, I kiss the spot where the metal has grazed him.

I feel him twitch beneath my ministrations, an involuntary spasm at the feel of my mouth. Lifting my eyes, I look at his beautiful face. He's panting, looking down at me, lips parted in expectation, waiting, willing me to continue.

Taking his stillness as a positive confirmation, and keeping my eyes securely on his, I place my lips on the tip of his penis, kissing it gently. The satisfied groan he omits, leaves me in no doubt I'm on the right track.

Unable to support his head any longer, he exhales on a juddering breath and drops back onto the bed and stares at the ceiling... desperately awaiting my next move.

This is easy. Straddling his thighs, I place my palms on his chest as I stretch the full length of his body. Cloaking every inch of him with mine, I writhe above him, barely touching him, my nipples stroking his chest so lightly, the friction delivers bolts of static, causing us both to shiver.

"Edi, bury me!" he growls his command.

"Inside me..." I tease as I rise and hover above him.

"No messing... get me inside you... now."

Grabbing onto my hips, he yanks me down onto his waiting arousal, knocking the breath clean out of me as I'm impaled on his huge manhood.

"Oh, my!" I just about manage to exclaim, before I'm lifted up, and rammed back down. "Oh, ouch!" It's my turn to complain...though I'd never complain about this; not truly. It hurts, but it hurts so good!

"You go..."

I'm released, and given free reign. Bending my knees, I rise, so I hover above him. Taking hold of his hands, I place them on my breasts, guiding him, showing him where to touch me. "Here, tight…" I hiss.

Lowering onto him once more, I circle my hips, gyrating and grinding down, ensuring maximum penetration. "Ohmmm," I fling my head back. Closing my eyes, I allow myself to drift into a trance like state. I feel every movement, every inch and every powerful surge as we writhe together in a beautiful undulating rhythm.

"Christ, you are one beautiful woman," he grunts, "I could watch you like this all day, ride me baby…"

I don't need to be told twice. I'm tantric, my breathing becoming erratic, our connection, cosmic.

"Oh, Fuucckk!" he wails to the ceiling.

I know I have him, I need him to release so I can find my own. "Silas, come…" I demand. With the tables turned, he has no control over his impending climax, he can't hold back.

Now!" I scream, unable to stop my own orgasm from surging forward. I lift, once more, then drop, hard, grinding. Smashing my clitoris against the rigidity of his pubic bone, I explode into a rainbow of coloured lights; a firework, a roman candle.

Silas too has erupted, shooting round after round of steaming cum directly into me, hitting my g-spot, prolonging my ecstasy.

"Damn woman!" he gasps, wrapping his arms around my waist and pulling me into him. "Still… stay still… lie with me."

"I love you," I mumble, barely coherent.

I'm completely spent. I can't even lift my head, choosing instead to blindly grope around with my hand in search of the duvet. Dragging it over myself, I remain prone atop of Silas. I've had it. That was incredible, but now I can't move.

Gradually, my eyes drift closed. I'll move in a minute, I tell myself; just one more minute…

CHAPTER 41

"Well, this is interesting," a sleepy, gravelly voice disturbs my peaceful slumber.

I'm lying on my front. It's comfortable. Beneath me is a solid mass of something and I seem to be straddled!

"Mmm, are you still asleep?"

"Yes," I mumble, into the solid mass.

"Do you want me to wake you up?"

"No." I want to continue sleeping. This rock is extremely comfy.

Recovering my sense of wakefulness, I'm aware not only am I straddled; I'm full! Oh boy! I've never woken up feeling like this before. Instant arousal, and a need to tilt my pelvis and rub against whatever it is that's filling me. It's very satisfying.

"Well, if you don't mind, I think it's time to rearrange things," the gravelly voice rumbles.

Before I know it, I'm flipped from my nestled position, and whipped onto my back. Whatever I was lying on, is now pinning me down and my legs are spread; and I'm still full!

My eyes spring open, instantly gratified at what I see. Silas looms above me with the most glorious smile on his face. "Lift up." His arms loop under my knees, and my lower body is boosted into his awaiting lap.

Once he has my legs where he wants them, the rest of me is hauled up, so I'm straddling his hips, clinging to his front. "Shower time I think," he says as he rises from the bed taking me with him.

Pulling back so we're at a 'v' shaped angle from the waist up, I smile at him. "Were we… coupled all night?" I ask, knowing full well that he's been asleep, buried to the hilt.

"We were; and if I had my way, we'd remain 'coupled', as you so eloquently put it, all day."

"Suits me, Boss-man."

"Me too, but I think we pong a bit… I don't mind, but we should really have a shower."

"Okay, just don't drop me," I giggle as we exit the bedroom… bumping directly into a very bemused Gerard!

"Mon, due!" he exclaims, not sure where to put his eyes. In the three seconds it's taken for us to cross the landing, his gaze has travelled from my exposed breasts to my arse, where Silas is cupping my butt cheeks tightly to him, and finally ending on Silas's passive face. To say he's shocked is putting it mildly. He doesn't know where to look.

"Good morning, Gerard…" Silas booms as he strides by him and into the bathroom - giving me no time to digest the embarrassment or raise even the palest of blushes - kicking the door closed behind us.

"He saw us," I squeak, unnecessarily – of course he saw us, he isn't blind!

"Yep, he did…"

"Oh, my… what will he think?" Now I'm bothered?

"Who cares… he could see I'm balls deep, it isn't rocket science."

I'm confused. "But yesterday you were so cross when he mentioned my name… you know… Honey-bee… yet today, you don't seem to mind he's seen my… well… my everything!"

"Edi, you know I don't care what people know or hear. And for your information… as I've said before… they can look, but they don't see… he didn't see 'everything' as you put it."

I'm uncoupled from him and immediately feel empty and bereft. I understand what he means. Though we were exposed, Gerard couldn't really see. It was like in Paris… we were visible, but not. It was clear what was going on, but our actual intimacy was hidden.

"People enjoy titillation… it can be thrilling to be the source of it. I love it when people know were enjoying each other… perhaps it's my thing… but I'm pretty sure, you enjoy it too?"

He's right, I do enjoy the thrill. Or rather, I'm beginning to enjoy the thrill. I just don't understand why he was so upset with Gerard yesterday.

"Edi, you and me… it's the most special thing… ever. I love you. When you love someone, you make love with them. People know. They understand. They covet what two people in love have… but your name… that's for me alone. Only I know that part of you, and that's a part I'm not willing to share with anybody… do I make sense?"

"Yes… no… actually… I'm not sure," I reply honestly. He's a conundrum alright.

"Get in the shower miss stinky; you smell of cum and spunk and of being fucked and it's as hot as Hell. I need you to wash it off before I lose control."

"Idiot…" I laugh as I climb into the steaming jets.

At breakfast, Gerard is struggling to meet my eyes. Good! I feel as if I have one over on him at last and it's empowering. I'm not embarrassed. Not in the least. It wasn't anything like it used to be all those years ago when I was being gawped at. This was different. The control was mine and it was Gerard who was embarrassed. It's an interesting counterpoint.

"What are you doing today?" Silas asks Gerard as he fills Bear's bowl with some tasty dog biscuits.

"I 'ave to fly 'ome. I promised my mozzer, we'd 'ave lunch. And you know 'ow French women love to lunch…" he shrugs as if we should indeed know this.

"Well…" I don't get to finish as my phone starts jumping all over the worktop. "Sorry, I'll… err!" Slipping from my chair, I pick up my phone and head into the garden. It's Lizzy…

"*What the ever-loving fuck!* Have you seen this place? Where are you? It's incredible… I mean… really… *fucking hell*… the view, the bed…"

"The pool!" screams Sammy from somewhere in the background.

"I can't believe you live here… bugger me!"

"And a jolly good morning to you too, my sweet, sweary little ray of sunshine!"

"Jesus, Joseph and Mary… I mean… how the Hell?" her words fade. I can imagine her walking from room to amazing room, absorbing the grandeur and loving it.

"I'm pleased you like it…" Silas has followed me outside, accompanied by Bear, who immediately trots off to do his business. "Here, give it to me…" he snatches the mobile out of my hand and swings away from me. "How would you like to be my tenant?"

229

What? He's offering her his apartment?

"I mean, you need somewhere safe to live, and your mum is here with me," he seems confident I'll be staying; "at least I hope she'll stay?" he adds, raising expectant eyebrows in my direction. My head concedes, nodding in response, before I can question it.

"Look, we'll come up with a tenancy agreement, but as far as I'm concerned, you and Sammy are welcome to use the apartment indefinitely. It'll save me having to go through the whole process of finding a suitable tenant. And besides, I know your mother!"

Lizzy's muffled squeals are an indication that, yes, she would love to stay… Sammy too.

"Great; here's your mum…Bear!" Handing me back my phone, he calls for the dog, who charges, sneezing and snuffling, from the long grass. His coat is peppered with sticky-buds from the overgrown garden. "Well, someone needs detangling!" Silas shakes his head, "I'll see you inside. He needs a brush."

"He's gone," I mutter into the receiver. "You didn't fight very hard, did you?"

"Well, why would I… you've seen the place. I just hope we can afford it?" I sense her initial excitement at the prospect of living in such luxury is beginning to wane at the thought of a hefty monthly rent!

"Perhaps you should have discussed that before you accepted the tenancy… I'm sure it'll be favourable. You need somewhere to live, and Silas needs a tenant. We'll work something out. What are you doing today?"

"I have an interview. Sammy said she'd come with me. Can I borrow the rusty bucket?"

"Yeah, sure. The keys are with me, here, but I'll drop them off on the way to the office. Look, Lizzy…" I hesitate, not wanting her to be upset with me, "just… what I said about Gerard, yesterday… please be careful."

"Oh God, not this again… Mother, I'm a grown woman," *yeah, but not a mature one.* "I can take care of myself… you know I can."

"Okay… it's just…" Seriously, I don't really know what it's just… I only know I'm terrified of her getting hurt. I couldn't bear it.

"Mum… I'm not you…" her voice is small and soothing. She's right. She isn't me, but that doesn't mean she can't suffer the same fate or be hurt in the same way. "Stop with the overprotective shit… please… if I make a mistake, it'll be *my* mistake… okay?"

"Okay," I sigh in concession. I need to let her grow up. I need to let her be free. "I'll bring the keys. See you in an hour or so."

"Yeah, see you soon. Oh; and I'm visiting David this afternoon. We'll go after my interview. I need to meet this Wendy of his!"

Lizzy is waiting for me at the front entrance. Sam is nowhere to be seen. Silas waits in the car for me as I hand over my keys.

"No Sammy this morning?" I drop my car keys into Lizzy's outstretched palm.

"God! She's in the pool. I can't get her out. She said something about a mile a day! It'll take her forever; she can only manage doggy paddle!"

I laugh at the image. The last time we went swimming, we were at Uni' and spent the day at a local indoor Waterpark. While Lizzy, David and I splashed around on the water chutes, slides and rapids, Sammy spent her time in the kid's pool, complete with armbands and noodle floats. The thought of her attempting a mile a day is worrying, though I can't knock her intention or determination. "You'd better get back before she drowns!"

"Oh, she's fine. She's made a new friend. Some old bird who's taken her under her water wings! She's teaching her how to swim breaststroke."

Ah, I wonder who that could be? "Hmmm, well, break a leg at the interview. You'll be brilliant. Let me know how it goes will you?"

"Yeah." Her smile is overly confident.

I know how good she is. She aced her exams and her degree is First-Class Honours, so she really knows her stuff. She's a fabulous accountant, but it won't prevent me from being anxious until I'm sure the job is securely hers.

"Morning darlings," Christina murmurs from reception. "Sleep well?" She has a pencil sticking out of her messy bun.

Skirting the counter, she grabs her navy folder and fountain pen, along with her two mobile phones, before edging towards the rear of reception. "I'm in a meeting this morning and I've a conference call with the people who are planning the Gala... which is in less than a week by the way! Walk with me..." she waits for me to follow.

"See you later Baby, I'll be in the hangar if you need me." Silas and Bear exit the electronic door and head off to where the Chuckle Brothers live... with the planes and all the other boy's toys and grease-monkeys.

"Morning." I manage to get a word in before she sets off speaking again.

"Err, yes... well, as I said, I have an interview this morning, and then a call later on to discuss the Gala. If you could take a look at these notes, it'd be a real help."

"No problem." I trot alongside her in an attempt to keep up with her leggy stride.

She hands me the navy folder. "All you need is in here," she says, pulling up outside the Board Room. "Read through it, note your amendments and I'll catch up with you later." Pulling the pencil out of her hair, she pushes her way into the Board room.

"Okay," I say to the closing door.

Tucking the folder under my arm, I head to the main office. The team should be in by now, so we can have a quick briefing and catch up before we start the day.

Nasima and Susan are ready and waiting for me. Susan has made us a pot of coffee, and Nasima has a glass of water. Jasper is sat adjacent to Susan, which I suspect is so he can look at her without appearing to be staring... which of course he is.

I try and hide my mirth at his attempted smartness. He's found a tie from somewhere – perhaps his dad or grandad – the knot looks as though it's been tied and loosened over a number of years, and the pattern, purple paisley clashes ever so slightly with his green and white dogtooth checked shirt. If I didn't know differently, I'd swear he was colour-blind!

"Good morning people," I cheer as I enter the office.

"Morning," they chorus.

"I made coffee," Susan says. She's not sucking up, just being factual.

"It's really good," Jasper stammers, squirming in his chair and taking a huge gulp from his mug – he is sucking up – to Susan!

"Okay, so, what's on the agenda for today?"

"Well..."

We have a really constructive meeting. The girls are working together as a team and have built an excellent rapport.

Susan is taking the time to call all our current clients, issuing invitations to the pending Gala and acquainting herself with their businesses.

Nasima has created a new database for our billing system. Book keeping and invoicing seem to be her thing. She's even chasing up on overdue payments. Small she may be, but timid, where work is concerned, she's most definitely not.

Jasper is busy networking the drives and enhancing the thingumajigs in the comms room. I've no idea what he's doing, but as long as it runs smoothly, I'm happy!

"Okay then guys, let's do this." I dismiss them to go about their tasks, secure in the knowledge all's well.

After I've completed Gerard's departure, I settle in my chair to review the notes Christina gave me this morning. I'm looking forward to the Gala. It should be a brilliant evening; combining networking of some of the most prestigious businesses and high-profile VIPs with a fundraising event for a worthy charity.

Flipping to the first page in the folder, my chin drops. Gala my eye! The contents couldn't be less than a million miles away from the expected event details. There are pages and pages of what appears to be evidence and data... about Bobby!

Initially, I think there's been a mistake. She must have handed me the wrong folder. But then, as I start to flip through the damning and incriminating evidence, I wonder at her intention; was this deliberate, was this what she wanted me to see?

My interview with the TV people is in two days and to say I'm ill prepared is a vast understatement. But the stuff in the folder is incendiary. Explosive; it will blow the lid off all of his current activities, exposing his various business interests to unbelievable scrutiny. Surely, she can't mean for me to disclose this information on TV?

All I want is for him to leave us alone. Give my version of events. My story. That's all. Slamming the folder shut, I make the decision there and then not to disclose or discuss any of this in the public domain. I won't stoop so low. If they expect dirt, they'll need to dig for it themselves.

I drop the folder into my out tray. Christina can have it back after her call. I'll tell her myself. I don't want the interview to turn into a three-ring circus. It isn't an interesting story anyway – just a way of getting my privacy back and sending Bobby packing. No, I'll do this my way... the boring way!

CHAPTER 42

"Hello? Anybody around?" Deciding to hunt down Silas for a quick Boss-man fix and a boost of confidence, I've headed for the hangars.

The sound of the radio is blasting from somewhere in the back. Rick Astley's *'Never gonna give you up,'* is ricocheting off the corrugated walls. Beneath his voice, I can hear another one, far less tuneful, my guess it's Spanners, adding his own tone-deaf twist to the chorus.

"Hello? Sparks? Silas?" I wander towards the internal office. The door is ajar, but I knock all the same. No answer.

Giving the door a hefty push, I bob my head in, searching for my Boss-man. I know he's around here somewhere. "Silas?" Nothing. The integral strong room door is also ajar – he must be in there.

Stepping into the internal office, the smell of diesel and engine oil hits me. It's weird how I associate the smell with sex! It really gets to me and I find the chemical tang coating the back of my tongue and my taste buds oddly arousing – how bizarre.

I'm musing quietly over my new-found fetish as I wander over to the open strong room door. It really is a heavy metal door; more fitting to an old-fashioned Bank safe than a store room.

"Silas…" I try once more.

"Edi?" It's Spanners. He's followed me into the office and is currently standing behind me in the doorway, wiping his hands on an oily rag. "Are you lookin' for Silas?"

Halting in my tracks, I turn around. "Yes, have you seen him?" Jim doesn't need to know I'm looking for a bit of afternoon delight! "It's just something about work!" *What else would it be – idiot!*

"'E's gone out." Spanners looks shifty, he isn't fooled. "Can I 'elp yer darlin'?"

"Ummm, no, it's okay. I'll come back later."

As I say this, a shift in my peripheral vision catches my attention. The strong room door has begun to move, heavily, silently and ever so slowly. There's somebody in there and they are trying to close the door on me!

I'm beginning to smell a rat. Something is going on here and I'm suspicious. "Where's he gone?" I ask, stalling, taking a step backwards towards the closing door.

"Err, 'E… err?" Jim struggles to come up with a creative excuse. "It's Christina… 'E… er…'ad to see 'er for somfink," his eyes flick to the metal door, which has now almost closed.

"No, Christina is on a conference call. What's going on Jim? Where's Silas? Where's Bear?"

At the sound of his name, Bear snakes around the closing door and into the office, standing before me, all innocent and light, wagging his tail as if butter wouldn't melt.

"Jim!" now I'm annoyed. "What's going on? Where's Silas?"

"Woof!" Bear gives out a loud bark. Jim has taken a step towards me, and Bear, taking his role seriously, is warning him off.

Spanners stills. "Now, don't be 'asty, Edi. Come away from there, 'e'll be out in a minute." Spanners' voice has gotten louder, almost a stage whisper, projecting over my head and into the strong room. It isn't for my benefit.

"Oh, I've had enough of this," turning on my heels, I make a nimble sweep round Bear. I know he won't hurt me; his default setting is to protect me from pending danger.

Grabbing hold of the door, I heave it open, swinging it wide. "Silas...?" My words freeze on my tongue.

The walls of the room are arranged with metal shelves, drawers, and glass-fronted cabinets. It's a very orderly room. One wall has been designated to an array of photographic portraits. Some grainy, as if taken with a long-distance lens - reminiscent of the recent images in the tabloids of me and Silas - and some are clear, like mug-shots or passport photos. Some have red crosses slashed through them, some do not. And some have green lines, draw diagonally through the centre.

Silas is here, and has his back to me. He's standing towards the rear of the cell-like room examining something in his hand.

I stand silently taking it all in. At first the room is puzzling. It should be a safe. You would expect it to contain expensive tools, valuable components and costly equipment. It contains all of these things. But none of them bare any relevance whatsoever to aviation or aircraft!

Guns!

Scopes!

Knives!

Grenades!

Ropes!

Cuffs!

Masks!

More guns!... What the FUCK!

I stand, unable to comprehend what I'm looking at. What the FUCK is all this... stuff? Moreover... WHY is all of this stuff here?

"Silas... I'm sorry... she just..."

"It's alright Jim." Silas doesn't move. He remains stoic. His back to me, facing the cabinet. His shoulders are hunched and tense and he's looking down. "Jim... I said it's okay... go and take Bear outside."

"Well, if you're sure... c'mon, lad." I hear him shuffling away.

"You shouldn't have come in here."

"No shit Sherlock!" I'm aghast. So shocked my heart is hammering. I can't fathom what I'm seeing, my brain rejecting the images and unaccepting of what's laid out before me. What the Hell is going on?

"This isn't how I wanted you to find out."

"Find out what?" I look around me at the mass of killing machines. *Jesus!* "That you like to play with guns?" These can't be real. It's just a collection, surely? *Please* let that be it – yes – that's it – he's a collector.

Turning towards me, Silas's eyes are soft, but wary. "Edi, Baby... this isn't what you think."

Phew! Relief floods my system. Thank goodness for that. I can cope with the desire to collect stuff; although weapons seem to be a dangerous passion. I know there are people who do this. After all he was in the special forces... yes, of course, he's a collector!

Silas continued. "I mean... it isn't just a collection or hobby."

I place my hands over my ears and close my eyes... *No!* My heart rate accelerates and my innocent assessment disintegrates into dust. It's as though the rug has been pulled from beneath my feet revealing a mire of deadly quicksand, just waiting to suck me under and suffocate me. *No!*

If I can't see him and can't hear him, it isn't happening!
If I turn around and leave the room, this will all be a dream.
If I walk away and step outside, this isn't real!
Why I'm bargaining again? ... I'm so stupid!

"Edi?" My wrists are clasped very gently. Slowly, he draws them down and into his chest. "Edi... look at me," he whispers, "you need to know the truth about me... us... who we truly are."

No!" the sob escapes my throat; unable to prevent the tears, they tumble down my cheeks. This isn't happening. It *can't* be happening! "No... please... don't tell me... let it all just... be a bad dream!"

"Edi... you know me better than anyone. But this part of me... you need to understand."

My terror at what I'm seeing swings to fury at his placid tone. *I* need to understand? I'm both fearful and livid at the same time. With tears streaming down my face, my anger wins and boils over and before I know it, I'm screaming into his face. "What Silas? How am I supposed to understand... *whatever* this is? It's sick! If these aren't a collection," I gesture around me at the disgusting assortment of firearms and weapons, "why the fuck do you have them?"

"They're the tools of my trade," he answers calmly and clearly.

My stomach turns so violently, it causes me to retch. My heart is galloping so alarmingly now, I feel light-headed and not in a good way. Bending double, I clutch at my chest; my breathing has accelerated and I'm beginning to hyperventilate... Shaking my head in denial; I think I'm going to faint.

Tools of his trade? *What the Hell?*

Oh God! I *am* going to faint. My knees buckle and everything goes black.

"You're a fucking idiot!" My head is spinning, I can hear hissing and whispering... but it's loud. "You did this on purpose! Poor Jim is beside himself. He knew you were in there. Why the fuck didn't you lock the damn door?"

"She needed to know."

"No! Silas, she didn't!" Ooh, Christina sounds mad! "Fucking pigs in Space!"

"Oh, they're fucking now, are they?"

"Silas! This isn't funny! For Fuck's sake; this woman may be the love of your life, but it won't prevent her from blowing the whistle on our operation..."

Operation?

"Christina. Calm down. Try and remember why we do what we do and why you wanted Edi here in the first place."

"Oh, don't you dare!"

"What?"

"Don't you dare try and make this my fault! You were careless. You wanted her to find out, didn't you?"

"Yes!"

The sudden silence jolts me around. Opening my eyes, I find myself lying on the sofa in Christina's office. It's a strange Deja-vous, we've been here before, only last time it was my secret we were debating.

I feel the uncontrollable urge to laugh. The absurdity of the circumstances hits me and I need to release. A torrent of unrestrained laughter leaves my throat and sitting up, I double over, clutching my stomach in a sickening mirth.

It's hilarious! What an utter shambles! It's an unbelievably ridiculous situation; you couldn't make it up if you tried! Here I am, a recovering victim of abuse, and then there's Silas, a recovering father of a murdered child. And Christina, out of control and bent on revenge... that's it...revenge! *Oh, sweet Jesus!* So that's what this is all about! They're a vigilante group?

"The Rose Council" I splutter, at their astonished faces. "The Rose, Bloody, Council!" I stand. My legs are like jelly, but I stand anyway. The hysterical laughter has turned to uncontrollable sobbing. "You're in this for revenge, aren't you?"

Christina and Silas stare at me. Their expressions unreadable, sombre, stonelike.

"See..." Christina turns on Silas like a viper, "she's going to ruin everything. All the good work we've done."

"Good work?" I can't believe what she's saying!

"Yes, Edi... good work," she spits, directing her icy glare on me. "This isn't just about our personal losses. We make a difference. We aid society," she looks at Silas, pleadingly.

"Edi... come and sit. You need to understand this."

"Oh, I think I understand alright... you lost your daughter... you had guns... so you decided to take the law into your own hands," I accuse, vehemently. I'm forming opinions as I go along... whether they are right or wrong, I'm spouting whatever comes into my head. My thoughts and imagination are running wild!

"Close but no cigar... now sit the *fuck* down!" Christina has rounded on me like a tigress. She's terrifying. With no way to exit the room I do the only sensible thing. I shut up and sit down.

If I have to listen, I will. But as soon as I can, I'm out of here!

My heart is still clattering and my breathing ridiculously erratic; I need to at least try and remain calm but my mind is a whirl of indecisive thoughts and notions.

Each time I define a reason to justify what I'm about to hear my logic produces another counteraction to dismiss it. Each time I formulate a viable excuse for what they're doing, my brain objects and just as swiftly rejects it.

The absurdity of the situation is playing havoc with my sanity. My natural sensibility tells me this is all a huge joke, an outrageous and elaborate ploy to test my compliance and loyalty; yet I know unequivocally, this is real.

There's no denying what I've seen and there's no escaping what I'm about to discover; the man I love without measure or condition is involved in some seriously dangerous and highly perilous activities. I can't even bring myself to ask the true nature of his involvement, or just how deeply he's associated, or even what level of authority he has over what they're doing. I need to sit, listen and try not to implode.

"We seem to be doing this a lot, don't we?" Christina hands me a glass of water. "Drink this."

Wishing it was whiskey, I accept it with shaky hands, managing to touch the glass to my lips before gulping the cold liquid on a splutter. "Try not to choke," she quips before grabbing her packet of cigarettes from the top drawer of her desk. "I need some fresh air," she says as she snatches up her lighter and storms out of the room.

"She's stressed." Silas takes the half empty glass from my hand, tipping the remaining inch of water into the base of the spider plant then placing it on the desk. "She resorts to solitude, pacing and smoking – her way of defusing, I suppose."

Reaching into the cupboard, he extracts a bottle of Scotch and tilts it at me. I nod once in approval. I need it. Unscrewing the top, he grabs a second glass then pours us both a generous measure of the good stuff.

Taking the glass, I knock it back in one. The amber fluid scalds my throat and the sudden intake of alcohol, hits my brain like a slap to the head fuelling my ire.

"Really... and what am I supposed to do with that information, hmmm? How am I supposed to calm down?" The moment I say it, my stomach twists and I lurch forward; the Scotch I swallowed barely seconds earlier threatening to reappear.

Silas is kneeling by my side in an instant, his warm hand stroking my back. "Hey, shhh, you'll be okay... just breathe... in... out...in...out," he coaches, "that's it... in... out..."

"I don't know what to do," I wail, the cry startling me as much as him. "I don't know if I'm dreaming; it's crazy... I'm crazy... Oh God... it's too much." I'm folded over at the waist clutching my stomach. A rhythmic rocking has started and I tilt forwards and backwards in a desperate bid to escape from the hideous thoughts bombarding my mind.

"Who are you?" I snap, my eyes full of seething accusation. "I can't believe this." The rocking becomes even more extreme.

"Edi... stop." Sitting beside me on the sofa, Silas wraps his arms around me in an attempt to still my lurching form. "Still, shhh? I'll explain, but you need to calm down."

"AND HOW THE FUCK AM I SUPPOSED TO DO THAT?" I start to fight against him, desperate to remove myself from his hold.

"Edi... please... stop... no... you'll hurt yourself..."

He's far too strong for me. All he does is tighten his arms, encircling my body, trapping me in his vicelike grip.

"Gerroff me!" My squirming and wrestling, does little to budge him. I'm going nowhere.

As abruptly as it started, the fight leaves me and all I can do is slump against him. Turning my face into his neck, I bawl my eyes out. Shuddering and heaving sobs; an uncontrollable torrent of ugly, snotty tears that just flow and flow.

I can't cope. How can my life have come to this? How have I gone from a hundred years of normal? A million days of ordinary? Being nothing more than an unassuming, boring mother and student, to this? To keeping company with… I don't even know what to call them…

"Tell me…" I sniff, not really wanting to know, but all the same needing to validate what I've seen with this man I've come to love so much. "Explain it to me. I *need* you to explain."

"I don't know…" he mutters, stroking my hair. "It's a lot… are you ready to listen?" Softly, he kisses my forehead. "Can you be calm?"

"I doubt it… but I need you to tell me everything. If I don't know the truth, how will I know how I feel or if I can remain calm?" How will I know what to believe?

"Just promise me one thing?"

"I don't think I can make any promises right now Silas."

"Okay then, no promises, just a condition."

"What if I can't keep it?"

"I think you will be able to."

"Okay then; what is it?"

"Edi, just listen… please listen… and try not to run."

I look up into his sincere but wary eyes. How can this man, who has suffered so much loss, and demonstrated such compassion, be anything but good?

"Okay, I'm not sure I can promise, but I'll try not to run."

CHAPTER 43

Silas releases me and seemingly needing the distance, he sits down in a separate chair.

"When we lost Maya, we were in unimaginable Hell." There's no preamble, he just launches into his explanation. "Unless you've been there, experienced the loss of a child… it's visceral, an indescribable pain. You just can't envisage a way through it. The weight of grief is inconceivable.

"It hit Christina like a tidal wave. She was distraught, unable to function on any human level. Her depth of despair was so deep, for a while I thought I would lose her too. She was so bad she was sectioned and put on suicide watch; her behaviour became erratic and she began to self-harm."

After a small pause, he continues. "Because she was so ill, she was unable to visit Nic in the hospital, which only compounded the situation. However, it meant that my own grief had no outlet, no vent. I had to be strong, I had to cope, and find a way to look after Nic and Christina."

This much I know; it all came spilling out the day he broke down in front of me and told me about that dreadful event. He had bottled up all the grief and personal emotion for years. I don't voice this thought; I just allow him to continue in his own time. So far, I've heard nothing that particularly shocks or concerns me. It was understandably a human reaction to the most horrific incident.

"It took months of counselling before Christina's mental health began to improve. I was living in a vacuum, on auto pilot, a surreal plain of existence. As Christina gradually recovered, I withdrew. I became a shell of myself, incapable of feeling anything other than a debilitating hatred for the people who had ripped our lives apart. Any love and compassion I held on to was solely for Dominic; nobody else mattered, only him."

Taking a deep breath, Silas retreats in on himself, visibly sinking into his chair. Swallowing heavily, he gulps back the wave of emotion threatening to overwhelm him. All I can do is listen, now I'm enthralled at what I'm hearing, and I allow him to continue uninterrupted.

Closing his eyes, as if to recall the exact series of events, he sighs. "It was my father who had the initial idea for *The Rose Council*. Of course, he and my mother had suffered the same blow we had. My immediate family were dealing with their own personal grief but watching the way Christina and I were imploding was as if they were losing everything again. We were destroying ourselves over it and they were front line observers. Honestly, they just couldn't stand by and watch it happen."

Barely pausing for breath, he continues. "Dad was in the Diplomatic Service for years but prior to that he was in the Air Force Department Constabulary. Because of this, he had all the right connections, internationally as well as here on UK soil. In 1971, the AFDC merged with the Army Department Constabulary and the Admiralty Constabulary to form the Ministry of Defence Police. At that time, Sir Geoffrey Whittham was in command."

The name is familiar but I can't place it. He must see the puzzled look on my face because he smiles softly. "Yeah, Elaine's late husband. He was Chief Constable."

Ahh, so that's where the indefatigable Mrs Whittham fits in!

"Elaine and Geoff were involved from the outset; Geoff was my Godfather, in fact. Dad wanted to create a taskforce or a council, who had diplomatic immunity and could work hand in hand with the Government to 'right wrongs' or 'redress the balance' as he put it. That's when *The Rose Council* came into fruition.

"But isn't that what MI5 is for?" I ask naively.

"What, like James Bond and Q and M?" he shakes his head. "They're all fictional characters. In the real world, there's no such thing as a *'licence to kill'* - not in any real sense - anyway. And even if it did exist the Government would refute it! Plausible deniability, I think is the term!"

"But you do though… don't you?"

"I'm coming to that." Silas sits forward, resting his elbows on his knees, folding his fingers together; at last, he's beginning to relax a little, though there's still tension in his jaw. "*The Rose Council* is more of a judgement chamber, a courtroom if you will. My mother was a QC - I don't think I've mentioned it - and Charles is a retired litigator. Johannes has worked in security and law enforcement and you know about mine and Christina's history. Together, we review cases. Or I should say, we re-review cases and judge them accordingly, passing the 'appropriate' sentence."

"I don't follow."

"Well, for example, if someone is found not guilty, due to a technicality or some loophole in the law, we conduct a judicial review of the case."

"I still don't follow; I mean how can you review the case if you don't have all the evidence?"

"We use the transcripts." He looks at me with a 'don't ask' expression. I decide I don't need to know – not yet anyway. "The transcripts include the evidence. But this is also where Elaine comes in. She's our secret weapon. She has contacts." I still don't want to know!

"Okay, so you conduct a review of the case… then what? You just go out and… murder them?"

"It's not quite that cold-blooded and uncivilised," he says, his brows knitting together as though considering my evaluation. "Do you remember back in the nineties, there was a spate of high-profile assassinations? About ten or so; they were Politicians, Army Personnel, even some celebrities and Royals were targeted. They were indiscriminate. Anybody who was deemed a threat, or who had the means to destroy their operation had a price on their head. Geoff was one of those killed." His eyes reflect his sadness.

"I remember… it was awful."

At the time the media was awash with it. Even the doorstep ambush and murder of a prominent newscaster was attributed to the vicious, faceless gang responsible for the killing of so many prominent figures.

"This so far unknown cluster of criminals and terrorists, they were my target; my assignment was to infiltrate, isolate and eliminate. It went terribly wrong. I became the focus of their attention and you know how that ended," he says this last part, eyes downcast.

"The *Bastards* who murdered my daughter and disabled my son," he swallows; the memory of that fateful day agonizingly raw. "The animals responsible for all this murder,

240

hurt and suffering… they were eventually caught." He grits his teeth, grinding the words like gravel in his throat.

"They were brought to trial and we expected to accomplish justice. However, due to a loophole in the law, certain evidence was not permitted in the courtroom. Previous convictions of which there were many, were deemed irrelevant to the case and therefore not permissible and couldn't be disclosed. Moreover, because the only prosecution evidence was from me, and the only eye witness was Christina - who at the time was deemed unreliable due to her mental state - all charges were dropped and they went free."

Christ!

"What happened?" It's like listening to an audiobook.

"*The Rose Council* happened." Releasing his hands, he once again sits back in his chair. "We simply couldn't allow it. If they walked free, the reign of terror would continue. Drugs would flood the streets; kids would die from badly cut heroin and cocaine. People would be trafficked – girls as young as five and six would be sold to the highest bidder – and more of our good and prominent people would be killed. We just couldn't let it prevail. We had to do something."

Raising his eyes to mine, I sense the depth of his despair and vulnerability. "Licence to kill!" he whispers.

"You… you…did you?"

"Yes; and with no sense of remorse, or guilt. They got what was coming to them. The whole lot of them. By the time we organised ourselves and had all the right people onboard, they were scattered to the four winds. It took years to tracked them down, but we prevailed. One by one, we weeded them out; uncovered their hiding places, figured out their new identities; traced their new businesses."

I feel him brace, ready to gauge my reaction to the next bombshell. "The most recent one was in Paris."

"Pierre Adrax? He was one of them?" I'm aghast, "but he was a fashion designer… those models, he adopted them… he died of natural causes."

"Yeah, convenient, wasn't it?"

"What? Are you saying it wasn't natural causes?"

"I'm saying nothing… other than the world is a much better place without him."

"What about the others? What happened to them?"

"Some had accidents, some were 'commercially disposed of' or so it seemed. You remember back in July? The news headline about a gangster who'd been reported missing?"

"Found in the boot of his own car with a bullet in him?" I remember this because it happened on the very day I graduated. "Yes, I do," I whisper.

"Ta-dah!" Silas holds his hands up, palms facing forward, "guilty!" he announces, completely unashamed and undemonstrative. "He was the lowest of the low. A paedophile, a pimp, a trafficker and a murderer. I have no regret whatsoever in assisting his passing."

"How can you…?" Words fail me.

"It's taken me nearly fifteen years to come to terms with the loss of my daughter. The way I've got through it was by the *Hammurabi Code*." I look at him completely blank.

241

"Hammurabi, the king of righteousness?" he explains. "'An eye for an eye'. Let's just say it's got me through some very dark days."

Explanation at an end, he leans against the chair. Unwavering brown eyes hold my attention. He's waiting for my reaction, what I'm going to do; am I going to run?

Well? Am I going to run? I contemplate my new-found knowledge. His reasoning for what *The Rose Council* is doing, as unbelievable as it may seem, makes sense to me.

Although I have a million questions, I can understand why they do it. Reconciling their actions is easy, just by imagining myself in his position. BUT, if *anybody,* no matter who they were, threatened the life... or God forbid... took the life of one of my children... would I be capable of such vengeful retaliation?... would I be able to take a life? - *'An eye for an eye'* - it doesn't bear thinking about.

What I do know with unwavering certainty is I still recognise Silas as the man I love; yes, despite all this. I still love him... unconditionally. He may not be the man he was sixteen years ago, but I didn't know that man. The man he is now, brimming with integrity, justice and honour was hewn from his own life experiences and losses. Undoubtedly, he has his imperfections. But I love him, warts and all.

So, no... I won't be running... not today.

"It's a lot to swallow," is all I can think of to say, whilst remaining as still as I can, so as not to reveal how truly nervous I am at this overload of information. I stay put, demonstrating my decision not to run in the only way I know how; sitting calmly and observing him as he's observing me. "What now?" I add, endeavouring, but failing to keep the giveaway tremor from my voice.

Blinking several times, he appears to grasp I'm not running. "What do you want to know?"

Though barely definable, the slight shift in his body language is obvious. He's still sat in an open and honest pose, his legs spread wide in apparent relaxation, and his arms resting loosely, one on his knee, the other across the back of the chair; the adjustment is subtle but I notice. His shoulders lower a centimetre; his breathing steadies slightly and his fingers, previously drumming a silent rhythm on the chair-back, cease to move for a fraction of a second before resuming the soundless beat.

After giving his offer some serious thought... *what do I want to know?* That's the six-million-dollar question. "Everything... I want to know everything." The words are out of my mouth before I can stop them.

"That's a lot to want to know," he says calmly.

Choosing not to speak, I hold his gaze. My wayward leg is desperate to jiggle nervously, I consciously battle the urge to let it go and give myself away. I'm far from cool and calm, but I'll be blowed if I'm going to give him the satisfaction of knowing it!

Finally, he comes to a conclusion. Removing his arm from the chair-back, he slaps his thighs in what appears to be a final decision. "Okay then. If you want to know everything, you'd better come with me."

He stands and holds out a hand. Now it's my turn to decide... do I stand and take it and discover the full extent of the truth; or decline and walk away, having only partial knowledge?

It's an easy decision… getting to my feet I take his hand. What else could I do? There's no going back for me now - I have to move forward into whatever murky waters await me - I need to know…. everything.

CHAPTER 44

With her unerring talent for precision timing, Christina chooses this exact moment to re-enter the office, and offering barely a glance in our direction, heads to her desk.

"I take it you've explained?" She directs her question at him. Her focus, at first landing on our clasped hands, drifts levelly up to Silas. She sounds a substantial number of degrees calmer than when she went outside to indulge in 'fresh-air'.

"I've explained some; and now I'm going to explain more." Silas meets Christina's stare with what appears to be a challenge in his eyes. Softly, he blinks, turning his head in my direction. "There's a lot more."

"Should I apologise now?" Her demeanour is anything but contrite.

Choosing not to answer, Silas just keeps his concentration directed to me; demonstrating that stoic expression I've come to know so well.

"Oookaaay..." Rolling her eyes, she flicks her perfect hair and drops her carton of cigarettes into the top draw of her desk. Picking up the file I'd previously dumped in *my* out tray, she gives us a last onceover. "Well, let me know if you need me..." she smiles, disingenuously, then sashays out of the office.

"C'mon, I can't say any more in here." Taking my hand, he leads me out of the office and through to the foyer.

There's no sign of life anywhere. The building is as silent as a church. "Where is everyone?"

"They've left for the day."

I don't question this. I expect my discovery of an arsenal of weapons may have earned the team an early finish.

We cross the tarmac and enter the hangar. Once inside, it's clear the only staff still working are Spanners and Sparks. Bear comes trotting over to us, tail wagging in greeting. My heart quietens at the sight. Merely being in his company is a calming influence. I don't mind him tagging along. He makes me feel safe.

We enter the inner office and I inhale on reflex, my nasal passages immediately assaulted by that heady tang of fumes, oil and musty paper. My heartrate increases, and my libido is stimulated. It's ridiculous under the circumstances, but the aroma ignites a chemical reaction I'm powerless to control.

Later..." Silas mumbles, completely in tune to my body's impulses. He's noticed it too.

Closing my eyes on my inappropriate response, I propel any indecent thoughts to the back of my mind. This isn't the time or the place to be getting horny... well, it may be the place... but it certainly isn't the time.

"The code is 7386AZRAEL."

"Why are you telling me this?" I don't know when I would ever need access to a room full of guns and bullets!

Silas shrugs. "You never know," he says, nonchalantly hauling the strong-room door open. "After you," he gestures.

"No, after you…" I respond. There's no way I'm walking into that room in front of him. I'll follow. He can be my shield.

Shaking his head, he allows Bear to enter first. He doesn't seem in the least perturbed by the room's contents. I suppose that's one major advantage of being a dog. A master's trust is without question and a dog's loyalty is unwavering.

Once we're inside, he draws the door closed. The latch clicks into place with a heavy clunk and I'm immediately unnerved. Suddenly the area seems confined, and claustrophobic.

"Don't panic," he soothes. "Look, this is the internal mechanism." He points to a keypad and bulky metal lever on the wall beside the door. "The handle will release the door, look," he demonstrates, easily lifting the lever, the lock releasing and the door's hydraulic hinges whirring into action. "It's quite safe. You can open it from the inside, or you can lock it down completely using the same code, making it impenetrable from the outside. It also serves as a safe-room. You can't get locked in by accident."

"You have a bunker?"

"No," he laughs, "it's just a way of remaining secure. If you need to, that is… We've never needed it yet."

On the wall above the door lock is a small security monitor. It shows an image of the outer office… the thought crosses my mind; *he must've known I was outside earlier.*

"Humm," I murmur, looking around me, desperately trying to assimilate everything.

This is all very surreal. I'm surprised at how swiftly I've accepted this new part of who he is; as if it was somehow expected. I must be completely obsessed with him; so much in love my brain will shrug off anything remotely distasteful as relatively normal. Idly, I wonder how far will my acceptance extend?

"Okay." He's brought me to the wall of faces.

Standing before me, he shields me from the array. Placing his palms on my upper arms, he slides them down until he's holding my hands. I gaze up at him expectantly. The last time we stood like this; he was about to kiss me. This time, I doubt it's the case.

"I'm going to talk you through this. There may be faces you know, recognise, and there will be faces you don't."

"Alright."

"Edi, when I say there may be faces you recognise, please try not to freak out. Okay?"

I look at him, completely befuddled. "Okay!" I'm not a complete baby! I doubt I'll recognise any of them.

"Alright…" he sighs heavily, clearly nervous.

Stepping away, he takes a stride to the side, revealing the rogue's gallery. Keeping hold of my left hand, he gauges my response as I scan the wall of photographs, seeking out any recognizable faces amongst the jumble of indistinct features.

Observing so many of them, side by side, I'm immediately struck by how different they all are. Some have bulbous noses, others small and pointed. Some have thick lips, then there are those with thin, mean mouths. There are bushy eyebrows, receding hairlines, spectacles.

There's the diversity in skin tone and ethnicity. Young and old too are represented. There seems no discrimination to creed, colour, age or gender, they're all characterized here. Each of them is so markedly diverse and yet, each of them exudes a haunting similarity; a kindred likeness or essence; it's extraordinary. There's an inextricable ghost in their expressions, linked by their chosen career paths within the criminal underworld.

I stare at each face in turn. "They look like ordinary people. Like anyone you would pass in the street and never look at twice."

I'm mesmerised by how unremarkable they all seem when viewed en masse, until, that is, I spy a picture of an incredibly beautiful woman, filed in amongst the gallery of mostly male faces. "But then…who's she?" I turn to Silas, lifting a finger at the portrait. And it is, most definitely a portrait.

The image is strategically posed, almost a glamour shot, and I should know. The photograph depicts a blonde woman of about forty, dressed in a couture evening gown and wearing some seriously expensive diamond jewellery. A white mink stole is draped around her smooth shoulders, her head is tilted and she's smiling with perfect, pearly-white teeth at the camera.

The only thing spoiling the portrait, apart from the thick red line, drawn diagonally, corner to corner across the photo and straight through the centre of her smiling face, is her eyes; they're the eyes of a calculating person; cold and devoid of compassion. They are eyes that would make you shudder, eyes that could turn you to stone... Medusa's eyes. "Who is she?" I repeat.

"Ah, yes. The stunningly beautiful Maria Devine. Or, Astrid Bouton. Or, Freya Martinez. Whatever name she went by, her real identity was Mara Goolde. Or as Christina called her, 'The Ghoul'. She was pure evil. Married to this charming man." Silas draws my attention to a very suave looking middle-aged chap, also, with blonde hair and a winning smile. Side by side they look like a formidable couple; movie stars. "Don't be fooled by their charming looks. That's how they lured their victims. A latter-day Hindley and Brady. They were a sickening pair. Mara and Faraday Goolde."

I'm stunned. I've never heard the names before but I'm familiar with Myra Hindley and Ian Brady, the notorious child killers in the 1960's. My wide-eyed horror at their innocuous pictures is real. I can't believe people like this exist outside of a horror film.

"You won't have heard of them… they were South African and notorious."

That tells me enough, I don't think I want to know the extent of their crimes. "What happened to them?" My morbid curiosity gets the better of me.

I look at Silas. He's sneering with contempt at the pair as if they're right here in the room with us. Lifting a hand, slowly he draws his fore-finger across his throat from left to right; leaving absolutely no doubt as to their fate. "We got them," he announces. "Or rather, Marc and Johannes got them."

My eyes flick to him, startled. I know Marc was the brother of Gerard and the son of Charles and Katherine. "Marc?"

"Yeah, he got them. They just disappeared one day; from their Chateau in France. Odd that…" he winks at me indulgently.

"Did… did… what happened to Marc have something to do with it?" I'm reluctant to ask, but it would make sense. After all, the *'Eye for an eye'* philosophy would fit right in here.

"Marc was an adventurous man." Silas sighs, remembering his old friend. "While it would be convenient to attribute his accident to these two pieces of shit, it isn't so."

He steps to the side, moving one portrait along. "This gorilla, however, is another matter." The man in the picture does indeed look like an ape. A huge barrel of a man with a wide, deeply wrinkled forehead and beady little black beetles for eyes. With his shaved head, decorated with swastika tattoos, he oozes evil from every pore. "This is the creep who killed Marc. This guy, Otto Tooms… known as *'Le Mécanicien'*, or *'The Mechanic'*. He built bombs, handled explosives and 'fixed' vehicles, including aircraft, so it looked like an accident. He's the one who took out Marc."

"Did you get him too?" I have an inkling, as his portrait, like that of the Goolde's, is defaced by a red diagonal line.

"Oh yeah, we got him," he nods sagely at the picture. "Gerard and Charles. It was Charles's last deployment into the field, but he was insistent. They took him down with one of his own devices. A trap which worked like a dream. He'd planted a bomb on a luxury yacht belonging to this man." He taps an image of an older man wearing a Keffiyeh, with kind eyes and a mild expression. A green line bisects the photograph this time.

"His name is Sheikh Zain Bin Maktoum. An Arab Prince and businessman and one of the nicest people I know. He foolishly got involved with the underworld after Nine-Eleven, determined to help track down those responsible. It was incredibly naïve of him. He wasn't a wealthy man, not in the realms of real wealth, only worth about thirty million."

"Thirty million!"

"Believe me, in the oil industry, thirty million is pocket change… anyway, he was way out of his depth. He meant well, but the hornet's nest he kicked almost brought down the entire operation. When they discovered his intentions, they sent *The Mechanic* to 'remove the obstacle'. Once we knew their strategy, it was simple."

"Simple!"

He smiles down at me, his eyes telling me it was anything but. "Charles and Gerard managed to decipher the encrypted code used in the remote device. Once they isolated the radio frequency, they could use the code to detonate the device early… and… BOOM! Bye-bye, Mr Tooms."

"Oh no… what happened to Sheikh Thingummy, Maktoum?" I'm morbidly engrossed!

"Green tick…" Silas says, pointing to the picture. "He's fine and well and living at his palace in Bahrain. Last I heard, he'd got married to his third wife and has ten children."

"Huh… a happy ever after ending." The barbed retort slips from my lips without filter.

"There are some, believe it or not," he accedes, "some even owe the fact they're still breathing to us." He taps the photograph of the very lucky Sheikh. "Without our intervention, he'd most certainly be pushing up daisies."

I move along the line of notorious villains, absorbing each face with a new found dark curiosity.

"So, all of these people, are people who have committed a crime and for some reason or another were let off?" It sounds simplistic, but I'm sure the reality is far from simple.

"I'd have to correct that; the multiple crimes these people committed were complex, making evidence difficult to obtain and proof of guilt even harder. They were vile... heinous - but for the purpose of explanation - mostly, yes - let's say we redressed the balance."

"Why are they all still up here? I mean if you've... eliminated them; why are they still on the wall?"

Silas remains silent, choosing to keep step with me as I pace slowly from face to evil face. I don't press him; I know he'll explain in his own time.

We move along to the next batch of pictures; on this section, there are only two with red lines through them, a couple without any lines at all, and one, which is just a black silhouette, a shadowy image of a person as yet unknown. "So, are these all connected then?" I ask, the system becoming clearer.

"Yeah..." he sounds apprehensive. "Edi, this is really complicated and I don't want you to freak out."

He's said that before, but that was when I was blissfully unaware of how highly dangerous his clientele is. So far, he's revealed some pretty scary shit, but I've managed to take it in my stride and stay calm. I don't know why he'd expect me to start freaking out now.

"Do you think I'm going to freak out?"

"You might," he pulls us up short, turning to face the latest batch of pictures. I gape as I see front and centre a photograph of Pierre Adrax. "Remember this guy?"

"Err, yeah!" I roll my eyes at him in mock distain. "He only turned up dead the morning we flew home from Paris, and apparently, you did it!"

"Well," he says, resting his palm on his chest in a modest gesture, "I had some help; but yes, as I said before; guilty."

I can't believe he's making light of the fact he took someone's life. "Are you *fucking* kidding me?" I'm appalled by his lack of contrition. "You're a killer!" a fact I'm sure he doesn't need reminding of, "you kill people..." and again; I'm quite sure he knows this fact too.

The pain that washes over his face is obvious. My harsh accusation has hit a raw nerve. "Edi," he whispers softly, "a moment ago you asked me why the pictures are still up there, even after... the event."

"Yes."

"It's so I never forget." His eyelids lower, closing on the images and the pain they conjure. "What we do - what I do - when we... I, take a life; even the most evil and deplorable. It's still a life. What we do is necessary but it is far from easy, no matter who it is, and we should never forget that. Regardless of how heinous the crime, how despicable the individual, it is still the life of another human being that's been ended. I don't ever want to get comfortable with it – I want to still feel – and that's why the faces remain on the wall. As a reminder that I need to stay human."

My heart breaks for him. Clearly this path is not an easy one to tread but he seems to have managed to negotiate a way through so far.

248

I shut up before I say something really regrettable. Clearly, he's struggling with whatever it is I need to know. I'll let him come clean before I decide if I can deal with all this, or if I'm just going to explode with this overload of information.

Facing the wall his eyes become clouded. I have an overwhelming feeling I'm not going to like the next revelation - not that I've liked any of them thus far - this time though, he's chewing his bottom lip as if contemplating how to drop the next grenade.

"Okay, I'm listening. I'll try to be objective," I offer; although I have no idea how I'm going to pull it off. Currently, I'm reeling. I'm determined to remain detached and look at this in a clinical way; basically, I'm pretending it isn't really happening. Once I allow myself to believe it's all reality, I'll crumble into a heap. "Tell me the worst," because I know, he hasn't, not yet.

Swallowing deeply, he inhales and squares his shoulders. "This group," he touches each face in turn; there are five altogether, including the dark silhouette, "Adrax was their ringleader; well, he was for decades, but up until a couple of months ago, we had no idea as to the extent of his operation."

"Him?" I indicate the innocuous looking man.

"Yes, him," he says. "Like all people in that 'industry' he was incredibly charming. But the silver tongue and charismatic manner were all a well-rehearsed persona. Outwardly, the perfect smokescreen veiling the true nature of the beast within; one who's capable of the most odious crimes. Behind the mask, he was vindictive, ruthless and brutal."

Silas demeanour worsens. "The models he 'adopted'. The fashion he promoted... all a legitimate front shielding the true landscape of his more lucrative endeavours. Adrax was in the business of people; but not in the way the world knew him. His interest was in the value of people as a commodity. Adrax was a modern-day slaver, dealing in people trafficking and prostitution all under the guise of a warranted designer and mogul; and all played out beautifully right in front of the world's stage."

Now I'm perplexed. "Yes, you explained all that before. What am I missing?" I'm not sure what else there is to know about this loathsome excuse for a human being.

"He didn't work alone, Edi."

"Well, clearly not, otherwise all these other pictures wouldn't be here." I shake my head, still not certain where he's going with this. All the people in the pictures either have a red cross through them, which I now know means they're dead, or a green one, which indicates innocence... or so I was led to believe.

"Okay, I can see I'm not doing a very good job of this." He rubs his hand over the stubble covering his head, dragging it over his face in frustration with himself. "This one," the picture shows an extremely unkempt guy, he looks like a vagrant, "is 'car-boot' man. As you know, we got him back in July; and this one," he slaps his palm on the silhouette photograph directly to the right of Adrax's image, "this is the one we need now, the one we've been seeking to identify for month's... years in fact." His hand completely covers the photograph, effectively, obliterating the outline of the unknown male. "You know him," he whispers softly.

My questioning eyes instantly flick from the hidden portrait to Silas. "Me? How... who..."

"Take a closer look at 'Car boot man,'" Silas encourages, gently, "notice anything?"

Returning my attention to the previous picture, I re-examine the face. There is a familiarity about him. His overgrown hair and stubble, along with the greying complexion and wrinkles give the impression of a vagrant. However, when studied more closely not all is ringing true. His hair, while scruffy is clearly well cut. And his clothes, although worn are of good quality. If he were tidier this'd be very different image.

"Do you see it now?"

"Oh!" It's as if a blurred image has morphed into focus, "Waylon?" I'm stunned. Waylon Price is, or was, Bobby's father!

Finally, Silas inclines his head towards the last portrait.

Returning my gaze to the picture, I scrutinise the back of Silas's hand as if the answer will somehow magically reveal itself.

"It's him."

I know immediately who he's speaking of, but it doesn't compute. Shaking my head in denial, I retreat from the display of offending images, my eyes unable to look away. I raise my hands to my mouth to stifle the cry as it leaves my lips, "Nooo!" It can't be!

"Yes, Edi... it's him."

My back collides with the high cabinets which flank the opposite wall, and I slide down, hitting the floor, still with my focus on the blacked-out silhouette, still with my hands covering my mouth.

Silas moves to crouch before me. "Come on, I need to get you out of here. All of this isn't helping." He looks about him at the masses of lethal weapons. In close proximity to so many, I wouldn't be surprised if he was expecting me to pick one up and bludgeon him with it out of sheer shock. "Let's go."

Dragging me to my feet, he hauls me to him, then as if I weigh nothing at all, he scoops me up, and carries me out of the strong room and into the musty smelling office.

CHAPTER 45

"Here, Honey-bee, sit down. Are you okay?" He places me gently on the old office chair.

Am I okay? Well, that's the burning question, isn't it? What am I supposed to say to that? I drop my freezing cold hands in my lap.

Am I okay?" I stare into space, unfocused. "Well, let me see…" I close my sightless eyes in an endeavour to form the right words.

My boyfriend has just informed me that he's a hit-man," I know this isn't strictly true, but I'm paraphrasing, "the job I have is fake because apparently the man I love runs a clandestine business, tracking down bad guys and bringing them to justice. I'm incriminated in a murder in Paris, just because I happened to be present at the time. There's a trial by a clandestine jury of someone who is deemed to be guilty even if they were found innocent. And the father of my children turns out to be the faceless, unknown final piece of the jigsaw linking it all together. And on top of that; your best friend calls you *'Black Tudor'*. What's that all about?" The last bit I added for good measure.

I'm enjoying my rant; it's cathartic but it still leaves a myriad of unanswered questions; questions which are flooding my brain at a rate of knots and threatening to send me crazy. I'm unable to keep pace.

Silas tilts his head, mulling over my proclamation as if he's deciding which shirt to wear today. "Succinctly put," he nods, "however, there were a few elements missing in that assessment."

"Would you like to elaborate? Which bits did I miss? That I was deceived from the start… there you go… how about that?"

"Will you just calm down? You promised not to freak out." He moves so he's sitting on the desk in front of me, effectively locking me in place in my chair.

I'm not going to flee; for one thing, I don't have the strength to stand up, let alone bolt, but Silas seems to think this is a good move on his part.

"Up until a couple of months ago, we had no idea who the mystery man was. He was illusive, skilled at deception and remained invisible to our investigation." I must admit, that does sound like Bobby, he was certainly skilled at deception.

"We knew about Adrax. We'd managed to open a dialogue with Django. Christina posed as a scout from a rival agency and approached her directly. It was a risk, because we knew Adrax watched her like a hawk. She and Liam were his top models, the main event, the real thing. With the media focussed on them, it meant he could hover in the background and his illegal business dealings were concealed.

"After we disposed of 'car-boot' man, or Waylon Price - we finally knew the connection to the UK division, but frustratingly we couldn't infiltrate deeply enough to find the missing piece. We needed to know who was number one; who was in control."

"Bobby?" I know he had ambition, but this?

"Yes. Eventually there was a call. It came to Adrax's phone. With assistance from Django, we'd managed to hack into his line and place a trace on all his calls. That's how the French Gendarmes caught him. However, we still needed proof of the UK arm."

"Adrax was becoming careless. He thought he was so well respected, nobody would believe the horror stories if they came out, and he was proved right in his assumption. He was eventually arrested and put on trial in France. Gerard attended the hearing. The jury was unconvinced. They didn't believe the evidence and delivered a unanimous verdict of not-guilty."

"We had to act. We had no choice but to convene *The Rose Council* and review the trial. It was a travesty. The judge wouldn't hear testimony from the under-aged kids, saying they would be unreliable as witnesses. Django's statement was disregarded because she was, to all intent and purposes, his daughter, and the judge refused to hear it on those grounds."

"When Adrax went free, we knew it would only be a matter of time before Django and Liam turned up dead. It would be made to look like a double suicide, of course – the distraught children – he had the manpower."

"We had to act. Paris Fashion Week was our chance and we took it."

"Where does Bobby fit in to all of this?" I'm still confused.

"When Adrax was arrested, Price didn't for a minute think he'd be found innocent. He expected Adrax to be imprisoned for a long, long time; life in France means life. As you know, his ego knows no bounds." Silas looks at me for validation and I nod in agreement. This is true, Bobby is nothing if not confident.

But his arrogance made him sloppy. He saw it as an opportunity to stake his claim on the remaining business. With his own father gone, he was the newer, younger protégé. All he was doing was biding his time to strike, and with Adrax out of the picture, he jumped at it. However, in his haste to overthrow the King, the Jester inadvertently revealed his hand. His big mistake was making direct contact with Django and offering her a place in the new structure. Once he did that, we had him – finally we knew the leader of the UK division."

"So, you knew who he was all along?"

"After the trial, yes."

"Before Paris?"

"Yes… and this is the bit where you rip my head off; because we've always known who you were too. That's why you got the job. That's why we needed you. Edi, baby… it was no coincidence your professor recommended you apply for a position with us. We needed you to flush him out."

NO… I press my back into the chair, retreating and shaking my head.

"We knew, once you were working here, he wouldn't be able to resist approaching you. He hates to lose. And you were the one that got away."

I'm dumbfounded. The revelation hits me like a sledgehammer; unable to digest it all, I sit in a catatonic stupor, staring at the wall.

"Edi? Did you hear me… Edi… baby?" His arms lift to embrace me. The subtle movement startling me back to life. All along, I was nothing but… *bait?*

"Don't *fucking* touch me… leave me alone!" I screech. My focus has returned, and with it an abundance of humiliation like I've never experienced before. All the information I've been hit with has bombarded my brain like a scattergun; infiltrating the corners of my mind with shards of silver bullets. But the one stark reality I'm finding the most abhorrent is I was deceived.

"I mean it Silas... if you lay one hand on me... I'll... I'll..." I don't know what I'll do, but it will be violent.

My hysterical screams, ricochet off the walls, echoing through the office. The sheer volume brings Bear careering into the room, flying to my defence.

In his haste to protect me he leaps at Silas, snarling and growling, hackles raised. His crazed attack on his master stuns us both in to silence. Only when I stop screaming, does Bear back down.

Silas has retreated from my personal space; the opening allows Bear to stand guard before me; effectively shielding me from Silas. I'm in no doubt where his loyalties lie; with the person who needs protection, and in his opinion, at this moment in time, that's me.

I can't believe you lied to me," I hiss as I sit, poker-straight, trembling from head to foot and reeling in indignation at the sheer callous audacity. "You purposely lured me into this false relationship."

"No... Edi, it really wasn't like that."

"Yes, it was... what else could it be? You must think I'm so naïve. You used me!"

They did. They must have thought I was such a soft target. Pliable enough and weak enough to be manipulated into doing whatever was required to flush Bobby out of the woodwork. "It must have been a dream come true when you found me!"

"It was... it is... but not in the way you think." His voice is rasping with raw emotion. "You *are* a dream come true. An impossible dream. I can't lose you."

"You should have thought about that before you tricked me into loving you." My tears are scalding my face, my freezing hands a true indication of my state of mind. "You deceived me in the worst way. I was as much a target as those people on the wall." I point towards the locked room. "I may not have a gun to my head, or a red line through my picture, but that's where I belong... on that wall!" I feel violated. "I love you; but how can I forgive you?" There, I've said it. It's the truth. I can't forgive him for using me.

"Edi... please!" he too is crying. This man who is fearless in the face of unimaginable levels of danger is crying. "I can't lose you." He repeats.

"I know..." The situation is impossible, I need him and he needs me, but if this is the level of deception which is going to define our relationship and dictate our lives, then we can't be together. It's destructive on an atomic scale.

"I love you!"

"I know..."

"Call him off." He asks softly. "He won't disengage fully until you call him off."

"Bear, still..." I give him the command to withdraw and he visibly retreats in deference to my order.

Dropping his head, Bear looks towards me, his sixth sense ensuring I'm alright, before he eventually takes a step towards his master; leaning his head in Silas's outstretched palm, a gesture of submission and forgiveness.

"Good boy." Silas fusses over the dog, praising him for doing his job – protecting me.

"I don't know what to do," I say as I watch the unconditional affection which flows between them.

"You'll stay. You can't leave me." The matter-of-fact way he says it is far from the outward display of uncertainty betrayed in the set of his shoulders. "You can't leave me... not now I've found you."

"I don't know what to do," I repeat. I truly don't know.

"We'll figure it out." He sounds so sure.

"How? How are you so sure? How can we figure this out?" I'm exhausted just thinking about it.

Suddenly the fatigue engulfs me. I'm shattered. Managing for a second to look out of the window, I see its night-time. The sky is dark. I have no idea where the time has gone.

I look at my watch. The beautiful watch he bought me in Paris; it's stunning, but the sentiment behind the gift is now marred by the knowledge it may have been given to lure me into a false state of compliance. "It's late." I say on a sigh. "I'm very tired."

"I'll take you home." Making to rise, he stands before me, the Grecian godlike creature he is.

I shake my head as it fills with the many images it holds of him. All the beautiful images of my Boss-man in all his imperfect perfection. I'll never forget them.

"Remember when I said, I would still want this? Even when I'm old and fat and it takes me hours to pee?" he draws the sincere words from my memory and I scoff sadly. "I do... I still do... and I always will. I love you... you're my life."

I hear him. "And you're mine too... but all this... it's a lot to digest. I need to sleep on it... Christ... I need a week to sleep on it!" But I doubt if a year's worth of oblivion will be enough to get my head round all of this hurt. "Take me home." I whisper as I stand, willing my weary legs to carry me out of the office.

The look on his face is one of great relief. I don't know why. He hasn't heard the last of this. The only reason I'm acquiescing now is because I'm so exhausted.

We exit the office and walk through the hangar in a veiled silence, which is unusual for us. Both of us are reluctant to strike up a conversation, preferring to err on the side of caution, should we inadvertently trigger another inflammatory outburst.

"Where do you want me to take you?" He's giving me an option to escape his presence.

"I'm fine with the barn – thank you." I add as an afterthought. I don't want him to think I need to avoid him. "I'll be more able to think without Sam and Lizzy in the way; and anyhow, I don't want them to know... ever! And I think if I went to the apartment now, I wouldn't be able to keep this to myself."

"Edi..."

"No; Silas please. Just give me some time to get my head around this."

"Just remember, whatever you decide, I love you."

He isn't making this easy, it's bad enough he's a... I can't bring myself to use the word, murderer, but he is; and that's without the confessed disclosure and devastating truth that our meeting was contrived from the outset.

As the drive home progresses, I allow the sway of the vehicle to lull me into a light subconscious slumber. I can't fully rest but I close my eyes against the night's black, preferring the darkness of my own thoughts.

"How did you know? How did you find me?" I ask eventually.

"I recognised you as soon as I saw you," he answers honestly. I have my eyes closed, but in my minds-eye, I know by his tone, there's a trace of a smile on his mouth.

"When? Where did you see me?" Resting my head against the seat, I allow my eyes to open a fraction and I squint over at him. My head is so heavy, I can barely move it.

"The first time I saw you was at The Beeches. You were in the garden and you were laughing with David over something. It was the day Christina and I were viewing the facilities for suitability for Nic... and there you were; I couldn't believe it. You looked so beautiful that day."

"You recognised me?" This is unnerving. I didn't think anybody recognised me from my old glamour days. I look nothing like that now. "But I've changed so much."

"You may have changed, but you're still the most beautiful woman I've ever seen. I'd recognise you anywhere."

"Oh!" Was he a fan?

"You don't get it do you? We knew we needed to find you, but it was impossible. You'd done a really great job of disappearing you know?" His smile is back; is he impressed?

"I meant to. I couldn't risk Bobby finding us. I thought it was all in the past. It was years and years ago." I still can't believe he recognised me.

"I was there, with Christina, just mooching around the place. I heard someone laughing outside and it caught my attention. I looked out of the window, and there you were. Call it fate, or kismet or a coincidence; call it whatever you wish, but there you were. After all these years of searching, you just fell into my life."

"So that was it?"

"That was it. After speaking to Mark - and before you go getting him sacked - he was discreet and didn't give away much detail, we knew you were attending Uni' and your chosen field of study fitted perfectly. We had no need to engineer a meeting."

"But you did. You fabricated the whole job thing, didn't you?"

"Only insofar as we decided to employ you; the role was real enough. The interview was real too."

"I got the job." From one online interview! Now it makes sense.

"You were uncontested... it was never in doubt."

"Huh! I was the only applicant you mean!" It's easier to be successful if your only opponent is yourself.

"We needed you. But the fact you were completely qualified and perfect for the position was an added bonus," he says honestly. "Seriously, I could not have prepared my heart for the moment I walked through those doors and there you were; looking beautiful and flustered. I'll never forget the flush in your cheeks. My heart exploded. I couldn't breathe. I'm sure you noticed?"

"I just thought you were an arrogant arse. You were very rude and abrupt."

"Didn't you at least think I was a decent looking bloke?" He's grinning now. I suspect the direction of the conversation has eased his mind somewhat.

"Decent... yeah, you were okay." Lord have mercy! The memory of that first unforgettable meeting washes over me like a warm breeze. He was magnificent – still is.

"Edi. I'll never be able to apologise enough for what we did; how we deceived you. I see now how ruthless and dispassionate it was. We were wrong to treat you so dismissively. Never once did we take your feelings into the equation; we were so wrong." He's ashamed, and so he should be.

"But you still did it…" I whisper, closing my eyes against the hurt. "I'm not saying, I'll never trust you again, or even that I don't trust you now…" even as I say this, I realise the trust is still there; I'd trust him with my life. "It's just… a lot to come to terms with." I let the bland statement speak for itself.

"I know, but please believe me when I tell you… everything I've ever said about the way I feel about you is the whole truth. I said I love you and I mean it."

I don't want to be distracted by his sweet talk so I divert the conversation to the current matter in hand. "Why does Gerard call you Black Tudor?"

"He doesn't."

"But I've heard him. Several times in fact." I swivel in my car seat; I know what I heard.

"Tueur Noir?" he says it, using the same inflection as Gerard.

"Yes, that's it."

"It means *'Black Killer'*, it's an in joke."

I'm appalled. "Well, it's not very funny!" I exclaim. "It's a horrid thing to call someone!"

"Ha, don't be offended on my behalf." We pull into the driveway of the barn. Silas stops the car and turns to face me. "I call him much, much worse."

"What on earth could be worse than being called a *black killer*? It sounds like you specialise in murdering… well… black people!" It's horrible.

"No, it doesn't mean that. Look at me, it's a joke. I'm black and I'm a killer – and Tueur is very similar to Tudor – it fooled you."

"It's still horrid," I shudder. I'll never accept the label. "Tell him I don't like it and never to use it when I'm around." He salutes his agreement. "And anyway, what could you possibly call him that's worse?"

"Renard Sournois," he growls, wiggling his eyebrows, as if I'm supposed to understand. "It means Sly Fox. He's sly like a fox, and the word's assonance to Gerard; Renard, Gerard, see? – they sound similar – he quite likes it."

I shake my head in distain. "Never in my company!" I affirm. The way these people address each other; it's disrespectful.

Reaching for the door handle, I pull, but it slips from my tired grasp. "Ouch!"

"Here, stay put, I'll come get you." He's out of the car in a second, rounding the vehicle and opening my door. "Give me your hand," he offers.

Tentatively, I place my small hand in his, it's the first time we've touched since he carried me from the strong room.

The sizzle is instantaneous. A jolt of electricity runs up my arm and slams into my heart as if I've been shocked by a defibrillator.

My feet slam onto the gravel; I lift my eyes to his. Yes, he felt it too. There's no denying it. That irrefutable fizzing of static, which flows between us when we're close.

Again, I shake my head. Looking down at my shoes I force myself to leave the relative security of the Range Rover. I know this discussion isn't over; but for tonight, I just want to close my eyes and sleep.

"I need to go to bed," I mutter, walking by him and up to the front door. Fishing in my bag, I find the loose key Christina gave me, and let myself in. I'm so weary, I barely notice Bear skirting his way around me and into the kitchen.

Slowly I climb the stairs. Entering the bedroom, I kick off my shoes and pull my shirt over my head. I can't be bothered to remove anything else, I'm too exhausted. Throwing open the duvet, I climb in and bury my head beneath the pillow. I'm asleep before Silas enters the room.

CHAPTER 46

Birdsong filters into my ears, gently urging me awake. Reaching my arms above my head I stretch out in the bed. The knots in my spine crack as they mobilise and my muscles ache from a lack of movement in the night. It must have been a very deep sleep.

Turning on to my side, I find I'm alone. Shaking the cotton wool from my fuzzy head, I check the time; Seven am.

Sitting up, I spy a customary mug of hot, very strong, builder's tea waiting on the bedside table. I swing my legs off the bed and use my toes to seek my slippers, which are hiding under the cupboard. Sliding my feet into them, I pick up my mug and take a sip. The tea is almost teak in colour and I can smell the bitterness of the tannin before it even hits my taste buds. "Mmmm," I sigh in deep appreciation.

Hearing the mumble of muted voices coming from the rooms downstairs, I can only assume it's the TV or the radio. I stare around the bedroom, unwilling to move and start the day. One thing is for sure, I'm certainly in no hurry to face Silas.

Yesterday was one of the worst days of my life. Insofar as bad days are measured, it is currently riding high in the charts and is number two on the hit parade of bad days; second only to my failed suicide attempt all those years ago. That dark reminder causes a shudder to run through me; my body involuntarily cools at the chilling recall. It feels like it's going to be another hideous day and I'm barely out of bed.

Everything I've discovered seems surreal. Emotionally I have no notion how this will affect me and I can't for the life of me, see how to begin processing all I've learned.

The only way to approach this is by breaking it down into bite-sized portions, small enough to digest, methodically dealing with one problem at a time. And the first problem being; what the fuck am I going to do today?

"Good morning."

I look up from where I've been focussing on my slippers. Apparently, they're the most intriguing thing I've seen in ages. They must be, because it's now 7:28am and I've been rooted in the same place in the bedroom, holding my empty mug and staring at my feet for nearly half an hour!

"Oh, hi," I blink as I realise it's Christina and not Silas who's come to wake me.

"So, how're you this glorious day?" Marching by me, she flings open the curtains revealing what is, indeed, a glorious day. "Edi? I said how are you this morning?"

"Oh... yeah, fine," I answer, not really sure how I am. Several words spring to mind, like, stunned... bemused... suspicious... doubtful... foolish ... suckered... idiot... all of the above frankly, but I stick to fine, knowing if I open the floodgate of feelings now, I'll never close it.

"Well, tomorrow's the big day!" she says, as if yesterday wasn't just so damn peachy!

"What do you mean... big day?" My interest is piqued, even though I don't want it to be... and anyway... where does she get off acting all bright and breezy like yesterday didn't happen?

"We need to prepare for your interview." She flashes her beaming pearly whites at me, as if butter wouldn't melt.

Oh, I can't deal with her!

"I'm going for a shower," I say as I pass her my empty mug, and stomp out of the bedroom. Perhaps a blast of hot water will wash the scales from my eyes and allow me to approach today with clearer vision.

Standing under the searing jets, I certainly feel better. I allow the healing water to pummel my skin, massaging my shoulders and easing my aching muscles.

I take my time, washing and conditioning my hair, until the water begins to run cold and I can stand it no more.

Swathing my head in a towel, I pat myself dry, then rub in a couple of layers of body lotion, before pulling on my fluffy purple dressing gown. I don't bother getting dressed. I just traipse downstairs with every intention of making my second brew of the day and disappearing into my bedroom for a good long sulk.

But I don't get very far with my plan. Christina is sitting at the kitchen table, seemingly engrossed with a mass of files and a pile of paperwork spread out before her.

On hearing me, she lifts her head. "Ah, nice of you to join me," she remarks with some sarcasm. "I thought for a minute there, you'd given up."

"Why would you think that," I answer, sliding into the chair opposite. There's no point in pretending, I do feel like giving up. I don't know why they need me to go through with the whole charade now they finally have the proof they've been seeking.

Sighing, Christina looks at me reproachfully. "Edi, I'm sorry you had to find out about us the way you did. Silas had no right really, we…"

I cut her off. "Where is Silas?" I had a belly full of sorry yesterday; I don't need her bleating on about how sorry she is too. It won't wash.

"He's at the airfield," she replies. "He wasn't sure how to deal… approach… he…"

This makes a change… Christina lost for words. I use her light fluster to my advantage; I'm not prepared to let this opportunity escape. "Why, what's he afraid of? Does he think I'll reveal your 'operation'? Is he scared I'll still be angry with him?"

I rise from my chair, making a show of filling the kettle, slamming on the tap so violently, the pressure of the water hits the sink and flies back up into my face, soaking the front of my dressing gown in the process. Thrusting the kettle under the deluge, I slow the flow of water to a more acceptable level, ignoring the fact I'm now drenched. "He should be concerned," I snap.

"He is," she responds, picking up a pot towel, and handing it to me.

"Thank you…" I wipe my face and brush the front of my robe. "Do you have any idea how it makes me feel?"

"No." She's nothing if not honest.

"I can't even begin to describe it." I turn to face her, my fist digging into my hip. "It was like a knife in my heart." I go on, "I know I'm nothing… a nobody, but you can't expect to treat people this way and not live to face the consequences. You hurt me…"

"I know," her expression is soft, "and if I could take it back I would; but I can't."

259

Rising from her chair, she approaches the boiling kettle. Taking down two mugs from the cup holder, she scoops four large heaps of coffee into the cafetiere then pours on the water. She seems tense.

Finally, she speaks. "And you're wrong... you aren't a nobody," she says softly.

Leaving the coffee to brew, she turns and leans her lower back against the worktop. "You mean so much to me, you know."

"You have a funny way of showing it." I fold my arms across my chest. I'm not ready to relent.

"I know, but you do... I don't have many female friends. I'd like to think you and I are now far more than work colleagues." She turns and places her hand on the plunger, forcing it down. "I know it didn't start out that way... but you know more about me than anyone; other than my family... and Silas, of course." She pours the coffee. "I don't want to lose that. And Silas loves you... I mean he *really* loves you. As in unquenchable love. He's *madly* in love with you, and I've never seen him this way, Edi... ever.".

"I know that too." The feelings mutual. But it's devastating to hear the hint of sadness in her voice; sadness because he never quite felt the same way about her.

"Look, I know I can come across as cold and calculating. And it's hardly surprising, because I am... cold and calculating I mean." Walking to the refrigerator she removes the milk and splashes it into the coffee. "I struggle with closeness. Since... losing Maya, I..." she visibly wilts, "I find it more tolerable if I don't have relationships complicated by feelings." The softer demeanour doesn't last, however. Quickly recovering her composure, she continues. "But I do care about you and I do care deeply about Silas."

"What about Johannes?" I remember the tall blonde handsome man she introduced me to as her lover. "Don't you care for him?"

"Edi," she passes me a coffee cup, "Johannes is a lovely man. We have an understanding and it works... and besides, he's married."

"What?" I nearly choke on my coffee. "Seriously... you're having an affair?"

"I'd hardly call it that. We barely talk unless it's about business. It is what it is. We give each other comfort when required, but yes, I suppose it could be classed as an affair; but it's all out in the open. We don't hide anything. His wife knows and she's fine with it."

I doubt that!

"She's an acquaintance of mine and we share similar views. She has lovers and Johannes has me... and I have him." Blinking her eyes several times, the involuntary flutter of her eyelashes betrays her. She doesn't fool me, I know she has deep feelings for him, but she'll never dare admit it. "In all honesty, the only person I truly love is Nic." She says it meaningfully. "It's easier to be a heartless bitch. It makes me better at business."

"You mean, better at making tough decisions... regardless of whether it could really crush someone," I correct. I have no doubt she wants to shield herself from the truth, and appear ruthless, but I don't buy the veneer.

"It's all bullshit, Christina," I say, deciding to call her out. "You want the world to believe you're the epitome of the successful business woman. Calm, collected and steadfast, completely unaffected by stress. And to everyone around you, you are. You're amazing. A workaholic. But I know differently. This granite exterior you portray so effortlessly is beginning to crumble. It's exactly what it seems, it's nothing but rendering.

It's all fake, an act. A shield against being hurt again. I know you better than you think. I know you have a huge capacity to love and I know you feel things. You couldn't be the woman you are if you didn't."

Her shoulders sag a little. She looks at me through her lowered lashes, she knows I have the measure of her. "Well… there's the surprise… you do know me after all," she smiles softly in defeat. "Just promise me one thing," she raises her cup and takes a sip of coffee, "keep it under your hat, I'd hate them to think I had a soft centre."

"I promise. I won't tell anybody how loveable you really are. As far as the world's concerned, you're a Hazelnut Whirl. If they find out you're really the Silky Caramel, it won't be from me." I smile at her with a new found fondness.

"You know, I think you're my new best friend," she says. "Cheers, and here's to girlfriends… you and me."

"You and me," I echo. I have to admit having a girlfriend would be nice. I think of the bond between Sam and Lizzy and smile. Yes, I quite approve of the idea of having a girlfriend all of my own. And Christina is available for the position. And besides, I really do like her; even with her contrary ways and scary attitude. Perhaps today won't be as bad as I thought.

I've written off going into the office. A quick phone call with Susan confirmed everything is under control and I'm not required on site. If they have an emergency, they'll ring. Anyway, Silas is there and he managed long before I appeared, so a couple of days absence isn't going to matter.

After I got dressed, we brewed another pot of coffee and headed into the garden to mull over the details for my interview tomorrow.

The schedule is strict and the timeslot allocated is between the hourly headline update and the daily sport feature. It's the slot usually held for celebrity gossip and common interest stories. I've been given ten minutes, which sounds like plenty enough to me. I just want to get in there, say 'no comment' and get the Hell out.

The interview should be informative, by filling in the missing blanks, yet tedious enough for the press to consider me as a nonentity, and thus hopefully leave me alone.

However, I don't see hope alone as a good enough strategy, so we agree some forward planning would not go amiss. Last thing we want is to be caught off guard by any out of left field questions.

So, the main approach is to get in, say as little as possible, closing them down by either agreeing to their assumptions, where it suits us, or giving them a simple yes or no answer. In other words, a classic Meg Ryan style interview! Basically, sound dull, reveal little and leave them wondering why they bothered in the first place.

If things take an unexpected turn, I should then, and only then, divert the conversation towards Bobby. We've agreed, now *The Rose Council* has the physical evidence they need to go and engage with the legitimate authorities, there's no need to rake up any dirt on National TV, if I can get through it without doing so.

The facts are simple; I was a glamour model, then a mother, and I wanted to change my lifestyle. I needed to get out of the business so I left – end of.

Christina has chosen my outfit. A pale blue Ted Baker midi-dress. No frills or fuss, just a beautiful light blue silk, that matches my eyes and sets off perfectly the colour of my hair. I've asked Morgan if he'll pop round first thing to blow dry it and Angie will manicure my nails and tidy my eyebrows. The studio insisted on their own make-up artist as the TV lighting can be harsh, so expertly applied foundation is a must.

As the day marches on, I can't help but wonder if I'm being coddled in some way; as if the revelations of yesterday have deemed I require kid-glove treatment.

The interview strategy hasn't taken long to prepare, and the beauty arrangements were no more than a five-minute phone call to the salon. Now I'm wondering if I should show willing and head to the airfield for the rest of the afternoon; even if it's only to clear my emails. I'm beginning to feel restless just vegging out here in the garden.

"Well," Christina leans back in her chair. Folding over the cover of the large notebook she's been using to keep track of our plans; she reaches over her head and stretches. "I think we deserve a break." Glancing at her Breitling, she raises her eyebrows at the time. "Pigs in space!" Employing her unique expression, she smiles broadly at me. "It's two o'clock, so you know what that means?"

"We've missed lunch?" I say, grinning back at her.

"It means, it's seven o'clock... somewhere," she drops her arms and pushes back from the table. "I'm having a glass of wine. Would you like one?"

"Why the Hell not." A glass of chilled wine in the sunny afternoon would be most welcome. Perhaps I won't bother going to the office after all. I'll stay here and get pissed instead, with my new best girlfriend.

"I'm going for some fresh air," she announces, grabbing her pack of cigarettes. "The wine is on ice in the fridge. Large glasses please!"

While I find the wine, I can see Christina through the kitchen window. She's speaking on her mobile as she indulges in her 'fresh air'. Drawing deeply on her cigarette, she blows out a stream of blue smoke before absently kicking one of Bear's tennis balls she'd spied lurking in the uncut grass.

Keeping one eye on Christina, I locate the corkscrew and uncork the bottle. I know Christina can exist on fresh air and alcohol, but I can't. I need sustenance so I cut a chunk of bread and slather it with butter. Slicing a wedge of cheese, I place it on one half of the bread, then fold the other side over, creating a doorstep sandwich. That should be substantial enough to see me through until dinner time and the bread will help soak up the wine.

I head out into the garden, carrying two wine glasses in one hand, the bottle of wine in the other and the huge sandwich clenched between my teeth.

As I approach, Christina ends her call, and drops the cigarette stub on the ground, stepping on it to put it out. When she sees me, her brow furrows in distaste at the sight of the giant cheese sandwich gritted between my teeth, but she doesn't comment.

"Let me help you." Taking the bottle from my hand, she leaves me free to take an almighty bite and remove the offending bread from my lips.

Oh, that's good! Crusty bread, butter and cheese... delicious.

"That was Silas on the phone," she says as she pours the wine. "He's running late, but he asked me to tell you he'd pick up a takeaway on his way home."

"Why didn't he ring me himself?" I wonder out loud. "Why did he call you?"

Christina hesitates, her wine hovering in front of her lips. "He wasn't sure you'd want to speak to him, after… you know…" she gestures with her glass, "yesterday." She takes a sip and closes her eyes. "Mmmm, that's good."

"Why would he think that? I mean, we came back here together – I was tired, but we weren't arguing." I'm puzzled. I know I still need to get things straight in my head, but after a good night's sleep, and a day with Christina, the impact of yesterday's discovery has faded somewhat. It's still there, but the distractions Christina has presented seem to have worked. I'm no longer obsessing over the events.

"He was worried you would still be in shock and thought if he left you alone to mull it over, you'd be able to come to terms with things better."

"So, what you really mean is, he was checking up on me and was too much of a chicken to ring me himself?" This should make me angry, but strangely, for some bizarre reason, I find it oddly endearing. He's worried I'd be angry with him. "Is he afraid of me?" I blurt the question out before I can apply my filter. "Bloody Hell! He is… isn't he… he's afraid of me?"

"It's more he's afraid of what you'll do rather than physically afraid of you, per se." She lights another cigarette.

I observe her closely, she never usually smokes more than one or two a day. She's now lit up another, only minutes after stubbing out the first. "What?" Catching me looking at her, she picks up her glass and takes a drink.

"Oh, nothing," I smile. I do believe she's a little scared of me too. This is an interesting twist. "So why do you think he's afraid of me?" If I ask in this way, I may be able to fathom out why both of them seem to have developed this sudden concern.

She takes another deep drag. "I told you. He's worried you'll do something rash," she answers vaguely.

"Like what?" I have her on the ropes and I'm not relenting. I need to understand why they feel like this; not to mention the sudden realization they've obviously discussed it…well, me. That thought ruffles my feathers. "Christina, I don't like being the subject of a private discussion. If you've been talking about me, I want to know what about," I assert myself. "Tell me… now!"

"It's this," she gestures with her cigarette, "this way you have of flipping from calm, to hissy-fit in a split second. We don't know how to deal with it and when you're in this volatile mood, we don't know what you're going to do next."

I'm floored. They are afraid of me. Moreover, they're afraid of what I'll do now I have the full picture.

Standing, I watch Christina slump in defeat. Dropping into her chair, she looks deflated, beaten. "We're concerned you'll be so disappointed, you'll… I don't know… do something."

"Like what?" This is rich. What can I do?

"I don't know… tell someone… blurt it out on the telly. You weren't supposed to know the details of the operation until after your interview. The plan was to explain everything then. But now you know, were worried it will all come out on National TV."

I laugh, it's insane. "Why would I do that?" Seriously! "I have much more to lose than you do. At least you're working for the Government, albeit clandestine, what you do is endorsed by the authorities in some way. The country already thinks I'm a nutjob who went missing and has resurfaced after all these years. Can you imagine what they'd think if I started spouting off about my boyfriend and his ex-wife being undercover assassins; I'd be straight down the loony bin." It's ridiculous. "They'd lock me up and throw away the key and Bobby would get his dearest wish."

"And what's that?" she looks really concerned now.

"His daughter," I say with conviction. "Christina, to you I may look like a crazy woman who can't control her emotions. I might flit from mild mannered to screaming banshee, but believe me, this is normal for most women who have endured an abusive relationship and are protecting their children. Remember when Nic was on the treadmill? What did you fear?"

Her face drops and her brow puckers at the recollection of her poor boy; pounding away, unable to thwart the uncontrollable urge to run.

"That he wouldn't stop. That he would have a seizure, that he would end up in a coma." She looks at the ground. All the pent-up agony she must endure on a daily basis, rushes to the surface, threatening to break through the tough shell. "That he'd die," she whispers the last words as a solitary tear rolls down her cheek.

Finally, she gets it. "Exactly, and that is what I've feared every day for the last nineteen years. I know what Bobby is capable of. I know he only wants Lizzy for one reason. He doesn't love her. He doesn't even *know* her, and he certainly doesn't understand what it is to be a father. All he wants is a fresh, beautiful face to add to his brimming portfolio of beautiful faces. And now I know the true depth of his depravity, it just compounds the issue."

Pausing briefly, I continue. "I'm terrified, and we all know how he treats the things that belong to him. I'd never disclose your operation because the one thing I can't risk is not being here for my children. Bobby would disown David, and abuse Lizzy and I can't... won't allow that to happen. I'll die before I let him near them."

Taking a healing gulp of wine, I drop into the chair beside Christina. The revelation scares me too much. "You see, my children are my world. If they were taken away from me, I don't know what I'd do. You of all people should understand. I'm in awe of you. You're so strong Christina. In your shoes, I think I would have been driven crazy by now."

Christina straightens her back. Looking at the lengthening ash on the tip of her cigarette, she flicks it off and drops the spent filter onto the floor before picking up the carton and lighting yet another smoke. "I'm not that strong," she exhales a blue plume. "When we lost Maya, I wanted to die. I didn't have the guts to do it or I swear, I wouldn't be here today. The only thing that stopped me, was the knowledge that Nic needed me."

She pours us both more wine. "It's ironic. The one thing that kept me alive was the one thing I was afraid I'd lose. I even contemplated putting us both out of our misery." Her eyes are moist as she nods her acceptance.

"That's how deep my depression was. But I was lucky, I had Silas and he took control of everything. It meant I was able to grieve properly. He put his own grief on hold so he could support me through mine." She draws deeply on the cigarette, clearly the memory of her recovery still raw.

"I dealt with my loss. I had years of counselling – still do in fact. Silas swallowed his anguish. Kept hold of it, clung on to it like a talisman. He grew bitter; became bent on revenge. A hallow man, incapable of affection for anything or anyone other than his son, or that damn dog. The wall he built around him was impenetrable. He was stone cold. It ended our marriage. He wouldn't get help. He just threw himself into work. He became vengeful, heartless and uncaring."

It's unbearable to hear. The man I love was hurting so insufferably, he became buried beneath an avalanche of unimaginable torture. The only way he could deal with it was through vengeance and retribution. In his battle to right the wrongs of the world, be was destroying his own humanity.

"*The Rose Council* became his anchorage, his reason for existing. I say existing because that's all it was. He didn't live. He filled his time seeking out the depraved and the corrupt and eliminating them from society. That's not living," she lights another cigarette from the stub of the last. She's really going for it today. "As the aviation business flourished, *The Rose Council* also established its reputation. We are good at what we do; in both areas. Silas was especially good at it. There were times I half expected him to drop the flying altogether and concentrate solely on the... on... well you know on what. He was descending deeper and deeper into a very dark pit... and then you arrived."

CHAPTER 47

As the light begins to fade, I stroll around the garden searching for the innumerable cigarette dimps hidden in the stubbly grass where Christina stomped them out.

She's chain-smoked most of the afternoon and divulged some pretty undisguised truths about the past and her uncertainties for the future. Her opening up to me as she did, revealing her vulnerable side, has wiped her out and after finishing the last of the wine and smoking one final cigarette, she called a taxi to take her home.

It's great to finally know you have a confidant you can pour your heart out to and they won't judge you, but it's a new and raw experience for us both and while productive and informative, today has proved quite draining in its intensity.

"Woof!" a familiar bark fills the silence, and immediately my heart lifts as a very waggy-tailed Bear appears, charging around the side of the house, his one mission, seeking me out. "Woof, woof, woof!" he shouts, as he dances around me in excitement.

I love his greetings, and after shoving the collected cigarette ends into my pocket, I drop to my knees in gratitude, only too willing to give him a huge fuss.

"Hello, beautiful boy... I missed you too," I coo as I rub him all over. His silky fur is heated to the touch, I suspect from being in the confines of the Range Rover. "Would you like a drink? Hmmm, I bet you would... I bet you would..."

Releasing Bear, who wanders off to his outside water bowl, I rise slowly to my feet. My heart, previously skipping in joy at seeing Bear, slows to a different familiar rhythm at the sight of Silas. A rhythm which reverberates into every nerve; a resounding pulse I feel throughout my body ending at a deep quickening inside my core. Oh, this man is so bloody handsome.

We stand quietly, neither of us prepared to look away; as if doing so would cause the other to disappear into a puff of smoke, never to be seen again.

A light breeze, absent for most of the afternoon, picks up and ruffles my hair, fanning it across my face and into my eyes. Lifting my hand to brush it away, I'm beaten to it, as Silas gently strokes the wayward tresses from my cheek.

"You look beautiful," he whispers, his tone low and rich. "Come inside."

I don't speak to him, choosing to acknowledge his request by slowly moving beyond his reach and stepping by him in the direction of the house. I'm aware he's following me. I can feel his eyes bore into my back.

"Edi?" I'm unable to resist him. Halting, I turn to face him, waiting, pensive. "Don't shut me out."

"What do you want me to say?" I shrug my shoulders; I really have no clue what to say to him.

"I'm s...."

"Stop!" Holding my palm so it's level with his lips, I silence him. "Don't say it." He knows I hate *'sorry'*; a trite word covering a multitude of guilt - used as a salve and applied to appease any situation from spilled milk to a black eye - bringing little solace, it means nothing to me. "I know what you're going to say... but... just don't. Okay?"

"Okay... but Edi... I..." the words die on his lips. There's no other term he can think of to apologise for the situation.

"Did you bring food?" I remember Christina mentioning a takeaway and I'm suddenly starving.

"Chinese," he points towards the kitchen, "if Bear hasn't nicked it." It's his attempt to thaw the atmosphere and I'm grateful for it.

"Well, we'd better get in there before he helps himself to the crispy noodles, hadn't we?" Turning on my heels, I continue to the house, Silas following in my wake.

We arrive in the kitchen in the nick of time. Bear has his front paws on the oak table and is sniffing eagerly at the brown paper carrier.

"Er... excuse me?" Silas gives him the beady eye, and Bear reluctantly drops down, sulking at being caught in the act of such blatant thievery. "I should think so..." Silas admonishes as Bear, tail between his legs in doggy embarrassment, crawls into his basket, demonstrating puppy-dog eyes to perfection and the 'starving canine' act to a tee. "You can forget it, mate. You've let yourself down big-time. You're on the Kibble and biscuits."

Knowing when he's beaten, Bear yawns exaggeratedly on a whine and drops his head to his paws; never once taking his eyes off the brown paper bag.

"What did you get?" It smells fantastic. I don't blame Bear for succumbing to his doggy instincts.

"Beef in black bean sauce, chicken and broccoli in oyster sauce and a special fried rice," he says whilst lifting each foil container out of the bag.

The smell intensifies, and Bear sits up in his basket, ears pricked, paying close attention and licking his lips. "No," Silas informs him. Drawing a huge bark of protest and an annoyed growl from the normally placid dog. "He's impossible," he says. "I had to strap him into the back seat otherwise he'd have stolen it and scoffed the lot before I got it home!"

"WOOF!" Bear argues back.

"What's that?" Another bag has appeared alongside the others.

"Spring Rolls." He empties the bag onto a plate revealing four giant, crispy, golden pieces of yumminess! "Want one?"

"Ummm, yes please." Picking one of the steaming rolls off the plate, I dip the end into the plumb sauce and take a bite. It's scrumptious, brim-filled with beansprouts and spicy pork. "Oh, that's good."

"Yeah, you like it?"

"Mmmm," I mumble with my mouth full.

Before he can stop me, I toss the half-eaten roll towards Bear, who leaps at it and catches it mid-flight.

"Whaa...?"

"Oh, shut up. Half a spring roll won't hurt him. It must have been torture in that car... poor boy!"

"Well, it's on your head," he finishes plating up and hands me my dinner. "Would you like a glass of wine?"

"Umm, no thanks. I'll have some orange juice." I've drank enough wine today and I'd like to keep a relatively clear head. "I've got that interview in the morning and I don't want to be fuzzy." It's a fair excuse.

"Do you mind if I have one?"

"No... you go ahead." If he's had a day similar to mine, he'll need it.

"So... what did you and Christina get up to?" he asks as we carry our plates outside. It's uncanny, this way we each have of divining the other's instincts. It's natural.

I walk over to the garden patio set and pull out a chair. "It was an interesting day – I discovered quite a lot about my new best friend." I notice my voice sounds a little off, a little sullen. *Am I sulking?* Yes, I decide I am. Christina scuppered my plans for a morning sulk with her distraction tactics. I may as well do it now.

"What's up?"

Shaking my head at his perception, I sit, drawing one leg up so my foot rests on the iron chair. I balance my plate on top of my raised knee and dig in. "Nothing... I'm just hungry," I mutter as I begin to twirl my fork in my food. Mixing the beef and rice and delicious sauce, I settle in to enjoy my dinner.

"Edi... I'm not an idiot – tell me – are we still fighting?"

"I don't know... you tell me?" I say without making eye contact.

"Pfft!" He ignores my ambivalence on an eye roll, picks up his fork and starts in on his own plate. "Silence it is then," he counters under his breath.

I don't want to argue, but for some reason I'm feeling particularly petulant. It could be the day I've had, or it could be the findings of yesterday, or it could be nerves due to the pending TV interview tomorrow. Most likely, it's a combination of all three.

But I can't let it lie. I need to clear the air. What with everything I've learned this week, I need to talk about it or I may just explode through sheer information overload.

I put my half empty plate on the table and push it away. The food is lovely, but my appetite has plummeted through the floor and I know if I eat any more, I'll either suffer an upset stomach or, more likely, throw up, and I don't want either.

"So, now you're not hungry?"

I offer him an uncompromising expression as I lower my foot to the floor, shifting my weight to the back of the chair.

Christina was quite forthcoming earlier, hinting they both were a little afraid of me, and of my apparent mood swings. I may as well use his uncertainty to my advantage while I have the opportunity.

Swirling my tongue around the inside of my mouth I check along my teeth for any stray bits of rice. Then I pick between my lower front teeth with my little fingernail for any grains of black pepper, which may have lodged there. I'm stalling for effect, attempting to make him uncomfortable.

"Why did you leave me alone this morning?" I dismiss his comment about the food, in favour of my own more important question. I'm leading this discussion.

Silas places his empty plate on the table; evidently, the strained atmosphere hasn't suppressed his hunger. Taking up the challenge, he presents me with his own rigid demeanour. Lifting his chin, he sets his jaw and gritting his teeth, his mouth forms into a harsh line in direct defiance to mine. We're heading for a standoff.

"I had to work," he answers, flatly. He's giving me nothing to battle against.

"So did I, but you still left me alone; why?" He's not getting away with that.

"You were tired; you needed to sleep." *Nope!*

"It's never stopped you waking me before." It's true, there's been countless mornings over the past few weeks where I've been woken from a deep slumber to find him hovering above me. "You like to wake me up." He does… I realise this is one of his favourite things… waking me in the morning. "In fact, you love waking me up, so that one won't wash either. So, I'll ask again… why did you *leave* me alone this morning?"

"I didn't *leave* you alone… Christina was here."

Ooh! This is just making me mad now! Closing my eyes, I work hard to retain my composure. I can see what he's trying to do. He's attempting to provoke me into an explosion, so his assumption of me can be confirmed. Mood swings, see-sawing emotions and a crazy out of control bitch woman. But that's not the real me. My emotions only race to the surface under duress, threat or frustration – *Keep calm Edi, don't rise to it.*

"Okay." I drop my gaze to the table. I need to think and the easiest way to do that is to keep on the move. Standing, I snatch up my half-empty plate and stack it noisily on top of Silas's.

He follows my actions, a hint of smugness on his face. He thinks he's won round one – a little victory – we'll see about that mister. "Do you want a refill?" I gesture to his empty glass, keeping him off-balance, interjecting an element of domesticity; that should tilt the scale in my favour.

It works. I detect a trace of scepticism in his eyes, just a glimmer, but it's there.

"Umm? Yeah… please." He proffers his empty glass and I take it with a smile. 1-1, we're even.

"Of course, if you had taken the trouble to waken me; things may have been favourable for you." Flicking my hair over my shoulder with a sweep of my head, I allow that thought to hang in mid-air as I sashay away in the direction of the kitchen; exploiting his view of my retreating behind with maximum hip-sway and an arched back. I'm taking that one as well, 2-1 to Edi… score!

Leaving him in open mouthed contemplation at my sassy exit, I enter the kitchen to find Bear sulking in his basket. He didn't even join us in the garden, poor scolded boy!

Checking over my shoulder, I can see Silas through the doorway, still lounging at the patio table, his hand rubbing at the scar on his chin. He's in deep thought; no doubt planning his next move.

Quickly placing the wine glass on the counter, I tip-toe over to Bear's bowl and swiftly scrape the remnants of Chinese food off my plate and into his dish. He's beside me in a flash, but as usual, he awaits my command before digging in.

"There you go." I allow him to dive in on the food. There's not too much, but having an ally is well worth it. That has to make it 3-1 to me, surely?

"You'll regret that," Silas drawls from the kitchen door, causing me to jump about six feet in the air; he moves like a panther. I though he was still brooding in the garden!

"Oh, you startled me!" No point in feigning awareness when he can see I could've just cleared the high jump! "He looked so sorry for himself. It's only scraps."

Silas levers himself away from the door frame and moves into the room, his hands draped casually in his jeans pocket. "Yeah, well…" he shakes his head knowingly, "as I said, on your head be it," he muses as he wanders by me into the living room.

I look down at Bear, who's licking the bowl clean. There's not a morsel left. His tags clink on the side of the dish as his pink tongue laps enthusiastically at every millimetre of the bowl's surface in an attempt to taste every last bit. Oh well, he enjoyed it.

I rinse the empty plates under the hot tap and stack the dishwasher. Pouring Silas a fresh glass of wine, I decide one small drink won't hurt me. Taking a clean glass, I pour one for myself too.

In the lounge, Silas is relaxing on the sofa, flicking through the latest Aviation magazine. I place his wine on the coffee table and sit beside him.

He looks at me as if he wasn't expecting me to place myself so close. Tentatively, he drapes his arm around my shoulder, and pulls me even closer. I snuggle in and he kisses the top of my head and relaxes; refocussing his eyes on the article he's reading. I, however I'm ready for the next round.

Contemplating my approach, I look at the words on the page; I'm not really paying attention, and nurse my glass of wine to my chest whilst curling my legs up onto the sofa.

Bear wanders in from the kitchen and flops down on the rug in front of the unlit fire.

"I thought you weren't drinking." Silas's hand strokes the top of my arm tenderly, as he drops yet another kiss on my hair.

"I changed my mind," I say coolly.

Silas stiffens. My actions have lulled him into a false sense of security. However, my tone denotes he's not out of the woods yet.

"Okay… if we're going to do this, let's get it over with." He closes the magazine and tosses it onto the table beside his wine. Removing his arm from my shoulder, I'm forced to sit up, or risk collapsing in an undignified heap.

Finally, we're actually going to have a frank discussion about all that's gone on and how we move forward.

Turning to me, he removes my glass from my hand and places it beside the magazine, "Hey… I was…" I begin to protest, but the words are cut from my lips as he grasps my shoulders and smashes his mouth on mine with such force our teeth clash.

"Mmmm!" I try and push him off, flattening my hands on his pecs, I heave with all my might against the ferocity of his kiss, but he's too heavy.

Unfolding my legs, I kick out, but catch my toe on the edge of the table. The pain shoots through me causing me to groan and bite down, trapping his lower lip between my teeth. The taste of blood fills my mouth and I realise I've bitten him. But he doesn't relent, he just continues to kiss me, feverishly, hungrily.

My arms buckle, and instead of pushing him away, they drift around his chest and onto his broad back, pulling him into me. Oh, this man knows how to kiss!

His growl of approval at my submission is faint but noticeable. Easing back, he softens the kiss. His hands release their vicelike grip on my shoulders and drift to the back of my head, his fingers entangling in my hair.

"Gotcha!" he breathes in heady triumph as his tongue sweeps through my mouth. "I know you're keeping score... 3-2, to you I think."

He plays with my lips, caressing his full mouth lightly against mine, teasing the kisses from me. I'm sunk. I can't fight against his intent and my body finally gives out and relaxes in total acceptance. I go lax in his arms; my own arms dangle freely, no longer able to hold onto him as I give myself over to the waves of pleasure washing over me.

At the exact point of my submission, he frees me. Just like that. I'm dropped. His hands untangle themselves from my hair and he rears away, separating our bodies, breaking the kiss and releasing me so I'm falling backwards like a boneless ragdoll onto the sofa.

"Ooof!" I can't believe it! He didn't just do that?

Without leaving the settee, he leans forwards and picks up his wine. Taking a large sip, he raises the glass to me in salute. "Cheers," he nods. "Three-all, I think... now we're even again."

I stare at him in disbelief. What an arrogant arse! And why didn't Bear jump to my defence when he was lying right there as Silas pounced? *Because he knew you weren't really in danger... that's why!*

"Traitor..." I scowl at the dog – unbelievable – I've just gone against his master's wishes and fed him leftover Chinese food and he can't even raise an eyebrow, let alone a growl. Suddenly I know why! An unholy putrid stink fills the air! "Ugh! What the Hell!!!"

"I did warn you," Silas smirks. "There's only one thing worse than doggy farts; and that's Chinese food doggy farts."

"Oh *Jesus*... It's rank," I choke, holding my nose and trying not to retch at the stench." Oh, God! I think I'm gonna be sick!"

"Bear, out." Silas commands and the disgraced canine, skulks out of the room. I don't know if he's embarrassed or proud; Lord that's foul! Silas rises from the sofa and opens a window allowing the air to chase away the noxious fumes.

"Now, can we call it a draw?" He returns to his place beside me, where I reluctantly nod up at him as I sit holding my nose.

"Yes," I squeak, still afraid that if I remove my hand, I'll pass out from the fading pong. Risking a sniff, I drop my hand. "Oh Lord, I didn't realise it would have that effect on him. That's gross!" I try not to giggle. I need to remain moody.

But it's a pointless exercise, what with the kissing and the farting, it seems futile to keep up the pretence. Who am I kidding? I love him and no matter what he is, or does, I can't be without him; it's a sobering thought.

I need to grow a pair and deal with this rationally. Okay, so he has an unusual side-line, but the positives really do outweigh the negatives. What he does, makes life so much better for so many people.

I worry about the affect it has on him mentally and emotionally, what price he must pay each time he steps into that world; but if it is part of him, then I need to learn to accept it. I don't have to like it.

I fling my arms around his neck and bury my face in his sweater. It's inevitable. I will always return to him, no matter what, so it's futile trying to justify my reasoning. He's mine and he happens to be a Vigilante in his spare time! He's James Bond - If I endeavour to approach it from that angle, I may be able to validate it.

"Am I forgiven?" he asks from somewhere above my head.

"Always," I answer, honestly. "It was a gigantic shock and it'll take some adjustment to come to terms with your... side-line... but I'll get there... you're worth it." I know I can do this; I just have to change my way of thinking.

"That's good... because I quit."

"I know, it's going to be an adjust... wait a minute..." I pull away so I can see his face. "What did you just say?"

"I said, I quit. I'm out. Resigned, retired, finished... call it what you like, but I'm done." Loosening his arms slightly, he leans back so I have his full attention. "I've had it. Honey-bee, It's over. I can't spend the rest of my life tilting at windmills... won't do it anymore."

"Wha..." I'm lost for words. This I didn't expect.

"Come on, let me explain."

He takes my hand and leads me upstairs to the bedroom. Once inside, he strips us both down and we climb beneath the soft cotton sheets. Turning on our sides we face each other.

Bending my arm, I tuck it beneath the pillow, supporting my head and stay quiet. He needs to explain this in his way.

Shuffling closer, so we're almost touching, we lie face to face. Lying like this is incredibly intimate. Our breath is heated, I can smell a hint of spice as he exhales, a vestige of his digested meal.

"You made me think," he speaks, his eyes drifting to my lips.

"Me? What did I make you think about?"

"Life, and what it means. About the value of life, and how brief it is."

"How did I make you think about that?" I return his soft gaze.

"When... I..." he's struggling to find the words.

"It's okay... go on... just say anything. It'll come," I encourage gently.

He sighs deeply, composing his thoughts into words. It's a couple of minutes before he speaks again.

"When we lost Maya, it was the worst thing to happen to me, ever." He stares at me, his pupils dilated and huge; so huge his eyes are deep black glittering pools. "You are the best."

My heart leaps. A resounding thud in my chest so loud, he surely heard it. I hold my breath, choosing to listen rather than respond.

"You made me think..." his voice is so low, it's barely audible. "What if, the best thing can reverse the worst thing?"

"I'm sorry, I don't quite..." Oh, he's trying so hard to get this out.

"I mean, when Maya... was taken away..." he starts again. "All I wanted was to get her back," he blinks away a tear. "I know that was impossible, she was gone. But until you've lost a child, you don't know the depths you will go to, just to have them back with you. To hold them once more, or hear them laugh." A second tear joins the first. He allows them to flow freely.

"She was gone, but I couldn't truly let her go. I didn't. Wouldn't. The creation of *The Rose Council* was something I could do to get closer to Maya. While I was working with

The Rose Council, I could convince myself I was doing it for her. It was all for her... and Nic," he adds. "My world was filled with thoughts of revenge and pain. Every day was the same. But, after each job, there were a few moments of peace when I could feel her presence. I could physically sense her there beside me. It was like an addiction.

"All the joy I used to feel when I was flying, was nothing... gone. I was consumed with guilt. I know that now. You made me see that."

"I'm pleased I could do something," I whisper. Although I'm still not sure where these ramblings are going, he has to get there on his own.

"In the years I've done what I've done, I never really understood, there's no real gratification in revenge. Those moments, where I could feel Maya beside me, was an illusion. Revenge is like an empty pocket, a bottomless pit and once you start on the way down, it's almost impossible to claw your way out.

"When you came into my life, I began to realise there was something more. I'd wasted so much time trying to forget the bad stuff, I didn't realise I was missing out on the good stuff."

"Okay."

"When you showed me the photograph of David, in Paris, do you remember?"

"Yes." How can I forget? It was the morning after we'd made love for the first time.

"It was your face... the look of pure joy on your face when you gazed at his picture. I remembered that look. I used to have that look when I saw Nic and Maya. You reminded me. There's still joy in the world.

"That was when I started to think differently. That was when I realised what I'd been denying myself. By blocking out my acceptance, my loss, I was only delaying the inevitable. I could never truly recover, until I could accept, she's gone.

"All those times, when I felt her there. They were bad times. I should be associating her memory with joy, not resurrecting it in the wake of taking a life. The bad was marring the good... do you see?"

I smile softly at him. His tears have dried, leaving streaks of silver salt on his cheeks. "Yes, baby... I see it."

"I can't keep thinking about her in those terms. I can't keep her as a memory only to be drawn upon to validate the deaths of others. It shouldn't be that way. I want to remember her as she was, or as she should be now; she'd be a young woman, happy and vibrant... like Lizzy, even."

Reaching out, he strokes a stray lock of hair behind my ear. "You... you made me realise. I need to stop now. I need to call a halt to all thoughts of revenge and start living again.

"Maya's life was pitifully short, but at least she lived and I can't allow the brevity of her existence to be a reason for retribution. I haven't lived properly for the past fifteen years. I've missed so much. Nic was a boy... now he's a man. I can't miss any more. Will you help me?"

"Anything, I'll do anything..." he knows this. I'd do anything for him.

"Will you help me to live? To find the joy again? To remember Maya how she should be remembered?"

273

"Oh baby, the joy is in here." I cover his heart with my palm. "It never left; it just got a little misplaced. Hidden for safe-keeping in your heart. Secure until you were ready to find it again." My face is wet too, "we can find it together... even if it takes a lifetime."

"Thank you. Thank you for helping me," he whispers, closing his eyes.

I trace his brow with my finger, smoothing along the deep river of frown lines, soothing the tension gathered in his face until, eventually he relaxes. His skin is smooth, all evidence of the strain he's been under has melted into softness; the only tell-tale sign of his age is the scattering of fine wrinkles fanning his eyes.

As he sleeps, the tautness in his body dissolves away releasing the weight of his burden. A burden he's carried for many years. Yes, I will help him... we will help each other.

CHAPTER 48

The studio is a seething hive of activity. Runners, doing just that, are rushing here and there like headless chickens. I'm sure there's a method in their madness, but I'm blowed if I can understand it. Shouting into walkie-talkies, headphones cover their ears as they ignore all of the activity going on around them, responding only to the demands of the Directors ensconced somewhere in an invisible command centre in the sky.

Huge tripod camera dollies are being wheeled into place, aimed at a cherry red sofa. There's a break in the live feed. The hourly update review of the pre-recorded morning headlines is streaming on the myriad of monitors strategically placed about the studio. The host for the day is having her makeup retouched. A huge green screen fills the backdrop behind the interview area and the black-painted ceiling is littered with what look like round shooting targets, lamps and arrays of spotlights, suspended from what appears to be scaffolding.

I stare around me in awe. The state-of-the-art TV studio is a million lightyears away from the seedy photographic workrooms I was used to in my old modelling days. They were no better than a rundown office or draughty warehouse space, usually filthy dirty and often freezing cold.

This morning, we rose early. Silas looked a hundred percent better than last night; far more relaxed, calmer and certain. His decision to leave *The Rose Council* was a huge relief to me, although how he will go about it, I'm not sure. I'm apprehensive they won't allow him to 'retire', as he put it. I don't even know if people *can* retire from such a career. It never seems to be allowed in the movies.

Silas was very reassuring, explaining he'd already had the initial conversation with his dad, as a precursor, testing the water at how the rest of the Board might react to the news their number one agent will be hanging up his weapons.

Apparently, Leon wasn't at all surprised. He said he saw it coming on the day of his Birthday party, when Silas was vehement, we were together and nothing was going to change it.

All that's left now is for Silas to officially meet with the rest of the Board to formally terminate his affiliation. When I asked if they would continue without him, he just smiled and shrugged his shoulders, saying, *'who knows and who cares?'*

This was wonderful to hear because it's unqualified proof, he most certainly *is* out. The appetite and drive for any form of revenge is gone completely; literally disintegrated overnight. And without the desire to avenge injustice, he would be useless in the field; even I can see that. I know nothing about the world of secret agents and from my experiences over the last couple of days, I never want to.

Morgan and Angie had come to the barn to make me presentable and Christina arrived with both Lizzy and David in tow, which was a lovely surprise.

Lizzy is still waiting to hear the outcome of her interview, so a morning of distraction at the TV studio seemed a good call from Christina. David has made friends with a member of the crew, and is currently standing on a box behind one of the cameras receiving instructions on how everything works. He's absolutely loving it. Lizzy on the other hand, is more interested in the celebrity photo's adorning the walls of the corridor backstage. She's been squealing and pointing out people I've never even heard of, and she almost fainted when one of the *Strictly* dancers winked at her and started chatting her up. Apparently, his name is Curtis and he was on *Love Island!* It's all over my head! It was all I could do to remain calm and stay focussed on my interview notes.

But now I'm caked in makeup. I was given a small dressing room; more like a cupboard, to get ready in. The girl really went to town, even fitting false eyelashes. When I looked in the mirror, I was quite taken aback to see how much of my old self was still there. The glittery eyeshadow, heavy eyeliner and red lips are reminiscent of my old persona and completely different from the current me; the real me. When I protested, asking her to tone it down, I was informed there wasn't time. Now I feel completely sick, and just want to get it over and done with.

"Edi, we'll be ready for you in ten minutes," the runner informs me, popping her head around the dressing room door.

"Oh... thank..." she's gone. "Oh God, oh God... what am I doing?" I shake my hands, loosening my wrists and trying to get some circulation going.

"You'll do fine." Silas sooths me by rubbing his hand over my back to ease the building tension.

"But what if I'm not... what if it all goes tits up?"

I'm deprived of his answer, by a knock on the door. "Come in," we chorus, expecting one of the children. But when it opens, it's not Lizzy or David, but Montgomery Phillips who graces us with his presence.

"Hello, hello... just bobbed in to see how it's all going?" He shakes Silas's hand and gives me a peck on the cheek. "Goodness, don't you look a million dollars," he sleazes, not bothering to disguise the lecherous way his eyes rove openly all over my face and body.

"Yeah, but it's not Edi." Silas hasn't missed Monty's libidinous manner. "As soon as this is over, the Ice Queen, is back in the box," he says with marked hostility.

"Oh, I hate this," I wail, making a grab for the box of tissues. "I can't go out there looking like this; everyone will think I'm a right old tart."

"Hey, it's okay. Think; if you go out there as Meredith, there's less chance of you being recognised as your true self. You look fine, honestly," Silas nods his reassurance.

"Well, if, you're sure?" It does make sense. The public want to see Meredith not Edi.

"I'm sure, Hon..." He's about to use my pet-name, but manages to stop himself. He won't say it in front of Phillips.

"Well, as they say... *'break a Leg!'*" Monty chuckles at his own pathetic joke, then ducks out of the room.

"Five minutes," the runner is back.

"Lord, it's like fucking Piccadilly Circus in here," Silas grumbles. "Are you okay?"

"I will be once this is over. Where are the kids?"

"They've been given a spot behind the cameras so they can watch. I'll be with them. Don't worry." He kisses my forehead where it's creased with worry lines!

"Is Christina still here?"

"No, she's gone back over to the Beeches; She had a call. I think Nic's fretting over David being away. He seems to be struggling since the treadmill incident." He frowns slightly, but just as quickly shakes off his concern. "It'll be alright; she'll calm him down. They'll watch it together in the TV lounge."

"Oh no… she should have brought him. I feel terrible now!"

"No, it's fine. All this would've just made him anxious; you know how he gets. Best to let him watch it on the telly in the comfort of familiar surroundings. He'll be calmer with his mum and Wendy."

"Okay, we're ready for you," the young blonde girl who's been bobbing around like a jack-in-a-box gives me my final call. "If you'll just come with me, we can get you mic'd up and introduce you to Marina," she enthuses.

"Oh, okay." I swing my chair round and stand. The nerves are really kicking in.

"Just breathe," Silas says. "You'll be grand. Fifteen minutes, and you can scrape that muck off your face and we can go for a well-deserved lunch."

"Yeah… wish me luck." I kiss him, leaving a huge pair of red lips imprinted on his cheek.

"Out, stop stalling." He slaps my bum and we leave the confines of the small dressing room.

CHAPTER 49

The runner leads me along the corridor and into the large brightly lit studio. "If you'll just wait here, the sound assistant will need to wire you up and then we can do a quick sound check."

She leaves me standing among the cables and wires, waiting for a spotty youth of about twelve to shove his arm down the back of my dress, where he places a transmitter; then blushes scarlet as he attaches a microphone clip to my neckline. I get the impression he may be a trainee! Once all the tech is attached, I'm led to the sofa, where I'm introduced to Marina Esposito.

"Hi, Edi, isn't it?" She shakes my hand warmly. "Call me Marina," she says, smoothing the creases out of her toffee pink designer skirt and sitting decorously on the sofa.

I can't help noticing how flawless her complexion is even beneath the heavy studio makeup. She has absolutely no lines, not one, and her chestnut brown hair is glossy and sleek, tumbling lustrously around the shoulders of her cream satin blouse.

"Nice choice," she smiles, aiming her pretty almond eyes at my feet and winking in admiration of my Paris shoes.

"Huh, er… Hi, and thank you," I mutter inadequately, as I follow her lead; nervously perching on the end of my seat and demurely crossing my ankles. I may be wearing far too much make-up and my CFM shoes but I'll be buggered if I'm going to act like cheap trash.

"Okay, yes… yes… got it." I'm about to answer her, when I realise, she isn't actually speaking to me. She has her hand to her ear, listening to someone in the director's gallery. "Would you say something please?" This time, she *is* talking to me. Oh blimey, this is so confusing.

"Err, what should I say?"

"That's fine, they've got you; is that okay Tessa?" She flips her attention between us as if it's the most normal thing in the world. "Can you run the auto-cue? Yeah, that's fine… roll it back… yeah, ready to go. Just relax… I don't bite." She gives me one last genuine smile, then squeezes my hand encouragingly.

"Ready to go in… 3… 2… 1…" The floor manager signals to Marina. As the title music for this section of the show strikes up, she preens in her seat and looks at the camera, where a green light indicates we're live.

Oh, shit! Here we go!

I've not been this nervous since my first day at RTC.

"Good morning, everyone!" Maria launches into her seasoned broadcaster persona as if she's slipping into her most comfortable woolly cardigan.

While Marina addresses the Nation, I risk a transitory glance around the studio seeking out the reassurance I so badly need. Sure enough, there they all are, standing on the periphery, watching intently. David waves and grins while Lizzy gives me a cheery double thumbs up. Silas, solid and steadfast, nods his head once, mouthing *'you'll be fine; I love you'*, then he winks and puckers his lips, blowing me a kiss; delivering with it a huge wave of well needed courage.

I can do this!

"... and that was only three weeks ago at Paris Fashion Week..." Marina finishes her introduction, reading the rolling transcript expertly from the teleprompter.

"So," turning to face me, she smiles, "I must start by thanking you for joining us today, Meredith." She sounds delighted I've made the effort to be here. "It must be a great feeling, knowing you've been so missed?"

Err? How do I answer that? "It's Edi, and um, well, I wasn't aware I *was* missed."

"But surely Meredith, after all this time, you must be delighted with the rise in publicity?"

"Edi..." I remind her then, "I... I'm... I..." I look over to Silas, who nods encouragement.

"Oh, you must be aware the public interest in you has never dwindled. The story was quite a sensation back in the day. One minute, you're on top of your game, then next... gone!" She tilts her head in expectation. I sense movement, and turn to look at the monitors showing the live TV feed. Projected onto the greenscreen behind us is a running montage of my old glamour modelling pictures – the same ones they used during the interview with Lynda – seeing them unnerves me.

"There was more to it." I mumble quietly, my train of thought distracted by the display of moving images.

"Can you elaborate? Meredith, please, tell us, tell the people... we're all dying to know. Why did you disappear and where did you go?"

Turning away from the photographs, I'm searching my mind for my prepared answers. What did Christina coach me to say? How am I supposed to behave? I can't remember, I've drawn a blank.

Think Edi!

"It's Edi!" I repeat; my nerves are jangling at the persistent use of my old name. I still can't find any words. "Err," *Jesus, I sound like an imbecile!*

Marina is clearly becoming frustrated with my lack of verbosity. Her smile tightens and her eyes flash in warning. "Well, *Edi*... you certainly aren't giving too much away are you. Can you at least tell us why you returned? What is your intention now your back?"

Ah, now I understand her strategy, she's baiting me; trying to rattle me into saying something provocative.

In an instant all of Christina's sensible advice comes flooding to the fore, restoring my self-confidence and with it comes a new found determination. I refuse to be provoked. I *can* do this, and I *will* do this, but it'll be on *my* terms. Straightening my back, I draw a cleansing breath, and arranging my face into a benign expression, I offer her my most sincere smile.

"Actually, Marina, the truth is I didn't come back," I say calmly. "As far as I am concerned, I don't want or *need* any publicity. The only reason I'm here today, is to set the record straight in that regard. The recent tabloid intrusion has been exactly that... an unwelcome, unwarranted infiltration into my personal life and a complete invasion of my privacy. I didn't court or seek attention; it was forced upon me unsolicited. And that's the *only* reason for this interview."

Her face faulters as she flicks her eyes to the autocue. My upfront reply has knocked her off balance. "But you did attend Paris Fashion Week with Lynda Summers, your old modelling partner, did you not?" Now the TV monitor cuts to an image of me at the fashion week closing party wearing my vivid green dress!

For God's sake!

But instead of ruffling me, as is the intention, this just fuels my anger.

"No, I did not."

That's enough, don't give more unless she asks. Let her struggle.

"According to Lynda Summers, you attended together, isn't that true?"

"No." I'm smiling on the inside, watching her squirm. My 'Meg Ryan' tactic is beginning to have the desired effect.

"Are you denying you were there?"

"Well, I can hardly do that, now can I? There are photographs of me in attendance. I'm just saying, I wasn't there with Lynda Summers."

Her face lights up at this information and the veteran interviewer comes racing to the surface. Sensing an easy kill, she formulates a completely different approach; off come the kid gloves and on go the boxing gloves.

"So, you don't deny you were there?" she looks down the camera lens triumphantly. "If you weren't with Miss Summers, who did you attend with? Is it someone interesting? A new celebrity suitor perhaps? Hum?" She smiles coquettishly, playing up to the invisible audience.

But I won't be her punchbag. "Marina, as much as you'd like to link me romantically with some outlandish scandal, there honestly isn't a story here. But if you really must know, I was there in a business capacity." The minute the words are out of my mouth, I realise my mistake. *Fuck!* I made it sound like I'm on the game!

Her face is an absolute picture at this faux pas; she doesn't miss a beat, diving on my slip up like a panther. "And what kind of business would that be? Have you diverged into something... a little more lucrative?" Oh, the nerve!

Rallying my reserves, I quickly attempt to execute a recovery. "Certainly not in the way you're insinuating. If it's any of your business, which it isn't, by the way, I was there with my boss. He is the owner of an elite aviation company and we were attending as guests of Montgomery Phillips, perhaps you've heard of him?"

There, she can't twist this one. He'll have her job if she attempts to link us in anything other than a legitimate way.

"Okay, so… Meredith," she regroups, reverting back to use of my old name. "If you weren't there with Lynda Summers, what truth is there in the news, the two of you will be working together again in the very near future?"

My lips purse, I'm beginning to feel a little railroaded here. She's determined to drag me through the mire but I have no intention of succumbing.

"Marina, that is complete nonsense. Allow me to set the record straight once and for all so we can all get on with our very busy lives." Here goes nothing. "I left a controlling husband and a degrading career – for want of a better word – for the sake of my children. I was determined they wouldn't be brought up surrounded by the seedy world of topless models and adult magazines. To be honest, I detested every single minute of it, it was demoralising and humiliating. It just wasn't for me. So, I left." Offering only the fundamentals, I stop speaking.

A couple of seconds skip by. She's waiting. If she's expecting to hear the specifics, she can get lost. Realising I've said my piece, she stutters back into action.

Her next question is the one I've been dreading; it's the left field question, but I'm well prepared.

"So, when I interviewed Lynda, she was quite forthcoming. She was unbelievably excited to reveal the exclusive news that you will be working together again."

"N…" I try to cut in.

"Collaborating on a brand-new calendar for next year."

"Rubbish."

She won't be deterred. "And she mentioned that you and your husband, Bobby, or Robert Price, the well-known entrepreneur, will be reunited in both business and in your personal life… you're getting back together."

"Utter garbage!" I clench my teeth at the mention of his name. How *dare* she? How *fucking* dare, they?

"So, there's no truth in this information?"

"Not a single word." I chance a sideways glance at Silas and the kids, they look concerned. Deciding to end this ridiculous farce, I start to unclip my microphone from my dress.

"I've had enough of this. It's total nonsense, and I'm not wasting any more of my time on it. It's done, in the past and I'm out of here."

"So, you and Bobby aren't reconciled?" She throws the grenade and it begins to tick its warning, loudly. Her eyes are gleaming in exhilaration. Something's going on.

I stop fiddling with my mic, "No! Never!" Again, I glance at Silas, unsure of where this is leading.

"Well, this is going to be interesting." She reclines against the sofa, and holds out her arm to the side stage, indicating I should follow her gesture; my heart stops! Walking purposefully towards me is Bobby. He's beaming from ear to ear and he's focussed directly on me, as he enters the studio from the wings; the camera follows his progress as he approaches.

CHAPTER 50

"Hi Meredith," he leers menacingly, leaning in, invading my personal space and forcing a hard, predatory kiss on my mouth. His rough hands find my shoulders and I tense in response to his unwelcome touch as he maliciously applies a vicelike pressure. It's subtle enough for the camera to miss, but severe enough for me to know it'll leave a nasty bruise.

The terror which I feel in this moment is paralysing. I can't move. Can't respond. I'm frozen, unable to respond. This cannot be happening!

"Hi, Mr Price, and thank you for joining us," Marina simpers. The woman is an idiot.

"Oh, believe me… the pleasure is all mine." He gives her his most ingratiating smile. It's sickening.

Ignoring my obvious repulsion at his presence, Bobby sits beside me. He's so close, our thighs are touching. Involuntarily, I jerk my leg away in protest at his unwanted proximity. All he does in response, is drape a proprietary arm around my shoulder, his hand finds the top of my arm and he grips hold tightly, pinching the skin, leaving me in no doubt at his intention towards me.

Placing his right arm across the front of my body he takes hold of my left hand, drawing it towards him and resting it beneath his in my lap. Looking at this book cover from the outside, it's a romantic epic; a harmonious display of reunified domestic bliss; a tale of sweetness and light. But this side of the page tells a different story. It's one of abject horror, control and domination.

Encircling my wrist, completely so he's covering my watch, he begins his invisible assault. Once he has hold, he squeezes, increasing the pressure so the metal strap bites deep into my flesh and the small bones grind together painfully. It's his way of demonstrating his fury.

I'm in far too much turmoil to respond. I'm trapped in the prison of his arms and I won't be able to release myself without a violent struggle.

Okay… if I play along, he'll believe I'm submitting and calm down.

If I remain passive and pretend to be happy at seeing him, he'll relax and release me

Oh, *fuck it*… why am I bargaining? He has absolutely no power over me! What the *fuck* am I doing?

The children… my immediate thought is for their benefit. That's why I'm sitting here like a subservient chicken, allowing him to reign his authority down on me. It's for the children.

As soon as I realise this, my blood boils and my temper flares. I have no idea what's being discussed between *him* and Marina; my mind is elsewhere. But I do know I need to get him the Hell off me!

Glancing towards Silas, I'm alarmed to see he's nowhere in sight. He's disappeared. I look at Lizzy, who's face has turned as white as paper, her eyes wide. She shrugs exaggeratedly and shakes her head in distress. She's totally shocked at the turn of events but I can tell she's fighting against showing her fear so as not to upset her brother.

David looks totally puzzled; he keeps turning towards Lizzy, clearly agitated at the sight of a strange man with his arms wrapped so possessively around his mother.

Bobby must sense my attention has shifted and he lifts his head to follow my line of sight. "Is that? Oh, my goodness!" he exclaims loudly.

"Yes!" shrills Marina, clearly thrilled, the prospect of an impromptu family reunion having the potential to send the program ratings soaring through the roof. "Yes, it's your children; or young adults as they are now," she waves, beckoning them over.

"Children...?" momentarily, he drops his guard and the mask slips. But only for a split second; his face switching from fake delight, to guarded uncertainty... as far as he was aware, he only had a daughter; now he's just discovered he has a son too. "Oh my, how wonderful." The guise quickly returns sweeping away the hesitation in favour of an overenthusiastic, artifice.

"Yes!" Marina is beside herself. "If you can bear with us for a moment, we can ask them to join us." She's clearly receiving messages from the gallery, because a frown puckers her brows. "Ummm, I'm sorry, but I seem to have lost contact with the Director. But, not to worry, we can still work with this... here they are," she rallies, pulling out all the professional stops; she's winging it.

To my utter horror, Lizzy and David are looking bewildered as the young sound technician faffs around, hastily trying to attach microphones in preparation for them to join us on the sofa!

No fucking way!

Instinctively I jump to attention; I'm not going to allow this – and certainly not on National Television. "No," I say loudly. "No, they won't be coming on screen," I assert my defiance.

Marina looks about her in alarm, touching her ear, desperately seeking guidance from above, which clearly is not forthcoming. she shifts uncomfortably in her seat, flustered by the sudden change in direction. The whole interview has gone from scoop to poop in a nanosecond!

"Err, and here they are," she tries again to encourage Lizzy and David to join us. "Elizabeth...David?"

Distracted by the presence of his daughter, Bobby's attention momentarily lapses and I seize the opportunity to escape his clutches. "NO!" I yell, startling both Bobby and Marina with my fury. "Get your f... filthy hands off me!" I scream, as I wrestle myself from his grip. The kids look on aghast!

With the programme swiftly morphing into an episode of *Jeremy Kyle*, Marina has no option, but to end the segment. Turning to the camera and switching on her most sincere persona yet, she looks ardently at the lens for the autocue, which has ceased running. The floor manager is looking on, clearly agitated, as it seems he too has lost contact with the control booth.

284

"Well, exciting times... exciting times. It's been a great pleasure to have you here today, Meredith."

"Stuff it up your arse," I grind, throwing my microphone onto the floor in rage as I finally alleviate myself from the tangled wires and Bobby's leaching grasp. "And you... you can fuck off too, you *Bastard*!" I hiss into his shocked face.

Never in all the years we were together did I dare to defy him, or speak to him with such disrespect. But today, I'm letting him have it, both barrels. "If you *ever* dare to lay so much as a finger on me again, I swear to God, I'll cut the fucker off and make you eat it!"

"Aaaand cut," the distressed floor manager comes running over in a feeble attempt to quieten the ensuing commotion and mollify Marina, who's threatening to attain total nuclear meltdown at the way the segment has degenerated. The monitors have conveniently segued to a natural history piece on whale watching.

"Lizzy, David, come with me... NOW!" I bellow, marching off in the direction of the green room, removing the false eyelashes as I go.

"Mum..." David canters after me, desperate to catch up. "Mumm... wait," he pants, urging me to slow my pace.

I can't be mad at him; this isn't his fault. Easing my stride, I turn and enfold him in my arms. "David, that was very wrong of me."

"No mum," he speaks into my neck. "That man was hurting you, I could tell. You had to stop him."

"*Meredith!* ... please ... Meredith! ..." the floor manager has chased after us, "you need to return to the floor, the interview isn't over." He indicates behind him towards the sofas, where Bobby and Marina are getting quite cosy, having their make-up retouched in preparation for round two.

"It is for me..." I snap, throwing him daggers over the top of David's head. "Have you any idea of what you've just done? Have you any idea, who that man really is? What he really does?"

The floor manager looks at me indifferently. "I don't care," he says, shaking his head in sarcasm. "I'm a programme maker and all I know right now is you're ruining one of the best public interest stories we've had in years."

"If you're so curious about public interest; go and investigate the real issues. Then you'll know exactly who you're dealing with and why all those years ago it was imperative I left. That's the story you want... not me. Now leave me alone."

His expression morphs from indifferent to intrigued. He doesn't speak, but I can almost smell the wood burning as he processes what I've said. Looking over his shoulder, he makes a decision. He knows there's not a snowballs chance in Hell of me returning to the studio to finish the interview.

"Alright... clearly you won't be persuaded?"

"No," I affirm.

"Alright then," he concedes, holding out his hand in a gesture of good will. "Thank you for your time... and I wish you well with all your future endeavours."

"Goodbye," I mutter, ignoring the handshake in favour of holding David close to me. As the floor manager walks away, I detect a spring in his step. Good. I hope he finds what he's searching for.

Sniffing, David shifts his face, so he can breathe. "Was that man my dad?" Mumbling the question from the security of my bosom, he lifts his head to look at me. "I mean... you said *he* wasn't a nice man. And *that man*, wasn't a nice man... was it my dad?"

Oh lord! 'That man' How on earth can I explain?

"Oh darling," I cradle his head pulling him into me. "Yes son, that was your dad. And no, he isn't a nice man," I sigh.

What a nightmare morning this has turned into. Taking David by the hand, I lead him towards the dressing room. I can't wait to get this shit off my face, it's cloying. I can feel my pores suffocating with the weight of the foundation. "Where did Silas go?" I wonder, suddenly remembering his absence.

"He went to tell them off. He said, 'I'm shutting this Pantomime down,'" David quotes verbatim. "I didn't think it was a pantomime, I thought it was a news programme?" he continues innocently.

"It's a figure of speech," I say, all the while wondering where Silas has got to.

I don't need to wait long, because as we arrive at the assigned 'broom cupboard', we meet Silas, coming the other way. "There you are!" he sighs in relief. "I thought you might have left."

"Oh, Silas, I'm so stupid! Why didn't I see it coming?"

"What's going on... what was *he* doing here?" Lizzy has joined us in the narrow corridor. "He just tried to give me his calling card!" she exclaims.

"Oh no! You didn't speak to him did you." I feel sick at the thought. "Lizzy, please don't be taken in by him. He's into some really horrendous stuff." Looking at David, I daren't elaborate in front of him, but I can't risk her getting involved with Bobby! No way!

"Are you serious! Why would I?" She's disappointed with my lack of faith in her. "As far as I'm concerned, he's just another stranger; I ripped it up."

"Oh, Lizzy... It's..." I cover my face with my hands, the whole debacle has been a nightmare.

"Look guys... I think we should leave. There's nothing we can do from here. The damage is done. Let's just get our things and go home."

Taking control, Silas shoves open the door to the dressing room and we all pile inside. There's barely enough room to swing a cat, but we manage by shuffling about, choosing to remain together in the confined space rather than risk being separated again.

"Where did you disappear to, anyway?" I ask Silas as I pile my belongings into my tote bag.

"I had a little meeting with the Director," he says, confirming my suspicions. "Let's just say, she won't be trying that trick again anytime soon."

"You shut it down?" I feel the trace of a smile on my lips. He's incredible.

"Hook line and sinker. C'mon, let's go." He grabs his jacket from the hanger on the back of the door, and with a last check to make sure we have everything, we exit the tiny room and leave the studio.

CHAPTER 51

The drive back to Cranleigh is quiet, apart from David's excited description of the camera operating system; and whilst he's regaled us with every detail, we're all lost in our private thoughts.

I rest my hand on Silas's knee, needing the physical contact and to feel his solidness. The last few days have on both sides been a minefield of revelation. If I knew the interview was going to manifest into a long-lost family reunion, I'd never have agreed to take part.

Fucking Bobby!

I'm exasperated by how he can still affect me so badly after all this time. I know he has absolutely no interest in me; his focus is on Lizzy. And that's what scares me the most.

Her gentle innocence is ripe for exploitation. I've kept her so protected and out of harm's way; she has no worldly skills to speak of; she just isn't streetwise, and that's my fault for being so overbearing. I would never forgive myself if she succumbed to his lies. He's a master of deceit and manipulation and now he has full control of the 'business' Pierre Adrax left behind; my fear is only magnified...

"I messed up..." I sigh, looking at Silas as he follows the steady stream of vehicles. Cranleigh is only forty or so miles from London, but the flow is at a snail's pace this time of day.

"What makes you say that?" he glances at me as he pulls up; the crawling traffic reduces to a stand-still.

"It was... I lost it completely." I did; the whole thing was shambolic.

"It made for good telly though!" he smiles, giving me a flash of his perfect white teeth.

"Don't make fun of me," I huff.

"Honey-bee, I would never..." he scolds. "Look, if the desired effect was to make him come across as a wanker; I think it worked. The country could see from the way you responded; it was a set up... all a load of bull-shit."

"Language," David mumbles from the rear.

"Really?" I'm not so sure. I think the one who looked like a wanker was me. I was the one who ripped off their mic and stormed out of the studio cursing like a fishwife. The jury's out until the public votes are in.

The traffic starts moving and he slips the shift into first gear. "We'll see. Let's not discuss it now." He tilts his head in the direction of the rear seat, where two interested parties have pricked up their ears and started eavesdropping on our conversation.

"Yeah, okay."

"Guys?" Silas changes the subject, drawing their attention. "As the traffic's so bad, how about we pull off the motorway for a while and go and grab a bite?"

"Sounds great," Lizzy shrugs.

"Can we have a MacDonald's?"

"Yeah, no problem, buddy… next junction, is that okay?"

"Yay! … I'm having nuggets," David announces, his mind already diverted to his favourite fast food.

"Veggie Burger, please," says Lizzy, "and fries," she adds.

"And a milkshake," counter's David.

"Well, if you're having a milkshake, I'm having a diet cola." She won't eat the burger and I imagine she'll only pick at the fries, but at least they're distracted from this morning's fiasco.

Our stomachs are satisfied as we enter the Beeches. We dropped Lizzy at the apartment on the way. She was continually checking and rechecking her email; but still no reply.

As I suspected, the veggie burger was barely touched and she took it away with her, for the ride, offering a promise she'd *'finish it later for supper'*. David is still tucking into her leftover fries as we walk into the conservatory.

"Hey, hey, hey…" Christina greets us as Nic jumps to his feet and wanders over to greet his dad and David. "He's been waiting for you," she smiles at David as he offers Nic the remnants of the chips. "Wendy's making drinks in the kitchen. Why don't you two go and help?" Christina urges gently.

"Okay, c'mon Nic, let's go and help Wendy… I've really missed her," David says pointedly, I think, specifically for my benefit.

As they head off in the direction of the kitchen, Christina sighs deeply. "God, Edi… I'm…" her words trail off, knowing how I feel about apologies. "That must've been horrible for you."

"Well, let's just say, it wasn't my finest hour," I grimace.

"I didn't exactly mean that," she says. "You were amazing actually. You came across as extremely genuine and articulate." Her face falls slightly. "It was only when that piece of shit came on, I could see how frightened you were. It was completely out of order. They had no right to drop you in it like that."

"Well, they did," I say stiffly, looking around me for somewhere to sit. I pull out one of the dining chairs and flop into it. Silas and Christina take my cue, joining me at the table.

"It wasn't too bad, you know," Christina pulls my hand away from where it's massaging my aching forehead. "Hey… you did good," she squeezes my hand in encouragement. "Really good Edi."

"God, the way she kept calling you Meredith…" Silas bristles. "I wanted to yell at her for that."

"I sorted it. Anyway, it's only a name." But as I say this, I realise, it's not only a name, it's an identity; my identity.

"They, can call me Meredith as much as they like… but Meredith doesn't exist anymore. She can't hurt me," I affirm, "and neither can Bobby!" His hold, I once thought so imperious, has gone. I've finally escaped from his shadow.

289

"Now, I've broken my silence, he has no power," I say a little doubtfully. "Anyway; how will you approach this with the authorities? The interview went fine for him... nothing was revealed. He won't be getting away with... all the other things?" I add, not wanting to speak of *those other things* in these surroundings.

"Don't worry; it's under control," Christina reassures. "Let's just say, the interview didn't end when you left... in fact, it got quite interesting," she raises her eyebrows. "But we can discuss that later... ah, here's the tea." Releasing my hand, she leans back in her seat making room for Wendy to lower the tray onto the table. "Lovely, jubbly..."

"Oh, puh-lease!" I laugh, shaking my head at her overzealous appreciation.

"What? It looks absolutely delicious guys," she praises the cakes and biscuits, while Wendy pours and David and Nic take their appointed places around the table.

"Berrr!" Nic mumbles.

"He's at the Barn," Silas says, taking his China cup. It looks like a child's tea-set in his huge meaty fist. "If you're up to it on Saturday, we can take him for a run on the field in the morning; what do you say?"

"Berrr, runnn, yesss!" Nic rocks, back and forth, indicating his approval of Silas's suggestion.

"Anyway, I think we'd better get going. Are you coming with us?" Silas poses the question to Christina.

"Err, no, I'll stay for a bit I think." She looks fondly at the group of young adults around her. It's the softer side she rarely shows, but I suspect she needs the down-to-earth comfort of their warm company. It's so far reaching from the demands of her regular day to day life, the atmosphere here must be a balm to her overactive mind. "We'll pick up tomorrow, if that's okay?"

"Yeah, no worries. Thanks for the tea, Wendy." He winks at her, causing David to sit to attention and Wendy to smile modestly.

"You're welcome," she grins, sneaking a cheeky sideways glance at David. *Oh, how I love these two!*

"See you in the morning, Tina" Silas nods, "... and we'll see you lot on Saturday?"

"What's Saturday?" they all chorus, looking excitedly around at each other then back to Silas, who smiles indulgently. "After we walk Bear, let's just say, you'll all need some party clothes," and he leaves it at that.

"Bye, then," he waves. As we leave the room, the excited chatter has ensued about the prospect of needing 'party clothes.'

"What was all that about?" My curiosity is piqued.

"The Gala; didn't Christina mention it? It's on Saturday evening. Surely she told you?"

"It must've slipped her mind," I say tartly, unsure as to why she's failed to mention it. I knew it was happening soon, I just didn't realise it was this weekend!

290

"It's a nice excuse to buy something new to wear," he jiggles his eyebrows suggestively.

"Oh yeah," I say as I open the car door, "and what exactly did you have in mind?"

"Oh, I don't know…" he counters, climbing into the driver's seat. "Something as sexy as Hell," he growls, "with underwear to match!"

"You're incorrigible," I laugh, relaxing fully for the first time since this morning. Perhaps I could pay Oreille a visit?

"And you're beautiful," he plants a soft kiss on my lips, "and if that Bastard ever comes within an inch of you again," he grates, "I'll fucking kill him!"

Perhaps a few days ago, I would have regarded this declaration as simply an overprotective boyfriend issue; staking a claim and flinging out a subtle warning to the opposition. But now I know different. There's absolutely nothing veiled about this threat; it is much more than an overprotective boyfriend; he's delivering a clear statement of intent. If Bobby dares to harm me in any way… he's a dead man. Literally!

CHAPTER 52

The following morning, after evading yet another media van at the perimeter fence, we join the rest of the team in the board room for a rundown on the day's activities. I don't miss the subtle looks passing between Susan and Jasper. I suspect something's happened there; the furtive glances speak volumes.

"So, do we all know what we're doing today?" Christina asks the team.

"Yeah," they chorus enthusiastically.

"Yup!" Jasper salutes. "All systems go… literally!"

"Okay then guys, there's just one more exciting piece of business to deal with and I'll let you all go," Christina looks expectantly at Silas, who shrugs, indicating this is her meeting, her forum. "Alright, then… today we welcome another member to the growing RTC team. Please meet our new company accountant, Elizabeth!"

My mouth drops open as I turn and watch my beautiful girl sashay through the heavy oak door. As always, she looks a dream, in her simple navy-blue shift dress, her blonde curls piled atop her head in a messy bun. Her skin is still glowing and lightly sun-kissed and but for a minimal sweep of mascara on her upper lashes to emphasise her toffee-coloured eyes, and a coating of nude lip-gloss, her face is bereft of make-up. She looks stunning.

"Hi everyone," she smiles broadly, flashing me with an even brighter grin when she catches the look of sheer astonishment on my face. "Surprise!" she quips on a breathless giggle.

"Oh… you…" I'm lost for words. Her new job is *here?* She's our new accountant?

"I warned you…" Silas shakes his head at Christina, his perception at my reaction, as usual, is bang on the money. "I told you she wouldn't be happy," he warns.

"Hiya, I'm Sue and this is Nasima." Susan, sensing the subtle change in the atmosphere, and eager to meet the new girl, seizes the opportunity to jump right in with introductions.

"Hello, welcome to the team," Nasima waves shyly.

"And Jasper." Susan beams at her workmates, encouraging them to welcome their new colleague into the fold.

"'sup?" Jasper drawls at Lizzy.

"Hi, hi… hi…" she greets each in turn before returning her eyes to me. "Hi?"

She has got to be kidding me!

I'm completely gobsmacked.

Pushing away from the large oval table, Silas rests his hand on my shoulder, before whispering, "go easy on her; c'mon guys!" and kissing me once on my crown, he exits the room; the rest of the team follow in his wake like a row of baby ducklings, and I'm left alone with Christina and Lizzy.

"Was it something I said?" Lizzy speaks through her fixed smile; her eyes follow the mass exodus as they file through the door.

"No darling," Christina purrs, "they're just busy. Now, would…"

"Hold on… just hold your blooming horses there," I cut her off, raising my palms to make my point. "When were you going to tell me?"

"Um, now?" Lizzy offers with her most innocent air.

"Seriously? You're working here?"

"Edi," Christina cajoles, "Lizzy is perfectly suited to the role, and as the Air Business is … evolving… we need her… you and Silas need her," she says pointedly.

"Evolving… I…" I'm confused.

Christina faces Lizzy, and placing an encouraging hand on her arm, she turns her and guides her through the boardroom door. "If you just follow the others; Susan will show you around the rest of the building. I'll be out soon to settle you into your new office."

"Oh, okay… see you later." And away she goes; positively skipping in joy.

"Would you care to explain?" I ask, leaving no room for procrastination I dig my knuckles into my hips and tap my foot impatiently.

"Silas told you, right?" she puzzles on a furrowed brow; clearly doubtful of how much I'm party to.

"Told me what?" In fact, he told me plenty, but he failed to mention my daughter was starting work here today. Now I come to think of it; when I'd asked Lizzy for details about the interview, she was pretty vague on the topic. I'll be having words with that little madam.

"I mean, he told you the 'Business' was changing?"

"No… well, I mean yes… he said he was out… of the *other Business*'… you know?" It's so difficult to discuss this as if it's nothing more than closing down a branch of a shop or moving offices… this is sooo not like closing a shop!

"Well, then you know." She starts to gather together her paperwork and tidy it away in the buff folders.

"Yes, I know… he's out." But there seems to be more I'm not party to. Or am I just being dense?

"Edi…" she sighs, patiently, as if she's placating a small child. "Just because Silas is out, doesn't mean *The Rose Council* is at an end. We're continuing… Our mission is too important. Only, with Silas gone, it means we can't remain here. We need to relocate our headquarters."

"Oh." I hadn't even given it a second of thought… of course, just because Silas was leaving, doesn't mean they all are. "I didn't think," I say quietly.

"No… well… the transfer is fairly easy to be honest. In a business like ours, there's always the possibility of discovery; we have contingencies. We'll convene in France to begin with, pending authorization from Interpol and the UK Home Office." She has her head down and her back to me. "Leon will liaise with the relevant authorities." She's simplifying for my benefit.

"I..." I don't know what to say.

"Edi... this job we do is so important to me personally. You know my reasons. I can't walk away; not yet."

Turning towards me, she looks ardent in her commitment. "The global ambition to rid the earth of these sorts of people will never cease. As long as they're filling the world with their evil, *we* will exist to counteract them; International collaboration is the only way forward. We need to work together so we can stop them in their tracks and slow this growing pandemic. Unfortunately, like every virus, the minute you control one outbreak, a mutation occurs and a second, more resilient wave usually follows. That's why we will never give up. They evolve," she shakes her head.

"I know for Silas the battle is over; finished. I knew the moment he set eyes on you; he'd lose his drive for revenge. And that's a good thing... a great thing... believe me..." she entreats, resting her hands on my shoulders and looking directly into my eyes. There's no hidden agenda, no visible malice, just honesty in her blue depths. "He loves you... I'd go as far as to say, he can't live without you. He has to leave. Remaining would make it far too dangerous for him. To do what he does... did; you need to remain detached, keep focussed on the goal and be ruthless and selfish... Silas isn't capable of that anymore... because of you."

The sincerity almost brings me to tears. "But, what will you do? Where will you go?" I hadn't given her own circumstances a moment's consideration in all of this. If anybody is going to lose here, it'll be Christina.

"Me? I'll be fine," she says puzzled. "Why shouldn't I be? As I said, *The Rose Council* will continue... I'll still be needed, here in the UK; just not at this location."

"Oh?"

"This site will revert to a legitimate Airport... that's all there is to it... I'll become a sleeping partner and Royal Tudor Charters will carry on as normal. Besides, my son is here. I could never move too far away from Dominic, and I'd be a fool to remove him from The Beeches. It's his home."

Patting my arms, she turns and carries on with the job in hand. Picking up her stack of folders and holding them to her chest, with her free hand she checks her pocket, ensuring her cigarettes are where they should be before handing me my empty coffee cup. "Now, you're in need of a caffeine fix and I'm in need of some fresh-air." She sidles past me to the door. "After you."

Collecting my own files, I tuck them under my arm as I heave the heavy door open. "So, Lizzy then?"

"Oooh, yes..." she changes subject like the snap of her fingers. "She's amazing. If the business is growing, we need an accountant and she's perfect."

"Hmmm, I just wish you'd had the guts to tell me."

"We did... just not directly!"

We separate. Me heading for the kitchen to replenish my coffee cup and ponder over Christina's news, and her, to the foyer, where I'm sure she'll be marching to the field for a quick smoke. I stare out of my window at the runway beyond. Everything *looks* exactly the same, but it's not. The landscape has changed.

I now know the grey corrugated aircraft hangar, standing out there all innocent looking, is actually housing a strong room containing hundreds of lethal weapons. I know Silas, himself, is a lethal weapon. I know *The Rose Council* exists, the reason why they exist, and I know who their next assignment is. I know who the members are and that they are affiliated with the International Crime Agency. And more importantly, I also know why they do what they do.

I know so much but have little or no control over that knowledge. I'm glad Silas is out. He deserves some peace; some normality. Christina seems content with her decision to remain with the Council. I suspect Johannes has something to do with that. I just hope and pray she'll be happy.

"Hey there… truce?" Lizzy enters my office, sheepish and bearing gifts. Two large mugs of builder's tea. Extra strong, extra dark and completely capable of supporting a colony of small rodents; let alone a solitary trotting mouse! Just how we northern lasses like it.

"Thank you… how was your first day?" I've managed to get over the initial shock at discovering my darling daughter is now an official member of the RTC team.

"I'm sorry I didn't say," she blows a stream of cooling breath over her tea. "I didn't want to jinx it."

"It's okay; I'm fine." I am *now*… I cool my own tea before taking a welcome sip, "Mmm. That's good."

Christina pop's her head around the door. "Okay, I'm off…See you tomorrow?"

"Yeah, bright and early," Lizzy beams.

"See you." We wave her off.

"She seems really nice?" Lizzy poses the question without a hint at discretion or embarrassment. "She was the bird who was married to Silas?"

"Yep!" I drain my tea and hold out my hand for Lizzy's mug. "And I wouldn't call her a 'bird' within earshot… she's your new boss." Sometimes, Lizzy will speak first and engage brain later. "I'll just drop these in the sink, then we can go."

"Are you not going with Silas?" she asks. "I can take Rusty-Bucket. I think me 'n' her are on a celebratory takeaway tonight," she says. "Sam wants to have a picnic on the roof. Hot tub and bubbles – both kinds."

"Ooh, Champagne and farting, sounds lovely; excuse me if I decline to join you." I drag on my jacket and pick up my bag and lap-top.

"Hah! I meant hot-tub bubbles and Champer's, 'though after a takeaway, you never know with Sam."

"Well," I flick off the office lights, and pick up the cups as we head for the foyer. "If it's anything like the effect it has on Bear, God help you." Reaching round the kitchen door, I place the mugs on the counter. I'll wash them in the morning.

"Hiya, gorgeous," Silas meets us in reception. "Ready to go?"

"Yeah, I'm in need of a bath and a large glass of something cold!"

Kissing my lips, he relieves me of my bags. "And how was your first day?" he asks a delighted Lizzy – I smile, musing how it must have been so very different from *my* first day, when he was gorgeous but rude and brooding, relentlessly stalking me to the gym and around the supermarket!

"It was really good; thank you for the opportunity," she replies in genuine appreciation – that's my girl.

We head outside to where Bear is sitting patiently beside the Range Rover. The dark transit from this morning has gone. Turning to Lizzy I give her a tight motherly hug.

"See you tomorrow. Don't drink too much..." I warn. "Remember, you're a working girl now …"

"Yeah, you too and I won't, and I know!" Rolling her eyes in mock exasperation at my fussing, she jingles the car keys and traipses off to where my old trusty BMW is parked.

"Home James… and don't spare the horses." Contentment envelops me and I smile at Silas as we climb into the car. Bear, in his usual fashion, snakes between the front seats and settles into the back, flopping down onto his tartan rug.

"I'm starving. What're we having for supper?"

"Well, I know what I want to eat," Silas grins suggestively, "but after that, I quite fancy lasagne."

"Sounds good to me," I agree, fastening my seat belt. We head off home.

CHAPTER 53

"So, how did your dad take the news?" I lean back, patting my full stomach. Silas's homemade lasagne was unbelievably good. We sit in semi-naked comfort on the living room floor. I've had a double helping of Silas, followed by a double helping of lasagne but now I'm regretting the second portion. Pasta is so filling.

"He was good." Silas isn't giving much away about his conversation with his dad. If I want to know more, I'll need to keep digging.

'He was good.' "How do you mean?" I'm not letting this drop. There're loads to consider. An International Anti-Crime Organisation can't just disassemble from one location one day then the next reassemble somewhere else - possibly in a different country - contingency plans or no contingency plans. Surely there's tons to do regarding logistics and transfer. Not to mention the restructure of the board members!

"I mean just that... he was good... really happy." He peels an orange delicately. I'm transfixed as I watch his giant hands, deftly pull away the skin from the juicy flesh without breaking it so the long curl of peel remains in one complete piece. He drops the skin onto the coffee table and breaks the orange in half. "Want some?"

"Thanks." I take it and tear off a segment, popping it into my mouth. "So, what did he say, exactly?"

"He said, it was about time." Silas eats his own slice of orange.

"And?... Silas, come *on*... it's like pulling teeth!" I exclaim, shifting on the sofa so I'm more comfortable. I really shouldn't have had that second helping.

"Okay," he teases, tenderly stroking my inner thigh, all the same aware I'm impatient to hear the finer details of their conversation. "He said, he was delighted I'd made the decision to leave." He swallows the last piece of juicy orange.

"He said, he and mum, would take the opportunity to 'retire' fully. Apparently, the only reason he remained on the Board was because of me. Now I'm out, there's no reason for him to stay... he's out." A smattering of guilt puckers his brow at the realisation, his parent's 'retirement' was delayed because of him, but it's only a temporary frown; he's soon smiling again.

"Really? Oh, Silas, that's wonderful. All of you!" It really is. It means the connection to *The Rose Council* will be severed for the Tudor family... they've served their dues.

"Ah, not quite all. Tia isn't ready to quit yet."

"Tia?" what's she got to do with it? "I thought she's a cleaner?" I state questioningly.

"Yeah, exactly..." he leaves it hanging, allowing me to get there on my own... I soon make the connection.

"Ooh, you mean she's an actual *'cleaner'*! I emphasize the word, with invisible quotation marks, "like, she cleans the... like in... like *Winston Wolf!*" I remember him using the analogy. I thought it was tongue-in-cheek at the time. Talk about dropping hints!

297

"Yeah, only better," he nods. "She earns a fortune; she's the best in the business, there's no way she's leaving."

"How did your parents take that bombshell?"

"What can they do?" Landing a playful slap on my leg he stands, picking up the orange peel. "She's a big girl, she has no dependents and what she does isn't strictly dangerous; she'll hang up her marigolds one day." He leaves the room, heading for the kitchen. "Tea?" he asks, clearly ending the conversation.

"Please."

There's loads I still want to know. But I realise, by continuing this thread, he'll be forever discussing the one thing I want to put behind him. If I keep raking over the coals, the embers will continue to smoulder; best to let it fizzle out rather than risk a reignition. With this in mind, I heave myself off the sofa and go and help with the washing up.

After we've cleared everything away and got dressed, we take Bear for his favourite evening stroll across the open fields behind Silas's barn. I cling onto Silas as if there's no tomorrow; content to be doing something so perfectly simple - just to be walking with this man - my thumb hooked through his belt loop - in these beautiful fields at sunset.

I'm not naïve though, I'm aware there's still plenty of loose ends to tie up. Bobby, for one. I know Christina mentioned the interview carried on without me, but I can't bring myself to watch it on catch-up TV.

"Your miles away," he pulls me close so our bodies jostle together as we walk. I love it!

"I'm in Heaven…" I purr. "Is that far enough away?"

"I'm in Heaven too," he sighs. "You know, I can't remember the last time I felt like this."

"How do you mean?"

"I mean, this calm… this content… this happy…" he pulls up short, dragging me into his arms.

The dying sun is setting behind us and the whole world is bathed in an iridescent burnt-sienna glow. A slight breeze ruffles through the long grasses generating wave after wave of rippling wheat; it looks like the whole meadow is coated in shimmering gold flames, a living breathing entity of the sheerest beauty.

"You make me so happy… you're my life… I love you Honey-bee."

Taking my wrist he unfastens my watch, removing it, placing it into his jean's pocket. Lifting my hand to his lips, he breathes, "this represents your life so far." He kisses each small bee with reverence, my pulse ignites and my heart swells.

"I want to have my place, I want to belong here," stroking his thumb over the void; the space in the string of fluttering insects, he places his lips to my heated skin. "Here, this is my place; will you add me to your life?"

"Yes; I will," I whisper softly. He's already indelibly cemented in my life; I can't imagine my life without him in it but he needs to know he's permanent. "I will add you to my life."

The tattoo isn't complete; not yet. I don't know why I left the void. Maybe on some subconscious level I was waiting for something incredible to fill it. Silas has filled the void in my life; a void I was unaware existed until I met him. Now I have, the emptiness I didn't even know was there has dissipated, gone forever. Now I'm brimming full, overflowing with happiness and indescribable joy. It's time to demonstrate it... so, at the earliest opportunity, I will add one more bee. The one special bee that's been absent for so long... my Silas, bee. My Boss-man, bee.

"I love you too," I whisper.

"I know." He kisses me slowly. "Let's go home, Honey-bee... Bear!" He calls, and the beautiful creature appears, bounding gracefully through the golden ears of corn; his coat aglow with the scattering rays of the setting sun. "C'mon lad, let's go."

I don't know how I'm awake so early? I'm refreshed and thoroughly revitalised, which is a complete miracle considering we made love for most of the night. Silas was insatiable, no sooner did we finish one steamy session, he started again, barely waiting for me to recover my breath before he was growing hard inside me once again. It was as though his body was driven by an invisible, unquenchable force, fuelled by the potent combination of both freedom and desire.

I was a more than willing participant, more than happy to bend to his wishes. My own thirst for fulfilment was quenched over and over until finally, sleep overtook me and, exhausted and sated, I rested peacefully in his arms.

This morning, I have neither stiffness, sickness nor any aches and pains. I'm supple, as if I've completed a relaxing Bikram Hot Yoga session, rather than a midnight marathon of scorching, mind-blowing, delicious sex!

I stand at the kitchen window in my fluffy dressing gown while nursing my first inky brew of the day, watching Bear snuffle around the garden. He's in his element, sniffing out where the visiting foxes have scented a trail and re-marking the boundaries of his territory by cocking his leg on the trees, overlaying their scent with his own. I get the impression it's a never-ending morning ritual, a battle of wills and territorial one-upmanship that will be ongoing for years to come.

Smiling, I put my cup in the sink and go and fetch his bowl, ready to make his breakfast. Rummaging in the cupboard, I find his biscuits and unfastening the bag, locate the measuring scoop inside.

Silas is still sound asleep. Without him here and Bear still concentrating on his doggy security patrol in the garden, I'm in need of some background noise so I switch on the small kitchen TV.

Counting out the scoops of Kibble, I'm distracted by the breakfast presenter. Her voice grates on my second nerve after our brief encounter a couple of days ago. Gritting my teeth at the vacuous, self-important whine of her over-the-top jabber, I place Bear's breakfast on his mat. There's no need to call him in; he has a sixth sense like Radar where foods concerned. Garden detail complete, he's already sat expectantly waiting, licking his lips.

"There you go, boy," I stroke his head. His coat is warm, an indication we might be in for a lovely sunny Friday.

"So, on Wednesday," Marina squawks, far too gleefully, "we had a couple of very interesting guests in the studio." *Oh please!* "If you recall, I interviewed Meredith Frost, which unfortunately wasn't the best interview…"

"Cheeky cow," I mutter under my breath, while pouring a second cup of tea.

"Morning," Silas wanders in, looking sculptured and edible. He saunters over and kisses me as he passes on his way to the coffee machine. "Who's a cheeky cow?" He fiddles with some switches then joins me in front of the TV while he waits for the machine to perk up.

"That bloody woman," I gesture with my mug. "She's in the process of explaining to the whole world what a disaster my interview was… it was her bloody fault in the first place!" I moan. "Cheeky cow!" I repeat for emphasis.

"I doubt this will be on the BBC world news," he quips as he fills his beaker with hot, strong coffee.

"Shhh," I hush him. "I want to listen to this bit."

The vapid chatter continues, "We have some very fascinating developments in regard to Mr Robert Price," she beams in delight. "If you recall, on Wednesday, he denounced the fact he had a son… letting himself down quite badly in reference to the young man, who has Downs Syndrome."

"Why is that *all* everybody sees? *Why* do they have to label David like that? It's disgusting!" That was a low blow; she's really annoying me now, bloody stupid woman!

"Shhh, let's hear it then…" he soothes.

The screen segues to a replay of Wednesday. It's the second part of the interview; the piece after I'd left the studio, the piece I'm yet to see.

Bobby is looking decidedly flustered and angry. I know he's seething; I can see the muscles twitch as he clenches and unclenches his jaw.

"So, Mr Price, that was an eventful reunion." Marina, clearly shaken at the unexpected turn of events, valiantly attempts to rescue the segment… there are still a few minutes left to fill.

"It's all a complete lie… she's lying… that… that… *'bleeep'*… has nothing to do with me!" Bobby spits in utter fury, raking a shaking hand through his hair. Clearly, he's unaware he's still live on air! Thankfully they've managed to mute the more repugnant language in this replay. But it doesn't prevent the audience from reading his lips.

"Jesus!" I gasp, disbelief and revulsion overwhelm me in equal measure… could I detest this man more?

"Shh," Silas places his arm around me as if to protect me from the nasty bastard on screen. "It's okay Honey-bee, he's one incredible shit… we know that; what did you expect?"

"Er…" Marina can't quite believe what she's just heard, neither can I quite frankly… I'm bloody livid! "Mr Price, we're still rolling, perhaps you're just in shock to discover you have a son?"

"What? No… listen…" Gathering himself, as bold as brass he faces the camera. "Is this on? We're live?" he barks at Marina, who nods, visibly shrinking away from him, her eyes darting across the studio to where I know the floor manager to be. Bobby faces the camera and launches into his vengeful attack.

"That woman is nothing more than a lying, conniving *'bleeep!'*" He's raging live on breakfast television. "I've *one* daughter… I *don't* have a son… especially not a… *'bleeep'*… one!" In the background, I hear Marina's sharp wince of disgust at the offensive expletives.

Glaring with icy menace down the lens I feel the punch in my gut as if he's right there beside me. I go cold with fear as he drives his threat home.

"Meredith, I'm speaking directly to you now. I'm coming for you," he snarls, jabbing his finger at the invisible enemy.

"You can't escape me… you and Elizabeth, you belong to me; you're mine! I know where you are, and I'll get you for this, you *'bleeep'* Bitch!" His breathing is even and measured, there's not an iota of tension or unease about him. He's utterly calm, collected and terrifying… he's revealed live on television his true colours without a hint of remorse or regret. He means business.

"Jesus!" Silas whispers, "fucking Hell…" instinctively, he enfolds me in a protective embrace, as if to remove me from Bobby's verbal threat.

"Well," the screen has shifted back to a far more composed Marina, now live in the studio. "That was the shocking moment Mr Price issued a warning to his ex-wife live on air." Marina becomes sincere. "I must apologise to everyone who was affected by Mr Price's comments; comment's which are not upheld by the corporation." They're covering their arses. "In direct response to this outburst, we have received several complaints and the BBC wishes to apologise unreservedly for the remarks made."

Yet they still repeated it! WTF!

"I can also confirm, following information received from an unnamed source, the Metropolitan Police are very keen to speak to Mr Price, in relation to this and a number of other, unrelated incidents…"

I go from fuming to stunned at the news. *Fuck a duck!* This changes things, I can't believe it… they're really going after him!

"Couldn't happen to a nicer guy!" Silas grinds. "The supercilious bastard just can't keep his powder dry. This is what I mean… he's so self-assured, he honestly believes he's untouchable; the arrogant prick – his ego will be his downfall!"

301

"…leading to a dawn raid on a property in East London this morning; I can confirm that a thirty-eight-year-old man has been remanded into police custody and is currently assisting with enquiries into several incidents relating to a known Organized Crime Gang."

Shuffling her papers, she smiles, directing her attention on the second camera; the well-rehearsed segue, effectively realigns the angle – drawing a line under the whole sordid item in favour of a new more palatable subject. "Now… have you ever thought you were being scammed? Our next guest is…" I pick up the remote and cut her off.

"They've got him?" I spin around breathlessly. "They've really got him?" I can't believe it! The terror I felt at his threat has been eased by the knowledge he's finally locked away.

"It certainly sounds like it…" Silas confirms my suspicions.

"Did… did you do this?" It has to be the work of *The Rose Council*, surely? "Who made the call?"

"I told you; he got what was coming to him." Silas is unforthcoming, he knows who it was but isn't saying. "Now we just need to make it stick, and Mr Price will be facing a very long holiday at Her Majesty's pleasure!" He places his mug in the dishwasher. "Shower?"

"Err, yeah… yes," I'm bewildered. "I'll be up in a minute…" I can't believe it; it's over… finally he's out of my life.

Bear whines, attracting my attention. I shlep over to his mat and pick up his empty water bowl still reeling from the news; Bobby has been arrested! I place his fresh drink on the floor, then take myself upstairs, where I can hear Silas's singing along to Tom Petty's *Free Falling,* as it blares from the radio. He sounds happy and that makes me happy too.

CHAPTER 54

"Okay guys," I smile at the team, "it's over to you." The day is going to be busy. Christina is at the Café Royal, organising the finer details for tomorrow night's Charity Gala. It should be a fabulous evening and I'm really looking forward to it. With Bobby securely under lock and key, I can truly relax for the first time in years.

This morning, I was visited by the CID, who wanted to interview me in regard to Bobby's past. Thankfully the interview was very short. There was nothing new I could add to what they already knew; we were together for just over three years until I was eighteen, and I left following yet another violent attack.

Looking back, I had no real evidence to offer them, other than the old photographs of me with covered up bruises and an historic hearsay account of physical assault, which bearing in mind I never actually reported it to the police at the time would be my word against his.

As there's no other proof to the beatings, the only thing they can do is introduce a further count of historical rape in addition to the numerous citations against him, which should help to substantiate one of the more recent charges of sexual assault against a minor.

In this instance, we have the physical proof in the form of Lizzy. Paternity will be easy to confirm with a DNA test. Along with her date of birth, and my own, it's conclusive evidence of statutory rape.

I've been advised I won't be required to testify as my statement isn't relevant to the current case; but as it is pertinent to the facts, it can be disclosed as a witness statement in open court adding context and corroborating recent findings. This comes as a huge relief, as it means I won't need to face him in court. I just hope the discoveries of the investigation are solid enough to stand up and he goes away for a long, long time.

I'm taking a well-deserved tea break. Silas is in the hangar with Gerard. They're conducting an inventory of all the 'hardware' in the strong room. Everything needs to be logged, checked and packed securely away, ready for removal and transport to the new secure location. I wish they'd chosen a different day to do it; perhaps Sunday when nobody is around. I know it all has to be removed. I just think it'd be better done under the veil of darkness or something, not in broad daylight when some unsuspecting soul could see it and end up having the fright of their life! I'm still struggling to come to terms with it all myself. I find the whole situation bizarre.

Lizzy has settled in really well. Last night's celebration takeaway was consumed, by all accounts, both guilt and wine free. One small bottle of prosecco followed by a couple of beers was all they drank before they spent the remainder of the evening making 'bubbles' in the hot tub. This morning, she was here before I was, settled in and with the assistance of Nasima, familiarising herself with the spreadsheets, customer invoices and accounts. I'm so proud of her.

I've updated her about Bobby's situation but she already knew. At first, she appeared upset and even concerned by the news and I expected question after question about what his dealings were and how he's involved. But I needn't have worried. Her concern was more for me and her brother. Apparently, Sammy had watched the whole interview and was so utterly incredulous at the content; she was barely coherent by the time Lizzy arrived home. Screeching so loudly in protest at the TV. Lizzy had to threaten to douse her in cold water if she didn't calm down.

The grubby details were all over the tabloids this morning. Bobby is in prison awaiting his Arraignment. He has a shit hot Barrister, well known for his association with some of the more notorious criminals and underworld bosses. Just the sheer fact he's managed to retain his services is enough evidence for me to confirm his guilt.

Silas expects him to plead guilty to some of the lesser charges, a calculated ploy to dilute the possibility of being found guilty to the more heinous ones. I just hope they throw the book at him. I'm not going to the initial hearing. I don't want to see him again; ever. They have my statements and that's enough.

My main concern now is for David and Lizzy. Lizzy understands, but David? I just hope and pray he didn't see the rest of the segment. Mark gave me his word he'd make sure the TVs were programmed to a different channel; however, I know, word or not, the staff will have had a field day watching my unladylike outburst on National Television.

I've made arrangements to visit The Beeches tonight. Using the Gala as an excuse, I'll pop in to see Mark, test the water and see how the land lies in relation to my now known identity. I can't imagine it'll be anything like favourable, especially with Wendy's parents. I expect her stuffy mother will be beside herself. By way of an olive branch, I'll offer them invitations to the Gala.

We have several guests from The Beeches coming and I'm sure they'll enjoy the evening, especially with the local celebrity attendees. We're promised a couple of premier league footballers and their model wives who've endorsed our business through their continued custom. Rubbing shoulders with millionaires, Lords and Ladies as well as members of the government have ensured the sale of over two hundred and fifty tickets. Christina has worked tirelessly to promote the fundraiser. It should be a fantastic night.

"Daydreaming?" Christina wanders into my office, carrying her customary stack of folders and files.

Plonking them down on my desk, she pats her pockets. I know she's looking for her cigarettes. It's amusing how this tiny mannerism of hers has become so noticeable to me. She never reveals anything; remaining cool and calm under most situations. However, this small trait has become somewhat of a 'tell' with her. I know she does it when she's distracted by something. Of course, today I expect it's the close proximity of tomorrow night's Gala that has her hand stroking the well-tailored pocket.

"Oh, you know… thinking about the boys, the girls, Silas… Oh and a certain low-life scumbag who shall remain nameless and hopefully locked up," I muse.

"Hope is not a strategy," she asides knowingly as she flops into the chair next to mine. "Now, have you got your outfit sorted?"

She's said this before, about hope… or Silas has… or somebody has. It makes me wonder if the anonymous call came from Christina? I bloody hope so.

"Hmmm." I draw my mind away from the horrible and focus on the enjoyable. "I think I'm wearing the green again," I say abstractly.

"Oh no you're bloody not!" she scorns me. "You will be wearing red, and you will be wearing something new!"

I'm taken aback by this revelation. Was I supposed to know? Is there some significance to the red I am unaware of?

"Tudor roses are red…" her smile is sly and seductive. "He'll love it if you wear red."

"Ah, okay. Then I'll wear my red dress. It's newish; it's never been worn." That's one less thing to worry about.

"Huh!" Her eyebrows shoot up towards her hairline in astonishment. "Err, you certainly won't… I said new and I meant it, now pack your bags and get your coat on because we're going shopping!"

"Ughh," I groan, grabbing my hand bag and jacket. I know there's no point arguing with Christina when she's in this mood. "I have to be at the Beeches at seven," I remind her, "so we haven't got all evening to be leisurely shopping."

"Oh, I know… I'm coming with you. I want to see Nic to make sure his tuxedo is clean and ready for tomorrow." The joy in her voice is infectious. "What will David wear?"

"Probably a tee shirt and jeans," I ponder. Try as I might, I can't seem to interest him in anything else. He loves his slogan tee's; especially the red one, which states in yellow letters, *'Keep Calm It's Only an Extra Chromosome'*. Perhaps he should've worn it on Wednesday.

"No, it's black tie… he'll need a suit."

Oh Lord, no. I can imagine the drama. "Leave it with me," I say with some concern as we jump in Christina's car.

"Hey… wait!" Silas is running towards us, dressed in his stained, grease-monkey overalls. Bear gallops by his side. "You didn't think you could leave without saying goodbye, did you?" Sticking his head through the open car window he lands a huge passionate kiss on my mouth, taking his sweet time, sweeping his tongue against mine.

"Mmm." I don't think I want to go shopping anymore.

"Enough," Christina laughs. "If you don't put her down, she won't have any new knickers for you to admire tomorrow!"

"Oooh! We can't have that." Silas pulls his head out of the way as Christina depresses the switch causing the glass to ride up and shut him out. Silas mouths *'I love you'*, blowing me a kiss as we squeal out of the car park.

My thoughts return to David and the dilemma of the suit; there's no way I can get him one by tomorrow. Suddenly having a brainwave, I grab my phone from my bag, and ring Sammy. She'll be more than happy to assist and if anybody can persuade David to wear a suit, it'll be her. With Sammy on the case, I can relax and enjoy the experience of shopping for something new and red to wear for the Gala.

CHAPTER 55

"I can't believe you," I say to a grinning Christina as we drive to The Beeches. "The underwear was expensive enough," it was ridiculous, two-hundred and fifty pounds for knickers and a bra! "But I've never spent that much on a dress." I still can't bring myself to say the price aloud. It could feed a small Principality for several years I'm sure... "If you just donated the cost of the gown to the charity, you wouldn't need the Gala," I complain, feeling uncomfortable by the vulgarity of the hefty price tag.

"Seriously? If you're going to work in this industry, you need to understand that to get some of these disgustingly rich buggers to part with their lolly, you need to splash some cash yourself... speculate to accumulate!" She's adamant.

"You have to establish the impression of wealth; show off a little, flaunt it." She gives me a mischievous, sidelong up and down, then winks before turning her eyes back to the road. "If they think you only paid twenty quid for a frock, it won't impress them and that's all they'll give in return, but wear a six-hundred-pound gown, and you're on to a winner. It's all about one-upmanship with these fellows. You know how it is...I have a larger yacht; my dad's bigger than your dad... or in this case, my wallet is fatter than your wallet...

"It's a pissing contest at the end of the day; none of them have any idea of how nauseatingly wealthy they really are, so the odd couple of grand here or there is just a drop in the ocean to them, pocket change. Remember Monty and Victoria? He must've bought the entire Versace line for her at fashion week and she's never worn any of it."

Turning into the Beeches driveway, she adds, "just think of it as a means to an end; to energise the charitable donations... and besides, after your performance on the TV this week, they'll no doubt be falling over themselves to get a look at the *'back from the dead Meredith Frost'*."

"It's still obscene," I grumble reluctantly. "And *that's* staff exploitation," I add for good measure but understanding her point entirely.

"Oh, get over yourself!" she snorts. "Look on the bright side... Silas is going to be walking around the *Café Royal*, sporting a stiffy all night!" She finds this image hilarious for some reason, and I shake my head on a wry smile; she's incorrigible.

We're distracted from our girly chatter by the sight of an ambulance outside the main entrance. The rear doors are open and a paramedic is wheeling an empty gurney down the ramp, he's in a hurry.

"Oh no!" I exclaim. "It looks like someone's had an accident."

In unison, we leap out of the car and rush towards the door. I'm feeling relieved that neither of us has received the dreaded phone call. However, my comfort is short-lived, as on cue, Christina's phone begins to ring.

She looks at me with bewildered eyes as she notes the number... The Beeches... Something's happened to Nic.

"*NO!!*" she wails as in the wake of the paramedic she dives forcefully through the front door. I dash in, behind her, my heart in my mouth.

Inside is little short of organised pandemonium. The residents are standing around restlessly, looking anxious, lining the corridor, refusing to be escorted back to their rooms or the lounge. They're aware something is happening to one of their friends and nobody wants to leave in case they're needed.

"Please everyone, can you just go back into the lounge... we'll let you know as soon as we can, but please keep the corridor clear. The doctor needs space." Mark patiently and gently convinces the concerned residents to return to the sitting room. Several members of staff are assisting those who are more upset and unnerved into their chairs, giving comforting hugs and reassurance.

"Oh, Christina, thank God." Mark spots us and comes hastily forward. "He's in the gym," he announces, taking her elbow. I follow, frantically searching for David among the distressed faces in the living room. He's not there.

Christina is as pale as a ghost as she turns to me, choking back the fear in her voice. "Call him."

Nodding, I draw my phone from my bag and dial his number, he answers on the second ring. "Honey-bee, how're the new knickers? As sexy as all *fuck* I hope."

"Silas, baby, you need to come to The Beeches." I'm not going to sugar-coat this, it's serious and he needs to get his arse here, right now! "It's Nic."

The phone goes dead before I can say more. I know he'll be charging to his Range Rover; I can't have him driving like a lunatic, so I call him back. This time he answers on the first ring.

"What happened?" he bellows. I can hear him opening the car door, jumping in, starting the engine.

"Silas, calm down... I'm not sure of the details, but the ambulance is here. I think he's been running and they didn't know!"

"Fucking Hell," he yells, as I hear the wheels screeching on the asphalt. "If anything happens to him, I'm gonna be cracking sculls!"

"Just... just drive carefully... we don't need you in the hospital as well!" I plead, hoping he listens. "I love you," I whisper.

"I know," he returns, his voice only slightly calmer but still urgent. "I'll be there shortly." He hangs up.

The distraction of the conversation has interrupted my focus. I need to get to Christina and I need to find David. Quickly, I pocket my phone and head towards the gym. The sight which greets me is heart-wrenching.

Dominic is lying on the floor. David is kneeling by his side with his arm protectively round Christina's shoulder as she holds Nic's hand.

The Doctor has his head bowed in observation as he moves his stethoscope from place to place, examining Nic, listening to his heart, checking for his vital signs. His facial expression is grave; I can't really comprehend what's happening.

Searching the room, I see Mark speaking in low tones with the two paramedics; explaining the circumstances. Wendy is crying in the arms of the gym instructor, who is also sobbing lightly.

"Please," the Doctor is speaking, "could anybody who isn't immediate family, step outside. I need to assess this quickly before we can move him." He doesn't look up, but expects his instruction to be followed to the letter.

Mark, Wendy and the trainer slowly start to exit the gym. As they reach me, I turn, ready to join them.

"David," I whisper, trying to call his attention, "you need to let the Doctors help Nic," I say, opening my arm for him to accompany us.

"No!" Christina answers. "Please... stay... you *are* family... they're family," she stutters at the Doctor, who without breaking concentration, nods his approval. We're allowed to stay.

Relieved, I sidle closer to where they're all looking at Nic with great concern. This is unreal. It can't be happening, just when everything was beginning to go right.

"Did you call him?" Christina asks quietly.

"He's on his way," I answer, noting the break in my voice. "David, are you alright?" I need to know my boy is coping.

"Yes, mum," is his solid answer. I'm unable to hide my relief at hearing the strength in his voice.

"Mrs Tudor?"

"Royal," she corrects automatically. "But please call me Christina."

"Ms Royal, I'm afraid your son is in a serious condition. We need to hospitalise him urgently," the Doctor says without preamble. Christina will appreciate his directness; she deals better with straight talking. "The paramedics will be careful. We need to put him in a brace and collar, please don't be alarmed, it's for his safety."

"O... okay."

"Where is he?" Silas runs into the room. "My boy, what happened to him?" Kneeling beside Christina on the floor, he takes in the sight of his one remaining child and the depth of anguish in his eyes is suddenly unbearable. "Will he be, okay?"

It's the million-dollar question nobody has dared ask until now, and now it's out there, the room becomes chilled with a quiet dread at the possible answer.

Raising his head, and looking directly into Silas's eyes, the Doctor can't hide his own uncertainty. "Honestly, Mr Tudor, I don't know. It appears Nic has suffered a cerebral haemorrhage; it's stabilised enough for him to be moved to the hospital, but until I complete the scans, and have a clearer picture of the damage, I can't say for sure if he'll recover."

The wail Christina issues is the cry of a wounded animal caught in a trap. Frightening, unbearable to hear, devastating to witness. "Nooo!" she rocks back on her heels and cries to the ceiling, calling out beyond the rafters and up to the heavens, blindly seeking out something, pleading to the almighty to spare her the anguish of losing another child.

I can't bear it. This is a vengeful reminder of what it must have been like all those years ago when they lost Maya, and Nic received the devastating injury that damaged him forever... this can't be real... they don't deserve this twice.

"Please, if you can move aside. The sooner we have him at the hospital, the sooner they can help him."

Silas's eyes are wide with shock and worry as he assists Christina to her feet. David, relieved of his role, comes to me, his eyes swimming with tears, and wraps his arms tightly around my waist.

"Mummy, he just fell." Guilt tinges his words. Bewilderment and distress radiate from his concerned face. "We hadn't even started our workout... he fell and didn't move."

"Oh baby." Unable to bear his pain, I pull him into me offering comfort; kissing his hair as we helplessly observe the paramedics gently lift Nic onto the stretcher. "You did great, David. You'll see, he'll be okay."

He has to be...

"Okay, mum and dad, only one of you can come in the ambulance," the paramedic says as he passes us.

"Christina, you go, I'll follow." Silas releases a sobbing Christina into the custody of the Doctor, who gently takes her arm as they follow behind the stretcher.

"Car keys," Christina says as she passes me. I take them with what I hope is a comforting smile.

"We'll be right behind you..."

Silas doesn't look at me as he heads out of the door.

Taking hold of David's hand, I follow, keeping my eyes on the small procession before me. "C'mon, he'll be okay." I attempt to soothe David as we make our way to Christina's car.

Please, please, please... let him be alright...

CHAPTER 56

We've been here for over five hours now and Silas is so tense he's almost scaling the walls. Pacing the floor restlessly, his anxiety manifesting in agitation at the time it's taking the medical team to update us on Nic's condition. I watch him with concern, anxiously biting my lower lip. I'm unable to imagine the level of fear they both must be experiencing.

Christina sits beside me, uncharacteristically silent. Folded in on herself she seems shrunken somehow; her unfocussed eyes staring vacantly at the mustard-coloured gloss painted wall; seeing nothing but whatever horrors her imagination is conjuring. She must be petrified. I perch beside her with my arm around her shoulder, veiled in the echoing sense of wretched helplessness. Impotent. I have no words of comfort. Every time I try and compose something in my mind it just sounds trite and hollow; so, I sit here, mute, allowing them to digest what's transpired and prepare for whatever is yet to come.

David, desperate for something to occupy his mind and unable to remain still, has gone to fetch coffee from the vending machine.

I telephoned Lizzy and Sam to explain what's happened, though I omitted the more controversial details... they don't need to know everything... not yet...

Silas's parents and his sisters are waiting at home for an update. I can imagine the tension in that majestic place. They wanted to come to the hospital, but there isn't enough space in the waiting room for everyone so they've very kindly said they'll stay at the house and field phone calls, until they hear otherwise. It's very kind of them; they're wonderful people.

"Tomorrow..." Christina says suddenly, her voice ringing clear in the small room.

"What about tomorrow, sweetie?" I ask gently.

Silas has returned to his pacing. Every now and again, he stops and draws aside the small blue curtain, checking the window in the door for any sign of the medical team.

"The Gala..."

"For *fuck's* sake," Silas hisses under his breath. "They *must* know something by now." Frustrated, he opens - then finding the corridor deserted - closes the door, turning his back on it and landing dull frightened eyes on mine.

"What about the Gala?" I ask Christina gently, at the same time offering Silas a pacifying look, willing him to sit down, even if it's only for a couple of minutes. "You're going to wear the carpet out babe; they'll update us when they can." I endeavour to console them both... it's harrowing to see them so desolate and hopeless.

"You'll have to host it..." Christina's mind is still reeling in shock, but the thought of the pending charity Gala has given her something tangible to focus on. A diversion.

"No... no, sweetie, we'll cancel... I'll get Susan on to it..."

"It's too late... people are flying in from all over; there's no time. No, you'll have to host it... Elaine and Johannes can help you." The practicalities of work have straightened her back and I notice a solid tension creeping into her shoulders as the steely

311

businesswoman endeavours to claw her way out from beneath the weight of the concerned mother.

I don't want this unnecessary debate to deteriorate into a full-blown argument… I can see where this is leading. I understand fully, it's Christina's way of coping with her turmoil; a distraction from the battle going on in the operating theatre. Her armour plating.

As soon as we arrived at the hospital, we were ushered swiftly to the family consultation room while the medical team whisked Dominic away for further scans and tests. Eventually, after what seemed like decades, the consultant joined us.

"Good evening," he smiles mildly, his soft Indian accent soothing his deep voice. "I'm Mr Zaman, the consultant neurologist. I'm pleased to meet you." He holds out a meaty hand to Christina and Silas in turn, then extending his greeting to David and I in the form of a curt nod.

"What's happening?" Silas demands, politeness aside. "Where is he?"

"Mr. Tudor, please …" Without adjusting his tone, Mr Zaman indicates we should all take a seat. I watch his hand in awe - a huge hand - so large yet so talented. I'm momentarily transfixed by the improbability of those enormous digits ability to perform such delicate surgery. I shake the image away and resume my place beside Christina.

Once we're all settled into the adjacent sofas, he pulls over a wheelie chair and places it before us, leaning forwards to ensure we're fully engaged before he starts to speak.

"Currently Nic is stable. We've conducted some preliminary tests and we're satisfied, although there is some evidence of swelling, the bleed has stopped and there's *currently* no significant lasting damage." He pauses for a moment.

"Oh, thank God…" Christina exhales, clasping her hands in a preying motion.

"Thank you," Silas mutters under his breath, and my heart thumps in grateful relief at the news.

Yes, thank you Lord…

"Is that it?" Silas queries, lifting his gaze to the learned man who's waiting patiently for this piece of information to sink in.

"I don't know how much you know about your son's condition," he opens. "I'm sure you are fully aware of the 'complications' resulting from his … *accident…*" Wincing at his own choice of language he looks down at his shoes.

"That was insensitive of me, of course you do," he says this more to himself, as if he's scolding himself for being careless with his words. After a short interlude, he begins again.

"As you know, Dominic suffered severe brain trauma due to a bullet, which lodged itself in his Temporal Lobe," he says, tapping his right temple for emphasis. He looks to each of us in turn, evaluating our individual levels of understanding. Our collective silence is confirmation enough for him to gauge our awareness of the situation. He proceeds.

"In cases such as Nic's, there's no reason why the brain, after time, can't begin to recover some of the more cognitive functions originally believed lost for ever." He leans closer and drapes his arms loosely on his thighs, leaving his hands free to gesture.

"Scientists now know that the brain has an amazing ability to change and heal itself in response to mental experience. This phenomenon, known as neuroplasticity, is considered to be one of the most important developments in modern science for our understanding of the brain."

"So, what happened then? Is his brain healing... is... is that what you're telling us?" Silas demands, becoming agitated, confused. His eyes blaze with intense hope.

Christina stares wildly at the consultant in an attempt to absorb what she's hearing. "But he collapsed..."

"Please, Mr. Tudor, Ms. Royal... allow me to explain." Mr Zaman remains calm, intimating by his steady demeanour, that Silas should try to do the same; he continues swiftly with his clarification. "With a brain injury, circuits can become... dormant. The brain needs time to recover, build new pathways."

"Okay, that would seem to make sense, but why did he collapse then?"

"Over time, a foreign object, such as a piece of shrapnel, a bullet or even in some cases a splinter of wood, lodged in place for a number of years, can begin to move... we believe this is what's happened with Dominic." Again, he leaves time to gauge our perception. The man is attentive, which is encouraging.

"Go on..." Christina urges, impatient to know the details.

"It would appear the bullet has shifted from its original position. It's encapsulated in a pocket of tissue, which has formed around it; protecting his brain from further damage."

Mr Zaman lifts his hands, cupping his fingers and gripping them as if to demonstrate the physical process of forming a protective barrier. "However, the density of the tissue has increased over time and is now becoming a problem."

"How do you mean?" Silas asks, anxiously.

"I'll explain," Mr Zaman says patiently. "So, while the tissue initially provided a cushion against the bullet itself, it is now applying pressure which has resulted in the bleed and subsequent swelling. This is the cause of Dominic's sudden collapse."

Silas passes a furtive glance at Christina, who's sitting to attention, hanging expectantly on the Doctor's every word.

"What can you do?" Christina asks the obvious but terrifying question.

Zaman looks down at his shoes again, as if composing his reply with extreme care. However, when he eventually re-engages and looks up to continue, he doesn't immediately answer Christina's question.

"May I ask," he enquires gently, "have you noticed any differences or changes in Nic's behaviour recently? Nothing major, they would be very subtle variances, something only those who know him really well would notice." He searches our faces in turn for any clarity.

"He likes to run…" David interjects before the rest of us have even had time to think. As one we all turn our attention to my son.

"Is that new?" Mr Zaman looks to Silas and Christina for confirmation.

"Y…" Christina and Silas, barely utter their responses as David, once again jumps in with his.

"Yes," David replies eager to help. "He always liked to run, but now he runs more… like he knows it helps him."

"That's true… he does enjoy running, but we always assumed it was a symptom of his condition…" Silas confirms.

"Ah." David has the full attention of Mr Zaman now. "David," he engages him fully, "this is very important. Can you tell me of any other new things Nic has been doing lately?"

David's freckled brow puckers in deep concentration as he searches his mind for the subtle changes in his best friend. "He doesn't like jam," he states adamantly, "I mean, he won't eat it anymore. He always used to like my jam, but now he doesn't."

"Wonderful," the Consultant smiles widely, "this is the kind of thing I mean. It indicates changes to his perception of taste and emotion."

That he doesn't like jam? I'd have thought that was more of an indication to David's cooking rather than a sudden dislike for strawberries!

"What does it mean though?" Christina asks. "He collapsed," she repeats, still with a grain of confusion.

"Yes, he collapsed, but that in itself doesn't indicate further damage… it could just as easily be a minor shift in the position of the bullet, which resulted in the pressure that in turn, triggered the incident."

"I don't understand…" Christina frowns. "How…?"

"Brain healing is the process that occurs after the brain has been damaged," Mr Zaman explains. "If an individual survives the initial trauma, the brain has a remarkable ability to adapt. When cells in the brain are damaged and die, for instance by stroke, there will be no repair or scar formation for those cells. The brain tissue will undergo liquefactive necrosis, and a rim of gliosis will form around the damaged area. A pocket…"

This sounds bad, not good…

"The fact that Nic suddenly has an aversion to jam and an increased desire to run, is an indication of the subtle changes in his Hippocampus," he says this as if we should understand. We don't.

"Okay," Zaman ponders for a moment, searching for a clearer approach. "Let's look at the jam for example," he says, patiently. "Has Dominic always liked it?"

"Yes," says David…"

"No," chorus Christina and Silas.

"No, I mean, he never liked jam when he was small, before the accident," Christina clarifies. Silas nods his affirmation.

"So… after the accident?"

314

"I…er?" Christina looks from Silas to the Doctor and to me and shakes her head. "I guess his tastes changed?" She poses it as a question.

"Ah, it could be so, but it's more likely he was conforming to a new behaviour. He probably still didn't like jam; he just couldn't remember."

I think I'm beginning to understand. "Are you trying to say, his brain is remembering it doesn't like jam?" I ask, "even after all this time?"

Zaman nods sagely. "Yes… that's exactly what I'm saying. Time is indeed a great healer," he adds. "There's an abundance of truth in that phrase."

Silas takes a sharp inhale, boosted by the news his son may be experiencing some kind of delayed recovery. No matter how slight, this is a hugely positive step.

"Oh, my!" Christina sobs. "He's remembering?"

"Well, part of his mind is," the doctor smiles, at last offering the fragment of hope we've been waiting for.

"The temporal lobe, where the bullet is lodged, is located behind the temple, sheltering the auditory cortex, taking care of comprehension, and acting over emotions and memory. The Hippocampus is the area located within the temporal lobe. It's central for cognitive processes as well as integrative functions such as language etc. Most patients who suffer from this form of brain damage lose some cognitive capability. Cognition allows people to understand and relate to the world around them."

"So, what exactly is happening in there?" Silas asks, suspiciously.

"Mr Tudor, to tell you the whole truth, at this moment we don't fully know. We can only surmise." He looks at Silas with what appears to be an element of what? Encouragement? Optimism?

Where's he leading with this?

"What are you asking? Why are you looking at me like that?" Silas checks Christina's worried face. She too is looking earnestly at Mr Zaman, they're back to being scared.

"I need to ask your permission to operate." Zaman states bluntly. "If the bullet has moved, we need to know what, if any, danger there is of further brain damage… or to life expectancy," he adds gravely.

Silas's face crumples, all hope seems to melt away, leaving behind it the pain of facing another devastating blow.

"Mr Tudor, Ms Royal," Zaman pleads with them to look at him, "as I said, *currently* Nic is stable. For the time being at least. However, that situation could change and if it does, there's no telling at the moment if it will be for the better."

"So, you mean if you don't operate, he could deteriorate? He could die?" Christina's voice tremors, choked with suppressed tears.

Oh no…!

I hear David sniffing quietly beside me and reach for his hand.

"Yes." His abrupt response is jarring. Hearing it like that makes it all *real*. Nic could die… they could lose their son!

"I'm sorry, but surgery is the only real option for Nic. If we can successfully isolate the area of the brain where the pressure is building, we may be able to stem it. Inserting a shunt, will relieve it, but all surgery contains an element of risk, and brain surgery holds more."

"What are the chances of him surviving?" Silas is calculating the possibilities; he won't even contemplate the alternative.

"At the moment, I'd say we have a thirty percent probability of success."

Those odds don't sound promising.

Silas is silent. Pondering, weighing the barely non-existent alternative. The choice seems to be no choice at all, Hobson's choice. If they don't operate, he could deteriorate, or worse. If they do, he could still deteriorate. All I can see is bad news. It doesn't bear thinking about.

"Christina?" Silas looks at his ex-wife with unveiled tenderness. Their relationship is still one of true affection. They will always have a connection and that connection is currently lying in a cold, sterile hospital bed waiting for them to make a decision that could affect the rest of his life.

"Go ahead." Christina whispers before burying her face in her hands as if she can't come to terms with the decision, she's faced with.

"Where do I sign?" Silas looks resigned. He's always vowed to protect his family from whatever evil lies in store but this is beyond his control.

Mr Zaman passes Silas the paper and Silas scrawls his name, and with one stroke of the pen, he places his son's future in the hands of the neurologist.

"Thank you," Zaman says shaking Silas firmly by the hand. "You have my word; we'll do everything we can."

"I know you will." Silas turns to look out of the window.

"How long before you'll know?" I ask, noticing the weakness in my own voice.

"A few hours. Please, if you need to wait here, you're more than welcome."

"Can we see him?" Christina asks anxiously.

"Of course, but only for a moment. I'd really like to start the procedure as soon as possible. Please remember, Dominic is sedated so he won't be able to respond."

"We'll wait here." I stand, taking David's arm, hindering him from following Silas and Christina out of the room. They need some precious time alone with their son.

"Thank you," Silas whispers, placing a protective arm around Christina. I offer him an understanding smile… this is something they will always share, only they can truly comprehend.

"But mum?" David begins to protest, but a slow shake of my head is all he needs to understand.

That was five agonizingly long hours ago…

CHAPTER 57

Reaching for Christina's hand, I find myself replaying the details of the meeting with Mr Zaman. We wait patiently in silent contemplation, each lost in our own thoughts; all conversation has been muted, apart from Christina's sudden urgent need to discuss the finer details of tomorrow night's Gala.

Under duress, I've agreed to host the evening. Not that I'll need to do much. I have a schedule of events and a script and that should be enough. And if it isn't, I also have the support of Gerard, Johannes, Susan and Nasima to fall back on, not to mention the Chuckle Brothers and the indomitable, Elaine Whittham. But under the circumstances I can't rely on Silas's family attending.

Thankfully Christina had the forethought to hire a professional M.C, so really there's very little for me to do other than greet people, appear welcoming and apologise for Christina and Silas's absence. Oh, and get them to part with their dosh... piece of cake! I'll be relieved when it's all over.

"You'll need to organize the donation envelopes," Christina says, ticking off yet another item of her mental list.

"Yes," I answer, knowing I'm just paying her lip service.

The door opens, and David reverses into the room carrying a tray of coffees. "There's a doctor coming," he announces flurriedly, quickly placing the tray on the table.

No sooner has he said this, when there's a polite knock at the door and Mr Zaman enters, looking... well, looking no different than he did earlier. His demeanour gives nothing away.

Silas swings towards him, an expression of concerned expectation on his face. Christina stiffens, as if braced for bad news. David sidles up beside me, taking hold of my hand for comfort.

We all turn our eyes to the man who has just walked in.

"Well, here we are again," he muses mildly; still with an absence of disclosure in his manner... he's good. "Please, sit."

As one, we resume our places. I see Silas close his eyes, as if offering a silent prayer.

"Okay, I have some positive news."

The overwhelming collective sigh of relief reverberates around the room.

"The operation went very well... very well indeed... We managed to relieve the pressure and the swelling is in retreat." He allows himself a small gratified smile.

"Oh gosh!" Christina launches herself at the unsuspecting doctor, flinging her arms around him in utter gratitude. "Thank you, thank you, thank you," she repeats, over and over.

Mr Zaman, taken by surprise, blushes beneath his tan complexion, his eyebrows shooting up to his hairline. Taking hold of her arms, he gently untangles them from around his neck, giving himself some room to continue.

"It's early days of course, but all the signs look… encouraging." He takes a step backwards so he's out of her reach.

Silas draws Christina into his arms, relief written all over his beautiful face. He looks at me from over her shoulder as he holds her sobbing form tenderly; his swimming eyes say it all as he pours every ounce of love into me.

"Mr Tudor?" The consultant draws Silas's attention. "There's one more thing."

Silas wipes away a wayward tear as he turns to face the doctor. Christina continually pats at her damp cheeks, breathing jerkily beneath the weight of her emotions, vying to regain composure.

"You may want to take a look at this…" Sounding slightly self-satisfied, he proffers his hand, opening his fist to reveal a small glass vial with a red screw cap.

Silas tentatively takes it from his palm, lifting it to the light so he can see the contents better. A compressed, black, raisin-like object is floating in a couple of inches of pinkish solution.

"Is this…?" His eyes widen, as he looks to the Doctor.

"Yes." Mr Zaman flashes a broad white dazzling smile, for the first time that day. Suddenly it's as if the sun has come out from a dusky cloud. "And it's all yours, to keep."

"Oh, my God!" Silas reels towards Christina and I, wide eyed and amazed… "The bullet… he removed the bullet!"

"Oh!" Christina's hands fly to her face, unable to comprehend what she's witnessing, the tears begin again, this time unrestrained.

"I know," Zaman grins. "I didn't want to get your hopes up earlier, but I was pretty sure the movement had placed the bullet in a more accessible position." He's beaming like a delighted schoolboy.

"As I said, the brain is an incredible organ and were still learning so much about it. Dominic's system had created a protective pocket around the bullet, it was attempting to push it out of his body, as it would a splinter in a finger, or grains of gravel in a grazed knee… amazing, eh?"

The metaphors hardly compare, he's so unassuming. This man has just performed the most complex, extraordinary, life changing brain surgery on a young man, and he could be talking about applying a band-aid to a paper-cut! He's remarkable.

"And… and… the outcome?" Christina can barely dare to ask.

Mr Zaman softens his smile, his eyes full of compassion for this amazing mother and father, aware he's given them the best possible gift… their son.

"At the moment, Dominic is in the recovery room in the intensive care unit. He needs to be kept in an induced coma until we're certain his vitals are steady. We'll know much more in the morning, but as I said; things are positive."

"How can I thank you?" Christina cries with relief.

"No need… The result is thanks enough." He pats her shoulder gently.

319

"Now," he returns to the business at hand as if embarrassed by the praise, "we only permit one visitor at a time. I would prefer it if you would wait until tomorrow morning, but I know you're anxious to see him. You can look through the window," he whispers conspiratorially. "But don't tell Matron, I said so." He widens his eyes in mock horror... and I suspect only partially in jest. "However, you can't enter the unit for another few hours yet."

"I need to see him." Christina declares, her eyes dry for the first time in hours. She won't be deterred from seeing her boy, even through a window.

"You go, I'll make the calls." A relieved Silas urges her to follow the doctor. "Mr. Zaman, one more thing..."

Zaman turns expectantly. I get the feeling he knows what's coming.

"When will you know if he's... okay?"

"In time..." he answers, still smiling, "in time... For now, he needs to rest and recover. But, either way, that thing," he points to the mangled bullet with obvious distaste, "has gone and Nic is recovering nicely." Turning his attention to Christina, he places a guiding hand in the small of her back and opens the door. "Shall we?"

"Thank you, Mr Zaman." Silas's voice is clear and genuine in acknowledging the talented consultant.

Zaman smiles, announcing it's all in a day's work and leads a very wobbly Christina down the corridor to the ICU.

CHAPTER 58

Leon points to the small vial Silas is holding. Silas tosses it to him, and Leon catches it deftly, enveloping it in his fist. Gripping it between his finger and thumb, he rolls the small glass tube, disturbing the contents a little then tilts the container beneath the bulb of his desk-lamp so he can examine it more closely.

"Looks like some kind of hybrid. I'd say five millimetres. Flat-base with a hollow tip. Homemade I'd wager; harder to trace." Leon squints his eyes as he expertly scrutinizes the distorted lump of metal.

"He was lucky," adds Leon, standing the vial on its end; the mangled bullet descends to the base of its new home and sits there benignly. *Lucky* is an understatement.

Now I've seen the evidence with my own eyes, I'm amazed Nic survived the impact at all. I shiver at the thought.

"Yes." Silas stares at the bullet. His face is blank, but I know better than to think he's calm.

"Come on son, your mother needs a hug," Leon drawls as he rises from behind his desk. "Seriously, this is wonderful news, son." He snatches up the ampoule and heads to the corner of the room. "I'll look after this for you."

Stepping towards a painting of a voluptuous, Victorian nude in an ornate gold frame, he swings it aside to reveal a hidden safe. He winks at me as he swivels the combination lock. "I know, it's a cliché, but where else would it be? There." Placing the vial inside, he secures the handle and replaces the painting. "Safe and sound. C'mon, I don't know about you but I could do with a drink."

Sylvana, Chloe, Tia and Jasmine are seconded in the family room. Sylvana, though externally exuding serenity and calm, is relentlessly pottering about, moving from coffee table to mantlepiece to shelf, adjusting the ornaments a fraction here, and swiping at an invisible speck of dust there.

"Mum, come and sit down," Tia urges. "You're as bad as Silas." This is true. Silas's incessant pacing at the hospital was distracting and unsettling; it appears he inherited the trait from his mother. "Nic's going to be fine."

Christina called from the hospital a couple of hours ago to update us. Apparently, Matron was no match for her tenacity and after a frank discussion, where Christina explained exactly what would be acceptable, and Matron, explaining exactly what would not... they agreed that Christina could stay overnight. This means we are receiving regular progress reports. So far so good. Nic is comfortable and sleeping. All his vital signs are stable and his brain activity displaying good readings.

"I just want him to come around," Sylvana relents and allows her husband to envelop her in his bear-like arms. "Oh, *Log*, our boy..." she sighs burying her face in his substantial chest.

"*Log?*" I mouth at Silas.

321

"Don't ask…" he whispers. "Mum, Dad, if you don't mind, we'll go." He takes his mother's distraction as a means of escape. "It's been a hell of a long day; and I doubt we'll sleep much."

Using Bear and Lizzy as an excuse, he nimbly sidesteps Sylvana's insistent protest we should stay here tonight. One needs to be walked and the other needs to be called.

"We'll be back first thing in the morning," he says, moving between each family member depositing kisses. "We'll drop the dog off on our way to the hospital."

"See you tomorrow Bro'," Chloe says, picking a dancing Margo up from beneath the many shuffling feet. "Edi, if you need help, just call me. I don't think there's room for everyone at the hospital and I'll only worry if I have to stay home," she offers kindly.

"I think I'll take you up on that offer," I smile and give her a tight hug.

"Yeah, I'll help too," says Jasmine.

"I won't…" I didn't expect Tia to offer. Of all of Silas's family, Tia is the only one I struggle to connect with. "See you later, Brother," she hugs him lightly, and heads off to do her own thing.

"C'mon, we need to sort that dog out."

"Yeah." I have a million things to do before tomorrow. I daren't think about any of them.

Why did I agree to host the Gala?

"We could have cancelled you know," I mutter as we climb into Silas's car. "It's not too late?" He gives me a sideways glance as he hauls the door shut.

Waving to his family, huddled on the doorstep, he turns to face me. "It is too late, and no… we couldn't. Christina's right. It needs to go ahead." He straps himself in. "And besides, once the fat-cats are full of champagne, they won't care where they are. Just keep the bubbles flowing and the donations will roll in."

"You have a lot of confidence in me," I grumble, unable to unearth an iota of confidence in myself.

"Every confidence… look at you…" he exclaims as we drive away. I'm aware the concerned father is simmering under the surface, but this is the calmest I've seen him since we were at the hospital. "You're as sexy as all *fuck*…you'll walk it."

I know he's convinced I can do it. He's always had complete faith in me. And all I'm doing is being negative, thinking of myself and my inadequacies when I should be supporting him through this difficult time.

C'mon Edi; grow a pair!

"I know… look at me." I feign bravado. "I'm Edi Sykes. I go on TV programmes and hold my own against nasty bastards and nosey-parker reporters. *I don't take no shit brother!*"

"Oh, for *fucks* sake…" he groans on an exaggerated eye roll.

"Too far?"

"*Too* far," he laughs. But at least he's laughing.

Oh God, I love him! Today's outcome could've been so different if it wasn't for that ridiculously talented team of neuro-surgeons. Yes, today ended well.

The barn is in complete darkness when we arrive home. It's been a stupidly long day. I check my watch and I'm surprised to find it's almost two am.

Silas unlocks the door and we're greeted by a whirlwind of tan fur. Poor Bear has been inside since about five o'clock, with his legs crossed; he must be bursting.

Quickly charging to the front, Bear relieves himself before galloping back for a proper welcome. Lithely bouncing between us, he alternates his affection equally; glad to greet us both, delighted that we're home.

"Just this once," Silas says to him and Bear flies up the stairs and into the bedroom.

"He's happy," I smile as I climb the stairs, bone weary.

"I'm happy." Silas kisses my crown as we navigate the winding staircase side by side.

"Me too... I love you, Boss-man." I squeeze him tightly around the waist. "You make my heart happy."

"You make my heart happy. Let's go to bed."

"I hear you!" I yawn, as I enter the bedroom. I doubt I'll need much rocking tonight.

Bear is snuggling atop the duvet, nose between his paws feigning sleep.

"Er, I don't think so..." Silas scolds, and the dejected dog, knowing when he's beaten, sneaks off the bed and onto the rug, circling once before flopping down with a huff. The bedroom is allowed, but the bed is off limits to canines.

"Strip..."

"What?" I'm aghast, he can't be in the mood, not at this time; especially after the day we've had.

Clarifying his meaning, his soft eyes find mine. There's a familiar smoulder, but even Silas is exhausted. "I just need your nakedness beside me, on me, beneath me... anywhere... just be naked... please." He undresses and leaves his clothes where they land, crawling beneath the duvet, opening his arms to me needfully.

"Your wish is my command." Pulling at my clothes, I can't shed them urgently enough. "Smother me," I groan as I crawl in beside him.

His lean body is strong, hard and warm. His long limbs embrace me, tangling with mine, drawing me to him and holding me as close as he can get. "Thank you for today," he mutters quietly. "I don't think I could have remained calm without you being there."

"Calm? I'd hardly call that calm. But you were fantastic with Christina." I snuggle in, and breathe in his musky scent. "You love her." It's a statement of fact.

"Yes, I do," he admits. "She's the mother of my children and I'll always love her for that."

"I think that's commendable," I say, wondering at my own circumstance. "Bobby is the father of my children, but I could never love him..."

"You didn't know."

Lifting my head, I look at him in the semi-darkness. Behind the curtains, the sun is beginning to rise. "I didn't know what?"

"There was a beast within…" His eyes drift closed and his breathing becomes steady. He's right. I didn't know when I met him there was a beast lurking beneath the suave exterior, but I should have. I should have known from the first time. That first time at my friend's birthday party where he unapologetically raped me, then acted as if it was the most normal thing in the world. I should have known then, there was a beast within.

Well, now he's gone. Out of my life and behind bars, exactly where he should be. I allow myself to be thankful and snuggle deeper against Silas's sleeping form.

I drift off, counting my blessings… Nic is recovering, Lizzy and David are safe. Christina is happy and best of all, Silas is out of *The Rose Council*. It's been one hell of a day!

CHAPTER 59

"*Morning has broken, like the first morning…*" Silas is singing. His baritone reverberates through the room as though he's had the longest and most restful sleep of the century.

"I'm knackered!" I moan from my nest, beneath the warm, fluffy quilt.

"That as may be, but we have a full day today and it's already…" he looks at the bedside clock, "Seven am."

"Oooh, God! Are there really two, seven O'clocks in one day?" I grumble as I reluctantly crawl out of my hidey-hole.

"Yes, this is the first, and if I'm lucky, I'll get to see your new knickers by the second."

"Won't you be at the hospital?" I question as a flush of self-doubt floods me. The thought of hosting the Gala tonight has me feeling inadequate and queasy again.

"Probably; but I won't turn down a quick preview…" he jiggles his eyebrows and I chuck my slipper at him.

"I need a shower…"

"Don't be long, we need to get moving."

"Yes Boss…" I yawn as I shlep my way to the bathroom.

Commencing my shower routine, I check my mental list of everything I need to do today.

Shower – Tick

Shave – Ummm!

Hair.

Dress.

Breakfast.

Hospital… Nic… Lizzy… David… Dog… Gala… Oh, it's too much. If I carry on like this I'll implode before I get downstairs. Best to let it happen organically. Grabbing my shampoo, I lather up in an attempt to quieten my reeling mind.

Less than half an hour later, I land in the kitchen. Dressed for speed rather than seduction, I'm in my leisure gear; my new grey marl leggings and a lightweight pink DKNY sweatshirt.

"You look nice." Silas kisses me as he places a steaming cup of rodent-proof tea on the breakfast bar before me.

"Any update from the hospital?" I ask, while tying my hair in a sloppy bun.

"No, not yet," he murmurs. "Bacon alright?" Flipping off the gas hob, he tips the sizzling contents of the frying pan onto absorbent kitchen roll. Dropping the pan into the sink, where it hisses, releasing a cloud of steam, he grabs two soft floured baps from the breadbin. "Barm-cake?"

"Ohh, yes please." My stomach makes an appreciative growl. I can't remember the last time I ate. "Brown sauce please."

"Philistine…"

Standing, I go and flick on the radio - Saturday morning music is a must - and I fiddle with the dials, searching for Radio 2. Once it's located, I settle into my barstool to the dulcet tones of Glen Campbell's *'Wichita Lineman.'* Humming along tunelessly, I take a huge bite of my breakfast. "Gawd, this is *good!*" I mumble appreciatively through a full mouth. "You can cook, boy!"

"Mamma teach me," he sings in a fake Jamaican patois, shaking his booty. "Every-little-ting she know, baby…"

"Yeah well, she didn't teach you how much sauce you should use… epic fail on that one… pass the HP please."

As he reaches across with the bottle, his phone starts to ring. "This'll be Christina." He stands, fishing his phone out of his jeans pocket. Checking the name, his puckered brow doesn't escape me. "Johannes? What's up mate?" he queries, walking away from the table, taking his empty plate to the sink.

I watch him as his pace slows and his shoulders stiffen, squaring up, tension building. Something's happened. I listen intently, trying to get the gist of the conversation.

"When…" It's difficult when it's one sided.

Raising my leg, I bend my knee beneath me, and slow my chewing, trying to figure out what's going on.

"Do the Council know?" It sounds serious. "No, I can't come in; you'll have to deal with it…" There's a long pause and a stream of indecipherable squawking from the other end.

"Yes, she's at the hospital."

More squawking…

"He's doing well so far." This is so frustrating. "I'll let them know. Ring if you hear more… I will… cheers mate… I owe you." And he clicks his phone off.

"What was *that* all about?" He's still facing away from me as he drops his phone into his back pocket.

"Oh… er… nothing… just some Council business."

"But you're not on the Council anymore," I remind him. "What's so urgent Johannes has to interrupt your breakfast?" Not to mention a trip to the hospital.

Slowly he turns to face me, and leaning against the kitchen sink, he lifts his head. His expression looks both angry and wary… "What?" I demand. "Tell me."

"He's out." His teeth are clenched, grinding and his jaw is ticking with tension.

At first, I'm elated… Nic's out of hospital… but I realise, that can't be right… it's far too soon. Then it smashes me in the face like a base-ball bat. He doesn't mean Nic, he means Bobby!

"How?" I'm mortified. How the hell did this happen. They had him, bang to rights. How can he be out?

"He made bail," is his hostile whisper. "His solicitor pulled a few strings with the right people. Bent Judges… it happens."

"But where… when… how?" There are too many questions fizzing around in my head to string together a coherent sentence. "Is he free? I mean, is he off the hook completely?"

Silas is thoughtful and pondering. Biting his lower lip, he looks down at the floor, seemingly reviewing all the evidence for any flaws, for the small loophole that has allowed Bobby's lawyer to exploit the system and secure his release.

"No… he's on remand. He's been released into the custody of his barrister. He'll remain under house arrest until the trial. He's tagged, he can't go anywhere without them tracking him." His troubled expression tells me he believes this as much as I do… I'm not convinced.

"Look, there's nothing we can do about it now. We need to leave it to *The Rose Council* to decide. He's still officially under lock and key and *if* anything happens, Johannes will be the first to know." Shaking his head, he moves to the hook where he keeps Bear's lead.

"C'mon, let's get this dog to my parents and go visit Nic. We have better things to think about." The thought of visiting his son, is paramount. He's right… let Johannes worry about it. But one thing still bothers me…

"Should I tell the children?" The notion of explaining things to Lizzy and David is sickening.

"No, not yet. You shouldn't worry them unnecessarily," but again, he doesn't look entirely convinced. "Bear, come," he calls for the dog. "Grab that carrier bag will you," he says abstractly. "It's got all his food and stuff… he hate's that poncy grub they feed to Margo."

With my mind still reeling from the news Bobby is all but free, I stand and leaving my empty breakfast things where they are, grab the bag and follow them out into the hazy daylight.

It looks like it's going to be a glorious day. Well weatherwise… only several hundred metaphorical clouds are threatening to ruin it.

There's an abundance of activity going on at the Tudor residence; all Gala related. It appears to be chaotic, but Chloe convinces me they have everything under control.

"We're good… we've had plenty of years to practice… now go and see my nephew and tell him I love him…" is her parting instruction to me.

Bear and Margo are happily getting under everyone's feet. It's a scene of surreal festivity; it's so misplaced.

"Here we are." Silas parks in the overspill carpark, collecting a ticket from the machine as we walk holding hands to the intensive care entrance.

We've heard nothing from Christina all morning. Adopting the adage, 'no news is good news,' we refrained from talking about Nic all the way here; choosing instead to go over the finer details for the evening… even though it was a redundant conversation… I'm assured Chloe has got it in hand and there's absolutely nothing I need to do until the doors open later and the guests walk in.

The doors to the intensive care unit are sealed. We have to buzz to be let inside and once there, we sign in with strict instructions, only two visitors at a time per bed.

David was bouncing to come with us this morning, but I managed to hold him off, telling him he was needed to assist Sam and Lizzy with some important Gala stuff… that appeased him. I have no idea how they'll keep him busy, but I trust them.

"Ah good morning, Mr. Tudor." Mr Zaman is as fresh as a daisy and still beaming his sunny smile. "Please, come through."

Noticing some uncomfortable looking plastic chairs lining the wall, I leave go of Silas's hand and start to walk towards them. "Please, Miss…Err…"

Realising he has no idea of my name; Zaman's words melt away. "You may join us." Smiling directly at me, he indicates I too, should follow.

"I have a certain, authority here," he explains, adding, "but don't tell Matron." He really seems scared of her. She must be a formidable woman. I get an image in my head of Mrs Whittham in a Matrons uniform, hands on hips, issuing out stern orders. The picture makes me smile.

"What're you grinning at?" Silas whispers as we head down the corridor.

"Oh, nothing," squeezing his hand, bringing the subject back to the present. "I'm nervous."

"Me too," he squeezes back. "Look, there's Christina."

CHAPTER 60

Walking towards us, in her immaculate cream suit, and looking decidedly rested and uncrumpled, is a vision of sheer happiness. If you'd tried to tell me Christina had spent the night in vigil, scrunched up in an uncomfortable hospital chair, I'd have laughed and deemed you a liar. She's radiant. Increasing her speed, she's almost but not quite running, trotting towards us on clicking heels.

"He's awake!" she exclaims ecstatically as she reaches us, stretching her arms as wide as they'll go, capturing us both in a tight, euphoric embrace. "He opened his eyes and looked at me…" She's joyous.

Stepping back, she beams at Silas who gapes back at her in wide eyed bewilderment. Instantly, the shocking news of this morning melts away into insignificance at this fantastic revelation.

"Yes," Christina nods fervently in answer to his silent question. "He *looked* right at me…"

"Seriously?" Silas's breath is laboured, he's struggling to take in oxygen at this incredible news.

I would not have thought it possible, but feeding from our reactions, Mr Zaman's already dazzling smile becomes wider and brighter than ever.

Without warning, Silas tips forward, doubling over, gripping his knees, his breath now coming in great heaving gulps. "Oh Jesus…, thank you," he pants, towards the floor, "thank you…"

"Si?" I lean towards him alarmed at his reaction. "Silas… Baby?"

"Fine, I'm fine." He straightens up, inhaling deeply, gathering his equilibrium. "It's just… I can't believe it."

"It's true," Christina's voice is pure wonder. "It's a miracle." I'm sure, in her eyes, it is. "He *looked* at me… properly."

Shifting my questioning gaze to the eminent Consultant, I try and understand the real significance of what I'm hearing. Have I missed something?

Zaman responds. "Eye contact, especially sustained eye contact is an indication his condition has significantly improved."

Now I understand. Before, Nic barely made eye contact with anybody and when he did, it was fleeting, as if it caused him some internal pain or discomfort. One of the signs of autism.

"I need to see him." Silas is on the move, quickly heading in the direction from which Christina came; a man on a mission.

"Yes, he's in here," Christina strides ahead, pausing outside the door to a private room. "Silas, listen to me," she asserts. "Steady yourself and take a few breaths, don't go in there all guns blazing, he needs calm… breathe Silas." Resting her hand on his arm, she bars his way until she's sure he's sufficiently recovered enough to cope. Only then does she step aside, indicating that I too, should join them.

I look at the doctor for confirmation. "Don't tell Matron." He grins, before turning towards the nurse's station. "I'll be here when you come out. No doubt, you'll have questions."

The room is comfortably warm, not too hot or cold. The intermittent bleep, bleep, bleep, of the monitor is comforting and the lighting is not the usual harsh fluorescence I'm accustomed to in a general ward. This lighting is soft, subdued and gentle; restful even.

Nic is lying still and serene; one arm resting on the bed on top of the covers. It's the arm nearest the guest chair. I suspect it's the hand Christina has held onto all night. The other arm is draped loosely across his torso.

There's a canular attached to a drip taped to his wrist and his head is swathed in bandages. Even with all the complicated monitors, medical equipment and paraphernalia filling the room, he appears comfortable and relaxed. His eyes are closed in sleep.

Silas stands rooted to the spot as though in awe, absorbing what he's seeing. His wonderful, brave, boy. Christina moves quietly around to the side of the bed. Picking up her bag, she turns to me. Every trace of the worry clouding her stunning face yesterday has dissolved. She looks tranquil, content, happy.

"If you don't mind, I'll go and freshen up," she smiles, "and I could do with some 'fresh air'." She winks, knowing I understand her need for a cigarette. "Silas?"

Not removing his eyes from his son, Silas inclines his head in her direction in acknowledgement. "Uh-hu?"

"Relax... he's doing great," she says. Then, kissing my cheek as she passes, she adds for my ears alone, "you're so good for him," then exits the room, closing the door softly behind her.

"Silas, come and sit." I tug his arm, nudging him to the vacated seat. Without looking, he allows me to guide him into place as I would a blind person. He only has eyes for Dominic.

Once he's seated, I help him shrug out of his jacket so he can relax a little. Draping it over the back of his chair, I look around for somewhere to sit myself. Noticing there's another plastic chair next to the small cupboard on the opposite wall, I move to fetch it and Silas's head snaps up in alarm.

"Where are you going?" he frantically whispers, a slight panic at the thought I might be leaving the room.

"I'm just going to get that chair," I point to the blue inanimate object standing in the corner. "Is that okay?"

"Sorry, I'm just a bit freaked out." Visibly, he eases and returns his attentive gaze to Nic.

I place the chair beside Silas and take my place, in silence, waiting patiently for him to feel comfortable enough before I contemplate engaging in conversation.

330

"Talk to me," he says after a couple of minutes. "Tell me something."

"Like what? What do you want to know?" I'll tell him anything to make him more at ease.

"I don't know… something about the children… when they were younger… something… family."

I consider this for a while. In the few weeks we've known each other, our time together has, to say the least, been eventful. A relationship, initially founded on work, became overwhelmed by an unexpected mutual attraction, which knocked us both off our feet and shook *my* small insignificant world to its foundations.

As we became overwhelmed by the power of those feelings, desire soon blossomed into love and with that love arose the irresistible headiness of our instant bond. That closeness and intimacy forged a deep trust, which allowed us to reveal secrets of past lives; things we'd never share, other than with a soulmate.

Yes, we know about the big things, the life changing things, which have moulded us into the people we are now. But the small minutiae, the glue, the trivial but important, almost insignificant moments, the links in the chain, that make up the bits of life in-between, we know so little of. I trawl my memory for one such moment and come up with a corker. I laugh softly as the images process, bringing the dormant story to life.

"What's funny?"

"I have one…" I say fondly. "It's a Lizzy story."

"Go on… I'm listening." Though he doesn't remove his focus from Nic, I know I have his attention.

"It's nothing major, just funny. Even as a little girl, she was… inventive. She knew her own mind."

"Why? What happened?"

"She was in the first year of junior school, so I reckon she was around eight or nine. It was a school trip, to Chester Zoo. All the kids were excited. It was the first school trip without a parent – apart from the escorts. The children were allowed to take some spends, but because there were so many of them and they were so young, there was a limit of two pounds. Not much I grant you, but the teachers didn't want to waste the day in the gift shop."

Smiling, I continued. "Anyway, I dutifully made up a packed lunch, and secured her two-pound coin in the little purse attached inside the pocket of her back pack and off she went; all blonde curls, long gangly limbs and enthusiasm for her first trip to the zoo."

Silas is listening, while keeping an intent eye on his sleeping son. I notice his shoulders beginning to relax as some of the tension is abating, so I continue my silly tale.

"Well, I hear nothing all day, which is a really good thing. Although I was worried, it was without reason, she was safe with the teachers. But she'd never been away from me like this before so when six o'clock came and it was time to collect her, I was the first parent at the school gates waiting for the coach to return.

"When it arrived, all the children disembarked, looking tired, but happy. They'd had the most wonderful time. However, as I waited for Lizzy who was saying her excited goodbyes to her friends, her teacher came over to speak to me. Apparently, Lizzy and one of the other children had managed to become separated from the rest of the group, in the reptile house of all places. Luckily, a diligent keeper spotted them dawdling at one of the exhibits and managed to join them up with the rest of the party. No harm done."

"Ha… that sounds like Lizzy… adventurous."

"Yes," I mused at his perceptiveness of my daughter. "Well though, that wasn't quite the end."

"Oh?" For the first time in about half an hour, and for a split second he briefly flicks his eyes away from Nic, before resuming his intent vigil. "What happened," he asked, intrigued by the antics of my girl.

"Well, when we arrived home, I was unpacking her back pack. You know, throwing away the uneaten bread crust, the apple core, the half empty crisp packet… the tomatoes she'd picked off her sandwiches," even then she was a fussy madam, "and I came across the little purse."

"Oh, what did she get you? Don't tell me… one of those fat chunky foot long pencils that say *'I've been to Chester Zoo'*." He's grinning at the image.

"Well, no, actually," I shake my head at the vivid memory coming back to me in full colour. "Even at the age of nine, I could have told you she'd be an accountant or something to do with money," I announce, waiting for his reaction.

"Huh?" Now he's seriously hooked.

"Yes… when I opened the purse expecting nothing but coppers and small change, there were *three* pounds in there. The original two-pound coin and another two fifty-pence pieces."

He looks at me now. Fully focussed, and questioning. "She came back with more than she went with?"

"Ummm, yes," I nod, dryly. "Apparently, when they 'got lost' in the reptile house, the other child was inconsolable, frightened they'd be lost forever. Lizzy, ever practical and inventive said she would give him a kiss… if he stopped crying… and if he paid her fifty pence!"

"Ha!" Silas barks a laugh, Nic stirs at the sound then settles. "*Hah!*" Silas whispers, in delight. "Little entrepreneur, even then."

I wait for him to work it out…

"Hang on; you said she came back with a pound more, not fifty pence?"

"Yeah, I did… When young Steven Doyle - I'll never forget his name - agreed to her suggestion, she took advantage."

"Huh?" he's perplexed.

"She did it twice!" I pronounce, shaking my head at the end of the story. "Honestly, for a while I was really worried, she might make a dubious career choice, if you get my drift."

Silas is laughing, silently, his shoulders shaking in mirth. I'm pleased.

"I was so cross with her, I insisted she gave the money back. She was grounded for a month without any sweets or TV. But she was absolutely unrepentant. To this day, she doesn't believe she did anything wrong."

"What a girl," Silas shakes his head. "I love it," he smiles; then, "I wonder if Maya would have been like Lizzy? Fierce, intelligent, beautiful." His face morphs into deep thoughtfulness, his caring eyes back on Nic.

Initially I'm berating myself for using this silly example; possibly I've raked up some raw memories or notions. But then as I look closer, I see there's no pain in his expression, just a longing, an imagining of what might have been if she were still here. But there's no hurt or agony, just a curious wistfulness, and I'm glad I chose that story after all.

As if on cue, Nic stirs. His hand moves from across his chest and drops to his side by the edge of his bed. His head turns towards the window, as if seeking the natural light behind the blinds. His face, at this angle is angelic, a cherub. There's little sign of the trauma he's suffered or the discomfort he must be enduring from the operation. His eyelids begin to flutter, his eyes moving rapidly behind the delicate film of his lid, his long lashes fan his cheeks.

"Mmmm," he hums, restlessly. The sound is coarse due to the dryness of his throat.

"Nic?" Silas murmurs, leaning closer to his son's side, closer to his ear.

I hold my breath.

"Mmmm," Nic mumbles again, clearer this time, turning his head in the direction of Silas's voice.

We both remain immobile; waiting, watching.

In the flicking of a switch, Nic's eyes snap open, instantly focussing on Silas's. I expect the glance to be transitory, for him to look away as he always has done in the past, but he doesn't. He remains transfixed, agaze, unyielding.

For a terrifying moment, it crosses my mind he can't see, that the operation has rendered him sightless, blind... but as swiftly as the thought enters my head, it evaporates. There's clearly no doubt. I know he's looking directly into Silas's wondering eyes, deep into his troubled soul.

I watch intently for some inking of recognition. He always recognised his dad; they had a tight connection, the head-butt thing they did.

"Daaa," a discernible croak...his voice a deep gravelly, susurrate murmur. I squeeze Silas's shoulder. He's stopped breathing.

"Nic?" Silas's speech is as gruff as Nic's, though I don't think it's through aridity of the vocal cords.

"Daddd!" He says again, still staring intently, still absorbed and focussed. "Dad?" This time it's pronounced with complete clarity and recognition. "It's you?"

"*Huhh!*" Silas gasps in shock. "*Agh*... Yes! ... yes son, it's me..." Recovering quickly, Silas expels a rush of air and weeps in disbelief. "Nic... Nic... my boy..."

"Daaad. d... don't... c... cry, it's g... g...girly." Nic manages a full sentence before his eyes drift closed and he's once again sleeping peacefully.

"Hah!" Silas barks, half laughing half crying, leaping to his feet, then abruptly sitting again as dizziness hits; then finally standing on wobbly legs, his hands fly to his head, his face is filled with unbelievable joy. "He spoke to me..." turning towards me, he yanks me from my chair swathing me in his arms and I enfold him in mine.

We weep together, clinging on for dear life at the wonder and miracle, which has just occurred before our very eyes.

CHAPTER 61

"Did you hear that? He actually spoke to me… really… he spoke … words…to me?" Silas is beside himself in awed wonder. The magnitude of what's just occurred; an event so utterly incredible that could only have been imagined at yesterday. A hopeless, helpless dream that Nic could one day recover from the horrific injuries, which robbed him of so many formative years… has come to fruition. A towering phenomenon almost too great to accept.

"Oh, God!" Silas is weeping openly and without any desire to stem the gushing tears. "Oh, my Lord… *God!*" he repeats, over and over. "*Did you hear?*" There's an element of doubt in his tone, a niggling uncertainty jabbing away at the tender edges of his fragile trust. He's beginning to doubt his own sanity; to think he imagined the whole episode. The range of emotions passing over his face are a manifestation of physical pain and sheer impossible astonishment.

"Yes… baby… yes! I heard him. He knows you… he *looked* right at you… *properly.*" Desperate to give him the affirmation he so badly needs, I endeavour to suffuse him with comfort and encouragement, but it's so astoundingly difficult when I can scarcely comprehend it myself.

"Look, he's sleeping…" Nic looks serene and peaceful, his smooth untroubled face the polar opposite of his father's creased, worried countenance. "Let's go and see Mr. Zaman, he'll be able to explain it." I pertain little hope of removing Silas from Nic's bedside, he's steadfast, but we need to speak to the consultant. We need to know if what just occurred is real.

"Come on." Gently, I give his arm a small shake of encouragement. "We can come back later. Let him rest for a few minutes."

Silas is like a granite boulder, solid and unyielding. "Silas, please," I try again, tugging harder this time. "Christina is waiting for her turn…"

That draws his attention. "But she was here all night, can't I…?" He's hesitant, nonetheless I can hear the waver in his voice; he's generous and would never monopolise this priceless time with Nic, he'll share.

"Okay." He's reluctant, but at last he submits. "Only for a few minutes… to speak to the consultant," he adds.

"Of course," I smile softly, reaching up to brush the wetness from his cheeks. "Here," I offer him my used tissue. "Sorry, it's covered in mascara." I don't know what I was thinking applying makeup this morning. I should have known I'd spend the day blubbering.

"It's okay, Honey-bee… It's quite apt really… you have stripes…" he jokes at the state of my streaky cheeks, then balls up the tissue and dabs his own damp face. "Is that better?" he asks, loath to look at himself in the small vanity mirror, which hangs pointlessly on the wall.

"You'll do." I reach up and kiss him lightly on his full lips. "Oh, how I love you, Boss-man," I sigh, allowing the joy to fill me up.

"You are so beautiful… even smeared with black gunk." He kisses my nose, then my hair then my eyes, before turning his gaze back to his restful boy and very gently, presses a paternal kiss to his bandaged forehead. "Sleep well, son," he whispers. "C'mon," he sniffs once, clearing his throat. He rolls his shoulders composing himself. "Let's go and speak to this genius of a surgeon." Placing his hands on my waist I'm manoeuvred gently so I'm facing the door and his doubting eyes drift sideways. He's unable to resist one longing, wondering, adoring look at the handsome young man lying peacefully in the hospital bed.

"Well?" the moment we re-enter the main reception area of the unit, a fresh-faced Christina removes herself from the intense conversation she's having with Mr. Zaman and rushes towards us in a flurry of fervent anticipation. Mr. Zaman, his gleaming smile still plastered to his face, follows casually in her wake. Honestly, if I were that man, I don't think I'd ever stop grinning in self-satisfaction at my own incredible achievement.

"He spoke to me," Silas, says, the wonder still evident in his tone. "He looked directly at me and he spoke… to me." His eyes drift between Christina and the consultant.

Christina's mouth forms a silent 'O' at this development and they both shoot anxious faces to the doctor; barely daring to ask the questions they so desperately wanted answered, for fear it might be a cruel illusion to all but disappear in a moment of ruthless fete.

Mr. Zaman very gently raises his arm, indicating towards the quiet side room. "I think we all need a few moments," he sooths, "to digest and understand."

Placing his arm around Silas's shoulder, the visual is completely at odds, an unbalanced tableau. The doctor is barely the same height as Christina, easily five or six inches shorter than Silas, and he has to stretch his arm up high to offer the avuncular comfort. It doesn't bother either of them. Silas accepts the support willingly, allowing the good doctor to escort him into the homely reflective space.

Christina, still reeling, links my arm, looping hers through mine tightly and rests her head on my shoulder. This too, must look lopsided… she towers over me. "Come on, Edi, you need to hear this as well," she says giving my arm a little squeeze.

"Please, take a seat." Mr. Zaman must have used this line a million times over the years. Once again, we settle into the soft chintzy cushions and even though the questions are bubbling up and threatening to spew out like an erupting volcano, we focus all our energy and pay attention.

Silas is unable to hold his tongue. "Mr. Zaman…" he starts.

"Please, call me Ali," the Doctor says, "Mr. Zaman is my dad!" His smile is encouraging and kindly.

"Mr. Z… Ali…" Silas looks uncomfortable dispensing with formality, but he pushes through. "What's happening?" His face crumples at the banality of the question, though, what else could he ask? How else could he put it?

"Mr. Tudor…"

"Silas," he returns the gesture. "Christina," he nods to us in turn, "Edi," he smiles warmly when saying my name.

336

"Silas, Christina, Edi…" he begins again. "This is an extraordinary phenomenon. As I said previously, we still know so little about the brain, but we are discovering more and more and learning new techniques daily. When Dominic first had his accident, there was no probability of operating to remove the foreign body. Its location was inaccessible… the risk to Dominic was far too great."

The way he terms the disgusting object seems apt – not naming it takes away its power.

"The accomplished advances made in recent years have been unparalleled. That, together with the brain's ability to heal itself over time, has resulted in what has happened here today. His recovery is without doubt, truly remarkable. Never in my twenty years as a neurosurgeon, have I seen anything quite so extraordinary and unexpected. I have read of it happening in medical journals, but this phenomenon is so incredibly rare," he says earnestly.

"Following a discussion with a colleague of mine at The John Hopkins Hospital in Baltimore, we concluded that most of Nic's initial *'symptoms'* pointed towards an unusual form of 'Locked-in Syndrome'." We share puzzled glances, not quite understanding.

"But… when it happened, we were told the accident had left him with a form of Autism… are you now telling us he was *misdiagnosed*?" Silas is becoming agitated. The thought this could have been resolved years ago is unbearable. Could Dominic have been leading a normal life, had it been diagnosed something sooner?

Mr Zaman drops his eyes, searching for the right words to explain. Eventually he takes a soft breath and refocuses on his audience.

"Usually, Locked-in Syndrome is characterized by complete paralysis of voluntary muscles in all parts of the body except for those that control eye movement. It may result from traumatic brain injury, such as Nic's. However, Nic wasn't affected that way. In Nic's case, we now believe his brain reacted differently; only partially locking down, in an effort to protect those areas that were truly injured in an attempt to heal." Sensing Silas's frustration bubbling up, Zaman continues.

"I understand your frustration, Mr. Tudor, but believe me when I tell you; Nic's recovery could not have been expedited, even if we'd possessed the technology, back then. Any operation would most likely have rendered him severely brain damaged… leaving the object where it was, is the reason we have this level of recovery now." I can see by his sober expression; he solemnly believes this to be the truth.

He continues. "His mobility remained relatively unaffected, leading to the diagnosis of Autism. All the signs and all the test results were indicative of that diagnosis at the time. There was no evidence it could have been… something else… until now."

"So, what does this mean… moving forward?" Silas's confusion is evident in his expression. "Does this mean the *recovery* is only temporary?" A flash of fear widens his eyes.

Mr Zaman slowly shakes his head. "I can only speculate at this point, but I have to say, once recovery begins, it rarely regresses. It may stall, or faulter, but a full relapse is highly unusual."

We all sit in dumbfounded silence for a moment, absorbing this information.

"Mr. Tudor… Silas… as I explained earlier to Christina, this is marvelous news. The likelihood of a deterioration, now the foreign object has been removed, is minimal. Nic's recover will take time, but if he continues to follow his current trajectory, and with the right kind of support and therapy, I see no reason why he can't, eventually, lead a full and happy life… Silas, Christina… you have your son back."

"See!" Christina is ecstatic. "Silas, he'll recover… he's come back to us. Our son is going to get better!"

Silas can't speak. He sits, staring at the floor, wringing his hands, his features, transforming from delight, to apprehension, to disbelief and finally bewilderment.

The last few years have been a form of never-ending torture for him; I understand this now. Forever culpable, he was persistently seeking to atone for his mistakes; choosing a life he didn't want in order to castigate himself for what he perceived was his responsibility, barely able to live with what he felt he'd done to his children; tarring himself with the same filthy brush as those who so cruelly ended Maya's life and ostensibly destroyed Nic's.

As if an oppressive veil has lifted, I see it now with crystal clarity. The pain, radiating from him like a pulsing aura, the invisible crushing weight that he bore on a daily basis… is no more… I vow, if it's the last thing I do, to make it my life's mission to rid him of the wicked debilitating torment marring his existence.

"Silas, he's going to get well," I whisper, taking his hand in mine. "He's going to be better… baby?" In a bizarre reverse twist, I note his hands are freezing, where mine are warm. He stares deeply into my eyes. Where once his were haunted by sorrow, I see a flicker of hope.

"He's going to get better," he exhales, and he bursts into sobs of utter overwhelming release, dropping his head, his brow resting on our joined hands. My whole body is flooded with a sense of love, so intense I almost expect the room to blaze in a glowing light and fill with angel-song….

A weeping Christina is offering her own comfort, crouching beside him, her arm tight around his heaving shoulders, her swimming eyes, gazing in awe at the eminent surgeon. "Silas, he's going to be fine…" She roughly shakes his shoulder so he's swaying in the chair. "Love, he's going to be okay."

"How will we ever repay you?" she whispers to Zaman.

"Heh, heh…" Ali rises from his chair, an air of acute embarrassment in his posture. It's unbelievable that a man so talented can be so humble.

"Well, I have other patients to see. Nic is well tended, but I'll visit him again tomorrow, and if his improvement continues so rapidly, I expect he will be moving to a general ward within the next few days."

Silas is on his feet in an instant. He grabs the unsuspecting doctor by the hand and shakes it, before giving up and pulling him into a forceful bear-hug. Mr. Zaman's face floods beetroot red, as he clambers to breathe under Silas's vicelike hold.

"We're forever indebted to you, Silas growls, through clenched teeth, anything... absolutely anything..." he promises, and I don't doubt it.

A sudden inspiration strikes me... "The Gala..." I raise excited eyebrows at Christina. She understands immediately.

"Yes... of course... the Gala," she coughs once, clearing her tight throat. Silas and a very crumpled, but now released, Ali stare at her as if she's grown a second head.

"The 'Fund Raiser'," she spells it out, wiping her eyes dry. Now that she's occupied by business she can cope better. "There's absolutely no reason why we can't split the donations." She looks eagerly between Silas and Ali, who are still trying to shake off the awkwardness of their clumsy man-hug.

"Not following... sorry," Silas sniffs.

"How about, we split the proceeds raised, between the Neurological Department here, and the other charity?"

It's a wonderful idea. If the evening is as profitable as she expects and the donors are generous, there should be enough for two major donations.

"Well... I'm... err... thank you?" Ali Zaman is back to beaming his dazzling smile, though somewhat strangely bashful. "That's incredibly supportive of you, we're always seeking contributions to fund research; all gifts are very well received. Thank you," he adds.

"Anything..." Silas concludes. "Let's go and see our boy, and I can't wait to tell my parents the news. Thank you so much Mr. Zaman. We'll make sure tonight's fat-cats are separated from plenty of their cash."

339

Nic was still fast asleep when we returned to his room. The nurse in attendance was gently performing routine observations and replacing his drip. She tutted once in annoyance at the mass invasion but was happy to work around us as long as we remained out of her way. That was though, until we were caught by Matron, who's ferocity at our presence was terrifying enough even for Christina to relent and leave Nic alone in relative peace for a few hours.

We used the time to update everyone. Silas's family were exuberant, cheering so loudly on the end of the phone, they barely needed one.

Christina called Johannes, intermittently sobbing and laughing as she spoke; her head shaking continually in a subconscious portrayal of amazement. Her face has always been stunning, but now her beauty is elevated to a dazzling, spectacular loveliness I can only marvel at. Johannes said he was delighted to relay the messages to the international team.

Unable to stay away for long, Christina met up with Silas's parents and returned to the hospital at noon; they'll spend a quiet hour or so with Nic, before visiting ends.

My own calls were just as moving. Mark at the Beeches was crying openly on the other end of the phone, so much so, I worried for his sanity. Once he'd gathered his wits, I asked him to put David on, having forgotten David was spending the day with his sister and Sam.

To be honest, I was quite pleased, as it meant I could cut the call short, giving Mark the opportunity to communicate the good tidings to the staff and residents. He'll be at the Gala tonight, so I'll be able to speak to him less frantically and in more depth later.

After we were all kicked out by Matron, it made sense to regroup at the airfield. The agency crew were already busy, managing the influx of VIP private jets, in preparation for tonight's attendance. Christina wasn't exaggerating when she said they were flying in from all over. Spanners and Sparks were in complete control, overseeing the whole operation; directing the process with a level of competence I never knew they possessed. Clearly, when required, they can pull the rabbit out of the hat.

Susan, Jasper and Nasima had also come in to lend a hand. Incredibly, everything was so totally under control there was barely anything left for us to do. All outstanding tasks were evenly distributed as I should have realized they would be. I guess it was only to be expected they'd want to be in on the action, buoyed by the amazing news about Dominic.

"Silas, I need to try and get hold of Lizzy. They've taken David and Wendy out for the day, but he'll be desperate for an update," I say as he ends yet another call. He looks exhausted but happy.

"But my battery has just conked out," I grumble whilst impatiently rooting for my personal mobile. Locating it in the bottom of my handbag I find it also has only one bar of power left. "God, I'm so useless… this is dying too; can I borrow your charger please?"

"Yeah, there you go, Honey-bee." He chucks the tangled cable across the desk towards me.

"Ta, babe." Catching it, I blow him a kiss as he starts yet another call.

Hunting around for an empty socket to plug in my dead phone, I notice yet another sleek silver jet has parked on the apron beside the others. Distracted and fiddling with the knotted cable, I casually notice the aircraft doors open and the internal steps lower to the tarmac. I idly wonder who it'll be this time? A sports star, perhaps; a footballer maybe, or a rich business man?

I'm intrigued when a very elegant, long slender jean-clad leg appears, swiftly followed by a tall willowy body, swathed and wafting gracefully in varying layers and shades of cream cashmere ... Django... the supermodel ward of the late, Pierre Adrax, is descending the steps of the plane, closely followed by an identically dressed Liam Zaio. Mesmerized I cease my inept attempt at unknotting and watch them gracefully alight onto the apron, striding towards an awaiting navy-blue Jaguar.

"What's so fascinating?" Silas's call has ended and he's joined me at the window, snaking his arms around my waist from behind and nuzzling my ear. "Hmmm, you smell amazing," he croons, not really interested on the object of my fascination.

"I didn't know *they* were coming." I lean against him, allowing the heat of his breath to wash over my neck.

"Who?" Now he's entirely distracted. "I think we should go home," he mutters suggestively, pulling me against him.

I'm not totally unaffected myself, and I wouldn't say no to some hot and steamy afternoon delight, but at the moment my curiosity has got the best of me. I'm intrigued.

"*Them*, look... Liam and Django..." I point through the window, expecting him to snap his head up in interest.

But he just nuzzles deeper, bending his knees so he can better thrust his groin enticingly against my bottom. "Guest speakers," he answers, clearly preoccupied and completely uninterested at the new arrivals.

"Oh, I didn't know..." I hum. I'm getting sidetracked. His teeth grip my earlobe and bite gently down, I'm losing all interest in the knots in the wire and the beautiful ones standing on the tarmac. "Ooh," a delicious shudder runs through me at the pleasant pinch, shooting straight to my apex and igniting the dormant embers that simmer there.

"Elaine's picking them up," he reveals, as his rough hand circles my throat, tilting my head and allowing him easy access to the delicate skin of my ear and neck. His lips are burning. "Now... I think I was promised a preview..." he growls, through clenched teeth; and I feel his nip morph into a sexy grin as his lips travel along my pulsing vein and land in the sensitive hollow of my collarbone.

Swirling his hot tongue in the shallow concave, he licks hungrily up the side of my neck and I'm done for. The cable slips from my fingers and my hands fly out to support myself against the plate glass. Panting heavily, I close my eyes and allow the sweet sensation to overtake me. My forehead connects with the cold window pane and I wheeze in anticipation as I absorb the attention of his mouth.

"We need to stop," I heave, reluctantly. Ideally, I want nothing more than for him to take me, right here, right now in the office; but common sense prevails… everyone is milling around outside and they only need to look up to see us at the window.

"No, we don't." His palm flattens and skims down the gentle hillock of my stomach; long capable fingers in search of the scorching heat between my legs. "They're aware your here," he hums, darkly as his agile fingers gather the material of my skirt, "but they can barely see you… remember? They *can* look, but they *won't* see." I feel his mouth twitch as he grins knowingly at his pointed mantra.

"But they'll know," I state breathlessly, my heavy panting is misting the cold glass.

"And?" is his barely intelligible question. "What if they do?"

"I have no idea." And I don't… all reason for remaining discreet has vanished and I whip around, pressing my back against the window and with all my strength, heave my legs up, clasping them tightly around his neat waist and crossing my ankles; clinging to him with a fervent, feverish want as the stress and strain of the past twenty-four hours dissolves into the most incredible flood of intense desire I've ever felt in my entire life.

All I know, is if I don't have him, or rather let him have me, right this instant, I'll spontaneously combust from a combined overload of deliverance, passion, longing, relief and downright unadulterated lust.

"Grrrr," I growl into his neck, forcing my soaking groin into his hardness. "Fuck me… NOW!" The demand surprises even me… a minute ago I was obsessing over a knotted phone cable and some pretty people; now I just need to feel his hardness and the pounding of his body against mine as he slams into me. "Silas," I beg, as I'm pressed up against the window.

"Oh, yeah, baby…" he grimaces, dropping one hand and squeezing it between our heated bodies, releasing his belt and unzipping his fly. "You're gonna get it… hold onto me, I'm about to explode and I want to be deep inside you when I do."

I hear a rip as my knickers disintegrate, and the next second, I'm full to the hilt with what feels like a solid length of smoothly crafted, warm, hard mahogany.

"Oooh, Lord!" I heave, gripping him so tightly, he's unable to draw back and thrust. I need to hold him inside for a moment. Savoring the glorious sensation of fullness, reveling in the sweet sting as my muscles contract greedily around him. "God, this is gooood," I groan incoherently.

"Baby, I can't move… you need to at least allow me that…" he murmurs, desperate to draw back his length.

"Soon," I murmur, "just let me have this," and I squeeze my muscles so forcefully, I feel him gasp at the vicelike grip my internal walls have on his huge length. "Yesss," I sigh, tilting my head back so it collides with the windowpane behind me.

Fractionally, I unflex the muscles in my thighs and uncross my ankles, finally permitting him some much-needed movement. The muscle tension transfers from my thighs to my belly, as my weight, no longer supported by my legs, descends; the pressure shifting into a delicious, deep ache at the tip of my sex. Once it begins, it grows and I heave myself over and over, rocking against Silas's granite body, urging him to join me in my frenzied movements.

"Jesus," his curse is loaded with seething pleasure as at last he can release the pent-up power of his thrust against my open frame. "Fuck, yeah…" grabbing my thighs and hoisting me higher before slamming his palms either side of my head on the window, he grinds, deeper and deeper.

My head is rebounding with every hit, my bare bottom, rubbing against the glass, a scourging, friction, bringing with it an audible screech as I ride up and down the clear pane.

"Silas, I'm coming," I yell, there's no way I can stop this, my release is imminent and I'm about to explode. My fingernails dig into his shoulders. My legs tremble with the strain of being so wide apart and unsupported. My stomach muscles tense and ache with the unrelenting drive of his cock inside me and with that pressure, I'm aware of a familiar wetness building, ready to gush at the point of shuddering, looming detonation… I can't hold on any longer and I cry to the ceiling, all the tension, fear, joy and craving, erupt out of me like a rocket leaving a launchpad. I'm vaguely aware of a deep roar, resounding close to my ear; then I'm instantly soaring, up, up, up and away… toward the black velvety void of space, higher and higher on the way to the twinkling stars.

"Honey-bee?" unsteady hands are cupping my cheeks. Honied, heated breath, skims my face and I appear to be lying on the floor in a moist puddle. I'm disorientated, but not uncomfortable.

My eyes, flicker open, and I'm puzzled as to why Silas is hovering over me, nestled between my naked thighs… then I remember… "what was that?" I exhale the faltering question fearful I've been injured in some way. "Why am I on the floor?"

"Whew!" His relief is palpable. "You're back… I think you fainted," he tells me on a satisfied smirk. "I knew I was good, but that has *never* happened before," he drawls, clearly satisfied his skill has rendered me so breathless it caused me to pass out at the point of ecstasy. "Are you back in the room?" he smiles.

"Yes," I sigh. "That was the most…" words fail and I inhale deeply, filling my lungs with a much-needed influx of oxygen and gathering my splintered wits from where they're scattered on the damp carpet like my destroyed underwear. "You got me…" I affirm.

Tentatively, Silas withdraws, removing himself from my now aching channel, and I wince a little at the deliciously bruised sensation of my body regaining its natural balance. Beneath me, the floor is soaked and I realize the responsibility for that lies with us both.

"Ugh, yuck…" I complain, as when I go to support myself, my hand lands on a very soggy patch indeed. "Do we have any tissues?"

Silas stands, unaffected by the squelchy wetness. Tucking himself in, then dropping back to his knees, and nestled between my open legs, he smirks, "no, I'll do it my way." Dipping his head, he tenderly administers to my needs - in his way - gently lapping away the river of cum, tidying me up before finally, kissing both of my inner thighs and my sensitive clitoris.

343

"Mmmm, good," I croon. Lying there open and available, ready to go again.

"There, as good as new, you can close your legs now," he jokes, licking his glossy lips. Surely, it has to be a joke, because I'm feeling unkempt, ruffled and so, so used, I feel second hand! "Here." He hands me his mobile.

"Thanks, Boss Man... for the amazing orgasm and the phone," I grin, satisfied and sated. Finally calm and relaxed, I'm feeling ready to deal with whatever the rest of the day chucks my way.

CHAPTER 63

For some unknown reason, the only number I can remember off by heart is Sammy's. I rake my fingers through my tangled hair and wait for her to answer. The first time it rings off, and I realize, she won't recognize the number so has probably ignored it. I quickly compose a text, telling her it's actually me using Silas's phone and I'll call her back. This time she answers on the second ring.

"Hello, hello, hello..." she greets with a cheer. "We've heard... Chloe rang us from the hospital, isn't it fabulous?" her voice is trilling with joy.

Chloe? "Oh, yes... it's just fabulous isn't it... look if it's okay... can I speak to Lizzy?" I know she's aware of the brilliant news, but I'm desperate to speak to my daughter directly and hear her voice.

"Oh, well you could, but she's taken The Carrot and Wendy back to The Beeches. Sorry, Edi." I can hear her grimace at the inconvenient twist.

"Oh." I didn't expect that. "When did they leave?" I ask. Surely, I must have just missed them. After all, I spoke to Mark barely an hour ago.

"Ummm," she's checking her watch. "About twelve thirty... it was after lunch anyway... a couple of hours?" she says, questioningly.

"Oh, okay... well, I'll try again later. My phone died," I say unnecessarily distracted.

"Oh, hey... Edi... wait until you see the Carrot tonight," she announces excitedly, "he looks *suh-weeet*! Even though I say it myself. The boy scrubs up well when you can prise him out of his jeans and tee-shirts." I hear the distinct sound of airbrakes. "Edi, I've gotta scram-diddly-am ... the bus is here. I'll see you later on... okay? Hope you catch the kiddies. Love-ya." And she's gone.

"What's up?" Silas has reentered the office with two steaming mugs of tea.

My puzzled expression hasn't escaped his notice... "Oh, nothing really... it's just Sam said Chloe rang from the hospital a couple of hours ago, to update them about Nic, and that Lizzy has driven David and Wendy back to the Beeches."

"Well, ring them there... surely Mark can track them down."

"Yeah, I will, thanks," I add, taking an appreciative gulp of my tea. "Are we done here? If we are, I'd love to return to the barn for a long soak in the bath before tonight's party."

"I think so... look, would you mind if I dropped you off? I can call at the hospital for an hour. It looks like everyone has finished here anyway," he says, glancing out of the window as the last of the cars leave the car park.

"I didn't realize the time." Glancing at my watch, I notice we've managed to lose a couple of hours.

"Don't panic," he laughs, glugging on his own mug. "It's not that late, but everything is in order here. I just bumped into Gerard in the kitchen and everyone who's due in has landed safely and left for their hotels. There's nothing more to do.

"I didn't know Gerard was here?"

He frowns at me and rolls his eyes like I'm dense. "Edi, babe… the world and his *dog* is here!" Scratching his chin he adds, "which reminds me, I need to fetch Bear; are you coming?"

"Just did," I smirk cheekily.

"Honey-bee, you are incorrigible…" but his wide smile, says he's not at all disappointed by that notion. "Shall we?"

"Lead on MacDuff." I slide my arm around his slender waist, linking my thumb through his belt loop.

Bear is ecstatic. For almost twenty-four hours he's been in doggy limbo, wondering what he's done to deserve all this time with Margot Leadbetter! She's cute to look at, I'll give her that, but annoying doesn't cover the half of it.

Bear offers contrite apologetic eyes which clearly say 'release me from this purgatory' and 'whatever I did, I'm sorry, I promise I'll never do it again!' The poor dog is the epitome of penitence.

"Oooh, come on you." Silas kneels and roughs around Bear's head and neck, effectively tussling the grumps out of him. Before long, the beautiful creature is his usual happy bouncy self… Silas is forgiven for leaving him with the 'sitter' and Bear is bounding around us in desperation to be home.

"Thanks for having him, Chloe." Silas tentatively kisses his youngest sister, who's standing on the doorstep, wearing a pink satin dressing gown, a moisturizing face mask, hair in rags and toting a wiggly, yapping Margo, under her arm.

"See ya later Bro'… and brilliant news about Nic," she adds through clenched teeth, without moving her face. "I'm smiling under here, honestly…" she waves as we climb into the Range Rover.

"Right, home," Silas sighs.

"Just drop me off… I need to get ready and I really do need to get hold of Lizzy and David." The pair of them are still illusively dodging my calls. I'm beginning to think they're doing it on purpose.

"Look, don't stress, Honey-bee," Silas sooths. "Have a soak, do whatever you need to do… then ring them. Take some 'me' time… you deserve it. They're both big enough to take care of themselves for a couple of hours while you relax."

'Me time' - I think the last time I did that was … I can't remember… he's so unbelievably kind. He's right of course. They're both of an age where I shouldn't worry, but after the course of the last day and a half, I've missed them terribly. I know I'm being irrational, but there's an unsettled feeling in the pit of my stomach and until I speak to them both, it won't subside.

"They'll be fine," Silas reassures. Sensing my apprehension, he rests his hand on top of mine and gives it a squeeze. "Silly sausage."

I smile weakly across at him. I agree, I'm being silly; I'm seeing them in a few hours anyway. I can talk to them properly then. Shaking my head, I widen my smile and try to relax for the remainder of the journey home.

I feel much refreshed following my soak in the tub. Silas has gone to the hospital; though he's promised he'll be back in time to change for the Gala.

My nerves have started to kick in big style. This kind of event is so far out of my comfort zone, it could be on the moon. I could barely stand my graduation ceremony and the ensuing drinks party was excruciating. I hate being the focus of attention.

Once I've delivered the opening welcome speech and they've savored the news about Nic the party can get under way. This should mean the spotlight will be deflected away from me, and all being well onto all the other fancy people in attendance.

I walk to the kitchen, with my damp hair wrapped in a turban, and wearing my trusty purple fluffy dressing gown. My phone is fully charged, so I try, for the umpteenth time to phone Lizzy and David.

Lizzy's goes straight to answerphone. I quell the twinge of annoyance by telling myself she'll be too busy getting herself ready for tonight; although deep down I know, all she needs to do is put on a dress and finger-comb her wavy blonde locks... my girl is a walking, talking Vogue advertisement for pure perfection. She doesn't need to try to look fabulous... it's a natural talent.

Grumpily, I walk to the fridge and pour myself a glass of sparkling water. Dropping in some ice for good measure, I watch as Bear, now very happy to be home, abuses his rubber chicken with great gusto. I don't know what's happened to the squeak? He must've swallowed it. He eyes me with a canine nonchalance of the purely contented; raising an eyebrow and tilting his head as I approach him.

Leaning down, I give him a gentle stroke and in turn, he thumps the floor with his feathered tail. "Come on you, I think you need to go outside for a wee." Opening the door he trots obediently into the garden, rubber chicken suspended from his smiling jaws, looking for all the world like a giant Timber Wolf carrying its slaughtered prey.

As I push the door to, leaving it slightly ajar so Bear can get back inside, my phone beeps a message. It's a text from Lizzy. For some reason I'm flooded with relief when I read it.

Sorry I missed your call. I'm beautifying. □

I heard the fantastic news about Nic... Sam told me.

See you l8ter Mater

ILY

Lizzy xx

Hmm? Sam told her, that's odd. I was under the impression they were together when Chloe rang. Clearly, I misunderstood.

While, I drink my water and wait for Bear to finish his business, I try David. Surely, he'll be able to talk now.

"Hi mum!" His excitement has me grinning from ear to ear. "I'm nearly ready. Wendy is wearing a *Ball Gown!*" Oh David, just the sound of his voice is a balm to my shattered nerves.

"What happened today kiddo?" I ask, dropping my empty glass in the sink and tapping on the window to call Bear inside. "I tried to call you about a million times but you didn't answer."

"Oh mum, it wasn't a million!" he laughs. "We were… driving, and then Lizzy needed to get back, and then I needed a shower and how's Nic? It's brilliant that he's okay, isn't it?"

A crease puckers my brow as the frown forms. Instantly I'm worried whether this is what I feared all along. Nic is recovering. He's going to get well, and if all goes as expected, he'll be, for want of a better word, 'normal'. Is this why I'm feeling off kilter? Is it because of how David will take the news his best friend isn't going to be so dependent on him anymore?

"How do you feel about that?" I turn the question to David, probing for some insight into his own perception of this revelation.

"It's great," he enthuses. "I know he'll be different, but he'll still be Nic," he explains. "It's just that he'll be able to talk to people… not just me… but to other people too…" God love him. "It's fantastic. Wendy's dress is blue… she looks beautiful," he spirals off on a tangent as usual. "We'll see you later. I need to put my tie on." And the phone flips off.

Tie?

"Honey I'm home," Silas trills as he enters the kitchen, Bear trotting at his heels, rubber chicken now consigned to a shallow grave beneath the oak tree. "Wow! You look ravishing!" He eyes me up and down sarcastically then kisses my nose and pats my bum. "Go and get dressed; we only have," he looks at his watch, "an hour," he widens his eyes in mock horror.

"Shut your face… how's Nic?"

"Oh, Edi," he melts and sighs in wonder, stealing the glass of water from my hand and downing it. "He's doing brilliantly. He opened his eyes and said, 'Grandpa', to my dad, then smiled at mum!"

I know this is significant too. Nic's facial expressions were empty and blank for so long, merely daring to dream he'd one day regain the ability to smile was like wishing for a celestial miracle; but it's happened…the miracle of a smile.

"Oh, that's wonderful. How did they react?"

"Mum cried… dad cried… I cried… and Nic rolled his eyes!" He grins in awe at the notion. "It was amazing. He's asleep now and we've been chucked out again. That Matron's a bloody horror!"

I smile widely, I can't help it. My children are okay, and Nic is improving by the second, it would seem.

"I'll go and get dressed." Reaching up on my tip-toes, I kiss him and turning on my heel, sprint off upstairs, feeling about a thousand times lighter than I did half an hour ago.

CHAPTER 64

As requested, Silas had a preview of my new *red* lingerie, complete with sheer stockings and suspenders, not to forget the *'come fuck me'* Paris shoes. And, as the discerning connoisseur he is, physically demonstrated his gratitude while stood in the bedroom doorway, gawping hungrily dressed only in a tented, waist draped bath towel. Then he expertly scrutinized every minute silk stitch, every inch of luxurious satin and every delicate whisp of lace, before deeming the ensemble *'fucking perfect'*, and telling me to get the hell out of his sight before he *'shagged me stupid'* and destroyed my new knickers.

Silas and Christina have gone back to the hospital. The wonder and excitement of seeing Nic is all they want right now and they trust the team to manage everything here. As is the rule for these occasions; the event will run on until the last guest leaves, and as the 'stand-in' hostess, I'm expected to remain here until they do.

Silas expects they'll be asked to vacate the hospital around 10pm. They assured me if that happens, they will show their faces for a few minutes as it's only proper they thank everyone. Personally, I hope he changes his mind and goes straight home to rest. He needs a good long sleep after the week he's had.

I'm nervous, but my scarlet velvet Bardot-style gown and pinned up hair have miraculously instilled a boost of much needed confidence. I'm quietly quaking at the thought of public speaking, but I'm no longer feeling nauseous. I stand on the periphery of the splendid room and endeavor to quieten my racing thoughts. *Just enjoy it...* I tell myself, over and over... *you'll be fine...*

The Pompadour Ballroom at *Hotel Café Royal* is stunning. I've never seen anything quite like it before. The Louis XVI style room has a series of fluted Corinthian pilasters and mirrored panels with gilded frames, accented further by a rich decorative ceiling, ornately decorated, with scrolls and pillars adorned in sumptuous gold leaf.

The lighting is subtly muted. The music, set at an unobtrusive background volume ready for our guest's arrival, plays a mellow blend of modern and traditional swing - Robbie Williams, Sinatra and Bublé in equal measure - ensuring all audible tastes are catered for - as long as you like swing.

Our guest's filter in, in dribs and drabs; many of the women seeming to glide effortlessly on impossible skyscraper heels. Most of them tower over their male companions; I'm struck by the visual similarity to the Paris Fashion Week After Party, and the way the models, designers, rich and the famous, wafted by in a cloud of narcissistic indifference.

Tonight however, there is a pronounced variance; these people, while clearly beautiful, wealthy, glamorous and... *tall*... are here on invitation, by Royal Tudor Charter's, for the distinct purpose of parting them from their hard-earned cash; and every one of them seems to be thoroughly delighted at the prospect.

Even Spanners and Sparks are looking dapper arm in arm with their wives Vera and Margaret. Both ladies are dressed impeccably. The chuckle brothers have certainly made an effort, especially Jim, in his fifties-vintage brocade trimmed tuxedo.

Susan, Nasima and Jasper are an ill-assorted trio with their wildly diverse fashion styles, but in the scheme of things, the combination doesn't look out of place.

The room is filled to the brim with beaming smiles and friendly faces. There's a smattering of cheerful laughter, a murmuring of happy chatter, and an abundance of social camaraderie and warmth, which was entirely absent from the Paris party. Yes, while these people are here to be seen they are also here to do something for the common good. The irrefutable difference in intention is as far detached as the opposing faces of the Grand Canyon.

"A quoi pensez-vous?"

"Gerard!" I turn to come eye to eye with the soave Frenchman, looking absolutely drop-dead-gorgeous in a stylish Armani Tux. "How lovely to see you!" I exclaim in utter delight… and I'm quite surprised to realize, I totally mean it. It's so nice to see someone I recognize as a friend, rather than just from the TV.

"Edi, once again, you are magnifique." Taking my elbows, he kisses me on both cheeks. "Zis news of Nic is incroyable, non?"

"Yes, fabulous news," I gush, brimming with enthusiasm.

"I am, 'ow you say, joyeux, for my best friend, Silas." He's beaming. "And you, looking so belle, J'adore ta robe écarlate." *He's a smooth-talking bastard…*

But I too can play! "Pourquoi, merci gentil monsieur," I stumble through my reply in finest high school French. Gerard roars with raucous laughter, clearly relishing in my ineptitude with his beautiful language and terrible accent; I hope there isn't an inquest into the murder!

Dipping his head, he turns momentarily serious as he says, "I was very impressed wiz your interview ze ozer day." Glancing around us, he checks for eaves droppers before continuing even more quietly. "It was, as you say, made for good TV, but more importantly, it 'elped us get anozer *notoire* Porn Baron, locked away," he mumbles under his breath. "'E was a complete… *Ordure,"* he frowns, searching his brain for the appropriate English translation. "Scumbag… yes a scumbag," he nods, satisfied.

"I… er… thank you." I'm not sure what to say. His assessment of Bobby is mild to say the least. Slimeball, Crook, Thug, all of these descriptions come to mind plus a whole load more, which I'm far too ladylike to even think about, let alone speak aloud! "Did you know he was out?" I'm concerned he's not privy to this news.

His warm expression fades to one of gritty consternation, his heavy brows drawing together in a tight brooding frown, tinging his usually affable features with a menacing edge I've never seen before. "I know…" he mumbles, "but 'e won't be out for long. As I understand, 'e's under 'ouse arrest, non?"

"Yes, according to the reports." I have concerns as to exactly how well guarded he is; but I trust the authorities… I have to.

"Alright, zen," he cheers instantly. "We will not let such trivial matters concern us this fine evening." His gleaming smile is back in full force. "We need to 'ave a good time, soir?"

His grin is infectious, and I detect my own lips twitching at the corners in response. "Yes, yes; look… thank you for your support, Gerard, I mean it. You're an incredible friend to Silas and I'm eternally grateful."

"Edi… beautiful lady, it is I who should be obligé." Taking both my hands between his he looks at me squarely and with complete sincerity he says, "you have given me back my best friend; my brozzer. You make 'is 'eart 'appy… and 'zat makes me *very* 'appy… you bring 'im back to life." Kissing my cheek affectionately, he nods once and lowers my hands, focusing on the wider room.

"'ere! is zis a vision?" Abruptly, his solemness dissolves and his expression switches from pensive to intrigue; his attention is seized by a group of people entering the ballroom. "Mon dieu, mon cœur est en train de mourir," he gasps in awe, his hooded eyes widening in rapt appreciation.

I too, look in interest towards the group, noting the handsome young man in the striking tuxedo, arm in arm with a pretty young lady dressed in a prom gown of Royal blue taffeta. Walking alongside them are two young women, one wearing sexy black velvet and the other in gleaming gold sequins, both are giggling and pointing at the ornate murals on the ceiling. Then, following demurely behind, is a stunning girl in a simple pale grey satin slip dress, which clings silkily to every curve of her slim figure. Her hair is an unruly abundance of golden curls framing a barely made up, porcelain face; and every single head, including Gerard's, has turned to watch as my gorgeous, oblivious girl enters the ballroom.

"Mum!!" David is the first to spot me and comes bowling across the plush carpet, waving and dragging a very overawed Wendy in his wake. "Hi mum, you look beautiful." He kisses me lightly on the cheek. "Isn't this great?" he sings, staring around him in wonder. "Wendy," he gently draws her attention. "Doesn't my mum look nice?"

"Bonsoir, David… Veuillez m'excuser." Gerard, apparently losing the power to speak English, touches my elbow lightly and extracting himself from our midst, steps away, his eyes permanently focused on Lizzy; my own eyes accompanying his every determined step towards my precious girl.

"Wendy, darling, you look gorgeous," I smile, forcing my concentration on to the two people standing with me.

She blushes a very fetching shade of rose at the compliment. "Thank you, you look lovely too," she grins. "Mum and dad are just on their way; look," she points, towards her mother and father.

Mr. Prestage looks rather distinguished in his white dinner jacket and Mrs. P. is wearing a chartreus green gown, embellished with pale yellow and pink sequined blooms. On anybody else it would look wildly over the top, but Mrs. P. carries it off spectacularly. "I'll go and talk to them," she says kindly, leaving David with me, sensing I need the support of my boy right now.

"This is wonderful, mum," David says again looking around us at the now full room.

"I know, but I'm shitting it…" I grimace, flashing my teeth and aiming for humour. I'm starting to fidget, absently fingering my bumble-bee bracelet, and adjusting my watch. "You look fantastic by the way," I aim to change the subject and distract myself.

"Thanks," he beams. "It was Squirt and Lizzy really." His red hair has been trimmed and styled in the latest fashion; he really does look fabulous. "But they couldn't get to change all of me," he winks, then points down to his feet.

Following his jabbing finger, I shake my head and laugh at the battered old trainers, which surprisingly give a funky edge to the otherwise sophisticated ensemble.

"You can say that again," I grin. "You look magnificent," I concede. "I'm so nervous."

"Oh, don't be daft… you'll be great… where's Silas?"

"Oh, he's at the hospital, darling," I answer, unnecessarily straightening his bow-tie; more fiddling. The opportunity to just be mum, has dulled the sensation of anxiety at my pending speech.

"Why does that man like Lizzy?" He bats my fussing hands away impatiently. "And who's that girl with Squirt?" He's looking over my head at the small crowd near the bar. "She's nice," he pronounces.

Grateful for the distraction, I pay notice to his point of interest. On a second look, I realize the 'girl' is actually Chloe, and she look incredible. Her hair is a mass of frothy afro-curls and the black velvet one-sleeve mini-dress clings to her body like a second skin, accentuating her athletic build and shapely legs. Hanging on to her every word and smiling from ear to ear is a diminutive, curvaceous, golden, glitter-ball… Sammy!

"Oh!" The exclamation is out of my mouth before I can stop it. "Ummm, it's Silas's younger sister, Chloe," I say, aiming to keep the surprise from my tone. "Have you met?" Clearly, they haven't otherwise he wouldn't be asking me who she was! "Come on, I'll introduce you."

Keen to know more, I tug at his hand and eagerly lead him towards the small cluster of people, which now includes Wendy and her parents. This is the perfect excuse to interrupt Gerard from his Gaelic seduction of Lizzy; they're looking decidedly too cozy for my liking.

However, before we reach the bar, the M.C. is tapping on a glass and calling for attention.

"Ladies and Gentlemen."

Halting mid-stride, I turn to see I'm being beckoned towards the front of the room by a man in red livery. A lectern has been set up, in front of a white screen. My heart sinks at the sight.

Seriously! We're going to look like a pair of Chelsea Pensioners, in our matching scarlet!

"Ladies and Gentlemen, please take your seats. The evening shall begin in a few minutes, but first we have a few words from our hosts…"

Oh, shit… here it comes.

Gritting my teeth, I release David's hand and start to make my way over to the M.C. when he announces: -

"Mr. Silas Tudor and Mrs. Christina Royal."

The room erupts into an enthusiastic peal of applause, as Silas and Christina walk, hand-in-hand into view. Greeting people as they pass, it's like watching the President and First Lady enter the room.

Initially I'm eased at the relief of knowing I no longer have to stand at the front of this crowd and speak. But as I watch the pair of them together, my stomach lurches and I'm flooded with trepidation at the sight. They look unified, as one… and I instantly feel sidelined.

Silas is in a slick Black Tuxedo, white tie, a black silk fringed scarf, draped artistically beneath his collar - looking for all the world like a Hollywood movie star; but Christina, *oh my*, Christina is absolutely stunningly breathtaking. There's no other comprehensive way of describing how radiant she looks; she's literally glowing.

Dressed in pure brilliant white - virtually bridal - satin, she shimmers beneath the golden lights like a celestial angel descended from the heavens. There's an aura about her and it's an aura of complete unbounded happiness. My heart sinks and a vicious stab of pain reminds me, he was hers long before he was mine. They look so good together, so unbelievably devoted… the perfect couple.

But, as they approach the lectern, I notice Silas's eyes as they traverse the room. His smile holds, but his eyes are sweeping through the crowd intently… and I know, he's searching for me.

The moment he spots me amongst the crowd, my heart arrests and my surroundings are promptly forgotten. His eyes are hooded and dark, the deep caramel of his irises flecked with gold. Filled with moody intention they seek and find mine and, suddenly I'm floating.

Drawn towards him by an invisible cord which links our hearts, I glide freely, weaving my way between the stationary bodies of the people around me. All I'm aware of, is him, as he wills me to his side.

Christina is speaking. All the while as I wend my way across the floor, Christina commands the hub of the room. But, as two spirits in their midst, Silas and I just fixate on each other's gaze, until, finally, I'm safely beside him. Only then does the sound unmute and Christina's voice penetrate my hearing.

Retraining his eyes on his ex-wife, Silas inconspicuously takes my hand and squeezes it tightly, causing my frozen heart to jolt awake in my chest, restarting its steady drumbeat.

"And, without the skill of Mr. Zaman and his talented team, I don't know what we would have done. So tonight, with your permission, any proceeds will be equally divided between our chosen charities. *Liberty from Trafficking* and *Brain Trauma Medics*… Thank you in anticipation for your generosity."

The room explodes into an abundance of applause and whistles.

Johannes has arrived to escort Christina. He too is dressed in brilliant white.

354

"Liberty from Trafficking?" I gasp as Silas and Christina take a bow and wave to the cheering guests. "I thought... I thought... tonight was for *The Beeches?*" I'm utterly confused; but in hindsight, it makes sense now I know that Django is a guest speaker.

"I wasn't at liberty to say," Silas explains. "We weren't sure if we could announce the true cause of the evening, or how you'd react. But as everything is in the open now, and you know what we do, there's no need for pretense."

"So... all these people...?"

"No, no, don't get me wrong... the illusion remains intact for the wider public," he clarifies. "To them, we will always be Royal Tudor Charters."

"Woah, for a moment there, I was worried..." I hesitate, thinking aloud. "But what about The Beeches?" If the money is going to the victims of sex-trafficking and the hospital, what about The Beeches...?

"Oh, Honey-bee," Silas grins. "The Beeches is well funded, believe me." He joins in the applause, as the guests' troop in an orderly line towards the stage, where a white HM Royal Mail letterbox, decorated with red Tudor roses, stands loud and proud, waiting for the fat envelopes and cheques to be posted.

"But?" No, I can't think of a question. "I'm confused," I concede.

"The Beeches receives an annual donation from Royal Tudor Charters. We subscribe to the upkeep of the home and its facilities. Honestly, they really don't need a charity fundraiser. But the poor kids affected by the likes of Price," he sneers his name through gritted teeth unable to hide his distaste, "and Adrax and the like; those kids need all the help they can get... Look, the band are here." Squaring his shoulders, he whistles at the arrival of a four-piece taking the stage to even more applause.

"Ladies and gentlemen, please take your seats as dinner is served," the M.C announces.

During dinner the guests are encouraged to fill the gold envelopes at their place settings to donate generously, either in cash or by cheque. The band are taking requests at a charge of twenty-pounds per tune and have so far managed to perform abridged versions of songs by the likes of, *Florence and the Machine, The Vamps, The Rolling Stones and The Beatles.* No-one requires much encouragement to make a request, and everyone seems determined to outdo each other with the diversity of their musical taste and knowledge. They're all trying to find something the band won't know and so far, failed spectacularly. Up to now, the most diverse request was for *The Ting Tings 'Shut up and let me go,'* which the band performed brilliantly.

"How's your food?" Silas asks.

"Fantastic, thank you." It's Chicken Supreme with julienne carrots, dauphinoise potatoes and shallot puree. "I didn't expect to be hungry," I say looking at my almost empty plate. "It was delicious." I place my knife and fork down, as the band strike up yet another classic, *'Sit Down' by James.*

"How was Nic when you left?" We haven't really had a chance to talk as everyone is so keen to speak to Silas and offer their best wishes and congratulations. Christina has been consistently engaged by a steady stream of well-wishers and is thoroughly enjoying the experience. Silas, on the other hand, is barely tolerating the attention, with a modicum of good grace. Not that he's irritated by the constant interruptions, it's more that he's embarrassed by the fuss. He doesn't enjoy being the center of attention as much as Christina clearly does.

"Sleeping, peacefully. Guarded by that Rottweiler of a nurse."

"Oh, that's so good to hear." I'm relieved. We've been advised that his recovery will be a steady progression, and could take time but all the current signs are very encouraging.

He places his knife and fork on his empty plate, then laces his fingers through mine where they lie in my lap, giving my hand a small shake and nudging my shoulder. I'm staring at the table across the room, where Gerard and Lizzy are sat in a close huddle, heads almost touching as they engage in quiet conversation. Judging by the body language, they each appear to be equally enchanted by the other's company.

"Hey," Silas whispers. He's followed my disproving gaze and can no doubt read my thoughts. "Edi... Honey-bee?" He removes his hand from mine and places warm tender fingers beneath my chin, encouraging me to turn away and look at him. "She's a big girl," he reminds me.

"But..." I protest, although I know he's right.

"Edi..." His eyebrows raise in mild caution. "And anyway, Gerard is well aware that if anything should happen to Lizzy, if she's hurt in any way, he knows it'd be more than his life is worth."

"It's..."

"*Edi!*" he scolds, shaking his head for me to relax and leave it. "Come and dance with me."

Crap! Is he serious? I look at him in askance. It's only now I realize; we've never danced together before.

"You can dance, can't you? Or am I wasting my time with an uncoordinated klutz?"

Ooh, the bloody cheek of him!

"I'll have you know you're looking at the winner of a bronze medal in Ballroom and Latin dancing... Junior level," I stand superiorly, and hold out my hand. He doesn't need to know it was at my dance school presentation and there were only ten couples participating.

"Well then," he stands too, accepting my challenge. "Bring it on, '*Ginger'!*"

"After you, '*Fred'.*"

Laughing, he scoops me up and twirls me around as I squeal in delight.

"Come on, they're playing our song." Dropping me to my feet, he grasps my hand and leads me to the dance floor.

"*Whah...?*" It takes me a second to recognize the music, but when I do, I'm pulling against his hand, desperately trying to halt him in his tracks and return us to our seats... *I'm not dancing to this!*

"*Nooo, Silas... we can't...*" I wail in sheer embarrassment; *there's no way!*

"Oh yeah... you'd better believe it Baby... show me what a Bronze medal in Ballroom can do to this rockin' tune." He reaches the dancefloor and with one swift yank, I'm hauled against his chest. I can feel his body heat radiating through me, he must be boiling in that suit.

Cupping my bottom, he grinds against me, urging me to do the same. I'm mortified and clasp my hand over my eyes in embarrassment. I know everyone, including my kids, are watching. I can feel their eyes burning into me; what must they be thinking.

"Everyone's staring!" I wail in justified mortification, as he grinds away. His hands are everywhere.

"Honey-bee," he murmurs in my ear, "what do I always say?"

"They can look, but they won't see..." I repeat his mantra, breathless now, my hips beginning to circle, in time with his, performing a gentle sway of their own volition.

"Yeah, you're getting it." One hand travelled up the center of my spine, until it landed on the bare skin at the nape of my neck. The heat leaves a blistering handprint all the way to my core. "Let it go, Honey-bee, just move, baby. Feel it..." He kisses my ear and I implode.

Although we're undulating like it's a slow dance, the music is the same explicit bump and grind, Hip-Hop they played at the Paris Party. *Snoop Dog's 'Drop it Like it's Hot'.*

"It's hardly a romantic song!" I pant, leaning back and tilting away so I can see his glorious face.

"Of course, it is." He pulls me upright and steps away. "Show me..." Extending his arms, he puts distance between us so he can watch me move. Rippling his finger like a pianist, he mimes to the lyrics and makes a parody of Snoop and Pharrell by blatantly clutching his crotch and licking his lips. Arrogantly jutting his chin, he rolls his shoulders.

"Dance for me woman!" he demands with a suggestive growl.

As if his words are an incantation, the undulating throng of people surrounding us vaporize into a swirling cloud of mist and disappear until it's just, him and me... me and him... Us!

I stare unashamed into his blazing eyes, and let the music take me. The finger snapping, the tongue clicking, the heavy, reverberating, throbbing base... all of it. I allow it to penetrate my being, and as the beat kicks in, I start to writhe and sway along with it; gently at first, then, as it continues to pulse and the song progresses, and the lyrics become more explicit and suggestive, so do my moves.

I touch myself, stroking up and down my torso, and placing both hands around my neck I tilt my chin, swinging my hips and gyrating to the throbbing rhythm. All the while, Silas nods along, unwilling to take his eyes off me as I dance for him alone. Yes, they can look, but they can't actually see. People blindly think what they see on the surface is all we are; what they perceive us to be. But what truly lies beneath, the reality, is for our eyes only… for Silas and I alone. Now I understand what he means and it's liberating.

As the song comes to its conclusion, I spin, raising my arms aloft; I feel like I'm on a fairground ride. My stomach somersaults and I'm engulfed by a vertiginous rippling wave. My breath escapes in a heavy whoosh as I whirl dizzily around the floor. Ascension accomplished!

All too soon, the music changes and I descend back down to earth feeling a little self-conscious and embarrassed by my wanton display. However, Silas has no time for that, he's delighted. Grinning a megawatt smile from ear to ear, he grabs me around my waist and draws me close.

"I knew it," he growls into my ear, "you're a dirty dancer." His arms are so tight around me I can barely breathe. "It follows… you're a dirty girl in the bedroom… you couldn't fuck the way you do and not be able to dance like that; when we get home, you're gonna do that again and I'm gonna watch you. And you're gonna do it naked."

"Anything you say Boss-man!" I laugh and drape myself all over him, all trace of embarrassment washed away by his unapologetic boldness. At this moment, I'd rip this dress off right here and do it all over again. Who'd have thought, that would be 'our song'?

The dance floor has filled up considerably. Everyone is having a fantastic time. The band have satisfied all requests, no matter how obscure or cheesy, and performed every tune and song perfectly; even some awful, moody, indie dirge requested by Jasper.

"Silas, I need to get a drink." I'm parched. We've been on the dancefloor for about six songs and I need a break. I've bopped with David and Wendy to *Chumbawamba 'Tubthumping'*, I've grooved to *'Groovejet' by Spiller*, with Lizzy, and the rest of the girls but best fun of all was boogieing on down to *'Relax' by Frankie Goes to Hollywood*, with Mrs. P and Mrs. Whittham! Those broads can't half shake a tail feather with the best of them!

"Okay, Honey-bee; I'd better have a dance with Christina. You go and get a drink. It's a free bar." Silas kisses me and I wander off the floor, leaving him to sway with Christina to *Lionel Ritchie*.

Reaching the bar, I wait in line for my turn. Leaning against the brass rail, I take the opportunity to flex my aching ankles and massage some blood back into my feet. Standing on one leg, I bend my knee and grip my toes, willing them back to life. These shoes are comfortable, but after an hour on the dancefloor, my insteps are aching a bit.

"Well, that was quite a performance you put on out there." The slurred sneer at close proximity to my ear has me flinching away; recoiling at the sour stench of alcohol-breath filling my nostrils, Affronted, I turn to challenge whoever's dared to invade my personal space.

CHAPTER 65

"What the *Fuck* are you doing here?" I blurt in utter shock at the sight of an inebriated Bobby... "How the hell did you get in? This is a private function."

My illogical fury at his sheer audacity and boldness has momentarily superseded my fear at the knowledge he's actually standing bold as brass before me. But the flush of anger just as abruptly fades as the gravity of my current situation takes hold. Suddenly my eyes are darting around, desperately trying to attract the attention of someone, anyone who can come to my aid. Unbelievably, even in this crowded room, there's nobody close enough to notice what's going on.

My initial rage has evaporated, giving way to a sickening dread; a much more sensible response to the danger I unexpectedly find myself in as he looms closer and leans, breathing rancid fumes in my face.

"I've just come to check on my investment..." Looking me up and down he smirks openly. "You must think you've won the lottery; you can't help yourself, can you?"

I try to back away but I can't because the Bar is behind me and Bobby has somehow managed to maneuver himself so he's pinning me in place, hemming me in with my back against the cold unyielding metal.

"You think you've won. But look," he veers backwards, half a step and gestures about him, "nobody's watching." Leaning back in, he leers and whispers, "we're all alone."

Holding my nerve, I grit my teeth and hiss vehemently, "*you,* need to leave," whilst dodging left, seeking to get away.

But as drunk as he is, he anticipates my move and with precise cobra-like timing, positioning himself so his arms are two rigid barriers, either side of mine, ensnaring me within the circle, and foiling my escape.

"Oh no..." he snarls. "You're not going anywhere."

Staring into his eyes, I open my mouth to scream, but he's swiftly up in my face, so close I can see the broken thread-veins feathering his cheeks and nose... *alcoholic*... I'd recognize the signs anywhere. His eyes are bloodshot and rheumy, he must have spent the last couple of days swimming in vodka, drowning his sorrows and building up the courage to turn up here tonight.

"You think you're so *fucking* clever..." His putrid breath almost knocks me out and I close my eyes against the desire to vomit.

"Look at you..." one hands leaves the brass rail and lands heavily on my breast. "Ooops, sorry," he sneers, "I forgot, I mustn't touch the merchandise." But instead of removing it, he grips tighter, squeezing with all his strength. His face grimaces a vindictive smile of satisfaction as I impart a little cry of pain.

"Take, your, filthy, hands, off me," I hiss through gritted teeth, all the while glaring at him, willing myself not to break, to have the bravery to stand up to him.

"Leave now; and I won't make a scene," I demand with a determination I don't feel. "GO!" I want to scream, but I stand my ground, refusing to give him what I sense he really wants; tears and begging. But it's in vain. In a split-second and with a whip-like motion, his hand travels upwards, from my breast to my throat, encircling my windpipe in an unrelenting choke-hold.

Before I know it, I'm clawing at his wrist, digging my nails into his forearm, scratching at his hand, desperately attempting to prize it away from my neck so I can take a breath. From behind, it looks like nothing serious is happening; just two people chatting, friendly, intimately, so skilled is he at disguising the truth.

"Oh, I could do it you know. It'd be so easy and so much fun. Don't think I couldn't."

He leans even closer, increasing the compression until I'm no longer gasping, but opening and closing my mouth in a silent scream against the unrelenting pressure on my throat. My eyes are watering and a red mist is blurring my vision… he's going to kill me… right here and he's going to get away with it because everyone thinks he's just chatting.

Opening my mouth once more, I try in vain to make a sound but only a choking gulp comes out. Using my eyes, I plead with him to release me, to let me go, but I'm struggling against consciousness. Why can't people see what's happening?

Gripped by terror, my lids begin to droop, and my flailing hands lose their grip as he squeezes my life away… then instantly, I'm free. My breath whoops in, in a heaving rush and the sudden influx of air clears my head. Brilliant white flashing lights blind me as my eyes fly open and my ears ring with the piercing blend of rushing blood and loud music.

"That was just a little taster." Excitedly, his greedy hands trail all over my torso as he leeringly observes my recovery. "A *reminder* of the good old days. Something for you to think about."

Swaying back on his heels, he checks out his handywork. "Ooh," he tuts, as if concerned. "There might be a bruise tomorrow," he chuckles. "But you know how to hide them, don't you?"

"Fuck you!" I manage to hurl the words through the pain in my damaged vocal cords. "FUCK YOU!" The yell is louder this time… loud enough to summon the attention of the barman.

Activity in my peripheral vision, causes me to stand stoic against his threat. "Fuck you…" I hiss in his face. "Get away from me you *Bastard!*" Though I'm riddled with fear and gripped with pain I don't move, standing firm my ground.

"Hey!" The barman, at last, has noticed there's something wrong and is heading in our direction. "Are you okay Miss?"

"You just wait…" His eye's flick to where the server approaches. Knowing he needs to get out and quickly, he leans even closer and issues one more final threat.

"I'll get what I want, one way or another…remember *who* you are…remember *what* you are…remember you're *nobody*…you'll always be nothing but a cheap little tart, worth nothing to anybody unless you're on your back."

His words are scalding, a bitter reminder of the years enduring his degrading comments on a daily basis. But still, I don't retreat. I remain unmoved and upright, defiantly frozen into place.

"You're worthless." He tries again to intimidate me, but the barman is approaching now, tentatively creeping nearer…I wonder idly, what's keeping him.

"Remember who you're dealing with." He jerks his head, as if to headbutt me; this time I do flinch. Oh, I know only too well who I'm dealing with.

"Be careful…because…one day…when you least expect it… '*SNAP!*'" He clicks his fingers menacingly. "I'll be only too happy to finish what I started, and you're out like a light…hunt the shark and risk the bite…and this Great White is deadly!"

"Leave!" Finally, the barman is here. Standing safely protected behind the barrier of his bar, he points towards the exit. "Sir, I think you need to go before I call security."

"Oh, don't worry, I'm going." He staggers backwards, remaining focused on me. "Don't bother to call for help, I'll be gone before they get here." And he lurches away, far more agilely that the level of alcohol in his system should allow.

As I watch him lumbering through the doors, my legs begin to shake and I can no longer bear my own weight. Collapsing to my knees, I stare unseeing at the vacant space once occupied by the vilest man alive.

"Miss? Miss…"

"Edi?" Strong arms are tight around me and a concerned, baritone voice is urging me to stand. "Honey-bee? Baby, I'm here…" I'm trembling so violently; my teeth are chattering.

"Help me! Help me to get her up," I hear Silas command. "You…what the *fuck* happened?" He's yelling at the barman. "I'll have your job for this."

"No, it wasn't his fault," I manage to mutter, my senses returning to the here and now. Looping my weak arms around his solid body, relief surges through me at his closeness.

A rushing sound fills my ears as I realize the party is still continuing around me. It would appear my collapse has gone relatively unnoticed by all, except the barman, Silas and Leon, who are now assisting me to my very wobbly feet.

"I'm fine." I shake my head, trying to clear the fuzzy feeling. "Really, Silas, Leon, please. Is there somewhere I can talk to you in private? I don't want the whole room to know what just happened. Especially the children." *Oh no, Lizzy and David…* my concern is once again heightened.

"Sir, you can use the snug." The barman aims to redeem himself by offering us the small quiet lounge beside the main Ballroom.

Nodding to Leon, Silas takes my waist and gently guides me towards the ornate double doors.

"Check on the kids please dad, will you? I don't want them freaking out. Just tell them we're having a quiet five minutes."

"Will do son," and without question, he heads back towards the main party, acutely aware any unnecessary ruckus will do no good.

"In here sir." The simpering barman, clearly more concerned for his job than my wellbeing, is overly attentive, as he holds the door to the snug. "Can I get you anything? Brandy perhaps?"

"Whisky," we chorus.

"Talisker, if you have it," Silas instructs.

"We have a 25-year-old single Malt?"

"Yes, yes… perfect, and bring the bottle," he adds as an afterthought, "and glasses."

As soon as the door swings closed behind him, Silas kneels, switching his full attention to me. Lowering me onto a plush dark blue sofa, I recline into the cushion, lying still.

With tender fingers and concerned eyes, he examines my injured throat. A flicker of murderous vengeance ripples his features, but right now he's far more concerned with the damage done to me, than contemplating chasing down my assailant.

"Does it hurt?"

"Only when I laugh… or scream," I quip sarcastically. "Yes, it bloody hurts."

"Honey-bee…"

The door flies open and Christina hurtles through, swiftly followed by Johannes and Leon, and the bemused barman toting a silver tray with six crystal tumblers and an unopened bottle of whiskey.

"I'll take that…" Christina dismisses him with one of her 'not to be messed with' looks; unstoppers the bottle and pours generous measures into each glass, handing them around.

Before I can think, I'm surrounded by a group of solicitous, attentive faces all keen to know what reduced me to this state.

"What happened?" Christina is on the seat beside me, handing me a Scotch, her arm protectively swathing my shoulders.

"The children?" I ask. Before I tell them anything, I need assurance David and Lizzy are alright and out of harm's way.

Christina glances furtively at Johannes, who in turn, bites his lip and looks to Silas.

"Don't look at me, this was your assignment…"

"I…, just…" Johannes stutters, looking uncharacteristically sheepish for him.

My heart races, something's happened to the children. Abruptly, I sit up, needing to distinguish the extent of my fears. "What's happened, where are they?" I panic, ready to leap into action and do, I don't know what, but I'm ready to do something.

"Calm down, Baby, it's okay… Lizzy is with Gerard and David is with Elaine, Wendy and her parents. They're fine." Silas is too quick to dispel my initial worries.

"Gerard and Lizzy, err," Johannes, already a man of few words, seems completely at a loss.

"What?" I demand, annoyed now.

"They left. They went to the airfield. Lizzy wanted to see Gerard's plane!" Johannes cringes, knowing full well I'll be seething at this information.

Turning on Silas my eyes are ablaze, with delayed pain from my near choking and in utter disbelief he's allowed his *'hound'* of a mate to take my daughter on a magical mystery tour of his private jet!

"Silas! How could you?"

"Me? Oh no, this was nothing to do with me, and anyway, as I said, Johannes was supposed to be babysitting."

"Some baby," Johannes mumbles – then whispers, "so not a baby," under his breath.

"I heard that," I snap, my voice breaking at the energy required to keep up this level of crazy.

"She's safe," Silas soothes. "I called him and let him know, in no uncertain terms… a reminder of what I'll do to him if she isn't."

That little speech, has me blanching. *A reminder…* the same exact phrase Bobby used not ten minutes earlier.

"Edi?"

I deflate against the cushions and swallow, flinching against the discomfort. My eyes are dry, but my throat aches with the kind of choking agony you only get when you're suppressing howling sobs.

"*He* said that," my voice cracks on a whisper. "He said, it was a *reminder*, of the good old days and that he'd be back to finish the job once he had what he wanted."

Four pairs of anxious eyes exchange worried glances.

"What did he mean?" Silas responded.

"Lizzy." It's the one word which causes my eyes to moisten and the tears to brim unrepressed. One glittering sphere spilled over, blazing a scalding trail down my cheek.

"Lizzy," I say in utter defeat. "He wants her… then once he has her… he'll kill me."

CHAPTER 66

Things speed up considerably, but it's still not fast enough for me, as Silas, Christina, Johannes and Leon discuss a plan of action. Nobody knows the exact whereabouts of Bobby, but someone must know which direction he went.

"I'll speak to the manager… get the tapes from reception." Johannes swiftly disappears; relieved, no doubt, to be away from Silas's accusing glare and to have a focus.

Within minutes, we're all looking at the monitor in the Managers understated office. The CCTV shows Bobby exiting through the main lobby doors and colliding with the doorman, before assertively striding away, dodging the after-Theatre throng on Regent Street and disappearing into the milling crowd at Piccadilly Circus. He's heading for the tube.

"Can we pick him up anywhere?" Leon is pacing, thinking, planning. "Should I call my contact in Whitehall?"

"No, no…" Silas shakes his head. "Not yet…"

"But, son… we can track him with the street cams, the underground system…"

"No," he looks at me in earnest. "Edi and the kids come first. Let's ensure they're safe before we do anything rash. We'll wrap this up and head to base… the airfield. Gerard's already there. Lizzy will be safe." His look tells me they'll protect her with their lives if they have to. He'll lock her in the panic room until the coast is clear if necessary.

"I'll take Edi back to the Barn; she'll be secure there with Bear on guard – David can stay with you?" He looks directly at me for confirmation.

"Yeah, God, yes of course," I nod. Having David with me will be a huge comfort. "Bobby won't come after me again tonight."

For all his bravado, Bobby's basically a coward of the worst kind; he'll wait this out until he's clear headed enough to be efficient. He's not stupid, even he would recognize when he's blind drunk.

"He'll sleep it off somewhere. He won't come back tonight."

"If, you're sure?"

"I'm sure."

"But we can't just wait…" Johannes is champing at the bit to give chase.

"Edi knows him best… she knows his character, and if she says he'll lie low, we need to trust her instinct," Silas says with little conviction.

"Johannes, take Dad and go and round up Gerard. I don't want Lizzy scared, so don't mention what's gone on here. Christina, can you speak to mum and gather up the rest of the family?"

"And Sammy," I add. We mustn't leave her behind.

"No problem. I'll take them to the apartment; I'll suggest they carry on the party there. I'll instruct Elaine. They won't know what's gone on but they'll be closely chaperoned."

"What about Wendy?" I'm panicking about everyone, my overactive brain and mother-hen instinct is kicking in.

"Mark will make sure everyone gets back to the Beeches safely; stop worrying. You're not the only one who can organize and multi-task you know. Pigs in space... I'm a mum too," Christina admonishes lightly. Her affected eye-roll and warm smile are a balm to my shattered nerves. I know she'll deal with everything.

"Thank you... I was just..."

"I know... C'mon, let's get this show on the road. I'll go and thank everyone for coming. Django and Liam gave a fantastic speech by all accounts; it's a shame we missed it!" In a blink, she's gone and I'm left alone with the man who holds my world in balance.

"I'll get David." Silas makes to follow her.

"No; no, I should. I should show my face, otherwise people will suspect something's up. We need to play this as normally as possible so as not to raise suspicions. I'm okay." Silas doesn't look convinced, but he doesn't argue either; knowing I'm right this time.

"Okay, but here, wear this." He passes me the black silk scarf from his Tux, and drapes it around my injured throat. "Just until we can get you away from prying eyes."

"Thank you," I nod appreciatively as he tenderly drapes the silky material around my bruised neck.

Back in the ballroom, Christina is finishing a rousing closure to the proceedings by announcing the total raised by the evening.

"Before I send you all on your weary way; I'd like to thank everyone for their incredible generosity and contributions to tonight's event." Turning, she nods to the band and on cue the drummer picks up his sticks and begins a steady drumroll.

"It is with great pleasure; I can announce the grand total raised this evening is... One million - Six-hundred and fifty-seven thousand pounds!"

Sheesh! These people are seriously wealthy!

The drummer smashes his cymbal and the room at once explodes into peals of piercing whistles, raucous cheering and loud applause.

Christina raises her voice over the din. "This means we can not only fund a new shelter for the victims of trafficking, we can also donate a substantial sum to neurological research... you did this..." She holds her arms out to the audience and picks up the applause, saluting in turn their generosity and kindness. The band joins in with a jaunty version of *'Congratulations'*.

Turning towards us, Christina lifts the hem of her skirt, and climbs elegantly down from the stage. "Now, let's get out of here."

Smiling for the benefit of the congratulatory crowd, Christina walks over to Elaine, and whispers swift instructions in her ear. Elaine, unphased, turns herself towards Chloe and Sam, who are gleefully hanging onto each other, boisterously singing along to the music, which has morphed into *'New York, New York'*, and performing a high kicking routine. Gently rounding them up, she shepherds them, still singing and dancing towards the exit.

David, dickie-bow askew and cheeks glowing a rosy pink, runs to my side. "Mum, it was brilliant!" he beams. "Mark's taking Wendy and the rest of us back to the Beeches."

"Oh, David… would you mind staying with me tonight?"

David's brows pucker and he gives Silas a suspicious look. "Ummm, okay?"

"Hey, buddy," Silas winks at him. "I need to get some stuff done – you know – for Nic; and your mum would really like to spend some time with you." Leaning in, he stage-whispers in David's ear, "can you look after her for me?"

Chest inflating and bristling with pride, David soon forgets his suspicions and consents to keeping me company. "At the barn?" he asks, brightening at the prospect of sleeping over.

"Yeah, if that's alright with you… and Wendy?" Silas nudges his elbow, ensuring his compliance, before heading out. "I'll get the car."

"Thanks for this David," I smile. "We've not had much time alone for ages; it'll be fun."

"Yeah. Let me tell Wendy. I'll be back in a jiffy."

I watch as David heads over to where Wendy and her parents are gathered with a group of her friends.

"Interesting evening." Tia has sidled up beside me, still looking magnificent with her inch-long silver acrylic nails tapping the side of her Martini glass. "I see my sister and your dear little friend have hit it off," she raises a well-groomed eyebrow at the state of Sammy and Chloe. "Jaz is stoked, you know?"

Searching the room, I spot Silas's middle sister standing quietly beside her mother. The resemblance between the two is striking. I've not noticed it before.

"About what?"

"You, and Si', and the *'businesses.'*" Dexterously, she picks the cocktail stick from her glass and removes an olive with her teeth.

Twisting side-on to give her my attention, I'm puzzled. "But I thought the younger two weren't aware of… the other things." I don't know how to phrase it. "You know… the airfield."

"Oh, well, they have an idea." She replaces the remaining olive, and takes a sip of her dirty Martini. "You don't live in a family like ours all these years without an inkling… no, she's happy… you got him out. Now she can concentrate on fulfilling her ambition of becoming a legitimate pilot. It's all she's ever wanted."

Tia has never demonstrated any warmth towards me. It's only now, I see it. This *is* her warm side, frigid though it appears. She's much more like her father than any of them; Silas included. In this moment, I completely understand why she's committed to remaining in the other side of the 'Business'.

"You're good for him. I like you," she pronounces as if she's been deliberating her appraisal for a while; weighing me up before concluding she's on my side after all.

"I like you," I say, still a little perplexed.

"I need to find Mark before he leaves. Do you think he's in to me?"

I have no idea! I remain mute.

"Never mind… I know he'll like me… Ciao!" She waves her ridiculously long nails and turns on her five inch stilettoes, her focus clearly on a very unsuspecting Mark.

Luv-a-duck! Poor Mark.

I'm staring after her, when David arrives back at my side. "Ready?"

"Yeah, ready. Wendy's going to stay over at her mums tonight too," he grins.

"Okay, let's go."

The room is almost empty. Everyone else has filtered out and the band are beginning to pack away. Linking arms with David, I'm beyond relieved he's coming home with me. All I need now is a call from Johannes confirming Lizzy is okay and I can rest a little easier. Well, for one night anyway.

CHAPTER 67

The forty or so mile drive to the Barn takes a little over half an hour. The road from London to Cranleigh is pretty clear at this time of night. By the time we reach the outskirts of the village, David has dozed off and is snoring gently in the back seat.

He's folded Bear's tartan blanket and has it wedged against the window as a pillow. Each time we pass beneath a streetlight, it reflects on the silver threads of dog hair that have brushed onto his tuxedo jacket.

There's a muted buzz from Silas's phone. Retrieving it from the dashboard where he's left it, he passes it to me so I can read the message.

It's from Johannes: It reads

L safe. No sign of the mark. Awaiting instructions. J

"Oh, thank God!" Flooded with relief, I exhale softly so as not to disturb David, and read the text to Silas.

"That's good news," he nods sagely. I can literally see the wheels of his mind spinning, calculating and planning.

"It still doesn't excuse Gerard's behavior though – taking her away from the party was a stupid risk. Text him back. Tell him to take Lizzy to safety and for Gerard to wait at the airfield for the rest of the team; I'll be having strong words when I see him," he concludes.

Turning into the driveway of the barn, Silas affirms. "Wait here. I'll do a quick sweep of the grounds then let you in."

I tap out the reply as he leaps from the Range Rover. David, wakened by the slowing vehicle begins to stir.

"Are we here?" Stretching and yawning, he straightens up. The folded blanket slips, leaving yet more dog hair in its wake.

"Yes, darling… we're back. Silas is just opening the door and letting Bear out for a wee," I explain with more detail than necessary.

Within seconds, Silas returns. "Okay gang, out you come." Bear is on fox patrol, stopping every couple of paces to sniff the scent and make his own mark. "Let's get you inside and settled. It's been a long night."

"Can I play with Bear?" David asks.

"Not tonight, love. I think we all need to get some sleep. You must be dead on your feet. I saw you dancing with Wendy and her mum. Come on. Inside."

David reluctantly saunters in through the front door. I know he's shattered. Blue-grey circles are forming beneath his eyes, a sure indication of fatigue.

"Can I play with him tomorrow?"

"Of course, you can. You can even take him for a walk. But tonight, what we *really* need right now is a cup of tea and PJ's… Deal?"

"Deal," David concedes defeat. Thankfully, he's far too knackered to argue the toss with me over this.

"Okay Honey-bee," Silas says. He's already changed into dark jeans and a black sweater. My red dress is in a heap on the bedroom floor and David and I are snuggled on the sofa, in our pajamas, nursing our mugs of steaming tea. "I'll be back as soon as I can. You'll call if you need anything, yes?"

"Yes." With Lizzy out of danger, David and I locked safe and secure in here and Bobby in hiding under some slimy rock, I can't think of any reason I'd need to call him, but I'll agree anyway.

"See you later... leave the internal doors open where you can so he has the run of the place for a couple of hours... Bear... On Guard!"

I swear, Bear grows six inches at Silas's command... On Guard! And my goodness, does he just. If he's not sitting to rapt attention in his basket when he's in the lounge with us, then he's patrolling diligently through the house every few minutes, making a circuit of the downstairs rooms. He's trained to an exceptional level; this dog takes guard duty extremely seriously.

"Mum," David yawns. He's barely conscious. "I need to go to bed," he mutters, lifting his weary head.

"Okay darling, you're in the downstairs annex room, is that okay?"

"Yeah. Can Bear sleep with me?"

"Well, he'll probably want to wander around, but if he's tired, I'm okay with him sleeping on your bed. Just don't tell Silas!" I'm fine with that. Bear can watch over David down here.

"I won't... Bear come."

For a moment, Bear hesitates, looking at me for instructions, unsure whether his guard duty is complete. Rising from the sofa, I tilt my head, giving him the signal he's relieved, for now, and he can go and have forty-winks with David. At least I know David will be protected with Bear beside him all night.

As David and Bear head off to the downstairs guest suite, I step into the kitchen to rinse the mugs and generally tidy up before I go to bed. I'm exhausted both physically and mentally, although I doubt if I'll be able to switch off and get any decent shut eye.

All I keep thinking about is Bobby, and where he could be? I know he has contacts - and many of them - but whether they'd be prepared to harbour him for a few days is questionable. After all, he's a wanted man now he's broken the rules of his parole. But he's crafty too, and I'm in no doubt he'll have the ways and means to lie low.

Reaching the stairs, I can hear gentle snores coming from the guest bedroom and resist the temptation to check on David, reminding myself he's an independent adult and quite capable of putting himself to bed.

"Silly woman," I whisper to myself, ascending the stairs with tears filling my eyes.

369

My hands are trembling as I clean my teeth. The welt on my breast, which I daren't show Silas, is a livid reminder of my recent assault, and the bruise on my throat is beginning to colour where his fingers so viciously threatened to squeeze the life out of me.

I attempt to divert my thoughts to lighter things, to stop my overactive imagination from replaying the trauma. But even now I'm safely holed up at the barn, I can't suppress the flashbacks; the rancid smell of his breath as he bore down on me, the sweat on his brow, the bloodshot eyes, the heat and pressure of his hands… STOP! I scream in my mind, as the floods of tears stream relentlessly from my eyes.

Don't cry. It's what he wants. Don't give him what he wants.

Dwelling on what has happened is futile. I Need to look forward. But I can't help it. And although I have every confidence in the abilities of Silas and his team, it plays on my mind he could once again be placing himself directly in the cross hairs – and it's all because of me.

Burying myself beneath the covers, I listen to the pings and ticks as the old house settles into sleep around me. Each quirk and creak a reverberating echo, which under normal circumstances, provides a familiar comfort. Tonight however, the tick of the clock in the hall, the drip of a tap in the bathroom, the air popping of the radiators; all disquieting, all of them reminiscent of a time bomb, primed and ready to explode like my frayed nerves.

'Okay… ten drips from the tap and they'll find Bobby tonight…'

I listen, starting to count the intermittent droplets as they land in the basin. *'One… two… three…'* There's a long pause, before drop four.

'Alright… if Silas comes back before…' I check the time on the bedside clock, it's two am, *'four o'clock, Bobby will be caught and rearrested.'* I can't believe I'm laying stupid bets and bargaining with myself again.

Drip… drip… dri… dr…d…

BUMP!

My eyes fly open… I must've drifted off because there's a sliver of light seeping under my door. I don't recall closing it but in my befuddled wakefulness I'm sure I left it ajar. There's only one logical reason it's closed now; Silas must be home. That must be it. Bear would be barking his head off otherwise. Relieved, I relax and lean over to check the time. Three-thirty am. I've slept for an hour and a half.

THUD!

Another disturbing noise, coming from downstairs. Now I'm fully conscious. Perhaps Silas isn't back after all? There's only one rational explanation - it must be David - he's woken up and forgotten where he is.

HISSS!

What the Hell's that?? It sounds like a hose pipe in the yard? The back-door bangs shut and suddenly… Bear starts to bark. Ferociously, vigorously and loudly. Freaking out. His growls and snaps echo through the night.

He's outside at the rear of the house. I can hear him scampering in all directions. Silas can't be home. Bear wouldn't behave like this if he was. I listen, trying to discern the course Bear's taking; he's darting all over the place. The barking is intermittent and scattered. Sometimes distant and sometimes it sounds like it's directly beneath my bedroom window.

My immediate concern is David. If he's awoken, disorientated and wandered outside, he could be in danger. In the past, he's been prone to sleepwalking when overtired... if he manages to get out of the garden, Lord knows where he'll end up.

I leap out of bed with one objective, to locate David and get him back inside. Ignoring my slippers and dressing gown, I fly out of the bedroom ... and stop dead. There, blocking my route down, standing a couple of steps below the top landing, is Bobby.

CHAPTER 68

"What've you done with David." I have no fear for myself anymore...I need to know what he's done to my boy.

"Who? ... the retard? Oh, he's away with the fairies. Sleeping like a baby." He appears sober. Evidently, the last three or four hours have cleared his head sufficiently; he's lucid, livid and terrifying. He tilts his chin and takes another step closer. "Nice place this... difficult to find, mind you... off the beaten track you might say." He takes another step; now he's on the top riser.

Bear is still going nuts outside. I can hear him scratching and scrabbling, but it's distant, so he's not scraping at the kitchen door.

"Although, looking at those newspaper clippings, it's not too hard to locate, if you know what you're doing. A Google search here, a Companies House check there, and hey presto... here we are!"

He's lying. There's no way Silas would have left himself so vulnerable to outside scrutiny. "Who told you how to find me?"

"Hah." He knows I'm onto his deceit. He can't fool me anymore and he's momentarily rattled. It's the unconscious licking of his lips that gives him away.

"It's surprising what a little bribery can do. The girl at the restaurant, wasn't very helpful." *He has been following me!* "But the guy at the gym... he couldn't tell me enough about their new 'celebrity member.'" *Alex!* "After a couple of drinks and a fifty quid bung, he was all for spilling the beans."

"He did, did he, what did he say?" All I know is, the longer I keep him talking, the greater the chance of Silas returning.

"It won't work." Catching on to my attempted diversion, he steps onto the landing, and I take a stride backwards, into the bedroom doorway. If I can just grab my phone, or lock him out, I may be able to call for help.

He tries another approach to unnerve me and pick on my rawest fears. "The *retard* is locked in. I think he's asleep... do you want to know how I know?"

No, I don't...

"I heard the dog barking..." I won't use his name.

"Not much of a guard dog," he smirks. "It was easy to lure it outside. All I had to do was make some noise, and he ran out like a rocket. If you listen hard enough, you can hear him trying to get to that *ginger* prick."

Now I know how he's got inside. He's entered through the guest annex after luring Bear out. I groan internally when I realise David can't have locked the exterior door properly. I should've checked it.

Bobby's desperate to induce a reaction; to provoke me into retaliation. I grit my teeth, compelling myself not to take the bait. For my own sanity I have to believe David is safe - but I'm rapidly losing it.

"Where is he?" I ask again. I'm fully aware Bobby has absolutely no interest in David, he's made his feelings very plain.

"God, you really do care about him don't you?" Dubiety clouds his expression. "Why? He's not worth it. He should be locked up in an institution somewhere," he laughs. "Oh, yeah... he is, actually!"

"What have you done with him?" If Bear's outside and not scraping at the annex door, he's obviously locked him somewhere else in the grounds.

"Where, Bobby?" I utter his name intimately, as a weapon to try and defuse him.

"Oh, get over it. He's alright. There's no fun in harming someone like him." He's so disparaging of David, clearly, he's decided he's not worth the effort. "In the shed," he concedes. "Someone will find him," he adds dismissively.

Bobby tilts his head sideways, observing me, almost wistfully. "How did you ever get away from me?" he ponders, inwardly. "You were *mine*... my first, and I have to say, the best... I can't believe you left me." His voice has taken on an odd cadence; almost a sing song element. It's chilling.

"Bobby, what are you doing here?" Softening my voice, I try reason. "I know it's Lizzy you want to see but she isn't here."

A muffled scourging sound comes from outside; a door or heavy object being dragged or pushed across the ground perhaps? I aim to distract him, hoping he hasn't heard it, convinced its David endeavoring to free himself from wherever he's imprisoned.

Bear continues to whine and scrabble.

But he has heard it. "He can't get out." Clearly, he's unconcerned they'll escape anytime soon. "He might be a little on the warm side though!" he huffs a laugh.

Warm?

His eyes are glassy and glittering in the semi-dark. It's only now it occurs to me why; he's ingested something. Some Amphetamine; a line of coke maybe, to give him the shot of boldness required to do what he aims to.

"Bobby, what've you taken?"

At my repeated use of his name, his eyes flash. "Oh, you know... a bit of this... a sniff of that... it'll kick in soon."

Jesus... kick in soon... what the fuck is this then?

"Bobby, you need to let me get you some help." I step backwards, another stride into the bedroom and towards my phone.

"Looking for this?" He holds my mobile at arm's length so I can see it's definitely mine. "You won't be needing it."

Having realized he must have been in my room while I slept, I can't avoid him seeing my shocked expression. Clearly taking sadistic delight out of this, he swings his arm and opens his fingers, dramatically releasing my phone over the banister. It lands with a splintering crash on the tiled hall floor below.

"I went to the airfield." The subject change switches my attention from thoughts of my shattered mobile, to Lizzy. "She wasn't there. The *Frog* was, but he couldn't tell me where they'd taken her."

Oh, shit! Gerard...

"What have you done?"

"Oh, he might still live. I have to hand it to him though. He didn't crack; even when I broke his fingers. Even when I sliced his pretty face to ribbons. I can only conclude; he was telling the truth."

My stomach flips. *Oh Christ, No...*

"Where is he?"

"Hah, you concerned about the little *frog* prince? I left him there, sprawled beneath the wheels of that absurd plane of his. He'll be okay if they get to him before he bleeds to death. 'Though, I suspect that's unlikely. I left him with a knife in his gut, just to be sure."

My hands fly to my mouth - *Oh Jesus! He's lost his mind!*

"It matters little to me. He couldn't give me what I wanted." His voice is becoming thicker and more agitated. The drugs are kicking in. "You know, though, don't you?"

Trembling, I try hard not to show any fear. "I told you... she's not here." I've never been more thankful I have no clue where she is. I can only pray Silas has managed to conceal her at one of his safe houses.

"Hmmm." As much as I can see through his lies, he knows when I'm telling the truth. Nodding, he acknowledges. "Well, in that case," he sighs and wipes the back of his hand across his dribbling mouth, "I'll have to make do with the consolation prize. I can find her later, and then we'll be free to start our new life... she can join the family business."

"NO!" My heart lurches with adrenalin and I scream defiantly in his face. "NO! you stay away from her. She's good and kind and free. You keep away from her!"

"And who's going to stop me once you're out of the way, huh? That arrogant bastard you've been sharing your bed with? He's as crooked as a bitch's hind leg. He doesn't want you... he used you." Seething with loathing, he spits his words. "He got what he really wanted... ME!" screaming the last bit with unmitigated wrath. "He killed his own child and disabled the other."

"NO! It wasn't his fault," I shake my head.

"What conceit, what contempt to believe he could evade us... he got her killed... Him!"

Motionless, I stall, playing for time; attempting to measure the significance of what he's saying. Is he confessing to murder? Silas said *'they got them'*, but what if he was mistaken? Was Maya's death Bobby's doing? Is her blood on his hands?

"Was it you?" My voice is suddenly small in disbelief. I always knew he was an unimaginable bastard, but I never believed him capable of such a heinous act.

Shrugging, as to dismiss it as nothing, he clicks his fingers like he did earlier, "Snap! Gone!"

"You... y..." The words choke me. There aren't enough adjectives in the world to describe the kind of monster he truly is.

"Now, I'm getting bored. If you don't know where she is, then I've only one more thing to do here tonight." Twitching in agitation he steps up one more stride and he's standing barely two feet from the threshold of the bedroom.

"I think we'll finish what we started earlier - in there," he gestures towards the room behind me. The room where Silas and I have made love so many times.

"Poetic justice, don't you think? He'll come home, and there you'll be. On the bed. Defiled. Raped. Dead!" Manic delight is radiating from him; the Devil incarnate.

"I'd so love to be a fly on the wall when he sees the surprise gift, I'm going to leave for him." He wrings his hands together, "and when I'm done, I think I'll dress you in those nice red shoes he loves so much!"

His momentary fantasizing is enough to distract him from the present; a precious second of hesitation is all I need to make my move. Lunging backwards over the threshold, I make it into the bedroom. Stretching out my arm, I locate the handle and yanking the heavy wooden door, slam it against the jamb and lean my full weight against it.

Although he sees my intention, Bobby's reflexes are sluggish. Over confident and dulled by the drugs and fantasy, his reactions are too slow.

Fumbling, I manage to turn the key, locking him outside. All he can do is vent his frustration by banging wildly on two-inch-thick, solid oak.

I don't know how long the lock will hold. His pounding and kicking are so violent, I expect the door to come crashing down at any moment.

Scanning the room, my eyes fall on the heavy chest of draws beneath the window. Risking leaving the door unattended, I leap into action, sweeping the ornaments and toiletries off the surface, before opening the top drawer enough to slide my hand in and purchase a grip on the upper lip.

It weighs a fucking ton. Summoning all my strength, bracing my bare feet on the carpet, I heave with all my might on the chest. It shifts fractionally. It's all the encouragement I need. I grit my teeth and heave again, lugging it inch by inch across the floor, dragging and pulling until it stands before the bedroom door barricading it from within.

"Open the *fucking* door!" He's incandescent with rage. "Mare! Get the *FUCK* out here now!"

BANG, BANG, BANG!

Does he really expect me to open the door? He's crazy.

I back away gasping, until my calves collide with the bed. Keeping my focus on the door, I sit and listen to his incessant, hammering against the wood.

"MARE... Open up... you'll be sorry..."

"I'm already sorry, you fucking pig!" I whisper under my breath, my chest heaving from the effort of exertion and terror. There's no way he's shifting that chest; no matter how crazy he gets or how much sub-human strength is derived from the drugs.

Now I have a moment to breathe, I need to think. If he's locked David in the Annex, there's a chance he managed to free himself and raise the alarm. Darting from the bed, I ignore the continued screams and shouts coming from the landing and approach the window. It overlooks the rear garden.

Across the yard space, the out buildings, the shed and the Sauna, can just be viewed where they mark the perimeter to the woods beyond. Directly below me is the apex roof of the downstairs annex. Adjacent to the kitchen, it juts out at an 'L' shape from the main body of the house. I can't see inside, but I can see the separate exterior door standing half open beneath the tiled canopy covering the porch.

All I can hope is David and Bear are either safe inside an outbuilding, or have somehow managed to get away. My mind flips to something Silas had said numerous times before. *'Hope is not a strategy.'* How right he is… my situation isn't going to improve by doing nothing. I can't just sit here, praying and hoping help will come; I need to act.

CHAPTER 69

"Think, think, think…" Frantically I pace the room, searching in earnest for something I can use to my advantage. The discarded items on the floor bring no joy – not even a pair of tweezers.

The land line is useless. Bobby has cut the cables. I look out of the window again just to check, but there's no sign of David or Bear.

"Meredith?" Bobby's still on the landing. Although he's tempered his approach and stopped hammering on the door, I'm under no illusion he's given up.

This is a game of wits; me against him and I won't allow him to get the upper hand.

Dawn is breaking and a milky, hazy light is seeping through the window. I check the clock – is it really only four in the morning? – It feels like I've been under siege for hours, not thirty minutes.

"Meredith? Or should I call you Edi? That's what you like to be called now, isn't it?"

"Shut up, you fucking arsehole," I mumble to myself as I pace the floor, one hand on my forehead, the other on my lower back. "Think, Edi… think."

"Oh well! This isn't getting us anywhere, is it?" I hear a brushing scraping sound, against the door. "Don't worry; I'll be right back."

The loose floorboard on the top stair creaks as he descends. I'm not sure if he's actually leaving, or trying to fool me into thinking he's leaving. Tentatively, I creep to the door. Removing the key from the lock, I bend and peer through the keyhole. The landing is empty. He's gone.

A distant slam draws my attention and I charge across the room to the window. Bobby's walking away from the main house, striding purposefully across the back garden towards the outbuildings. Bear is nowhere to be seen, and it's only now I realise, the dog is silent and has been for quite some time.

I watch cautiously as Bobby approaches the sauna… *Christ!* He must've locked David in there. That's what he meant by him being warm!

"Mum!" I'm startled out of my observations by David's small voice calling my name from behind the door.

Oh my God! He's somehow managed to get free and is inside the house.

"David!" I exclaim, "how did you get out?" I rush to the bedroom door, and start the mammoth task of heaving the chest away from it. "Where's Bear?"

"He's with me. He was wonderful, mummy. He showed me where the window was open. I climbed out. I've been waiting for *him* to go away, so I could come and rescue you."

"Guughh." I can't answer him. I grunt and groan and shove with all my might and after a couple of gargantuan attempts, I manage to shift the chest about eight inches but it wedges on the carpet, refusing to budge another centimeter.

"David, I can't get the door open. I blocked it with the chest and now it's stuck. It won't move any more. Go and check the landing window… make sure he's still outside."

"'kay." I hear his footsteps cross the landing.

"Be careful, don't let him see you."

"I'm back…" he whispers. "He's checking the sheds."

Has he realized David's escaped and is now searching the other outbuildings for him? Silently I thank God for his narrowminded underestimation. He wouldn't expect him to come back inside to find me, he'll assume he's hiding.

I abandon moving the chest, it's well and truly wedged and I don't have time to wrestle with it. Turning the key, I open the door. The gap's wide enough, but barely. If I squeeze hard and breathe in, I might be able to wriggle my way out. But there's absolutely no way on God's green earth David is getting in.

"David, I'm going to try and get out but you're gonna' need to pull me, okay?"

"Yes, hurry up. I'm scared. He locked me in and it was too hot."

"I know baby, but please… try and help me now, okay? I'm here."

I press up to the door, and push my left arm and leg through the narrow gap I've created. Then I wrestle my shoulder through, but the space is a fraction too small. I can't get my head through the small space. I need more room.

"Meredith?"

"Mummy!" David whines and Bear lets out a low grumbling; the beginning of a growl deep in his chest.

"Shhhh… Hush…!" I warn them both. "Quickly… David, get in the bathroom … now… take Bear and lock the door – here, take this as well."

I don't know why, but I toss the duvet through the gap. "Get in the bath and hide underneath the covers… go… go!"

With a petrified glance at me, David grasps the duvet and he and Bear quickly enter the bathroom.

"Shut the door, and lock it," I say to his pleading face, peering at me from across the landing. "NOW!"

"Meredith, I told you I'd come back." By the volume of his voice, I can tell he's searching the downstairs rooms. He's not yet started up the stairs. He's looking for David. I pray he doesn't check in the bathroom.

STOMP!

Once I'm certain David and Bear are inside, I close and lock the bedroom door again. Kneeling and tugging at the rucked-up rug I attempt to straighten out the folds of carpet, so I can move the chest. To my surprise, the piece pulls away slightly and flattens. Turning my attention to the edges of the rug, I can see the border beneath the bed. Quickly crawling across the floor, I sit with my back against the divan and gripping the fringe tightly, heave with all my might. From this angle, it moves a lot easier than I expect it to, and reveals four lovely inches of polished wooden floorboard, directly in front of the chest. Perfect!

"Oh, Meredith." His voice is getting closer.

STOMP!

Clearly abandoning his search of the lower rooms, he's coming up the stairs. No matter what cost to me, I have to prevent him from finding David.

"Come out, come out, wherever you are… I'm coming to get yooo…"

BANG!

Something heavy and forceful hits the wood. He's trying to beat the bedroom door down.

BANG!

"OPEN THIS DOOR! You *fucking* stupid bitch, or I swear to God… I'll burn you out!"

Oh Jesus! I know him… he'll do it!

"Okay… okay… I'll open the door." It's my only option. I can't risk him setting fire to the place. Gripping the chest of drawers, I push against it. Free of the carpet, it moves more easily this time and in a couple of shoves, I have a gap wide enough for me to get through, but not quite wide enough for Bobby to fit.

Opening the door, a fraction, I look out.

"Oops… I lied!" he grins manically. Held in his hand is a box of matches.

The first thing I notice, is a bluish fug in the air. A hazy mist of vapor on the landing. Then I smell it; smoke. There are no flames visible so it could be a ruse; a ploy to make me believe the place is on fire, panic and let him in.

"I reckon you have about ten minutes," he sneers, "before the roof catches."

This part of the barn is thatched. I'm under no misconceptions. It'll go up like a tinder box if it catches alight.

"What've you done?"

"Well, just look at this place. It's a death trap. And I thought… if I can't get to you, I might as well, leave you to burn instead… either way *you're dead!*" He strikes a match and drops it on the floor at his feet. It lands on the carpet and fizzles out.

"Bobby, stop… I'll come out." Nervously, I grapple to maneuver myself through the gap, it's smaller than I thought so it takes some effort.

Ignoring my struggles, he strikes another match and lets it fall. Once again, the flame smolders weakly before fading.

"I'm not having much luck here am I?" he sighs in disappointment. "What about over here?" He walks across the landing towards the bathroom.

My heart leaps and I struggle, fighting harder to get myself free of the doorway.

"Bobby, no… look, help me out!" I reach an arm to him, hoping he'll come to my aid, or at least change his mind and direct his focus on me.

Halting mid stride, he half turns so he's side-on between me and the bathroom. With a twisted grin, he strikes another match. Observing my fruitless struggles, he winks, purses his lips in a parody of a kiss and holds out the match at arm's length towards the hem of the curtain. "Will this work, I wonder?" he taunts as the third match flickers and dies.

"Bobby…. *Please!*" I beg, dragging myself through the tight space until I'm standing barefoot on the landing.

"And, there she is!"

We regard each other with mutual contempt. I can't believe I was ever in awe of this malicious man. He's odious to me and the more cruelty and sadism I recall, the more my revulsion and guile builds; gathering with it my courage.

Bobby remains in place, beholding me with an expression so dark and scornful, I'm chilled by his malice. With one scathing glance, he turns his back, enforcing his utter disregard, and strikes the fourth match.

Consumed with rage, any remaining measure of self-preservation diffuses and, in its place, arrives sheer unadulterated fury. I roar in vehemence, and charge at him. Raising my elbows, I collide with his solid form like a human battering ram. Hurling my full weight into his back, the impact knocks him forwards and off balance. Before he can save himself, he stumbles and dives head first into the wall. The sudden collision and subsequent bone crunching thwack, cause his legs to buckle and he plummets like a stone to his knees.

My attack completely took him by surprise, and for a moment he's dazed; confused by both the force of the impact and my audacity to retaliate.

Using his disorientation to my advantage, I pummel him, forcing him to cower into the corner. If I can disable him further, we might just have a fighting chance. But the smoke on the landing is getting thicker. Somewhere downstairs, something is burning. If he's set light to the curtains in the lounge, the flames will spread quickly into the hall and from there to the kitchen, blocking off our main means of escape.

In this frenzy of activity, my mind starts working logically. I'm thinking more clearly than I have since he first invaded our space. I know the drill when there's a fire, I just need to remain calm. The urgency now is for us to get out of here while we still can and raise the alarm.

Rearing back, I retreat. Bobby remains sprawled on his hands and knees, still stunned by my impulsive attack. Seizing the opportunity, I hammer on the bathroom door.

"David, open up!"

The door swings open, and I'm confronted by the tearstained frightened face of my son.

"David, listen to me… quickly…" His terrified eyes dart to where Bobby is stirring, woozily shaking the dizziness from his head and attempting to struggle to his feet.

"David…" giving his shoulders a little shake, "David… run the bath, put the duvet in and get yourself in. Get wet… soaking wet… both of you." Bear is peering from behind David, desperate to get out. He's no longer quiet but barking furiously, at the prone intruder.

David nods his understanding and slams the door closed again. I hear the tap running. He's doing as he's been told, filling the bath with water.

Once I'm satisfied David is engaged, I return my attention to Bobby. He's managed to stand but he is unsteady and swaying. With one hand resting on the wall to support himself, the other rummages in his pocket. He looks for all the world like a drunkard, rooting for small change. But when his hand comes free, it's not money he holds, but a cigarette lighter. With one flick of his wrist the flame ignites... and so do the curtains!

"Noooo!" I yell, springing towards him, but I'm too late. Dropping the lighter, he turns, victorious; the lighted curtains ablaze and licking a tongue of flame up the wall.

A trickle of blood is running down his face from a nasty gash in his forehead and his eyes are glazed. Clearly concussed from the collision, his vision has to be affected.

His arm shoots out towards me, attempting to grab my arm, but a swift sidestep on my part has him reeling and flailing, staggering on the landing towards the stairs. He's struggling to remain upright and walking appears to be a problem... good!

Returning to the bathroom, I once again hammer on the door. "David, let me in."

Following a series of sloshing and splashing, the door opens and a bedraggled David appears. Pushing past him, I dive inside and he closes the door behind me. Now all three of us are locked into the smallest room in the house. "Bolt the door," I instruct, and he does.

Climbing into the bath, I immerse myself in the water, soaking my hair, my pajamas. Grabbing the duvet, I drag that in too so it absorbs almost all the remaining water into its stuffing, rendering it so heavy I can barely lift it.

"Help me, David..." David hauls the sopping duvet out of the bath and I leap out behind it.

"We need to wrap ourselves in this and get out of here," I say with a level of controlled authority I don't feel.

"Mummy... Nooo!" he wails.

Bear is barking nonstop. He senses the danger and is keen to get out as much as I am.

"David... listen." I dip so I'm in his direct eyeline. "I need you to be brave. Now isn't the time for chicken," I coax. "You can do it. We'll go together, yes?"

He's crying silently, his eyes scrunched with fear and denial.

"David," I scold, "you need to open your eyes and do as I say. Be brave and this will be over in seconds... you understand me?"

"Mmmm?" he nods, still reluctant to open his eyes.

"Okay." I swathe us in the waterlogged duvet. "Bear!" I call the dog to my side, who obediently joins us, still howling his head off. "Quiet!" He shuts up instantly.

"Ready?"

"Mmmm?" he mumbles a second time.

"Now!"

Turning the key, I yank on the door handle, pulling it open.

CHAPTER 70

The brief time I've been in the bathroom was long enough to transform the creeping blaze into a roaring inferno. The curtains are completely consumed and the rail is hanging down on one side. Where the drapes have fallen, the carpet has set alight and the flames are devouring what remains of the fibers and biting into the floorboards beneath.

There's no sign of Bobby. Characteristically, he's made a run for it, no doubt hoping the place will burn to the ground with us trapped inside.

Swallowing my desire to panic, I force myself to reign in my own fear so as not to frighten David. "Put your hand over your mouth," I instruct, firmly and calmly, hitching the sodden duvet up and over our heads, like a saturated, ton-weight cloak.

It's stifling, the smoke is black and acrid, billowing swirls are filling the landing but the stairs aren't yet burning. I have no idea in which downstairs room he's set the fire, but I do know we need to get down the stairs before they collapse. "Come on," I drag a coughing and spluttering David to the top of the stairwell.

Taking a moment to peer over the banister, I can see the hallway is filled with a choking fog, but I don't see flames. "Let's go. Take your time."

Steadily, but with determination, we take each tread, one at a time until all three of us are on the downstairs landing. From here I can see the front door. It's clear of flames and smoke, but it's locked. There's no key and I have no means of breaking it down.

Scanning about, I look towards the living room. That door too is closed. But I can hear the fire raging behind it. The only other option is the kitchen. I may be able to break a window. Maneuvering David, so we're faced with the length of the hall, I start to guide us towards the kitchen door.

"Wait!" David, suddenly lucid, halts as we pass the line of family pictures. "We can't leave these," he says.

Reaching out, he grabs the photograph of Silas and his children from the wall. "Maya," he sighs, tucking the frame inside the duvet and hugging it to his chest. "Now we can go."

The brass doorknob is scorching. Wrapping my hand in the duvet, I grapple with the handle, but it won't grip. With my hand swathed in the thick soaking fabric, there's no purchase and it keeps sliding off. I have no choice but to use my bare hand.

The pain is overwhelming, so hot it feels cold. There's a smell of burning flesh, but I force myself to hold on. With a will of iron, I manage against every rational thought, to turn it, and flinging the door open, we dive through into the smoldering kitchen.

The room is not yet fully ablaze, small areas of the worktops are alight and patches of flame are beginning to take hold here and there, but the room is mostly devoid of fire.

The path to the back door is clear, but our way is blocked.

Bobby is standing in the center of the space. Dazed and swaying and completely oblivious to the flames licking the walls around him. I can see his clothes are wet, the kitchen sink has been filled with water and an empty Pyrex measuring jug stands to the side. He's used it to soak his clothing.

"Get out of my way!" I yell.

Bobby just stands there stupefied, his head injury even more prominent now he's washed away the surplus blood. The wound is both wide and deep. There's a sliver of ivory bone visible. He must be in considerable pain. His glazed expression reflects the damage within. His skull is probably fractured, and the likelihood is, he's bleeding into his brain.

"Move." Knowing he's incapacitated, I barrage our way past him.

But he's faking it.

Just as we make it to the door, his arm springs out and grabs a hold of my wrist, spinning me backwards. The momentum knocks David, and he lurches, stumbling away from me, crashing through the door, which was on the latch the whole time, and out into the back yard and the bright sunny morning.

The door slams behind him, leaving me trapped in the now burning kitchen with Bobby.

"Get off me…" I yank at my arm, willing myself to find the remnants of strength I need to escape his clutches. The last few minutes have drained me. My arms are elastic and my chest is raw with the inhalation of pungent smoke, but at least David is free.

Choking, I splutter a cough as the heat rises and the smoke thickens. Something in here is giving off noxious fumes, my eyes are streaming and I'm struggling to see. "Bobby, please," I try begging, "we need to get out."

"No," he's emphatic. He may be injured and in pain but he's lucid enough. "No… it ends here. You and me."

Understanding he has no intention of our escaping, I yank once more on my arm, and to my surprise, he releases me. In the initial melee, the duvet has slipped off and landed in a heavy saturated writhing heap on the floor. My feet are bare and my hand is blistered from wrenching the door handle, but my resolve is strong.

I won't allow him to end my life. Not now. Not today. Not ever.

Silas…

My mind is inundated with a million images of him. How he took my breath away the first time I laid eyes on him. His beautiful face, his stunning body. The way he loves me, touches me, worships me, needs me. His voice, his unwavering belief in us. I can hear him, speaking to me, calling … *'Honey-bee… don't leave me…'*. I can't allow Bobby to take that away. I won't let him destroy the best thing that's ever happened to me.

"NO!" Screaming, I wipe my eyes and surge forwards. If I can only lever him out of the way. I've done it before; I can do it again.

Crashing against him, I'm winded as his solid fist plunges in to my stomach. The punch is vicious, stealing my breath. Gripping his shoulders, I raise my head so I can see his face. He's smiling that evil sickly smile. Lifting his hands, he takes my upper arms and shoves me hard so I reel backwards and into the burning cupboard behind me. Breathless, I slide to the floor gasping.

A deafening roar fills my ears, and a golden darting flash surges through the air across my path. Bear has launched himself at Bobby, snapping and snarling; jaws agape with rows and rows of razor-sharp teeth.

The dog, initially trapped beneath the weight of the duvet as it slipped from my shoulders, has wormed free and is hurtling towards Bobby like a bolt of deadly lightning.

"Aghhh!" Bobby screams and Bear barks menacingly as they disappear through the door to the hall and into the ever-blackening smoke.

I hear flesh ripping, the fire surging but I can see nothing. My head is fuzzy and my eyes are watering profusely. My stomach is cramping painfully from the cowardly sucker punch. The kitchen is now fully ablaze. The cupboard I'm leaning against has caught alight and I can feel the flames licking my shoulders.

I need to move while I can. While Bear is mauling Bobby, I can make my escape. Pushing back, I try to stand, but my feet slip. The wetness from my recent plunge in the bath has them sliding all over the slippery kitchen tiles.

I try again. And again, my feet skitter out from under me and I land heavily on my bottom. Moving my head, I search for a dry patch to place my feet, but am puzzled when the water beneath me appears dark, and oily.

Bobby's screams are ringing the air and the fire in the kitchen is now raging, licking up the side of the door. Another minute and I won't have a free path. I need to move.

"Bear," I manage to choke, "Bear, leave." He needs to come away. He can't die in the flames for the sake of that Bastard! *"BEAR!"* I manage to yell, causing a fit of coughing. I lift my hand and cover my mouth. When I pull it away, I'm startled to see it's covered in blood.

The oily patch on the floor is spreading. My head is swimming. I look down at where Bobby has punched me. Sticking out from my stomach is the handle of a wooden carving knife. It wasn't a punch...

At the sight of my own blood, bile rises in my throat and I'm no longer being choked by the thick smoke alone, but an ensuing nausea is building too.

I have to stand. I know if I pull the knife out, it will be worse for me, so I press my uninjured hand around the hilt. The feeling is one of tension, rather than pain. It isn't how I expected being stabbed would feel.

My head is reeling. I know I'm losing too much blood and I need to get help before it's too late. I can't get to my feet, so I crawl. Two knees and one hand supporting me, I move at a snail-like pace towards the door.

"Bear!" I call weakly. "Bear..." In my peripheral vision, I see a shape. Too small for a human, but large like a wolf. Bear is by my side.

The kitchen is burning all around us. The only area still devoid of flames is where the wet duvet lies smoldering on the floor; the fire unable to take hold due to the level of water saturating the filling. I crawl towards it, my strength dwindling with the effort and blood loss.

Bear is leaping at the door, hurtling his weight against it, in desperation to batter it down. The edges of his fur have started to singe. He's burning.

The heat of the fire has weakened the door frame, and with a final leap, he hurls his weight against it and it gives; flying outward on its hinges, the door blows open.

The daylight and oxygen rush in. For a surreal moment, it's like looking through a magical portal into another world. Then, the world I'm currently in explodes! The influx of fresh air instantly feeds the greedy fire and I'm engulfed in a blazing inferno.

Knowing there's no means of escape, I concede defeat. All my determination and fight desert me. I'm beaten, bleeding and choking. Unable to move, unable to breathe, unable to escape.

Acceptance.

Resting my head, I curl up into a ball on the now barely damp quilt and surrender to my fate, allowing the depths of oblivion to consume me.

CHAPTER 71

Intermittent flashes of blue, seep through the skin of my eyelids, and a wailing haunting scream emits from my lips. But I'm not screaming, I'm choking.

"Please, Mr. Tudor, we have her." A male voice is speaking in urgent tones but at the same time it's calm. "The bleeding is under control… Oxygen."

I feel tugging and something is placed over my nose and mouth. It induces a fit of coughing, but as I cough, I'm no longer choking. I can breathe, with some effort; but my screaming lungs are eased as the life-giving air infiltrates.

"Morphine," the voice commands. "Five milligrams," he instructs. "Increase Oxygen to forty percent."

"Edi baby? … Honey-bee?"

"Please Mr. Tudor, we have this."

I try and open my eyes, but I can't. They're glued shut. I can't move my head. In fact, I can't move anything.

"Little scratch," a female's voice this time. "You're going to be okay. We're going to move you now."

I'm unable to respond. I sense movement, lifting. Then my head clouds, the pain fades and I begin to drift.

"Doctor!" Someone is shouting, but it's far away in the distance… a fading record… "Doctor, quickly… Edi?… Edi? … Can you hear me?"

Bip… bip…bip…

It's dark. There's a strange smell; like stale disinfectant…

Bip… bip… bip…

Odd sounds, rolling wheels, swinging doors, mumbled voices…

Bip… bip… bip…

Sore, stiff, aching… need to cough…

Bip… bip… bip…

"Ummmm," trying to speak, choking, throat hurts. "M*mm,*" *dry, burning…* my eyes won't open…

Burning… smoke… pain… knife…

As the images flash in my head, the recall unravels thick and fast and I start to flail my arms in panic.

"Edi… Honey bee…" a soothing soft voice, one of the most wonderful sounds I've ever heard. "Edi, try and stay calm."

Buzz…

"Nurse, nurse, she's coming round…. Nurse!"

"Now, there you are… Please Mr. Tudor, let me through. Thank you… Edi? Can you hear me?"

I feel something peeling away from my eyes. It's sticky. A cool hand touches my forehead. "Edi, can you open your eyes for me?"

Squeezing my eyelids tightly, I brace myself for the onslaught of light, which will blight my vision. I blink my eyes open and they flicker. There's no sudden blinding flash, just a dull, grey muted semi-dark.

"Hey…," the perfect voice is near. I turn my head towards it and I'm surprised to see the outline of someone sat very close to my side. "Hi beautiful… welcome back Honey-bee."

"Shhhilllnnnss?" the sound startles me.

"Don't try and speak. You have a breathing tube. Nurse, can this come out?"

"I'll check her vitals, but it appears she's back with us. Edi, when I say so, I need you to cough… do you understand?"

"Yyyy."

"Don't speak sweetheart, I know, it hurts. It'll be out in seconds…"

There's some fumbling as the nurse reaches around me and presses a sequence of switches and some buttons. "Okay, now I'm going to support your head and then when I say so, you give me one good hard cough… now… and cough!"

"Hhuck…" I clear my throat, and for a few seconds feel like I'm swallowing a snake, then something long and slimy is knocking against my teeth, clearing my airway and exiting my mouth.

"There." My head is rested against the pillow and I get a front row view of the nurse's ample bottom as she squeezes from between the array of machinery beside my bed.

"Mr. Tudor, would you give me a few minutes to change her dressing and check her vital signs please?"

"Go ahead… I'm not leaving."

The nurse sighs, but doesn't argue. I expect she realizes how futile it would be to try and remove him from my side.

"Okay, well, if you could sit over there at least?"

"Humph," I hear a disgruntled acceptance. "Edi, I'm right here." He kisses a spot on my forehead, before backing away to the sofa in the far corner.

It takes about twenty minutes for the nurse to complete her ministrations. Waiting patiently, I observe as she gently removes the dressing from my diaphragm. The wound is small, only about two inches in length. And I'm fascinated at how neat the scar looks already.

"It was deeper, rather than wider," she explains. "You lost a lot of blood and we needed to give you several transfusions, but the scar has healed really well. In a couple of months, you'll barely see it."

"Mmm, huccch." My throat is killing me.

"I'll get you some water. It's best not to try and speak. Your throat will be sore for a few days and you inhaled a lot of smoke. The doctor will want to examine your chest." Turning to Silas, she gives him a stern look. "Don't upset or excite her," she warns... then winks at him and gives him a beaming smile...

"I promise, Sister," he beams back as he unfolds his long body from the dark blue sofa.

As the door swings shut behind her, Silas pours some water and places the thick rim of the plastic cup to my lips. Supporting my head with his other hand he offers me a sip.

It's tepid and has a metallic taste, but immediately I swallow, I feel it soothing my raw throat.

"Thank you," I manage to croak through sandpaper-dry lips.

Silas kisses my head again and a ripple of joy runs through me.

"How long..." I start but can't finish without a fit of coughing, which almost doubles me over in pain and breathlessness. I clutch at my wounded stomach as the coughing fit subsides.

Silas is fussing, supporting my back so I don't strain. "Shhh, don't try to talk. I'll explain everything. You need to rest." He lies me back against the pillow and straightens my covers.

"Wh..." I try again.

Taking a seat by my bed, Silas begins. "First things first..." He holds his hand up as if to tick off a list. "David and Lizzy are fine." He touches his first two fingers. "I'm fine..." though I'm not at all sure he is... he looks exhausted...I smile at him, and feel the weight of stress begin to ease. "So are you," fingers, three and four. "Christina and the team are good. And best of all, Nic is doing amazing... he's up and about and... he's home!"

"Ger..." Bobby was adamant he'd left him for dead.

Silas nods slowly, his expression pained but reassured. "Johannes got to him in the nick of time," he murmurs. "He'll be left with battle scars; his face will never be quite as handsome, but he's healing. He's in the next room actually."

It's a huge relief. Gerard is his closest friend. Another significant loss would have been too much to endure. I lift my head, needing to know more but am unable to speak through my ragged throat.

"A week." He answers my silent question. "The fire was a week ago. You've been in an induced coma to help you heal. The doctor will explain it better than I can."

"Bbb?" I try again. Bear saved me... I have to know if he's alright. The last thing I remember was his fur catching fire as the room was engulfed in flames.

"I'm sorry Edi," he says sadly. "Bobby didn't make it."

"N...n, no...." I couldn't care less about Bobby; the world is a far better place without him in it... "No... Berrr," I say, sounding like Nic that first time we met. But before Silas can answer me, the door swings open and the Doctor arrives.

"Good morning, Miss Sykes... how wonderful to see you awake."

388

Silas looks weary. His eyes, though bright with happiness are at the same time, heavy with fatigue. I wonder if he's been home at all this week? Then I realize, there's no way he could. The Barn was destroyed in the fire.

"Mr. Tudor. If you wouldn't mind, I'd like to examine Miss Sykes. Please, could you let us have the room?"

"Edi?" Silas looks at me in askance.

"Go…" I mutter, he needs to rest. "See later," I dismiss him with a confident wave.

"I'll go and get a shower. I'll be back in an hour or so… don't go anywhere," he says, much relieved.

"Now, let's have a look at you…"

The Doctor examines me thoroughly. Checking my blood pressure, heart and throat, listening to my chest and my lungs for crackles. He checks my scar and my mouth where the intubation tube has rested for the past week and the burn on my hand where I gripped the white-hot door handle.

Once I'm fully scrutinized from head to toe, he deems I'm well on the mend and orders me to sleep for a couple of hours. Quietly he exits the room and I'm left alone with only my thoughts for company.

By myself in the growing twilight, my mind replays the incident. After a week in a coma, I would expect the memory to be fuzzy at best, but I remember every detail in vivid clarity.

I remember the pain, the worry, the heat from the fire and the fear. I remember the terror of Bobby's wrath, his determined quest to destroy me and David. All of this is as clear as day. But what I remember most of all; *the* one thing… that will doubtlessly haunt me for the rest of my life, is the one ineffaceable, helpless, intolerable, unmitigated dread of never seeing Silas again. I close my eyes and let the tears flow.

I must have been sleeping. When I open my eyes again, the room is dark, except for a sliver of light seeping under the door, and a bluish glow, coming from between the slats in the window blinds.

Silas is snoozing in the chair beside me. He's changed into that light sweater I love and he has one long lean be-jeaned leg, resting on the knee of the other. His arms are folded across his chest and his chin is dipped; his head gently tilted to the side.

Turning my head, my neck is stiff. I could do with a sip of water. Trying not to disturb Silas, I reach out my hand to the bedside cabinet but misjudge the distance. My fingers collide with the plastic tumbler knocking it over and spilling water everywhere.

Silas jumps awake, suddenly alert to my attempt. "Hey, here, I'll do that," he croons, grabbing a handful of paper towels and mopping up the puddle on the floor.

The sight makes me want to cry again. I'm such a wuss; I never cried. I'm not a crier, yet here I am, blubbing over some spilled water.

"Hey… hey, it's okay." Leaving the wet paper where it is, he sits beside me on the bed and envelops me in his arms. "It's okay, Honey-bee… It's okay… everything is going to be okay." He rocks me, and holds me close as I finally permit myself the indulgence of tears… "Oh, baby… I've got you," he whispers gently, swaying me gently. "You're free."

CHAPTER 72

Two weeks later, Silas is wheeling me through the hospital towards the exit. I'm discharged, with a list of follow up appointments and a bag full of dressings and pain killer medication.

All in all, I've been extremely lucky. The knife missed vital organs, and the burn on my hand, while deep and leaving a scar, didn't require plastic surgery.

David and Lizzy are waiting in the car park beside the Range Rover. As we exit the hospital swing doors, they scream with joy and come hurtling over to me. It's the first time I've seen either of them in weeks. Silas felt their visiting would excite me too much and hinder my recovery.

"Mummy!" David flings his arms around me, but then thinks better of it and steps back cautiously.

"I'm fine," I smile, opening my arms wide for one of his special hugs. Lizzy stands back and observes, quietly.

"Lizzy?" I say over David's shoulder.

"I'm so sorry mum," she cries. "If I hadn't sneaked off with Gerard, this wouldn't have happened."

"I keep telling her it isn't her fault, but she won't listen," Silas explains as David releases me.

"It's not," I answer emphatically... how can it be her fault? "If you'd have been there, at the *Café Royal*, he'd have snatched you and things would've been even worse." I struggle to my feet, trying not to show how my scar twinges at the effort.

Silas cups my elbow as he wheels the chair away, and David pushes it back through the sliding doors and into the hospital foyer.

Using his absence, I reach over to Lizzy to curb her worries. "Darling, you did nothing wrong. He made it clear, he would have hurt you. It's over... he's gone and he can't hurt us anymore." I pull her into my arms as David returns from parking the chair.

Silas opens the car door and David and Lizzy assist me in. "Let's get out of here. There's a welcoming committee at my parents' house... I expect you to act surprised." He fastens my belt and circles to the driver's side, tipping his seat to allow Lizzy and David to climb in the back.

"My tuxedo was full of dog hair," David announces from nowhere.

"It's at the cleaners Bro'," Lizzy says on a smile as we drive away from the hospital.

Silas was right about the welcoming committee. His parent's home is filled with friends, family and colleagues. Everyone is here and I'm completely overwhelmed by the reaction to our arrival.

"Darling." Sylvana is the first to grab me and kiss me, swiftly followed by Leon, Sam, Jazz and Chloe.

"Come inside and sit down." Leon and Silas support me into the lounge, where a space is made for me on the sofa, beside a beaming Christina.

"Edi, it's good to have you back in the fold," she smiles, handing me a glass of Champagne.

"A toast," Leon calls. "To Edi, welcome home, and welcome back," he announces loudly, and everyone repeats the chant.

Raising my glass, I barely touch it to my lips before it's removed from my hand and replaced. "Ginger ale," Silas says. "No Champagne for you... not yet anyway."

"Cheers." Reluctantly I sip my ginger ale and lean back, enjoying the family atmosphere.

In one quiet corner, I notice Lizzy has located Gerard. His handsome face is partially hidden with strips of gauze; the dressings concealing the many injuries Bobby so callously inflicted. Lizzy doesn't notice. Sitting beside him, as close as she can get, she rests her head on his shoulder and takes his plastered hand in hers. Contentedly they sit; heads touching, in companionable silence.

On the other side of the room, there's a heaving table piled high with buffet food. Beside it stand Chloe, Jazz, Sam and Tia, laughing and joking together. A cheeky looking Margo dances at their feet, desperate for attention. They look happy.

Standing with their group, is a tall, slim young man with tightly clipped black hair. He's dressed casually in jeans and a sweater and his back is turned to me whilst joining the girls in their conversation. I watch, closely observing and I realise with some awe, that the young man in their midst is actually Nic!

The transformation is unbelievable. Since I last saw him in the hospital over three weeks ago, he's barely recognizable. Where once there was a damaged, shy boy, there now stands a confident, smiling man... yes... that's the distinct difference... he's smiling!

"Nic." David's deep voice hails from the doorway, and the young man I'm observing turns his beautiful green eyes towards the call. "Nic, my man." David raises his hand in a 'high-five' and Nic slaps it with his own, before draping it around his shoulder in a brotherly hug.

"Daaa...vid," he smiles widely, and pulls him in to join the group.

"Oh!" is all I can say.

"I know." Christina has the largest grin I've ever seen spread over her beautiful face. "I'm not a believer in miracles," she says, "but fucking, 'Pigs in Space'! If this isn't the best fucking miracle of all!" Pushing herself off the sofa, she turns to me, "welcome home Edi," she says with genuine warmth. "It's great to have you back."

"Penny for them?"

I've been daydreaming for several minutes; looking around me in delight at the huge gathering of people. Silas has dropped into the seat beside me. "Here, you deserve this," handing me a mug of strong hot tea.

"Will it support a mouse?" I ask, taking it from him with gratitude. "The hospital offering was pretty dire." I sip the warming liquid, allowing the tannins to coat my tastebuds before swallowing it down. My eyes close in appreciation at the delightfully bitter tang. "Oooh, that's bloody good."

"How're you feeling?" He drapes his arm around me and cuddles me close.

"Amazing," I answer truthfully and without any thought.

"Me too," he smiles, then kisses me deeply, ignoring the chorus of cat calls and cheers. "Are you tired?"

"'li'le, bit," I can't lie. I'm feeling it now.

"We're staying here if that's okay?" he wrinkles his nose in question.

Is he expecting me to reject the offer? Where else can we go? The girls are at the apartment and the barn is a pile of ash. "Yeah, that's completely fine."

"My old room." He jiggles his eyebrows in that suggestive way he has. "Though, there'll be no shenanigans," he says gravely.

"Why's that then," I tease, handing him my empty cup and struggling to my feet. "Oh yeah, I remember... ouch!" My scar twinges as I clench my stomach. This thing better hurry up and heal because there's a fine man with my name on him, waiting to be climbed!

"Good night, everyone... I'm putting Edi to bed. That's enough excitement I think."

The family chorus their goodnights and Silas leads me slowly up the stairs to his bedroom, which turns out to be a suite on the second floor.

"Wow, I love this room."

The huge windows overlook the rear garden and open out onto a balcony. I can see where he got his inspiration for the apartment and the barn. It's impressive.

"You can look at that in the morning. Come on, B.E.D," spelling it out as if talking to a young child. I don't mind.

"You never told me what happened to the barn?" I've broached the topic a couple of times in the past weeks, but he's always managed to evade the subject. He also won't speak about Bear. I still don't know if he was injured... or worse. I close my eyes on that thought. Now though, he has no escape.

"I'll run you a bath," he says in an attempt to divert the conversation.

"Okay, but you'll have to stay with me while I'm in the tub." That way he'll have no choice but to answer me.

"Alright," he calls from the en-suite. "Get undressed. Can you manage?"

"I'm fine." I'm not really, I could do with a hand, but if he starts to remove my clothing, there's no telling what I'll do. I haven't felt his touch for weeks, and I could possibly explode with desire if he touches me in the right way... or the wrong way for that matter.

Reclining in the warming bubbles, I ask him again. "So... the barn?"

A look of deep resignation shadows his features. "It's gone," he says as he gently passes the natural sponge over my shoulders. "Are you okay? Does your scar hurt?"

"No, I'm fine... what do you mean it's gone?"

"The fire damage was too substantial. Everything's gone. Apart from the internal structural beams, which remain, the rest of the building was too dangerous. It's a skeleton... gone."

Shocked, I turn to him, sloshing water onto the tiled floor and giving my scar a little tweak in the process. "All of it? Can you rebuild it?" I ask in alarm. He loved that place. His heart and soul were in that place... he has to rebuild it.

"Shhh, it's fine. I'm having an architect create some new plans." A frown puckers his brow. He doesn't look fine.

"Silas, what's wrong... tell me..." I demand, concern for him growing.

"I..." he starts then stops. "Pass me the shampoo will you and I'll wash your hair. Get rid of the hospital smell."

A peal of laughter rises up from downstairs, reminding me there's a party in full swing below us.

"Silas," I whisper handing him the bottle. There's no need to reject his offer, I too want rid of the medical stench.

Squeezing a yellow blob onto his hand, he strokes it into my hair, tenderly massaging my scalp and combs his fingers through the long, tangled tresses.

"Silas, please. I thought we could tell each other anything..." That does the trick. He's unable to deny we agreed to share everything, no matter how difficult.

"It's him, isn't it?" he blurts bitterly.

"Him?" I don't follow.

"It's where he died. The barn, he destroyed it. He ruined it. Him!"

For a moment he's still. His hands stop ministering to my hair and he stares stonily into the bath tub as if it has dark, hidden depths.

Now I see what he's been suppressing these last weeks. He's been so occupied with my recovery that I couldn't see how consumed he had become; a seething fury raging at what Bobby had done.

There was sadness in his voice when he told me he'd died, but that sadness was for me, not for Bobby. Ever compassionate, he knew I'd once loved him... or thought I did. He felt the need to soothe me because despite everything Bobby had done, he still thought I'd be upset by his death... I'm not.

"Silas, listen to me. I'm glad he's gone. Good riddance to bad rubbish... if you tell me where his grave is, I'll gladly dance on it. He was a pariah, a taker, a destroyer of the innocent and a truly heinous individual who got exactly what was coming to him... I hated him and I'm glad he's dead!" There... I've said it; out loud, openly and I mean it. When I think of all the terrible things he did, I'm only sorry he didn't meet an even more painful end.

"But the barn," his expression is pained. "Won't it ever be tainted by him?" His eyes are moist. "The bastard took everything from me. My daughter, my life, my son's health, my home, my sanity... and he tried to take y... y... you!" he sobs. Dropping his head, he rests his brow against the side of the bath. "He wanted to destroy everything..."

"But he didn't," I whisper. "He didn't, because... I'm still here, Nic is getting better, and the barn was only bricks and you're the sanest person I know. He may have tried, but he didn't succeed. We beat him and now he's gone... forever... we won." I stroke his head with my soapy hand knowing I'm right.

"I don't care that it's where he died. He can haunt us all he likes... there's no changing the fact we beat him. If his ghost is there, we'll exorcise it with our love, laughter and joy. He'll never taint our lives again. Let's show him. We'll rebuild the barn; we'll move in and we'll live happily ever after."

"I love you Honey-bee," he replied, looking at me with those dark chocolate eyes that are fathoms deep.

"And I love you too Boss-man... now wash my hair before this water gets cold."

CHAPTER 73

The following day Silas drives us to the Barn so I can see what remains of the carnage for myself. Climbing out of the car, I'm overtaken by a sweeping wave of sadness at the distressing sight before me.

The place is in complete ruins. Only the internal beams, slabs and lintels, though charred and scarred, remain defiantly intact as if their enduring years rendered them immortal and impervious to fire.

From here the site resembles an archeological dig, or an ancient, fossilized skeleton of an Elizabethan shipwreck rather than a once beautiful dwelling. Protruding ribs of the original building are stripped of their internal supporting walls and substance. A singed portion of the thatched roof remains, balancing precariously over what is left of the terracotta tiled apex roof.

I'm distraught that this is all down to me. Silas poured his wounded heart and soul into renovating and building this place; it was his solace and now it's gone. And it's all my doing.

One minor consolation in the profusion of devastation is all the internal furnishings have been cleared away. It would have been rubbing salt into his wounds and unbearably heartbreaking to see the scattered remains of Silas's carefully selected furniture and personal belongings rendered to nothing more than crumbling charcoal. I'm eternally grateful to David for remembering the precious photograph.

"Jesus, what a mess." The words escape my lips before I can apply a brain to mouth filter. "I'm sorry," I apologize at my stupid insensitivity. "Silas, I don't know what to say…"

"It's okay… you're right; it is a fucking mess."

I watch as Silas walks across the debris towards the crumbling structure. There are no words to make him feel any better. This is devastating for him. All I can do is stand powerless and guilt-ridden beside the car as he scuffs through the wreckage of his home.

"It's okay," he smiles softly at me. "Truly it is; the only thing that matters is you're safe. All this can be rebuilt. It's just bricks and mortar." He picks up a soot-blackened brick and examines it, before tossing it back on the ground.

Walking towards the front of the building, Silas suddenly comes to an abrupt stop. Staring down at the accumulated rubble and blackened debris, he stares into a pile of ashes before crouching to look closer at something. I watch as he clears away a few pieces of charred wood, clearing a space, until he finds what's caught his eye.

Only when he stands and turns towards me, can I see what it is… Bear's lead, or what remained of it, rests in his hands. The links of the silver chain have turned an inky black due to the heat of the flames. The leather loop is gone, destroyed by the fire.

"Oh!" My hand flies to my mouth, but I can't prevent the sob escaping my lips.

Winding what remains of the lead around his fist, he stares at it for a long time before dropping it into his pocket and lifting his eyes to the heavens.

The blueness of the sky is a laughable backdrop for the stark emptiness of the aftermath. From what was once a stunning home, only the outbuildings remain; forever stained by the acrid smoke, their wooden exteriors baring the scars of the fire.

"Silas?" Slowly, I walk over to him, mindful he poured his heart and soul into creating this place. After Maya died, this was his rationality, his sanctuary and now it's gone. "Babe?"

"Fine... I'm fine," he says sadly. "Now I see it with you here, it's not so bad. We can rebuild it." Although his smile is weak, I sense an underlying determination. "We'll make it better, more beautiful. We'll make it a proper home."

"We will," I atone with certainty. If there's one thing I can do to compensate for this disaster, it's to create something Phoenixlike and incredible out of the ashes of destruction. "I promise."

"Come on... someone is waiting for us." He grabs my hand and we head back to the car. We have a meeting to attend.

On the drive into town, I take the time to really look at my surroundings. This whole area is stunningly beautiful. I absolutely love it here. I don't think I've ever felt more at home anywhere.

"Silas?"

"Hmm?"

"Let's do it... let's rebuild it, better." I smile at him, knowing it's what he needs to hear.

Suddenly I'm filled with excitement at the prospect of creating our own place. Our own beautiful retreat, just for us. Somewhere to call our own.

"Really?" he looks over at me, his face almost splitting in two as we turn into the road which houses the carpark to our destination, and I nod like a grinning idiot. "Honey-bee," he laughs. "A wooden shack would be perfect, as long as you were there with me... you really want to do it?" His mood has lifted considerably.

"Yeah," I grin back. This meeting is going to be the icing on the cake... I can't wait.

We leave the car in the car park and walk round to the front of the terrace of shops and offices. The doorbell tinkles merrily as we enter the premises announcing our arrival. A pretty young girl sits behind the reception desk. Dressed in a pale green blouse, she's sporting huge false eyelashes, and a jet-black parting in her brittle yellow hair. She smiles in delight at the sight of Silas standing before her.

"Can I help you?" she asks in a friendly efficient manner.

"Yes, we're Bear's parents!" Silas announces with unashamed pride.

"Oooh!" The young girl, who I notice is wearing a name badge 'Polly' claps her hands in delight. "The hero doggy. Please take a seat, and I'll call the vet and let him know you're here." Jumping out of her swivel-chair, she skips excitedly through a door to the side of reception.

Silas nervously takes a chair. His hand drifts into his pocket and I know he's caressing the links of the destroyed lead. Encouragingly, I link my arm through his and rest my head on his shoulder. The gesture causes him to exhale and I feel some of the tension leave his body.

A sudden bark splits the quiet. A recognizable bark. A loud bark and a very welcome bark. Silas and I both leap to our feet. I've never felt so thrilled in my life at the sound of such fierce growling. I start to giggle.

The doors to the surgery swoosh open, and out flies a rocket! Poor Polly doesn't stand a chance... she's hauled through the swing doors, her trainers barely touching the floor.

Bear leaps at Silas, all four feet off the ground and I laugh hysterically at the horrified expression on Polly's face... I'm not concerned, it's not new to me.

"Hey boy, I guess your better then?" Silas laughs as he's smothered by a squirming, wriggling baby donkey.

The vet, who's followed poor Polly and Bear through the doors is smiling from ear to ear. "You could say that," he grins in a lovely Irish brogue. "He's a tough one, aren't you boy." He ruffles Bear's neck, and Bear reciprocates by snarling at him whilst baring his teeth. "Yeah, we're best bud's alright."

"How's he been?" Silas lowers Bear to the floor, who immediately leans against my legs, so I'm duty-bound to drop to my knees for a much-needed cuddle.

"Well, the fact that he survived at all is a miracle." The vet looks on astounded as if he can't believe his own capabilities. "As I said, he's a tough cookie." As if to demonstrate just how tough, he shakes his hand out, revealing a cluster of fresh puncture wounds. "He doesn't know who his mates are... do you?"

Bear, still seething, growls his reproach at the vet. Clearly, he's not his favorite person at the moment. God love him.

"Unfortunately, I couldn't save all of his tail." It's only now I notice a good quarter of the majestic rudder, which betrayed his personality, is missing. "The damage to his ears was considerable too, but he can still hear a packet of biscuits being opened from half a mile away, so there's no long-lasting damage."

Oh no! His poor silky ears are nothing but shriveled leathery shells!

"His paws have healed nicely and his fur will grow back eventually. It's just the scars on his face that might need further attention. I don't think he'll be quite as handsome as he was. But I'm sure the ladies won't mind."

Well, I for one still think he's the most handsome dog in the world. I hug him gratefully, thanking all that's holy goodness, we still have him.

The Vet wanders behind the reception counter, where Polly is checking out her make-up in a hand-held mirror. She looks fine.

398

"I've prepared your invoice and there's no need to return until he needs his boosters next year. Unless you have any pressing concerns, that is," he adds, giving Bear a hard stare that would match one of Lizzy's. I have the feeling Bear has outstayed his welcome. Yes, I expect he's made his presence felt and they're pleased to see the back of him.

Silas reaches out to the vet and takes his hand, pumping it vigorously. "I can't thank you enough," he enthuses. "He means the world to us... thank you."

"Err, no problem. Just keep him out of mischief, and he'll be fine." He dismisses us and walks back through the door, no doubt glad to see some of his more appreciative patients.

"Come on you..." Silas grins to a now, very half-waggy, Bear. "Time to go home. I think Margo is waiting to see you."

I can't describe how happy I feel in this moment as we walk out of the vets, Bear in tow, proudly holding his half-tail and scarred head high.

"You know," Silas sighs as we stroll back to the car, "I would never have believed my life could be like this."

"What do you mean?" I ask curiously.

"I mean, I never thought I'd be this happy again. I need to say something... it's going to sound really bad, but can you just hear me out?"

"Of course," my brows pucker into a frown. I'm not sure where he's going with this but I know I need to listen.

We halt by the small park adjacent to the car park and sit on the swings. Bear lies happily at our feet.

Silas swallows, bracing himself for what he's about to say.

"The first life I ever took was my own." Closing his eyes, he sighs, grasping hold of my hand and squeezing it tightly. My breath hitches and I'm stunned into horrified silence as he continues.

"Emotional suicide was the only way for me to move forward after Maya." His breath is juddering and harsh as he recalls the coping mechanism that technically saved his life.

"It was necessary." He shakes his head, battling with his internal daemons. "For me to become the man I had to be... to fulfil the tasks I had to do. I needed to die – emotionally I mean. I couldn't be who I needed to be unless I became someone else. So, I killed off Silas Tudor to become *Tuour Noir*."

Opening his eyes, he looks at me. His expression remains bland. Not questioning or pleading. It just is. This is what he had to do to get through it.

I look at him in awe, with an abundance of love; with complete and utter understanding and compassion. My heart breaks, aches and yearns for this beautiful man. At last, I get it. I know. I understand why he did what he did.

"Now you've killed the killer," he says, softly. "He's gone and he won't be back. Silas has been resurrected; raised from the dead – by you – my Honey-bee. You are... in more ways than one... the 'Goddess of small death.' Thank you."

My Silas is back.

The End.

EPILOGUE:

They say, 'where there's a will, there's a way' and it's true. The last three years have been a whirlwind. The inquest and post mortem found Bobby's death was accidental by means of asphyxiation. At the posthumous trial he was found responsible for the cause of the fire at the Barn and guilty of attempted murder. The ruling included a legal declaration that the deceased defendant was the one who committed the crime - to provide justice for society and family members of the victims. I'm grateful every day that now, in the wake of his death, the case is finally closed.

We took our time to rebuild the Barn. It was completed six months ago, and is a Haven of peace and tranquility, fitting to the future Silas deserves. Now we stand on the periphery of a new beginning and I can't wait to share the rest of my life with him.

"Are you okay?" David's voice breaks into my daydream. He sounds so happy.

"Yes, darling," I smile at him. He looks so incredibly handsome in his navy-blue three-piece suit.

"Well, you'd better hurry up. We can't be late," he grins indulgently. "You look amazing."

Looking at my reflection, I have to agree. My ivory silk suit is flattering and the covered buttons that run the length of the fitted jacket are just enough detail. I love the paneled swing of the skirt, which hugs my hips and accentuates my small waist. The fluted hem flutters around my knees, elongating my legs perfectly. I never did regain the stone or so I lost while in hospital but I like my new slimmer figure; although, Silas sometimes complains there could be more of me to hold on to, especially when he's buried balls deep inside me. Even the stress of living in a caravan on a building site for two and a half years didn't quell his passion. The caravan was rocking most nights… and afternoons for that matter.

"Mummmm!!!"

I've drifted off into my thoughts again. "Sorry, love. I'm so distracted."

"You can't be distracted. Not today! Come-onn-err!" David, sighs exaggeratedly. "You have fifteen minutes before the car arrives."

He's right. I need to pull my finger out and stop daydreaming. But it's hard not to when I remember how Silas touched me last night and brought me to explosion over and over again until we both fell into a sated, dreamless, blissful sleep.

Oh God! I'm doing it again!

Shaking away my wayward thoughts, I concentrate on the finishing touches. Picking up my watch, I lay it across my wrist, the dial atop the new tattoo that completes the band of flying bumble-bees. Smiling, I tilt my head to admire the delicate artwork. It's funny, I no longer feel ashamed when I look at it and I'm happy to show it off. What was once a very private reminder of a troubled time in my past has become a shining emblem of courage, perseverance and freedom for the future… since the addition of the 'Silas bee',

401

I'm no longer embarrassed for people to see it. I've developed a pride in my ink and what it represents.

I fasten the clasp, and pick up my favorite piece of jewelry – my bumblebee bracelet Silas bought me in New York, and place it next to my watch.

There; my diamond stud earrings are already in place and my hair is held to one side with a filigree pearl and diamond slide. The rest tumbles in auburn waves around my shoulders. The only thing to do is slip on my new shoes.

Kinky, shoe-fetish Silas will cream when he sees them. I laugh under my breath. He'll absolutely love them. Usually, I'm forbidden from buying shoes unless he's with me to supervise, but for today he had no choice in the matter. These beauties are my selection and I chose them for him. Cream, nubuck suede, with a half inch platform, slim heel and embellished diamanté straps; they are to die for and I'm hoping they do the trick when he sees me later, wearing nothing but these and my satin Basque, silk stockings, suspenders and a seductive smile. I'll be killing him softly all night.

"*Mum*, the car's here!"

"Okay baby," I say, picking up my matching clutch decorated with a pink and cream rose corsage. I take one last look in the mirror and leave the room sporting the biggest smile.

As the car pulls up at the door to the Beeches, everything looks immaculate. We were granted a special license to hold the ceremony here, in the walled rear garden.

A beautiful marquee with an abundance of floral bowers and decorations has been set up ready for the reception this afternoon, and a white alter stands in the center of the manicured lawn, the aisle leading to it flanked on either side by rows and rows of white and gold chairs. In the bright sunshine and with all the flowers in bloom, the place is a fairytale fit for a princess; the whole garden is vibrant and alive with the intense perfume of honeysuckle and jasmine. It's glorious.

"Okay, if you'd like to take your places. The guests will be arriving shortly." Mark is taking his usher duties seriously.

"Okay, thank you," I mutter. "Are you alright?" I whisper to David, who's sporting the biggest smile I've ever seen.

"Never better," he grins. "We'd better do as we're told." Together we walk down the aisle to our places at the front.

People start to filter in. First to arrive are Gerard, Christina and Johannes. They all look resplendent as they're directed to their seats.

Johannes and his wife called it a day over a year ago after admitting they preferred the company of their respective lovers, as opposed to each other.

I don't miss the gigantic ring on Christina's engagement finger. The huge pink sapphire was mined in South Africa last summer and Johannes was quick to bid on it and even quicker to get it on Christina's hand. I never thought I'd see the day. But it suits her, and they look deliriously happy.

Gerard is fidgeting restlessly, turning this way and that in his seat. It's strange to think how opposed I was to his union with Lizzy, but the pair are so inseparable they can barely function if they're apart for any considerable length of time. Their wedding in Paris two years ago was a joyful occasion, and was swiftly followed by the birth of their daughter.

My granddaughter is an absolute fireball. Little Isabelle-Edith has the same calm temperament as her father and the blonde hair, brown eyed, stunning looks of her mother. She's a sheer delight and every day I thank my luck stars for the joy she brings. She's already speaking, in both French and English. I couldn't be prouder of Lizzy and her little family.

"Mum, do you think I have time to go to the toilet?" David asks.

"If you hurry. Be quick and come straight back." I knew I should have checked. No doubt, he was so giddy, he forgot. Quickly, he paces off back down the aisle towards the conservatory. As I watch him, I notice the arrival of Silas and Nic, both in matching navy suits, heading in my direction.

As they approach, Silas shakes his head in heated warning. Bending towards me as he sidles into the row behind, he whispers intently into my ear. "I think someone is asking for a full body inspection later," he drawls. "You might be pushing forty, Granny, but you get more beautiful by the day… when're we going to do this?"

It's not the first time he's asked. He's wearing me down gradually. Eventually I may surprise him and say yes.

"Oh… one day maybe." I kiss him, drowning at the thought of promised pleasure.

"Daaad, where d… do I stand?" Nic snaps us out of our private moment.

"Ummm, next to Edi, I think."

"Yes, Nic you come and sit here. David's on his way back, see?"

As I turn, to watch David's return, I can't help but wonder if he orchestrated the whole 'I need the toilet' episode so he could have a 'center of attention' moment as he walked back between the guests.

He waves at Gerrard and the rest as he arrives back by my side.

"Hi D…d…avid…" Nic pulls him into an embrace. "I've got it all under c…control." This intrigues me and I look at Silas, who just winks knowingly. I narrow my eyes at him in warning and he shakes his head… I've nothing to concern myself with.

"Great, I'm so happy you're here." David and Nic lose themselves in gently chatter for a few moments.

A couple of minutes later, the registrar arrives, chatting to David, wishing him well. The next person to arrive is Mrs. Prestage, accompanied by Elaine. The pair have struck up a close friendship. The difference it's made to Jean, is amazing. Elaine's influence has really softened her and she no longer looks on disapprovingly when she sees me. I give them a little wave.

"Ladies and gentlemen. Please stand."

The music begins *'The One'* by Kodaline, and we all take to our feet and turn our gaze towards the rear of the garden.

Standing at the head of the aisle is a vision in pale pink silk. Calf length, perfectly cut, not too fussy. With a boat neckline and three-quarter-length sleeves. The gown was designed by Christina's favorite dressmaker especially for Wendy, and it's perfect; she looks incredible. Mid heeled satin shoes in the same colour and a simple headdress and bouquet of pink and cream roses complete the vision.

The bridesmaids are a spectrum of pastel shades, all dresses designed to flatter each individual figure to perfection. Lizzy in fuchsia, holding the hand of little Isabelle-Edith, in peach, with coral embroidered flowers as she toddles the length of the aisle towards her waiting daddy. Sammy is glowing in the softest pale yellow; Chloe, mint green; Jasmine, wears pale blue, Tia, a statuesque goddess in teal. And finally, Wendy's friend Eve, wearing lilac.

Wendy insisted on a theme of rainbows and unicorns and that's exactly what she's achieved. They all appear happy and smiling; even Tia, who winks at Mark as she passes. This makes me laugh. Of all his sisters, Tia is the most like Silas temperamentally. I imagine Mark must be completely knackered most of the time these days.

As I watch Mr. Prestage escort Wendy down the aisle towards my son, I'm filled with such love and pride I think I'm going to explode.

Months in the planning, the day has finally arrived and it couldn't be more perfect. David and Wendy are getting married, here at the Beeches. It's where they met and it is where they will live together as husband and wife. They have a new bungalow in the grounds and are so happy and in love it's almost unbearable.

"Seriously… when are we going to do this?" Silas mumbles in my ear.

"One day," I answer, honestly.

The speeches were hilarious. Nic and David performed a rap, of all things. The guests were overjoyed. I don't think I've been surrounded by so many happy people in my entire life.

Isabelle has fallen asleep and I'm using it as the perfect excuse to indulge in some quality 'Granny' time. Her cheeks are flushed, her breathing soft and even, as she slumbers in the crook of my arm.

Closing my eyes, I sniff her hair. Instantly I'm catapulted back to that fateful day when I fled my old life with my baby girl. Unvoluntary tears fill my eyes at the memory.

I know without doubt I did the right thing, but it still creases me to know it happened. Isabelle's baby smell is a huge trigger for my subconscious and I expect it always will be.

"Hi, Granny." Lizzy has crept over to the quiet side of the room to join me. She drops a kiss on Isabelle's head, and places a glass of champagne on the table to my side, before easing herself beside me on the sofa. "I got you this."

"Hmmm, thank you, sweetheart."

"Welcome... how is she?" Lizzy brushes a maternal hand over Isabelle's brow. It's a gesture so familiar, yet one I could hardly imagine my daughter performing. Gerard has been so good for her.

"Spark out. I think the wedding was far too exciting." I kiss her head again. It's irresistible. "Can I ask you something?"

"Yes, of course," Lizzy answers. Distracted by her sleeping baby, she's on autopilot; only half listening.

"Do you remember anything, from when you were small?" I don't know why I'm dragging all this up now. Perhaps it's the presence of a granddaughter, but the emotion is overwhelming. Far stronger than when I had my own children. It's strange.

"Do you mean from when we left?"

"Yes." I hope she doesn't.

"A bit... sometimes I think I can remember things... like the car and the radio, but it's only snatches. Why? What's brought all this on all of a sudden?"

"Oh, I don't know... the day... the baby," I shrug. I really don't have an answer for her.

"Are you happy?" Her question surprises me. I've never thought of my children having concerns about my happiness... it's always been my desire to see them happy; that's been my focus... until they were grown and I met Silas. It didn't occur to me; it would be reciprocated. It's unconditional. It's what parents do.

"I'm *very* happy. You know this... why do you ask?"

"Same as you really. I never gave your happiness a thought until this little one came along and I realized I'd do anything in the world for her. It made me understand you more, and why you did what you did; for me and David I mean."

"You always put us first..."

"Yes, but that's what every good mother does."

"No... I know... but... shush, a minute... It took having Isabelle for me to realize exactly how much you sacrificed to keep David and me safe. I was a selfish brat at times. We owe you so much, mum... thank you." She kisses me and reaches for her sleeping darling. "I'll take her to her Daddy. He's having withdrawals. I think there's a tall dark handsome man somewhere waiting for a dance with you. Seriously mum... I'm so glad you're happy. Silas is amazing. You really should marry him."

"Oh," I shoo her away with a flap of my hand. "Don't you bloody start! Did he put you up to this?" I laugh at her retreating back. But she's set me thinking. Perhaps I should make an honest man of him.

Unfolding myself from my chair I go in search of my man.

"There you are, I've been looking for you." Silas folds me in his arms as we stand with the rest of the guests on the edge of the dance floor. "The first dance..." he says happily.

"Ladies and Gentlemen, please put your hands together for your bride and groom as they take to the floor for the first dance as husband and wife... welcome...Mr. and Mrs. Sykes."

The ensuing cheer is deafening as David leads a beaming Wendy to the center of the floor.

The music starts. It's perfect. *'Nothing's Gonna Stop Us Now'* by Starship... so appropriate.

Silas stands behind me and we sway together as we watch the happy couple.

"Penny for them?" he asks.

"I'm just so happy. Will you marry me?" I don't know where it came from, but it's out now.

Silas stops moving and turns me in his arms; checking I'm not having him on. "You mean it?" The delight in his face is enough.

"Yes, I mean it. Nothing flashy. Just you and me, but yeah... I really mean it."

"I've already told you..." he whispers, his voice cracking. "I want this forever."

Dragging me onto the dance floor, he spins me around, and we laugh and twirl together. "We're engaged!!!" he yells at the top of his lungs and my heart burst with joy.

It's amazing... this feeling. It's as if for the first time in my life I'm truly awake. Looking around me, a flush of love overwhelms me and my heart soars. I realise now, I always had courage.

It was courage that allowed me to leave *him*. My courage gave me the resolve needed to protect my daughter from a world neither of us belonged in. And when David was born, it was courage that helped me accept him for who he was.

When I lost all hope, and everything in my world was collapsing so badly that I attempted the unimaginable; it was courage which brought me back from the brink and restored my faith in myself.

Courage gave me a glimpse of a future. Courage saw me through university and set me on the path to achieving my goals. And most significantly of all, courage brought me to Silas.

It's taken time; twenty-two years to appreciate, but I see it so vividly now; I always had the courage to fly. But it's Silas who's given me the best courage of all - the courage to fall...

Courage to fall in love with living. Courage to fall into a life filled with new and joyful things. Courage to fall into his heart and his arms and not be afraid he won't catch me, because I know, he always will.

But most of all, more wonderous than all of this; Silas has given me the courage to let go of the fear and fall in love with myself.

Thank you for reading my words.

...Falling is like flying, it can set us free.
We just need to have the courage to know; as we tumble through this
life, there will always be someone, somewhere, waiting to catch us...

Julie Anne Kiley

Printed in Great Britain
by Amazon

86837684R00234